PRAISE FOR *White Mare's Daughter*

"Tarr's faithful readers will cheer her latest, replete as it is with the results of minute research and distinguished by the finely wrought tale-spinning skills they expect from her. From the ancient Egypt and Rome of previous novels, Tarr steps back in time to a realm of goddess worship reminiscent of the setting of Marion Zimmer Bradley's *Mists of Avalon.*"

—*Booklist*

"*White Mare's Daughter* is a wonderful book, powerful and evocative. The characters come vividly alive and the clash and eventual melding of the patriarchal nomadic and settled matriarchal agrarian cultures is fascinating."

—Roberta Gellis, author of *Enchanted Fire*

"Culture clashes, war and goddess worship set the stage for Tarr's well-rounded and lively prehistoric epic. . . . Tarr's skillful juxtaposition of two vastly different, yet spiritually similar, societies gives a sharp edge to this feminist epic."

—*Publishers Weekly*

"This well-written novel about loyalty, passion, and the search for understanding between different kinds of people showcases Tarr's ability to create fascinating, passionate characters and to bring their unique cultures to life. Highly recommended."

—*Library Journal*

"Rich, meaty, and fascinating! Judith Tarr never fails to deliver the best in historical and/or fantasy fiction. *White Mare's Daughter* is her most ambitious book to date, and exemplifies Tarr's dedication to accuracy as well as top-notch storytelling. If you like Jean Auel's books, you'll love this one. . . . If you enjoy excellent historical adventure à la Mary Renault, this one will go on that special shelf that's all too short. Complex and realistic characters, and truly wondrous horses written by someone who really *knows* horses!"

—Jennifer Roberson

OTHER HISTORICAL NOVELS BY JUDITH TARR

✦ ✦

Lord of the Two Lands

Throne of Isis

The Eagle's Daughter

Pillar of Fire

King and Goddess

Queen of Swords

WHITE MARE'S DAUGHTER

JUDITH TARR

A TOM DOHERTY ASSOCIATES BOOK
NEW YORK

WHITE MARE'S DAUGHTER

Copyright © 1998 by Judith Tarr

A Forge Book
Published by Tom Doherty Associates, LLC
175 Fifth Avenue
New York, NY 10010

www.tor.com

Forge® is a registered trademark of Tom Doherty Associates, LLC.

Design by Michael Mendelsohn of MM Design 2000, Inc.

Library of Congress Cataloging-in-Publication Data

Tarr, Judith.
    White Mare's daughter / Judith Tarr.
        p.   cm.
    "A Tom Doherty Associates book."
    ISBN 0-312-86112-5 (hc)
    ISBN 0-312-87556-8 (pbk)
    I. Title.
    PS3570.A655 W48 1998
    813'.54—dc21   98-10290
                                                                         CIP

First Hardcover Edition: June 1998
First Trade Paperback Edition: June 2001

Printed in the United States of America

0 9 8 7 6 5 4 3 2 1

ACKNOWLEDGMENTS

THIS BOOK COULD not have been written without the help, advice, suggestions, and plain old aid-and-comfort of the following:

Professor David W. Anthony of the Institute for Ancient Equestrian Studies, whose work on the very early history of riding was the original impetus for this book, and who suggested a time and place in which it might be set;

Joanne Bertin and Sam Gailey, who trekked through a blizzard to hear and record a lecture that was critical to the background of the book;

Beth Meacham, who asked for it and, I hope, got it;

Jane Butler and Danny Baror, who leaned on me till it was done;

Russ Galen, who picked it up and carried it on;

the members of the Internet mailing lists Equine-L and Dressage-L, for daily, hands-on assistance and research;

the Internet "coven" who held my hand during the final throes;

and of course the three White Ladies and the famous Keed, and all the rest of the horses who provided the original and ongoing inspiration for the book.

THE
SEEKER

I

HORSE GODDESS' SERVANT

················ 1 ················

FROM FAR AWAY she heard them, echoing across the steppe: the drums beating, swift as a frightened heart. The voices were too far, too thin to carry above the shrilling of the wind, and yet in her belly she knew them, deep voices and high, strong and wild.

Blood and fire! Blood and fire! Fire and water and stone and blood!

They had made the year-sacrifice, one of many that they would make in the gathering of the tribes. On this day, from the rhythm of the drums, it would be the Bull. Yesterday, the Hound; tomorrow, the Stallion, with his proud neck red like blood.

She laid a hand on the Mare's neck. In the rolling of years it would be white, like milk. Now it was the grey of the rain that had fallen in the morning, shot with dapples like flecks of snow. The Mare snorted lightly and tossed her head. She could smell the stallions. It was her season, the strong one that waxed with the moon in spring, and would wax and wane slowly with each moon all the summer long, and in winter sleep.

She snorted again and pawed, impatient to be going. Her rider eased a little on the broad grey back, freeing her to spring forward. The wind tangled in thick grey mane and silver tail; caught the long thick braid that hung to the rider's buttocks and sent it streaming out behind. The pounding of hooves blotted out the drumbeats. They raced the wind then, swift over the new grass, into the westering sun.

✦ ✦

The gathering of the people spread wide in a hollow of the steppe, where a river ran through a cutting that deepened with the years. Winter's storms brought down the banks nonetheless, and the herds of horses and cattle made broad paths to the water.

The herds were the girdle that bound the camp. The center, the soft body, divided into circles of camps, each with the staff and banner of its tribe: black horsetail, red horsetail, spotted bull's hide, white bull's horns, and three whole handfuls of others; and in the center, in the king-place, the white mare's tail catching the strong wind of spring.

Agni was on his way to the king's circle, but taking his time about it.

The dancing, that had begun where the hill of sacrifice rose dark with blood, had wound away toward the river. He had been part of it when it began, before the king's summons brought him back in toward the white horsetail. His father was entertaining the chiefs of tribe and clan in the feast of the Bull, and had called on Agni to stand at his right hand. Rumor had it among the tribes that the old man was going to name an heir at last; and he had called for Agni, the avowed favorite of all his sons.

Agni was sensible of the honor, and of what it meant—how could he not be? But he dearly loved the dance, and the delights that came with it. He was none too eager to forsake it for the dull dignity of the elders in their circle.

As he made his somewhat desultory way past the tents in the center, a hiss brought him about. Someone had lifted the back of a tent. A white hand beckoned from beneath, and a slender arm heavy with ornaments: carved bone and stone, beads strung on leather, and one woven of horsehair that he knew very well.

His breath quickened. Completely without thinking, he dropped down and slithered into the tent.

It was black dark to his day-accustomed eyes, heavy with scents of musk and sweat and tanned hides. Strong slender arms circled his neck. A supple body pressed against his. Warm lips fastened on his own. They fell in a dizzy whirl.

She was as naked as she was born, slick with sweat, white glimmering body coming clear in the gloom; and her hair, her wonderful hair, like a pale fall of sunlight. He could drown himself in the stream of it.

For the dance one wore nothing but a kilt of fine-tanned leather—very fine, if one were a prince. It was no barrier to a woman's urgency, least of all if it were this one. She did not even wait for him to shed it. She flicked it up and opened her thighs and took him where they lay entangled. She was burning hot, as full of the god as any man, and imperious in her urgency.

He had brought with him the heat of the dance. The Bull was in him, driving deep. She gasped; then laughed. "Again! O beautiful! Again!"

He was the Bull, the god's own. He heeded no woman's bidding. But the god in her—that one he was glad to obey. He took her as the bull takes the heifer, but with a man's strength, and a man's endurance, too, riding her till her breath shuddered and a cry burst out of her—muted swiftly, but sharp enough for all of that.

He let it go then, with a gasp but no cry; for he was more circumspect than she. She locked arms and legs about him, took him as deep as ever she could, draining him of every drop of seed.

When he was all empty, she let him go. He rolled on his back, gulping air, quivering still.

She lifted herself over him, white breasts swaying. They were the color of milk, the nipples pale, like the sky at morning. She teased him with them, tormenting him, brushing his face and his sweating breast, knowing full well that he had no strength left to rouse. "O beautiful," she said. "O prince. Be like a god. Love me again."

He looked past her breasts to her laughing, mocking face. She was beautiful in everything, with her white skin and her delicate bones and her eyes the color of a winter sky. She could drive a man mad. Indeed she often had.

His eye followed the line of her shoulder to her arm, and down it to the wrist, to the one ornament of them all that mattered: the bracelet woven from the hair of a white mare and a red stallion, woven on her living arm, intricate and strong, to last lifelong. "The god is gone from me," he said, "and the king is waiting."

"Ah," she said without contrition. "Have you kept him standing about? For shame!"

"Sitting," said Agni, "in his circle as he always is, with my brothers on the edges, vying to catch his eye."

"But only you ever truly catch it," she said.

"You should have married me, then," said Agni, "and not my brother Yama."

Her face twisted delightfully, a moue of disgust. "That was my idiot of a father, insisting on giving me to the eldest, and not the one who would be king. I would have waited, and made him ask the king for you, once you were a man. I want to be a king's wife."

"You should be a king's wife," Agni said with sudden fierceness, seizing her and holding her tight. She laughed, fearless. Her hips rocked against him. He was reviving; but not enough to matter. Not yet. "When I'm king, I'll make my brother give you up."

"Oh, no," she said. "That would only be dishonor. I'd have to go back to my father; and I could never be the king's wife then. You'll have to kill your brother, my prince. Then I can be your wife."

Agni's stomach clenched round a small cold knot. But he managed to laugh. "Oh, you are a fierce creature! Come, give me a kiss, and let me go. I have to stand beside the king."

"Oh yes," she said sulkily. "Leave me for that smelly old man. And make me lie here waiting for my so-noble husband to remember that I exist."

"I don't see how he can forget," Agni said. Her kiss nearly broke his resolve; and her breasts rising as her back arched; and the hot moist valley of her sex, coaxing him to lose himself in it.

But the king was waiting, and Agni had dallied more than long enough. He slipped out the way he had come, biting back the smile that kept breaking out in spite of him. If he came flushed and disheveled to the king—well, and the dance was wild, and he had come straight from it. Had he not?

He glanced back once, half expecting to see her peering through the gap in the tent's wall. But the gap had vanished. She nursed her sulks in solitude.

✦ ✦

If the king had grown impatient, he did not show it. Agni presented himself in the circle of elders, bowed as was proper, and received the gesture that he had looked for: bidding him come in, even to the center, and wait on his father. His brothers were where Agni had known they would be, relegated to places unhappily distant, except for the lighthearted few who had gone off with the dancers.

Yama in particular glared poison at him. Yama was the eldest, though begotten of a mere prince and not a ruling king, and fancied himself greatly; but he was never the hunter nor the fighter that Agni was, and everyone but Yama knew it. No more did he know what was between Agni and the youngest and fairest of his three wives. That was a secret that Agni meant to keep— for Rudira's sake if not for his own. She could die for what she did.

Agni liked to think that what they had was in some way blessed, though the priests would have been appalled to hear it. Was he not the king's heir? Was she not the fairest woman in the tribes?

He would have been glad to be with her now, or with the dancers who had reached the river and begun the circle back. He could not help a longing glance or six toward the leaping, yelling skein of men and boys. They would dance round and round and inabout, weaving together every strand of the camp, till it was all bound up and blessed of the Bull; and then they would drink the strong dizzying *kumis* till the moon went down, and fall insensible on the ground, and so bless that. Agni was not so enamored of the headache afterward, but he did love the dance and the drinking, the laughter and singing, and maybe, if one was lucky, a willing girl creeping out of a tent to lie, as they said, with the Bull—meaning any young man full of drink and the god.

Not, thought Agni, that he had failed to give the gods their due. Maybe Rudira would quicken from this night—and maybe Yama would claim the son that came of it, but Agni would know, and she would know, whose it truly was.

He sighed and did his best not to look bored. The elders and the chieftains had little to say. Their mouths were too full of the Bull, their faces slick with grease. Their cups were kept well filled with *kumis* that he as servant was not permitted, and for the few who held to the oldest ways, the Bull's own blood caught fresh from the cutting of his throat.

"You! Boy!"

Agni started to attention. The old man glowered up at him—his wonted expression, and no more eloquent of disapproval than it ever was. "You, boy," he said in a somewhat milder tone. "Go on, go and play, I'll share a cupbearer with old Muti here."

Old Muti was, as far as anyone knew, some considerable number of seasons younger than his king; but it was true, he did look older, with his toothless grin and rheumy eyes. The man who waited on him had the same face, albeit much younger—and already gaptoothed when he grinned at Agni.

Agni's face flushed. Bored he might be, and desperate to be gone, but his brothers were watching. They would call it dishonor, to be sent away before the sun had touched the horizon. They would laugh among themselves and reckon that Agni the arrogant had had his comeuppance, summoned from the dance to be set above them all, but after a bare hour of such honor, sent off to play like a weanling child.

But one did not argue with one's father. No matter how one longed to cry a protest, one bowed low and kissed one's father's hand and went as one was bidden.

Agni put a swagger in his stride, lifted his chin and straightened his shoulders and took his leave as a proper prince should.

And by the gods, he was glad—though he should be stiff with shame. "Gods," he said when he was well away, "how crashingly dull!"

No one was near to remind him that he did, after all, want to be king when the old man gave himself up to the gods; then it would be his place to sit on the royal horsehide and be fed the flesh of the Bull and forswear the pleasures of the dance.

The dancers had passed the Red Stallion and the Black, and wound now through the Spotted Bull. That was not so far to go, if Agni would join the dance again. The tightness of shame eased in his belly. He was smiling as he strode in the dancers' wake. A girl of the Dun Mare leaned against a tentpole, her face wantonly bare, and smiled at him. But his mind saw another face altogether. He smiled because yes, this one was pretty, though never beautiful as Rudira was; and went on toward the line of the dancers. He did not look back to see if she shrugged and waited for the next handsome passerby, or if she stuck out her tongue and cursed him.

Between the tents of the Brindled Hound and the outriders of the Red Deer, a commotion brought Agni veering about. The dancers were close now, just beyond the next line of tents, invisible for the moment but clearly audible until a nearer clamor drowned them out. "Sarama! Sarama! The White Mare! Ai, she comes, the White Mare! Sarama!"

Sarama was not the name of the White Mare, who carried naught but her title and, on suitable occasion, her servant: but that servant's name, indeed, was Sarama. Agni forgot even Rudira the beautiful in a surge of pure and ringing joy. Of beautiful women the world had a sufficiency—but he had only one sister of the same mother, and they twinborn, blessed of the gods.

And there she was riding the Mare who was not yet white but dappled like the moon, with her hair as dark as blood under the moon, and her narrow witchy face. It lit with her broad white smile as she caught sight of him standing tall above the boys and women who flocked to her coming. That smile soothed the last of the tightness in his belly, and healed a wound he had not known was there: an old oozing scar like the stump of a severed limb. He thrust his way through crowding bodies into her opened arms and the familiar weight and smell of her, wind and grass and smoke and horses, slipping down from the Mare's back and standing—

"Little sister! You've shrunk."

They who had been eye to eye when she went away, were sore unbalanced now. She tilted her head back and laughed. "No," she said in a voice as new as her smallness, "*you* shot up like a tree on a hilltop. And your voice—what bull did you steal it from, eh, little brother?"

"What Bull but one, O elder sister?" he answered her, great daring on this day of all days, but Sarama was never shocked as other girls might be. Sarama was not at all as other girls were; not now, nor had she ever been. Sarama was the White Mare's child. She laughed at him and linked her arm through his, and with the Mare following in a ring of awe and quiet, went back the way he had come.

No woman but one might set foot in the feast of the Bull. That one had no delicacy, nor any hesitation. Even Agni was not so bold as to walk with her through the circle of chieftains, but hung back on the fringes. The Mare, unled, unbound, moved slightly ahead of her servant, so that it was the beast who led the woman before her father. No man presumed to lift a hand to the Mare, which was well: one who did not move aside swiftly enough had to scramble away from the lash of an outraged heel.

The old king's glower lightened as his daughter came to stand in front of him. She did not kneel as a woman should; she knelt to none but the Mare. Nonetheless she bent her head in respect as a son might in the privacy of the tent, and held up what she must have carried all this way in the fold of her coat: a cup of polished bone, the cup of a skull, carved with something that Agni could not see, but must be a skein of galloping horses. "The Old Woman is dead," she said in her voice that was deeper than he remembered, deeper and more still, as if the silence of the steppe had sunk into it. "The Old Mare has borne her into the place beyond the sun. Now I come back to you, I and the Young Mare, to take the place that they have left behind."

There was a silence. It was deep within the circle, thinning without, till far away one heard the dancers singing and stamping their feet. No one could have failed to expect it; the Old Woman had been failing at the last gathering, and the Old Mare had been thin and worn and lank of coat. And yet it shocked them, as the death of a goddess can; it shook the world a little. Not even the oldest of the old men could remember another servant of the White Mare than the Old Woman.

Now there was a Young Mare, and Sarama her servant, holding the cup that had been the Old Woman's skull. What had become of the rest of her, what had happened to the cup that she had carried in her turn, that had been the skull of the Mare's Servant before her, was a mystery. A shiver walked down Agni's spine, a chill of awe.

Sarama looked no different than she ever had. Thinner, perhaps, and finer-drawn, but she was herself still. There had always been a god in her, a strangeness that to Agni was as familiar as the wayward curl of her hair.

She lowered the cup and secreted it in the folds of her coat, took the old king's hands and kissed them, and received a kiss on the brow. Then she turned, and the Mare turned with her, departing from the circle as she had entered it, with the aplomb of one who may go wherever she pleases. No one moved to stop her. The elders and the chiefs would drink tribute to the Old Woman, but after that they would forget her. She had served a goddess, but she had only been a woman after all. Men had little to do with the likes of her.

+ +

Sarama was rather too glad to leave the old men's circle. It had always been the Old Woman's part to enter it when rite or the Mare's will ordained; doing that, walking where and as the Old Woman had walked, brought back the grief and some of the chill of winter, the black days of the Old Woman's sickness and the blacker ones of her death and consecration to the goddess. Alone in the freezing cold, Sarama had performed the rite, all of it, every step and word and gesture, no matter how terrible, no matter how grim the task. Clean white bones lay under the earth in the Mare's Place, half a moon's ride from the place of gathering; the Old Mare's white tail fluttered from the summit of her hill. Other, far older bones lay beneath those that Sarama had laid there, bones on bones from time before time, mares' bones and women's bones laid one atop the other till together they had made a high and sacred hill.

"You are the last," the Old Woman had said before she died. "You, and she"—tilting her age-ravaged chin toward the Young Mare. "Her blood continues in certain of the herds, but of her servants are none left, save only you. Once we were a tribe, a great throng of us. Then the tribes of men ran over us, outnumbered us, diminished us into veiled and feeble women. Your line we kept pure, as pure as it could be; but it dwindled and faded, and now there is but one. Be strong, my child. Be mindful. *Remember.*"

Sarama had promised to remember. She had made other promises, too, promises that she must keep or her soul would die.

But now, this moment, having done her duty by the old man her father, she was free to be a part of the tribe again. The Mare nipped lightly at her shoulder, bidding Sarama recall her presence. Might she not go now? The wind was calling her.

"The stallions, rather," Sarama said. The Mare flattened her little lean ears and snapped with temper. Sarama laughed, which made her wheel and lash out with a wicked heel; but Sarama was too quick for her.

She went to torment the stallions in their tethered lines. Sarama lingered till her brother came loping up beside her, all long limbs and young male arrogance. He made her think of a stallion himself; but she was not minded just then to torment him.

He dropped an arm about her shoulders, easily, as if they had been parted only yesterday and not a year and more ago, and swept her toward the tents of the White Horse. "You'll be hungry," he said, "and thirsty—*Aiiii!* such a thirst as must be on you. We have a new thing that came from the sunrise countries, a drink that the gods must drink in the houses above the sky. Come, I'll fill you a cup."

Sarama had no desire to dizzy and fuddle herself with strong drink, but she let him have his way. With Agni, as with the fire he was named for, that was always a wise thing.

Their father's tent was kingly broad, housing as it did all the wives that he had won in battle or in debts of honor, with their daughters and their youngest sons, and such of the grown sons as were either unmarried or unbound to one of the companies of young men. It surprised Sarama, somewhat, to find that Agni had not gone off to run with a pack.

He did not explain or excuse himself. All the brothers were gone, and many of the sisters, too, on this night of all the year; but the wives were there still. They could go nowhere, do nothing, till their husband gave them leave.

Sarama's arrival sent them into a flurry. She had never understood them, never comprehended minds and spirits so utterly encompassed by the walls of a tent. That there were factions among them she knew; she had been subjected to no few of those in the times when she was sent to visit her father's tent. But she was part of none of them. In time and with her silent persistence, they had learned to keep a respectful distance; to conceal either envy or rancor, and never to bid her choose sides in one of their wrangles.

They knew in their bellies what she had had to tell their husband in raw half-shaped words. The women always knew. Each met her eyes boldly or looked circumspectly away, as her character dictated. No one fell in worship at her feet. Such was not done in the tents among the women.

They brought her the new thing that Agni had spoken of, the thing called wine: dark and potent and richly sweet, almost too sweet, and headier by far than *kumiss*. Sarama was not sure what she thought of it. It was too strong, maybe. Too full of the spirit that reft men of their wits.

Agni drank as little as she did, she noticed, though he had made great vaunt of its excellence. Agni was not the toplofty young fool he too often liked to seem.

He caught her staring at him; stared back hard, eyes gleaming amber beneath ruddy brows, and laughed for gladness. "Ah, sister," he said. "It's good to have you here again."

Sarama could not say that it was good to be in this place; not with such tidings as she had brought. Still she could say, and say truly, "I'm glad to rest eyes on you again, my brother. Even if I do have to crane my neck to do it."

He grinned, inordinately proud of himself.

He might be as tall as the sky, but she knew a trick or two. She fell on him while he basked in his own grandeur, toppled him with gratifying ease, and sat on him till he cried for mercy. Which he did soon enough: and that was all as it used to be, as it well should be. Even he, in the end, was persuaded to admit to that.

.... 2 ....

Sarama woke with a sour taste in her mouth and a sour scent in her nostrils: the scent of too many people crowded too closely into too small a space. Instinct bade her leap up and flee; but awareness dawned, holding her still. She lay in the camp of the gathering, in her father's tent, surrounded by her blood kin. No one pressed up against her, for a marvel; even if the grownfolk would not do it, the children always seemed to pile like puppies wherever a newcomer was. Maybe the goddess had protected her, for once. Or maybe they had chosen another instead.

She did not know why that should irk her as strongly as it did. She hated to be roused by the weight of a bare-bottomed infant bouncing on her breast, choking the breath out of her. She was glad to wake of her own accord, in a quiet place near the tent's wall. Still she felt alone and oddly bereft, left to herself.

Two of her father's wives were whispering nearby, giggling over ripe fruits of gossip. Sarama did not will to listen, but she could hardly avoid it, not with them so close. The names and scandals were much the same as always. This wife caught with that young bull, and ah! such a shocking thing, the husband had been so preoccupied with tupping his neighbor's wife that he had never even known of the transgression. "Not but that her brothers would have killed her for it, such dishonor as it was," the teller of the tale said, "but with him being caught and gelded by the husband he'd wronged in his own turn, and dying of it, they were all a little distracted."

"*I* heard," said her sister—and they were sisters; women of the Running Wolf brought from far away as gift and tribute to the lord of the White Horse: "I heard tell that after all that, she flung herself screaming on his body, and found his knife, and cut her own throat with it."

They shook their heads and clicked their tongues. "Ah well," said the first, "all the Dun Cow people are mad."

"And White Horse people?" the other whispered, furtive but not furtive enough.

"Ah!" said her sister. "Well. But they are prettier than Dun Cow people. All that red hair. Did you see the prince last night? Wasn't he lovely? That face. Those shoulders. Those yellow eyes. Now if I'd been married to *him* instead of . . ."

"Hush!" the other said, clapping a hand over her mouth. "Someone said to someone who said to me . . . but that's a dreadful thing, if it's true: that someone else thinks the same as you, but *she* does something about it."

"I wish I dared," her sister sighed. "It's said he'll be king when the old one goes to the knife."

"It's also said," said the other, "that Lord Yama will make sure that doesn't happen—and the other princes are eyeing the king's place, too. Remember when our king died? He wasn't even particularly old, but he had brothers and cousins enough to get a good war going."

"Prince Agni will win," her sister said.

"Ah, to be so certain," said the other with a touch of mockery. "Here, sister, did you hear what Dissa did with her hair? Can you believe it? By the Mare, washing it in henna to see what it would do!"

"She wanted to look like a White Horse woman," her sister said, "and maybe get Prince Agni to come and visit her during the Bull Dance."

"Then she should whiten her hair with lime and make herself all pale in the face," the other said. Her sister widened eyes as if at a scandal, but then, as if shocked into it, she giggled. Sarama would have loved to rise up and knock their heads together, but war in the women's tent was hardly a fit beginning for her return to the White Horse people. She yawned instead and stretched, waking for the world to see. The sisters fell abruptly silent. Sarama smiled impartially round the tent, and went to make her morning toilet.

✦ ✦

It was a fine morning, the sun still below the horizon but the sky full of light. A scud of clouds ran away westward before a fair wind, with a flock of birds in close pursuit. Geese, she thought, flying on some errand of the gods.

The camp woke around her. Veiled women tended cookfires. Their little children played at their feet, and older children ran in packs like the camp dogs. She could hear the lowing and snorting of cattle in the herds beyond the tents, the cry of a stallion, the shrill angry squeal of a mare. Scents of dung and spilled *kumiss,* grass and horses and humanity, roasting meat and baking bread, wrapped her about in warm familiarity. Home was the steppe, the Mare's back, the Hill of the Goddess under the sky, but this was a place she knew, and knew well.

She paused at the privy-pit and passed on down to the river, with a mind to bathe though the air was cool and the water would still be snow-cold. Horse Goddess enjoined cleanliness on her servants, whatever its cost. Sarama had grown accustomed to the shock of icy water on warm skin, till she could not wake fully without it, nor confront the day unwashed and unblessed.

No one else was so bold or so bound by duty to the goddess, although women came down to draw water, and once a gangling boy who saw her bathing there, went stark white, and bolted as if from a demon. She laughed at that. Women in the tribes were never seen naked, not even, if they were proper, by their husbands. Out on the steppe, in the company of the Old Woman and the Mares, one had no need of such foolishness. Did a mare go clothed, after all, while she grazed on the hillside?

Poor women, thought Sarama as she rubbed herself dry, eyed her too-well-worn clothes and marked them for washing, and hoped that someone in her father's tent would have garments to lend her while they dried. For the moment she put them back on. They were men's clothes, or near enough; practical if one lived as she lived, on the back of the Mare. She had never worn the skirts and shawls that so trammeled a woman.

It was not likely she would find what she needed among her father's wives and daughters. Agni however, Agni her womb-brother, would have clothes that she could borrow: gods knew he must have outgrown no few of them since she saw him last.

✦ ✦

He was still asleep, the lazy great oaf, but he woke quickly enough once she wrung water from the river onto his face. He woke fighting, too, but she had expected that. She danced back laughing, undismayed by the terror of his glare. "Wake up, brother!" she said brightly. "Greet the sun. It's a fair morning, and I need a new shirt and a tunic, and trousers, too. Do you still have the red tunic I liked so much?"

He growled, but he answered her almost civilly. "I still have it. I thought you'd want it. It's over there." He tipped his chin toward the bag of dun horsehide that had housed his belongings for as long as Sarama could remember.

With his leave freely if not joyously given, Sarama dived into the bag. The red tunic was there, a wonderful thing, made as it was of cloth woven in the sunrise countries and brought far out into the steppe to clothe a prince. She found leather trousers, too, that fit not badly, and boots, and a belt with a clasp of bone carved in the shape of a running horse. She put them all on, wrapped her old clothes into a bundle and thrust it into his hands while he stood swaying, still half asleep. "See that these are cleaned," she said.

That woke him to indignation. "Am I your servant?"

"I am the goddess' servant," she said, "and all men are mine. Go on, see who'll do the cleaning. Then we'll find someone to feed us breakfast."

He growled again. She grinned. He stalked off to do her bidding, as she had known he would.

✦ ✦

They made the sacrifice of the Stallion as the sun touched its zenith, all gathered on the plain beyond the camp. Herdsmen kept the lesser horses and the cattle and the goats well away. The women and girls kept to the tents, for it was an ill thing to see a woman's face in the rite of the Stallion.

Unless that woman was Sarama. She was the Mare's child: not a man, no, never, but not a woman either, not as other women were. It was not given her to speak or perform in that rite, but neither was she forbidden the sight of it. Her place was just outside of it, on a sudden rise of ground, sitting the Mare without bridle or saddle. The two of them were preternaturally still.

Agni could see them from where he stood, again and by his father's will in a place of honor. He had begun to wonder if the old man might not be playing a game, taunting the sons of other mothers with this one who had no womb-brothers, only the sister who belonged to the Mare. Their mother had been a strange one by all accounts, born to the tribe and yet outside of it, suckled it was said by the Mare herself. She had died bearing her children, as a mare might die in bearing twins. He had never known her. Other wives had suckled the two of them, passing them from hand to hand till the Old Woman came and took his sister away. He had not understood then why she must go and he must stay. He had been furiously angry. He had screamed, he remembered. Screamed till he had no voice left. But the goddess had never cared for mere male rage.

Odd, he thought now, and yet wonderful, that they had grown up as close as they had, though parted so often and for so long. The womb was a potent place. Sarama said she could remember it: dark and warm and close. He was less blessed, or perhaps less cursed. His first memory was of her being taken away, and of his fury—not that she was going, but that he could not go with her.

She sat on her hilltop, mounted on the moon-dappled Mare, high and remote. He down below, hemmed in by the men of the tribes, wondered if she was happy; if she knew what it was to be part of the people. He would ask her later. Not now. Now was the chanting of the priests in their tall horsehead masks, the beating of the drums like the thunder of hooves on the earth, the dip and sway of the dance. He as an initiate, new come into man's place, might wear the horsehide tunic but not the mask—not yet. Not till he passed the test of the hunt, caught a stallion wild on the steppe, tamed him and conquered him and brought him home to be his mount.

He shivered a little, thinking of that. After the gathering, when the tribes had gone on the summer wanderings, each apart from the other on the broad breast of the world, he would go out. This was his consecration, this sacrifice. The tunic was heavy on him, heated by the sun, chafing the bare body beneath. His palm was slippery on the haft of the knife that he must carry, the black stone dagger honed and polished till it gleamed, its edge so keen that it could draw blood from air. He was terrified; exhilarated. Excitement raised his shaft as it had risen for Rudira, hard and aching, yearning toward a woman.

And there was none here, none but Sarama. He sighed faintly. Tonight, yes. Rudira would be waiting for him. Maybe even she would come to him, impossible boldness, but utterly like her. His breath came a little quicker, thinking of it.

The priests' chant wound on, now deep as the drums, now shrill as a stallion's call. Their dance had drawn in close to the altar, the sacred stone that the gods had laid down, high as a man's waist, level as if smoothed by a monstrous hand. They linked hands in a circle and stamped, beating the earth, now with this foot, now that. The drum pounded with them.

Down the way that the men had left open, treading the trampled grass, the Stallion came in his glory. A priest led him, a man without a face, masked and clothed in undyed horsehide. The eyes behind the mask were hidden in shadow, as if he had none at all; as if the mask and the garments were empty, and inside them naught but air. Nameless, faceless, silent, he led the Stallion toward the circle.

It was a red Stallion always, unblemished, unscarred, with no mark of white upon him. Agni's father, as chief of the priests, had chosen and blessed him, and whispered in his ear the secret name, the name that he would bear before the gods.

Sometimes the beast did not go willingly to his sacrifice. Then, Agni knew, the priests fed him herbs to calm him. It was not a thing anyone talked of, but everyone knew it was done, and knew the look, too, the slight stumble in the gait, the slight clouding of the eyes.

This one had been fed no herb. He walked calmly, head up, alert, looking about him with interest but no fear. The scent of blood was sunk deep in earth and altar. His nostrils flared; he snorted, but did not shy away. He was bold, this one, and beautiful, as red almost as the tunic that Sarama wore on her hilltop—Agni's tunic that had been, that she had made hers. The gods would love him; he would speak well for the tribes, and his strong back would bear the weight of their prosperity in the year that would come.

No wise man spoke as the Stallion approached the altar, yet Agni heard the hiss of a whisper behind him. "That's a fine one, that is. The Old Man chose well."

"Of course he did," someone else hissed back. "He knows he should be going to the altar with the horse. It's his time, and past it. Did you see how he stumbled just now, and forgot the word he was about to say?"

Agni stiffened. The king had hesitated, yes, but who would not? It was a long rite, and the words were difficult, some so old that their meaning was forgotten. And if he had misstepped slightly—well; and the ground was uneven, much trampled from the day before. The Bull had not gone quiet to his death. One of the priests would be a long while recovering. Another would be laid in the earth when all the sacrifices were done, with great reverence, for he had died on the horns of the Bull.

The Stallion offered no such violence. And the king was not ready, not yet, to mount the back of the sacrifice, and to offer his own throat to the knife.

"It is a Ninth Year," said the hissing voice behind him. He could not turn to see who it was, but he had his suspicions. "Everyone forgets, or chooses to; but this is a year when a king should go with the Stallion into the earth. We'll pay for that, you'll see. The gods don't like to be deprived of their due."

Agni, who had been born in a Ninth Year, the year his father had risen from prince to king, was well minded to whirl about and ask the one who was so eager to see the king die, whether he would offer himself instead, as the royal born well might. If it was Yama as he suspected, he would win naught but a glare for his pains.

But he could not so disrupt the rite. The Stallion had nearly reached the altar. The scent of blood had roused him at last. He was sweating and snorting, stepping uneasily, but he did not stop, did not pull back rearing and fighting as the Bull had done the day before.

Agni loved him for that courage. As he reached the ring of priests, the ring broke; the priests drew back. Agni did not need the stroke of the drum to know that it was time. He stepped forward from among the youths who were not yet men. His fingers were locked tight round the knife's hilt. He could not have let it go even if he willed to.

He was aware, keenly, of the eyes on him. He was the chosen one, the one blessed, the instrument of the sacrifice. None of them moved, none spoke. The wind blew away the sound of their breathing.

The faceless priest stood in front of him, holding out the cord of braided leather with which he had led the Stallion. Agni took it blindly. His eyes were full of the beast. The proud head lifted, ears pricked, nostrils fluttering as they drew in his scent. He laid a hand on the soft muzzle. The Stallion breathed deep, feinted a nip, looked at him with eyes that laughed, stallion-laughter, as fierce as it was joyful.

"Ah beautiful," Agni sighed. "How the gods will love you!"

The Stallion tossed his heavy mane and pawed.

Yes, thought Agni. Yes. Get on with it. He could have wept for the beauty and bravery of this creature, this child of the gods, whom they called back to themselves.

Perhaps it was the gods who spoke, bidding him do what he did. He dropped the cord over the Stallion's neck, left him loose to come or to flee, as he willed; then walked forward through the broken circle, onto the holy ground before the altar.

And the Stallion followed. Calmly, sweetly, as—yes, as the Mare followed Agni's sister Sarama, he followed Agni to the altar of his sacrifice. Later Agni would marvel; would mark the omen as they all did. Now it was only as it should be, like the sun overhead, the grass underfoot, the wind in his face. He could smell the smell of the Stallion, the warm slightly pungent scent, and hear the soft thud of his footfalls.

Before the altar Agni halted, and the Stallion halted with him. He took the cord then. He looked into the dark bright eye. "O beautiful," he said, crooning the words. "O blessed." And with no more words than that, though the priests were full of them, chanting the death-song all about him, he lifted the knife gripped still in his hand, and thrust it deep in the gleaming red throat.

Blood was redder far than any stallion's hide, even if he were the get of a god. It sprang forth in a fountain, flooding the dark stone of the altar. The Stallion sank down in it, slowly, as if lying down to sleep. Yet there was no sleep in his eyes. He was wide awake, seeing through the veils of the world, looking with wonder on the gods' country. Almost Agni could see it, almost know the light of it, almost walk where the Stallion walked.

Death took the Stallion as he touched the altar's stone. The light in his eyes went out. The breath departed from him in a sigh. His soul fled away, bright airy thing, head up, tail up, galloping swifter than mortal horse could gallop, vanishing into the endless vault of the sky.

.... 3 ....

Agni's half-dream shattered in a roar of sound: the shout of exultation at the Stallion's sacrifice. He wobbled in his place, the knife slipping in slackened fingers, till he tightened them with a convulsive movement. He would re-member, later, how very red the blood was, and how very different a red was the Stallion's body; how the hair whorled on the broad brow beneath the tumbled forelock, first sunwise, then, above it, the opposite. There should be a white mark on that forehead, he thought, curved like a crescent moon. He did not know why it should be so; and yet it was.

He fell back into himself all at once, into consciousness of the priests dancing and swirling about him, and the people calling out, and the rest of the young men, the hunters who would seek their horses between now and the summer's end, running forward to finish the sacrifice.

His part was done. He hated to see that beautiful body cut, the hide stripped off and carried away to be made into the king's new year-seat, the flesh sundered from bones, the fire lit for the feast. And the head, the splendid head, cut off entire and buried in the holy place, to watch over the tribe till the year should return to its beginning.

But he could stand apart from that, nor need he watch it unless he wished. People let him be. Maybe they could see the gods' hand on him. He could feel it, strong as a stallion, heavy as worlds.

He bowed and laid the knife on the altar's edge and backed away as one did before the gods, letting the crowd of people surge past him to the conclusion of the rite. In a little while they were all gone ahead of him and he was alone on the trampled grass. He looked up. His sister was gone from the hill, and the Mare with her.

He shed his robe of ceremony, let it fall on the grass. The trews underneath were all he wore. The wind was chill, but he barely felt it. He walked back slowly to the ring of tents, the women and the children and the blessing of quiet.

✦ ✦

Sarama tended the Mare with her own hands. That was as it should be, and as it had always been. People knew better than to interfere, though children hung about and watched, fascinated as children always were by the sight of a woman in trousers tending a horse. Sometimes one of the boys would strut and fret and disapprove, though he never spoke directly to her. Rather he made sure that she could hear: "Look at that! A woman without a veil, and with a horse. Horses are for men. Women belong in tents."

Sarama never had to respond, even if she had been inclined. Another of the boys was always there to hush the arrogant one and warn him: "That's not a woman like other women. That's Horse Goddess' servant. She lives to serve the goddess."

"Women live to serve men," the arrogant one would often retort.

Sarama had been angry at first, long ago when she was still a child. She had been the Old Mare's lesser servant then, fetching and carrying for the Old Woman. Then it had mattered that she dressed more like a boy than a girl, and that the boys teased and tormented her behind the Old Woman's back. Boys had no respect for the gods, or the goddess either.

Since then she had learned to ignore them, and to resist the temptation to teach them manners. The gods would see that they learned proper respect, sooner or later. Today, even as she combed out the Mare's long mane with her fingers and fed her bits of honeycake from breakfast, the loudest of the arrogant ones tripped and fell over his own feet and split his lip on a stone. She happened to be watching him just then. He raised himself on shaky arms and happened, by the gods' will, to catch her eye. She smiled sidewise. His face went white under the scarlet stain of blood. She was merciful: she looked away, and let him make his escape in peace.

They left her alone after that. Boys were cowards, when it came to it. Girls could be bolder. It took great courage and no little ingenuity to escape the stifling confines of a tent and creep out to the horselines. There with hunter's stealth they eluded the boys' watchfulness and lurked in shadows. She would feel their yearning on her skin, their eyes fixed on her, wanting what she had: free air, white Mare, open sky. She never betrayed them, not even when their mothers or brothers came hunting them, cursing their impudence.

There were two in shadows now, two pairs of eyes watching her. She could not acknowledge them, but she could teach as the Old Woman had taught her, by singing the songs that had come down from the time long ago. Today it was the Song of the Mare and the Woman, how the Mare had come to the Woman in the dawn time, spoken to her in the voice of the goddess and called her most beloved of servants.

Men sang that the Stallion had come to the Man, that there had been no Mare, no Woman; that horses were men's province and men's alone from the long beginning. But the Mare and the Woman lived and endured, and proved them false. She sang that, too, how men had seized the power of horses, claimed the Stallion as if he and not the Mare were the lord of the herd, and wrought a whole world of clever lies to keep the Mare and the Woman forever bound and mute.

It was terrible, that song, sung soft and sweet as a woman could sing it, as if she sang her child to sleep. It was never sung where man or boy could hear. It was a woman's mystery, and a woman's remembrance. *Let the men remember as they please,* she sang. *We women—we remember as it truly was.*

Some girls fled then in fear, because in the world that they were bound to, the men's world, it was blasphemy. But these were of a rarer, bolder sort. They lingered after the song had ended, silent in their patch of shadow, waiting to see what she would sing next. She considered for a while, but in the end chose silence. Leave them hungry, the Old Woman had taught her. Make them yearn for more. Then they come back. Then truly they begin to learn.

Sarama hummed softly to herself as she made the Mare's coat a smooth and shining thing, and stroked mane and tail till they ran like water. The Mare's beauty was a great weapon in itself. Sarama did not wonder that men had seized on it and claimed it for their own.

Somewhere, she thought, must be a world in which a woman could speak freely as a man, and not only because Horse Goddess had commanded it; where every woman walked free, nor had to creep and whisper and hide lest she be caught and shut up in the tents again. Such would be a marvelous world indeed. Then she could teach the girls and the young women what she best knew to teach, and no need to conceal the truth in riddles or in songs.

Old Woman had known no such world, not in this age. "Long ago," she had said, "such things were so. Now the gods will otherwise; and Horse Goddess in her wisdom permits it."

"But why?" Sarama had demanded. "Why does she allow it? It's not fair."

"Nothing is fair," Old Woman said, "nor simple, nor easily comprehensible. Particularly when there is a god in it. What is, is. That is the most that one can know."

"I would know more," Sarama had said, but Old Woman had told her to hush and set to work peeling roots for dinner. When Old Woman spoke in that tone, Sarama had learned to obey. But the questions lingered, though she never gained an answer.

A shout brought her about. The men were coming back from their feasting, bearing the head and hide of the Stallion, and well gone in *kumiss*, too. She whose sacrifices were secret things, who had laid the Old Mare to rest in clean bones and tanned hide, looked on the men's poor likeness of the true sacrifice, and sighed. There was another incomprehensibility, another folly of the gods. Horse Goddess took no joy in stallion's blood, though the milk of a mare and the caul of a newborn foal gladdened her greatly.

Still, the men's gods seemed pleased by the rite, as by the rites of Bull and Hound; and without them the tribes would suffer. Sarama had heard too how people whispered that more than beasts should have died in this festival, that the king held on past his proper time, that he should have offered his own throat to the knife, and ridden the Stallion into the gods' country. And perhaps it was so. It was a Ninth Year. Horse Goddess had taken Old Woman and the Old Mare, had accepted their lives and blood as was her due. What the men's gods wanted, was not for Sarama to know.

The Mare was clean, shining, and sulkily uncomfortable. She would roll in the grass when Sarama left her, staining her grey hide green. "Yes," Sarama said to her, "and my sacrifice becomes your sacrifice, and all is well in the world."

The Mare snorted wetly. Sarama leaped back laughing, slapped her neck and let her go. She danced away with head and tail high, beautiful and knowing it, though beauty to a horse was dusty and filthy and thick with burrs and mud and tangles.

✦ ✦

Yama the king's eldest son set himself across Sarama's path as she returned to the circle of tents. That they were begotten of the same father meant little to Sarama. The mother's line was strongest, the Old Woman had taught her. It was the mare who conceived and bore and raised the foal, not the stallion who mounted her when she came into season. But among the tribes the father meant much; and one's father's son was one's brother, and if one was a woman one must yield to his will as if he were a god.

Certainly Yama expected as much, though he should long since have known better. He was a big man, bigger than Agni but not as strong to look at. There was something soft about him, something not quite firm; a weakness that he concealed with bluster.

The path was narrow but there was space enough on either side. Nonetheless she stopped, because clearly he expected her to. It was a form of contrariness.

She was supposed to cower, she could see. She kept her head up, and though she was much smaller, she refused to be diminished by his lordly bulk.

"Sister!" he boomed in his deep voice that sounded so well in the circle of the men. "Here, I've something for you. A returning-gift."

Sarama's brows rose. Now that was something new. Yama had never tried to buy her before. He set in her hand a thing that, shaken out, showed itself to be a woman's veil.

She kept her expression still, her eyes level. "I thank you," she said. She gave him no title, nor any name of kinship.

Either he did not notice or he chose not to care. "You are welcome home," he said, "where indeed you belong. Our father will have arranged for your housing, I'm sure, and your welcome among the people. Still, if you have need of hospitality, my wives have been instructed to welcome you into my tent."

Sarama inclined her head as she had seen Old Woman do. "You are generous," she said. "Again I thank you."

"Remember," he said, "that I offered this. It may serve you well."

"I shall not forget," murmured Sarama.

He nodded as if pleased, and went on his way.

Sarama went on hers, somewhat less content within herself than she had been. Yama had not accosted her out of the goodness of his heart. Oh, indeed not. His gift was meant for a message, and his offer for a sign—and a warning.

Some perhaps might have scorned him for a fool, to so insult Horse Goddess' servant: to give her a gift that was proper to a woman, and to imply that she would enter the tents as a woman of ordinary lineage should. Sarama was no veiled or tentbound creature, nor would ever be, by the goddess' will.

Yama knew what he did. He was telling her somewhat that Old Woman had warned her of long since. Sarama was the last of Horse Goddess' lineage, last of what had in the old time been a great tribe. After her, if Yama had his way, would come no other—not of her likeness. She was rather surprised that he had not offered to find her a husband. That would come later, she had no doubt. Yama meant to be king, he had told her as clear as words. And when Yama was king, such oddities as Sarama would be disposed of, made a proper part of the people.

"Lady," she said to the bright depths of the sky, "whatever you will, I obey; but it would serve us very well if yonder bullcalf failed of his ambition."

She received no answer. She had not asked for one. It was enough to know that she was heard.

.... 4 ....

After the third of the three great sacrifices, the clans and tribes lingered yet a while in the place of gathering. Spring, which could be capricious, showed one day a blast of winter in chill rain and a spit of snow; the next, a coy face of summer in warm breezes and cloudless sky. The herds were yet content though they had wandered somewhat afield in search of grazing. When they had gone a day's journey, then the people would disperse to their summer runs.

They were not so far out yet, and the people, freed of the obligations of the high festival, mingled freely among the tents. Then marriages were made, alliances promised, feuds made and broken. One of Agni's brothers by a mother of the Spotted Bull took to wife a woman of the Dun Cow—and not a madwoman either, that Agni could determine. She seemed a meek enough creature, demure in her veils, with wide-set brown eyes like a doe, and a voice like a dove's call.

She was said to be beautiful. Muriadni would know for certain this night; and he was eager for it, between *kumiss* and his brothers' teasing. He had been kept away from any woman through the gathering, particularly in the dances on the days of sacrifice, housed in a tent apart and kept under strict if laughing guard. He looked, Agni thought, like a young stallion kept penned during the mares' season: ready to batter down the walls and leap on the first mare he saw.

Weddings were grand occasions among the people, rich with gifts and feasting. Strangers would come from far away to partake of a great lord's bounty, bringing songs and tales and sometimes a marvel. When Yama took his first wife, Agni remembered, a traveller had had a wondrous thing, a knife made of smooth shining stuff both softer and keener than stone, which he called copper. He had not given it to anyone though many sought to trick him out of it, nor offered it as a wedding-gift, which had been reckoned rude. But Agni rather thought he understood. This copper could take an edge that would draw blood from air, and bore a sheen on it like sunset on water, red and golden and faintly green. He would not have given such a thing away, either, though he be thought mean for it, and less than princely.

There were no such wonders at this wedding, though someone was showing off a mare born all white and not, he swore, greyed as the children of the Mare were. And indeed she was a strange thing to look at, her coat pure blank white, her skin pink beneath it and not the black of the Mare, and her eyes blank and icy blue. Those eyes had a demon in them, people said. Maybe so; but there was none in the mare. She was a placid thing, inured to stares and exclamations and strangers' hands running over her.

Agni found Sarama not in the crowd about the white mare, where he might have expected, but hovering on the edge of a taleteller's circle. This was nothing so wondrous as a horse born white; simply a man in travelworn clothes, one eye blinded in an ancient knife-fight, with a strikingly clear voice for one so apparently ravaged by age and wandering.

"Yes," he was saying as Agni came up beside Sarama, "I traveled toward the setting sun with the people of the Black Mare and the people of the Red Bull and many another people, westward and westward, till I found the Golden Aurochs that some had told me were long vanished into the grass. But they were very much alive, and they were riding westward, seized by the desire of their king and drawn by tales of wonder—just as I had been, who came from so far to find them. They were camped by the edge of a great and terrible place, a forest of trees such as none of you has ever seen, trees so tall they touched the sky. Beyond those, their wise men knew, was treasure; but they had failed of their courage, and would not venture the trees.

"But I was only one man, and men have called me mad before. I said my prayers to Skyfather and to Earth Mother and to Horse Goddess, too, and sang myself a beast to carry fodder for my horse, and rode into the dark place. Oh, it was dark, my children! Dark as night, full of whispers and rustlings and the flutter of wings. And there was no sky to see, no stars to light

my way, and hardly the sun by day. Yet the gods guided me, sent game to
my bow, kept my horses on a path as straight as it might be, till I came to
the light again.

"It was a beautiful thing, my children, beautiful and purely strange. For
there was the grass that grows in the world I knew, and a great river that was
still, after all, a river; and the sun over them, and rain when the gods willed
it, and night with moon and stars. But all on that plain of the river, as far as
eye and mind could perceive, were the habitations of men.

"And such men! Men, my children, who live in tents built of earth and
wood and stone, that never move, but stand fast from life to life. Cattle they
know, and goats, and sheep, but of horses they know nothing. They walk
where they must go, or float like logs on the river, nor think to mount one
of their cattle—strange people, fools one might think, but such treasures as
they amass, such wonders as they make, how could they indeed be witless?
They clothe themselves in all the colors of earth and water and sky, and
surround themselves with the work of their hands, wonderful things of wood
and stone and pottery, and a thing that some call metal, and when it is red
they call it copper, and when it shines like the sun they call it gold. This is a
rarity, and a sign of great wealth, but is neither a wonder nor a thing to
remark on there, no more than their garments or their pots or the music they
make with pierced reeds, that sounds like the voices of the gods.

"But strangest of all, and most remarkable, my children, is that no man
rules there. No, not one. Their kings are women, my children. Yes, it is true!
Women rule them. Women walk boldly, with faces unveiled, and speak as
freely as men, and men not only listen; they bow their heads and obey."

But for the respect every civilized person owed a teller of tales, he would
have been drowned out then by a tide of disbelief. As it was, people murmured and nudged one another, and someone laughed, almost loud enough
to overwhelm his voice. He jabbed his chin at that one, not at all dismayed,
and nodded broadly. "Oh, you laugh, do you, little man? So did I, long and
loud, in my disbelief. And yet it was true. They know nothing of Skyfather.
Earth Mother only they know, whom they call Lady of the Birds, and they
worship her in every dwelling, in every place in which they gather. Men, too;
men there submit in all things to the women, nor carry weapons, nor know
the arts of war, except to drive off the wolves from their flocks. And that, my
children, the women also do, strong tall creatures whose hands are hard and
whose hearts are implacable.

"Still," he said, and there he sighed as if at a memory, "not all of them
are as men, or as stones, either. They are free of themselves; aye, very free.
Nor do they scorn a half-blind traveller, if he come mounted on a beast they
reckon impossible, and bearing gifts from far places. My knife they had little
use for save for cutting meat, but my bow they loved, for they had nothing
like it. It would wage great war among the wolves, they said. I gave it to
them. How was I to refuse? My horse I would not give, nor dared they ask
for her; but when she foaled, they kept her colt. It was tribute, they said, to
the Lady of the Birds. I thought that they might sacrifice him, but they kept

him, the daughters of the she-king of that place, and made a little king of him, feeding him the choicest grasses and garlanding him with flowers."

There was more to his tale—a great deal more, from the look and sound of him—but Sarama, it seemed, had heard enough. She wandered off as if in a dream, and Agni followed.

When she stopped, she had left the tents and found her way to the horselines, though not as far as the Mare. Agni did not know what stopped her there. Probably nothing but the turning of her thoughts, and perhaps the sight of a mare with a new colt at its side. He had been born in the night from the look of him, tiny and spindly and down on his pasterns but bright-eyed, curious, coming to investigate the strangers while his mother grazed nearby. She was an old mare, a mare who had borne many foals; she was far too wise to guard her child against the goddess' children, though she favored them with a long glance before she bent to her grazing.

Sarama knelt in the grass, making herself smaller so that the foal might not take fright and flee. But he was a brave one, a mouse-colored creature who would, Agni judged, be black when he was grown. He approached her boldly, neck outstretched, ears pricked, tiny nostrils flared, till he touched her with his nose. She knelt motionless except for her hand, which came up slowly to stroke the soft newborn fur of his neck. He snorted and shied a little, but he came back. By degrees and with a bit of snorting and rapid retreating, he suffered her to stroke him from ears to tail, lift his feet one by one, breathe into his nostrils and, Agni had no doubt, lay the goddess' blessing on him.

It was nothing that Agni himself had not done, and yet he watched, fascinated. Sarama was Horse Goddess' servant. She spoke for the goddess to the people, on those rare occasions when the goddess might choose to speak. Not all those people, he could see, walked on two legs.

Sarama let the colt go. He went direct to his mother and nursed hungrily. Sarama straightened. She was smiling. "That one will be a hunter's mount," she said. "He's small but very brave, and he'll be strong and sure on his feet."

"Maybe I'll lay claim to him," Agni said.

She slid her eyes at him. "You? No. Your horse is waiting for you." Her chin tilted northward, away from the camp. "There. You'll leave soon."

She was not asking. She was telling. From anyone else he might have resented it, but Sarama was Sarama. "And you?" he asked her. "Will you stay and wait for me?"

"I'm not your wife," she said. It was quick, and no thought in it, he did not think; she softened face and voice when she spoke again. "You know I go where the goddess bids me."

"I thought the goddess bade you come home, now that Old Woman is gone."

"To do what? Sit in a tent? Wear a veil? Be someone's wife?"

Agni did not see why she should be so angry. He certainly had said nothing to merit it. He chose to be calm, to say mildly, "Old Woman sat in the king's council and spoke when the goddess moved her to speak. Sometimes she stayed for a whole round of seasons. Isn't that what you came to do?"

"I came to show the king the cup of her skull," Sarama said, soft and too still. He read grief in it, and more of that inexplicable anger. Sarama was always angry at something. It seemed to be her nature—as it was with young mares, never a quiet moment, ears flat and teeth bared and hind feet restless always.

Stallions learned to avoid the mares when they were in such a mood, but Agni was a man. Men did not run away from women, even women in a temper. "So where will you go?" he asked. "Back to the goddess' hill?"

"No," said Sarama, again too quickly. "There's too much memory there."

"So you'll stay with us," he said. "Heal. Speak for the goddess when she asks. The people will be glad to have you back. They've been too long without Horse Goddess' word on them. Not all the foals are as fine as this one. Too many are born weak or dead, and those that live are too often flawed."

Sarama tossed her head in annoyance. "What, don't you so-wise men know how to breed horses? I saw the stallion who's been covering so many of the mares. Am I the only one who can see how poor a beast he is? His front legs are crooked and his hindlegs too straight. He's pretty, to be sure, with that sun-colored coat, but there's nothing worth keeping beneath it. It doesn't take the goddess to tell you to keep the hide and be rid of the horse, and find another sire for the herd."

"I said much the same," Agni told her, "and the men bade me mind my business. *You* could speak with honest authority."

"I'll speak," she said, "but I'm not staying here."

"So? Where will you go?"

"West," said Sarama. "Toward the setting sun. To the country in which women rule, and men bow their heads and obey."

.... 5 ....

Sarama had not truly known what she would say until she said it. That she could not stay—yes, she had known that, had known it since Yama accosted her and made her too keenly aware of her position among the people. Old Woman had had great power, that had kept the men at bay. Sarama was too young yet; and she had been born into a strong clan. Too strong, Old Woman had said. It had thought to master Horse Goddess through Sarama's mother. She had died in the battle. Sarama might not live, either, or live in captivity.

Then who would serve the goddess? Who would ride and love and tend the Mare? Not a man. The Mare would never suffer that. But the men might imagine that she would.

Sarama was not the people's servant. She had had to learn that. The goddess was her own self. The people of the White Horse were hers by virtue of their sign and symbol, but her servant did not belong to them. Just so did Sarama belong to the Mare, but the Mare did not belong to Sarama.

Now came the sign that Sarama had been waiting for, the words of a traveller who might be mad or a liar. Agni said as much, as she had expected him to do. Agni was her brother and she loved him, and he often understood her, but he was a man. In the end he thought as a man thinks, of owning and mastering. Even when men prayed, they bargained: this for that, prayer and worship in return for success in the hunt, perhaps, or strong healthy sons, or power among the people. They did not simply lay themselves open to the gods, to be done with as the gods willed.

The goddess had willed that she hear the tale of the sunset people. A land of women who were kings—yet a land that knew no horses. Sarama's heart beat faster at the thought of it. Surely these people would welcome her, and the Mare whom she served, whose lot in this place would be only to fade and vanish among the herds. Men never saw how the mares ruled, nor cared. They could only see the stallions' noise and vaunting.

Agni's voice startled her. She was halfway to the sunset already. "You can't go. What if you die on the road? You're the last of the Mare's people. What will she do without you?"

"Better than she would do here," Sarama said. "I met our eldest brother yesterday. He informed me that when he is king, I shall learn to be a proper woman. Our time is over, he meant me to understand. His time—the Stallion's time—is long since begun."

Agni's face flushed; his fists clenched. "And who says that Yama will be king?"

"Yama means to make sure of it," she said. "You have to go away—unless you win your horse, you can't claim authority over the White Horse people. Yama won his a good while since."

"Oh yes," Agni growled. "And it's said he did it less than honorably, too, by trapping a herd in a barren valley and starving it into submission—and the stallion died rather than submit; so he came home with a yearling colt. For certain the poor thing didn't last out the year, in such state as it was when he brought it in."

"Still, he won it," Sarama said. "The winning is all that matters. And he'll be here with the people while you wander far and long, hunting an honorable prey."

Agni did not look as if she had surprised him, except with her perception of things as they were. He must have thought her ignorant, or innocent at least, as far from the people as she had lived for so long. He said, "I have friends here. They'll be on watch. Our father will be alive when I come back, alive and in possession of the kingship. Then what will happen, will happen."

"Pray that it be so," said Sarama.

+ +

Muriadni's wedding was as wild as one could ask, even as wearied as people were by three days of festival and sacrifice. Agni whirled back into it from his conversation with Sarama, seized a cup as it went past and found it full of *kumiss*, drank it down and went in search of another. They had put the bride away once the marriage-words were spoken, hidden her in her tent as was proper, but the young women were still out and about, dancing their ring-dances and teasing the men with the flash of slim ankles and the clatter of their little finger-drums.

One pair of bright eyes called to him from a fall of shadow. They were not Rudira's, no, never; Rudira was a married woman. She must keep to her husband's tent. She would expect him there—but later. Not so early, not yet.

And these were very fine eyes, as green almost as grass. She who owned them wore the devices of the Red Deer people, and splendidly too, as if she were a chieftain's daughter. Her tunic was rich with beadwork. She glittered with gauds, brow and throat, ears and wrists and ankles. She might have been the bride herself, save that the hair unbound beneath the headdress with its disks of carved and painted bone, proclaimed her both unwed and unbetrothed.

She was hunting a husband, then, and from a covert, as it were. Agni was not hunting a wife—oh, no; not for a long while yet. Still they were enchanting, those eyes, even if they were not Rudira's, and he was warm with *kumiss*. What harm after all in honest worship of the gods? This at least was no man's wife, least of all his brother's.

She saw the light in his eye. The dance whirled him into her reach. He did not recall stretching out his arm, and yet she was caught in the curve of it, rich with the warm scent of woman.

She could not suffer that, not and be proper; indeed she must gasp in outrage and whirl out of his grasp. But not before she had whispered in his ear, "Out behind the tents. Come!"

He had to keep his face blank as the game required, and join in the dance for a while longer, then drink from the cup that was handed him, exchange a pleasantry with someone whom he forgot as soon as he was done. Only then might he begin to wander away.

The sun had set a little while since. The sky was wild with stars. The moon was waxing, a bright half-moon. Agni with his hunter's eyes needed no aid of torch or firelight to find his way out past the tents, out where the wind blew untrammeled across the world of grass. It was soft tonight, soft and cool, no winter in it.

She was waiting for him in the place that everyone knew, a hollow just far enough from the camp that no one could hear what one did there, and yet close in if there should be a raid—if there had been a war, which this year, by the gods' grace, there was not. She had spread her mantle on grass well beaten down by assignations before theirs, and arranged herself on it in all her finery. She had even—wise lady—brought a skin of *kumiss* and a pair of cups.

There was nothing either modest or shy about her. No dove's voice, either. Hers was clear and perhaps a little sharp, though he could tell she strove to soften it. "Good evening, my lord," she said, "and welcome."

"Well come indeed," said Agni. He was looming over her. He dropped to one knee, to bring their heads more level. Even in the dimness her eyes were bright. Fevered, he would have said; but was it not a fever, after all, that ran in the blood?

She let fall her veil. He was not greatly disappointed. Her features were like her voice, a little sharp, but well-shaped. She was not a beauty, not as Rudira was. Neither was she ugly.

Once her face was bared, her eyes seemed to grow shy. They lowered. "Am I ill to look at, my lord?"

"No," said Agni. "Oh, no. Not in the least."

"Perhaps," she said, "the rest of me will suit you better."

He drew breath, to protest perhaps; but the swiftness of her movement startled him into silence. She was on her feet, looming as he had loomed a moment before. She took off her garments one by one. It was a dance, meant to warm a man if he were not warmed to burning already. She danced it well, and yet she did not linger. As each garment fell, more of her revealed itself under the moon. Indeed she was fair, deep of breast, broad of hip, with strong round thighs: made for bearing sons.

At the last garment, the thin brief tunic of fine-tanned hide, she paused. Agni knelt unmoving. Too late he saw what she had wanted: for him to rip the tunic from her, to prove his passion.

Passion he had. His rod was stiff under his own tunic. Yet he was not quite reft of his wits. He was remembering a body far more slender, far whiter of skin, white as milk, as snow; but hot as the gods' own fire. This beside her was an ember among ashes. He began to think perhaps—after all—

Before he could finish the thought, she had caught the lacings at her throat and tugged them free, and skinned the tunic over her head. She stood naked before him. Her breasts were full double handfuls, the nipples as wide as a child's hand, and dark. Her hips were full as broad and deep as he had expected, centered with the triangle of her sex, thick hair and crisp like a horse's mane, strong with the scent of musk and woman.

A heat came off her, as if she were an open fire. The scent of her was dizzying. She lifted her breasts in her hands, weighed them as if they had been twin kids. "Am I not beautiful?" she demanded of him. "Is there a goddess who is as fair as I?"

A shiver ran down his spine. Even Rudira had never dared to speak so— though she had mocked her mortal husband often enough. His rod was as stiff as ever, as if a spell lay on it, the spell of those heavy breasts and that potent scent. Ill might a woman speak so of the immortals.

Maybe there was a goddess in her, possessing her. She advanced upon him. He did not move. No spell lay on him: he was sure of that. He liked to play before he mated; to laugh, to kiss, to tease, till they were both half blind with wanting one another. She seemed to know nothing of play. For her this was as grim as duty.

She did not wait for him to undress as she had done, as he might have liked to do. She caught at his belt, fumbling the clasp. It slipped free. She tugged down his trousers. Her breath came hard, as if she ran a race. "Come, my lord. Why do you dally? Am I ugly after all?"

"Not ugly in the least," he said, and that was true enough.

She bore him backward. He fell hard, hard enough to jar the breath from him. "*You* are beautiful," she said. "I've seen you, wanted you—oh, how I've wanted you! Have you wanted me?"

He did not answer. His voice was not back yet, though his rod had barely softened. She clasped it in her hand. Her grip was firm.

There was no way to tell her how he liked to do it. She would not listen. She bent over him, those big breasts swaying, veiling him in the curtain of her hair. Her breath was strong with *kumiss*. She had been drinking deep of it, perhaps to gather courage.

He wanted to laugh, but laughter would have offended her terribly. It did not do to offend a woman with one's manly staff in her hand. She rubbed and squeezed, squeezed and rubbed. What she roused was rather too much like pain.

His breath had come back, though it was caught in his throat. He used what there was of it to lift himself up, bearing her with him, till she lay beneath, he atop her. Her legs had locked about his middle. His shaft found what it had wanted, armed itself, plunged through a wall that tore, shredded, was gone.

She cried out. He nearly fell backward, but her arms were about him too, arms and legs pinning him, holding him fast. He was deep in her, the first that had ever done such a thing.

No wonder she had been so maladroit. She had been a maiden.

He was appalled. Of course every girl went virgin to her wedding, though the blood on the coverlet might be calves' blood, and even her husband might know where she had been before. But he had never danced this dance with a true maiden, a woman who had never known a man. That she was as old as she was, his own age surely or near to it, and so new to the dance—either she had father and brothers of exceptional ferocity, or she had kept herself for some useful purpose.

To snare a prince, perhaps?

She would not let him go. And all the while his thoughts raced on, frantic as a startled colt, he rode her as a man rides a woman. His body knew well what it should do, though the soul within it was all scattered and gone.

Ah well, he thought with what wits he had left: a shrug of the mind, accepting what he could not help. Let this first ride be as pleasurable as it could be, since she had forced it on him. He smiled down at her and stroked her hair, and was almost dismayed at the light in her eyes. He did not want her to love him; only to remember him with fondness. "There," he said, crooning it. "There now. Steady, steady."

So he would have spoken to a filly whom he was taming. She responded as the filly might, calming, easing into the dance, which was the oldest of all. She was well made for this, deep and strong, not small and tight as maidens were said to be. She had pleasure, he thought, or feigned it well: breath that quickened as his stroke quickened, and broke into soft cries, and of a sudden, as she arched beneath him, a muted shout.

His own breath caught just after, and he stilled, locked body to body.

She was, he realized without surprise, sobbing into his neck. Women did that, he had heard. Never women he chose—but then he had not chosen this one.

He freed himself carefully. She clung with desperate strength, but he was stronger. "You should have told me," he said as gently as he could.

It was not gentle enough. "Now you hate me!"

"I do not." But, he thought, he well could, if she kept on. He softened his voice as he might with a particularly aggravating filly whom he had in mind to train. "Come, sit up, wipe your face. You chose this. Are you truly sorry that you did it?"

"No!" she wailed. But she did sit up, and she did wipe her face—with her hair, which was nearest to hand.

He smiled at her. "You see? It only takes courage."

"I am a woman," she said. "I have no courage to find."

He snorted. "Oh come! It takes all the bravery in the world to face what women face, bearing and bringing forth children. They are the honor of their tribe, the good name of their family. They are a great thing, a strong thing, and let no man tell you otherwise."

"You are very strange," she said.

Yes; and she had stopped blubbering, which was a great relief. He shrugged. "I'm who I am. My mother wasn't . . . like other women. Nor is my sister."

"Ah," she said. "Yes. The Mare's servant. She rides about like a man, and has no modesty. All the girls are jealous of her."

"She would be amazed to hear that," Agni said.

"No, really! They are."

"Are you?"

She smiled a slow smile that reminded him of the girl who had so allured him, back among the tents. Then indeed she was beautiful. "I might be. But could she be here, where I am?"

Not naked, no, and not still warm with his loving. Agni conceded her the point.

He helped her up, helped her dress. She had recovered some of her bold spirit, he was pleased to see.

They could not go back together; that would betray too much. He left first, walking quickly. He did not look back.

Only when he was long gone did it strike him. He had never asked her name.

✦ ✦

Rudira could not have known what Agni had been doing. Nor did he think it wise to tell her. He went from the place of the lovers all the way to the river, and scrubbed himself clean before he went to her.

She was waiting where they had agreed, out beyond the tents, but far away from the place where Agni had gone with the woman of the Red Deer. She was wrapped in a mantle, a shadow in starlight. When he went to fold arms about her, she slipped away. "You're late," she said. Her voice was petulant.

"I came as soon as I could," Agni said.

"That was not soon enough," said Rudira. "There's no time to do anything now. I have to be back in the tent when *he* comes back. He asked for me tonight. He told me to wear the amber that he gave me."

"I thought," said Agni, "that we agreed: you'll not be going to him."

"I never agreed to that," she said. "He's my husband. When he asks, I have to obey."

He seized her shoulders before she could escape, and held her tight, though she made no effort to resist him. "You don't have to let him ask you!"

Somewhere in the flurry of movement, the mantle had slipped from her hair. Her face was a pale glimmer, her eyes paler still. She looked like nothing mortal. But her voice was altogether of earth. "He is my husband."

"That never mattered to you before."

"And did it matter that I was waiting, when you went into the night with that slut from the Dun Cow?"

"She was never from the Dun Cow," Agni had said before he thought. He bit his tongue, but the words were out.

She hissed and sprang. He caught her before her clawed nails could rake his face; caught her and fastened his lips on hers. She twisted, but he was stronger. With a sound like a moan, deep in her throat, she set about eating him alive.

This—oh, gods, this was fire. With the woman of the Red Deer he had known but a glimmer of warmth. This was a white heat. The touch of her lips, of her hands, roused him as none other ever had. Or, he thought— wished, vowed—ever would.

They tumbled in the grass, reckless of any who might hear. She was naked under the mantle; wonderful, wanton creature. Her white body glimmered in the starlight. His own, darker, heavier, joined with it. Her eyes gleamed silver. "You," he said, or gasped. "You are—"

"I am all that is," she said, calm as one may be at a truth that is inarguable.

"Gods," he said. "Oh, gods."

"Goddess," she said. And when he would have said more, she swooped and seized him and drowned him again, and yet again, in her kiss.

.... 6 ....

Sarama lived in the camp as one who both belongs and does not belong. She had a place to sleep, she was fed, more often than not she knew the names of the people who greeted her when she went here or there. That she knew more of the horses than of the people did not concern her greatly. Horses were more interesting by far than the run of human folk.

Those who were her kin, or rather her father's kin, his wives and children, had little to do with her. Except for Yama her brothers did not trouble her; the sisters and the wives mostly let her be. The children followed her about,

but children always did that; and them she would speak to. They were eager
to learn, pelting her with questions, which she was glad to answer.

Of the king her father she saw as little as any woman did who was not
one of his wives. Even they, unless they were favorites, saw him only when
he called for them, and then only to wait on him of a day or to please him
of a night. His daughters were never regarded. She doubted if he even knew
how many he had.

He was reckoned merciful, perhaps too much so, for that he suffered
them all to live, nor had commanded that they be drowned in the river or
set out on the steppe for the wolves to dispose of. Sarama did not know if it
was mercy or simple absentmindedness. She did not know him, not well. He
had always had eyes only for her brother.

Men and their sons, she used to think. Then she had seen other fathers
doting over their daughters, and decided that her father was odder than most.
Maybe it was that he was a king; a king must be unlike other men.

After she knew in her heart that she must go to find the sunset people,
she knew another thing, a thing that pleased her rather less. She could not
simply ride away. She must stand face to face with the king, and understand
. . . something. What it was, she did not know; only that she must do it.

In the end she went to him not as a petitioner while he sat in the circle
on his royal horsehide, nor as a feaster among feasters in the firelit evening,
but as a daughter to her father. She approached him as was permitted a
woman, in the morning after he had risen and been dressed but before he
went out among the men. Then he would summon this or that wife or daughter to keep him company, and would break his fast, sometimes with a friend,
sometimes alone.

Today he had with him his eldest wife and a handful of her daughters—all
sisters of Yama, daughters of his mother, and one strikingly pale creature
whom she remembered, vaguely, as one of Yama's wives.

His sisters and his mother were as large as he and as good to look at,
but none of them had his half-finished look. They eyed Sarama narrowly as
she approached the king's dining place. There was no friendship in their gaze,
but no enmity either. They were reserving judgment. The wife was slender
and icily lovely. She might have seemed a pretty fool, vapid with her white
skin and her wide colorless eyes, and yet Sarama thought that there might be
more to her than met the eye.

Here, thought Sarama, was the strength that she had not seen in Yama.
She would have been willing to wager that these women had set Yama on
her, and told him what to say.

This was not the wisest or best time, perhaps, to speak to the king. But
nothing would free her from the intrigues of the women's side; and while
she had these in front of her, she could know precisely what they knew.

She inclined her head therefore, first to the king and then to his wife and
daughters, and last, but not least, to Yama's wife. They inclined theirs in
return. It was simple courtesy, nor could they properly refuse it.

The king smiled at her. In the tent's dimness, without the high horned
headdress to lift him up above simpler men, she could see how old he was,

how grey and worn he had become. The long braids of his hair were thin and dulled to ash. Deep lines were carved in his cheeks, cleaving into the grey-shot beard. His eyes under the heavy brows were clouded.

Perhaps, she thought, and that thought was cold and still, Yama had had the right of it. This was a Ninth Year. A king who faded, whose strength was failing, should mount the Stallion and ride him into the gods' country. He should not linger, should not weaken the tribes with his weakness.

No. The man was aging, no one could doubt it. But his shoulders were straight. His eyes though dimmed saw clear enough. His voice was strong, his mind unblurred. "Sarama," he said. "Daughter. Are you well?"

"I am well," she said.

He smiled. "Good," he said. "Good."

Sarama fought the urge to wriggle as she had done when she was small, when her father had summoned her for this reason or that. Their conversation then as now had proceeded in fits and starts, in twitches of discomfort. They had never known what to say to one another.

She wished that she had brought Agni with her, though he might well have chosen to hinder her. Agni was his father's favorite. Anything that he asked, the old man would grant.

But Agni was off doing whatever a young man did in the morning. Sarama had only herself to look to. She drew a deep breath. "Sir," she said, "I'm going away."

He blinked at her. Whatever he had expected her to say, clearly it had not been that. She fancied that she could see Agni in him then, in the startled expression, perhaps somewhat in the line of cheek and jaw under the grizzled beard. "And where will you go?" he asked, much as Agni had before him.

"West," she answered, "where the goddess leads me."

"West? To the sunset countries?"

Sarama half-smiled. So he did listen when people talked around him, though he never seemed to. "To the sunset countries," she agreed, "where they know nothing of Horse Goddess. She calls me there."

"We had thought you would stay here," he said.

"I go where the goddess bids," said Sarama.

He nodded. He looked senile then, falling asleep where he sat, with his gimlet-eyed wife and too-silent daughters about him, staring. But beneath the thicket of grey brows, Sarama saw the gleam of his eyes. He was watching her.

Old fox, she would have said had they been alone, *you watch us all, don't you? And what do you think of your sons who would be king?*

But she could not say such a thing in this company. She said instead, "Your blessing would set me well upon my way."

He stirred as if she had roused him from a doze, but it was as she had suspected: his eyes were bright, no sleep in them. "And what would you do with my blessing, goddess-child?"

"Be glad of it," she answered, "O my father."

"You look," he mused, "like your mother. Oh, indeed, very like her.

You think as she thought, too. She was a most interesting woman, was my beautiful Surti."

"She was the last of her people," Sarama said. "Now there will be no others."

"There is you," said the king.

"And is there none of your blood in me?"

"Some said," said the king, "that she conceived of the dawn wind, as mares are said to do—as if the stallions had no part in it. But the boy is mine. There was never any doubt of that."

"So too am I," Sarama said. "The goddess made me, but your seed was her instrument. Of that she has assured me."

He regarded her in silence for a moment. "You believe that you speak truth," he said. "Perhaps it is so." He lifted his hand, she thought to bless her—she bowed her head for it—but he waved her away, irritably. "Go. Go! Do as you must. I was never given authority over you, not even as a father. Horse Goddess took all of you from the moment you were born."

But she would not go, not without what she had asked. "And your blessing?"

"You have it," he said. "Now and always. Now go."

Then she went, not for obedience, but because she had what she had come for. Not only a blessing. An acknowledgment.

✦ ✦

The king did not walk out and about, not in these days. Therefore it was a profound shock to Agni to be minding his business near his father's tent, fletching a quiverful of arrows, and to look up as a shadow fell over him, and to see his father's face bent down. The king regarded his work with interest. He took up an arrow that Agni had finished, weighed and balanced it, nodded. "Good work," he said.

Agni considered various forms of obeisance, settled for the inclination of the head that he had seen his sister use. It seemed his father knew it: that was a smile lurking under the beard. He sat on his heels with none of the stiffness that one might expect, took up one of the arrows as yet unfletched, began deftly to cut and fit the grey dove-feathers to the readied shaft.

It was strange, Agni thought, and perhaps intended; but the king was alone. He was dressed like any man of the tribes, no mark on him that he was king. The many who saw him only seated in state with his tall crown on his head might never have known him as he was now, crouched companionably with the prince, performing a task that any mortal hunter could do. He was good at it, too. Agni wondered if he practiced when he was shut up in kingly solitude, making and fletching arrows that he would never use, simply for the occupation they gave his hands.

Agni wanted to be king. But not for a long while yet. Not till he was old himself, and weary of the hunt and the raid, and ready to sit on a well-tanned horsehide and wear a tall heavy crown and be father to the gathering of the tribes.

They worked in silence. Agni was quicker but the king was surer, his skill honed with years and patience. When the last pair of arrows had gained their wings, the king said, "Your sister is going away."

Agni nodded.

"She has never been here," the king said. "Never in spirit. She was always with the Old Woman, being servant to the goddess. Odd that it matters now, how far she will go, and where."

"She wants to bring Horse Goddess to people who never knew her," Agni said.

"So she told me," said the king. He paused. "And where will you go, my son?"

So, thought Agni. That was his trouble. "I have to hunt my horse," he said, "or never be reckoned a man."

"Indeed. And will you hunt westward?"

"There are no free horses in the west, Father," Agni said.

The king sighed. "No. There are not. You would do well to hunt north; there's a herd, an old one, that some say descends from stock that bred the Mare. For all that any of us knows, the Mare herself came from it."

Agni bit his tongue. The Mare came from such a herd, he had no doubt; but not the one his father spoke of. There was a band that ran the steppe near the goddess' hill, a band of greys, with here and there a black or a bay. But he could not speak of that. It was a mystery. He only knew it because he had crept out there when he was supposed to be hunting, and he had found the herd and known it for what it was. He might have died for that, but he was twinborn with Sarama. The stallion did not fall on him with battering hooves, nor did the Elder Mare leave him broken in the grass. She chased him off as she might a stranger of her own kind, a yearling colt who had gone prying into things that were not fit for him to know.

He had never told anyone of that. He did not tell the king now—no, though this was his father and his king. He said, "Yes, perhaps it could be, that the Mare knew that herd. I'll go hunting there, though it's a stallion I'll be hunting."

"That is well," the king said. "And yet—I could wish that there were horses in the west."

"Pray I find my stallion quickly," said Agni, "and I'll go after her, if it will please you, and see that she's safe."

The king's face lit, but then it darkened. "No," he said. "No. She'd hate us both for that. Horse Goddess will protect her. Hasn't she always been so guarded?"

"Always," Agni agreed.

They sighed together, the old man and the young. Agni feared for his sister, and yet it warmed him, to see that his father shared his fear. If prayers could guard her, she would go warded as if with an army.

He laughed inside himself. *She* would never believe it, nor welcome it either. She was too fiercely her own creature, like a boy who must always be proving himself a man. Small enough wonder, that, since she was what she was; but she should trust in the goddess. She had more power than perhaps she knew, and more influence among the tribes.

Someday she would know it. Then Agni would be king, and would have to contend with her. He almost dreaded it—and he was almost glad of it.

If Yama seized the kingship instead . . .

As if he had spoken the thought aloud, the king said, "Your brother Yama is an ambitious man."

Agni's hands clenched into fists. "Yes," he said. "He says—he is the eldest."

"And some say that the eldest born should inherit, and not the firstborn of a man's kingship." The king's eyes glinted. "And you? Do you say as much?"

"I say," said Agni, "that in our tribe a man may choose his heir. In other tribes, the law may differ."

"In, for example, the tribe from which Yama took his wife?"

Agni did not know why his heart had begun to beat so hard. No one knew what he did with Rudira. That was their secret, between the two of them. No one had ever seen them, or caught them, or guessed—

He mastered himself. He was calm. He said coolly, "Which, Father? He has several."

"I think you know," said the king.

Agni held tight to his expression of innocence. "If I do, then I don't know I know it."

"Liar," the king said mildly. "Some say she's a witch, did you know that? Perala's white-haired daughter, with her skin the color of bone, and her eyes of winter ice. When he came looking for a husband for her, he asked for you."

Agni's breath hissed between his teeth. "He did not!" he burst out, and not wisely either.

"Oh, indeed he did," said the king. "But I refused. You were too young, I said; truthfully enough. I offered him my eldest in your place."

Agni sat where he had been sitting for the past hour and more. He could not breathe. Just so it had been when he was thrown from his pony, when he was young and uncertain of his balance. The wind struck out of him. No air, no breath, no life. And no thought either, except an echoing emptiness.

Words rushed to fill it. "Why? Why did you do that?"

"Because," said the king, "she was not good enough for you. Not for your first wife. For a second or a third wife, for the likes of Yama—for that, she served well enough."

"There may be more to her than you think," Agni said, almost too low for the other to hear.

But the king heard it. He laughed: light and free and surprisingly young. "She is a beauty, isn't she? Beauty can make up for much. But intelligence and wit—those are rarer."

"Rarest of all," said Agni, "is the woman like a creature of fire."

"Not so rare," the king said, "or even so wonderful, in the cold light of day. It's not the wildfire that makes a chief of wives. That's for the lesser wives, or for the women one takes on a whim."

"Not always," Agni muttered.

The king fixed him with a keen and all too piercing stare. "You are young," he said, "and your blood is hot. Have a care how you let it burn."

Agni had no answer for that. Evidently the king expected none. He rose, stretching as a young man stretches, no stiffness of age. "Look to yourself," he said, "and be prudent. Few wars are more bitter than the war of brother against brother."

"If there is war," Agni said, "it will not be I who start it."

"No?" asked the king. "Perhaps you already have."

While Agni sat mute, the king left him, walking back straight and tall to his tent. Only when he was near to it, as he came in sight of a circle of hangers-on, did his head bow, his shoulders droop, his firm steps shorten to a shuffle.

Senile, was he? Weak and wandering, had Yama said? Yama would be most dismayed to discover his error. Nor did Agni have any doubt that he would. The king had as much as promised to make sure of it.

It would please Agni greatly to see his brother discomfited as he himself had been. By the gods, how had the king known? Unless Rudira—

And if not Rudira, then who? Who else could know? Would that one betray him to Yama as to the king?

The world was a dangerous place. Agni had known it when first he met his brother's youngest wife, when their eyes had met and he had felt the fire wake in her; and known, quite simply, that he would have this woman. Honor, prudence, even life be damned. He *would* have her.

.... 7 ....

Sarama left without ceremony, packed up her few belongings and saddled the Mare and rode away. But her leaving did not go unregarded. When she sought the Mare, she found another beast there also, a thick-legged sturdy gelding, and a laden pack with him. Her father's gift, and his blessing.

It was strange to know so late that her father had some care for her existence. It warmed her a little, more than the sun could account for.

Agni was not there to see her go. No one was. Only the two horses amid the many, and the wind and the sky. She slipped the bridle over the Mare's ears and smoothed the heavy forelock, and fastened the girth tight, binding the saddle-fleece to the broad dappled back. The Mare lipped her palm. Sarama had brought her a small dainty from the king's tent, a bit of honey sweet. She took it greedily but did not protest when Sarama sprang onto her back. The steppe called her as it called Sarama, luring her away from the rising sun.

They left without regret. The Mare had no herd here. If there had been a stallion, he was forgotten in the passing of her season. Sarama had not even that. Only her brother.

Well. She had left without speaking to anyone, packed up and simply

gone. Yet if her father had known that she would be going now, surely
Agni—

Foolishness. They had no need of words, they two, least of all words of
farewell.

She tightened her grip on the packhorse's lead and urged the Mare to a
quicker pace. It was a long, long way to the sunset country; the sooner she
was set on it, the quicker she would come there.

The camp of the tribes sank swiftly behind her, vanishing into the sea of
grass. She followed the line of the sun, at first behind and then before her.
By that and by subtle changes in the land, the lift of a hill, the curve of a
valley, she knew her way. When night came, the stars would guide her.

She fell into an easy rhythm of travel, a rhythm that she had learned long
ago under the Old Woman's tutelage: sitting easy on the Mare's back, letting
the long smooth strides carry her through the ripple of grass. She could
drowse so, if she had need, or ride in a half-dream, resting her spirit while
her body was carried onward. Then she was the Mare, and the Mare was
herself, running light, skimming the earth with her hooves. The wind was in
her nostrils, streaming in her mane. The myriad scents of the world flowed
through it. They told her stories, whole cycles of sagas. She could lose herself
in them, give herself up to them.

The Mare snorted. Her head lifted. She was walking just then, resting
from an exuberant gallop. The wind brought her a tale that made her prick
her ears and call out.

A call rang in reply. The Mare rounded the curve of a hill, ears pricked
forward, dragging the packhorse behind her—he was not as sure as she was,
that this was anything he wanted to see.

And there they all were, a swirling, whooping crowd of them, the young
men of the White Horse, with Agni in their midst, whooping the loudest of
anyone. A few had won their stallions. Most had yet to do it, and rode their
geldings with a grand insouciance.

Sarama laughed to see them, laughed till the tears ran. It was not mockery. It was joy. Her brother had always known how best to surprise her—
and this was wonderful.

They had made a camp on the steppe, a hunting-camp: stone-lined square
of firepit, tethered or hobbled horses, cloaks spread to mark each man's place
and his weapons and his belongings. To this and in her honor they had added
a spit on which turned a fine young buck, prize of someone's hunting; and
there was *kumiss,* and a skin of sweet berry wine.

Sarama burned to be going, but she could not refuse such courtesy. Not
when they sat her in the chieftain's place, plied her with cups of wine and
kumiss, and fed her morsels of venison wrapped in flat bread that they had
made of wild grain and baked on stones in the fire. She ate till she could hold
no more, remembered almost too late a politeness of the men's side, belched
enormously to signify her pleasure in the feast. They cheered her every move.

And in the camp, she thought somewhat wryly, they had barely acknowledged her presence.

Her eye found her brother. Agni had been sitting beside her, but had got up to fetch another skin of *kumiss*. It was for him they did this, because she was his sister. The worship they accorded her was in part for the goddess, but in much greater part for their prince.

They would make a fine warband, come the day, puppies though they were now. Those overlong legs and great clumping feet and patchy beards would not persist forever. One day soon, these would be men, good men, men whom a king might delight to call his own.

She had not drawn a circle or cast the bones, nor done anything to call up the spirit, but it had entered her nonetheless. The goddess' closeness opened the door to the lesser power. Her body had gone numb as the spirit took it, raising it to its feet, standing till the laughter and shouting stopped. All the *kumiss*-blurred eyes had caught and held. That was the spirit, too, possessing them, a little, through the gate of their drunkenness.

When she had silence, she took it to herself for a while, cherishing it. Then she let it go. She said, "I thank you, men of the White Horse, for the honor you show me. Now I go—but where I go, I bid you not follow."

She glanced at Agni as she spoke. He was clearer-headed than the others, watching her fixedly, as if to remember every line of her.

"Do not follow me," she said again. "Your place, your world, is here. If I can come back I will. Never come looking for me. If you must hunt men, for men are great prey—hunt east and south and north. Shut your eyes to the west. What is there belongs to another. If you presume to reach for it, you may win a victory. For a while. But in the end the west will conquer."

"In the end," said Agni, his voice soft and slow, "the west will be conquered. You look too close, sister. Look far, and see how it must be."

Sarama frowned. So. Her spirit had a rival, did it? And speaking through her brother, too. She had not known that Agni had the gift. As far as she had ever known, Agni was a prince, a leader of men, a tamer of horses—but of the things that Sarama did and understood, he knew nothing.

She should have looked closer when she was with the tribe, to see what in truth her brother was. He made her a gift of it now, a gift of defiance. "I see," she said to him, "how far you look. Ages, my brother. Years out of count. I speak of *now*. I speak of what will happen to you, to your living self, if you do what you more than half think to do. Were I marching against these people with intent to conquer, I would welcome your army. Yet I am not. I am following where my goddess leads. She has not called you, nor given you leave to go."

"I am not her servant," Agni said, "though I honor her as she deserves."

"You will stay," she said. "You will be king when our father is dead. That is the fate laid out for you. Mine is another entirely."

"Maybe," Agni said. He shrugged, sighed. She saw how the spirit ran out of him as if drained from a cup. It was not defeated, she was not fool enough to think that. It had simply said all that it wished to say.

The spirit in her was inclined to linger. But she was not. She bowed to her brother and then to them all, a slow sweep of the body. She smiled, because after all they had meant well, and they were a fine pack of hunting hounds. "You have given me a great gift," she said: "such a leavetaking as even a king might envy. I'll take it with me into the sunset country. And if anyone asks what courtesies the young men of the White Horse know, I can tell them an honest truth: that you are courteous and most kind. These virtues will serve you well."

She feared for a moment that Agni might press her to take them with her after all, but he refrained. She was proud of him for that. "Go with the gods, sister," he said, "and come home safe again."

Neither would know after, which of them began it; only that they embraced and kissed each other on both cheeks, as close kin might do. Agni did not at once let her go. He held her in a fierce grip, strong enough almost for pain. "Come back," he said. "Please. Say that you'll come back."

She could not say it. But she could say, "Wherever I am, whatever I grow to be, I'll always remember you. Tarry well, brother. Be king for me."

"I do intend to," he said.

She laughed at that, with a catch in it, which they all pretended not to hear. "The gods love a man who knows his mind," she said. She kissed him once again, for luck, and slipped out of his grasp.

Even after she had reclaimed her horses and sought again the westward way, he stood where she had left him, with his friends about him. He looked like a king: a very young one, but surer of his strength than anyone knew, least of all himself.

The gods would protect him as they chose. She turned her back on him and her face toward the westward horizon. There she must go. There she would go, of her own and the goddess' will.

II

LADY OF THE BIRDS

.... 8 ....

EVERY MORNING THE Mother went out, soft-footed in the dawn, and sang the sun into the sky. For all the years of his life the sound of her voice had roused Danu from sleep, that high sweet singing, calling the light back into the world. When he was small he had thought that no one was alive or aware till the Mother sang; that the night was a vast emptiness shot with dreams, and only she could make the world real again, or give life to the people in it.

Now that he was a man, he knew that he had seen true—but that it was also true that people could lie awake in the dark, beset with this fret or that, and wait for the long night to end and the sun to come back. The sun would do that no matter what the Mother did. She was a great witch and priestess, and magic was the air she breathed; but the sun was a god, and greater than she.

Still he was comforted by the sound of her rising, the soft pad of her bare feet on the floor, the opening and shutting of the door as she went out to the Lady's place. Sometimes he would rise from his bed and stand in his doorway and watch her go. She would smile then, beautiful and serene, with her great breasts that had nourished a round dozen children, and her ample belly, and her huge round thighs. And he would smile back, content with the ordered round of his world.

On this morning, a clear morning of spring with the promise of summer in it, Danu woke gasping from a dream of fire. Fire and shouting, and thunder, and a bright river of blood. He lay for a long while, struggling to breathe, to fit the world about him again. Dark world, gentle world, cry of a night bird, rustle of the Mother's pallet as she rose to greet the sun.

There was no haste in her movements, no tremor of fear, no sign that she had dreamed as he had dreamed. It had beset him with the force of a true-dream, or such as he had heard they were. But the Mother had not dreamed it. How then could it be true? Men did not see past the veils of the world. That gift was given to women.

He wished that he could be surer of that; that he could thrust aside the conviction that this dream came not from the night spirits but from the Lady herself. It was terrible arrogance, to think such a thing.

He stumbled to his feet. His skin felt too thin, as if a breath would tear it.

The Mother passed by, soft padding of feet, faint ripple in the door-curtain. Danu moved without thought, softer even than she, following her out into the chill of the morning.

The light was dim and grey yet oddly clear. The stars were fading. Light glimmered along the eastern horizon, over the walls and roofs of the city. It was the greatest city of the Lady's country, where one could stand atop a roof and see a city on every side. Her people were rich in cities, rich in copper and gold, in fine weavings and work of hands, in songs and magic. This was the richest of them all; and the Mother was lady of it, in the Lady's name.

She walked down the street from her house to the Lady's shrine, that stood higher and prouder than any other. Its walls were painted with holy things, wings and eyes of birds, fishes, shapes of women and does, she-goats and ewes, and over and over, the image of the Spiral Dance. Strangers grew dizzy at sight of it. Danu had been born inside it, had grown up with it before him. To him it was merely itself.

The Mother entered through the lesser door. Danu was a man grown; he could not follow. He sat on the doorstep, shivering slightly with the morning's chill, clasped his knees and rocked and waited till she should ascend the tower.

Then it came, the thing that he had waited for. The high clear call like the cry of a bird, and the ripple of pure notes thereafter. Words grew out of them. They were older than anyone living could remember, as old, some said, as the world. The meaning was all worn away from them.

But not the power. That was strong with the strength of ages. It rang in her voice. It hummed through Danu's bones and thence into the earth. It called the sun into the sky.

The blaze of it, the pure daily glory, made Danu weep. It washed away the memory of fire, and stripped the dream of its terror.

The Mother's voice fell silent. Danu sighed faintly. Well before she came out of the temple, he was gone.

✦ ✦

His sister was waiting for him, sitting on his rumpled bed in her fine red skirt and her striped shawl. She had been gone the night long—dancing the dance with Kosti-the-Bull, Danu could well guess. Women always had that look of creamy contentment after a night with Kosti.

Danu ignored her in his quest for a clean tunic. She was sitting on the one he had wanted, but he had another, if he could remember where he had put it.

"In the chest," Tilia said. "Under the cloak with the hole in it."

Danu shot her a burning glance. Of course the tunic was where she had said it was. "You've been in my things again," he said.

She shrugged, unrepentant. "I was looking for a shawl to wear to the Planting Dance. What did you do with the one Mother made for you, with the birds woven on it?"

Danu showed her his teeth. "I hid it," he said. "I'm keeping it for a morning-gift."

"Oh!" she said brightly. "Are you going to get Chana to ask for you, then?"

He flushed hotly but kept his head up. "Chana doesn't want *me*. She's after Kosti."

That was nasty, but Tilia only laughed. "Oh, is she? Poor Chana. Such a stick of a girl, and Kosti, as everybody knows, prefers a woman with substance."

Danu thought Chana lovely as a willow is lovely, lissome and slender, but he was not going to say so to Tilia. Tilia was beautiful as a woman well should be, as the Mother was beautiful, great-breasted and broad-hipped, with wonderfully potent thighs. She would be Mother in her own time, would speak before the goddess for the people of this city, and the Mothers of the lesser cities would look to her for wisdom.

But that was far away in the round of years. She was young yet, and neither as wise nor as imposing as she fancied she was. Danu pulled the tunic over his head and raked fingers through his wild curly hair, taming it somewhat with a bit of leather wound and knotted at his nape.

Tilia watched with frank appreciation. "You really are a pretty thing," she said. "Why would you want to waste yourself on Chana? You could have yourself a woman of worth in the world. It's only right, after all, since you're the Mother's son. You owe it to her name."

Danu had not the faintest intention of wasting himself on Chana, who was pretty to look at but dull to listen to—unless one was fascinated by minutiae of trading in fine clay pots. Chana meant to be very rich, and likely would be, though her family was nothing in particular.

Because it would drive Tilia wild, Danu said, "Chana will be richer than the lot of us. Wait and see. And shouldn't I be looking for a woman with ambition?"

Tilia snorted in disgust. "Oh, you men are always thinking—with your manly parts. It's well women speak first to the goddess; if it were left to men, there'd be nothing in the world but mating and squabbling."

"You mate well, I'm told," Danu said sweetly, "and you squabble famously." He ducked the blow she aimed at him, laughed and danced aside and out the door, and left her cursing his impudence.

＋ ＋

In some parts of the Lady's country, young men were given nothing to do, or were cast out to run in packs like dogs. Not so in the Mother's city. There everyone, even the least regarded boychild, had a task and a place. Danu's was to tend the Mother's house and to run her errands as she required of him. It was a great task, and a great trust. He was well aware of the honor she did him.

This morning there was considerable to do: it was a washing-day and a baking-day, and later a guest would come, the Mother of a city to the westward. Danu roused the Mother's acolytes: new since the Planting Dance, awkward and sullen, resentful that they must do the bidding of anyone but the Mother herself. The menservants were at their tasks already and long since.

The last of the ill dream faded beyond recall, lost in the day's brightness. When the washing had been brought up from the river smelling of sun and of the grass it had been spread on to dry, and the bread and honeycakes and the guest-cakes were made and set to cool, Danu sent the acolytes to wait on the Mother, and the menservants to take an hour's leisure, and set himself free to wander down to the market. It was, after all, a duty of his. He brought a little wool to trade, a bead or two, even a bit of copper if he should find something irresistible.

At this hour, just after noon of a fair day in spring, the market was humming. A trading party had come in from the east, bringing furs and tanned leather and ivory; and there were weavers with fine wool of the northern cities; and it was a day for the livestock market, a tumult of lowing and bleating, haggling and crying of wares. Danu loved the liveliness of it, the babble of voices, the unexpectedness of a new thing and the familiarity of an old one side by side in the broad market square.

He bought a thing or two that he or the house had needed, and a frippery for Chana, mostly to spite his sister; then in a fit of remorse he bought another for Tilia.

Some others of the young men were out and about, freed or on errands. Danu wandered past a favorite place of theirs, a stall that offered middling bad wine for a middling decent exchange. A twist of wool gained him a cup and a sop of bread to dip in it, and a place on the bench between that stall and the next.

One or two others were there already. They slid down to make room for him, smiling or lifting a cup in greeting. He settled into their companionship, which was mostly silence, with lowered eyes when a woman walked past. Sometimes she would stare, and they would try not to look as if they noticed.

Danu ate his bread and drank his wine, and sat for a little while, enjoying the contentment of full stomach, warm sun, leisure that must end soon—but not yet.

Others had come while he ate, till there was a fair gathering of them, the sons of the elders and such of the weavers and potters who could escape for a little while from their labors. With so many, the silence could not last; ripples of chatter ran down the line, rumors, gossip, snatches of stories. Of late it had too often been the same story, one that had come out of the east.

A stranger had come to the city called Running Waters, near the wood that rimmed the world. He had come through the wood, he said in signs and gestures and snatches of traders' speech, he in his leather and furs, with his stone knives and his bold manners. The people of the wood had let him pass, as sometimes they did, on a whim or for curiosity: to see what the cities would make of him.

He was a savage, ignorant of true speech, and he reeked like an ill-kept animal. But savages were not as uncommon as that, though mostly they came from north or south rather than from the east. Strangest and most wonderful were the beasts that he brought with him, huge creatures, hooved like cattle but shaped to carry a man on their backs. *Horses,* he called them.

"Great as a bull," Kosti was saying; and he would know, since he was himself. "Strong as one, too, but fast—faster than any man can run. Whole tribes of them ride on these *horses,* the savage said, racing the wind across their plains of grass."

"I think they're the dead," said Shuai, whose mother was one of the singers before the goddess. "Only the dead can outrun the wind. That was a ghost come to trouble us all."

"Ghost or dark spirit," someone else said; Danu did not see who it was. People murmured, agreeing, disagreeing. No one argued. They did that in less public places, where the women could not hear and disapprove.

Everyone was full of this story of the stranger and his beasts. Ghosts at least one could believe in. Savages, surely. But horses? What sort of animal was as tall as the temple, as swift as light on water, with a hide like living copper?

"Like fire," Kosti said. Kosti had not seen the horses, but he had been sopping up stories as bread sops wine, and remembering them all. It gave him something to do, Danu thought uncharitably, between flexing his muscles in the smithy and being a bull for the women. "Red as fire, and gleaming like copper in the forge. They're gods, it's said, or the children of gods."

"Goddess," Rami said. "That's what I heard. He said *Horse Goddess.*"

"How could he say that," Shuai demanded, "if he didn't speak any language of the living?"

"He had a few words," said Rami. "Traders' words. And he saw an image of the Lady, and he kept pointing to it and saying *Horse,* and then a word nobody knew. Why not *Goddess?*"

"She is everywhere," Kosti said. People nodded, agreeing with him, as was proper piety.

Danu stood up abruptly. "I believe there was a stranger," he said. "I believe he came out of the wood, and the people of the wood let him pass. I do not believe he brought anything with him but a cow or two, or maybe a deer. A tame deer—my sister had one once. What's so remarkable about that?"

They stared at him. He was not given to sudden speech or to outbursts of temper. But something about this story, endlessly repeated, put him straight out of patience. "It's a story," he said, "told and retold till there's no telling truth from wild rumor. Ghosts!" he snorted. "Spirits—yes, spirits of folly. What does any of it have to do with us? What should we care?"

He left them still staring, with a new tale to tell among themselves: how the Mother's son had lost his temper over nothing at all. They would wonder, he had no doubt, which woman had provoked it, and laugh behind their hands, and look to see who singled him out at the next fire-dance. Then they would think they knew why he had been so unwontedly cross-grained.

It was nothing to do with women. He disliked the story, that was all, and the monotony of its repetition. There was something else, a memory that fled before he could grasp it, a flicker of fear from nowhere that he could discern.

"Savages," he muttered. "Horses. Who dreamed such a word? It doesn't mean anything. It's air and nothing."

He did not feel better for having said it. But duty—that calmed him. He had delayed unconscionably. The Mother from Larchwood city would be here, and nothing would be ready for her. He quickened his pace even as he stilled his mind, putting aside both temper and fear. By the time he came to the Mother's house, he was almost his quiet self again.

.... 9 ....

The Mother from Larchwood city arrived in state, well before sundown but well after the Mother of Three Birds was ready for her. She did great honor in the size of her company: not only a fair handful of her daughters but even a few of her sons, with acolytes and servants, friends and companions, and a flock of sheep and goats to aid in feeding them all.

The Mother of Three Birds received her guest at the edge of her city, where the last houses looked over the green swell of the fields. She had her daughters with her, and her acolytes, and such of the elders as could be spared from duties about the city.

Tilia held the place of honor at the Mother's left hand, her heart-hand, as befit the one who would be Mother in her time. She had not met the Mother from Larchwood before. Larchwood was far away, almost to the eastern edge of the world. It was a remarkable thing for a Mother to come so far simply, as the messengers had said, to visit and pay respect to the greatest of the Mothers in the heart of the world. Remarkable but not, thought Tilia, incomprehensible. Everyone knew that Three Birds was the greatest city in the world.

She kept her place and a properly respectful silence, but her eyes and her mind were well occupied. The stranger-Mother was older than her own, and never so vastly beautiful. Nor were her daughters as lovely as the daughters of Three Birds. The one who stood in the heir's place was a slender whip of a thing, hardly more substance to her than there was to Chana. Surely a Mother's heir should be an image of the Mother, not of the young larch-tree from which her city took its name.

The stranger was eyeing Tilia, too—admiring Tilia's beauty, surely, and judging her fitness to rule. Mothers' heirs must do such things. It was their duty.

Tilia smiled at her, because that also was duty. She barely smiled back. Either she was a sour-faced creature by nature, or something troubled her almost beyond the bounds of politeness.

Mother embraced Mother with much ceremony. They blessed one another in the goddess' name, spoke the words of greeting and of welcome. The Mother of Three Birds took the Mother from Larchwood by the hand then and led her into the city, a gesture that made her free of it, and named her friend and sister.

Tilia took the daughter's hand in turn. It was thin and rather cold. Tilia could read nothing from it or from the face beside hers, except that this Catin's mind was troubled.

There would be time to ask. Now was time for ceremony, for procession through the city to the Goddess' house, for the blessing and the solemn dance that would bind Larchwood and Three Birds in amity thereafter. One might converse in the processional, but Catin appeared to have no conversation. She walked mute at Tilia's side, hand limp in Tilia's. If Tilia had been a bit of a fool, she might have thought that Catin did not want to be here. But that was ridiculous. Who would not want to be a guest in Three Birds?

From the eastward side of the city one walked past the Mother's house to reach the shrine. Tilia saw her brother standing in the door as the procession passed by. As idle as he was managing to look, as if he had leisure to hang about in doorways and stare at strangers, she did not doubt that he had everything in hand within. Danu was an admirable keeper of the household, though Tilia would never have told him she thought so. It was best to keep a young man humble. Otherwise he got too full of himself.

He was in very good looks today. He never seemed to be aware of his fine dark eyes or his fine olive skin, or of his lovely broad shoulders and his long clever hands. Women could never forget; they were all a little in love with him.

Tilia watched Catin out of the corner of her eye, to see if she noticed how beautiful the young man was. Indeed she must have seen him: her eyes passed right over him. Passed, and went on. They never even paused.

Tilia's own eyes narrowed. Ignore him, would she? Tilia would see about that. This was a Mother's daughter: she was worthy of him. Quite unlike that little nobody he was chasing after.

Then they were past, and Tilia could not in propriety crane over her shoulder to see if he stayed to watch the rest. Catin, she was deciding, was an odd and anxious creature—quite alien to the serenity that a Mother was supposed to cultivate. And she had no taste in men at all.

✦ ✦

The Lady's house was full of birds. They came at her will, some to nest, some to eat the fruits of her garden or to be fed at morning and evening by the Mother's acolytes, some even and occasionally to die. They were all sacred while they lived in the shrine. No hunter might follow them there, no cord or cage compel them. This was their free place, their goddess' sanctuary. Therefore she was called the Lady of the Birds.

Tilia told all these things to Catin, aware that the others listened, the sisters and brothers, even the Mother of Larchwood once she had paid tribute at the Lady's altar. "I suppose," Tilia said, "that you worship the Lady of the Wood, since you live so close to it."

"The Lady of Wood and Water," one said, but not Catin. It was one of the sisters, a tall gawky child with a bold manner and a direct stare. "Yes, we worship her, but above all we give our hearts to the Lady of the Deer."

"And aren't they all one?" said Tilia.

"One may hope so," the girl from Larchwood said.

Her Mother spoke with ponderous serenity, in the voice that Mothers could put on with the power of their office. "We have walked far today," she said, "and rested seldom. It would be great pleasure to sit in a place both cool and welcoming, and to listen to the songs of the birds."

The Mother of Three Birds betrayed no sign of annoyance at what was almost an insult to her hospitality. She simply said, "Ah, sister; so you have heard of the Lady's bower. Come. All has been made ready for your comfort."

✦ ✦

The Lady's bower was her garden, a place of water and of greenery set beside her shrine. There were trees there, tall and rich with shade, trees so old that they were more than holy. Once, Tilia had heard, they had been worshipped as goddesses themselves, till the Lady came to teach the truth. They were still much revered, great-trunked broad-crowned oaks standing in their circle, and in the center, in the sunny space, the dance of a stream and the Lady's pool, and a riot of flowers.

There the Mother's acolytes had spread the feast of welcome. By ancient custom they had prepared no flesh of beast or bird, but of bread and cheese and fruits of the earth, sweet honey and the nectar of flowers, herbs and grains and green things, there was enough and more to sate the most avid appetite.

Tilia forbore to regret the lack of coarser dishes, and the absence of men, too. This was a women's feast. Men were not allowed in this place, not even to serve the feasters. Any man who dared it would have died.

It was very good, she thought, to be a woman.

✦ ✦

There were times, Danu reflected, when it was a great burden to be a man. The women's feast was theirs to trouble with, and he was glad of it, but he had had to see it prepared, and when the remains came back, they were his to dispose of. If such things had mattered greatly, he would have been glad that he had taken that moment to see the procession pass; he had had no opportunity since, to be sure, to look on the Mother's guests. He was immersed in kitchen duties when they came in from the feast, nor could he escape till long after they had been shown to their beds.

It was nothing, he told himself. There were no great marvels among them. They were strangers, and from farther away than any he had seen before, and they spoke somewhat oddly, with a hint of a burr; but they were women and men like any in Three Birds. He did not know why he should have expected anything extraordinary. A Mother might go on pilgrimage, might she not? Or she might choose to visit a sister, if that sister happened to be Mother to a great people. Mothers did such things. It was expected of them.

Nevertheless he wished he could have been a woman, to sit at the feast in the grove where he was not allowed to go, and to ask these strangers why they had come. The few men who had come with them, sons and servants, were taciturn, and not inclined to conversation. They were a dour lot; the women too, from what the servants and the acolytes said. "As if they travel in the shadow of the Wood," said Riki, who was given to fancies.

Her sister acolytes hushed her, but Danu reckoned hers as good a guess as any.

✦ ✦

Danu woke the next morning to two voices, two Mothers luring the sun from its lair. He had not heard such a thing before, a mingled beauty, and perhaps a greater richness to the day, for having been called forth by so much power.

This morning the sun was wan, veiled in cloud. The air bore a scent of rain. Well for the household that yesterday had been the washing-day. Today should have been a day for scouring out the house, but the guests needed looking after, feeding and plying with warmed wine and honeyed milk. The Mothers lingered long in the shrine, sharing such wisdom as Mothers shared. Their daughters and sons and servants mingled uneasily in a house grown small in the embrace of the rain.

When guests were congenial the house would ring with laughter. When they were dour as these were, uneasiness grew to annoyance, and then to barbed silence. Tilia had taken a clear dislike to the stranger Catin, and was not trying overly hard to hide it.

She caught Danu in the weaving-room where he had sought refuge, threading a loom. It was niggling, eye-wearing work by the light of a lamp-cluster and such dim daylight as window and doorway let in. She blocked much of that, so that he had to stop, squinting up at the shadow of her.

Tilia never wasted time in preliminaries. "Come out of here," she said, "and rescue me. I can't get a word from her, not even yes or no. You're much more charming than I am, and prettier too. See if you can't get her to talk."

Danu did not move. "Why? What do you want her to say?"

"Anything," said Tilia. "She's not mute, I heard her mutter something to one of her sisters—criticizing my manners, I don't doubt. Do you think she's annoyed because we didn't offer her the pick of our men to keep her warm last night?"

"It was a warm night," Danu said.

Tilia stamped her foot. "Oh, you! Come out here and stop being contrary. I'm at wits' end."

"You are not," said Danu, but he rose stiffly, stretching the kinks out of his back. "You want me to do your duty for you. Is she as unpleasant as that?"

"She's not unpleasant. She's not anything, that I can tell. None of them is. You'd think they were traveling to a funeral, they're so sour in the face."

Danu sighed. "Someday you're going to have to learn to be charming yourself, and stop expecting me to do it for you."

"Why? Because you'll run off with Chana and be a trader?"

"No," said Danu. "Because I'll run off with this Catin and never see Three Birds again."

"She's not good enough for you, either," Tilia said. She clasped him by the hand and pulled him out into the soft drizzle of rain. "I'm going to find you someone nearby, with pleasant manners and some small acquaintance with laughter. But until I do, you can charm Catin into something resembling a smile."

"And what will you give me if I do that?"

Her eyes narrowed. He smiled sweetly. She hissed at him, but she said, "My necklace with the blue beads."

"Oh, you hold me cheap! Make it your golden armlet and I'll do it."

"I can't do that," she said. "It's *gold*."

"So," said Danu, slipping free of her grip and turning back toward the loom.

She sprang after him and spun him about. "What will Mother say if she sees you wearing her gift to me?"

"She'll know you bribed me again," Danu said calmly. "She won't say a word. She never does."

"All *right* then," Tilia said. "You can have it. But not till you've done what I ask."

"Now," he said, and held her glare until she gave way.

She slapped the armlet into his hand with stinging force. "Now *do* it!"

He took his time in putting on the armlet, turning it to admire its golden gleam, stroking the richness of its surface. A pattern of spirals wound along it, the Lady's roads weaving one into the next. His fingers loved the feel of it.

Just before Tilia would have struck him to make him move, he sauntered past her into the rain. The armlet was like a cool hand clasping his wrist. It held him to a promise. Not one he hungered greatly to fulfill, but word once given was sacred. The Lady heard it, and remembered; and if one chose to forget, she well might choose to punish.

10

Catin, who would be Mother of Larchwood, occupied herself in this strange place and on this day of rain, by sitting in a corner of the gathering-room while her sisters chattered among themselves. The names of their gossip meant nothing to the sisters and acolytes of Three Birds, but scandals were much the same everywhere.

If not a congenial gathering, it had become a moderately friendly one. There was wine and honey mead to help it, and bread and sweet cakes at Danu's order. The menservants knew what else they should do, the courtesy of their city to guests; and not an unpleasant one, either.

Danu brought cakes and mead to Catin. She seemed wrapped in herself, rocking slightly, eyes fixed on nothing. She had the look of one who dreamed dreams, but all those dreams were ill.

He knelt in front of her and poured a cup of mead, lifted the hand that lay slack in her lap and wrapped her fingers round the cup. He held them there, cold and thin as they were, until a semblance of life came back into her eyes.

She looked at him as if she had never seen him before. Perhaps, at that, she had not. He could not tell what she thought of him. Mostly women's eyes lit at sight of his face. He was beautiful, they said. He supposed that he was, since they all agreed on it.

Her eyes blinked. "Here," he said in the voice he used with animals and children. "This is honey mead, warmed over the fire. Drink. It will sweeten your spirit."

She drank as if he had given her no choice, a sip first, then rapid swallows, draining the cup.

He smiled. "More?" he asked.

She nodded.

She drank the second cup more slowly, holding it in both hands, not pausing or lowering it till it too was empty. She did not surrender it to him to be filled again.

He offered her the basket of cakes. She ate two as she had drunk: the first in a single bite, the second less swiftly but steadily. Again she did not wish a third.

Tilia had had the right of it. This Catin was a dull creature, no life in her. In Three Birds, even if she was the eldest daughter of the Mother, she would have been passed over as heir.

Larchwood was not lacking daughters with wit and intelligence. One of them had taken Beki's hand and led him away. That was an interesting choice. Beki was neither the youngest nor the prettiest of the menservants, but he was known to be a wise and careful lover.

Catin's sisters were lively enough with wine and mead in them, though they laughed less often than the women of Three Birds. Catin seemed to gain no benefit from the mead.

Danu did a thing he might never have done if Tilia's wishing had not compelled him. He did a bold thing, a thing a respectable man might shrink from doing. He took Catin's hand and met her eyes, and said, "Come with me."

She did not respond at once. He held his breath, braced to be struck, cursed, flung away for his presumption.

She sighed a little, just enough to hear, and rose. It looked, perhaps, as if she led, and not the opposite.

If it had not been raining they could have gone to one of the gardens or the bowers that were blessed by such things. As it was, with the house so full, there seemed no better place than Danu's own cell of a room. It had a window, which he opened to the rain, and a lamp-cluster which he had had the foresight to light before he fetched the cakes and mead for Catin.

There was nothing particularly beautiful about the room, though the bed's coverlet was well woven, and there was a rug on the floor. The lamps were plain, without adornment. The chest of his belongings was carved with the Lady's spirals and a hatching like the feathers on a bird's wing.

Catin seemed barely to see it, as she had barely seen Danu till he gave her no choice but to see him. She sank to the bed as if her knees had failed her. He began to wonder if she was one of the Lady's children, so ridden with dreams and sendings that nothing in the world of flesh was real to her.

He knelt at her feet, carefully, and took her hands in his. "You dream dreams," he said. The Lady set the words in him; he felt her, a presence so strong that his soul reeled. But she held him steady, and let him meet the eyes that raised to him, startled, coming awake again and fully. Catin was no dull creature then, nor ill to look at either.

"You see," Catin said. "You can see."

"She lets me see," said Danu.

"I do," said Catin. "I dream . . ." She shivered. She reached for him, drawing in his warmth, taking him as a woman should take a man. He was glad to wrap arms about her, to give her what she was seeking. Warmth he had, of his own and of the Lady's giving. He was not the lover that Beki was, nor had he Kosti's bull-strength, but such as he was, he gave to her.

She took it as if she had been starving. She did not want gentleness, nor the subtle turns of the Lady's dance. She wanted swift passion, white heat, and rhythm so rapid that she ran him out of breath; nor would she let him stop, only slow a little, till he could breathe again. He had never run so in a woman's arms. He had not known he could.

Her grip on him tightened suddenly. She rocked and spasmed, locked against him. Just when he must breathe, must break free, she fell back.

He gulped air. His sight had begun to go dark. Light came back, too bright almost to bear. He was in her still, though she lay limp, unmoving. He could not move himself, to finish it. His will was lost somewhere, perhaps in her eyes.

She stirred. He slipped out of her, limp, unsatisfied. She drew into a knot and began, piteously and horribly, to weep.

Danu was too numb to be dismayed. He gathered her into his arms as if she had been one of the children, and held her till she quieted.

✦ ✦

Danu had never danced so odd a dance with a woman before. Nor had he known so odd a woman. When Catin had done weeping, she did not pull away as another woman might, nor flay him with embarrassment or injured pride. She looked up into his face from the circle of his arms. Her eyes were wide and dark and very calm. "I hope," she said, "that the women of Three Birds know what they have in you."

He blinked. That was not what he had expected, either. "Are you mad?" he asked her. He meant it as a question to be answered.

She took it as he had intended. "I don't know that I am," she said. "The Lady's hand has been heavy on me. You . . . I see that she loves you."

"I'm not a woman," he said.

"Is that what they teach here?" she asked.

"What, that woman is the Lady's first and best creation? Isn't that truth?"

"No," she said. "The way you say it—as if you were something lesser. As if she could never love the likes of you."

"I'm not—" He stopped in confusion. "I don't understand you."

She smiled. It was a dazzling smile, astonishing, wonderful—terrible. "You don't need to understand. Come here."

When a woman spoke so, a man had no choice but to obey.

She had exhausted him short of the finish, and now she asked him to rouse again. No man was strong enough for that.

She made him so. This time she took him with both power and gentleness, soft as water, inexorable as the river wearing away stone. She did nothing for herself. She roused him again, cradled him inside her, brought him the gift that her desperation had denied him. It was quick; it took him by surprise. He cried out.

She held him till the gift was all given, the song all sung. He did not weep as she had. He was too astonished.

He must look a perfect fool. She laughed at him, but gently, too light to wound. "I owed you that," she said, "after what you had done for me."

"I will never understand you," Danu said.

She shook her head, but this time she did not respond. She sat up. Her hair had fallen out of its braids. Her face was vivid, no dullness in it. She was staring at him, so hard that he blushed and tried to turn away, but she would not let him. "You dream, too," she said.

"No," he said. He meant it; but something caught his throat. He had forgotten—he had willed to forget—

It came back in a black flood, memory that he had buried deep, a dream of fire and shouting, blinding fear, and the terrible beauty of blood.

"Yes," she said. "Yes. You see. You know."

"I don't know anything!"

Danu pressed his hand to his mouth. He did know—he did not want to, but he did. He knew what she knew.

"But what are we seeing?" he demanded of her. "What has the Lady given us?"

"Fear," she said. She did not, in spite of that, sound afraid. "Something is coming. It comes from the east, from the rising sun. It is like a flood, but a flood of fire."

His belly knotted. "Fire in the wood? But that could never come as far as Three Birds. Even Larchwood might escape it in such a year as this, with the rain coming so often."

"We thought so, too," she said. "But the dreams have never stopped. They've only grown stronger. Something comes. I think . . . did you hear the tale people are telling? Of the stranger who came through the wood, and the beasts he brought with him?"

Danu stiffened. What? Was he never to be free of this thing? "You saw him? You saw his beasts?"

She nodded. "He came to Running Waters, and its Mother sent to ours, because she's reckoned wise. She sent me to see what it was that so troubled her sister."

"They were real? They weren't deer, or ghosts, or shadows?"

"They were as solid as you beside me," she said, resting her hand on his shoulder as if to make sure of it. "I've never seen a creature quite like them. They're a little like cattle for size, but like deer for grace, a little. Their hooves are round, and not divided. Their eyes . . . they aren't quiet, as cattle are, or placid like sheep. They think. They know when a person is looking at them."

Danu frowned, listening to her. It made no sense, and yet in a strange way it did. He could not see the beasts, but he could feel them. They were caught in the fire somehow, in the memory of his dream. "Horses," he said. "They are called horses."

"Yes," said Catin.

"But," Danu said with a flash of impatience, "what harm can an animal do? They're the Lady's creatures. The stories never vary. They all say that the stranger was excited when he saw the Lady's image; that he called her Lady of Horses. How can her own creatures be a threat to us?"

"I don't know," Catin said. "That's what we came for, to ask your Mother. She's the wisest of all the Mothers. She must be able to answer. Why we all dream so black, with so much blood. Why when we look ahead down the round of the years, we see darkness."

"All of you?" Danu whispered. "Every one of you?"

"Most of us," said Catin. "I worst, I think; or the Mother, who is too strong to show it. My sisters once or twice. They're young. They forget. My brothers have been spared it."

"Here," said Danu, "no one else admits to dreaming of it."

"Maybe no one remembers." Her hand lay on his shoulder still. She let it wander up to stroke his cheek, then down to rest over his heart. "Maybe the Lady favors you."

He shook his head. "No. I'm only the keeper of my Mother's house. I have no greater place in the world, nor do I want one."

"The Lady doesn't care what a person wants," Catin said. "And why should she? She has her own purposes. We live to serve them."

Danu bowed his head in reverence at a truth he had been taught. But it did not prevent him from saying, "My Mother must be dreaming, too. It can't have come only to me."

"Then she'll know what to say to my Mother," Catin said, "and we'll discover what it is we have to do to turn this flood aside."

"Yes," Danu said in a kind of desperate relief. "Yes, that is how it will be." He paused. He should not say it, but it was in his heart, and it would not let him rest till he had let it out. "I thought . . . that you were less than you were. It was the Lady's burden on you. So heavy—it's a wonder it never broke you. And yet you're strong."

"You have made me strong." She silenced his denial, fingers pressed to his lips. They were warm. He could feel the Lady's strength in them. "No! Don't refuse it. I was wandering in the dark places. You came, and light came with you. The Lady sent you."

No, Danu wanted to say. *My sister did. My sister who has never known the name of fear; who commanded me to make you speak.*

Ah, but had she expected such speech as this? A Mother might. But Tilia was far short of becoming a Mother.

Maybe the Lady had spoken through her, after all. The Lady used such instruments as she pleased to use.

Even Danu. Even the keeper of his Mother's house, whose ambition rose no higher than that.

"And maybe," said Catin as if she had never paused, "the dream itself will fade in daylight, and the terror turn aside."

"The Lady will protect us," Danu said. He willed himself to believe it. Willed so strongly that he almost laughed, dizzy with the effort.

She did laugh, perhaps at his expression, perhaps for plain relief. Then laughter turned to something else; and he was ready for her: marvelous, the Lady's hand in it surely, and her blessing.

✦ ✦

"Well?"

Danu was doing his best to walk steadily, let alone to think clearly. He ached to the bone, and the manly part of him was the worst of it. But he kept smiling, and trying to hide it, because he was supposed to be overseeing the baking.

Tilia trapped him in a corner of the kitchen, blocked his escape with her ample body. "Well?" she said again. "Did she? Did she talk?"

Danu knew a brief, appalling impulse to deny it—to lie. To his sister. To the Mother's heir. That was so horrifying that it emptied him of words.

She took his silence for answer. She snorted in disgust. "And they made *that* the Mother's heir of Larchwood. Imagine it!"

Danu could, easily. But Tilia knew what she knew. He did not try to convince her otherwise.

She went away. He was glad. It saved his lying—and why he felt he should, he could not think. He could not think clearly at all. He kept remembering blood and fire, and Catin.

·············· 11 ··············

Danu performed his duties as he always had, or so he could hope. He was startled therefore, toward evening, to be summoned into the Mother's presence. The acolyte who brought the message seemed rather too pleased with her errand, by which Danu presumed that he had committed some infraction. He could not imagine what it might be—unless Tilia had complained to the Mother of his apparent failure with Catin.

He was not given time to make himself properly presentable. The acolyte was insistent. "She asks for you *now*." In his ragged and flour-stained shirt, therefore, he went from the baking to the Mother's presence.

Every house of any size or style in the Lady's country kept a room apart, a shrine of the goddess like an image of the great one in the city's heart. Yet while men were forbidden entrance into the temple, the shrine was open to any who wished to address the Lady face to face.

The shrine in the Mother's house was old, as old as anyone living could remember. Its altar was small, the image of the Lady ancient. Its stone was worn smooth, but its shape was clear still, great fecund breasts and huge thighs. Her signs were drawn about her, the magic that only Mothers knew.

There was an offering of flowers in front of the image, and all the lamps were lit, burning sweet-scented oil. No memory here of blood and fire, death and terror. Only peace.

The Mother sat before the altar, an image in living flesh of the stone-carved Lady. Her face offered Danu nothing. It was serene as always, the dark eyes focused inward, contemplating the Lady's wisdom. She was the wisest of the Mothers in this corner of the world; she heard the Lady's voice clearly, as few ever did, even those who were Mothers.

Danu knelt in front of her, bowed his head and waited. He did not allow himself to be afraid. If she wished to rebuke him, she would.

She laid a hand on his head. He bent beneath the weight of her benediction. "Child," she said in her beautiful voice. "If I bade you leave this city, would you do it?"

He did not move, though his body stiffened. He had learned somewhat from her: how to discipline himself. How to be still. "Have I sinned so terribly?" he asked, very low.

"Oh, child!" said the Mother, and for once she seemed not so serene. She sounded, strangely, like Tilia; which made him wonder—

But he could not let his mind wander, not now. "Child," said the

Mother, "you have done nothing at all to offend me or the Lady who speaks in me. Never fear that. I ask again: would you do it?"

"I do as the Lady commands," Danu said.

She made him look up at her, took his face in her hands and raised it whether he would or no. He met her eyes, dark eyes, tilted up at the corners as Tilia's were. They were not so serene now, and yet they were full of the Lady's presence. "You know why the Mother of Larchwood came to Three Birds," she said. And of course she would know that; she was the Mother. "The way of your knowing . . . did you like Catin?"

He flushed in spite of himself, but she would not let him look away. "I like her well enough," he said.

"I see that you do," said the Mother. He could hear no irony in it. "She has asked for you—to go with her on her return to Larchwood. Not bound to her; simply to go."

"Why?" It was the only word in Danu, the only one he could utter.

"You dream dreams," she said.

Danu shook his head. "No. I know that. I meant—what is in Larchwood, that I must be there to see it?"

"She said," said the Mother, "that you would understand when you came to it. But you must go to Larchwood."

Danu sat on his heels. Only her hands on his cheeks held him up. Of all the things she might have asked of him, this was the last he would have expected.

Leave Three Birds? He had been outside of it, of course he had: hunting, herding, traveling about visiting this city or that. But to leave it truly, to dwell somewhere else, that he had never imagined, nor wished for. He had been born in this place. He hoped to die in it. He had no desire in the world to leave it.

Unless the Lady asked. "Do you wish me to go?" he asked the Mother.

"What I wish matters little," she said. "The Lady wishes you to go. There is somewhat that she would have you do, some thing that she requires of you."

Danu closed his eyes. Yes, he knew that. It was a fullness in his belly, a hammering in his heart. And, though it shamed him, a kind of dizzy excitement. To go so far on the Lady's errand—to live in Catin's city, among her people—how many of his people had ever done so much?

He wanted to go. It shocked him a little; it was too much like disloyalty. But he wanted it.

The Mother knew. When he opened his eyes, she was smiling. There was sadness in the smile, but pride too. "You will matter in the world," she said.

That took him aback. "But I don't want—"

"Of course you do," she said. "Everyone does. Go, prepare. There's much to do; and the Mother and her children depart in the morning."

"So soon? But—"

"They have what they came for," she said. She set a kiss on his forehead. "Go now. Be quick."

He had obeyed her before he thought; before it dawned on him what

she asked. To set this house in order—to find someone to take his place—
to see to the guests meanwhile, and the servants, and—

They all knew that he was going. It was always so. Servants were keener-
witted than their masters, more often than not; and quicker to understand
subtle signs. These seemed actually to regret that he must go, though that
perhaps was fear for their leisure. He had set Beki over them, Beki who
neither knew nor understood the meaning of idleness.

But even they did not know why Catin had insisted that he follow her
to Larchwood. It could not be the spell he cast in the night. He was no such
sorcerer, nor had any wish to be.

"They have a secret," Col said. Col had come from a city far to the west,
long ago; he saw deeper than some, and his ears were keen. "None of them
will speak of it, but they all know. It haunts them. I heard the Mother's heir
speak of you. 'He is the one,' she said. 'He knows what no one else knows.' "

Danu was aware of no such thing, and would tell her so at the earliest
opportunity. But he was trapped in the bonds of his duty, and when he could
escape it was deep night. There was no one in his bed, no sign that anyone
had been there. He fell into it exhausted; was asleep before he touched the
coverlet.

✦ ✦

He woke shivering. The air held the chill of dawn, but the house was silent
still. The Mothers had not risen yet, nor gone to call the sun.

The lamp that he had left lit when he fell asleep was still burning. It
illumined the pack that he had made, the belongings that he would take; and
the many that he had left behind. He was not going away to be a woman's
chosen man, to remain with her in her city and never return to the place
where he was born. He could come back. He would, he swore to himself.

He rose and washed and dressed, too restless to lie abed; though it would
be full morning before they set out for Larchwood. He kept having to pause.
His heart kept hammering; dizziness kept swaying him as he stood or bent.

He straightened, at the last, closed his eyes, breathed deep and held it.
Just then he heard the sound that had comforted him all his life, the Mother's
tread as she went out to call the sun. That steadied him. He could open his
eyes, let go the breath, go out to hear the morning song.

✦ ✦

Danu had not troubled to tell anyone that he was going. The servants knew.
He had presumed that everyone else did.

But when at last, after what seemed an unconscionably long while, he
came out with his pack and his walking-stick to take his place among the
departing guests, Tilia stared at him from among the acolytes and the younger
sisters. Her expression was shocked—too shocked at first for anger. Danu
stared at her, shocked himself. Tilia knew everything. She always had. Then
how—

There was no time to ask, nor was this the place to do it. Tilia might
have cared little for that, but the Mother had come between. Her presence

filled his vision. She embraced him and held him till the world shrank to the circle of her arms and the softness of her breast. She did not speak. All that was necessary had been said.

She let him go. He maintained such serenity as he might, walked to the place that waited for him among the travellers from Larchwood. He did not glance at Tilia. Still he could feel the heat of her temper, as if he passed a new-lit fire. She would never forgive him this, he knew in his belly. No more could he keep from doing it. This was the Lady's will.

She should listen, he thought. She should still that tongue of hers and quell that temper, and let the Lady speak to her. Then she would have known as the Mother did, as Danu himself knew, that he must do this.

He had never let himself think such thoughts before. They came of his leaving, of the shock and the suddenness of it. He could see more clearly than he had before, or less kindly. And yet, for that, he could look on his sister with more compassion than he might have mustered before. She would be Mother in her time, but not until she learned to be quiet. To listen.

While he wandered inside himself, the drums had begun to beat, the pipes to shrill, beginning the song of farewell to honored guests. As was both polite and proper, the guests—and Danu in their midst—danced to the music, a sweeping, swaying step that carried them lightly forward. The people of Three Birds, gathered along the eastward way, raised their voices amid the music.

Even the Mother of Larchwood was dancing, ponderous in her dignity. Danu found himself handlinked with her, and Catin on his other side, and the rest in a skein winding along behind. Step and sweep, dip and sway, while the drums beat and the pipes called, and the voices of women wove in and about them. This was the way he wished to remember Three Birds: this bright morning, these people singing, and his body caught up in the dance. He would forget, for the moment, his sister's anger, his own fear, the dark thing that called him toward the rising sun. Time enough later to remember. Time enough and more, to learn what the Lady intended for him.

############### 12 ###############

Past the outermost limits of Three Birds, after the last excited child and barking dog had retreated in search of other entertainment, the travellers dropped out of their dance and settled to a firm and steady walking-pace. Danu was breathing lightly. The wind felt cool on his sweating face. He was still, he noticed with a small start, handlinked between the Mother and Catin.

They slipped free together, as if in the last movement of the dance. Danu would have been glad to hold back, to let the rest of the walkers pass him, but they made a wall behind, kept him irresistibly in front.

It was not so ill a place to be, once he resigned himself to it. He had walked as far as they would walk today, hunting or visiting cities eastward of Three Birds. Tomorrow again he would walk roads he knew. Thereafter would be all new, all unfamiliar.

For now, and for tomorrow, he would let the walking be all he thought of. He did not look back to the city. He let memory limn it for him: the houses in their circles, the rise of the Lady's house above them, and the birds that nested in the eves, hunted and mated and played in air blessed with their presence.

Other cities were never so full of birds. Danu wondered if Larchwood would be blessed with trees. Here on the plain, trees were precious, cherished where they grew, worshipped as the Lady's own. Larchwood was near the wood that walled the world. It might be all made of trees. What a wonder if it was.

The farther the people from Larchwood walked, the nearer they came to their own city, the less dour their faces grew. Danu was the stranger now, the quiet one. They seemed to have taken heart from their journey, though it had accomplished nothing that he could clearly see.

The first night they stayed as guests in a town called Two Rivers. Its Mother was young, almost as young as Catin, and uncertain of her powers as yet. She knew Danu, had been his sisters' companion when she was small; but he had not seen her since he grew to be a man. Her eyes lingered on him at the feast that she had spread for the travellers.

He did not know what to do with himself. Ever since his voice broke he had looked after his Mother's house and taken charge of such occasions as this. He had never been a guest, never had to sit while others waited on him. A woman wanting him—yes, he knew the way of that, but not when he was twofold guest, of this house and of the company in which he traveled.

At the time when it was proper, the Mother of Two Rivers rose and held out her hand to him. It was his place to take that hand, to go where she bade; but he glanced at Catin.

She was not watching him at all. Her eyes were on her fingers, which had locked in her lap. She dreamed again, or remembered: blood and fire, present always just behind her eyes. He at least could forget. She never could.

With a faint sigh he turned back to the Mother of Two Rivers, and clasped her hand just before it dropped. He had barely escaped impropriety. She smiled at him, a quick smile, as if she were uncertain, too; and led him away from his uncomfortable companions.

There was comfort, yes, in one who had known him so long, who could ask after his sisters and recall with him this escapade or that. Her name had been Sana then, but all names vanished when a woman became the Mother. She gave them to the Lady with all of herself that had gone before.

But this young Mother, who had been Sana not so long ago, still carried a memory of the self who had been. She did not ask him why he had come here, or what he did with the Mother and the people from Larchwood. She was content to remember things that had passed long ago. One thing only she touched in the time that was now. "I hope," she said before she slept, "that this night's work will make an heir."

He bowed his head at that. Some of the elders still maintained that men had nothing to do with the making of children; but anyone with wits could see that a woman who took men to her bed had children, whereas one who did not remained barren. What was a man meant for, after all, if not to complete the Lady's dance?

The Mother slept as soon as she was satisfied. Danu lay awake. Her body against his was warm and ample. The room was strange and yet familiar. The bed with its leather lashings and its warm coverlets, the little shrine of the Lady with its lamp that was never suffered to go out, the chest for clothing and the table for oddments, were all as he had known it in his own Mother's chamber. The coverlets here were woven differently, the oddments on the table less numerous and less varied, and these walls were bare where his Mother had hung a fine bit of weaving. This was a younger Mother of a lesser city. And yet, and no doubt of it, a Mother.

In the morning he would leave this place. Maybe he would come back. Maybe he would not. And maybe, come winter, this Mother would bring forth an heir. It was all in the Lady's hands.

✦ ✦

Catin said nothing to Danu when they took the road again come morning. They left Two Rivers quietly, no dancing, no song, simply a murmur of fare-wells as the morning brightened around them. When the full light of the sun struck the road and burned the last of the dew from the fields, they were well past Two Rivers.

Danu carried the blessing of the Mother of Two Rivers, and a wheel of cheese from her own goats. The scent of her went with him, and a memory of her hands on his skin.

He walked in the lead again today, where the people of Larchwood seemed to have decided he belonged. The Mother walked ahead of him, Catin just behind. The Mother's strides were strong, her pace steady, swift but not too swift, shortening the way eastward.

After a time Danu dropped back a little till he walked side by side with Catin. She did not acknowledge him. He thought of words that he might say, but none seemed worthy of the moment. He settled on silence.

At length it was she who said, "The Mother of Two Rivers likes you."

Danu shrugged.

She shot him a glance. "And did you like her?"

He shrugged again.

Her glance heated. "You did!"

"Is that so terrible a thing?" he asked.

"No," she said quickly. "No. Of course not."

"So," said Danu. He relented somewhat, then, though why they should be quarreling, he was not entirely sure. "We knew each other when we were children."

"Ah," said Catin. "And . . . you never knew me."

"No," Danu said.

"Tonight," she said, "I may ask for you first. Will you refuse?"

He shook his head. He did not need to hesitate, or to think about it.

"And tomorrow night, too," she said. "And the night after that. Will you still assent to it?"

"Am I allowed to refuse?"

Her face tightened. He had not meant it that way, but once he had spoken, he could not unsay it. "And what would you do," she asked, "if I said that you were?"

"I would assent," he said.

He had not hesitated. She had seen that: he read it in her face, in the light she veiled quickly, because it might betray her pride.

He let go a breath he had not known he was holding. It was difficult—because, after all, he had not known her since he was a child. With the Mother of Two Rivers he had had a kind of comfort, a sharing of memory; likewise with the women of Three Birds. But this was a stranger. Everything she did and said came from a world that he did not know. They shared three days' memories—that was all.

It was fascinating, when it did not utterly dismay him. He managed a smile. She looked away hastily. She did not like people to see how gentle a creature she was beneath the prickly pride.

In that, she was quite like his sister Tilia. He smiled to himself, thinking that; because Tilia would be furious if he told her.

He walked with Catin in silence, comfortable in it. The sun rose overhead and sank behind them, its path measured in their footfalls. When night came, and a city that welcomed them as all cities would in the Lady's country, it was Catin whose body warmed him, and her presence that he woke to, for she had not left him in the night as a woman might choose to do.

She honored him. That honor gave him a place among the travellers, a presence that he had not had before. They greeted him in the morning, smiled as if at one of their own. When they shared out the morning's bread, his share came to him; he did not have to fetch it for himself. He was a person of consequence, because the Mother's heir had made him so.

He could hardly quarrel with it, though he might have wished to have had some consequence in himself. Was he not the Mother's son of Three Birds? But sons were little regarded, except for the women who might be drawn to them for their beauty or their lineage.

It was the way of the world. He could be content that Catin had chosen him, that she favored him above the sharing of an ill dream. It made his way easier and his journey more pleasant, to be part of the conversation and the laughter; to be one of them, though he had been born in a city far to the west of theirs.

⁜ ⁜

They were nine days on the road, nine days of steady walking, nine nights of resting in cities that, past the second, Danu had never known before. The country did not change overmuch at first, but on the sixth day he began to see a shadow on the eastern horizon. That grew clearer with each hour's passing, till the whole of the world's edge was lost in darkness.

Where they walked was still sunlight and open sky. But the wood loomed in front of them. Danu had never known or imagined the size of it.

Larchwood lay well outside of it, a solid day's walk to the edge of the trees. But already the land had changed; had grown less level, opening into hills and valleys, sprouting copses of trees. The sky closed in here. One could no longer see along the whole valley of the river. One's sight was halted by hills and by the crowns of trees. But one was aware always, and never more than on the hilltops, of the wood that walled the world.

The city of Larchwood was as Danu had imagined it, a city of trees. Its houses were made of wood, set among the trees of the grove. At first it was difficult even to find them; the eye kept rising into the branches and ignoring the walls and roofs below. Not only larch-trees grew here. There were oaks, too, and the trembling of aspens, and other trees that he had not learned the names of, child of the plain that he was.

The city welcomed its Mother with singing and with gladness, with skeins of dancers and with garlands of flowers. Danu was half drowned in them, handlinked between Catin and the Mother as he had been when he walked out of Three Birds: made perforce a part of them, acknowledged and given a full welcome. It was a great honor, and seldom given to a man.

He would happily have dispensed with it. His place was more often in the quiet, ordering the festival; not in the midst of it with others waiting on him. But he had to endure it, for the honor of Three Birds and in gratitude to the Mother and the heir of Larchwood.

He hoped that he acquitted himself well. It was all a whirl, city and people, feast and dancing and the Mother's entry into the Lady's shrine. That at least he could not enter. He stood outside with the men who had gone to Three Birds, briefly and blessedly forgotten, before the women came out and swept him up again. None of the rest was closed to him, feast or city, nor could he in propriety refuse to be shown it.

So many strangers. Not one face that he had known since before this moon was new. Nothing familiar, not even the Lady's face. Here she was Lady of Wood and Water, crowned with young leaves and mantled in the running river.

She was still the Lady. He clung to that, as he clung to the place in which he sat, the bowl that he had been given. It was fine pottery ware, painted with the waves of the river and filled with a stew of herbs and—yes, spring lamb. It was savory and sweet, hot and rich in his belly. It was, in its way, the Lady's blessing.

············· 13 ·············

The morning song was different in Larchwood. Some of its words were strange, some of them turned in ways Danu had not heard before. Oddly, it did not unsettle him. He had slept little in the night, had kept waking, looking about to assure himself that he was indeed in Larchwood next to the Mother's heir, falling asleep again. Near dawn, sleep deserted him. He heard the whole of the morning song, the last of it from outside the Mother's house.

It was strange to see the morning from beneath the branches of trees.

The light fell scattered, bits of gold and green dappling his face and hands. He wanted half to rip the veil of leaves away and uncover the open sky; half to draw it over him and wrap himself in green twilight.

As the last notes faded and fell soft to the leaf-strewn earth, Catin came out of the house behind him. He knew her step already, light and firm, and the way she had of drawing a breath before she spoke. "Do you ever sleep?" she asked him.

"Often," he said. He turned to face her. She stood against the house-wall. Its wood was dark and old, worn smooth with years. She looked some-how a part of it, as if she had grown there, like a branch on a tree.

He wondered how he looked to her; if he seemed all out of place. He read nothing of it in her eyes. She caught at his hand. "Come," she said.

She led him not into the house but away from it, down the tree-lined ways of the city. Past the Lady's temple the trees thickened into a wall. She drew him straight toward it.

He dug in his heels. He knew a sacred grove when he saw one, though this was a thicker, wilder one than he had ever known. And like the temple, it was no place for a man.

But Catin would not let him stop. She was strong. He could be stronger if he set his weight into it; he was larger, heavier. But a long habit of obe-dience warred against old fear, and lost.

Surely, he thought as she dragged him into the thicket of trees, she had not brought him all this way only to be the death of him. One heard of such things among savages; not among the Lady's people.

Light blinded him. From the near-darkness of the woven wood, he half-fell into the full flame of the morning sun.

He blinked, eyes streaming tears. Slowly his sight came clear. He stood in an astonishing place, a circle of grass that seemed as broad as a city. No trees grew there. Something had been built near the center: roof but no walls, such a shelter as a shepherd might build for the lambing, or to shelter his sheep from the rain. It was so commonplace a thing, and so completely un-expected, that he stood gaping like a fool.

Catin let go his hand. She walked a little apart, not very far, and seemed to be searching for something.

Under the roof of woven branches, a thing moved. It went four-legged like a deer, and high-headed like one, too; but something about it was heavier, less delicate in its grace.

It stepped into the light. Danu knew, then, what it was. The tales had said too much, and yet too little.

"It's smaller than I thought," he said. His voice sounded faint and far away.

Catin did not seem to hear anything odd in it. "It's young," she said. "It was born in the last spring. It will grow, the savage said, two more springs, three, four. Then it will be as tall as your shoulder."

"So tall?" Danu looked at the creature anew. It came perhaps to his breast: taller than a deer, and heavier, with a longer, more massive head. Its ears were small. It had no horns, nor space to grow any. Its color was odd, between dun and ocher. A dark stripe ran down its back. Its upper legs were striped, its legs dark to the knee. A thick dark mane fell over its neck and between its little lean ears. A thick brush of tail fell below its hocks behind.

It raised its head as he stared at it. Its nostrils flared. It snorted. Without thinking he snorted back. It pawed the grass. Its hoof was undivided: hard, round, black, a single thing. Again as his body bade him, he eased forward. The creature—the horse—did not retreat. It watched him alertly, eyes bright under the thick forelock. It reminded him, suddenly and incongruously, of Tilia. Just so would she eye him when she had a mind to test his patience.

He had never been afraid of Tilia. Nor, for that matter, had she ever feared him. This creature seemed of the same mind. It stood still even as he came within reach.

He laid a hand on its neck. The fur was soft and rather thick. Winter fur. It was coming out in patches, showing a lighter, far thinner coat beneath. It itched, he knew without needing to ask. He rubbed the broad flat neck, carefully at first, then more vigorously as the horse leaned into his hand. More, it told him. There. And there. And there: all over, shoulder and back, belly and haunches.

It was male. He was rather surprised. Here in the Lady's grove, male things were seldom welcome.

Well; and perhaps that was why Catin had brought him here. To show him the secret that she had promised. To . . . test him?

He turned to her. She had not left the field's edge. He had to raise his voice so that she could hear him. "And do the men of your city come here, too?"

"No," she said.

"Why?"

"The Lady forbids," she said.

"Yet you brought me," said Danu. "Shall I be condemned now?"

"No," Catin said. "The Lady asked for you. In the night she told me: *Bring the man here.*"

"In the night? And not before?"

"In the night," said Catin, "before I left Three Birds."

Danu lowered his eyes. "Does my Mother know what you keep here?"

"Yes," Catin said.

"It's not . . ." said Danu; and yelped. The horse had nipped him, caught him in the shoulder, painfully, and danced away with head and tail high. It was laughing at him.

He finished what he had begun, through gritted teeth. "It's not a spirit, or a thing of the dark. It's an animal. It bites."

"Yes," said Catin. He thought she might be laughing behind her carefully bland face.

"And you keep it hidden?" he demanded. "Why? What's there to hide?"

"Fear," she said. "Holiness. This is the Lady's creature."

"This is not his place," Danu said. He did not look at her as he said it.

His eyes were on the horse as it circled the field, snorting and shying at shadows. "He needs his own kind. Or failing that, room to run, and companions in his running."

"We have no other horses," Catin said.

"Goats," said Danu. "Let him run with the goats."

"And let him escape?"

"No," Danu said. He did not know where the words came from. They were in the turn of the horse's head, the flick of his heel. "He'll not run away. He was born here. But he was never made to live in solitude."

"And what of the people?"

"The people know," he said. "Don't they?"

"In Larchwood," she said, "yes. But the Mother—"

"I'll speak to the Mother," Danu said; and stood amazed to hear himself say it.

It was the horse. He did not know this thing called submission. He only knew the wind that called him, the earth under his feet, the blood that ran swift as spring waxed into summer.

He danced up to Danu, head high, half in play, half in challenge. He was heavier, less graceful than a deer, and yet beautiful, with a power that no deer ever had. When he was grown, he would carry the weight of a man, and never stagger nor stumble. Men and women mounted on the likes of him could outrun the wind.

Danu held up his hand, wary of wicked teeth, but unafraid. The horse blew warm breath in his palm. He worked a knot out of the thick coarse mane, and rubbed the neck beneath it. There was a great pleasure in that simple thing.

He hated to leave the horse, but the sooner he spoke to the Mother, the sooner the beast would be free. It followed him back across the field. On the wood's edge it paused. He fought the urge to hesitate; made himself walk into the shadow of the trees. Catin was ahead of him, leading him on the hidden path.

Behind him he heard footfalls, and a muted snort. He stiffened but did not turn to drive the horse back. If it followed—if the Lady willed—who was he to gainsay it?

Where the path turned, where it seemed to vanish into tangled undergrowth, the horse halted. Danu could not pause, could not turn, or he would lose his guide. It startled him, how hard that was, how much he wanted to turn back.

✦ ✦

"The Lady speaks to you," the Mother of Larchwood said. They had found her in the house of a friend, helping that one tend the kiln, for she was a potter. Danu had to move carefully in space shrunk small by the potter's wares, finished and unfinished.

The potter looked more like a Mother than the Mother did, a vastly beautiful woman with wonderful, delicate hands. Those hands shaped a pot on a wheel, while the Mother worked a small bellows, feeding the fire in the kiln.

Danu waited to be acknowledged. He had been seen, he could not doubt that: the potter had smiled at him, a smile of warm and open pleasure. But the Mother, preoccupied, did not spare him a glance.

Only when the fire was burning to her satisfaction did she leave the bellows and turn. Danu bent his head in respect. She smiled as the potter had: startling, because he had never seen her smile before.

He managed to smile back. Then she said it, the thing that he could not believe: "The Lady speaks to you." It was her greeting, and addressed to him, he could not doubt it: she met his eyes, and not her daughter's.

He was not fool enough to ask how she could know. Mothers knew. But he did say, "I hear no voice."

"She seldom speaks in words," the Mother said. The potter nodded. The wheel spun, the pot taking shape on it, a thing of magic and of the woman's hands. That was the Lady too, he thought. It was all the Lady.

He shook his head in confusion. "She speaks to the Mothers," he said. "She speaks to my sisters. She never speaks to me. Why should she? What can I possibly be to her?"

"Her child," said the Mother. "Tell me what she said to you."

She said nothing, Danu began to say, but stopped himself. "She said— she showed me—the horse—" He glanced at the potter. She listened without surprise. "The horse," he said. "It can't live as it is now, alone. It needs the sky. It needs companions. Goats, maybe—sheep are too dull, and cattle too slow. Since it can't have—"

The Mother nodded slowly, eyes on his face, as if she studied it. As if she had hoped to hear such a thing from him.

Catin spoke behind him. "Mother! Dare we? Can we? What if it runs off?"

"Then that will be the Lady's will," the Mother said, as serene as ever a Mother could be. "This was given to her, not to us, though we have kept it in her name. You know it was not thriving; it was running, endlessly, and tearing at its house, and fleeing from anyone who came to tend it."

Danu turned to stare at Catin. She had never said a word of that.

She seemed unaware of him. Her eyes were on the Mother. "It had calmed before we left."

"And your dreams were darker than ever." The Mother shook her head slightly, as if to silence Catin before she spoke again. "It is all bound together. The dreams, the horse. This one, this child of Three Birds. What did the horse do when it saw him?"

"It came to him," Catin said almost sullenly. "It spoke to him. It never spoke to any of us."

"Perhaps none of us knew how to listen." The Mother warmed him again with her smile. "And it told you what it needed in order to thrive."

He nodded. "You've been afraid of it," he said. "Haven't you?"

"It told you that?" Catin demanded.

He answered her, but spoke to the Mother. "It's neither dream nor demon. It's living flesh. The Lady speaks to you. Did she tell you nothing of this?"

"We were afraid," the Mother said. "It was born here, in this city, of one of the horses that the stranger brought. When he left us, the Lady asked that the young one—the foal, he called it; the colt—be left as tribute. He had no objection. It was young and small, he said, and would slow his return; but it was old enough to live apart from its mother. He told us how to feed and care for it. But it wanted none of us. We kept it in the temple for a time, till its pacing and fretting grew too much to bear. We coaxed it into one of the sheepfolds. It broke free and ran into the Lady's grove, and there stayed. We built the house for it. We fed it as we could. It let none of us near it, nor let us touch it. It might have been a wild thing, for all the trust it gave us."

"It smelled your fear," Danu said. "One of you could have gone in with courage in your heart, and it would have come to you. Then you could have led it out again. It can't live in so small a space, not if it's to grow and be strong."

"It will run away," Catin muttered.

The Mother ignored her; therefore Danu did the same. "Since it speaks to you," the Mother said, "then I name you its keeper. Do with it as the Lady bids you. I think that she brought you here for this, even more than for the rest."

Danu did not know that, but then he was not a Mother. He bowed to her, for respect and for submission. "May I do as—as the Lady tells me? May I command people if I must?"

"Whatever she bids," the Mother said, "you may do. My people will obey you."

They would do that. He saw the flash of her glance at her daughter, and the inclination of the potter's head. The rest would follow where those three led.

He bowed again, lower this time. As he straightened, he saw that the potter's wheel had stilled. On it sat a graceful shape, a vessel for oil perhaps, with a handle like the curve of a horse's body, and the rear of its head above. Power and grace. And no fear.

Yes, he thought. Yes. No fear. Without fear they could master anything; even a creature out of a dream. Even a horse.

·········· 14 ··········

The savage from beyond the wood had shown the people of Larchwood how one confined and led a horse: much as one did an ox or a sheep, with a cord knotted into a halter for the head. Danu might have trusted the horse to follow him at the Lady's bidding, but Catin was not so certain of the beast. Danu was not in a mood to contest with her.

The horse, it seemed, was; but while he would not come near Catin, he stepped willingly to Danu and suffered the halter to be slipped over his nose and ears. He had worn it before, Catin had said, when he was small; the savage had taught him to lead and to obey, though no one had succeeded with him since the savage went back into the east.

Danu did not see the difficulty. The horse—the colt—was large, but oxen were larger, and heavier too. He liked to dance and snort and threaten terrors, but so did a he-goat or even a young ram. Any shepherd knew to keep the will firm and the lead well secured, and the beast would give up its fighting and go where it was led. No beast could be as insistent as man or woman could, unless driven by fear or hate.

The colt had no fear, nor had ever learned to hate the people who tended it. That he had little respect for them, Danu could well see; but he had learned the art young, and Danu bade him remember it. The crooked-horned ram in Three Birds had been more obstinate by far, and more willing to wreak bodily harm on anyone who presumed to lead him. The colt would strike but not to wound, and bite, but not when halted by a firm hand and firmer voice.

The flurry of argument was brief enough by the sun's path, and ended in the colt's walking sweetly beside Danu to the grove's edge. The trees alarmed him; he pressed closer then, and paused often to arch his neck and snort. Catin's eyes would roll back then as she led them through the wood, white as the colt's. He could not stroke her neck and soothe her as he did the horse, but he pitched his voice to carry. And maybe it comforted her; or eased her fear at least, because the horse would do nothing that he did not allow it to do.

They came out of the grove into the full light of the sun. The colt threw up his head at the flame of it, braced his feet and opened his mouth and loosed a cry such as Danu had never heard. It was like the trumpeting of a stag, the bellow of a bull; but clearer, higher, more piercing than either. The force of it nigh flung him down.

Somehow he kept his grip on the rope, and kept his feet. Catin had clapped hands over her ears. The city that had seemed deserted when they sought the grove was suddenly full of people, peering out of windows and doorways, running into the streets, staring at the beast that had raised such a peal of sound on the edge of the Lady's grove.

Danu had never craved to be stared at as some people did. Kosti-the-Bull had loved it, had done great feats simply to draw the women's eyes. Not so Danu. He was a quieter spirit.

And here he stood on the edge of Larchwood, clinging to the lead of this great, trumpeting creature, with every eye on both of them. He felt the slow heat rise in his body.

The colt did not care how bitterly he embarrassed the man. He danced to the end of the lead, and pawed, impatient.

Danu scrambled himself together. It was some little distance to the goats' spring pasture. Danu would have to walk it through the much too richly peopled city, with the colt snorting at everything, dancing and shying, making a spectacle of itself.

"The Lady bids it," Danu said to himself, and perhaps to the colt. He stepped forward. The colt danced with him.

Step by step. The colt was quiet now. Amazingly so. Perhaps the Lady had calmed him. He offered no insolence. He stepped lightly among the trees and the houses, alert, prick-eared, but obedient.

A train of people had fallen in behind. Children mostly, but men too, and women. They followed without urgency, as if they had taken it in mind to wander down to the goats' pasture.

Danu could not look back to see who had come, or how many there were. It was a kind of pride. There were many, he knew by the sound. The horse was aware of them: his ears flicked back, then forward, uneasy but unafraid.

Past the last of the city's houses, the trees thinned and the land rose in a long stony slope. The goats, Catin had said, pastured on and about the summit and down the southern side, where the grass grew rich and sweet.

The colt was tiring a little, perhaps. He had been kept so long in so small a space, and naught in it but level land. The hill gave him much to think of.

He was not as light on his feet as a goat, nor as sure of himself on stony paths. Still he did not hesitate once he had begun, nor shrink from going where Danu led him. He had courage.

He saw the goats before Danu, or more likely scented them. He stopped on the slope just short of the summit, and stood staring.

Danu surrendered to the opportunity to rest. "Has he seen goats before?" he inquired of Catin.

She looked down from her perch on a stone above him. "No," she said.

He suppressed a sigh. As all Mothers were unshakably serene, all Mothers' heirs were impossibly difficult. The Lady made them so, he had concluded long ago, to try the spirits of lesser mortals.

He had paused long enough. He coaxed the colt up and forward, stepping carefully for the way was steep. If he slipped and fell, he would not fall far—the slope was crowded with people. But bruises were no pleasure. He scrambled the last of the way, with the colt scrambling behind, and stopped again to breathe and to stare.

It was a broad hilltop and nearly level, falling off less steeply to the southward. Goats grazed on it, watched over by a pair of shepherds. All of them were staring as the people of the city had, at the man and the horse.

Danu could bear a goat's slotted yellow stare more easily than a woman's brown one. He slipped the colt's halter free, conscious as he did it of a gasp that must have been Catin's. Yes: and if the colt had a mind, he could run away southward.

But not, thought Danu, while there was grass here, and companions who smelled strange and looked even stranger, but who ran on four legs, danced and leaped and played, and when they paused, cropped grass as the colt himself did.

The colt forgot the weariness of his climb in dancing toward the goats, neck arched, nostrils wide, drinking their scent. The youngest and boldest of them broke out of the herd to rear to their full height, leap and challenge and threaten him with their horns. He reared in startlement, taller than any of them. They leaped on their hindlegs. He tossed his head and pawed the air. They leaped higher. He wheeled and spun.

A young spotted he-goat stood his ground, shaking his horns. The colt's eye laughed. He caught a horn on his teeth. The goat butted and bucked. He held easily, till the goat twisted; then he let go. The goat reared. He snaked his head, aiming again for the horns.

"Dear Lady!" Catin cried. "He'll be killed."

"No," said Danu. "Look. They test. He plays. He's never in danger."

Catin glowered at him. Still she must have heard the Lady in his voice: she held her peace.

Danu held his own breath. He trusted the Lady. How could he not? And yet Catin had the right of it. Those horns could rip and gore, and the colt had no perceptible fear of them.

The goats pursued him, or he pursued the goats, from end to end of the hilltop, down the southward side and up again. Then at last—and none too soon for Danu's peace—they tired of the game. All together, as if at the end of a dance, they dropped their heads and began to graze.

Danu dared to breathe. The colt was unscathed, cropping grass with his strong yellow teeth, much as an ox would, while the goats nibbled and browsed about him. He towered over them. And yet they seemed to have accepted him.

A murmur brought Danu about. The people of Larchwood were turning away, descending the hill, going back to the city. None of them had spoken, to approve or disapprove what he did.

He had not asked them to judge. He remained where he was. The grass was soft for sitting, the sun warm. One of the goatherds sat quietly by him, produced a packet from the satchel that she carried, unwrapped a loaf and a cheese and a bowl of fruit stewed in honey. She spread them on the grass between the two of them.

It came to Danu as he sat there, that he had not eaten at all that day, nor remembered till this moment. The goatherd broke off a piece of the loaf and held it out to him, smiling. He smiled in return as he took it, and a bit of the cheese with it. His stomach growled like a dog. He laughed in startlement, and bit into the cheese. Goat's cheese, salty-strong, melting on his tongue.

Catin crouched beside him, broke off her own share of the loaf. She had a satchel herself, and in it a napkin of cakes, both sweet and savory.

It was a fine feast they had, there at the top of the hill, while the goats and the horse grazed. The second of the goatherds milked one of the goats for them to drink, and offered them herbs to cleanse their mouths after.

Danu had been a goatherd when he was younger. He remembered how it had been: hard work enough in season, but in the spring there was little to do but watch the goats browse, and keep count lest one of them stray. In Three Birds, people had come on certain days to milk the goats and to carry the milk away in jars for the cheesemaking.

If such was done in Larchwood, this was not one of the days for it. It was a day of lazy watchfulness, of the goats coming to accept the stranger among them, of the stranger finding his way in the order of their herd. The herders were not afraid of him as the rest of their people seemed to be.

"He's flesh and blood," said the woman, whose name was Nati. Her brother Lati seldom spoke, and then chiefly to the goats. She said all that was needful for both of them. Now she said, "It's the dream that frightens them. A living thing, walking on feet and eating our grass . . . that's nothing to harm us."

"He's very large," Catin said, eyeing him as he loomed over the goats. "He'll grow much larger before he's done."

"Never as large as an ox," Nati said: Danu's thought precisely.

"Oxen don't bite," she said, "and *look* at you while they do it."

"Goats do," said Lati, startling them. He got up from his place beside his sister, wandered along the hilltop. He paused to rub the big he-goat between the horns, and to dance a turn or two with the gathering of the kids.

He seemed to take Catin's objections with him. She rose after a few dozen heartbeats. "Come back to the city at evening," she said to Danu.

"And the horse too?" he asked her.

"No!" she said, too vehemently. "Leave him here. Nati will see that he comes to no harm."

Nati did not seem to mind this burden that the Mother's heir had laid on her. She raised a brow, that was all. Catin turned, rather abruptly Danu thought, and set off down the hill, back to Larchwood.

She had not asked Danu to follow yet. Nor was he moved to do so. He lingered in quiet but for the wind and the bleating of goats, and the high far singing of birds.

✦ ✦

At evening Danu left the hill as he was bidden. He was not averse to a night in a soft bed, after a dinner cooked and served under a roof. And yet he was reluctant to leave the colt.

The colt hardly knew that he was there. Replete with grass, content with four-footed company if not of his own kind, with playmates who could run nigh as fast as he could himself, he needed nothing that Danu could provide.

Lati laid a hand on Danu's arm as he hung back, eyes on the horse. "Go," the herdsman said. "I'll look after him for you."

Danu nodded, but slowly, and turned more slowly still, and made his way down toward the city. His shadow paced beside him, looming huge on his right hand. The sun hung low. He should not dally; not if he hoped to be in Larchwood by dusk. He knew the city's ways by daylight, easily enough now he had walked them, but not in the dark.

It was absurd, so to loathe leaving an animal, and one that had forgotten him besides. And yet the Lady had set this beast in his charge. If it came to harm while he lolled in a soft bed, he would bear the burden till he died.

Foolish. Whatever would attack a horse-colt would strike the goats first; and the goatherds would defend him. They had promised.

He straightened his shoulders, firmed his strides. It was dim dusk as he came under the trees. He directed his steps as he could best remember, trusting in the Lady to guide him. As in the morning, the city's ways were empty, as if this were a city of trees and not of people. And yet, tonight, lights glimmered in windows and in open doors. People were watching him, waiting for him to come back as the Mother's heir had commanded.

Almost he did not know the Mother's house as he passed it; but the spiral dance carved on the door, and the young tree in front of it, touched his memory. He was half a dozen steps past before he paused. He turned, to find himself face to face with Catin.

"You came late," she said.

He bent his head. It was neither submission nor reply, but she seemed to accept it as both. She took his hand and tugged him through the door, into light and warmth and the fragrance of roasted meat and new-baked bread.

She kept her Mother's house. He had known that. And yet it struck him as a new thing, a thing that he had not expected. It was a common thing; much more so than a son who saw to his Mother's care. While she was gone a younger sister had done duty for her. The brothers lived in the men's house, all but the one whom one of the elders had chosen. In and from the men's house they did what men did in the Lady's country: tended children, spun and wove and stitched clothing for the people, or went out to the herds, to hunt the woods or fish the river, or to bear messages for the Mother and the elders to this city or that.

Danu's place was in the Mother's house, beside Catin; and, while the sun was high, on the hilltop with the colt whom he had taken out of the grove. Whatever he had come to this place to do, he had not expected that.

Tonight he could eat, drink, rest as much as Catin would allow. She seemed weary herself, though never as dulled of spirit as she had been in Three Birds. They were all quiet: the Mother, the sisters, one or two elders who had come to share the fine roast of lamb. Danu, the only man not a servant, could not wish himself one of them. Not tonight.

It was the horse's pride, perhaps, working in him. They all looked on him with respect. Even the elders. Even—and that was more remarkable— the acolytes who brought the wine.

They all finished at once, and parted as if by agreement. He, too. He went where he had learned to go the night before, to the room farthest back, with its window on the kitchen garden.

Catin had duties still to perform. Danu well knew; in Three Birds that would have been his to do. Still with the horse's pride, he did not go in search of her, nor offer his help. She would not have accepted it.

He undressed and washed in the basin that was set for them both, slowly, all over; a luxury of time that he was seldom given. In the morning, he decided, he would go to the river and wash his hair. Tonight he only combed it out, plaited it and bound it, or by morning it would be one great knot and tangle.

Clean, warm, and naked, he lay on the bed. It was a broader bed than he had had in Three Birds, a woman's bed, with room for the man she chose and for her own comfort. Its coverlet was richly woven but worn, as it had come to Catin from an elder sister. Or perhaps, he thought, her Mother.

He had meant to keep himself awake until she came, but his body betrayed him. He roused, perhaps, as she slid into the bed beside him, but the memory did not linger. Another thing drove it out.

Blood and fire. A roaring as of wind, and a sound like thunder, that broke into shards, and those shards were the sounds of hooves on earth. Horses, horses in multitudes, tossing manes, pounding hooves, bodies jostling as they swept onward. The light on them was blood-red: sunset light. Already the east was dark. And still they came, horses beyond number, streaming out of the night.

And he was not afraid. The fear that had ridden his dreams before was gone. In this one he stood on a high place, and the young horse stood beside him. Its presence made him strong.

That was the secret. That was the thing for which he had come to this place. Not only the horse. The strength that the horse carried. If his mind could encompass it, if he could understand it—he could mount a defense against this thing that came upon them. He, and every one of the Lady's people who could learn not to fear the horse.

Even in his dream he knew the difficulty of that. Catin was the proof: stubborn in her terror, persistent in her refusal to cast it down. If he could make her strong, the rest would follow.

The Lady never asked for easy things. He laughed in his sleep, since if he did not laugh he would cry; and that would do him no good at all.

III

THE SUNSET ROAD

·············· 15 ··············

SARAMA RODE AWAY from her brother and his companions, toward the sun's setting. It was morning still; her shadow rode ahead of her, laying down the path. She did not look back. The Mare was fresh and eager. Even the packhorse danced a little under his burden.

She was no stranger to long journeys. She had traveled the steppe since she was a child, in service to the Old Woman and to Horse Goddess. She set a pace that would not tax the packhorse unduly, but swift enough that by sunset of that first day she was far out of sight of the place where her brother had met her. She camped in a place that she knew, a hollow rich with new grass. A circle of stones marked a firepit, for the place was well known to hunters and walkers abroad.

Such camping places traced a web of roads and hunting-runs across the steppe. They marked the nearness of water, or a place of truce between two tribes, or a resting place on the path of the wild herds.

In this one was a spring welling up from beneath a rock, and a warren of rabbits that yielded a sacrifice for Sarama's pot. She ate to repletion and slept well under a vault of stars. Far away she heard the calling of wolves, but none came near. She lay safe in the goddess' hand.

This was White Horse country in a year when no wars raged. She had cause to hope that none would begin, not after a mild winter. The grass was thick and green, the streams and rivers running high yet no longer in flood. The hunting was good: herds of deer and antelope with fine crops of young, rabbits springing underfoot, birds flocking till they darkened the sky. She hardly needed pause to hunt for the pot. The gods' blessing lay on the earth.

While that was so, the tribes would share the steppe in peace. There was grazing for all their herds, and hunting enough to occupy their young men who might otherwise begin to think of raiding.

Nonetheless a woman alone was prey. Sarama did not creep and hide like a rabbit making its way through a wolfpack. Neither did she ride the ridges, or pursue the tracks of hunters or herdsmen. She cherished her solitude. The wind's song bore her company. Sun by day, stars and moon at night kept watch over her.

Thrice she slipped round camps of the tribes. Red Stallion and Dun Cow looked for kingship to the White Horse. Black River tribe had long been a rival of the White Horse; its young men raided White Horse country in fiercer seasons. They were much given to stealing women and mares.

Even in this rich spring they would look on Sarama and the Mare as ripe fruit fallen into their laps. She took great care to conceal her traces, slipping through their lands like a wind through the grass.

She gave due thanks to the goddess for keeping her safe, and so again each morning and evening, as she passed unmarked into the west. The steppe rolled under the Mare's feet, changeless and yet endlessly, subtly different. The color and flavor of the grass, the flowers that hid in it, the earth and stones beneath it, changed in ways that she had learned to see. Thus she knew when she had come to Red Sand country, and when she left it for the Tall Grass: grass that waved and rustled above her knees as she rode the Mare, and nigh engulfed the smaller pack-pony.

This was country she had not traveled in, that she knew only from tales that she had heard. She had to hunt now for water and for camping places, trusting in her craft and in the noses of her horses. They could always find water. It was her part to keep them more or less on the westward way.

✦ ✦

For all her craft and art and her trust in the goddess, still one day her vigilance failed her. She had known that she was on the track of a hunting party, but had seen where the herd it pursued had veered aside from an outcropping of stone. The hunters had followed it, hot on the chase. It was still some distance ahead of them; therefore when she came to the remnants of the hunters' camp, she had no fear that they would come back to it.

It was well before sunset still, but late enough in the day that she chose to stop rather than to go on. There was grazing in plenty—the hunters had not paused overlong, nor suffered their horses to strip the hillside of grass. Sarama hobbled the pony and turned the Mare loose and bade them take their ease, and built a fire of dried dung that she found near the firepit.

Earlier in the day she had shot an antelope, cleaned it and skinned it and wrapped it in its hide to roast for her dinner. All of it that she did not eat tonight would dry and smoke over the fire, and feed her for days thereafter. With herbs and cresses that she had found by a little river, it made a feast, the best that she had had since she left her brother's camp.

She had the habit of watchfulness, but this day she was at ease. It was, she calculated, another half-moon's journey to the wood that rimmed the world. She had traveled swiftly, without hindrance even from the weather; when it had rained, she had gone on, undaunted by a little wet.

She lay by the fire while her dinner cooked, contemplating the sky. Rain again tomorrow, she thought. Maybe she would linger here, rest, let the packhorse graze and restore its strength. It was looking a little ribby.

Rather to her surprise, she fell asleep. Some last remnant of sense pricked at her to rouse, to mount a better guard—at least to call in the Mare and bid her stand watch. But sleep came on too swift.

+ +

Sarama woke abruptly. It was still daylight; still some time indeed from sunset. The place in which she lay was quiet—too quiet. No wind blew. Nothing stirred the grasses.

The sound when it came was thunderous after the silence, and yet the part of her that measured such things knew it was soft, barely to be heard: the shift of a foot on cleared ground.

Her skin counted them before the rest of her woke to awareness. There were a dozen, perhaps more. A dozen young men afoot, standing in a circle, staring at her as she lay like a child in its mother's tent.

As if her awareness gave them leave to move, to breathe, to be audibly and visibly present, they roused to the myriad small sounds of men gathered together. Feet shifted, weapons clattered, someone coughed. Farther off, a horse snorted. She should have heard those coming—must have, in her sleep; but she had been too great a fool to rouse for it.

She had not, yet, opened her eyes or stirred. She ventured a slit of sight under her lashes. A pair of legs rose next to her, booted and leather-trousered. By the embroidered loin-covering and the broad tooled belt she knew it for a man, though of a tribe she had not seen before—unless the devices on covering and belt were his alone.

No: they all had some form of the same symbols, a burgeoning of cloud, a slash of rain, a creature that must be either wolf or dog. Not all were as rich or as elaborate as that which she had seen first. He had splendid embroideries on his loincloth and his leggings, much tooling on boots and belt, and a shirt so fine he might have worn it to a festival.

He was a handsome creature, too, even without the pretty clothes: a big man even if he had not been looming against the sky, broad-shouldered, with hair as yellow as sunlight, and a thick, curling red beard. If his beauty had a flaw, it was that his hair had thinned somewhat at the temples. But that was little to the whole of him.

She pretended to wake slowly, with much blinking and yawning, as much like a child or a harmless creature as she could manage. That was not as easy as it might have been, what with the knives she wore at her belt, and the bow in its case near the fire. But maybe these strangers had not seen that. It was hidden, somewhat, by the bulk of her pack.

The stranger-chieftain watched her with the dawn of a grin. Any hope she might have had that he would think her a boy on stallion-hunt vanished as he said, "Good evening, beautiful lady. Your man has gone away and left you. That's a poor protector he is, and it so close to sundown, too."

Sarama bit back the first retort that came into her head. They were poor trackers indeed, if they could not see that she had come here alone.

And she was an idiot if she let them know that. Let them think her man had gone off hunting—then they would be wary of his return, and be less inclined to trouble her.

She sat up therefore and stretched, which was perhaps a mistake: eyes widened, tongues licked lips. She had never thought herself particularly good to look at. Certainly she had little by way of breast and hip, and no softness; she was all bones and angles.

She was still a woman, and that, so far out on the steppe, was a great rarity. She rose carefully. No one moved to hinder her. Two of the strangers, she saw with a flare of temper, had crouched by the fire and were hacking off a collop from her antelope. "Good!" one said, with a grin and a leer.

As if that had been a signal, the rest sauntered over to share the feast. Their chieftain made no effort to stop them.

Sarama's anger carried her straight through them, elbowing them aside, kicking the laggards, making a weapon of their openmouthed surprise. The last one, the one who had tasted first, she heaved up by the scruff of the neck and dispatched with a swift kick to the seat of his trousers. She planted her feet in the space that he had left, set fists on hips, and glared at the lot of them. "This is *my* dinner. If you hunger for a share of it, ask. Were you raised in a wolves' den? Where are your manners?"

She had taken them completely off guard. The lesser ones shuffled and muttered. Their chieftain wavered transparently between wrath and laughter. By good fortune and by the goddess' will, he settled on the latter. He threw back his great golden-maned head and roared.

The others followed suit, some hesitantly, some faintly—but they were all their prince's men. He strode through them still laughing, swept a bow

as if she had been a king or a king's son, and said with elaborate courtesy,
"Lady of the hearth, great queen of the steppe, if your generosity can spare
a traveller's portion, we would be glad of it."

"Your hunt fared ill?" she asked him. That was not courteous, but she
was in no mood to indulge his fancy.

His eyes flickered. She was put in mind again of the horses hidden away
out of sight—and, no doubt, the quarry that they carried. He had seen that
this place was occupied, had marked the lone woman, had come to prey on
her.

Wisdom would have put her to flight while he was still off guard. She
would lose provisions, bow and arrows, blanket—but she would have the
Mare and the pack-pony, and she could hunt for what else she needed.

Unless the horses had been captured.

No; she would have known. And he would not have thought that she
had a companion.

But she was not wise. She was angry. This was her camp, her antelope,
her rest that these strangers had disrupted. Let them find their own camp
and cook their own dinner.

Her smile made the chieftain flinch. She did not pause to wonder why.
"That was a fine herd of deer you were tracking. Did they escape? My brother
would have brought home half a dozen, enough to feed the tribe. He's a
great hunter, my brother is. He killed a lion once, because he'd tired of lesser
sport."

The chieftain flushed. Sarama had told no lies. Agni was indeed as she
had said; though he would have growled at her for saying it so baldly. Sarama
had never learned the fine art of the vaunt.

Still it was enough, perhaps, to shame this yellow-haired prince. If he
thought that it was her brother out on the steppe, hunting new prey while
his sister roasted the old, then so much the better.

"Suppose," Sarama said, "that you bring one of those fat bucks, and
such bread and sweetness as you may have, and we feast together. Have you
kumiss? Or honey mead? My brother loves the honey mead—though he's
grown somewhat fonder of that thing called wine. You know wine, yes?"

"Wine comes from the west," one of the lesser strangers said. "She talks
like an easterner. What do easterners know of wine?"

Sarama forbore to upbraid him for speaking of her as if she had not been
there. Men did that in the tribes. And these did not know who or what she
was—nor, quite yet, did she intend to tell them. If they could not see Horse
Goddess' hand on her, so much the worse for them.

She answered him therefore, as sweetly as she knew how. "We know what
wanderers and traders bring, and what our king takes in tribute in the gathering of tribes. My brother is very fond of western wine."

"We have none of that," the chieftain said, and perhaps his regret was
genuine; perhaps he told the truth. "Mead we have. Rodri! Maelgan! Go,
fetch the horses. We'll feast here with this stranger, and with her brother
when he comes back."

The two whom he had commanded wheeled and leaped into a run. The tightness in Sarama's back relaxed the merest fraction. She was not at ease—not in the least. But she had passed a test of sorts. They had declared a truce. For a little while. Until the horses were brought, and indeed they were laden with fruits of the hunt.

Men set to work skinning and cleaning the kill. Others tended the horses, built a fire, made camp as the sun sank low.

Sarama sat beside her own fire, close by her pack and the shadow-hidden bow. The chieftain settled near her with an air of one who never thinks to ask another's leave. She wondered if he was indeed a king, or a chieftain of this Stormwolf tribe; or whether, at home among the tents, he bent his head to another, older chieftain. He did not look like one who had ever bent his head to any man.

He was protection, of a sort. None of the others would trouble her while he sat near her. She settled herself more comfortably, back against her pack, hand resting on the grass near the hidden bow.

The chieftain's name was Gauan. It was an odd name in his western burr, of which she heard a great deal as the camp took shape around them. Gauan was a talking man. He loved the sound of his own voice.

It spared her the effort of entertaining him. Every question that he asked of her, he answered for himself, without pause to let her speak. She had no need to lie, then, or to turn her words in ways that concealed the truth. She was traveling with her brother, he had decided, on some errand of dubious significance—hunting wine, he said laughing, or chasing the horizon. Or they were exiled from their tribe; sinners against the king, condemned for some infraction that would seem small in the eyes of a stranger. "Did you step in his shadow? Laugh at the wart on his nose? Offend him by being children of an elder wife?"

That last was close enough to the truth, if the king had been Yama, that Sarama let her eyes widen a fraction. He took it as she had hoped, for the ghost of a nod.

"So!" he said in satisfaction. "Children of an elder wife are a great inconvenience if one would be king. So your brother is still a boy, then? Still too young to contest his right?"

Again Sarama implied without speaking.

"Ah! Not so young then. But young enough. Not won his stallion yet? That's a pity. He'll not likely find one here. All the herds run northward, this time of year. There's one—it grazes in Raindance lands—its colts are strong and not too willful. But they go up around the Lake of Reeds and stay there summerlong."

"Is that a long way from here?" Sarama asked in what was, for once, space to speak.

He blinked at her, as if the sound of her voice had startled him. Nonetheless he answered her willingly enough. "Nine days' journey," he said, "if the weather holds fair. Longer if it rains. The Lake of Reeds grows then."

"Maybe," said Sarama, "we should go there."

"It is a strong herd," Gauan said. And was off again like a colt with the bit in his teeth.

She barely listened. The sun hung low. Of the Mare and the packhorse she saw and heard no sign. She could not escape yet; for all his endless blather, he never took his eyes from her.

It was full dark before the deer was roasted, the bread made, the mead brought out in its leather-wrapped jars. Sarama might have thought to ask what kind of hunters carried mead enough for a feast. The same kind of hunters, she thought, who dressed as if they were riding to a festival. Somewhere amid Gauan's babble she gathered that they were doing just that: riding to his wedding in fact. But he had ridden more swiftly than he meant, and must not, by the rite, show his face in the woman's tribe before the new moon, which was a hand of days hence.

"And so," he said, "we hunt the runs just past theirs, and wait to make our extrance."

Tonight they dined on venison and antelope and honey mead, on bread and herbs and pungent cheese. It would have been a pleasant feast if Sarama had not felt like a rabbit among wolves.

No, she told herself sternly. A she-wolf in the pack of the young males. She was not safe, no, but neither was she defenseless. She was armed with teeth and claws, and with the power of the goddess.

She drank little of the mead: a sip only. She ate lightly, as one should before battle. The others knew no such restraint. They gorged happily, stuffing in the meat till the grease ran down their sparse young beards, and drank in great gulps, vying with one another to see who could down the most the fastest.

Gauan could hardly do otherwise than be the best of them. It was a prince's duty, one that he could not shirk. And yet, as a prince should be, he was no soft-headed man. He could eat hugely, drink hugely, and keep a steady eye on Sarama.

The inevitable, when it came, was surprising in its gentleness. He reached in the firelight to trace the line of her cheek. "You are beautiful," he said.

She set her teeth and did not twitch away from him. The bow was out of its case, eased there by excruciating degrees. Four arrows lay beside it. The bow was unstrung; but she could string it at the run.

A run she could not make. Not yet. Her other hand, her free hand, rested near the hilt of her longer knife, the one that was almost a sword.

He swayed closer. She held her breath against the smell of him: mead, meat, leather and wool and unwashed male. He was vastly sure of himself. Softly, sweetly, he said, "I do not believe that there is a brother out there waiting to come to your rescue. If he exists at all, he's gone alone to find his stallion—or to capture himself a tribe. He'd not be glad of a sister's presence, not unless he hoped to trade her for power in the tribe."

Sarama smiled with sweetness to match his. "You don't know my brother," she said.

"I know men," said Gauan. "Come, beautiful lady. I'll protect you. No harm will come to you while you live in my tent."

"Your wife might beg to differ," Sarama said.

He regarded her in honest amazement. "How can she do that? She is *my* wife."

Sarama shook her head. "I have never lived in a man's tent. I never intend to."

"You are a woman," Gauan said, as if that ended all discussion.

"I am Horse Goddess' servant," said Sarama.

He laughed as if at a glorious jest. "*Are* you now? And I serve Skyfather and Earth Mother and the Storm Gods and the Ones below. Can your one goddess stand against all of those?"

"She can indeed," said Sarama, "if she is the goddess in her own self, and not merely names in a braggart's vaunt."

He sucked in breath, and temper with it. She rose above him. Her bow was in her hand: strung in a blur of motion, arrow nocked, aimed at his heart. She loosed a clear call. A second call came back: the full-throated neigh of a mare who finds that one of the herd is lost.

The Mare came out of the night into the red glow of the firelight. In that light her grey coat was gleaming white, her eyes blood-red. Her hooves battered men too drunk or too slow to spring out of her path. She leaped the lesser fire, on which the bones of the antelope lay like an offering, scattering bones and embers, and thundered to a halt before Sarama.

Sarama did not lower the bow nor shift her glare from Gauan's face. "I am the goddess' servant," she said.

Gauan was a fool, but not a blind one. He fell down before her—and all of his people who could, did as he did. "Lady," he said. "Lady. I never—I didn't—"

She almost took pity on him. "I do in truth have a brother," she said, "and he is in truth on quest for his stallion. Maybe he will find the herd you speak of. Maybe he'll find another. As for me, I ride at my Lady's bidding. She would not take it amiss if you were to ride with me to the edges of this country. But offer no insolence, and take no liberty. Surely you have seen how a stallion pays when he mounts a mare who has no desire for him."

Gauan blanched. The first gelding, it was said, had been made by a mare.

Sarama smiled. "I see you understand. And now I shall sleep, and in the morning I shall ride, and you and your men will ride with me. And when I have passed out of this country, you will go to claim your wife, and to dance at your wedding."

"Lady," he said, bowing to her will. Or at least, to the power of the Mare, who had raised her head to snap teeth in his face.

16

Gauan was not an ill companion, for a man. His stream of chatter had well recovered by morning, and he seemed to have bowed to necessity. Not he nor any of his people had offered the slightest insolence to Sarama in the night, nor cast a glance astray since.

In their company she had no fear of meeting strangers. They were a large and strong riding, and they knew all the best ways of their own country, the springs and streams that her craft might have missed, the hunting-runs and the paths of the herds. They made her think not a little of her brother and his friends.

But like her brother, Gauan could not follow her past his tribe's borders. He had a wedding to ride to, a wife to take.

"Be kind to her," Sarama said the night before they came to the edge of his people's country. "Listen to her when she speaks to you. She has a mind, too, and intelligence, though it's been stunted in the walls of her father's tent."

"But," said Gauan, whose awe of her had grown rather than diminished in the days of their riding together—and goddess knew why that was, but there was no denying it. "Lady, she's a woman. Everyone knows women are weak of wit as of strength, and sore in need of men's protection."

"So too would you be weak," she shot back, "if you were never let out of a tent nor allowed to ride or even walk."

"But women are weaker," he said, "and smaller. Lady, are you as tall as I, or as broad?"

"That is so," Sarama said willingly enough, "but I'm no weaker than a man of my size. I can ride and I can shoot, and I hunt not badly. You will be amazed, I think, to find that your wife has wits and will of her own."

Gauan frowned. At least he was willing to listen; that was more than most men would have done. Sarama sighed a little and let be.

There was little more they could have said in any case. Gauan's companions had conspired in a grand farewell, with the last of the mead, and dancing and singing and telling of tales. Some had music with them, pipe or drum, and one fine singer brought forth a tortoiseshell strung with horsehair that, plucked, sounded sweet and faintly sad.

They danced and sang for her as if she had been a king. It was in Horse Goddess' honor, of course. Sarama alone would have been raped or captured and carried off to Gauan's tent. Nonetheless it was a fine thing, and some of the singing was very good indeed. The dances were men's dances, with much stamping and shouting, exuberant as young stallions and quite as much inclined to fall into mock war.

For honor's sake Sarama must respond in kind. She waited till the dancers had dropped exhausted, and the singers paused to cool their throats with mead. The player on the tortoiseshell continued, and one or two of those with pipes. They wove a wandering melody.

Sarama rose from the place of honor beside their chieftain. One of the young men had laid his drum near her foot. She took it up. It was one of the small drums, easy to carry on a horse, skin stretched taut over a frame of supple wood. Its sound was rich for a drum so small. Sarama beat on it lightly with her fingers, striking a pulsebeat.

With that she drew all eyes to her, and silenced the ripple of chatter round the fire's circle. Still beating the drum, swaying slightly in time with the rhythm, she made her way to the cleared space. The grass was well beaten down by the dancers who had come before. She tested it with gliding steps, found it good.

The musicians had found the beat and made themselves part of it. She flashed a smile at them. Perhaps they smiled back. She could not see. She was in light, the rest in darkness, a ring of shadows, a flicker of eyes.

She danced slowly at first, little more than a step, a turn, a sway, over and over, round and round. The earth was firm and yet yielding underfoot. The stars arched overhead. She could feel the horses beyond the reach of the fire's light, some on guard, some grazing, some sleeping within the ring of their herdmates.

The fire cracked suddenly and shot sparks up to heaven. She leaped with it, and the music with her, swift as a startled mare. Like a mare she wheeled, stamped, veered. The music quickened. She matched it, swifter, swifter, till the long plait of hair whipped out behind her, and the stars spun, and the wind wailed in her ears.

She danced the Mare. That first slow meander had been the horse at rest, grazing on the breast of Earth Mother. Then the leap into flight, the mad gallop, the startlement turned to delight in her own swiftness. And then, as the music bore her onward, little by little she eased her pace, to canter, to trot, to walk again, to slow meander in search of the sweet grass.

The music softened and faded till it had sunk away beneath the wind's whisper. There was a moment's silence.

Shouts shattered it, whoops and roars and the drumming of fists and feet. Sarama dropped down beside Gauan. The young men cheered her on for a while, for the sheer pleasure of making the stars ring.

✦ ✦

Sarama rode westward again with a glad heart and a memory of the young men of Gauan's following, the whole rank of them, standing at the edge of their camp and singing her on her way. Their song followed her long after they had sunk below the curve of the horizon, borne on a wind out of the morning.

The wind carried her far before evening. As she rode she began to see a shadow in the west, like a low lie of cloud. At first she thought little of it. But it remained, motionless, while the sky shifted and changed, sun to swift scud of clouds to brief and startling spat of rain, and thence to sun again.

By evening she knew what she had seen, and would see until she came to the edge of it: the wood that walled the world. With each day's riding it loomed larger, and seemed darker. Night never left there; the sun never touched it. She began to understand the fear that had held back the tribes of the west, that made the wood a wall more forbidding than mountain or river.

In this season the tribes should be well scattered, seeking each its own lands. And yet as she rode she saw remnants of camps close together, signs of tribes moving as they did in the spring, as if to a gathering. It was not a war: in war, the women would not go, nor the herds. Something brought them together out of season.

Their path lay westward as did hers. Caution bade her move carefully, let none see her riding alone on the steppe. She could travel more quickly for that; could pass ahead of the clans with their herds, their laden beasts and women, their need to travel from water to water for the herds' sake.

She began to wonder—to fear—that they had determined, all of them, to venture the wood; to cross into that country to which Horse Goddess called her. If the goddess had willed such a thing, she spoke no word of it to Sarama. She was not mute—Sarama heard her voice in the wind, her blessing on the land; heard her song in the Mare's footfalls, and her will in the rustle of the grass. But of these tribes moving westward, she said nothing at all.

Perhaps, thought Sarama, it was Skyfather's doing. She knew little of him. He was a younger god, a men's god. Her people—her mother's people—had naught to do with him, or he with them.

She should go on, should take no notice of these tribes. They were none of hers, nor had the goddess bidden her trouble herself with them. But they held to much the same road, and their gathering would lie across her path. If they were preparing to brave the wood, their purpose well might run afoul of hers.

She would not be caught as she had been by Gauan's people. She rode as a hunter on the track of watchful prey. She pitched camp in carefully hidden places. She concealed her tracks as she might, passing like a wind through the grass.

❖ ❖

The clans and the tribes came together perhaps a day's ride from the wood, where they must gather in the spring: a wide well-watered place marked by a circle of stunted trees like an outrider of the wood that, now, filled the horizon. It was a holy place. Its earth had drunk deep of the blood of sacrifice.

Sarama walked there boldly, concealing herself in plain sight. People saw what they expected to see. A broad-striding figure in trousers, bow and quiver at back, knife at side, could be no woman.

Their dialect was odd, with words in it that she had not heard before, and cadences that made even the words she knew seem strange. And yet, listening on the edges of camps, just past the circles of men or boys, even, from a tree's shadow, within the grove where the elders met, she understood enough.

They spoke of the west. Of tribes pressing on them from east and south. Of clans growing, herds waxing, lands diminishing. "North," said one of the elders in the circle of trees. "Why not north?"

"North is Skyfather's country," the king said. He was a man of middle years, soft and thick about the belly, but the hands that gripped the haft of a spear were long-fingered and strong. The spear was his mark of office: its haft was painted red, its head of bone bound to the haft with an intricate weaving of cords. A black horsetail hung from it.

A small wind played in the circle, stirring the hairs of the horsetail. "North promises us nothing," said the king.

"West promises less," the elder said. "North are the tribes of the north wind, and the home of the winter snows. West is—that."

He lifted his hand, flicked a gesture that Sarama had not known before, but its import was plain. He averted evil from himself and his people.

The king sat still, though other hands flicked round the circle. His own were motionless on the spearhaft. "What fools are we, that we remember old fears and forget what every trader and youth on walkabout knows? West is rich country, tents that never move, people born to serve the lords of creation, and no horses. They make wine. They make the pots for which we pay so dearly in furs and hides and cattle. And they make copper, which is the greatest wonder of them all. All ripe for us to take, waiting for our coming."

Just so had people spoken in the gathering of the White Horse, far away in the east of the world.

But these tribes were closest. These tribes could, if they mustered their courage, pierce the wood like a sword, and take the soft country beyond.

Their king clearly had thought long on this, and prepared himself against the elders' fears. "The wood is full of demons—granted. Death walks there on its bony feet. Madness flits among the trees. *But*"—and that one word was like crack of thunder, snapping them all erect, even Sarama—"have we not Skyfather? Have we not our courage, and our horses? Are we not men? Men fear nothing while they work Skyfather's will."

"If it is his will," said the elder who seemed to speak for the rest. "What say the priests? Have they read the omens?"

The king's eyes flickered, perhaps. "The priests are as blind with fear as any of the rest of you. Skyfather has opened my eyes. I can see—and what I see is splendor."

"So is the gods' country splendid," said the elder, "but before a man may go there, that man must die. The wood is death, my king. Would you kill us all?"

"And when," the king demanded, "has any one of us died in the wood? The traders never have, nor any of the young men who dared to wander."

"They were few, or alone," the elder said doggedly. "They were no temptation to demons. Our whole tribe and nation, leaving the lands that we have held since the dawn time—us they will not only see but lust after."

"They lived," said the king, as dogged as he, and as unwearied in repetition. "So shall we."

Sarama could see that he was determined to have his way, but she could see with equal clarity that his elders would not hear him. A king was king, but without the elders his power was a shadow.

Among the lesser tribesmen it was much the same. A few of the younger hotheads were ready to take horse and charge into the wood. Most of the men were as the elders were, set in fear and unswayed by accusations of cowardice. It was not cowardice, as Sarama heard one say, to refuse a certain death for no useful cause.

She should have been comforted. The king had called this gathering to rouse his people to an advance on the west. But his people were not to be roused. It was a rich year. Their flocks and herds had pasture enough, though not as wide as in the days that their fathers remembered. They were glad of a gathering out of season, pleased to visit with kin and distant friends. They were not of a mind to venture a place of ancient horror, even for the hope of riches.

Nonetheless their king had heard Skyfather's will. On that he was adamant. Let the winter be harsh, the summer lean and poor of grass and hunting, and these tribes would forget their resistance; would turn toward the king's will.

Perhaps after all Horse Goddess had sent Sarama here, set this gathering in her path, as both lesson and warning. If the tribes did not brave the west in this season, they would do it before too many seasons had passed. It was as inevitable as the breaking of a riverbank in a flood.

•••••••••• 17 ••••••••••

Sarama slipped out of the gathering as unnoticed as she had slipped into it. She had been guided, and was being guided still, held safe in the goddess' hand.

The Mare waited impatiently for her, and the packhorse whose burden now was barely enough to notice. They were eager to be away. She had been thinking that the sun was closer to the horizon than to the zenith; that she might camp here, even as close to the gathering as it was. But the horses tugged at their leads, yearning westward.

If she had been a man, perhaps, she would have set herself against their will. But a wise woman knew to heed her horses. When the Mare glanced over her shoulder toward the direction from which Sarama had come, and snorted, Sarama wasted no more time. She sprang onto the Mare's back. The packhorse, for once, was happy to move at speed, moving swiftly under his much diminished burden.

The wood was a wall of darkness before her. As the Mare settled to a steady pace, she heard behind her the sound of hooves, and the yelp of a hound.

Hunters went out often from such gatherings as that of the tribes, and often in companies, the better to hunt down and bring back game for the pot. They would not pursue two horses, one ridden, one led, who might themselves be on the hunt.

And yet they rode on her trail; and the Mare had no desire to linger, even to greet the stallions.

Skyfather and Horse Goddess had not often been allies, nor had they ever been friends. Sarama, running as prey, hunted by men who should not have seen or known of her, felt keenly her own smallness and her solitude, and their strength and numbers. All her army was one grey Mare and a packhorse who could not, with the best of his will, keep for long to the pace that the Mare was setting.

She could feel him laboring through the line that held them together, straining for speed that he had never thought was in him. The Mare would not slow, though he dragged at her.

With a sound like a cry, he stumbled. The rope burned Sarama's hand, slipped and broke free. She nigh fell with it, but the Mare shifted as she slipped. She caught mane, gasping at the pain of her torn hand. The packhorse had staggered up, was struggling to follow. But he could not catch the Mare.

Once free of him, she stretched her stride. She was not running to her fullest, not she. And yet even at what was still, for her, a none too pressing pace, she made the wind her rival.

Sarama had lost even pretense of mastering the Mare. She crouched low over the outstretched neck. Mane the color of smoke whipped her cheeks.

She ventured a glance backward. The packhorse had dropped to a stumbling trot. A mob of yelling riders swept upon him. As if in surrender, he halted. They swirled about him, whooping and brandishing spears.

He did not even delay them. They had seen the greater prize: the lone rider, the fine horse. A god rode them, or gods: the gods of the hunt, of war, of the storm. Skyfather ruled them.

There was war in heaven. The thought was very clear. Sarama was astonished at its clarity. She had no wits to pray, still less to think past the next rapid heartbeat, but that one thing held fast within her. She must not let it go. Whatever she did, she must not lose it as she had lost the packhorse.

All her purpose now was to cling to the Mare's back, to let her run as the goddess guided her. There were no horses like her in this part of the world, none as strong or as swift, but she had traveled far and on short commons, and these horses were fresh from the camp.

They were gaining on her. Sarama crouched lower on the Mare's neck and prayed.

The Mare darted sidewise. Sarama's deathgrip held her on. She sucked in a startled breath, just as the earth dropped beneath the Mare's feet.

They fell for the count of eternity. And yet it was not even a breath's span. The Mare landed lightly, her stride barely interrupted, and ran along a steep wall of earth and stones. A little river ran on Sarama's left hand. The Mare ran on what must be its bed in the flood season, clear and solid sand.

The river bent sharply, and the cutting with it. The mare swerved round the bend, then slowed a fraction; and sprang into the water.

It was breast-deep, its current slow. The shock of cold water on hot skin made them both grunt. The Mare pressed doggedly onward.

The bank on the far side thrust outward somewhat, as Sarama saw when she came near it. Roots of trees hung in a tangle. A tree had fallen across the stream. It was not too much for a horse to cross, but the Mare had no intention of doing such a thing. She plunged into the tangle of roots and weeds and dead leaves.

Sarama wrapped arms about the Mare's neck and made herself as small as human form could be. Roots clawed at her back and her hair. The air was heavy with the reek of earth and mold and rotting wood.

Just as she knew she would be caught forever, and the Mare with her, the roots retreated. The Mare stopped. Her sides were heaving, wet with sweat. It had soaked through the saddle-fleece and through Sarama's leather trousers. Her buttocks and the backs of her thighs stung with the shock of salt on chafed skin.

Slowly, stiffly, Sarama unlocked her arms from about the Mare's neck, and straightened. No roof of branches stopped her.

She looked about in astonishment. This was no mere hollow made by the roots of a tree against a flood-carved riverbank. It was a cave. Light shone dimly through the tangle of roots, some distance ahead of her. She stood in a chamber in the earth. Its walls were earth and stone. Its floor was stone beneath a carpet of leafmold.

Sarama slid from the Mare's back. Her knees buckled, but she braced them. She cared nothing for that. The Mare's neck and flanks were crusted with foam; she was all dark as she had been when she was a foal, her grey coat darkened with sweat to uncover the black skin beneath.

Praise the goddess: there was room in the cave to walk the Mare till her breathing quieted, to pull saddle and saddlebags from her and leave them, and walk her cool and even dry. Her footfalls were silent on the leafmold.

When the Mare's gasping had ceased but before her skin had cooled, and well before she was dry, Sarama's straining ears caught what she had dreaded. Men's voices calling. But no hounds' baying. No sound of their having found the scent.

She walked the Mare round and round as they drew closer and closer. Her own breath had grown quick and shallow. She caught herself trying to hold it.

They were on her, voices as clear as if they stood in the cave, conversations mingling and tumbling over one another.

"Cursed sand won't hold a track."

"Bet your best arrowhead he went in the river."

"What do you think he was? Spy for the Winter Hawk?"

"Na, na; they never hunt this far north."

"They would if there was something worth hunting for."

"Horse like that, that's a prince's prize. What if he's a decoy?"

"They'd raid in broad daylight?"

"Why not? All the better to strut at home, how they lured off all the best hunters and fighting men with a grey horse and a lone rider, and walked in as free as you please, and took whatever they could get their hands on."

"Curse this sand! There's been a whole herd of horses through here, and that one without the sense to drop a pile and show us the way."

As if that had been a reminder, the Mare lifted her tail and deposited an odorous heap near the back of the cave. Sarama suppressed a spurt of laughter. The hunters had ridden past, but if she could hear them still so distinctly, then they well might be able to hear her.

"Hoi!" one of them called from well ahead. "Fresh sign!"

The hoofbeats quickened, the last of them passing at the gallop.

Whatever the one in the lead had found, it lured the lot of them onward, away from Sarama's hiding place.

The Mare was cool, her coat dry, her breathing at ease. Sarama brushed away the stiff salt sweat with a knot of roots, taking her time about it. It calmed her, too, let her rest a little, suffered her to think. She could not go on, not without danger of the hunt's return. She had no desire to go back. She could climb the bank and so escape, but the Mare was not so fortunate.

She grieved to lose the packhorse, but she would die before she lost the Mare.

The packhorse had carried most of what she owned, but she had a little with her: her bow and arrows, the spare bowstrings, her waterskin, a little dried meat and a few roots and herbs. She offered the Mare to drink from the waterskin. The Mare, accustomed to such courtesy, drank as much as Sarama would allow her: nearly all of it, with a swallow or two for Sarama. That was no cause to fret; there was a whole river to drink and to fill the skin from, once she dared venture out. The meat and herbs were enough to keep her fed till morning. Fodder for the Mare was a greater anxiety. There was nothing here, not even leaves; it was all rotted to mold.

Goddess in flesh the Mare might be, but that flesh was a horse, and horses must eat. Sarama moved with sudden decision. "Stay here," she said to the Mare. The Mare regarded her blandly, as a horse could when it had not decided whether to listen. *"Stay,"* Sarama commanded her. "I will come back. My oath on that."

Oaths meant little to a mare. But she did not try to follow when Sarama slipped out the way they had come. When Sarama looked back, she was hip-shot, head low, dozing as a wise mare might when she reckoned herself safe.

Sarama sighed faintly. It would do—it would have to do.

✢ ✢

The hunt had run far ahead. Sarama kept to the shadow of the bank, alert for hiding places if it should come roaring back upon her; but it seemed well gone. Perhaps it had found another hapless quarry, a deer, or a spy indeed from the tribe that seemed to be their rival.

The river bent several times more. It was flowing, she began to perceive, out of the wood. Its banks grew less steep as she went on. In time she could see where a horse might scramble up.

The light was growing long. The shadows down by the river were deep: night had already settled there. She could, perhaps, fetch the Mare and bring her back to this place, and ascend to the steppe; but then she would be caught in the open, fair prey for any hunter who passed.

After dark, she thought. There would be a moon tonight; the sky was clear, no threat of clouds or rain. Demons walked after the sun had set, but Sarama had less fear of them than of men under Skyfather's power.

Travel by night or travel at dawn and pray the hunt did not come back or find her, travel she must, and soon. The wood was close. She felt it on her skin, a darkness and a coldness beyond what grew in the river's bed as night came on.

She would travel by night, and trust the goddess to defend her. An urgency was on her, apart from simple fear. She must go westward. She must hang back no longer.

18

The Mare came willingly out of the cave. Sarama did not try to ride her; let her follow unled, while the shadows deepened, though the sky was bright above.

The hunt did not come back. She found the fallen place, the slope less steep though still punishing for woman and Mare alike. The Mare's haunches bunched as she sprang up it. Sarama, caught behind, scrambled after. The Mare did not slip or falter, but Sarama saw how those haunches trembled, how her breath came hard. She was touching the edge of her strength.

So were they both. And yet they must go on. Up out of the river's deep bed, on under a waning moon and the fields of stars, walking slowly through the tall whispering grass. Neither led the other. They simply walked toward the darkness ahead, darker than the night about them.

No hunter of this country would follow them into that place. But first they must come there. As close as it seemed, still it was a long stretch of steppe to walk, and demons and night-creatures between, and hunters perhaps, if they had laid an ambush.

Sarama did not know what Skyfather might do. The west did not worship him, from all she had heard. He would covet it, its tribes of people, their riches, their sacrifices. And his people would be his instrument.

But where a goddess could move a lone woman to do her will at once and in unquestioning obedience, even a god could not sway whole tribes together; not swiftly, and not easily. He could set a pack of young men on the track of the goddess' servant, but none of them had had the power to pierce her subterfuge, to find Sarama where the Mare had hidden her.

Skyfather would not be pleased this night, to have lost his quarry. Without the sun that was his all-seeing eye, he was blind; but some of his servants walked the darkness, too, and they could see as clear as if it had been day. Sarama heard them hunting at some little distance: wolves squabbling, it seemed, over prey.

If they caught her scent they would harry her. Wolves in this country were scavengers, hunters of carrion, followers after the lion's dinner, but a pack of them could pursue a weakened woman and a weary mare. And where wolves were, the lion was seldom far away.

She could walk no faster. Her strength was nearly gone. And still she had the forest to face.

The forest was not Skyfather's place. No, not his of the open sky. If she could pass under the trees, shut out the sky, she would be safe from him. His creatures would not pursue her. Not yet. They were not brave enough.

She did not know that she was, either; but like a rabbit running ahead of a fire on the steppe, she would leap into the wolves' den rather than burn.

Only a little farther. The Mare stopped suddenly. Sarama stumbled into her. She turned, ears flattened. *On my back,* the sharp gesture said.

Sarama drew breath to protest. The Mare's teeth snapped in her face. It was not so very far—and the Mare, even so wearied, could move far faster under Sarama than could Sarama on foot. With a mutter that might have been a curse, or might have been a prayer, Sarama pulled herself onto the Mare's back.

The Mare wasted no time in satisfaction. She moved into a canter, slower than her wont but swift enough to wake the wind in Sarama's face. Sarama strained her senses; but there was no sign of uncertainty in the Mare's gait. Her footfalls were steady, unwavering, though the ground rose and fell, the endless roll of the steppe.

The wolves caught them under the first eaves of the trees: a manifold ripple in the last of the grass, a gleam of eyes in the moonlight. The lion would be behind them, if he had followed. Lions were lazy; they waited for their lionesses, or even for wolves to make the kill for them. But if they lost patience, their strength was deadly.

Sarama's bow was strung, an arrow nocked. She would have given much for fire, for certain terror to her attackers. But there was no time to muddle about with the firestick. Her arrows would have to be enough, and her knife if they came so close.

The Mare carried her with no evidence of fear, straight toward the darkness and the cool breath of the trees. Sarama had twisted back, seeking a target; but the wolves, as if sensing her purpose, had hidden themselves and their eyes in the grass. But they were close on her track.

Tree-branches wove together, shutting out the starlight. The moon shone fitfully through, dappling the forest floor. Sarama, faced still toward the steppe, nonetheless felt the dark wrap about her.

Perhaps Skyfather drove them; perhaps the lion behind grew short of patience. Dark bodies burst out of the grass, running under the trees. Fangs caught a fleck of moonlight. An eye gleamed red.

A wind swept past the Mare, a torrent of motion. And yet Sarama felt nothing on her cheeks. It was all below, skimming the ground: dark bodies, soft feet, the mutter of a growl. A wolf yelped, piercingly sharp.

Wolves again, but of a different kind: bigger, darker, fiercer. The wood defended itself. It let Sarama pass. But the wolves it drove back, hunting them into the grass; putting even the lion to flight. No lion was a fool, or inclined to fight unless he must.

The Mare carried Sarama some distance into the wood. Without moon or stars she could not tell how far, or in what direction she went; only that it was away from the steppe and its dangers.

It was dark, dark and still, no wind blowing. Yet it was not silent. Whispers, rustles, the distant howl of a wolf; the murmur of leaves high overhead, and the hooting call of a bird, and a brief, blood-curdling shriek as something died for a hunter's dinner.

The Mare moved among the trees, treading softly on the mold of years. As she walked she snatched at leaves and bits of things growing along the ground: feeding herself as she had not been able to do in her run from river to wood. Sarama reflected on the bit of dried meat in her bag, but hunger had shut itself away. Far more urgent was the need to sleep.

As if it had known her desperation, the forest opened suddenly into a broad clearing. It seemed a memory of steppe: a roll of grass under the moon, a scattering of flowers. A stream ran through it from wood's edge to wood's edge.

Sarama pulled saddle-fleece and bridle from the Mare, and dropped them in the grass. The Mare grunted with pleasure, snatched great mouthfuls of grass, went down suddenly and rolled till every itch and ache was gone. Sarama loosed a breath of laughter and let her knees buckle at last, and fell headlong into sleep.

✦ ✦

She woke with a start. Guard—she should watch—

Sunlight dazzled her. She shaded her eyes against it, sitting up and peering about. The Mare grazed not far from her, peaceful, unafraid. Nothing had touched or harmed her.

Dimly Sarama remembered being hunted: men in daylight, wolves under the moon—and wolves hunting wolves, forest guardians driving the strangers away. There was no sign of wolf here. Only sun and grass and flowers, the stream that sang over its stones, and ripe sweet berries hiding in the grass. She ate till she was sated, then drank deep from the stream.

The water was icy cold. Nonetheless, after a moment's thought, she stripped and bathed in it, head to foot, scrubbing away the memory of hunting and hiding, running and fear. Sweet herbs that grew on the bank both cleansed and scented her, till she tingled all over, beautifully and blissfully clean.

She lay naked on the grass, letting the sun both warm and dry her. She should go on, she knew that. She could not know for certain that the hunters had turned back at the wood's edge. And yet she could not make herself rise, dress, move.

✦ ✦

It was hunger that roused her at last, a growling in her belly that would not be ignored. Berries alone had barely whetted its appetite. She fed it the last of the dried meat; she would have to hunt and kill more, if her body craved it.

Her courses were on her. She gathered grass from the meadow and moss from the treetrunks, to do what was necessary; then gathered up bow and arrows and set out to find what she could find.

As soon as the wood had surrounded her and the meadow vanished behind, she knew that she had erred. On the steppe she knew her way, even when the country was strange to her. In this tree-bound place, cut off from the sky, she could not choose right from left, forward from back. She was all out of her reckoning.

With an effort she quieted her thudding heart, breathed deep, willed calm. Her tracks were visible behind her, more visible indeed in the leafmold than they would have been in tall grass. If there were rabbits here, or deer, she would find them by sign or scent, and retrace her own path to the meadow. It could not be so difficult. She was a hunter from her childhood. She could learn to hunt here as she had on the steppe.

It was none so simple, but need drove her, the gnawing of hunger. Panic stood at bay. Foolish to be so frightened of these closed spaces, these rustling silences. If demons walked here, Horse Goddess would protect her from them. Was she not on the goddess' errand? Must she not live, and thrive, in order to perform it?

Perhaps it was the goddess who led her to a place crisscrossed with rabbit-sign. She shot two in quick succession, and a third after a not inconsiderable while. They were larger than their cousins of the steppe, plump and well fed. A deer would have given her more meat, to eat and to carry, but these would more than suffice.

She traced her way back with no more than a handful of mis-steps and pauses to calm herself yet again. The sun in the meadow, now much shifted toward the west, was a golden blessing on her face.

The Mare was grazing as she had been when Sarama left her. She raised her head and whickered a greeting, and after a moment's consideration came to investigate the quarry and to have her nape rubbed. Flies had been a great torment to her. Sarama wove an eye-fringe of grass and bound it to her headstall. She tossed her head to make the braided fringes fly, snorted disgust at the dead things swinging from Sarama's belt, and went back to her grazing.

Sarama caught herself smiling as she skinned and cleaned the rabbits by the stream, gathered bits of wood and grass for a fire, and waited with snarling stomach for the cooking to be done. A bit of liver, sweet and blood-raw, calmed the worst of the snarls, and a double fistful of berries from amid the grass.

She lay on her stomach not too near the fire, chin propped on hands. The Mare cropped grass with singleminded determination, her white tail flicking steadily at the flies.

She was beautiful, Sarama thought. She often thought so, but it was different to lie here, at ease, even content, and simply watch the Mare be beautiful. It was not so much the lines of her, though those were good, solid and yet elegant, or her coat like moonlight and rain, or even the way she moved, with both strength and grace. It was more than that; a way she had of carrying herself. She knew that she was beautiful. She took great pride in it. And she would be more beautiful still, when she was grown out of her dappled youth.

Sometimes Sarama wondered if she yearned for her people, for the herd that ran the steppe near the goddess' hill. She seemed content to be alone, if only she was near Sarama. And yet horses were herd-creatures; and these more purely a part of their herd than some, so that horses of other kinds were strangers, and only their own kind worthy of friendship.

"Horse Goddess blessed them long ago," the Old Woman had told Sarama, "and gave them strength and intelligence beyond the common lot of their kind. But for it she exacted a price. They have little patience for horses of other kinds, that to them are too patently lesser. And horses of other kinds look on them in incomprehension; find their language difficult, their spirits strange."

"And yet they come to us," Sarama had said. It was winter, she remembered, and she was still young enough that her breasts had not budded. She was grinding dried herbs by the fire, and the Old Woman was brewing them into a potion for the winter rheum. The Mare had not yet come to Sarama, but the Old Mare drowsed in her stall in the goddess' house, and a herd of her sisters grazed the winter grass of the hill just below. Sarama could see them from the Old Woman's house, through the door that lay open to let in the sun.

"They come to us," she said, "and give their hearts to us."

"Well, and so do we to them," said the Old Woman. "We were made for them, and they for us, by Horse Goddess in the dawn time. But they grow few, and we grow fewer. The lesser ones—horses and people—rule the world."

"Then will we all die out?" Sarama asked. She was calm; the calm of disbelief.

The Old Woman stirred her pot. When Sarama had thought that she would not answer, she said, "That will be as the goddess wills."

Often when she said that, Sarama knew not to press her. But the horses grazing in the windswept grass, the white Mare contentedly asleep in her stall nearby, struck her so strongly with their beauty that she could not keep silent. "What does she will? Did she only make them, and us, so that we could vanish into forgetfulness? What are we for, Grandmother?"

The Old Woman frowned slightly, enough that Sarama quailed. Yet she did not complete the rebuke. "We are her servants. What she does in this, that you are the last of us, and of the horses there are only these few dozen in the world—that is known to her, and will come clear in its own time."

"I think," said Sarama with shaky defiance, "that she means us to grow strong again. Someday. When the world is ready for us."

"Maybe so," the Old Woman said. *And maybe not,* her eyes said; but she did not say it in words.

+ +

Sarama sighed as the memory slipped away. Now the Old Woman was dead, and the Old Mare with her. The herd had gone away from the goddess' hill. It lived, she knew; she would know if it had died. But where it had gone, or why, had not been made known to her.

There was still the Mare, content as if Sarama had been her whole herd and the world about it. So had the Old Mare been. So—if Sarama admitted the truth—was Sarama with the Mare. That was all her people, and all the kin she needed, while she rode abroad in the world.

·············· 19 ··············

Past that place of open grass and clear sunlight was nothing but a wilderness of woven trees. Sarama could find her way if the sun was in the sky, by the wan shadow of it below. In clouds and rain, or by night when the moon was out of the sky, she could only stop and wait till she had her guides again, sun and stars that were the same over the forest as over the steppe.

No tale had told of people in this wood; only of beasts and birds. And yet as she picked her way, straining to keep the sun behind her in the morning and before her in the evening, she knew that she was watched. It was a prickling in her spine, a tautness in the shoulders.

Perhaps it was a wolf, or a forest lion, if there were such. But the pressure of eyes, the sense of watchfulness, had no taste of simple beast. This was a human creature.

Or creatures. It, or they, never made move against her, nor threatened her. They simply watched.

She laid traps for them. They were too canny, or she too unskilled in such things. She caught nothing; saw no track, heard no body passing. It was an awareness, that was all. A certainty that she did not ride alone.

Her wits were slipping. The trees closed in. She yearned with physical hunger for a stretch of open sky. But even clearings were few, and in those she felt the eyes more strongly than under the trees. They weighed on her even more heavily than the shadows of the branches.

Where people were, must be habitations; remains of camps at the least, or tracks on which they walked. Of beasts she found ample sign, but of men, nothing.

It must be that she was going mad. That the trees had taken the sense from her, and the darkness drained the light out of her spirit. She walked and rode westward because she could think of nothing better to do. She hunted and foraged when she must, as she must, because she must live to see the land that the traveller had said was beyond the wood. If there was any such land. If the wood ever ended.

The Mare was quiet, but Sarama could sense uneasiness in her, too; tautness in her body at the sudden flight of a bird or the leap of a deer, or a roll of eye at a wind-gust in the branches. She had never required a great deal of fodder, but here where grass came seldom and leaves were not always either sweet or safe to eat, she had begun to drop flesh. Sarama could first feel, and then see, the jut of ribs along her barrel.

Sarama was growing somewhat ribby herself. It was difficult to muster will for a hunt, or to lay snares when she stopped because of darkness or rain. Roots and berries were not as rare as grass, but she seldom knew if they were safe to eat. Rabbits semed to gather in tribes and clans in some part of the wood and not in others. Birds likewise: in one place the air would be full of their calls and the flutter of their wings; in another, not one could be seen or heard. Small things like furry-tailed rats that chittered in the trees proved not ill to eat, if she could catch them. Sometimes she could not. Then she went hungry, and told herself that she was fasting. She had fasted often enough on the steppe, in the goddess' name. She could fast here. Could she not?

On the steppe she had had the sun to nourish her. Here she had little of that. She caught herself more than once, stopping beneath a tree that had suffered a shaft of light to touch the ground, standing motionless, drinking the light as if it had been water. She was parched for it, starved for lack of it.

How many days she had been wandering in this place, she did not know. She had forgotten. The moon had waned, then waxed again. Was it waning now? Was it swelling to the full? She could not remember. On the steppe she would have known by the shifting of seasons whether summer had advanced or passed. Here the trees were endless, shadowy green. Their kind changed not at all from spring to winter. They were always the same.

+ +

She woke one morning from a dream of sunlit grass, to a green darkness and a shape of leaves and branches that looked remarkably like a face. It was a broad face, brown as a treebole, with dark eyes set deep in it, and wild tangle of beard. It was very real, very lifelike, staring down at her.

She blinked. It vanished. Yet she thought she heard the faintest whisper, as of leaves parting and then slipping together again.

It had not been inadvertent, she thought. He wanted her to see him. As to why—who knew? He might not be a man at all, but a spirit of the wood. He had a look as of something older and wilder, and perhaps darker too, than any man she had seen before.

Thereafter she caught glimpses of him, or of men like him, shadows flitting among the trees, faces in the branches, a gleam of eyes at dusk or at dawn. She wondered if she had wandered aside from her path to the westward, whether they would turn against her; or whether they only, ever, watched.

They could not bring back the sun or the sky. Only her will could do that, her feet walking, the Mare under her when the trees grew wide and high enough.

+ +

She stumbled into the camp as yet another day was waning. She had seen, with some startlement, that the trees were different in this place. They were a softer green, and that green was giving way to gold. So, she was thinking: it was autumn, or nearly. No wonder then that the nights grew chill. She had thought it was only the chill in her heart.

She was on foot, the Mare following. Then she was alone, and there was sunlight on her face, and a circle of green-golden trees about her; and in the circle an oddity of shapes. They were tents perhaps, tents woven of branches, each perched on a platform made of treetrunks.

People stood staring at her. They were thickset, broad-faced, brown-skinned people, strong and solid to look at, with bones as heavy as stone, and jaws like outcroppings of granite. And yet there was about them something wild and shy. They looked like the aurochs, the great bull of the woods; yet in their eyes she saw the timidity of the deer. There was a strangeness about them, an otherness. Earth Mother's elder children, she thought: people of earth and stone, born before the gods brought air and fire into Earth Mother's creation.

She should have turned and run. She was a woman, and alone. Any man who saw her would reckon her prey—and they did not know Horse Goddess here. But she stood where she was. She was not afraid. None of the men was as tall as she, though even the women were easily twice as broad. They could break her in two, she had no doubt of it. But that they would—no. There was no hostility in them. The Mare stepped delicately past her. The people's eyes widened. They muttered among themselves: low voices, words that she did not understand. She heard no fear. Only wonder.

The Mare found a patch of sweet grass near the outermost of the dwellings. The people drifted toward her, but not too close. They watched her as Sarama had watched her mother and her aunts once, for the pure delight of her beauty.

Sarama's body betrayed her without warning, and without great gentleness, either. Her knees gave way abruptly. The dark swooped over the sun. She cried out in protest. Not here—not when she had found the light again.

⚓ ⚓

Voices murmured. Someone was singing, or chanting: a kind of tuneful tunelessness. A manifold reek stung her nostrils. In spite of herself she picked out the parts of it. Smoke, mansweat, hides tanned and untanned; roasting meat, burning herbs, and the strong green sweetness of fresh-cut grass.

She was lying on the grass, that had been spread to make a bed for her. Walls closed her in. She lay inside one of the dwellings, lit by a fire that burned in the center. Some of its smoke escaped through a hole in the roof. The rest wreathed the people who crowded into the space, thick bodies, broad faces, bright eyes fixed on her as if they had been waiting long for her to wake.

One bent closest. The face made her think of that which she had first seen, but they were not the same. This one wore no beard. It could have been a man's regardless, with its wide cheekbones and heavy jaw, but the eyes were a woman's. The hair was thick and smoke-yellowed and grey with dirt, but had it been scrubbed clean it would have been as white as the Old Mare's hide.

Here was a woman who carried herself like a king. She put Sarama in mind of the Old Woman: the same steady gaze, the same calm surety of her place in the world.

She saw that Sarama was awake. Her eyes shifted; she beckoned. A younger woman, less strong-featured but still as heavy-jawed as many men that Sarama had known, came out of the crowded people, bearing cup and bowl. She filled the cup from the bowl and held it out.

The old woman lifted Sarama with an arm too strong to resist, so that Sarama could take the cup. She sniffed, trying not to seem suspicious.

It was milk. Goat, she thought. Nothing had been mixed into it that she could sense. It was warm and fresh, sweet and strong. She had not known how badly she needed it until she had drunk the bowl dry and been given another. That too she drained, with a sigh that ran round the circle, and sparked a flicker of smiles.

Whatever she had done, she had done it well. There was a great easing among the gathering. They began to chatter to each other, and at her too, though she understood not a word of it.

Somewhere amid what had become a kind of revel, a feast appeared: roasted meats and bread made from wild grains, milk and honey, cheese and fruits, more good things than she had known the forest could provide. What had seemed a barren wilderness, for these people must be a rich and pleasant country.

Surely they seemed at ease in it, and joyful, welcoming a stranger as if she had been both friend and kin. Her own blood had not received her so well or with such open gladness.

Sarama tested her welcome. She rose and walked out.

No one stopped her or tried to hinder her. She emerged from the close and crowded place into a startling blaze of light. It was full day, and cloudless, and the sun so strong that her eyes streamed with the shock of it. While she lay unconscious she had been stripped of all but her soft leather undertunic. Even that was almost too much for the heat of the day.

She stood on the platform of a house near the center, with the others in nested circles about it. People came and went among the houses. Beasts rooted in the shade beneath—pigs, but smaller and less fierce to look at than the wild boar that only the strongest on the steppe had dared to hunt.

Neither people nor pigs seemed dismayed by her scrutiny. The people, if they saw her, smiled. As rough as they seemed, with their heavy faces and their mossy tangles of hair, they were gentle enough in their manners.

Not one spoke a language that she knew. Even the traders' argot, of which she had learned a little, met with blank stares and uncomprehending smiles.

They seemed to be testing her mastery of tongues as well: people inside and now people in the street would stop and speak, sometimes in a quick light rhythm, sometimes in tones more guttural, buried deeper in the throat. None of it made sense to her.

Somehow she had not expected the people of the west to be so foreign that she could not understand them. The traveller had said nothing of that.

But, she thought, these were not the westerners he had spoken of. This was a village, and a small one at that, smaller than a clan-encampment of her own tribe. She saw no riches, no woven fabrics, no pots wonderfully and intricately made, no copper nor anything that could be the metal called gold. These were savages, hunters and herdsmen from the look of them, rich in contentment but in little else that the men of the steppe might reckon valuable.

There were, to be sure, no horses. Unless those were hidden in the wood and all signs concealed from her, then that much of the tale was true. This country knew nothing of Horse Goddess' children.

Sarama was not a prisoner here. She could descend the ladder made of a cut treetrunk with well-placed branches, and walk where she pleased. Children followed her as children loved to do, because she was something new to run after and stare at.

She could walk if she wished right out of the village, back to the wood again.

At the thought of walking in that green darkness, away from the sun, her body shuddered. She had to stop, to cling to the piling that upheld a house, to gasp till she could breathe again. The flock of children crept in close, staring and whispering. Their curiosity roused her somewhat. She pushed herself erect, made herself walk onward, round the camp to the place from which she had begun.

The revel was still going on, the revellers delighted to see her, calling to her in their incomprehensible language, offering hands to pull her up onto the platform. She set her heels when they would have pulled her inside. They laughed with no sign of offense, and brought the revel to her since she would not give up the sky.

•••••••••••• 20 ••••••••••••

Words were of no use, but the people of the wood spoke well enough by signs and smiles, inclinations of head and hand, and sounds that, though not words, had meaning enough. From them Sarama gathered that her kind was known to them; that the Mare was known, and looked on with reverence. As to how they knew without words to convey such things, they smiled and pointed to their breasts and bellies, and thence to the trees that ringed their village about. Their gods, they seemed to say. Their gods told them.

Her own goddess granted her the mercy of rest, for a little while. But after the day of sun and two days of cold driving rain, when the sun came back again, she saw how the trees had gone all golden. The day was warm, but the night had been cold, a sharp bite of chill when she went out late to relieve herself.

She gathered her belongings. The house in which she had slept, which she thought might belong to the elder of the clan—if an elder could be a woman—was unwontedly empty, but there were people enough out and about. The Mare, as always, had an entourage of the curious, the young and not so young. They watched as Sarama picked out her feet, combed mane and tail with deft fingers, and readied her to ride. Someone had bathed her this morning; she was damp and gleaming, and there was a garland of flowers about her neck, golden and red, the colors of autumn.

Courtesy of the steppe would have sent Sarama to the king to bid fare-well, but there was no king here. She wavered, not ready to mount, yet desperate to be away.

As she stood there, a small flurry brought her about. The old woman whose guest she had been walked toward her in a shifting crowd of people. They were dancing, almost, handlinked or alone, weaving in and out, laughing when they tangled.

The elder wore a crown of flowers. She smiled as she approached Sarama, spread her gnarled hands, bent with unexpected grace. One of the young girls with her danced forward, balancing a bowl in lifted hands.

It was goat's milk, again: their drink of parting, it seemed, as well as of greeting. The milk of greeting had been unadorned. The milk of parting was sweet with honey. Sarama drank it down, while the people smiled and nodded, and some of the girls giggled, and the boys scowled and thrust out their chests at one another.

The elder herself took the bowl from Sarama's hands, bowed over it and passed it to the girl who waited to take it. Then she took Sarama's hands in strong dry fingers, turned them palms up and looked hard and long at each. She seemed to read something there as a scryer might in a clear pool, or a priest in the stars. A sigh escaped her. She looked bright-eyed into Sarama's face, and said something in that guttural language which Sarama could not understand. It was a prayer, her manner said, or a blessing.

Sarama bowed to her in turn. For lack of greater inspiration, she said what her people would say on departing for a journey. "May the gods keep you," she said. "May Horse Goddess hold you in the palm of her hand."

The old woman nodded and smiled. She could no more have understand Sarama than Sarama had understood her, but blessings were much the same wherever one was.

In mutual amity, with smiles and nods and gestures of farewell, the people of the village sent Sarama on her way. Some followed her, as she might have expected; trailing after her far into the wood.

They helped her more than they could ever have known. While they were with her, she could turn her mind away from the wood, from the dimness that closed about her, from the dearth of sunlight that had driven her so close to mad before. It would do so again. She could feel the madness hovering.

These people held it at bay. Inevitably they fell behind, but some few remained with her, and one pair of sturdy young creatures, as like as brother and sister, seemed to have appointed themselves her guardians. They strode just behind the Mare when the track was narrow, beside her when it widened. One carried a bow, one a bone-tipped spear. They did not speak, to her or to one another.

When, near evening, Sarama looked about for a place to camp, the woman slipped ahead. The Mare seemed content to follow her. She led them to a clearing. A spring bubbled in it. A tree bent over the spring, heavy with fruit.

The woman had vanished. The man settled by a ring of stones, a fire-ring of evident antiquity, and set to kindling a fire. After a while, as the light faded from the sky, the woman came back with a young deer over her shoulders. They dined on venison roasted over the fire with herbs from the clearing, and ripe sweet fruit, some roasted with the deer, some fresh from the tree.

Sarama did not know what she had done to earn this guardianship. Perhaps, as with Gauan's people, it was the Mare. Whatever the cause, she was grateful.

She should perhaps be apprehensive; should wait to be waylaid, robbed and beaten and left for dead. But not here. Not these people.

If she was a fool, then so be it. If these guides led her astray, Horse Goddess would set her on the right path. She must trust in the goddess. Always; unshakably. Or there was no trust in the world.

✢ ✢

Her guides, guardians, whatever they reckoned themselves, continued with Sarama. They made no effort to divert her from her course, except when it turned aside from true west; as too often it did in the dark tangle of the wood. But they knew, perhaps in their bones, which way was true. So did she know on the steppe, from the angle of sun or star, or from the lie of the land when rain or mist or snow obscured the sky.

These guides were a gift. They hunted the wood, fished the rivers. They made her eat when she would have simply slept, and rest when she would have gone on too long or too far. Because of them she rode safe and she rode strong, and stronger as she went on, though she would never be wholly herself until she stood under sky again, unshadowed with trees.

She had thought them brother and sister, but that, it seemed, was only her eye that had not learned to tell one broad heavy-jawed face from another. In the nights she heard them together, sounds that she could hardly mistake.

That too was a comfort, warm and real and unmistakably human: all that the wood was not, nor for her could ever be. She wanted only to be out of it. If she could—if there was ever an end to it.

That was her great fear. That the trees went on and on. That there was no country of the west, no plain well watered with rivers, no great gathering of people who had never known the horse. That she would journey westward till she died, and never find aught but an endless tangle of trees.

✢ ✢

On the day when she knew that even for Horse Goddess, even for her soul's sake, she could not go on, on the day when she had determined that if the wood did not end by evening, she would give up her service and turn back eastward, the trees opened before her. That was nothing to astonish her. There had been clearings enough with her guides' help, even a village of people like them, who welcomed her as those others had, and showed no fear of the stranger.

But this light was brighter than any she remembered. It was evening light, red-golden, bathing the trees with a sheen as of copper, or of blood. Shadows of the trees stretched long behind her.

Her guides, always so silent, were murmuring to one another. She heard no fear in it; yet there was a kind of excitement, as if they had come on something new.

They had fallen behind her, rarity enough that she might have remarked on it. But she was too intent on the light. The Mare's head was up, her ears pricked.

The trees thinned. And then, all at once, they ended. A few stragglers wandered down a long hillside. Grass grew there, sere with summer's ending. A wide rolling country opened before her, so wide that she reeled, caught unawares after the stifling closeness of the forest.

Just as she willed to venture forward, the Mare essayed a step. Her nostrils were wide, her head high, drinking this new and wonderful air.

She was well away from the loom of the wood before Sarama felt any lack. Sarama turned to look over her shoulder. Her guides stood in the shadow of the trees, visible only to eyes that knew to find them. They did not move.

Sarama opened her mouth to call to them, but shut it with the words unuttered. So it always was with spirits of a place. They were bound to it. They could not leave it.

And perhaps she was a spirit of the steppe, a creature of sky and of open spaces. She could feel her heart grow wide, her soul unfurl. She could not make herself turn back, even if the Mare would have allowed it. Her thanks must go unspoken.

She lifted a hand. One of the woodfolk lifted a weapon in return: the bow, from the curve of it.

She blinked, or shifted slightly. When she looked again, her guides were gone.

It was night under the trees. Here under the sky, the light lingered. Sarama rode on in it, keeping the westward way. Somewhere on the hills in front of her, or in the hollows between, were habitations of men. If the traveller had spoken true. If he had not lied, or stretched the truth to breaking.

He had not spoken of the forest people; but perhaps he had not known of them. They were secret, and shy, though welcoming to one who had fallen into their midst. He might have passed through the wood without ever finding one of their villages.

But that he had found this country, she could hardly doubt. There it was before her, plains and rivers, and on the plains and beside the rivers, shapes that might have been crags, or heaps of stones, or dwellings of human people.

The Mare carried her through the waning light. The Mare was not weary, nor afraid of the night. Sarama, who must confess to both, lacked will to hold her back.

This she had come for. This she must face. Whatever it was. Whatever the goddess wanted of her. Was she not the goddess' servant?

IV

STRANGER IN THE
GODDESS' COUNTRY

.... 21 ....

IN LARCHWOOD IN the autumn, when they brought in the harvest, the young men danced for the goddess' glory—and for their own, too, while the women watched. After days of grueling labor, oftentimes against the threat of rain, when the barns were full and the winter's comfort secured, they bathed all together in the river, put on their best finery, plaited flowers and leaves and ears of wheat or barley in their hair, and came out in firelight to dance the harvest-dance.

In Three Birds it was much the same. Danu had left the horse-colt in the autumn pasture with the goats, entrusted him to the herders' care, and come down to the city to help with bringing in the harvest. On this last night, with every muscle groaning and his body yearning to fall into a bed somewhere and sleep till spring, he found himself as he always had before, armlinked with the rest of the bone-weary men. The drums beat strength into him. The pipes sent the blood coursing swifter through his veins. The singing—clear voices of women, deep voices of men—lifted him up.

The Lady's song was different here, but its rhythms were close enough. Her praises changed little from city to city. She was the great one, the Mother, life-giver, creator. She woke the earth in the spring, taught it to burgeon in the summer, made the harvest rich with autumn's coming; and when, with winter, the earth slept, she watched over it, guardian and protector, till spring should come again.

This starlit night, Danu felt her presence, the warmth of her smile. Or perhaps it was only the light of the great fire, the harvest-fire, built of chaff and of dry shocks from the fields, and blessed with its share of fruits and grains from the harvest.

He beat the earth with his feet. He leaped high above it, as high as the sky. He danced the circle-dance with these strangers who were never his kin, who from day to day and moon-phase to moon-phase had become familiar. Tonight he was one of them.

The circle spun, sunwise, goddess-wise, setting the seal on the harvest. With a roar of drums it broke, the parts of it scattering, only to bind together into a new whole. In this one women too took part, young women naked but for the Lady's garment, the skirt of woven cords that concealed nothing; that flaunted their beauty for any eye to see.

The night was chill beyond the circle, an autumn chill with the bite of winter in it. But here by the fire, in the whirl of the dance, it was as warm as summer.

Danu found himself dancing face to face with one he knew very well, Catin with her long hair unbound and her breasts gleaming. Her skirt was the color of blood, bright scarlet, cords whirling as she spun. Her teeth flashed white. She was laughing, somber Catin whose smiles were rare and precious things.

She linked hands behind his neck and bore him with her, dancing the sacred circle, round and round the fire. Somewhere he lost his tunic—so had they all, all the men, and trousers too, cast aside, forgotten. They unwound in a skein then, the spiral dance, the dance that wrought the world. Out and then in, in and then out, and fire in the heart of it, roaring up to heaven.

Danu fell out of it onto yielding softness. Later he would see that it was a haystack, one of many that ringed the dancing-field. It seemed, just then, made solely for him to rest in, and Catin laughing on top of him, wet wriggling body, dizzying scent of woman. She mounted him as he lay there, with urgency that had not a little of the Lady in it.

He was glad to worship the Lady so, and in such a semblance. Catin was strong tonight, stronger than mortal woman, and in her strength she made him, for a little while, more than mortal man.

But even gods could tire. Twice again the Lady roused him, but the third time, even her power was not enough. Catin sighed and shook her head and smiled, and kissed him on the lips, and went away.

Danu lay for a while, dreaming of sleep. But the hay was rough on his bare skin, itched and stung the tender parts of him. He staggered up. The cistern for watering cattle stood not too far away, almost farther than he wanted to walk, and across a cold stretch of night air, too. Nonetheless he did it, and bathed in the icy water, which woke him rather too well. He did not know where his clothes had gone.

It did not matter. The great fire had died down. A few shadowy figures danced still. The rest had sunk to the beaten grass, or found haystacks of their own, the better to worship the Lady. Catin was in one of them, no doubt, with a stronger man than he.

He was not going to think about that, or to let it trouble him. Walking as swiftly as aches and weariness would bear, warming himself with speed, he sought, not the Mother's house, but the autumn pasture.

+ +

The herdsmen's hut was warm. They had had their own festival here, and given their own gifts to the Lady. They greeted Danu without surprise. Nati left after a little while to keep watch over the herd.

Danu wrapped himself in a fleece and followed. Sleep was close, but not so close yet.

The colt was asleep, curled up in a huddle of similarly sleeping goats. He did not wake for Danu's coming, though his ear flicked: aware perhaps, but unwary.

Danu thought of making his bed in the midst of them, colt and goats both, but the herdsmen's hut tempted him. He chose a place between, a mound of grass untenanted by goats. Wrapped in the fleece, with the stars to bless his head, he slept as he had not slept since this year began. No dreams tormented him. His sleep was peace, there on the hillside, and he woke to the grey light of dawn, woke smiling, though it was a while before he knew why.

✤ ✤

Danu came to the Mother's house as she lifted the sunrise song from the summit of the temple. He had seen her there as he walked into the city, a dark still shape on the roofpeak.

Catin was not in the room that, sometimes, she shared with Danu. He had not truly expected that she would be. The stab of disappointment surprised him, and made him ashamed.

He folded the fleece that had kept him warm all night, and laid it by the bed. Later he would take it back to its proper place. He dressed in his own clothing, combed and braided his hair, and made himself fit to face the day.

Today the elders would shut themselves in the temple for a rite more secret and more holy than that in which he had shared yesterday. They would set the seal on the season, and bless the altar in the inner temple, and make it all secure for the coming of winter.

He had his own securing to do, the finding and strengthening of a place for the colt. The goats would go to the winter pasture, but that was far away, farther than he could easily walk from the city. He should be close to it. He did not know exactly why, only that he must.

It must be a good place, a warm place, but with room about it for a young thing to run. He would have to supply it with fodder as people did with cattle too greatly valued to trust to the mercy of snow and cold, wolves and hunger. It would be good, he thought, to wheedle a goat or two out of Nati and Lati, to keep the horse company.

It would take all the time he had, maybe, from now till the snow flew, to find and ready the place. He had one or two in mind.

Not the Lady's grove. Danu had decided that from the beginning. The colt would grow stunted if he returned there. He should have sky unwalled in trees, and space to stretch his long legs.

Danu walked the city's rim, round the outermost circle of houses, where the trees ended and open fields began. The barns there were full, the byres waiting for the cattle. But on the southward side, not far from the bend of the river, someone had built and then abandoned a house of wood and wattle over fitted stone. There were two parts to it, the open stone space below and two rooms above, walled and floored in wood. The roof was thatch and somewhat rotted. The walls were sturdy, and the door was only a little broken.

Better yet, whoever had built the house had raised a pen behind, for goats perhaps, or a cow; and from that a long meadow ran down to the river. It would, with time and a little effort, be a comfortable place to winter in, the horse below and he above. And Catin, maybe. If she wished.

He had not thought yet what she would say to his leaving the Mother's house. Still the horse was his charge, and he could not keep it in the city's heart. Either he went away to the winter pasture and returned seldom if at all, or he claimed this place and kept the horse in it, and himself perforce, since someone must tend the beast and see that he was fed.

He approached the house with respect, but with no expectation that anyone would be living in it. Its mother had died, Danu had heard in the city, and her daughters found homes elsewhere. Her son had lived there for a while, till a woman from Woodsedge chose him to raise her children for her.

The spirit-knot was still on the door, worn and frayed with weather; protecting the house and its memories, and putting dark things to flight. Danu brushed it with his fingers, taking to himself somewhat of its blessing as he passed beneath the lintel.

It was as he had been told, a broad open space of a fine size to keep a horse in; and the ceiling surprisingly high overhead. It was musty with disuse, but no evil lay on it, nor had anything fouled it.

A ladder led up the far wall to an opening in the ceiling. Danu climbed into a room that might have been pleasant once, and could be again. It was lower than the room below, but still high enough to stand erect, with a stone hearth that bore a memory of fire. It was divided in two, inner room and outer, the inner smaller, with a platform in it, and the remnants of a bed.

Danu nodded to himself. It would do. The more so for that, in the inner room, he found a chest, and in it an array of pots for cooking and for storing wine and food, and other oddments that would serve well for the keeping of a house. It was better than he had expected, by far.

He walked back lightly to the Mother's house, traversing the city's circles that had become familiar since summer's beginning; even the trees that defined and shaped them, and made it difficult at first to understand how the city was made. People called to him, waved or smiled when he passed. He paused to watch a weaver at her loom; to glimpse the potters in a lesser temple, making vessels for the Lady's rites. He surprised himself with contentment. Three Birds this was not, but he had a place here.

He came round rather indirectly to the Mother's house, past the temple and the grove that were the city's heart. As he drew near it he heard an odd thing. It sounded like the murmuring of a crowd of people. And in truth, but for the weaver and the potters, he had seen few enough in the streets. He had thought little of it. The day after the harvest had ended, after a festival that had kept everyone awake until dawn, of course there would be fewer people about than usual.

But not, perhaps, so few.

The murmur drew closer. Danu halted by the temple, craning to hear. He was aware of the walls rising above him, the peaked gable with its carved faces: Lady of the Trees with her crown of leaves, Lady of the Deer with a fawn in her arms. The door was shut, as it should be; the elders would have finished their rite and gone away, and left the temple to its solitude.

Someone was coming down the eastward way. The murmur followed. Danu's ear caught a sound that made his eyes widen. Hooves on packed earth, round hollow hooves. Had the colt come in from the winter pasture by himself?

That was not his dun colt, this creature walking toward the Lady's temple. It was a horse most certainly, but larger, taller, older, dappled silver and white, like the moon on new snow. On its back, half-fallen over its neck, rode a stranger. He could see no face, only garments of worn and dusty leather, and a plait of hair the color of rich red earth.

So it was true. One could ride a horse, if the horse were large enough.

This horse had a look to it, a light in the dark eye, a sheen on it that made the people of Larchwood murmur in awe. This was the Lady's creature. There could be no doubt of it.

It halted before the temple—as it happened, full in front of Danu, who lacked will to remove himself. The rider sighed and slid. With no thought at all, he reached and caught the body as it fell, sinking under the weight of it, till his knees stiffened. It was lighter than he had expected. Not a man's body at all, though quite as tall as one.

He stood with the woman in his arms and not the least conception of what to do next. The horse nudged his shoulder with its nose, snorted and pawed. It was imperious, that one. He understood it well enough. *Move!* it bade him. *Look after this my servant.*

He could think of nothing better to do than to carry the stranger-woman to the Mother's house. The horse followed, and the people behind. They had fallen silent, perhaps in horror at his presumption. But he had to do something. He had to hope that this was enough; that it would satisfy the Lady.

The horse could not follow him into the Mother's house, but it hovered near the door. Danu laid the stranger in the gathering-room, on the heap of rugs that made a nest to lie on in the evenings. It was a woman indeed, though thin and wiry like a man. Her face was all bladed planes: sharp cheekbones, sharp curved nose, sharp chin. Her breasts were small, all but invisible under her leather coat, and her hips narrow like a boy's. She was too peculiar to be ugly, but he could hardly call her beautiful. Interesting, that was the word.

He debated undressing her, searching for wounds, for some cause for her unconsciousness, but he could not bring himself to touch her clothing. That was clean enough, to be sure—and somewhat to his surprise; and she was no more redolent than anyone should be who had been travelling as far as she must have done. Still he would not take on himself the burden of tending her, not without the Mother's word.

He grimaced. And what had he done after all but take it on himself, by bringing her here? This was not his house. He had no authority to bring a stranger to it.

He looked up without surprise into the Mother's face, and Catin's behind, in a crowd of elders and their daughters. They must have been close on his heels.

He kept his head up, though he spoke humbly. "Mother. Honored aunts."

The Mother inclined her head to him. The elders were less courteous, more intent on the stranger.

"This is another of the savages," one said. She sounded angry. "How did she pass the towns and cities, if she came from the wood? How did she escape the watchers? We should have been warned!"

"Maybe she came from somewhere else," said one of the daughters.

The elders hissed at her. "Where else could she have come from?" demanded the one who had spoken first. "A horse brought her. There are no horses anywhere but in the east."

"The Lady brought her." Danu was astonished to hear himself speak, still humbly but with a firmness that he could never have mustered while his wits were about him. "She belongs to the Lady."

"So she does," said the Mother, forestalling the rush of protests. She came to stand beside Danu, looking down at the woman. Her face was calm, but her eyes were somber. "So this is the beginning of it," she said. "So soon. I had hoped . . ."

She stopped, shook her head. "No matter. Danu, Catin, see to her. The rest of you, go. When the time comes, I'll summon you."

This Mother seldom wielded her authority. Danu might have thought her weak, if he had not seen how well the city ran itself. Now he saw the strength in her, the will to command, that she used so seldom; but its very rarity made it stronger.

They all obeyed, even Catin who could be sullen and resentful of any will but her own. For her Mother she would bow her head and submit.

The two of them tended the stranger, undressed her and bathed her and made a bed for her in an inner room. There was nothing to do then but watch over her. Danu left Catin to it under the Mother's eye and went out past the clusters of silent people, to find the horse still standing by the door. No one approached it, or tried.

"It attacks when we come near," said a child who crouched in a doorway down the street, nursing an impressive bruise.

Danu nodded. The horse eyed him. Its ears were back, a mean look, like a dog that growled at an intruder. Horses did not growl, but they could wrinkle their lips and bare big yellow teeth.

"Come," Danu said, as if a horse could understand the speech of the people. "Be at ease. She is well, but she would be better if you would look after yourself."

The horse's ears flicked at the sound of his voice. He could not tell if it understood him. He ventured a step closer. The horse did not lunge at him. He ventured another. Its ears flattened. He halted.

"I can," he said, "find you a place to rest, water to drink, grass and comfort. If you will permit me."

The horse turned its head away from him, presented its broad rump. It was, he noted rather wildly, larger than the colt. Very much larger.

He backed away carefully. Some of the children were watching him. He caught the eye of the eldest. "Water," he said, "in a bucket, and all the grass you can cut, from the river-meadow. Can you fetch those for me?"

The girl's eyes narrowed. She nodded. In a moment she had the younger children running to do Danu's bidding, and quickly, too.

Danu had them set the water—three pails of it, no less—in the space between houses, and spread the cut grass beside it. The horse watched with interest, though its ears flattened again if it caught anyone's eye on it. When the children had retreated, leaving the space untenanted, it ventured forward warily. It sniffed the water, snorted, lipped at it but did not drink. The grass met with great approval: it fell to willingly, and hungrily too.

Danu watched it for a while. It wore a harness about the head, like a finished version of the knotted rope that Catin had shown him to use with the colt; and there was a fleece strapped to its back, a shaped thing, with an arrangement of pouches and bags bound to or hanging over it. The horse might be glad to be freed of that.

It glared at him when he came close, but did not threaten him as it had before. The fresh-cut grass distracted it well. He moved in boldly then, slipped off the headstall and the reins, found and unfastened the knotted strap that held the fleece about the horse's middle. The hair beneath was dark and matted with sweat. He rubbed it carefully, then more strongly as the horse forbore to object.

It was not so fierce a horse after all. The colt was trickier, with his penchant for nipping when one least expected it. This one was particular about its hindquarters, but loved to be rubbed and scratched along its back and nape and under its belly.

In the course of those explorations he discovered a thing: it was not an it but a she. It was made differently than the colt, such a difference as made a female thing.

No wonder then that she was so imperious in her manners. Danu bowed to her as to a Mother or a Mother's heir. "Lady," he said.

She ignored him, as a woman might. He left her to her dinner and went to see if her rider had roused.

·············· 22 ··············

Sarama had been ill. It was winter, she remembered, and she had fallen victim to a demon off the steppe, a small fiery demon that filled her lungs with spite and made her cough, and vexed her sorely with fever. The Old Woman brewed potions for it, kept her warm when she shivered and cooled her with snow when she burned, and nursed her till she was well again.

But if that was memory, and therefore distant, how could it be happening again? And where were the cold stone walls and the wuther of wind in the eaves? Here were warmer walls, walls of wood, and sounds as of voices from both near and far. The scents were all strange. No smoke pungent with the dried dung of cattle and horses. No cold cleanness of snow. She did not know what she smelled: some sweetness, some pungency, and one that was familiar after all, the ripeness of a privy.

She opened her eyes. Wooden walls, yes, and carved beams above her, so strange that for a while she could only stare. She was lying on softness, covered in the prickly warmth of woven wool. The room was small but well lit, with a window open to sunlight.

Before she thought, she was on her feet, clinging to the windowledge, yearning toward the sky. Walls closed it in and branches tried to bar it, but it was there, just out of reach.

A sound startled her. She wheeled.

The room was dim after the dazzle of sunlight. A shape stood in it, a dark looming figure. It was human. She heard it breathe. Heard it speak. A low voice, a man's, with a lilt at the end as if he asked a question.

She remembered then: the steppe, the journey, the wood; the people in the wood, with their strange tongue; and after that a blur of walls and faces, road and trees and river, and an urgency that had brought her to one place, a place in which the goddess wished her to be.

This place. Unless she had wandered astray, or lost her way in the fever.

The man spoke again. His words were no more comprehensible than they had been before. She could see him clearly enough now as he entered the shaft of sunlight. He was not of the same kin or kind as the forest people. His hair was as dark as theirs, his skin only a little fairer, but he was taller, as tall as she, and though broader far than Sarama, never as broad as they. Nor was his face so heavy, his bones so thick. His eyes were large and dark under level black brows, his nose blunt and straight, his mouth full, unsmiling, framed in close-cut curly beard. He made her think of a young bull, even to the slight lowering of his head as she stared, and the hunching of his wide shoulders.

She was, she realized, as nearly naked as made no matter. To reach the bed and the coverlet she must pass him—this stranger. This man. And he made no move. He simply stood.

He must be the master here, or the master's son. He was dressed more richly than she could have imagined, in weavings of rich fabrics and wonderful colors, red and blue and green and gold. There were bright stones in his ears, and on his arm a wonder: a curve of sunlight given substance, bright gleaming marvel. Could that, indeed, be the thing called gold?

She shut her eyes against the lure of it, and called her wits to order. A prince, yes. A lord of these people—no women kings after all; no gentle rulers. Only men, as always, as the men's gods had ordained.

This prince, if such he was, was pitifully slow to seize the advantage. A tribesman would have had her on the bed long before now, and been doing his best to prove himself her master.

She glanced from side to side. The window was too small to admit her body, even as slender as she was. The door was behind the man. There was no other way to go, no weapon, no escape.

The man moved. She tensed, but he backed away from her. He bent to the chest that stood beside the door, rummaged in it, grunted as if in satisfaction. He pulled out something soft and finely woven in stripes the color of summer leaves and of new cream. He held it out to her, bowing slightly over it, a gesture that might have been—respect?

Maybe they knew Horse Goddess, too. When she did not take the thing that he offered, he stepped closer, too quick to flee, and set it firmly in her hands.

It was a garment, of course, long and loose. She put it on rather defiantly. It fell to her ankles, which was well. Its sleeves were longer than they should be: perhaps it had been made for a man, even for this man. But it fit well enough. She scowled at him lest he think that he had bought her with the gift. She had covered herself, that was all.

He met her scowl with a bland look, turned and called over his shoulder. Commanding his servants, she had no doubt; and in short order they came running, dark-eyed young creatures of ambiguous sex, carrying plates and bottles and bowls. They spread a feast on the lid of the chest, with many glances at Sarama, but nothing that she would have reckoned an impertinence.

One of the last brought something that she was very glad of, but that she could hardly use under the man's unwavering stare: a chamberpot. Yet again he seemed to understand, though she had spoken no word. He turned his back and leaned on the doorframe, comfortably and thoroughly blocking it, but unable at all to see what she did.

She relieved herself as best she could, as a prisoner might. Even when she was done and had arranged her new gown again, the broad back did not move. She regarded it for a while, then shrugged and investigated the cups and the platters.

She recognized very little of what they carried. Meat, yes. Mutton, but roasted with herbs that gave it a green and pungent flavor, not unpleasant but a little too odd for comfort. Fruit cut and mixed together and drizzled with honey. Something cooked together, roots and greens as they seemed. And bread whiter and finer than she had seen, whose people made flour from the seeds of the wild grasses, but never flour as fine as this. The jar with it was filled with something sweet and strong—mead, or wine mixed with honey—but there was a jar of water, too, cold and sweet, and a jar of goat's milk.

If this was bribery, then she would take it, and pay such price as she might. She had not eaten so since she left the steppe. She ate carefully, wary as one should be after fasting, tasting only, and not gorging lest she cast it up again.

The man had turned back while she ate, and stood still leaning on the doorframe, watching her. He began to puzzle her. His stance was pure young male, and he was not a weedy or a weak one either, but she could find nothing dangerous in his expression. If he had been a woman she would have said that he was keeping her company, watching her in some concern, gratified that she ate and drank so well and yet so sensibly. But how could a man be that simple, and demand nothing of a woman whom he could simply have seized and taken at his will?

There was no desire in his eyes at all. And when she had stood in front of him with her breasts bare and nothing to cover her but a scrap of loincloth, he had shown no sign of lusting after her then, either.

She began to grow angry. Was she that ugly to him? Did she attract him so little?

That was folly. She should be glad. Unless of course he was preparing her for another, some greater prince or king.

Yes, that was it. He was the errand-runner. When she was done with her dinner, he would do as indeed he did: beckon her to follow.

She considered resistance. But the room was small and its walls closing in. Even if she had to fight for it, she would welcome a broader space.

He led her out into a larger room, and thence through a door into sunlight. She reeled and fell against the first thing that would hold her up: his warm and solid body. He caught her but did not do the rest of what a man might do. He held her till her feet were steady under her. Then he let her go.

There were people about. They did not crowd close, they did not weigh her down with stares, but they were watching, murmuring to one another, offering commentary on the stranger. There were a good number of women among them, and none crept or hid or bent her head lest a man think her haughty. They strode about like men, with bold eyes and proud carriage. It was the men who looked down when she tried to meet their stares, turned their faces and refused to confront her.

Sorely baffled but beginning to wonder if there had been some truth in the traveller's tales after all, Sarama followed her guide, guardian, jailer, whatever he was. He led her down and round by a way that was like the arc of a circle defined by the patterning of trees and houses; then inward to a place that was taller than any of the others about it, two tall stories high, and made taller yet by the carved peak of its roof.

They did not go in, though the door was open. They went round to a curving wall of stone, and through a gate into a circle of green.

There were more trees growing here, and flowers, ordered as she had never seen them. Hands had set them here, not simply allowed them to grow. They made a pattern of interwoven spirals, ringed on the outside with trees. In the center grew a single slender white sapling, ghostly and beautiful, bearing a crown of golden leaves. Under the tree sat a woman.

There were other women with her. Sarama perceived them, dismissed them. This was the one whose attention mattered, this elderly woman with her thickened body and her sagging breasts, whose face could never have been beautiful. She sat as a king would sit in the center of his tribe, erect and imperturbably calm.

A woman king. Sarama had not realized she was holding her breath till it cried to be let out. After all, a king who was a woman. The tales were true.

Then what was the man who had brought her here? He had not followed her into the walled place. She glanced back. He stood in the gate, arms folded, as if on guard.

There were no men here. They were all women.

Their king spoke. At first Sarama thought the words were addressed to her, but the man answered from behind her. His reply seemed to interest the king: her brows rose. She spoke again. Their conversation went on for a while, with Sarama in the middle, uncomprehending, and beginning to lose her temper.

At much too long last, the king turned her dark eyes on Sarama. She inclined her head. Sarama inclined her own in response. The king's lips curved slightly. She glanced toward the man in the gateway, and beckoned with the arch of a brow.

Not only he was astonished to be so summoned. The women about the king seemed shocked, and one or two protested.

The king ignored them. She spoke a word. *Come,* that must be.

The man moved stiffly, walking as if the grass were edged blades, or as if the sky would crack and swallow him. He came to face the king, went down on his knees and bowed his head and seemed to wait for it to be struck from his shoulders.

The king laid her hand on it and said something soft, with a smile in it. It did not comfort him overmuch, but it did bring his head up. She glanced again at Sarama, and signed with her hand: at Sarama, at the man. She tapped him briskly on the shoulder. "Danu," she said.

Sarama frowned.

He tapped his own breast. "Danu," he said. And reached, and not quite touched her, lifting his brow as the king had.

Name, she thought. That was a name. "Sarama," she said.

"Sarama," said the man, twisting it oddly but not unpleasantly.

The old woman nodded and smiled, raised her arms and waved them away. The audience, it was clear, was ended.

Sarama did not think to object until she had been swept in the man—in Danu's wake, out of the green place and into the street again, to his manifest relief.

Someone else was waiting there. The Mare, clean and brushed and evidently fed, and queenly glad to see Sarama again. Sarama had not known how lonely she was, until she wrapped arms about that warm horse-scented neck and buried her face in the Mare's mane.

Too quickly the Mare wearied of such foolishness, pulled away and went in search of grass. Sarama followed. Danu trailed behind.

He had been confirmed as her guardian: that much Sarama understood. That she neither wanted nor needed a guardian, nor intended to submit to one, seemed to have occurred to no one. She kept her back turned to him, shutting him out, but there was no escaping the awareness of his presence.

The Mare led them through the circles of the city, past more dwellings than Sarama had ever seen, even in the gathering of tribes. All the people here were like the man, shortish and solid, though he was more solid than some. The women dressed in weavings that would have done justice to kings' wives at a festival. The men were if anything more handsomely adorned. Many wore ornaments of copper, or wore colored beads or bright stones in their ears or about their necks or on their fingers. None but Danu wore gold. By which she was certain again that he was a prince, or a man of importance at least—though why he would be relegated to caring for a stranger, and a woman at that, she could not imagine.

They passed the last of the houses, and the people who stared or smiled but did not interfere. Sarama looked down a long green slope to a slow roll of river; and then up to the blessed sky. No trees here, just where she stood. Not even one.

The Mare had not paused with Sarama. She strode down a path that led to a house, the outermost of those that ringed the city, and rounded it, and found there, at last, the patch of grass that she had been seeking.

A soft snort of laughter brought Sarama about. The man Danu was watching the Mare with an expression of wry amusement, as if she had done something that he had not expected, but that did not surprise him.

He caught Sarama's eye on him. Did he flush faintly? She could not tell. His laughter died. He pointed to the Mare. "Horse," he said.

It was mangled and slurred, but there was no mistaking the meaning of the word.

Sarama set her lips together.

He pointed to her. "Sarama." To himself: "Danu." Stamped the earth. "Earth," he said; and plucked a blade of grass. "Grass."

So that was what the king had commanded him to do. Teach the outlander a civilized tongue. Sarama could admit the wisdom of it, but a wicked spirit was in her, a spirit of contrariness. She did not want to learn his language. Let him learn hers. She stabbed her finger where he had pointed: "Sarama. Danu." And in her own tongue: "Earth, grass, horse, river, hill, tree, sky."

"Earth, grass, horse, river, hill, tree, sky," Danu said as rapidly as she had, and with a spark in his eye that told her how well he understood what she was doing.

She narrowed her eyes at him. "So," she said. "You're a bard, or a singer of stories. Or do they have such, in this place?"

He did not echo that—somewhat to her disappointment. He listened intently, and no doubt committed the sounds to memory, but he was too canny to take them for aught but acid commentary. When she had finished, he said deliberately, in her language with his barbarous accent, "Earth, tree, sky." And turned his back on her and went into the house.

She stood staring at the space where he had been. Was she free, then? Could she go?

And where? She had come here at the goddess' bidding. Now that she was here, she must do what the goddess willed—whatever that was to be.

She set her teeth and squared her shoulders, and went into the house.

·············· 23 ··············

Danu did not like the stranger at all. He had been less than delighted to be given charge of her; but the Mother's logic had been incontestable. "She came with a horse. You speak the language of horses. Learn her language, too, and discover what she is and what she intends."

"I know what she is," he had said with a kind of grand defiance, because she was standing next to him, listening and, he hoped, comprehending nothing that he said. "She intends something terrible. Haven't you dreamed of it?"

"I dream men on horses," the Mother said. "This is a woman. You will look after her."

This was not Danu's Mother, but he was living in her city, by his own Mother's will. He bowed his head in submission.

It was not he who had brought the two of them, and her grey horse, too, to the house that he had decided to take for himself and the colt. The horse made her way unerringly there, and the others followed.

Danu had no doubt that the stranger resented his guardianship as much as he resented his charge. That she was quick-witted he could see, but he was just as quick. He had always been able to remember words when they were spoken to him. He took her aback with that, he suspected.

He had had enough of it and of her. He went to the work that he had set himself, cleaning and repairing the lower story of the house for the horses' habitation. Tomorrow some of the people of Larchwood would come to help him repair the pen outside.

He rather hoped that the stranger would go away, or at least occupy herself with her horse. Of course she did no such thing. She followed him into the house. She gaped about at the stone walls and the deep-set windows, stamped her foot on the packed earth floor, found the ladder and clambered up it and vanished into the rooms above.

He sighed faintly. Good; she was out of his way. He bent to the sweeping and scouring, clearing and tidying.

✦ ✦

Just as he tackled a spiderweb as large as a Mother's cloak, with the spider crouched furious in it, her voice rang out above him, calling his name.

"Danu! *Danu!*"

He started, tangling himself in sticky web. The spider scuttled up his body, scaled the crags of his face, and leaped for the safety of her torn and mangled weaving.

He bit back a shriek that would have done his people no justice, and extricated himself with taut-strung patience. She was still calling, and curse her for it, too. If she was dying, he could not come to her any quicker.

At last he was free. He ran for the ladder.

She was not in the outer room above. He strode toward the inner.

She was not lying dead or caught in a fit, nor had she met some enemy, ill spirit or living beast. She had flung open the shutters of the window and leaned precariously out.

He peered past her. The meadow ran down to the river, mellow with autumn gold. The grey horse stood in it, chest-deep in grass. The colt, who was nigh the same gold as the grass, stood nose to nose with her.

The tightness in Danu's throat eased abruptly. "Colt," he said. "Horse."

The stranger—her name, he reminded himself, was Sarama—wheeled on him as if he had uttered a blasphemy. *"Colt!"* She loosed a spate of words, too swift and too many to follow. The burden of it seemed to be that she was not pleased to see another horse in this place—or perhaps, a male horse. A young bull among the cattle, a yearling ram among the ewes . . .

A piercing squeal snapped Danu erect. The grey horse had put the colt in his place, and handily too.

Danu could not help himself. He laughed. He was still grinning as Sarama rounded on him. She was fierce: she scowled as terribly as his sister Tilia ever had. That perhaps made him less cautious than he should have been. He did not wipe the grin from his face in the teeth of her evident indignation. "Colt," he said.

Sarama muttered something that he doubted was complimentary. She pushed past him and out of the room, down the ladder faster than he was inclined to follow, and out into the sunlight.

He pursued her at his own pace. When his eyes had settled to the brightness, he found her beside her horse, glowering at the colt.

The colt regarded her with interest but no fear. The grey horse was busily ignoring him. He approached her again with every appearance of care, and did an odd thing: mouthed at her as if about to break into human speech. She flattened ears and snapped. He retreated hastily, settled to snatching bits of grass, but watching her all the while.

Sarama glared at him, but he would not let her near. They danced a pretty dance round the grey horse and the field, while the grey horse grazed in conspicuous contentment.

Danu watched until it began to pall on him. He stepped in then, held out his hand and said to the colt, "Come."

The colt considered disobedience. But he was a sweet-tempered creature despite his fondness for testing anything and everything with his teeth. Nor did it hurt matters that Danu had taken to keeping bits of fruit or sweet cake about him, for such moments. He stepped lightly up to Danu and thrust a soft nose into Danu's hand, demanding his bit of cake.

Sarama's renewed glare was gratifying. Danu smiled at her. The colt was in comfort; the grey horse seemed undismayed. Danu left them to return to his scouring of the colt's winter quarters—and the horse's, too, as it would seem.

+ +

The grey horse's name was Mare. Or rather, her kind and sex was called a mare, and her rider called her the Mare, as one might call a woman the

Mother. Sarama seemed insistent that Danu understand this. She was also unduly agitated about the colt, as if his presence might somehow defile her precious Mare.

The colt, whom Danu had not presumed to give a name, showed no sign of being a great burden to the Mare. If anything she seemed fond of him. She tolerated him near her, let him graze beside her. He was allowed no insolence: if he offered any, she fell on him with hooves and teeth and beat him into submission. He learned quickly to mind his manners, as a male should.

Well before the sun sank on that first day of the Mare's meeting the colt, Danu could see clearly that the two of them would do well together. Sarama however seemed convinced that something dire was going to happen. He caught her trying to drive the colt off, without notable success; and while the colt watched, not at all dismayed by her leaping and yelling and whirling her belt about her head, the Mare shouldered in front of her and moved her firmly and irresistibly away from the colt.

Sarama was taken off guard. She stared at the Mare. She spoke: a few words in a tone of disbelief. The Mare shook off a fly and went back to grazing—standing exactly between Sarama and the colt.

Even Sarama could understand that. She hissed, but she retreated.

Danu went back hastily to his task of sweeping out the house. When he thought she might not be looking, he let the grin loose. It was not at all proper of him, but he was glad to see this haughty stranger so neatly put in her place.

✦ ✦

By the third day of his guardianship, Danu was ready to hand it on to a stronger spirit. Sarama just barely tolerated his presence. She might not have done that much if her Mare had not insisted on living in the meadow by the river, next to the house that Danu had taken and was making ready for the winter. He kept on with that, particularly once it was evident that Sarama was not going to join with him in the task of teaching each the other's language.

He persisted doggedly: naming things as they came to hand, making brief stories of them, repeating the small words, the important words, over and over. If she listened at all, he doubted that she troubled to remember. She would not teach him in return, except sometimes to flood him with a spate of words; then to curl her lip in disgust when he did not leap to obey whatever command she had laid on him.

He was beginning, perhaps, to understand some of it: *come, go, stop, look, go away*. In time it would be clearer.

He would never, for the pride of his people, show the temper she tried so hard to rouse. It infuriated her if he smiled blandly after she had tried to drown him in words, or if he walked away calmly from some tantrum, some foot-stamping refusal to do somewhat that would have been helpful to his readying of house and horse-pen. He knew better than to ask her, ever, to lend a hand. But a glance, the tilt of his head toward whatever it was she might have done, would send her flouncing off in a snit.

She was indeed very like Tilia in the spirit, though nothing like her in face or body. Danu had grown up contending with Tilia. He could continue with this stranger, he supposed, since the Mother of Larchwood had laid it on him.

The Mare at least was no trouble, and the colt, though occasionally impertinent, seemed glad of another of his kind, and delighted with his new pen and his big stone house. The pen was handsome, the work of the people of Larchwood, who were greatly skilled with stakes of wood and woven withies. They offered of themselves to bring in fodder from the river-meadow, to cut it and cure it and store it in a little byre that they made, while the sun shone and the Lady held off the rain.

Danu thanked the Lady as he thanked the people who worked so hard for him in her name. She was a warmth in his belly. They were shyly pleased. "We'll help as you need us," they said. "It's for the Lady, after all, and the Mother."

+ +

"And maybe a little for you," Catin said to him as they lay together the night that the hay-byre was done.

It was his last night in the Mother's house, though he had not spoken of that, yet, to Catin. The house above the horses' house was ready, cleaned and repaired, with ample wood to burn on the hearth through winter's cold, and foodstuffs laid away, and comforts brought as gifts by people who just happened by: thick soft coverlets for the bed, rugs for the floor, a chest to keep his clothing in, and a table and a pair of stools and even, from the Mother herself, a little image of the goddess to preside from her niche above the hearth.

Catin had seen it all today, admired it and seemed delighted by it. "They do it for you," she said in the warm aftermath of loving, running fingers through the curly hairs of his chest. "They like you, man of Three Birds."

He shrugged past the weight of her head on his shoulder. "I like them. Your people are good people. They don't laugh as much or as often as mine do—is that the shadow of the wood on them?—but they have a bright spirit."

"You aren't given to meaningless laughter, I've noticed," Catin said a little dryly.

"Well," he said. "No."

"Then do you hunger for your own people? Do you hate it here?"

"No," he said again, but with rather more feeling in it. "No, I don't hate this place. My people . . . I'll go back to them when the Lady calls me. I'm happy enough. I've more to do than I could have thought, and some of it very . . . interesting, too."

Catin looked up into his face. A smile quirked her lips. It made her look much younger than she was, and delightfully wicked. "Isn't she, now? Has she learned a word of sensible speech yet?"

Not likely, he had been going to say, but something made him say instead, "She's learning." Catin's face fell slightly. He did not know why that should annoy him; he could well understand how she felt.

"Ah," she said. "Well. The other stranger, the man, learned rather quickly. He never spoke well, but he could make himself understood."

"Was he very like this one?" Danu asked, in part to distract her from his prevarication, but also because he truly wanted to know.

Catin thought about it for a while. He watched the play of thoughts in her eyes, like fishes in a deep pool.

At length she said, "He looked like her, a little. Narrow and tall—very tall, much taller than this woman. Hair the color of straw, but his beard was red: yes, like tarnished copper. His eyes were brown. Not like hers—green; what color is that for a woman's eyes? He had terrible manners, almost as bad as hers. He was always trying to coax a woman into his bed. He seemed to think that a man can demand it and be proper, instead of waiting for a woman to ask."

For some reason Danu remembered just then how Sarama had been on that first waking, the way she had recoiled from him. Was that why? Did she think that he had come to be importunate?

He shook himself slightly, almost a shudder. No. Of course not. That was a preposterous thing to be thinking. It did her no honor, nor him either.

She was rude, that was all. She did not know how to be polite.

Catin could not have followed his maunderings. He was glad of that. She said, "You must make this woman learn our language. The Mother has great need to talk to her."

Danu nodded. He did not want to compound a lie, but neither could he bring himself to confess it.

Catin fell asleep soon after, to his relief. He had not yet told her that on the morrow he would be moving his belongings to the house by the river. He was a coward in every respect.

·········· 24 ··········

As Danu prepared to depart the Mother's house for the house by the river, the Mother herself came to him and stood watching him knot the last of his bundles. He would have risen and done reverence, but her hand stopped him. After a slight hesitation, he went back to his packing.

She actually, with her own hands, helped him knot the bundle and fashion a carrying-strap from the loose corners of it. He murmured thanks.

"Don't be too submissive, boy," she said. "It looks false."

His head snapped up. He stared in flat astonishment.

She laughed at his expression. He had never seen a Mother like this. Not even this one, who had always observed a proper and Motherly gravity.

Here where there was no one else to see, she was as brisk and acerbic as her daughter could be, and as little tolerant of what she considered nonsense. "You are a beautiful creature," she said, "and well you know it. You should strut a little more, and creep about a little less."

He did not know at all what to say to that.

Nor, it seemed, did she expect him to. She shook her head and sighed. "Sometimes I wonder if we do well to teach our boys soft manners. They'd run rampant else, the wise women say, like stags in rut, or bulls in the spring. And yet a little cockiness is not at all an ill thing."

"I'm told I have rather too much," Danu said—softly, he could not help it; he was trained to it.

"You should have more," the Mother said. She prodded him with a hard finger, and laughed when he jumped. "There, there. I horrify you, I can see it. And I only came to see you off, and to ask somewhat of you."

"No," he said quickly. "She has not learned any useful speech."

The Mother's brow lifted. "Did I ask you that?" In the face of his abashed silence she said, "I would like to ask that you take her with you."

"Take—" He bit off the rest. "Take her where I'm going? Keep her there?"

"Keep her there," the Mother agreed. "Teach her what she will learn. Learn from her as much as you may about horses, and about these people who ride horses."

Danu nodded, swallowing protests. Of course that was the wise thing to do, and simpler than requiring him to come back every day to the Mother's house, fetch the stranger, and coax her to follow him about as he performed the rest of his duties.

Nevertheless he did not look forward to keeping house for that of all women. He had seen how she was in this house, how she must be taught every smallest thing. Whatever she knew, it did not encompass the ways of a Mother's house in the Lady's country.

Still, this was laid on him. He too was a stranger here, and he seemed to understand the language of horses. Maybe time would teach him to understand the language of the horse people, too, whether or not Sarama would deign to teach him.

✦ ✦

One of the youngest daughters and one or two of the sons brought Sarama's belongings, such as they were, to the house that Danu found himself thinking of as his own. Strange thought, to have a house and not to keep it for a Mother, or for a woman who had chosen him. He could hardly count Sarama in such company. She was his duty, as the Mother's house had been in Three Birds.

She was at the house already, as he had expected, doing somewhat with the Mare. The colt, who had been watching, threw up his head and called to Danu, and came on at the canter.

Danu stopped and waited. He heard a muted squawk behind him, and a scramble as the children fought to make of him a wall between themselves and the charging beast.

They were in no danger at all, no more than Danu. The colt danced to a halt in front of him, half-reared, met his glare, came down and stood and set his nose in Danu's palm. Danu let him draw in the scent, then stroked his neck where the coat was thickening with winter's coming.

When they had exchanged a full and proper greeting, the colt returned to his scrutiny of the Mare and her puzzling servant. Danu led his little company of retainers past them, up to the house.

He had not made space for Sarama. On the way to this place he had decided that she would have the bed, and he would spread a pallet on the floor. She was not a proper or civilized person, but he, after all, was; and that was as proper as anyone could ask for. For the rest of it, she could share the chest, and he would see that she was fed and looked after, as he had done for his Mother and sisters in Three Birds. Certainly it was nothing new to him, and nothing that he could not do.

He refused, even briefly, to regret the loss of his solitude. Solitude was not a natural state. He should be glad to be relieved of it.

✦ ✦

Once the children had set down their burdens where Danu directed, the eldest, the daughter, said, "We're supposed to stay and do what you need us to do."

"For now I need nothing," Danu said, "but I thank you."

She frowned slightly, very like her sister Catin. "We're to come back every day. This is our duty, Mother said."

"That's well," Danu said, and meant it, too. "Come back tomorrow, then."

She hesitated, as if she might protest; but she was no fool. She gathered her brothers and ran off whooping.

Danu laughed. With a lighter spirit and the remains of a smile, he finished setting the house in order.

✦ ✦

As the day grew old, clouds crept over the sun's face. A chill wind began to blow. Danu, stepping out to test the air, caught the scent of rain.

Sarama was still outside, still together with the Mare. She must have ridden: the Mare's back showed the marks of a rider, though Danu had seen her saddle-fleece and her bridle hung neatly in their places inside the house. It should not have surprised him that Sarama could dispense with such things.

It did surprise him that she was still there; that she had not simply ridden away. He had brought with him a bit of bread new from the baking and dripping with honey. He offered it to Sarama where she sat on the sere grass, watching the Mare graze.

She stared at him as if she had never seen him before. He held up the bread. "Bread," he said. "Honey." And mimed the word as he said it: "Eat."

She never had refused to eat what was set in front of her. She devoured the bread without a word. Her eyes had returned to the Mare. She seemed determined to ignore his existence.

He sighed. But for the rain and the threat of early dark, he would have left her there. But it would not be kind to let her find her way back to the Mother's house, only to find her belongings gone and her place filled.

He touched her shoulder. She started. He drew back quickly lest she strike; but she only turned again to stare, and in no friendly fashion, either.

"Come," he said.

She did not move.

"Come," he said again. "More food. Eat."

That roused her, though she took her time about it. When at last she deigned to rise, the first drops of rain began to fall.

✦ ✦

The house was warm, a fire burning on the hearth, the air rich with the scents of bread, sweet cakes, roasting meat, honey and spices. Danu had blessed house and hearth before he lit the fire, walked the four corners and cleansed them with the smoke of sacred herbs. Their scent lingered beneath the rest, a memory of benediction. The Lady was here, watching over the house, blessing it with her presence.

Sarama seemed oblivious. She ignored the Lady's image in its niche, even after Danu had done reverence to it; looked about in some surprise, as if she had not expected that bare and empty space to be made so inviting.

Danu left her standing beside the opening to the room below and busied himself about the hearth and the oven and the table. There was a surprising pleasure in it, in doing things that he had done so often in Three Birds, but not at all in Larchwood. He had been happy as keeper of his Mother's house. He had not known how much he missed it here.

Down below he heard the thudding of hooves on packed earth, and a squeal as the Mare let the colt know which heap of cut fodder was hers. The horses had found their way in as he had hoped, safe out of the rain.

Danu spread the table as he had been used to do in Three Birds, with grace that met with a flat stare from Sarama. "In your country, I suppose," he said with a touch of acidity, "one simply heaves the whole ox off the fire and hurls it in front of the guest."

She did not understand him, of course. He found he could not care. "Come," he said. "Eat. Ignore me if you like. I'll teach you in spite of yourself. I'll talk you dizzy. You'll speak our language for the pure pleasure of hearing it from someone else besides me."

She came, at least, and sat at the table. He served her as if she had been a Mother, with a flourish that was lost on her.

Or perhaps not. She did know how to accept service. He was mildly astonished. For all her sullenness and her difficult manners, she had, in that, a native grace.

When he had done all that he judged proper, he sat opposite her and fell hungrily on his own portion. She, having blunted the edge of her own hunger, watched him in—surprise? dismay?

"Yes, I eat," he said. "I, too."

"You," she said. "You—" She gestured, flick of wrist, dart of fingers: miming cooking, carving, serving.

She mimed it very well. He smiled at that; nodded. "Yes. I cook. I serve."

"You," she said. "Man. Man not—cook. Serve."

His brows went up, and not only at the proof that, after all, she had been listening to his days of chatter. "No? Then what does a man do?"

Her frown had in it less of incomprehension, and more of bafflement. "Man—horse. Man—" She spoke words then that he did not know, but committed to memory: *hunt, fight.* He thought he knew what they meant: drawn bow, hand raised to strike.

But as to that last: "Why would a man want to . . . *fight?*"

"Fight," she said. "Hunt. Not—cook. Serve. Woman cook. Woman serve."

He nodded. "Yes. Woman cook, serve, too. And hunt. But not fight. Fights are not proper."

Her frown deepened. "You are man. You do—woman do—"

"I do what a woman does." By the Lady; this creature thought him improper. He must not laugh; laughter would be perilous, just now. "No, no. I am a man, I am proper, but when a Mother tells me—"

She did not understand. He hissed in frustration. As simply, as clearly as he could, he said, "Man, yes. Mother say, do this. I do this. Woman cook, serve, yes. Sometimes man may cook. For Mother. If Mother say."

He felt like a fool, and no doubt sounded like one, too. But she understood him. "For Mother?" He nodded. She tossed her head in a broad mime of outrage. "Tell Mother no! *Woman* do this. You *man.*"

He would not grow angry. He would not. That she should demand a woman—as if a man were not good enough. As if his presence diminished her.

In some cities, he had heard, such things were considered, if not proper, then at least acceptable. But not in this part of the Lady's country.

He swallowed his temper, and held it down until he could speak calmly. "In the morning," he said, "I will tell the Mother. Tonight, you stay here. Do you understand? Stay here."

"Stay?" She looked about. "Here?"

"Here," he said.

He braced for further resistance. But one of the horses whickered below, a soft contented sound. She stiffened at it, then eased abruptly. "Here," she said, a little grudgingly, but that did not trouble him. She took the bed with an air that dared him to argue.

She stared when he spread his pallet. Had she expected him to be *that* importunate?

He did not linger to discover the answer. He was tired, and he was out of patience. He turned his back on her and went to sleep.

+ +

"No," the Mother said.

Danu had expected that. "My presence to her is an insult. Mother—"

"Let her learn to behave properly," said the Mother. "If she will not suffer a man to wait on her, then let her learn. We have our own ways here. She will accept them."

"Even," Danu asked, "though she is a guest?"

"A guest who is proper accepts the ways of her hosts." The Mother's voice and manner were immovable. "No, my child. The Lady asks that you do this. She is quite firm on the subject."

"So is Sarama," said Danu, but he could not resist further. Not once the Mother had invoked the Lady.

The Mother, who must know that very well, brushed his hair with her hand, as his own Mother might have done. "Child," she said, "remember what I told you of permitting yourself to be proud. Never let anyone scorn you. This is a child herself, rude and untutored, with dreadful manners. Let her learn to serve the Lady as a woman should."

Humility would not suit Sarama well, Danu thought but forbore to say. The Mother kept him for a while, for the apparent pleasure of his company; then sent him back to his less than pleasant duty.

·········· 25 ··········

"Mother says," said Danu, "no. You stay. I serve."

He sounded conspicuously calm about it. Sarama was learning to read him, or so she hoped. He was not happy. He yielded to his king as a man should, and did his king's bidding, but he was much too carefully obedient.

Sarama tried to imagine her brother Agni doing the will of a king who was a woman. The thought was too preposterous. Agni had no such compliance in him as this man seemed to have.

That he was a prince she had no doubt. She had seen how the king was with him. He had position here, and a place of respect. There must be council or gathering of the men apart from the women; if there was, he must be high in it.

And yet the king had him playing nursemaid to a stranger. Was he being punished? Or was she?

He seemed happy while he did women's work. That was most puzzling of all. He was adept at it. He did it well. He managed somehow to keep the house clean, the two of them fed, the horses tended, and himself in good order, without the slightest show of difficulty. The king sent him on errands, too, and the plain-faced young woman who seemed to be the king's daughter seemed often to be demanding service of him.

She was an odd one. Her name was Catin; she was called the Mother's heir—like, Sarama thought, a king's chosen son, who would be king after him. It did not seem to be as uncertain a thing as it could be among the tribes. Catin was settled in it, as solidly as Sarama had been in her place as the Old Woman's successor.

It seemed to Sarama that Catin was more to Danu than simple friend or kin. That they were not blood kin she had gathered. He was, it seemed, from another city—though why or how he had come here, she did not understand. He did not act as a husband should act, even a husband of a lesser tribe who had married into the king's tent. And yet there was something between them, something other than mere amity.

The day after Danu relayed to Sarama the Mother's refusal to give her a less uncomfortable jailer, Catin came calling at the house by the river. The night's rain had blown away, leaving a sky full of restless clouds, and a sharp chill in the air. She was dressed for it in a wonderful coat of woven wool, sewn with bright threads in patterns that made Sarama want to reach out and touch.

But Catin was not a person to invite such liberties. Sarama was going out as Catin came in, intending to ride the Mare along the river. Catin barely acknowledged Sarama. Sarama, who had grown to expect such of her, shrugged and went on her way. The Mare was eager for a run. The colt did not wait to be given leave: he was careening round the meadow, tail in the air, laughing as only a colt can laugh.

Sarama had not been pleased at all, at first, to see that after all these people did know of horses. It was only the one, the colt that the traveller had left behind as tribute to the Lady. He was far beneath the Mare, but quite out of the ordinary in that he seemed to know it. He kept a polite distance, he offered no insolence that the Mare did not permit, and he had perfectly reasonable manners, for a yearling colt. If it had not so evidently annoyed Danu, she would long since have stopped pretending to dislike him.

Away from the house and from Danu's watchful eye, she could let herself laugh at his antics. He ran rings round the Mare, danced, curvetted, did battle with air. He was a well-made colt, handsome, and very fleet of foot. When his time came, she thought, he would be smooth-gaited and sensible, but with ample fire.

He still was not good enough for the Mare; but he was a very fine colt. Though she would hardly say such a thing to Danu. Danu was besotted with him. Sarama wondered if he knew what he had done: found and claimed his stallion, and made himself a man after the custom of the tribes. They could not have such a custom here, where there was only one stallion in all the west of the world.

This very young stallion was swifter than the Mare, but he wearied much sooner. He ran beside her for a while as she skimmed the winter grass beside the river; then fell back, but following doggedly nonetheless, till the Mare took pity on him and slowed to a dancing trot, and thence to a walk.

Sarama walked them both till they were cool, well down the river and then back again. She had seen another town there, in a bend of the river; but she was not minded to go exploring. Time enough for that when she was surer of herself in that first city to which she had come.

Maybe in summer or in kinder weather there would have been people out and about. Today everyone seemed to keep to house and hearth. She blew on her fingers to warm them, and slipped her hands beneath the fleece of her saddle. The Mare's warmth seeped into her.

She would be glad of the fire that Danu always kept burning, of the warmth that would bake the chill out of her bones. The horses were in comfort in their winter coats and the warmth of their run. They were glad to run loose once she had come back to the house. The Mare waited impatiently to be stripped of saddle and bridle and rubbed dry where she had sweated. Just as Sarama finished, she pulled away, dancing and racing again with the colt, vying to be the first to fling herself down and roll.

Sarama was smiling as she climbed the ladder into the upper part of the house, though she meant to put on a dour expression before Danu could see. It was a game of sorts, to try his temper. He was unnaturally difficult to provoke.

The outer room was empty. The fire burned a little low, but not banked as it would have been if he had left. He would be in the inner room, then. She warmed her hands at the fire, content simply to stand in a place that was both warm and out of the wind.

At first she thought it was the wind muttering in the eaves. But no: there were voices within.

She had sharpened her ears before she thought. Futile, maybe, but she had been listening harder than she hoped her nursemaid knew. She could piece together enough of what they said, to hazard a guess at the rest.

"Do you like her?" That was Catin, and a note in her voice that told Sarama rather too clearly what they had been doing.

He laughed, richer and deeper than Sarama had ever heard him. "No, I don't like her. Do you?"

"I don't think she tries very hard." There was a pause. "You could come back to my Mother's house."

"The Mother said no." Was there regret in that? Sarama could not tell.

"She thinks that that one is the Lady's messenger. *I* think that the Lady could have better taste."

"Ah now," said Danu. "She's not so bad. I think she's testing me. It's very insulting, you know, for a woman as high as she must be, to be waited on by a man."

"She should not be insulted. You are the Mother's son of Three Birds. The Lady brought you here. She speaks to you. She gave you the horse to look after, and then this woman."

"Sometimes I wonder why," Danu said, almost too low to hear.

"Because she knew that you could do it."

"But can I?" He made a sound: laughter perhaps, or a snort of disgust. "She despises me, I think."

"The Mother does not," said Catin. "Nor I."

✦ ✦

Sarama had crept closer as she listened, till she stood barely breathing by the curtain that separated inner room from outer. With hunter's care, she parted the curtain a fraction, just enough to see what lay within.

They were wound in one another: rocking together almost idly, then with waxing urgency.

Sarama tasted blood. She had bitten her lip. She drew back as silently as she could, crept through the room, slipped down the ladder and made herself very busy with the horses.

At least, she thought as she scoured their beds and spread fresh straw, she need not wonder any longer what those two were to one another. Was Catin his wife, then? Or were they doing what sometimes people did in the tribes, and could die for it, too?

They had seemed to be making no secret of it. When she went back up again with some trepidation, they were in the outer room, decorously dressed, but Catin's hair was out of its plait and Danu wore a smile that was difficult to mistake. Sarama saw no shame in it.

He waited on Catin as he always did on Sarama. Catin acted as if that were only to be expected: that a prince, a king's son of another city, should be her servant. It was precisely as if he were a woman and she a man.

And what if . . .

Preposterous.

And yet.

There were no warriors in this country. No one carried a weapon. She had seen knives, but only for cutting meat. No swords. Hunters carried bows, and sometimes spears.

Danu had said that people did not fight.

How could anyone live in the world without war? Men conquered men. That was their gods' decree. One took what one could take, and not always because one needed it. War was glory. For a man, there was none greater.

She looked about her with eyes that had just learned to see. No weapons. No walls, no defenses about the cities. They were all open to any who might come.

A man of the tribes would look on this place with lust. The gold on Danu's arm, the copper of knifeblade and axeblade, ornament and binding, the beauty of the clothing that even the poorest seemed to wear, all the painted pots with their designs either whimsical or holy—these were riches beyond the dreams of a simple tribesman. And here they were taken for granted. No one stole them. No one thought of fighting for them.

These people knew nothing of war.

No; surely she was deceived, or had failed to see something of vital importance. And yet all this place was open to her. These people were without guile. They hid nothing, unless it might be in their goddess' temple.

Maybe that was their house of war. Tomorrow she would go there. She would see if she was let in; then she would see what was kept behind that door which so seldom opened.

It shook her to think such things; to feel the world unsteady beneath her. She ate what was set in front of her, blindly, and went to bed after. The bed on its platform was hers. Danu had insisted on it. She had thought it was his whim, atonement for a sin perhaps. She had been amazed that he made no effort to join her there; that he slept on the floor, as naturally and as calmly as he waited on her; as if it was only to be expected.

What if—

Again she shut down the thought. She would sleep. Yes. And in the morning she would discover the truth of this place.

·············· 26 ··············

If Catin stayed the night, Sarama was not aware of it. When she woke in the morning they were both gone. There was food on the table for her, covered in one of the finely woven cloths that were in such casual use here. She ate the cheese and the bread and the fruit stewed in honey, and drank the cup of water just barely sweetened with wine.

The horses were out in the meadow. The Mare barely deigned to acknowledge Sarama, which was her privilege. The colt called gladly as colts will, and came running to have his neck scratched. She went on, smiling, because after all he was an engaging creature.

It was a fair day, warm for this time of year. People were out and about, and children in particular, faces that she was beginning to recognize from daily familiarity. They greeted Sarama with courtesy, often with smiles. They liked to try words in her language, sometimes a fair string of them. One or two were growing frankly fluent.

Her own smile died as she reflected on what those easy, sunny smiles meant. Innocence. Ignorance of war.

There were so many of them, and all so rich. They did so many things. They worked copper. They made pots. They wove on looms and tanned hides. They made clothing and shoes. They ground flour and baked bread. They traded in wonderful things, bright stones, shells whole and carved, wine and sweet herbs from far away. They sang as they worked, many of them; as she had caught Danu doing when he made supper of an evening, singing to himself in his lovely deep voice.

No woman hid in house or tent here. Most of those in the streets, in fact, were women. Men seemed to keep to the houses, or else to be out hunting or herding—though always, that she had seen, in company with women. When she saw little children, as often as not the one tending them was a man. And that was a shock, too, now that she could see it. Women had to nurse the babies, that was nothing a man could do, but once they were weaned, they seemed to be given into the men's charge.

Sarama saw men walking about with children in slings on their backs, as women of low estate might do among the tribes. But these were men in profusions of copper ornaments, in beautiful coats, with strings of bright beads woven in their hair. Rich men, men of consequence, although they deferred to women as richly adorned as they.

It was true. Men were as women here, and women were as men. Everywhere that she looked, she saw it. It was not obvious, not at first. Only if she studied them could see how it was. Women ruled here. They ruled with a light hand, but rule they did. Men were the lesser, as seemingly content to be so as women were on the steppe.

✦ ✦

The temple rose in the heart of the city, center of all its circles. It was of two stories like the house in which Sarama was living, but larger, broader, and loftier. The peaks of its roof were carved in a strange fashion, huge bulging eyes in a face half human, half other: bird, fish, trunk and branches of a tree. Its walls were painted in white and black and red, a dance of spirals, of branches, of shapes like wings, and shapes that made her blush for all their innocence, because they made her think of a woman's sex. There was strong magic on those walls, magic that even she could sense, who knew little of the gods of this place.

Or perhaps there was only one goddess. This was her house, her dwelling in the city. From its summit every morning the Mother lifted her voice in an eerie shrilling cry, half song, half summoning. She was calling the sun, Danu had said once. Rousing the day. As if the sun could not come up of himself; as if he were not a god but a servant, and must do a woman's bidding.

The door of the temple was open, as if it waited for her. Sarama breathed deep before she ventured in. No guard prevented her. No bolt leaped out of the dimness to transfix her where she stood. A breath of cool air whispered past her face. The night's chill lingered within.

It was only a dim room with a lamp lit in it, flickering on a stone table. There were vessels on the table, fine work of the potter's art. In one, a great bowl, sat or reclined a circle of clay-molded people, women all, with little round breasts and great round eyes. A greater image sat beyond the table, a massive blocky thing rough-carved of stone. Its face was a blank shield with slits of eyes, noseless, mouthless, but its body was vastly, blatantly female: huge pendulous breasts, great swollen belly, deep-incised triangle at the meeting of its heavy thighs. There was nothing human in it, and everything female.

Horse Goddess, when she wore flesh at all, wore the semblance of the White Mare. She was nothing like this mass of stone. And yet, thought Sarama. And yet.

Sarama advanced slowly, lifting each foot and setting it down with a hunter's care. The floor was made of stones fitted close together, polished by time and the passage of feet. They were smooth, and cold even through the soles of her boots. Winter had settled in them, though autumn lingered in the world without.

Light came in through the open door. Where it ended, the lamp somewhat feebly began. Sarama halted in front of the stone table and looked up at the goddess. The image sat in a chair of darker stone, more smoothly carved. It made her think, somehow, of the Mother sitting in the room where they all gathered in the evenings. The Mother had perfected that same immobility, that same divine stillness. Perhaps it was the way of kings here, as kings on the steppe endeavored to be stern and strong.

Past the image Sarama saw a door. It was small, not deliberately hidden, but not wide open to the world, either. She bowed to the image, offering it reverence, and perhaps apology, too, for searching out its secret.

There was nothing beyond the door except a stair going steeply up. Sarama had seen such a thing in the Mother's house. Here as there, the stair opened on the roof, a flat space between the carved peaks.

Here must be where the Mother stood to sing her morning song. Sarama had no sense of sacrilege. This place regarded her with neither welcome nor hostility. It accepted her.

She rested her hand on the carving of the eastward peak. It was worn, as if many another hand had rested there. This place was old. How old she did not know, but she thought perhaps as old as her own people, as old as the dawn time.

From this eminence she could see all the circles of the city, ring upon ring of human habitation, shaded by trees, divided by roads, interrupted by the open square of the market and, behind the temple itself, the dark loom of trees that surrounded the goddess' sacred place. Through winter-bared branches she saw the house in which she had been sleeping, and the horses, tiny with distance, grazing together down by the river that touched the city's edge.

Even the great gatherings of the tribes had not so many tents, nor spread so wide. She had not seen how large the city was while she was in it. From above it she understood much that she had been blind to before.

The tribes arranged their tents in lines, straight for the most part, and in squares round the king's tent. Some, like those of the White Horse, even rode to war in ranks, which had proved useful against less disciplined tribes. These soft edges and nested circles, wreathed in branches and in faded greenery, would have struck them as very strange.

Sarama, raised on the Mare's hill, stood outside of both. She saw what she had come here to see. Truth. A country ruled by women, as men ruled the steppe.

She should have been more keenly struck with the wonder of it. She could only think of horsemen riding joyfully to war. And no one here knew how to fight. Their weapons were all for hunting, for slaughtering cattle, for harvesting the grain that they had made into a tamed thing.

The horsemen of the steppe could run over these peaceable people as if they had been grass underfoot. They had no defenses. They knew none, nor knew the need.

Soft people, rich people. People who had never known hunger or want, murder or rapine.

The men's gods had cast their eyes on this place. And Sarama had been sent ahead of them. This stone goddess with her monstrous breasts and her masked face was still the goddess of the horses, the women's protector, lady of the white mare. She looked after her own.

Sarama stood on the summit of the temple, gripping the head of the bird-faced roofpeak, and closed her eyes to the crowding world. In the darkness she felt herself below again in the lamplit gloom, standing near the goddess' image. Shapes moved beyond the stone table, glimmering naked woman-shapes, dancing a spiral dance. Their bodies were human, and not all young: huge sagging breasts, slack bellies, greying black hair between their broad thighs. But none of them had a face. They wore the goddess' own: the flat shield with its slitted eyes.

Masks. Sarama shivered at their strangeness. Priests on the steppe would dance masked in the hunting-dances, and in the dances before the tribes rode off to war. In wearing another face, they became other; became the gods in whose names they danced.

So too, perhaps, in this place. Every woman was the goddess, and the goddess every woman.

A mask would not save any woman from the tribesmen's swords.

✦ ✦

Sarama opened her eyes. The air had gone chill: a cloud had drifted across the sun. She had been waiting impatiently for the goddess' word; to discover her purpose here. Now she knew.

"Lady," she said, "I'm one woman alone. And you ask me to stand against all of the tribes?"

The goddess never answered such things. Sarama descended into the temple and thence to the city. She meant to return to the house by the river, but she took the long way round, circling the city slowly and more slowly. There was no wariness here. People made no move to protect themselves or their belongings. Everything was open, free for the taking.

It was growing late as she made her way back to the river. The horses grazed near the house as they liked to do in the evenings, the better to receive whatever dainty Danu might be persuaded to give them. He, knowing nothing of horses, treated them much as a man might treat a favorite hound. They took shameless advantage of him.

Sarama, whose hands were empty of fruit or sweet cakes, escaped with a nose-thrust from each and a flattened ear from the Mare. She emerged from the dark of the lower space into light and warmth and a deep voice singing softly to itself.

He was oblivious to her, stirring something wonderfully savory in a pot over the fire. It was more than strange to see a man so broad and strong, doing women's work with evident pleasure. It made her angry—and why it should do that, she could not think.

He was a tall man here, and no weakling even had he been a tribesman. She had seen him carrying half a slaughtered ox from the market, and watched him butcher it, too, dividing it half for the Mother and half for himself. He would have been a great warrior, had he turned such strength to the killing of men.

She had too few words yet to say what she yearned to say. To cry out to him that the tribes would come with blood-red war—and come far too soon for him or for his people. Winter would pass, spring would come, and the horsemen would dare the wood. Their gods would drive them on.

And there were no defenses here. No arts of war. Nothing to stop them, or to protect the Lady's country from fire and sword.

Nothing but Sarama.

She must have made a sound: Danu looked up. He smiled at her as if he were glad to see her. Perhaps he was only relieved that she had come back into his charge.

She stalked past him to the inner room. There was no Catin there today, and no sign of her. Sarama dropped her coat on the floor—knowing with a small stab of meanness that he would pick it up and lay it in the chest where in his opinion it belonged—and kicked her boots into a corner, and flung her cap after it.

Something was lying on the bed, something that looked like a field at sunset, a little green, a little gold, a little red. It was a coat. She lifted it and shook it out. It was finely made, bright-stitched with patterns that made her think of the play of wind in leaves.

So, she thought. Danu had a new coat. But it was rather narrow to fit across those shoulders. On a whim she slipped it on. It fit—not badly. Not badly at all. Its fastenings were of pale bone carved like little fat-breasted women. Each was carved with a different expression: mirth, contentment, comic surprise.

She looked up into Danu's face. He was smiling—again. "For you," he said.

Her hand ran down the front of the coat, loving the feel of it, the richness, the fine weaving. But the anger that was always in her when she looked at him made her say, "Why?"

"You were cold," he said. He picked up her own coat as she had known he would, and shook his head as he looked at it, prodding one of its many worn patches. "I can mend this. But you need a warmer coat."

"This is warm," she said.

"So," he said. "You do speak better than you would admit."

She shut her mouth and glared.

He laughed. "Come and eat," he said.

·············· 27 ··············

When Sarama came to Larchwood, Danu had stopped dreaming of blood and fire. But the night he gave her the coat that the Mother's daughters had woven and he had sewn, slipping her own coat out of the chest at night to match the size, the dream came back. Now the shadows had faces. Narrow sharp-boned faces, strange pale eyes. And all of them were mounted on horses.

They were riding, more of them than he could count, shoulder to shoulder, and in each hand a great long knife or a wicked-bladed spear. They were hunting. And what they hunted—

He woke with a cry. Something trapped him—he was hunted—

He flung it off. It fell hard, with a gasp that startled him into memory. He leaped from his pallet to kneel by Sarama.

She had had the wind knocked out of her, but she could still muster her wonted glare. He lifted her while she was too stunned to resist, finding her again a lighter burden than he expected. She had no more bulk to her than a bird. He laid her on the bed.

"You," she said, still struggling a little for breath, "are too strong."

He flushed. "I'm sorry," he said.

"Don't!" Her voice was fierce. It made him stiffen. "Don't say sorry. Stand up. Be strong."

"You said I was too—"

"I mean," she said, "very. *Very* strong."

Maybe, he thought. She was a difficult creature, more difficult than most.

Her hand darted out to grip his arm. "You had bad—" She groped for the word.

"Dream," he said, rather thick in his throat. "I had a bad dream."

"Very bad," she said. "Tell me."

"Why should I tell you?"

He bit his lip. That had escaped without thought, without any vestige of proper conduct.

She did not seemed appalled. "Because," she said, "I ask."

He almost laughed. Oh, *that* was proper: if one were, for example, his sister Tilia. Because she asked, then, and because he was reeling still from the memory of the dream, he told her what he had dreamed. Blood, fire. Men on horses. Knives and spears. And screaming. People screaming in an extremity of fear and pain.

When he stopped, because he had no breath or will to go on, she said a word.

"War."

He stared at her.

"War," she said. "Men fight, men kill. That is war."

"War." It was a brief word, to be so terrible. Its taste was oddly bitter. "War. You have a name for it."

She nodded. "We . . . have much of it."

"You *kill* each other?"

His horror must have struck her strangely: her eyes were wide, fixed on him. "Men kill," she said. "Men fight in wars."

"*Men* kill?"

Her eyes flickered. Was she laughing? "Yes," she said. "Men."

"Not here," said Danu. *"Not here."*

He did not know if she slept after that. He lay on his pallet, wide awake, staring into the shadows. Between his dream and her words, he did not know that he would ever sleep again.

✦ ✦

Danu had learned a new word, discovered a new thing, and it gave him no joy at all. In Three Birds he would have taken his trouble to the Mother. In Larchwood he should, and he did intend to, but he was slow to come to it.

He brooded on it as he went about his duties. Sarama, to whom this horror must be an old thing, hardly to be remarked on, seemed not to notice his silence.

What it must be to be one of her people, to have a word for the killing of men; to know at once what had so baffled the Lady's people, the thing that she had called, without hesitation, *war*.

At that, she seemed to have a trouble of her own, and Danu was a part of it. It was not his ill dream—or not only that. She watched him when she might have thought he did not see. Something about him perturbed her.

He could not imagine what it was. Perhaps, that he did not go out and kill someone? If men in her country were given to bloodshed, if they were not like men here but like young forest lions, or like wolves in a hungry winter—then well she might be looking for him to turn manslayer.

And was that, he wondered, why she had been so strange at her first waking? She had recoiled from him, had conducted herself as if she expected him to harm her. Was this what she had looked for? To be killed, because the men of her people were all mad?

If that was so, then her people were barbarous. And they were coming. This was the Lady's warning, this her messenger. The red thing, the thing called war, rode in her wake.

"Tell me about the women," he said to her of an evening, when the first snow hung heavy in the clouds, and the fire within held off the numbing cold without. "Your men kill, you say. What do the women do?"

She regarded him in some little startlement. He had not, he realized belatedly, said a word to her all day. Or the day before, either.

He was failing of his teaching. But she, somehow, had learned to speak more clearly, with fewer stumbles. "The women do nothing," she answered him.

"What, nothing at all? Not one thing?"

"They do what you do," she said with a touch of venom. "They cook. They clean. They serve."

"And they let the men kill? Why do they allow it? Where are the Mothers?"

"There are no Mothers," she said. "The men are—the men tell everyone what to do."

"And everyone listens?"

"Everyone obeys."

Danu blinked hard. Sarama was watching him again with that odd intensity. "You were afraid of me," he said. "Because you thought—because men in your country are not tame creatures."

"I was not afraid of you," she said, firmly but without anger. "I was . . . wary. Men don't ask. Men take."

"Here," said Danu, "we ask."

Her lip curled. "You are weak."

"Is that weakness? To ask before one takes?" Danu curled his own lip in his own flare of scorn. "Then I am weak. I would rather be weak than whatever you reckon strong."

✦ ✦

At least, Danu thought, Sarama had stopped pretending that she would not learn the Lady's tongue. She had learned it well. That it had taken a quarrel to reveal it . . . so be it. He was in no conciliatory mood himself.

She seemed startled in the morning when he would not smile at her, would offer her no more than the barest courtesy: silent service, averted eyes. After some few moments of it, she began to laugh.

Danu gritted his teeth and finished filling her cup. As he began to withdraw, she stopped him. He stared at her long pale hand on his broad brown wrist. She was stronger than she looked.

He could still have broken her over his knee.

"You are not weak," she said. "Is that why you're angry? Because I said you are weak."

He would not dignify that with a response. He pulled against her grip. She tightened it. "Let me go," he said.

"No," she said.

He stood still.

"You see," said Sarama. "Not weak. Not strong, either. You do not know how to fight."

"Fighting is for children," he said, "and for animals in rut. Not for men."

"Men fight better than any," said Sarama.

He twisted free of her. "I will not fight."

"Fight will come to you," she said. "They come. You saw in your dream."

"The Lady will prevent them," he said with more confidence than he felt.

"Lady—Horse Goddess—sent me," Sarama said. "I think—to teach. To fight."

To teach you to fight.

Danu shook his head. "No. Animals fight. Not men."

"Men," said Sarama, "and women. You can learn."

"I will not," said Danu.

"You will die," said Sarama. She said it dispassionately. "In war, you fight, or you die."

"That is not a human thing," Danu said, "or a thing of the Lady."

"It is what is," said Sarama.

He had never hated anyone, nor wanted to. He did not hate her. But the words she said, the things she made him think of, were terrible.

So too the dreams. They were true, a truth worse even than he had feared. Men killing men.

"Why?" he demanded of Sarama. "Why do they do it?"

"To get," she said, "to be—more. To be more. To have. To—win." Her hand swept the room. It was a simple room as he would think of it, but rich in comfort. "To have this." She touched the armlet that he had won from Tilia. "And for this."

"For this?" He smoothed the armlet. "They could trade for it. Why take it?"

She shook her head sharply, perhaps in disgust, perhaps in frustration. "Trade is not—trade is a small thing. War is great."

"I do not understand you," Danu said. "I do not want to understand you."

"You must," she said. "Or you die."

"I think I would rather die." He snatched his mantle off its peg, not even caring that he had left everything, breakfast half served, fire unbanked, nothing done that should be done to prepare for the day. It did not even matter what he flung himself out into: the raw cold of a snowy morning, snow underfoot, snow falling on his head. It cooled him. That was good. He only wanted to be away, to escape from the thoughts she forced on him, the words he had no desire to learn.

············· 28 ·············

Danu had gone out and not come back. Sarama might well have left the house—his house, which he kept as if he had been a woman—for him to look after, but a pot had boiled over, nearly quenching the fire. She leaped to its rescue. Once she had done that, it was not difficult to remember skills she had learned in the Old Woman's service.

It was rather more fitting she should do these things than that bull of a man. A bull who would not fight to defend his herd. What idiocy did they teach their men here? How had they lived so long, grown so rich, without ever knowing the meaning of war?

Their Lady had protected them. Danu had said so. But the gods of the steppe were coming, and they had no mercy on the weak.

"Animals fight," Sarama muttered. She spat into the fire. "Idiots!"

It took her a remarkably long time to perform the tasks that for Danu were so swift and so evidently easy. She was rather glad of them. They absorbed her mind; they shut out, somewhat, the clamor of the truth. That she was here for this. To teach the arts of war to a people who had never heard of war and did not wish to hear of it.

✢ ✢

As she finished the last of the sweeping and tidying, the ladder creaked. She looked toward it with something rather like gladness—that she told herself was relief.

The head that climbed up from below was dark, but its hair was almost straight and not richly curling, and its face was narrow as these people went, pinched narrower with hostility. Sarama set the broom in its corner, carefully, and put on a face of greeting. "Catin," she said, since she knew no other title.

Catin did not return the courtesy. She set fists on hips and glowered at Sarama. "What did you do to Danu?"

Sarama blinked. "What—" She mustered her wits. "I did nothing."

"You did something," Catin said. "He came to us like stormwrack. He sits in the Mother's garden by the temple, where no other man is allowed to go, and the snow heaps white on his shoulders, but he will not move. He will not speak. *What did you do to him?*"

Sarama did not understand every one of that spate of words, but she understood enough. "He sits in the snow?"

"He sits in the snow," Catin said, mocking her stumbling tongue. "Why?"

"You don't know?"

Catin surged forward. Sarama braced for a blow. But it seemed that even the women here, though they were like men in everything else, were taught not to fight. Catin stopped before she struck, stood with fists clenched, flung words in Sarama's face. "*You* know!"

Sarama very much feared that she did. She could explain war to this woman, too, and send her off to sit brooding in the snow. She would explain it to the whole city, to this whole country. Then maybe, just maybe, someone would wake to sense.

Or they would all freeze to death, and Sarama would await the coming of the horsemen in a land empty of people. That would please the men's gods to no end.

Catin had not moved, seemed disinclined to move until Sarama spoke. Sarama said, "I told him a thing he did not know how to hear."

"That is what he said," said Catin, almost spitting it. "He won't even talk to the Mother. He simply sits."

"Do you want me to be sorry?"

"I want you to bring him in out of the cold!"

Sarama raised her brows. "If you could not, and the Mother could not, how can I?"

"You caused it," Catin said. "You cure it."

Sarama set her lips together. If this man had been her lover, she would not have demanded that another woman beat sense into him. She would have been sure to do it herself.

People were different here. Everything was different. That was why Danu was sitting in the snow. Because he had seen a face of the world that he could not have imagined until she forced it on him.

Better he learn it now, and his people with him, than be taken by surprise. He had time to learn to defend himself. They all did. That was the goddess' gift.

✦ ✦

Sarama wrapped herself as warmly as she could, and rode the Mare, who was more than lively with the exhilaration of snow and cold. It was a fair procession: Sarama on the Mare, Catin trudging sullenly behind, and the colt running circles about them all.

The city was wrapped in white silence. Voices of childen pierced it: the young ones bundled to the eyes and tumbling in the snow while their elders stayed warm within. Most of them trailed after the women and the horses, curious as children always were.

The snow fell lightly. It was just deep enough to leave tracks in, but the storm had not passed: the clouds were thick with it. It would snow again, and heavily, before nightfall.

The children did not follow Sarama into the Lady's garden. Nor, somewhat to her suprise, did Catin or the colt. She rode into it without escort, slipped from the Mare's back and stood a little distance from Danu.

He did not acknowledge her. He huddled against a treetrunk, knees clasped tight to chest, scowling at nothing that she could see. Snow heaped his shoulders and melted in his hair. He looked like one of the old stone gods from a shrine on the steppe.

She squatted on her heels nearby, rubbing her hands together for warmth. She said nothing. The words she needed were more than she knew how to say in his tongue. Best to keep silence and wait. He might outlast her. He might not. She had no intention of lingering here till her feet froze.

The Mare nosed about, pawing snow from still-sweet grass. One particularly delectable clump happened to be that on which he sat. She nibbled round about him. He appeared oblivious to the snap and crunch of her teeth so close to his fundament.

She taught him the folly of that: a snarp nip that brought him cursing to his feet.

Sarama smiled contentedly. "You sulk badly," she said.

"I am not sulking." He stamped his feet as if he had only just noticed how cold it was, and brushed at the snow on his mantle. "I was thinking," he said with dignity.

"Thinking too hard," Sarama said, "and it's too cold. Why not do it inside a house?"

"Because I needed to breathe." He drew a deep breath, let it out again; shivered convulsively. "By the Lady! When did it grow so cold?"

"Last night," Sarama said.

He snorted and stalked away from her.

She followed, quiet again. The Mare followed her.

At the garden gate he halted. He stared at the flock of children, at Catin, at the colt who came at him whickering and trying to chew on his hair. He wheeled on Sarama. "I have not been in this place since yesterday!"

She arched a brow.

"You have been here since morning," Catin said, impatient. "Now tell us why."

"No," said Danu, and shut his mouth tight.

"Then tell the Mother," she said.

Sarama thought that he might refuse again. But the Mother's power was strong, as strong as a king's on the steppe. Danu let Catin take him by the hand and half-lead, half-drag him to the Mother's house.

Sarama was very glad of the warmth there, the wine heated with honey, the fresh hot bread with cheese melted on it. The Mare and the colt had been let in, too, if only into the first of the rooms, and fed bits of fruit and cut fodder. They would all have been well content, if Danu's mood had not been so black.

When Sarama had eaten and drunk her fill, though Danu had barely touched what he was given, the Mother sent the servants and the children into the outer rooms, and gestured to Catin to secure the door. "Now," she said to Danu. "Tell me."

Danu hunched into himself as he had in the garden. "Ask her," he said, thrusting his chin at Sarama. "It's her nightmare we've all been having."

"She hasn't the words," the Mother said before Sarama could speak. "You tell us."

"She has—" Danu broke off. Sarama had not found the Mother's expression particularly daunting, but then she was not a man in this backward country. Reluctantly but obediently he said, "Our dream is of a thing that her people know. That thing is called *war*. War is when men—it is only men, she says—kill other men, but women, too, and children."

Catin's breath hissed between her teeth, but the Mother's expression remained serene. She gestured to Danu to continue.

He gathered composure as he went on, as if the telling of the horror eased the force of it, a little. "War is killing. Men of her people—men of the east, horsemen—reckon it great glory. They fight one another, and they kill one another, and whoever lives is called the victor. And the victor takes everything."

Sarama had not told him that. Perhaps his goddess had.

"Are you saying that these people make a virtue of shedding blood?" Catin's voice was thick with disgust.

"They make a virtue of fighting," Danu said. "Fighting is the duty of every man."

"And the women? What are they doing while the men fight?"

"Nothing," said Danu.

"They *allow* it?"

"They are powerless," Danu said. "They are less than men are here—they are like children. Men command them. They have no choice but to obey."

"That is preposterous," said Catin.

"It is true," Danu said. "That is why I went—where I went." He did not mean the goddess' garden: not entirely. "It seems . . . she speaks to me. Even though I am . . ."

"Yes," the Mother said. Her voice was soft, but it silenced Catin. "She will speak to a man, if he will listen. Men seldom will."

"Yes," said Danu. "And those, the horsemen—they hear others than she. Gods, they call themselves, powers of the sky, of the storm. They deafen their servants to the Lady's voice. They call for blood, and not only the blood of her sacrifice, or the blood that women shed with the turning of the moon. Blood and fire. Killing. War. To take what they will to take, whether it be theirs or no. To kill any who resists them."

Catin opened her mouth. The Mother's glance stilled her. It shifted then, not to Danu but to Sarama. Yet she spoke to Danu. "Not all the horsemen are men."

"I am only one," Sarama said. "Horse Goddess' servant. My people—long dead. Only I. And the Mare. The gods are too strong."

"The Lady sent you," the Mother said.

Sarama nodded. "I don't know why. Look at him. If all are like him—"

"He is an extraordinary man," the Mother said, "but nevertheless, a man. Men are not as strong of spirit."

Extraordinary. Sarama committed the word to memory. It was a lovely word, which she hoped she understood. "The horsemen would be angry if they heard you," she said.

"I imagine they would," said the Mother.

"You must learn to fight," said Sarama.

"We will learn what the Lady wishes us to learn," the Mother said.

"The Lady says fight," Sarama said. She did not mean it to come out so flat, but she did not have the words of this tongue to soften it. "The men broke us, before. The gods fought the goddess. She lost. Now I am the only one. All are gone but me. I think—we did not know how to fight."

"How can the Lady lose?" Catin demanded. "The Lady is all that is. She cannot be anything else."

"She might change," Danu said. He seemed surprised that he had spoken, but he went on nonetheless. "She might wax and wane like the moon. Waxing then, for your people, until her time came to wane."

"We are not waning," Catin said fiercely. "We are as strong as we've ever been."

"You are not as strong as men who know how to fight," Sarama said.

"Fighting is ugly," Danu said. "It shames us."

"It will save you." Sarama fixed her gaze on the Mother. "Let me teach your people how to fight."

"I must think," the Mother said. "What you ask—what you say the Lady asks—may be too much for our people."

"Then you will die," Sarama said, "or worse."

"What is worse than death?"

Sarama turned to Catin. "War," she said. "War is worse than death. And worse than war—to lose."

"Defeat." Danu sounded weary. "To lose—that is defeat."

"Defeat," said Sarama. "Death in war is bad. Life in defeat—worse than bad. It kills the spirit."

"I will think on this," the Mother said.

·············· 29 ··············

"You people think too much."

Danu had been eager to return to the quiet of the house by the river. Now that he was in it, and surprised to find it clean and swept and the fire banked, too, he caught himself missing the Mother's house, the people crowded together, the warmth of bodies, even their pungent scent now that winter made washing difficult. This was too clean, too open, too empty—or not empty enough, since he must share it with Sarama.

She had no mercy. "You think too much," she said again. "You should not think. You should *do*."

"Is that how it is with your people?" he demanded of her. "You never think, you only do? No wonder you have this thing called war!"

She seemed taken aback. He had never lost his temper with her before— never been provoked truly beyond bearing.

Let her think him weaker than ever. He did not care. She brought the overturning of his world. He could not accept that quietly. No, not even for his pride, which the Mother of Larchwood insisted was greater than he knew or liked to think.

She rallied quickly. "*I* do not have war," she said. "Never say I have war. War broke my people. War will break yours."

"You are one of them," Danu said. "You have a horse. You know how to fight. You must, if you say you can teach us."

"We learned to fight," she said. "Too late. All are dead. I am the last."

"Perhaps we would rather die than fight."

"Then die," she said.

✦ ✦

She went to bed. For all he knew she lay awake nightlong. He lingered in the outer room till his back ached and his eyes were gritty with exhaustion. But even after he had spread his pallet and lain down on it, well wrapped in coverlets against the creeping cold, his mind would not rest. It spun endlessly on the same thoughts that had dizzied it since Sarama taught him this terrible lesson.

It was not that he feared he could not learn to fight. It was that he feared he could.

He lay on his face in the heap of furs and wool. Sometimes when he was younger—not so long ago, if he admitted the truth—he had felt himself a stranger in his body, a child who had fallen somehow into the shape and semblance of a man. Now as then, he was too keenly aware of the size that he had grown to, the strength, the width of his shoulders and the solidity of his arms. He would have given much to be a child again, slight and smooth-skinned, weak and gladly so, because a child's weakness could not do the harm that a man's strength could all too easily do.

Imagine a world in which a man was proud of his strength; in which, when his temper slipped its bonds, he could do whatever he pleased. Rage, strike, kill. And no Mother to stop him, no sister strong enough to stand in his way.

Sometimes the boys in Three Birds had whispered of such things, half in horror, half in desire. Every boy wondered what it would be like if men ruled. But it was not anything that they dared speak of in public, or even think of, much.

Now they would learn what such a world could be. A world in which the Lady was defeated and cast down; in which her servants were all gone but for one prickly-proud young woman with a stumbling tongue and an irascible temper.

+ +

Danu woke to familiar scents: fire burning, bread baking. He yawned and sighed. Such pleasure, to know that the house was well run, the Mother well looked after.

He started awake, was on his feet before his mind caught up with his body. He was not in Three Birds. That was not one of the Mother's servants moving in the outer room. It was Sarama.

He was scrupulously careful to wash and dress and make himself presentable before he came out to face her. She had everything in excellent order. Last night, too, he had come home to a house that was properly run, that had not suffered from his neglect of it.

He should be glad. He should not be resentful. He should not, above all, show her precisely how she had seemed to him every morning that she had been in his charge.

He could help none of it. She knew: there was laughter in her eyes as she waited on him. "Do you wait on men where you come from?" he demanded.

"No," she said. "I serve the Mare. Not men."

"So you are a proper woman," he said.

"Not proper," she said, "where I come from."

"Proper here," said Danu. And after a pause: "If you teach us how to fight, we'll never be the same again."

"If you die, you will not be at all."

He bent his head under the force of that. "For years out of count we have been the Lady's people. Now you say that we must change or die."

"The Lady keeps you," she said. "Always. Even if you learn to fight."

"I don't want to—" He bit his tongue. Swallowed hard. "Teach me."

"Here? Now?"

"Here. Now."

"No," she said.

"No? But—"

"Eat," she said. "Drink."

"Then fight?"

"Then begin to learn," she said. She thrust a laden plate at him. "Eat!"

✦ ✦

Danu ate sullenly, but eat he did. And when he had done that, she bade him dress to go out, found his hunting bow and his boar-spear and made him take them both, and led him into a world of white light and soft snow. The horses followed for a while, warm in their thick coats, snorting and dancing in the cold, but Sarama sent them back before they had gone out of sight of the house.

It did not take him long to understand what they were doing. He stopped short. "This isn't fighting. This is hunting."

"Hunting is the beginning," Sarama said. "I want to see you hunt."

"But—"

"Hunt," she said.

✦ ✦

Danu hunted. In any case they needed meat for the pot, and the snow offered clear tracks. He persuaded himself after a while to forget the silent one who followed him. She was light on her feet, quiet, and offered no interference. She knew how to hunt.

Anger might have sent him in pursuit of a boar or even an aurochs, the great bull of the wood, but Danu was only half a fool. He hunted the red deer, that was swift enough and canny enough to require a skilled hunter, but not so dangerous that it could cost him his life. No doubt this woman of the horsemen would have preferred more dangerous prey; but she said nothing of it.

There was little challenge in tracking a deer in the snow, but when the track was confused and tangled by a herd of them, and a pack of wolves had trampled through, and a herd of wild pigs, then it was not so easy to find one slotted hoofprint amid so many. They had gone well past the hill that sheltered the town of Running Waters, toward the wood itself. If the deer—a stag, from the size of his tracks and from the marks of antlers that he had left on the trees that thickened, the nearer they came to the forest proper— if the deer escaped into the wood, they well might be there nightlong.

So be it. He was being tested, he knew perfectly well. Women underwent such a testing in the Lady's temple, the rite that no man was allowed to see. He had seen his sisters coming from it, his cousins, the women of Three Birds and later of Larchwood, and seen how they had changed: how their eyes were deeper, as if they had looked into the Lady's heart. That light was on them ever after, though it sank beneath the surface of their ordinary selves.

For men there was no such thing. A boy grew up. His voice deepened, his manly organ grew large, his body thickened with hair, his face sprouted a beard. When all of that was done, if a woman had not chosen him, he lingered in his mother's house and did as she bade him, raised his sisters' children, faded into one of the grey uncles who sat in the market watching the youth of the world go by.

Danu did not want to be a grey uncle. Neither did he want to be this thing that Sarama had shown him, this horror, this slayer of men, this *warrior*. He wanted to be what he had always been. Loved, valued, given duties beyond the usual lot of a man. Could not the world go on as it always had? Why must it change, and change so terribly?

All the while his spirit ran on the dark tracks, his body ran in the light, seeking the red stag. He did not care if he outran Sarama—though in truth she kept pace with him, breathing as softly as she could while running through snow. He ran at the wolf's pace, long steady lope, alert to the shifts of the quarry's path.

They brought the stag to bay not far inside the wood, in a stand of young trees, birches, tall and white and slender. He was a great one indeed, with a lofty crown of antlers, his neck swollen with rut, and the musk of him so strong that Danu had caught and followed it easily the last few hundred paces.

The stag stood blood-red against the snow and the trees, head high, poised, motionless and yet vividly, vibrantly alive. Danu nocked arrow to string with a heartfelt prayer to the Lady, begging her forgiveness for the taking of this life, giving her thanks for the life it gave him. The arrow flew straight and true, and buried itself in the great beating heart.

The stag leaped, high and high, up to the sky. Even before he fell, he was dead.

·············· 30 ··············

"Out of death, life; out of blood, sustenance."

Sarama did not know what all the words meant. They were a prayer, she knew that much. Danu wept as he spoke them. Yet even as he wept, he was cleaning and trussing the stag, lashing together branches, fashioning a litter to haul the carcass home.

On the steppe one gave thanks to the gods for granting one success in the hunt. But one never mourned the quarry. Beasts were beasts, even those of sacrifice. Their lives were set on earth for men to take.

This man wept as if for a brother, and begged pardon for each stroke of the skinning knife, as if the stag could feel it even in death. Yet he had hunted as skillfully as any she had seen, and killed cleanly, with one beautifully aimed shot. He was not a weakling.

Nor would he make a warrior. Not as he was now.

She helped him drag the carcass the long way back to the city. It was dark before they came there, but there were stars, and a wan moon through scudding clouds. Those, and the snow, lit their way well enough.

The Mare and the colt met them well outside the city, bounding through the snow, the Mare quietly glad, the colt noisily so. They made a royal escort, and watched with interest and no little snorting as the two of them finished butchering the stag and hung it on the outside of the house, high up lest the wolves come.

It was very late when they ascended at last to the blessed warmth of the banked fire, took turns washing in water from the cauldron that Danu had hung that morning, and fell headlong to bed or pallet.

+ +

Morning came rather too soon for Sarama. This time Danu was up before her. The scent of roasting venison drew her out at last, to find him in his usual morning semblance, even to the murmur of song. The stag was all butchered, and roasting or smoking or drying; Danu was scraping the hide, readying it for curing. Its bones and antlers would be put to use, its hooves, its sinews, every scrap of it—and a great labor it was, too, but he seemed glad of it. His mourning had been brief. And yet she thought it was heartfelt.

He greeted her with the flicker of a smile, and tilted his head toward the table, where her breakfast lay safe under a cloth.

She realized that she was ravenous. She had eaten nothing since yesterday morning, nor noticed the lack.

When the edge was off her hunger, she looked up to find him standing over her. "Now tell me what hunting has to do with fighting," he said.

He was not going to be merciful. That was a good thing. A warrior needed to be relentless.

She lacked the words to say that. Instead she said, "Hunting and fighting are much the same. But in war, you kill men. And even weep for them, if your heart is soft."

"So you think me soft," he said. He seemed more amused than not.

She shrugged. "You need to be hard."

"That will come when it must," he said, "but I'll do my best to fight it."

"See? You can fight."

He snorted. She thought he might be annoyed. Or perhaps not. He could laugh, even when the laughter was at himself.

It struck her that she rather liked him. He was a bright spirit, and strong. He carried himself like a prince, light and proud—except when he was bowing his head to a woman. The tribes would never understand that, or him.

Somewhere amid this was a way to do what the Lady willed of her. A way to make these people strong as the tribes would perceive it.

She spoke rather abruptly, but she knew no other way. "What do you do when a—an animal attacks you? Do you fight?"

"We defend ourselves," he said. "But we never attack each other."

"Still," said Sarama. "If men attack, you can defend. Yes?"

He frowned. "You should know what Catin thinks. She thinks that you haven't come to protect us. You've opened the way. You'll bring the war that you say you come to prevent."

Sarama stared at him. She did not want to understand him.

"She says," said Danu, "that you came to lead your people against us. That your men's gods have overwhelmed the Lady, and therefore you, and sent you ahead in order to weaken us with fear."

"Catin thinks like a man of my people," Sarama said. "Where did she learn to think like that? She has never known war."

"She's afraid," Danu said. "Her fear speaks for her. That's what war is, isn't it? War is fear first of all."

"War is fear," said Sarama, nodding. "She is afraid. That is good. But I bring no war. War is coming without me."

"She says it follows you," said Danu.

"I do not lead it," she said. "The Lady leads me. The gods—the gods are angry. They talk to Catin. Fear opens the spirit to them. She listens."

Danu's brows had gone up. "Men's gods talk to a woman?"

"The Lady talks to you," Sarama said.

"So," he said. He went back to his hide-scraping, but not to shut her out. It seemed to help him think. "You know what this could mean."

"People kill for fear," said Sarama. "If she makes people afraid of me— maybe they learn to kill."

"My people don't—" He broke off. "She'd say the same of you."

"I am not what she says," Sarama insisted. "I come to help, not to hurt. Listen to the Lady! She told you. Do you forget?"

"I remember," Danu said. He sighed heavily. "The Mother will remember. But Catin is the Mother's heir. How can she be deceived? People will say, maybe you think you came to help, but the gods are using you."

"The gods are using Catin."

"I don't know these gods," Danu said. "I barely know you. The others don't know you at all."

"You must tell them," Sarama said.

He straightened, arching his back as if it pained him. "I'm a stranger here, almost as much as you. I come from another city. They'll not listen to me."

"They listen," Sarama said. "You hear the Lady."

He shook his head. "They won't want to listen."

Sarama could not contest that. She had seen how he was when she told him of war. If Catin had turned against her, then the people would follow. People followed those set over them. It was the way of the world.

She mustered all the words she could, though her head was aching with the effort. "You must tell Catin," she said. "Wake her up. Win her away from the voices she hears. They lie to her. She must not listen."

"What makes you think I can do any such thing?"

She touched his arm. She never had before, not of her own will. His warmth startled her; his solidity, strong as the earth under her hand. "You and she—" she said. It was too difficult. She did not have the words. "When a man and a woman are—like that—a man will listen to a woman. Sometimes. She might listen to you."

He looked from her hand to her face. "She says," he said, "that I would turn from her in a moment, if you but lifted your hand. I told her that she was jealous. She sent me away for that."

"When was this?" she demanded.

"This morning," he said. "She came while you slept. You were sleeping deep."

"Then she did not send you away."

He hissed; then snorted in the way he had, that made her think of the colt. "She went away. But she told me not to come seeking her."

"Ah," said Sarama. "We would say, she *put* you away. When a man grows tired of a woman, or she has no sons for him—he puts her away."

"No," he said. "No, it wasn't—she was angry, that was all. She'll come back when her temper cools. But I am not to go looking for her."

"Ah," said Sarama. She did not think he liked the tone of that. He bent to the hide again and attacked it fiercely.

She had been sorry when he slipped from beneath her hand. She did not try to touch him again. He was not happy to have been put aside—even if that was not exactly what it was.

She wondered anew what there was between those two. As far as she understood, a woman chose a man here. "Why did Catin take you?" she asked him.

He froze. For a moment she thought that he would get up and stalk out, which she would have done if he had been as impertinent as that.

He was too polite in the way of his people. He answered without looking at her, which was also courtesy, but might have held a hint of defiance. "I was the Mother's son of Three Birds. I dreamed the same dreams that tormented her. And maybe she thought that I was good to look at."

That last would have been cause enough for a man of the tribes. Sarama tried to imagine seeing a man so, as a man would see a woman. It was not difficult. Only strange.

"If you were a woman," Sarama asked him, "would you choose her?"

"I am not a woman," Danu said.

"If you were," she persisted, "would you?"

His eyes flashed up. "Why do you ask? What is it to you?"

She flushed—and that, she had not expected at all. "I want to understand."

"Understand this," he said with great care. "You are the Lady's child, and a woman, and she speaks to you. She has made you her voice in her country. This I believe. But what I am to Catin, or what she is to me—that is between the two of us and the Lady. Do you understand?"

"Yes," she said. "You wouldn't, would you? You'd rather be in—Three Birches?"

"Three Birds." She heard the sound of gritted teeth in that. "The Lady sent me here."

"Not Catin," said Sarama.

If he had been a man of war, he would have struck her long since. Because he was what he was, he stripped the hide with blinding swiftness and left it shining clean. She thought he might take it to the tanner then, but he chose to wait. Consciously chose.

A thought had been growing for a while. It was preposterous. Of course she would never utter it. Unless he provoked her.

Which he did, by insisting that today of all days he must scour the house inside and out, air the bedding, scrub down the floor, clear away the evidence of the stag's butchery. Not that Sarama had any objection to hard work and plenty of it, but he seemed to be flinging it in her face.

As they put the bed back together, with his strength and her balancing hand, she asked him, "What would you do if I chose you?"

He barely hesitated. The bedding settled onto the frame. He smoothed it with his big deft hands. "Would you do that?" he asked in return.

Of course not, she had meant to say. But her tongue ran on ahead of her. "I might," she said. "But it would have to be your will, too."

"What does my will matter?"

"Much," she said.

"You don't even like me."

"No," she said.

He faced her across the broad expanse of the bed. She had not thought till then what she had done in choosing this moment to speak. "Then why choose me?" he demanded.

"Because you hunt well," she said.

He snorted. "That's a poor enough cause to choose a man."

"Why? We'll always eat well, and be warm, and have needles to sew with and hides to trade and—"

"You're laughing at me," he said.

She was, but not as he meant. It was a dizzy laughter, as if she stood on the edge of a steep riverbank and contemplated the leap into the water below. "I never chose a man before," she said.

"Did a man choose you?" He said it as if he did not quite believe such a thing could be; but she had said it, therefore he indulged her fancy.

She shook her head. "I was not—I belong to the Mare. They were afraid."

"Should I be?"

She blinked, frowned. "Only if you force me."

"Force?" She saw the incomprehension, but before she could enlighten it, he understood. "To—make war on you? You alone?"

His horror was sweet to see. Nor was it feigned. "Yes, that is war, too. It can happen in war. Or a man can take a woman when she does not want it."

"And the Lady does not destroy him?"

"The gods help him. The gods love such things."

"Your—the men's gods are terrible creatures," Danu said after a pause. "I think we would call them demons."

"I do not love them," Sarama said.

Her head was throbbing. She had not been using so many words, but she had used nearly every one she knew, over and over, to say things that would have been hard in her own familiar tongue. She reached across the bed and seized his hands, both of them. He did not resist. "Show me why Catin is jealous," she said.

He could refuse. She knew that. Perhaps he considered it. But if he did, it was only briefly. His fingers tightened. He drew her to him lightly, easily, as if she had weighed no more than one of the blankets.

So, she thought. The man could take, when the time came; if he was given leave. Even here. And the woman could refuse to be taken.

She did not want to refuse. At all. And how she had come to this, from barely tolerating his presence, she could not at the moment understand.

He had somehow disposed of his garments while she knelt on the bed with her mind a-wandering. She had seen men before. How not? But not a man so close, with his dark eyes on her, and the lower part of him stallion-rampant, but never so very rampant as a stallion.

He would never forgive her if she laughed. She bit her lip. He was waiting for something. For her.

She knew a moment of piercing shyness, and ice-cold fear. If she turned and ran now, he would never mock her. Not he.

Which was, in the simplest of senses, why she was here, in this predicament, and determined after all to continue.

She scrambled out of her clothes and knelt shivering, bare and pebble-skinned like a plucked bird. No sleek brown-skinned beauty she, and no warmth of curly black hair, either. Yet he did not seem repulsed. He wrapped arms about her, enfolding her, shutting out the cold. His scent was pleasant, more musky than pungent, overlaid with something sweet: herbs and a suggestion of honey. She was keenly, almost painfully aware of his body against hers. And, with more than pain, of the thing that pressed hard and hot between her belly and his.

Any man she knew would have thrust it into her and had done. He simply held her, master even, it seemed, of that.

She did not know what to do. Her arms were more comfortable linked behind him, her hands stroking the smoothness of his back. There was a whorl of down in the hollow of it, soft as a foal's muzzle.

Her head fit tidily on his shoulder. They were precisely of a height. He was broader, much; of course. Had she been thinking of this, of standing like this, from the moment she saw him?

She had thought then that he would force her; had been astonished when he did not. She was still astonished. Such strength—such discipline. His breath came a little quick, she thought. And he was very hard. He must be in discomfort. But he made no move to take her.

Her hands explored what they could reach: shoulders, back, buttocks. He liked it when she ran her nails lightly down his back. She ran them back up again, and found the pin that knotted his hair at his nape. She tugged it free. His hair tumbled down, all the curling richness of it, softer than it had looked, and wonderfully thick. She wound her fingers in it.

He sighed. She stroked her cheek along his shoulder. Then, because it seemed worthy of the trial, she traced its line with kisses, tasting it, salt and warm flesh and that suggestion of honey.

No man that she had ever heard of would let a woman explore him so, and make no move to hasten the ending. And yet, as with the rest of him, it was not weakness. It was great strength.

He was hers to do with as she pleased. She lifted her head from his shoulder, tilted it back to meet his gaze. No mute endurance there. He did this willingly. Gladly? She rather thought so.

He was younger than she had thought. No older than she. His bulk and the richness of his beard, and the way he carried himself, had deceived her. The face so close to hers was little more than a boy's, still with a suggestion of the child that he must have been. Beautiful child, full-lipped and soft-cheeked, as lovely as a girl. Had he been glad to grow into a man, to lose that prettiness? Or had he been sorry for it?

Later, maybe, she would ask. He was beautiful now, as a man is, and as a bull, and as a strong young stallion. She had learned to see that beauty, day after day in this city of broad-built brown people.

"O beautiful," she murmured in her own tongue. "O splendid." She swooped with great bravery, set a kiss on his lips. They opened for her. He tasted of honey and of fire.

She burned herself, a white heat that burned without consuming. Her breasts were exquisitely tender, pressed against his broad black-furred chest. But the heart of it throbbed between her thighs. She had never—she had not imagined—

She gasped, half in impatience, half in protest; slid up the rock-solidity of his body; found the tip of his shaft—his gasp echoed hers—gritted her teeth and impaled herself on it.

It hurt. Oh, dear Lady, it hurt. She was too small. He was too—

But there was pleasure on the edge of pain. A whisper of something else that should be, if she passed this gate, if she endured this rite. It was no worse than fasting on the steppe, than suffering the numbing bite of cold, than riding till her tender parts were raw, all in the goddess' name.

He rocked gently against her, a rhythm she knew. She had danced it. The sensation of him inside her, sliding against her, was unutterably strange.

He was holding her up. She locked legs about his middle, sighing a little, for it made the pain a little less, the pleasure a little more. He betrayed no sign of distress. His face was intent, abstracted, but he smiled and set a kiss on her lips. For him, it seemed, this was indeed a dance. An art. A thing that he did as he hunted the red deer, or as he set his house in order: for the joy of it, and for the pride of a task well done.

Irritation pricked. She did not want to be a task. She wanted to be—by the goddess, she wanted to be the world to him.

There was another rhythm like this, another rhythmic rocking motion, as familiar as the breath in her body. A horse at the canter, long and easy, smooth, untiring. Once she had found that, she found the limit of pain, and passed it. It lingered, and more than a whisper of it, too; but it ceased to matter.

He had great endurance. Not that she knew much of this, but she had heard enough. Men came, took, left again. They did not go on and on.

This one did. But not forever. Not even he. His stroke quickened, his breath with it. She rode it, not quite comprehending, until he stiffened, gripping her tight enough to startle the breath out of her. There was something, a glimmer . . .

It was gone. A long sigh escaped him. She loosened her grip on him and slipped free. He sank to his knees on the bed. "Sorry," he said. "I'm sorry."

"What ever for?" Her own voice was if anything more breathless than his.

"I failed to pleasure you," he said. "I could not—I lacked discipline."

"Stop that," she said. He was trained to a woman's voice: he stopped. She bore him back and down, flat on the bed, and sat on him. "You were beautiful," she said.

"I didn't—"

"Stop!"

He shut his mouth with a click. She pressed her finger to it, to keep it so.

"Do not ever say sorry," she said.

His eyes begged to differ, but his voice was silenced, even after she had reclaimed her hand. She was aware, then, of the ache inside. She pulled herself somewhat stiffly to her feet.

There was blood on her thighs, and on him, too. He was staring at it—not appalled. But faintly horrified. "You have never taken a man before," he said, as if it were an accusation. "Where was your mother when it was time to teach you? How could she allow you to suffer this?"

"My mother is dead," Sarama said. "I was born, she died."

That silenced him, but only briefly. "Sweet Lady! Your people are savages." He rose as she had, but never as stiffly. If he was aware of her resentment, he did not show it. He wrapped her in a soft blanket, he made her come into the outer room, he bathed her with warmed water. His hands were gentler than his expression. He bathed himself, too, thereafter, and for all the ache in her outraged parts, she felt them begin to warm again, her breasts to tighten, wanting him.

If that made her a savage, then so be it. She had heard—not from men—that men had limitations, but this one seemed to have fewer than some. He was less swift to rise, but rise he did. This time she knew better what to do, and her body knew what it had wanted: the completion of the rite, the thing that had failed her before—and not by his fault, whatever he might choose to think. She had not known what to seek. No more did she now, except that there was something, and one reached it . . .

So.

So. Indeed. And indeed again. And . . .

•••••••••••• 31 ••••••••••••

Danu had heard many a sound from women in the throes of the Lady's gift, but that shout of triumph was wholly new. And, like Sarama herself, it was both marvelous and shocking. She clung to him, locked tight as he completed his own rite, and laughed like a wild thing.

It was impossible to resist that laughter. Even uncomprehending, even mildly appalled. She was the Lady's own—now, for his heart and soul, he had no doubt of it. Only the Lady's chosen could love as this one loved.

And she had chosen him. Had she known she would do it? Would she even want to have done it, once the Lady's presence was gone from her?

He did not wonder if he would. That doubt had lost itself somewhere, he did not remember where.

They lay tangled together in front of the hearth, warm where the fire touched, snow-cold where it could not reach. Danu groped for the blankets that had wrapped them both. She laid her head on his shoulder and sighed. She was asleep, the deep and sudden sleep that came with the Lady's gift.

He should be sharing it, except that his thoughts were in such confusion. He had never thought to be lying here, least of all on this day, after Catin had come and flung sharp-edged words in his face and gone furious away.

Blindness. Jealousy. Demons speaking in her? Perhaps. And what would she do now that she had cast him off?

He would learn the answer to that soon enough. But not now. For this moment he would be content, wrapped in the arms of this woman as she was wrapped in his; and if he could not sleep, at the least he could rest.

He buried his face in her hair. So wonderful, so straight and fine, like tarnished copper, or leaves in autumn. She smelled of leaves and grass and horses, and of clean musky woman. Astonishing, that she had never taken a man before. Miraculous, that she had taken him. He was blessed, twice and thrice blessed, to be so chosen.

+ +

He slept after all, and woke to the snorting of horses. Something had caught their attention; from the sound of it, they had trapped it in a corner below.

Sarama was still asleep. He left her the blankets, retrieved his mantle and wrapped it about him, and descended not too quickly, but not slowly either.

The horses had indeed cornered their prey; and a pitiful scrap of a child it was, too, white with terror and desperately glad to see Danu. "Ah, laddie," Danu said with rough gentleness, "they only want to be petted. See, here, stroke her neck, so—and push young impudence away; he *will* nip. But he'll never eat you."

It was, when he had got it up the ladder and pried it from about his neck, one of the children from the Mother's house. Its face was familiar. It must be one of those who was always about, watching and listening and parroting the words when Sarama spoke in the language of the tribes. It—he—had a message for Danu and for Sarama. "Come to the Mother," he said.

"Not without breakfast," said Danu calmly. "Here, stay, eat with us."

"You keep the king waiting?" Sarama wanted to know.

"She won't be pleased to see us if we're growling with hunger." And, he thought, it would be best if their strength was up. His belly had gone hollow when he saw the Mother's messenger and knew what he must be. Catin's words this morning, the Mother's summons—which a Mother almost never made use of—at noon: they might have nothing to do with each other. Or, far too likely, one might have bred the other.

The child, whose name was Mika, was not at all averse to being fed. Danu could remember when he was as young as that, when he had been endlessly hungry. He wondered if the uncles who fed him had been as gratified as he was now, to see his labor of hunting and cooking put to such very good use.

Sarama had retreated to the inner room while Danu prepared their noon-day breakfast. She emerged as the last of it went on the table, decorously and tidily dressed in the coat that he had made for her. She would not meet his eyes.

He forbore to press her. Perhaps she was simply preoccupied with the summons, and shy in front of the child. He knew how it was with a new lover, how one was inclined to wonder if people could see what had changed. For a woman who had not undergone the rite of womanhood, or been initiated by the Lady's chosen lover, it must be a stranger thing than he could imagine.

If he had known that her people did not practice the rite, he might have acted differently. But he could not regret what he had done.

They ate in silence. Mika ate as much as the others together, and again as much, and only stopped because the table was bare. He belched politely and waited as was proper, for Sarama to rise.

She obliged, perhaps blindly. "Best to go," she said.

✦ ✦

She intended to ride the Mare, which meant that the colt would come as well. Mika was wide-eyed with terror—and with yearning. Sarama blinked out of her abstraction. "You can ride behind me," she said.

Mika swallowed hard. Danu opened his mouth to rescue the child, but Mika had more courage than Danu had given him credit for. He scrambled up behind Sarama, clinging so tightly that he must have left bruises, but she said nothing. Danu smiled what he hoped was reassurance. Mika stared whitely back; and gasped as the Mare began to walk. But he kept his seat. After a few strides his terror turned to incredulity; then to a white-lipped joy.

Danu, perforce and contentedly afoot, spared him a moment's envy. But only a moment. Humankind were not meant to sit on the back of a horse; or why had the Lady given them feet?

The colt walked beside him, shoulder to his shoulder, with occasional forays afield. Danu was forgetting what it was to walk in or about Larchwood without his hoofed companion. It was like the dogs that people had in some of the western cities, but a dog grown as large as one of the cattle.

That was an alarming thought. Danu laid his hand on the colt's neck, tugging lightly at its thick mane. No, no dog; not this one, who for all his propensity for testing the thickness of one's hide with his teeth, was a gentle creature.

Strange that such an animal should be the sign and portent of that terrible thing called war. Gentle in itself, eager to please, nonetheless it offered great power; strength; speed beyond simple human feet. A man mounted on a horse might find his own country too small for his compass; be tempted to wander far, and perhaps, if he were of such a mind, to think of taking what he found and keeping it for himself.

Danu did not like to think such thoughts, or to imagine a person who would think them. And yet, if he was to understand what was coming, he must try to understand the people who came.

The city closed about them with its mingling of walls and trees. The colt moved in close. He did not like the city, but the call of his own was strong: the Mare from whom he would not willingly be separated, and perhaps, a little, the man who had brought him from confinement into the great world.

It came to Danu that he did not like this place. It was tolerable, its people likewise, and for some he felt actual affection. But it was not his city.

+ +

Mika had so far conquered his fear as to sit bolt upright behind Sarama and grin at his agemates as he rode by. They ran after, calling to each other, half in envy, half in awe. Sarama on a horse they had grown used to, but one of their own was a new and mighty thing.

Sarama sealed Mika's place forever when they came to the Mother's house, by slipping from the Mare's back but leaving Mika there, and saying, "Watch her for me."

Mika was too stark with the honor and the terror to do anything foolish, such as try to ride the Mare. He nodded stiffly and hitched himself forward till he could cling to the Mare's mane. Sarama's smile bound him there.

It nearly bound Danu. He could not recall ever seeing her smile before. It was wonderful, marvelous; luminous. Small wonder she was so sparing of her smiles, if they were all so potent.

The edge of this one snared Danu and led him into the Mother's house. It was crowded at this hour and in this season. In the outer room the daughters had set up a loom. They were laying threads for the warp as Danu passed, colors of summer and of autumn, as if to remember them in the grey winter. They stared openly at Sarama as she passed, and more covertly at Danu. He had not, in a long while, felt so much a stranger.

The Mother sat in the second room, spinning wool into thread, with her daughter Catin for company. Catin's expression held a secret, a dark look, darker as she looked from Danu to Sarama. He did not think there was anything to see; but he was not a woman, with a woman's keenness of sight.

And they said that men were jealous; that lacking power, they clung to what they had, which was the favor of a woman. Yet it seemed a woman could be jealous too, and perhaps with cause. Though what power Danu could give the Mother's heir of Larchwood, he did not know. The colt, perhaps? The friendship of Three Birds?

The Mother spun her thread, making them wait, as was her privilege. Danu, after some few moments, took up a spindle that lay atop a new basket of wool, and began to spin in his own turn. He had shocked Sarama: her eyes were wide. So; men did not spin, either, where she came from. Pity. It was useful, but none too taxing; one could do it while walking on a journey, or while tending children. Or, as now, while waiting to be acknowledged by the Mother of a city.

Sarama sat near him, watching him. Not the Mother; not Catin. He noticed that. He wondered if it was deliberate.

They spun in silence, the Mother and he, for a lengthening while. The Mother was quicker, but he spun a finer thread.

It was Catin whose patience snapped first. "Mother! Will you speak or no?"

"I will speak," the Mother said placidly, "when I am ready to speak."

"You've thought about war," Sarama said. "About what I told you."

"I have thought," the Mother said, "and others have been thinking. I have met with the elders of the women, and with their daughters. We are agreed that this thing called war not be allowed in our city."

"You can allow or not allow," Sarama said. "It will come."

"Because you bring it," said Catin.

"I do not bring it," Sarama said. Perhaps it was her shakiness still with the words of the Lady's tongue that made her sound flat, as if she felt nothing.

"Knowingly," said the Mother before Catin could respond, "perhaps not. But it comes behind you. Some of us think that it follows you."

"The storm follows the crow." It was not Danu's place to speak in such a meeting, and yet he could not keep silent. "The crow does not cause the storm. It comes with or without her."

"And yet with one comes the other," the Mother said. "Believe this, woman of the horsemen: I am not one who contends that you bear us malice. But a dark thing rides behind you. We cannot permit it here."

"You send me away." Sarama did not sound surprised. "How will you learn to fight? No one can teach you."

"We do not wish to learn fighting," the Mother said.

"You will learn it," said Sarama. "You will have to."

The Mother set her lips together. "That may be. But our people do not wish to learn it from you."

"Then you die," said Sarama.

Danu tensed, because she seemed about to turn on her heel and walk away. But she stood still. She met Catin's eyes. "This is not well done," she said.

"We do as we must," said the Mother.

But this time Catin was not to be quelled by the Mother's words or her will. "I told them what you are, but it's not my will that they let you go. You'll only go back to your horsemen and show them the way to our country."

"I will not," said Sarama.

"So you say," said Catin. "They won't have you here, but I won't have you going back. I persuaded them to send you elsewhere—an elsewhere of our devising. We'll send you where you can be kept out of the way and prevented from running home to your horsemen. We'll send you to Three Birds."

Danu stiffened. "If she is the stormcrow that you call her, then why do you send the storm to us? Are you so weak and so afraid that you can only think to lay the burden on my Mother, as you did before?"

He had never spoken such words in his life, words of anger without thought. No, not even to Tilia when she provoked him unmercifully. Tilia had never turned on him so.

Catin was gaping at him. He had taken her completely aback. "I think," he said, "that your fear for your people is honest, and so is your fear of the dreams that we both have had. But what you do now, these accusations, this hatred—this is not selfless. You do it for dislike of this woman, for that and for no other cause."

"And what if I do?" Catin flung back at him. "Tell me now why you defend her. If she chose you—if she knew how—you would accept her joyfully."

Since that was no less than the truth, Danu nodded. "Yes, that much is so. But desire can see more clearly than hatred. I see that you can think of nothing better to do than send her—and the war you say she brings—to my people, so that they may suffer what you are too fearful to face. Think if you can. See what you do. Larchwood is close to the wood. If it and its neighbor cities know how to fight, the war can stop before it goes deeper. But if you refuse to learn, if you send the war onward, many more cities will be endangered."

"Without this woman," said Catin, "the war will not know where to go. If you keep her safe, the horsemen may never come at all."

"The horsemen will come," Sarama said.

"They will not come for you," said Catin.

"No," said Sarama.

Danu drew a deep breath. "If you send her to Three Birds, then I go with her."

"Yes," the Mother said. "It were best."

Catin opened her mouth, but shut it again.

The Mother nodded. "Indeed," she said, as if Catin had spoken. "The Lady brought him here, but his tasks are done. It is time he returned to his own people."

"He came to wait for her," Catin said. "Did I matter nothing?"

"You mattered very much," said Danu. It was difficult in front of the others, but it would be no easier if he waited to say what he must say. "The Lady has much still for you to do. But my part here is done. I belong in Three Birds. You belong here. For good or for ill, whatever comes—this is your place."

"You came for her," Catin said. She was blind, and deaf to any words she did not wish to hear. Maybe it was as Sarama had said: the horsemen's gods had fuddled her spirit.

He could not say so in front of her. The Mother must see it. Mothers saw everything.

She said nothing. She suffered Catin to go on, words he barely remembered once they were uttered, accusations against Sarama, against him, against the Lady knew what. Could not her own Mother see that she was distressed in the soul?

When she stopped for breath, Danu spoke; perhaps unwisely, but he could not forbear. "You chose me," he said. "I went by the will of our Mothers and with the Lady's blessing. And yes, for you, because I had conceived a liking for you. Don't destroy that now."

Had he given her pause? He could not see it. "Go with this woman," she said, "since you have conceived a liking for her. Maybe in your arms she'll forget the war she tried to bring upon us all."

Danu did not try to protest. Not again. He bowed his head and set his lips together and was silent.

"Go," said Catin. *"Go!"*

Danu glanced at the Mother. She raised a hand slightly: conceding authority to her heir.

He swept Sarama out of that room too quickly for her to object, all but carried her past the daughters—who had made little progress with threading the loom since he went before the Mother—and deposited her on the Mare's back, displacing the startled Mika. The Mare knew her duty: she trotted off toward the house by the river, with the colt trailing behind.

Danu would follow in a moment. But first he had somewhat to do. He steadied Mika on his feet, smoothed the boy's ruffled hair, and said, "Remember when they come, the horsemen: that you are not afraid of horses."

Mika did not understand. Yet in time, if the Lady pleased, he would. Danu tapped him lightly on the shoulder. "Remember," he said.

············ 32 ············

Sarama did not need any great fluency in these people's language to know that she had been cast out by the king's heir. That it had little to do with honest fear of Sarama's treachery, and much to do with the man they had in common, Sarama did not doubt at all.

The man himself was visibly dismayed, but it was more anger than grief. He would make a warrior, Sarama thought, after all—as would the king's heir, despite the passion of her protest. That very likely was why she did it: because she was afraid, not of the horsemen, but of her own eagerness for battle.

Without Sarama to teach her and her people to fight, she well might die, or be raped and held hostage. But she would sooner do that than concede Sarama the victory. It was a madness of obstinacy, unshakable for anything that Sarama might do; and her king seemed disinclined to restrain her.

Maybe this Three Birds would be more amenable to reason.

"Is that your city?" Sarama asked Danu when they had returned to the house, while he gathered belongings, food, drink, supplies for the journey, with tightly controlled violence.

He shot a glance at her, hot enough to sting, but his voice was mild. "What? Three Birds? Yes, that's my city."

"You will be glad to go back."

"Very glad," he said, thrusting one last packet of meal into the pack that he had fashioned, and lashing it shut.

"Will your Mother listen?"

He paused as if to consider that. "One can hope so," he said.

"Then maybe not," she said. "Someone must listen."

"I listen," he said. He spread clothing—his and hers—on a pair of folded blankets and rolled them tightly. "I hate it, but I listen. Others may as well. Maybe enough to save us. Maybe not. Who but the Lady knows, or knows why?"

"Maybe you do," she said. "Are you sorry you go from here?"

He did not answer. She cursed her awkward tongue. She could not say the things she needed to say, in the words that she needed.

She was about to turn away, to see to the horses, when he said, "I am not sorry to leave. No. It was my Mother who laid it on me to come here, and Catin who urged her to do it."

"Always Catin," Sarama said.

He lifted his head. He was frowning. She did not know why he should be so struck by something so obvious. "Always Catin," he echoed. "I wonder . . ."

He did not go on, although she waited. He finished his packing instead, still frowning.

Sarama decided to relieve him of his burden. "Catin is a—" She paused. The word she needed, she did not have in his tongue. She said it in her own; then struggled in that other language again. "A—one who lets the wind blow through. The gods speak, they use her voice."

"That's what a Mother is," said Danu. "The Lady speaks through her."

Sarama shook her head. "No. Not just the Lady. Other gods, too. Any god. The Lady, for you. Then, for me, the gods who bring war. She doesn't know, I think."

"She would know about the Lady," Danu said. "But if other gods can speak through her—what if it happens to all the Mothers? How will we know which words to trust?"

"It's not the Mother," Sarama said. "It's only Catin."

"Can you be sure of that?"

She had frightened him. She had not meant to do that. "What I am—I know whose voice speaks. The Mother speaks with the Lady's voice. No gods. Catin speaks for whoever speaks through her."

"By the Lady!" Danu murmured. "We should warn—"

"They will not listen," she said. "Better go to Three Birds, see if your Mother has better ears."

"Or better stomach for what she doesn't want to hear." Danu was not happy, but he acquiesced. There were advantages, Sarama caught herself thinking, in a man who would do as a woman bade.

+ +

They were not, for all their speed, to go alone or unattended. On the road from the house to the city, they found a company of women waiting, tall women and strong, armed with hunting bows and boar-spears. They looked precisely like warriors, or like the escort of a king.

Catin stood in front of them. Now that Sarama knew what to look for, she saw the light deep in the dark eyes, the will that was Catin's own, but fed and nurtured by another altogether. "We honor you," she said, "with the companionship of our people. They go to protect you against beasts, and against the claws of winter. They'll serve you, feed you, look after you. And," she said, "make very sure that you go nowhere but to Three Birds."

Sarama inclined her head. "I understand," she said.

The light in Catin's eyes brightened briefly, a flare of white fire. "I see you do," she said.

And so, Sarama thought, did Danu. She wondered if he was aware, as she was, that perhaps these people could fight, if suitably provoked.

Catin was speaking to the women, to the tall dour-faced woman who appeared to be their leader. "Keep watch," she said, "and see that she doesn't escape. If she breaks away eastward—stop her. By whatever means you must."

She spoke the last words slowly, with a weight in them that raised the leader's brows. "By whatever means? Any means at all?"

"Any that is necessary," said Catin.

Even, Sarama could well see, if that means should require killing.

Not all the women understood. Some, the younger ones chiefly, seemed to look on this as a lark, though they eyed Sarama with mistrust. But a few went still. They knew what had been said, and what had been commanded.

Sarama smiled at Catin. "You learn," she said, "after all. Good. Learn more. Then when the war comes—fight."

"Without you," said Catin, "no war will come."

Sarama laughed. That was not wise, but she did not care. She touched leg to the Mare's side. The Mare was delighted to oblige. The women, and Danu, had perforce to follow—at a trot, to keep pace with the Mare.

Ahead of them all ran the dun colt, tossing his head and flinging heels at the sky. The city could not have kept him if it had wished to. He was Danu's now, Danu's stallion—though Danu might not know or accept it.

No one tried to trap or keep him. They were all afraid of him. Not too foolish, that, stallions being what they were; but it would not serve them well when they met a whole horde of his kind, with men mounted on them, armed with swords.

Still, there might be strength here. There might be will to resist—to fight. Sarama could only hope for it.

✢ ✦

It was a fine day for riding, clear and almost warm. The snow was melting in the sunlight. The rest, traveling on foot, must be less enchanted with the beauty of the day: the road was rapidly turning to mud, though not, to be sure, as deep or as forbidding as it must have been in the spring.

Sarama was not grieved to leave the city behind. If Danu had stayed . . . that, she would have minded. But he was walking beside her with his arm over the colt's back, settled into a long easy stride. He did not press his presence upon her, nor insist that anything had changed.

So, she thought. Had it? Riding was interesting; she was sore in places that had seldom heretofore made themselves known. If the Mare's back had been less round or her gaits less smooth, Sarama might have been in honest pain.

Among the tribes she would have been said to be dishonored. She had joined in the body with a man not her husband, whom she had chosen for herself, and not through the choice of her kinsmen. Yet among her mother's people it would have been her right to do as she had done, to choose the man who would take her maidenhood. The Lady had led her to him. He had been set there for her, to wait for her—as Catin had so clearly seen.

He could not by the courtesy of his people refuse her. That much she understood. And yet she did not think he had wished to. He was no spineless thing. He made his own choices, though he might seem to be accepting what was laid on him.

He sensed her gaze on him, and made her the gift of a smile. Her belly fluttered, startling her. It was not that he had beauty, though he had it in plenty. It was that he was himself.

She had never looked at a man so before, or thought of him so. This must be what the stories told of, this trembling in the belly, this weakening of the knees.

The Mare's servant should be above such things. The Lady's servant might well regard it as part of her duty, to worship the goddess with the body, to make it fruitful in her name.

Sarama had taken Danu in no one's name but her own. She wanted him again, now. If they had been alone, she would have flung herself from the Mare's back and borne him down, and had her way with him then and there.

But they were under guard, half a dozen women watching her every move. She would be fortunate if she could even share a blanket with him tonight, or be left alone to do what her body so urgently wanted.

The Mare's ears flicked back. She was laughing at Sarama. All too often she had been hot for the stallions, and Sarama had mocked her for it. Now Sarama knew what it was to be in season—well and truly and quite completely.

✦ ✦

Night found them in a small city—a town, Danu called it, hardly larger than a gathering of tribes. There had been a remarkable number of such towns along their way, more than Sarama could have imagined before she came to this country. Every hilltop, every patch of trees, every little river seemed to have its human habitation, its houses of wood or stone, and tilled fields round about, damp with melted snow. And, unfailingly, its flocks of children running after the strangers, marveling at the horses, spreading word ahead of them that strangers, and strange beasts, had come into their country.

This town had a temple, though not as tall or as grandly carved as that of Larchwood, and a Mother of divinely vast proportions. She looked like the image in the temple, enormous and fecund—for yes, she was bearing, and close to it. Stranger yet, her daughter and heir, who was nigh as vast, was also with child—perhaps by the same man; Sarama could not quite understand what they said of that. It seemed that they might not even know that a man could sire children. That was preposterous, surely. And yet, as far as she could tell, there was no word for father in this language. Only for mother.

They were all housed in a single room, all six of their guardian hounds and Danu and Sarama. People offered them food, drink, fire on the hearth. There was a feast of sorts, if a small one; a welcome, but subdued. It seemed this was a poor town as towns went here, and its harvest had not been of the best. There was still more to eat than Sarama could remember in winter among the tribes, in warmth and comfort, wrapped in beautifully woven blankets and secure beneath a well-thatched roof. Even penury here would have seemed luxury on the steppe.

They retired ungodly early if this had been a feast. The Mother was weary, she made that clear, and her heir was not bearing as well as she might. Sarama found her blanket spread by the inner wall, and Danu's beside it. If she had in mind to escape, a wall of bodies lay between her and the door.

As long as there was a pot to relieve herself in, she was glad to be where it was warm; for after the warm day, the night had turned to frost. Danu took his time in coming to bed, lingering with the women, combing and plaiting his hair, ignoring Sarama on her blanket by the wall. She waited as long as she could bear to wait, but he was not going to have mercy. With a sharp rush of temper, she jerked the blanket up over her head, rolled herself in it, and set her face firmly toward the wall.

A light hand ran teasingly down her back. She shivered in spite of herself, for the pleasure of the touch. But she set her teeth and refused to turn.

The hand slipped beneath the blanket that she had thought so tightly wrapped, slid round, cupped a breast. Through coat and shirt she felt the heat of his skin. His body fitted itself to hers, front to her back. His breath whispered in her ear.

It could have been anyone. But she knew the smell of him, the musky sweetness; knew his warmth, and the length and width of his body, as if it had been made for her own.

She whirled in his arms. If she had hoped to startle him, she failed. He grinned at her, white teeth in his dark face.

"I thought the woman chose," she said, not perhaps as angrily as she had intended.

"Yes," he said.

"Then why—"

He simply smiled.

He was naked in his wrapping of blankets—all bare warm skin. She found that she could slither out of her own clothing, if she had help; and that it made a wonderfully comfortable bed, bundled behind her against the wall. She took him inside her, more easily than she had thought she might, and with less pain. He was gentle, a slow swell, like a smooth-gaited horse. Her body knew how to match him, found the rhythm of the dance with new-found ease and a kind of grace.

As slow, as gentle as it was, the release when it came was breathlessly swift. It startled a cry out of her. She bit back the end of it, flushing hotly, suddenly mindful of the roomful of women beyond the bulk of Danu's body.

He seemed altogether undismayed, and well enough content. She buried her face in his shoulder. He held her with his quiet strength, wise enough not to speak, kind enough not to turn away from her and fall into the sleep that she had heard was all too common in men after the gods' dance.

She was—by the goddess, she was happy. She was content, even knowing how publicly she had betrayed herself. Here, with this stranger, this man whose tongue she spoke imperfectly and understood only middling well.

How very strange, to find such such a thing where she had never looked for it, nor known to expect it. It was as he said, the Lady's gift: wonderful, startling, and greatly blessed.

.... 33 ....

From town to town and from city to city, they made their way westward toward Three Birds. Word of them ran ahead, and people came out to see the horses and the stranger-woman who rode the larger of them. At first the sky was kind, sending no rain or snow, though the warmth of the first day lost itself in winter's cold. But with cold came increasing weight of cloud, and raw bleak rain that turned, mercifully, to snow.

Sarama could not persuade Danu to rest himself by riding on the Mare. He was horrified at the thought. No matter that the Mare was willing; "I belong on feet," he said, nor would he be shaken from his conviction. Even when Sarama threatened to dismount and walk beside him. "Don't be a fool," he said. "You aren't used to walking. Get on, ride. I'd rather not be tending blisters when I could be doing other and much more pleasant things."

That made her blush furiously, as no doubt he had intended. He found her shyness endlessly amusing. It had become clear to her that people here were not modest of their bodies as they were among the tribes; that while it was not excessively common for a man to walk naked through a stranger's house, he might do it if the house was warm and there was a bath at the beginning and a bed at the end of it. A woman might wear nothing more than a garment of knotted string the color of blood, shaped like a kilt or a skirt but covering no part of her that mattered, and the rest of her as bare as she was born. Exuberantly so, too often; for women here were only reckoned beautiful if they were vastly fat.

Sarama had been no beauty on the steppe. Here she was even less of one, too thin and tall and sharp of face to be reckoned even passable. And yet Danu professed himself well content. *He* had great beauty for a man in this country; women, now that she had eyes to see, watched steadily as he went past, and sighed that he was the stranger's chosen.

She was not forbidden to keep him to herself, but neither was she expected to do so. This she discovered on the fourth night, when they rested in a town so small it was hardly a town at all. Village, Danu called it. They came in in the midst of a festival, a dance of the young men that took no notice of the snow. They danced naked but for a patterning of ocher and red earth and white chalk, and masks of deer, crowned with antlers. It was a hunting festival, she gathered, a thanksgiving for a rich kill, with meat enough for the village for many a winter's day.

Danu was not expected to join the dance. But after it was over, when the men had gone off to some rite of their own, or perhaps simply to wash off the paint and put away the masks and go sensibly to sleep, the Mother of the village said to Sarama, "This is a very beautiful man, this of yours. Is he as beautiful in the Lady's dance as he is in the face and the body?"

Sarama did not know what to say. The women from Larchwood had never said a word to her that was not of duty or of necessity. The Mothers who had offered them lodging had refrained from speech with Sarama, past the most essential courtesies.

This Mother was warm with honeyed wine, which perhaps had loosened her tongue. She patted Sarama's arm and smiled a gaptoothed smile. "There, there. Just chose him, did you? That's the sweetest time, and well I know it. I'll not ask you to share him; not while he's still so new. Pity; he is lovely. But then you know that better than I."

Sarama mustered a smile and a word or two, and enough composure to finish out the festival. But when she could be together with Danu—with a whole house to themselves, for a wonder; a hut of a single room and indifferent cleanliness, but warm enough and dry—she let loose what had been vexing her. "Am I supposed to share you?" she demanded.

Danu had been undressing by the fire, after having succeeded, somewhat, in persuading the smoke to escape through the hole in the roof. He looked over his shoulder. His brow was up. "You can choose not to," he said.

That was not what she had asked. "Am I supposed to?"

He shrugged. It did lovely things to the muscles of his back. "It's reckoned polite." He paused. "Catin didn't like to share me, either. But she allowed it."

"That's what she did," Sarama said. "Yes? She shared you, but I chose you. Was that polite?"

"No," he said, and he looked as if he wanted to laugh but did not dare. "No, when I flung myself at you, she had already unchosen me."

"You did not—"

"I couldn't choose you," he said. "A man doesn't. But he can persuade a woman to choose him."

She drew a sharp breath. "You *wanted* me?"

"Is that so horrible?"

"No," she said. "Goddess, no! But—"

"Ah," he said. "I shouldn't have told you."

He did not sound remarkably regretful. She gave up her resistance, rose from the heap of blankets—yes, clothed in nothing but her hair—and wrapped her arms about him from behind and held tightly. "I don't want to share you," she said.

"I don't want to be shared." Was he surprised to have made such a confession? She thought he might be. "It's not at all polite of me, but I want to indulge myself in you. I don't want anyone else to take me."

"You people are very strange," she said. "Mine don't share. The men don't. Women must. Men take them, and take many."

"Truly?" He turned in her arms and folded his own about her, and regarded her with great interest. "That doesn't sound proper."

"Women choosing men is not proper."

"It is very proper."

"No," said Sarama.

He shook his head and laughed. "We are so different," he said.

"Men and women are," Sarama said. "I thought you were weak, at first. Because you acted like a woman."

"Like a man."

"Like a woman." His grin was irresistible. "Oh, you are beautiful!"

"They say I am," he said.

"Women are supposed to be beautiful," she said. "Men are supposed to be strong. You are both."

"I try to be as I should be," said Danu.

"They won't understand," she said: "the horsemen. You must learn to fight."

"I will learn to fight," he said. His face had gone dark. "They are coming. I see them in the daylight now, as we walk toward my city. I hope Catin's dreams are as persistent. She did well to send me home, but ill to send you away."

"She sends me where the Lady needs me," Sarama said.

Danu did not reply to that. In a little while there was no need for words.

✦ ✦

The farther they traveled, the more people seemed to follow. They were a processional through the cities and the towns and the villages, even in snow, or in black icy rain. Sarama had never seen such a country, nor dreamed of one, in which cities were as common as tents in a gathering of tribes. The spaces between grew smaller, till city seemed to beget city, and each had its own offspring of towns and villages. They were built in circles, all of them, and never a straight line or a corner. Everything danced the great dance, the spiral dance, inward and outward in dizzying progression.

Now Sarama could see that Larchwood, which had seemed so vast and so unimaginably rich, was a small and poor city. The great city, the king city of this country, was the one to which she came on a grey evening. It had snowed, would snow again. The cold sank to the bone and lodged there.

The city offered no warmth to weary eyes, only blank walls and shuttered windows.

But the people who streamed out of those houses, who ran through the snow, calling to one another, were as bright as birds in spring. Some carried torches, some clay lamps that sent beams of light across the snow. They were laughing, singing, dancing a long skein of welcome. It wrapped the newcomers about and drew them inward to the city's heart, to the place that was sacred, because it belonged to the Lady.

The Mare and the colt were part of it. The Mare, who did not like to be crowded, endured this with remarkable patience. The colt, having tried and failed to climb into Danu's arms, settled for pressing as close as Danu would let him, and keeping his teeth to himself. People should have been wiser; and yet Sarama could not help but be glad to see so little fear. These people were strong of spirit. These might, indeed, learn what they must learn in order to defend their country against the tribes.

•••••••••••••• 34 ••••••••••••••

The Mother of Three Birds, Danu's mother, was an imposing presence. She was not the most vast of the Mothers that Sarama had seen, but neither was she meager. She was the image of the Lady that was in every temple, great belly, huge buttocks and thighs, and breasts well fit to nourish multitudes. And multitudes she had, too, more daughters than Sarama could easily count, and a whole pack of sons. There was even a baby, a child no more than a summer old, wide-eyed and solemn in the arms of one of her brothers.

Danu was not the eldest of the sons, but the second or third. They must be children of different fathers: each was quite different as to looks, and yet they shared a common semblance, perhaps no more than a habit of expression, that spoke vividly of their mother.

A man of the tribes would not have been ashamed to boast so many strong children, all of whom had lived past infancy. And this was a woman. She was blessed of the Lady, visibly and palpably the Lady's own.

The eldest of the daughters, the Mother's heir, was named Tilia. She was going to be as vast as the Mother, Sarama could well see, but as yet she was merely imposing in her bulk—and very light on her feet. Her eyes were bold, raking Sarama and finding her too evidently disappointing. "People said that you were beautiful," she said, "like the new moon in autumn. You are thin and your nose has an amazing curve, but is that beauty?"

It seemed that Mothers' heirs were not subject to the same discipline or the same strictures of politeness as other women. Catin had been much the same, and had been likewise uncorrected. Sarama smiled at this one and said, "No, I am no beauty. I never was."

"You are interesting," Tilia said. She tilted her head to one side and studied Sarama's face. "Yes, interesting. Very. Don't you think so, brother?"

Danu did not answer. His cheeks were dark above the beard. He was blushing.

"Ah," said Tilia, looking from him to Sarama and back again. "So. Did she?"

He nodded. He seemed unable to do otherwise.

"I thought so," said Tilia with every evidence of satisfaction. "That was a venomous message the heir of Larchwood sent, though it was oh so polite."

No one censured her for speaking so openly of what might better be said in private, but the Mother intervened before Tilia could speak again. She sent the women from Larchwood in the care of certain of her sons, to rest and to be fed. Her son who had newly returned, and Sarama, she kept with her.

Danu did not seem overly pleased by that. His sister slapped him on the shoulder as she went to do their mother's bidding, and said, "There, there, brother. Tomorrow you can have it back again. But for today we'll wait on you, and you will undertake to endure it."

Endurance was the word for it. This Mother's house was larger by far than the Mother's house of Larchwood, and richer. Its gathering-room was large enough for a dozen people to eat in, and for a dozen more to wait on them. Woven hangings warmed the walls, and treasures gleamed in niches, beautifully wrought pottery, images carved of stone or bone, and even a shimmer of gold that proved to be the likeness of a bird. They were there, Sarama realized, simply because they were beautiful; not because they had any immediate or constant use.

What a strange thing: beauty for its own sake. Sarama needed to think on it, to understand it.

But not now. She was seated next to the Mother, a position of great honor there as it would have been among the tribes. Everyone watched her and judged her, and reckoned her people by the way in which she conducted herself.

She knew no other way than the courtesy of a tribesman, to partake second after the king, to exchange politenesses but no matters of state, and to leave a little on the plate, to be given to the women and the children. All of that did not appear to shock anyone, though they ate everything they were given.

It was a fine feast, with roast mutton and roast kid and a haunch of venison, and fine bread, and milk rich with curds, and finer wine than Sarama had tasted before. Then after it they were given cakes made with honey and nuts, and sweet bits of fruit. Sarama recognized the cakes from Danu's baking. This then was where he had learned the way of them.

He should have been in great joy to be home again, but he was clearly in discomfort, clearly distressed that he must sit and others serve. Sarama wondered if Tilia had intended that. Sisters took petty revenge sometimes, for brotherly slights.

It was all very different from Larchwood, where she had been thrust out to the city's edge and away from the people, and given little honor by the Mother or her heir. Catin might have said that these were rich people, sheltered people, who did not know what evil might come from the wood. And yet, thought Sarama, innocence was preferable to fear. Innocence might be amenable to reason.

She ate and smiled, smiled and ate, and said little; but no one seemed to expect her to babble excessively. Soon enough she was let go, shown to a room that though tiny was beautifully appointed. It came with water heated for washing—remarkable in winter—and a stone that had been warmed in the hearthfire and laid at the bed's foot.

It also, and rather to her relief, came with Danu, who was visibly glad to be away from the feast. "I hate to be waited on," he said.

Sarama dared not even smile. As soberly as she could, she said, "Sometimes one has to be a prince."

She had used the word in her own language, because she did not know what it was in his, or even if there was such a word.

He seemed to understand. "I would rather serve than be served. One waits so long, you see. And nothing is ever quite as one would do it oneself."

"I never thought of that," she said.

"People don't."

His tone was brusque, almost angry. Sarama had never learned to be conciliatory, but she could at least distract him. "Was this room yours?" she asked.

He nodded.

"Should I be in it?"

"I would go to yours," he said, "if you had one. But since you don't, and since this is not too uncomfortable—"

"It is most comfortable," she said. "I like it."

"Do you?"

Ah, she thought. Good. He had brightened. She judged it wise then to pull him down with her on the bed, and to distract him completely and most pleasantly.

✦ ✦

Either Tilia had mercy on her brother, or the Mother exerted her will. When morning came, Danu was keeper of the house again. He tried to look as if it were nothing more or less than he had expected, but she caught the spark of relief in his eyes. Had he worried that someone had supplanted him?

Clearly no one had. He muttered happily over the condition of the pots in the kitchen, and reckoned up the winter stores, and restored order among the servants. Not that Sarama could find any disorder; but this was a king in his domain, and he knew well how he wished it to be ruled.

For Sarama there was no such comfort. In Larchwood she had had Danu for guardian hound and teacher. Here she was kept under no watch, given no jailer. The women from Larchwood were gone; had left at dawn. Having delivered the outland woman into the hands of the Mother of Three Birds, they were done with their task, and freed to go home again.

Sarama did not miss them in the slightest. But her teacher she did miss—more than she had expected to. There were people to wait on her, but none to guide her or to tell her where she should best go. When she had risen, dressed, been fed, she found herself without duties, the only one of all about her who seemed to be in such a state. Even the children had tasks that they were given, or teaching-games to play before they could run off to freedom.

Sarama's own freedom had a slightly sour taste. She wandered out of the house and into the city. Everywhere it was the same. Men looked after the children, she noticed, as they so often had in Larchwood; even the smallest went about in the arms or on the backs of men who must be their uncles or brothers, since no one admitted to fatherhood. Though surely at least some must be fathers, if they were the mothers' chosen men; if they had been so chosen when the children were conceived.

It was oddly complicated to understand how these people thought of men and women, children and the getting of children. Sarama learned some-what by watching: that whatever these men were to the children in their care, they seemed to take pleasure in the office, and to gain no little respect for it. Children were greatly valued here.

Here, women bore children—whole tribes of them—and still ruled cities. They made pots, wove wonderful things, forged copper and gold, herded animals, traded in a market that seemed little diminished by the winter's cold, did everything that Sarama had seen a man do, and more besides; and often great-bellied with child. It was great honor here to be a mother; greater honor than any.

The Lady of this city, Lady of the Birds as Sarama heard her called, was a mother goddess. She sat in her temple, which was greater than any work of human hands that Sarama had seen before, squat and huge-thighed and huge-breasted as she always was, her face masked with the likeness of a bird's beak, and in her ample arms a sleeping child.

Sarama stood before her in the light of the lamps, with white snow-light slanting through the open door, and said as if to the Mother of a city, "I think I may be carrying a child."

She did not know why she thought it. Her courses had come and gone—when? Soon after she left Larchwood. That was not so terribly long ago.

Nevertheless she had said what came into her mind. Once the words were spoken, they felt somehow more real. More true.

"If I am," she said, "and it lives, will you claim it? And if you do, which face will it see? Lady of the Birds? Horse Goddess?"

The lamps flickered. The temple was oddly warm, though no fire was lit in it. The air held a memory of sweetness. Blood was not shed here, nor lives taken in sacrifice. On the stone table—the altar—lay bread and fruit, a beau-tifully painted pot, a cloth woven in the colors of milk and bone and snow. A bare black branch lay across it, and a single scarlet feather. Winter gifts, gifts of harvest past and of life asleep beneath the snow. As, perhaps, life slept in Sarama's belly.

It would be born in the autumn, if it was born: in the golden time, in the last warmth of the year before winter's coming.

If it was born.

She laid a new thing on the altar, a thing that she had carried for time out of mind: a small smooth stone from Horse Goddess' hill. It was grey like a young mare, banded with the white of the mare in her prime. Sarama set it on the cloth that was all white, but no two whites the same, next to the winter branch. She spoke no prayer. She let it shape itself as it would, as it chose to be. Let the Lady take it as she pleased, to do with as she would.

············· 35 ·············

Danu in Three Birds, returned to all his old places, still was not entirely the Danu who had left with Catin in the spring. First there was Sarama, who had chosen him for herself; and then there was the colt, who required housing, feeding, and care. Danu had not, in his eagerness to leave Larchwood, regretted the labor that he had devoted to the house and the pen for the horses, but in Three Birds he had it all to do again, and winter gripping hard.

Nevertheless there was fodder stored away for the cattle, and grain that Sarama said would do; and if he ate a little less bread this winter, then so be it. House and pen he had none, but the horses had found themselves a place that they liked well, a meadow and a copse just outside the city, which like the house in Larchwood lay beside the river. There was a stream that ran too swift to freeze, and ample grass beneath the snow, and on the trees still a remnant of frostbitten fruit. The colt and the Mare were if anything more content there than they had been with a house to retreat to; the trees sheltered them in ill weather, and they could come and go at will.

Danu's mornings now were marked first, not by the Mother's song, but by the sound of hooves on winter-hardened ground, and the colt's rattling of the shutters in Danu's room. Danu would stagger from his warm bed, gasping with the shock of the cold floor on bare feet, and open the shutters, and rub the colt's face and neck by way of greeting; and as he did that, the Mother would sing the sun into the sky. Then the colt would receive his morning handful of grain, and the Mare hers; and maybe they would linger for a while, or more likely they would go back to their meadow to graze until Sarama came to ride or to tend the Mare. If Danu was fortunate he might go with her; if his duties were too pressing, he could rest assured that at evening the colt would come back to be given his dinner.

Winter did not appear to dismay the horses. They had neither fingers nor toes to freeze and blacken. Their coats were as thick as a bear's. Snow made them snort and dance. Icy rain met with little more than a snort of annoyance. They were hardy creatures, though oddly delicate. Sarama had warned Danu strenuously against feeding them more than a handful of grain at a time, and had invoked the terror of the Lady on anyone who fed them but Danu. "They will die," she said, "if they eat too much."

That was a great trust, to be the guardian of creatures so strong and yet so strangely weak. Danu might have been glad to be free of it; but if he had been, he would have envied the one who bore it. It gained him, he could not help but notice, a degree of respect that he had not had even for being the keeper of the Mother's house. He was the one to whom the horses came, who could speak to them in their language of gesture and touch.

"And grain," he said when people ventured to marvel. "They do it for that. Not for me."

✦ ✦

"Yes," Tilia said on a day not long after Danu had come back to Three Birds. The horses had been fed some time since; Sarama was riding the Mare, to the manifest delight of a crowd of the young and the not so young. Danu was grinding flour for a sweet cake, a labor that he could well have left to the servants, but his body welcomed the simple exertion.

His sister perched on a stool, graceful as she had always been in spite of her bulk. She was more beautiful than he remembered, and also more aggravating. "They're animals," she said of the horses. "They live to eat. But they'd come to you even without the grain, I think. Now tell me about her."

"Her?" Danu asked, deliberately dense. "The Mare?"

Tilia rolled her eyes. "Of course not, idiot. The woman. You left with one, came back with another. That's fast work, little brother."

Danu's cheeks were hot. He bent more diligently to the stone, grinding the emmer grains white and fine.

"Tell me about the woman," Tilia persisted.

"What's there to tell?" he said, panting a little. "She comes from the east of the world. She serves the Lady, whom she calls Horse Goddess. She's bearing a message to the Mother, which she'll deliver when she's ready."

"I know all that," said Tilia. "Tell me about *her*."

He set his teeth and would not answer.

Tilia waited till all the meal on the stone was ground. When he reached for another bowlful of grain, she caught his hand. "Do you like her?" she asked.

He nodded.

"She's not beautiful," Tilia said, "but she's interesting. Different. Her eyes are almost alarming. They're *green*."

"There's nothing demonic about her," he said, perhaps more heatedly than he had meant.

Tilia did not tax him with it, for a wonder. "Kosti says the men are jealous. They want to know how you convinced her to choose you."

"They should ask me that," said Danu.

"They would, if you weren't keeping so close to the house or else to the woman."

"Her name," said Danu, "is Sarama."

"You like her very much, don't you?"

"You're talking like a man," he said.

She laughed. He had forgotten how difficult it was to prick her temper. "It's true, what Kosti said. Isn't it? In her country, men do the choosing."

"How does Kosti know that?"

"He asked her," Tilia said.

Danu did not know why he should find that objectionable. Kosti was a great master of attracting women. But Sarama had yet to order Danu out of her bed.

Tilia's eyes were dancing. She could see perfectly well what he was thinking. "So in the east, men do choose."

"It . . . was both of us," Danu said.

"Sometimes it is," said Tilia. "I'm glad you left Larchwood. The house
didn't like anyone else who tried to run it. The Mother was actually cross.
Nothing was really right, till you came back."

That was a mighty confession. Danu granted it a moment's silence. "So
you don't mind? That I came back with a stranger from so far away that she
doesn't even speak our language?"

"She does after a fashion," Tilia said. "I don't know that I like her. But
she brought you home."

+ +

"I don't know if I like your sister," Sarama said.

She had come in late, as the last light left the sky, windblown and with
her cheeks ruddy with cold. When Danu was done with all his tasks, he found
her curled in the bed they had been sharing, wide awake, with a cup of warm
honey mead that he had kept by the hearth for her. She insisted that he take
half of it. It was strong and almost unbearably sweet, and still warm enough
to startle his tongue.

"I don't know if I like her," Sarama said while he savored the mead,
"but I think she is very good as a—Mother?"

"Mother's heir," Danu said.

"Yes. She will be a Mother."

"People say," said Danu, "that she's too headlong and headstrong, and
knows too little of serenity. But I think Mothers learn that once they take
their places. It's something the Lady gives them."

Sarama nodded. "I—there was the Old Woman. Now there is only I. I
should know more, be more. But sometimes, I do know."

He could see how difficult it was for her, the words stumbling, perhaps
ill chosen, but she knew no others. Still he thought he understood. "You are
a Mother," he said.

She went white, as if he had struck her. "How did you—" She broke
off. The color came back slowly to her face. "A—a Mother. Like the Mother
of a city. No. No, I don't have everything that a Mother has. All the people.
The duties. The—everything."

"A Mother is the Lady's servant," Danu said. "You serve the Lady. She
speaks to you. You bear burdens—the whole world, your journey, the war.
That's what Mothers do."

"They rule cities," Sarama said.

"Sometimes," said Danu. "Not always. A Mother hears the Lady's
voice."

"Then you are a Mother," Sarama said.

He could not see that she was laughing at him. Yet she must be. "A
Mother is a woman," he said.

"Can't a man hear the Lady, too?"

"Can they, where you come from?"

She shrugged. "Men hear gods. I think—maybe—my brother could hear the Lady, if he would admit it."

"You have a brother?"

"I have many," she said. "But one—the same mother. We were born together. I was first. He is—the horsemen have men to rule them. Kings. He is the king's heir."

"King," Danu said, trying the strange word on his tongue. "A man who is a Mother?"

"Different," she said, "but maybe a little the same."

Danu's head ached. It often did, when he tried to understand her. "I am not a king," he said. "Nor a Mother either. I am something much less. Like a flute. It is not the music, nor does it make the music. The music sings through it."

"Maybe," she said, "a seer. A prophet. One who speaks when the gods speak, so that other people can hear."

He nodded. "Yes. Yes, that's it."

"Then I am that, too," she said.

"No. You are more." He spoke swiftly, before she could stop him. "Teach me your words. Teach me your language, as I've taught you mine. I need to understand. What your words are like. How you think them."

"You know some words," she said. "I'll teach you more."

"Yes," said Danu. "All the words you know. Even the ones that frighten me."

"That could take a long time," she said.

"I learn quickly," he said. "Or are you leaving soon?"

"Not unless your sister sends me away," she said.

"Tilia won't do that," said Danu. "Catin was afraid—terrified, all the time. Tilia is afraid of nothing."

"I think she is afraid of some things," Sarama said, "but she doesn't let them rule her."

"She doesn't know about war," Danu said. "When are you going to tell her?"

"When the Mother asks," Sarama said.

"She'll wait for you to tell her."

"She shouldn't wait too long," said Sarama.

"I think you should tell her," Danu said. "And soon."

"And if she sends me away?"

"She won't," said Danu.

Sarama's glance was doubtful, but she did not argue. There were advantages, he thought, in a woman whose tongue was not entirely certain, yet, of the Lady's speech.

Sarama had delayed in speaking with the Mother because—at last she would admit it—she was a coward. She did not want to be sent away from this place, from this man who had, somehow, become as necessary as the breath she drew. She did not need to be near him every moment, but when she was apart from him, she felt the lack more keenly, the longer they were parted.

He did not feel the same. She could tell that. He was home, among his people, in the place that was rightfully his. A prince indeed, and the heart and center of this house, too, though he seemed unaware of it. Everyone who came in, went inevitably to him, wherever he was. He was much too preoccupied to dream and sigh after a woman.

But he had forced her to see what she must do. She was not here simply to be his lover. She must speak to the Mother, must persuade her to listen as the Mother of Larchwood had refused to do.

This Mother was stronger, hardier, and less overtly fearful. And yet that strength might well betray Sarama; might persuade the Mother that she need not listen to a stranger bringing tales that, for all she knew, might be sheerest falsehood.

✦ ✦

Sarama did not need after all to seek the Mother. The Mother met her on the path that she had made from the city to the horses' meadow. For once there were no children about, and no curious elders. Only the two of them and the snow, and the low grey sky.

Sarama greeted her with wide-eyed silence. That she was well able to walk despite her massive bulk, Sarama had seen often enough; and yet it was startling to see her here, wrapped in a mantle like an ordinary woman, without escort or guard of honor.

She smiled at Sarama. Sarama mustered something like a smile in return. She began to walk, not toward the city but on the way that Sarama had been going, toward the meadow and the horses. Sarama had to stretch to catch her.

They walked without speaking. It was strange, because it was not an uncomfortable silence. No hostility. No tension. It had been so with the Old Woman; but Sarama had been of her own blood, her daughter's daughter. This was a dark-haired, dark-eyed, dark-skinned woman of an alien country.

The Mother spoke first, as would have been proper on the steppe. "Tell me, woman from far away. Are you well looked after here?"

"Very well," Sarama said.

"And my son: does he please you?"

Sarama choked, coughed. She must remember—she must—that a woman here was as a man. And a king would have asked such a thing of his guest whom he had given the gift of a woman. She tried to answer as such a guest would have done. "He pleases me well," she said.

The Mother nodded. "Never tell anyone, but he is the best of my sons—perhaps of all my children. The Lady loves him dearly."

"I . . . can see why," Sarama said.

"He tells me," said the Mother, "that you came here not simply to see our city."

"Did not—" Sarama stopped; but the Mother's level stare bade her go on. "Did not the people from Larchwood tell you why I was sent here?"

"I sent them home," the Mother said, "for they were ill for want of it. If there was a message, it was left to you to deliver."

Sarama could not believe that. As silent and forbidding as those women had been, surely they would speak to the Mother of a city. Or the Mother would command that they speak.

"My son tells me," said the Mother, "that your people have very different ways of doing things. Here, we cultivate patience. I'm not compelling you to tell me now why you came here. I only ask that, when you judge the time to be ripe, you speak and hold nothing back."

"They told you nothing?" Sarama asked.

"It is yours to tell," said the Mother. She could, it was clear, be greatly patient.

Sarama drew a deep breath and walked on. She had mustered words long ago, but it took a degree of courage to speak them. They were the same words she had spoken to the Mother of Larchwood, the same unvarnished truth: war, killing, the tribes of the steppe running over the Lady's country with fire and sword. She knew no other way to tell it, none gentler or sweeter to the tongue.

This Mother heard her in silence as they walked on the path that Sarama had made in the snow. Sarama finished just at the edge of the horses' meadow. They were at the far end, playing one of their games of circle-and-chase, but at sight of Sarama their heads flew up. The colt's call was piercing in the still, cold air. They wheeled and came on at the gallop, manes and tails streaming.

The Mother stood her ground beside Sarama as the horses thundered nigh on top of them and halted, snorting, churning the snow into a cloud about them. Needles of it stung Sarama's cheeks. She reached through it. The Mare lowered her head and blew warm breath into Sarama's hand.

"This is how they will come," the Mother said. "On horses, faster than any of us can run."

"Yes," said Sarama over the Mare's neck, for the Mare had slipped herself craftily between them.

"A horse is a beautiful thing," the Mother said, venturing to touch the Mare's mane. The Mare did not object. She recognized one of the goddess' servants. The Mother stroked her, gingerly at first, then with growing confidence. "It's rather horrible that these people should use them to make war."

"Horses are fast," said Sarama, "and strong. And they do a man's will. They don't know if that is good or bad. Only that it is."

"Perfect servants," said the Mother, a little wryly.

Sarama slanted a glance at her. "Not perfect," she said. "But—willing. For love or fear."

"Yes," the Mother said.

Sarama did not know if she understood. Perhaps she did. "Do you believe me? About war?"

"I believe you," the Mother said. "She of Larchwood sent you away. Why?"

"Fear," said Sarama. "Catin—the heir—said I brought the war. If I went away, the war would go away. She thought I was leading the horsemen, showing them the way."

"Are you?"

Sarama's lips twitched. "Catin said yes."

"What do you say?"

"Would I tell the truth?"

"You can't lie to me," the Mother said.

"Larchwood's Mother thought I could."

The Mother shook her head. "No. But a Mother's heir—she has to be heeded. If she believes a thing, even if that thing is not—what it should be, the Mother considers it. And, as now, may send the trouble onward, to a Mother who is stronger, whose people are more numerous, who can overcome it as she could not."

Those were a great many words, and some of them confusing. But Sarama comprehended enough. "You are stronger, and she was afraid. I understand. But she should have kept me. They don't know how to fight."

"Necessity will teach them."

"Necessity is not enough. They need—" Sarama groped for the word, could find none. She thrust up her hand, clenched into a fist. "They need to know how. The horsemen know. All their lives—they know."

"They are born to fight? To kill?"

"Wolves are born to kill. Lions. Bears. Men."

"Not our men," the Mother said.

"You teach them not to," said Sarama.

"Sometimes," said the Mother, "a person—not always a man, but often—goes mad, or loses his sight of the Lady. Then he takes up an axe or a hunting spear, and he takes a life."

"And do you kill him for it?"

"No," said the Mother. "We invoke the Lady's mercy. Sometimes she cures him of his madness. Sometimes she takes him away. Sometimes . . . she asks for his blood."

"You kill him," Sarama said. "I think you can learn to fight."

"Fighting is a terrible thing."

Sarama sighed. Again, it went round again. "War is worse," she said.

This Mother did not refuse to listen. She regarded Sarama over the Mare's neck, with her fingers woven in the smoke-grey mane, and said, "You know what you're asking us to do."

Sarama nodded somberly.

"And yet," said the Mother, "we have no choice. Do we? The Lady sent you to us. For this: to help us stand against the men's gods."

"Why couldn't she see?" Sarama demanded. "The other one?"

"I have no doubt she could," the Mother said. "But she was afraid, and her daughter was even more afraid."

"The war will come to them first," Sarama said.

"Yes," said the Mother. There was grief in her voice, but no yielding. "Each of us does as she must. It's no one else's place to interfere."

"That too you must learn," said Sarama. "To interfere. To help."

"Ourselves first," the Mother said. "The rest after."

"It will change you."

"Yes," the Mother said. Her calm had cracked, perhaps. It was difficult to tell. Sarama saw her then as a woman, and not vastly old, either; troubled as any other would be, and frightened, but determined to do whatever she must do, to keep her people safe.

She was very like her son.

+ +

Sarama did not ride long that day: the snow fell early and heavily, and drove her back toward the Mother's house. The horses professed no desire to follow. They were content with the shelter of their copse, and their heavy coats.

The house was wonderfully warm. It was full of people, but people who offered her neither suspicion nor dislike. They smiled and opened their arms and welcomed her as if—by the Lady, as if she had been kin.

This was not the Mother's doing. It had been the same yesterday and the day before. She was welcome, she was kin, because she had come with the Mother's son.

If they knew why she had come—

They knew. Tilia sat next to her, passed her a bowl of something fragrant and steaming, for which she had no word yet, and said, "Tell me what fighting is."

Sarama gaped.

"Yes, tell us," said one of the other daughters. "We need to know. The Mother said."

"Now?" Sarama asked. "Here?"

"If not now," said Tilia, "then when?"

Sarama drew breath to answer, but the words did not come. She rose instead and set the bowl aside, and said, "Somewhere open. With room."

There was no better place, in fact, than here, once the table and the benches and the stools had been pushed aside, and the makings of dinner covered or taken away, and space made that was, if not ample, then at least adequate. It was a strange army Sarama had begun to train, and by its own expressed will, too: a handful of women and girls, and a manchild or two, and Danu and a pair of the elder sons dragged in from the kitchen whether they would or no.

Sarama did not think that Danu was as willing as the women were. But he had asked her to teach him to fight. Now she could begin.

She caught his eye as she mustered her troops. Yes: he remembered. His expression was more rueful than sullen. She had not known she was holding her breath till she let it go; or that it had mattered so much that he accept this that the Lady, and now his own Mother, had laid on him.

If he accepted it, then so could she. Gladly, even. Even with war in front of them, and fear, and maybe, if the Lady willed, death.

So be it, thought Sarama. As the Lady willed.

THE
CONQUEROR

THE KING'S HEIR

W ITH THE COMING of full summer, the White Horse people settled into the chief of its camps, the high camp where the grass was richest and the water purest, springing from a cleft in the rock and spreading into a broad pool before it ran down to join a greater river.

On the morning after the tribe had come to this place, Agni, wandering in search of diversion, came on his pack of young wolves playing at the game of princes. It was a milling, tumultuous melee of men and ponies, sticks and clubs and no few bruises.

As Agni sat his pony, watching the uproar, the object of it flew out of the melee and fell ripely at his pony's feet. The pony shied. Agni urged him back toward the reeking thing: the goat's head long since burst out of its leather bag, and separated from the rest of the goat even longer since. Stick or club he had not thought to carry with him, but spear he had, and a good, thick one, too; he had been thinking somewhat desultorily of going after boar. He kicked the pony over, swooped and caught the goat's head with the butt of the spear, and hurled it back into the mass of players; and himself in hot pursuit.

It was a grand game, a game fit for princes. It distracted Agni rather admirably from contemplation of the steppe without Sarama on it, and the emptiness that opened in him; and from the fact that tomorrow he must go out alone himself, and find his stallion.

But a game could not go on forever. He drove the goat's head at last between two yelling players, straight at the peeled wand that was the goal of all their battle, and sent the wand flying. He whooped and whirled his spear about his head, calling out, "*Now* then! Who'll go hunting boar with me?"

They were all avid for it, even Tukri, whose head was nigh split: he had got in the way of a club. He had tied it up with a strip of his shirt, and he sat his pony steadily enough, though he had a drunken look in his eye.

Agni wheeled his sweating pony to lead them out of the camp. But someone was standing in his way. The boys and men tangled behind him, some pressing past before they could stop their ponies. Agni swept his arm at the rest. "Go." And when they hesitated: "Go! I'll follow."

They were none too reluctant, though a few went slowly, with many glances back. Agni let them go. His pony was glad enough to stand and breathe. Agni was not so glad to look into the face of his brother Yama. There was always that dislike which they had cherished since they were children; but leavened now on Agni's part with memory of the words his father had spoken, the secret that the king knew. That Agni was the hidden and frequent lover of Yama's youngest wife.

That did not suffer itself to be spoken, nor would it while Agni was master of himself. "Good morning, brother," he said lightly enough. "I trust I find you well."

"You've always had a glib tongue," said Yama. "Are you thinking to talk a stallion into your snare?"

"If it works," said Agni, smiling sweetly, "why not?"

Yama had always hated it when Agni refused to be baited. He snarled now, but would not move aside to let Agni pass. "Where are you going? Have you forgotten what you must do tonight?"

"Not for a moment," Agni said. "Why? Is it forbidden that we bring somewhat home for the feast?"

"It is rather expected that you remain in the camp until the feast," said Yama. "Others can hunt for once, and bring home the quarry. Or are you afraid you'll be outmatched?"

Agni smiled again, sweeter than ever. "I'm never afraid of that," he said. He urged the pony forward. Yama could have stood his ground, but he was not as brave in the body as he was in his boasting. He stepped aside hastily. Agni laughed—not prudently, but at the moment he did not care. Yama was a blusterer and a fool. Anyone with eyes could see it.

+ +

They tracked the boar to his lair and slew him there, and it was Agni—of course—who made the kill. Agni was the gods' beloved. There were few who could equal him in the hunt, and none who could best him.

It was a great boar, and old, with tusks so potently curved that they had pierced his lip thrice. Agni had met the little red eyes as the boar plunged upon his spear, and seen his own death there. But not yet. Not this day. The boar died with its breath hot and reeking in Agni's face, and its jaws gnashing impotently, snapping at his hands. He took no wound at all, and the boar died as the gods had ordained. They carried him back to the camp with singing and rejoicing, and laid him at the king's feet where he sat amid the elders.

The king bestowed on Agni a wintry smile, a gift so rare as to be beyond price. Agni took its memory with him when he went among the priests, he and those of the young men who would be sent out on the morrow to find their stallions.

The priests in their masks and their horsehide mantles would be the young men's guardians from now until morning. The feast was not for them: they would fast while the tribe gorged itself. They must go out empty, empty and singing, and find life and sustenance on the steppe.

Some of them had eaten heavily this morning, the better to endure the long night. Agni, who had been hunting, felt already the edge of hunger. But he would be strong. He would prove to the gods that he was worthy, and pray for a king of stallions, a horse fit for a man who would be a king.

There were half a score of them, a great number for a single tribe. They had all hunted and raided and fought with Agni. It was inevitable that he find himself in front of them, the first to be taken by the priests, and the first to go away with them, away from the tribe, down the river to the circle of stones that had been raised by the gods long ago. He had walked in that circle before: when he gave up the amulet of his childhood, when he slew his first boar, when he killed his first man in battle.

This, if the gods willed, was the last time he would pass the gate of stone as a youth not yet a man. He was nigh as tall as the lintel now, and nigh as broad as the two stones that held it up. That, people said, was the measure of a man; of perfect rightness, neither too large nor too small.

The space within was sunlit still, but the shadows of the stones were long. The altar stone was swept clean. A great basin had been set near it, a cauldron of boiled and tight-bound leather, broad enough and deep enough to hold the body of a man. It was full of water, and more in skins, waiting to be poured in.

The priests who had led him here took him by the arms. He stiffened; but made himself submit. They stripped him unresisting, lifted him into the cauldron and bathed him without gentleness. It was his pride to make no sound, even when they scraped his skin raw. They were scouring off the years of his youth and making him new. They took his beard with a keen stone razor and consecrated it to the gods. They lifted him out and bade him lie on the grass, while one by one each of the others was accorded the same ritual cleansing.

The wind was cool on his drying body. His cheeks felt strange, bared to the world as they had been when he was a child. The others as they came to lie beside him were unwontedly quiet. The usual badinage, the jests and the vaunting, were quenched.

The sun sank lower and the air grew cooler. Just at the fall of night, the last of the young men was brought among the rest. "Up!" commanded the priest in the mask and high headdress of the Stallion. His voice echoed hollow in the mask, as if it came from beneath the earth.

They rose in their various ways, with grace or without, smoothly or in an awkward, shivering scramble. Agni hoped he managed grace. The sky was full of light, the earth growing dark. They stood in a wavering line, white skin glimmering, hair hanging lank with wet.

The priests, who in daylight had been merely men in masks and the hides of beasts, in the dusk swelled to godly vastness. The Bull, the Hound, the Stallion, loomed over the naked boy-men.

A drum began to beat. Lesser priests, naked but for faceless masks, plain coverings of tanned hide over heads and faces, danced into the circle. Each bore the horn of a bull, carved and limned and bound with cords, filled to brimming with what proved by scent and color to be *kumiss*. There were ten horns, one for each of the young men. The priest who approached Agni was a thickset man, shoulders furred with hair, and very thick and short in the manly parts. Agni searched for the gleam of eyes in the mask, but found only darkness.

It was not Yama, surely. There were other men of such proportions in the tribe. Agni took the horn as it was proffered. The reek of *kumiss* dizzied him. Something else rode under it, something more potent still.

Others had recoiled from their own drinking-horns, startled as Agni had been. If this was a drug, then it was meant for them all.

Agni drew a deep breath and held it as he drained the horn. "All of it," one of the priests told someone else, down the line. "Every drop."

Agni's ears were ringing even as he lowered the horn. The priest took it, bowed—did his eyes gleam mockingly?—and wheeled away.

The stars were singing. The drum beat in his own flesh, in his blood. The Stallion reared over him: great crest, streaming mane. From a man's loins sprang a great black rod, the tip of it as broad as a man's hand, great as a club and hot as a brand from the fire.

Agni swayed between heaven and earth. Beneath him, before him, the Stallion mounted the Mare. His strong yellow teeth seized her nape. She squealed. The sound pierced Agni's skull. The Stallion's hammering strokes kept pace with the drumbeats.

They danced, the young men. There was no will in them. The drug, the drink, the drum, seized them and wielded them. They danced round the Stallion and the quiescent shadow of his Mare. Their feet woke the thunder. Lightnings cracked in their hair.

Agni felt his own growing long, sweeping like a stallion's mane. His feet were hooves, hard and stony. Strength rippled through his body, the strength of the stallion that acknowledges no limit. The sound that burst from him was a stallion's scream, both exuberance and challenge.

Another scream met it. His nostrils flared. He scented musk, male— enemy. Stallion trespassing on the herd that he had won in battle. Young stallion, bright-maned, heavy-shouldered—but never as heavy as he. He flung the mass of his body against the stranger. His teeth snapped, diving for the throat. Hooves battered, forelegs tangled. They reared against the stars; reared and wheeled and fell away, shrunken into human shape again.

Others danced that same dance, the dance of stallions doing battle for their mares. The Stallion was in them all. The Mare waited, a patient shadow. To the victor she would go. To the one who conquered; who was worthy to reckon himself her master.

Agni, mere naked man, looked about him at the warring stallions, and laughed. The one who had fought him would, with morning's coming, be Patir his friend and yearbrother, with whom he had hunted the boar. Tonight it was a fallen man-beast, man's body, stallion's eyes.

Agni danced past him toward the Mare in her solitude. She was silent, a thing of night and starlight. The scent of her dizzied even his human senses. He caught at mane like a fall of moonlight. Warm neck flexed under it. She wheeled, startled. He let the force of her movement draw him up and round, onto a warm living back, the back of a mare indeed, rearing under him. He rode with her. She tossed her head. He stroked her neck, gentling her, while the stallions fought and the stars wheeled over them all. He had the victory. He had the Mare—as man, and master.

·············· 38 ··············

The stars wheeled overhead. Agni was aware, dimly, of lying on the grass; of staring up at the loom of a stone. The others were somewhere in the circle, the priests, the mare who had been the Mare. But here was silence, as if the night had held its breath.

The stone moved; divided. The lesser part of it, the slender upright shadow, bent over him. It breathed. Eyes gleamed in it. He drew in a scent that he knew extraordinarily well, musk and sweetness and a faint, pungent hint of fire.

He sucked in breath to cry out: *You should not be here!*

Her hand stopped the words before they began. Her lips followed. He had no power to resist them.

She lowered herself on him, the folds of her mantle falling over him, veiling them both. Her body was as bare as his, and warmer by far. She coaxed and teased his shriveled rod, tormenting it till it rose in its own defense. When it rose high and rampant—and no will of his at all, to make it so—she loosed a sigh as of relief, and impaled herself on it.

She rode him as he had ridden the mare, smaller, lesser in strength, and yet by far the greater. The part of him that cried sacrilege was vanishingly small. Man had mounted man in the madness of the dance; Stallion had mounted Mare, and all the rest had caught the heat of his passion.

Now Agni shared in it. Rudira the headlong, Rudira the impossibly bold, took him in the shadow of the gods' stone, in the place to which no woman was admitted, and no female thing except the Mare. He believed then what his father had said, that she was a witch, a creature outside of simple human nature. Else how could she dare such a thing as this?

There was no woman in the world like her. That much the king had failed to see. In clasping her, Agni clasped a burning brand.

She fitted her body to his body, breasts to his breast, riding the last slow surging strides into a taut and ecstatic stillness. She slipped from him then, skin sliding on sweat-slicked skin, and lay on the grass beside him.

His head was full of the scent of her. He tried to shake himself free of it, to whisper urgently: "You shouldn't be here! Go!"

She ignored him. Her hand sought and found his shaven cheek. She peered at him, as if she could see more of his face than a dim blur in the starlight. And maybe after all she could. Witches had night-eyes, he had heard, like the creatures of the dark that they were.

And when had he last seen her in daylight, by any light but that of lamp or star?

He shivered. Her hand burned, but he had no power to thrust it away.

"I had forgotten how beautiful your face was," she murmured. "As beautiful as many a woman's. No wonder you were in such haste to hide it behind a beard."

He tensed at the sound of her voice, barely audible as it was. If a priest happened to be lying nearby, or one of the initiates—

She stroked the tension out of him. Her fingers were supple and strong. She had no fear, none of the shyness that was supposed to be proper to a woman.

When he was all slack on the grass, held back from sleep only by the heat of her presence, that presence left him. She melted into the night, dark mantle mingling with the darkness. He heard no sound of her passing. He might have thought that he dreamed it all, except for the scent of her that was on him still. That was real. That was incontestable.

❖ ❖

When he opened his eyes again, the grey light of dawn met them. Dew had fallen heavy in the night. He shivered with the damp and the cold, and no garment to warm him.

They were all rising in the circle of stones, groaning, shivering. The bravest of them washed in the dew, scrubbing away the excesses of the night. Agni, too; losing her scent that had lingered on his skin, making himself all new.

There were no priests to bid them do their duty. They did not speak to one another. Each was wrapped in silence.

For each, just within the circle, a gift waited: his own clothing made all new for the hunt, and boots for walking, and a pack laden with necessities for the journey. Agni scrambled hastily into the warmth of clean new clothes. He took up the pack and shouldered it, and followed the track that the sun showed him, shining through the stones.

Outside of the circle waited the men of the tribe. No woman, no mother or sister, for this was the men's rite. Each father or elder brother held the bridle of a horse, or more than one, if his son or brother could or would muster the wherewithal; and each horse was saddled and laden with supplies for the journey. They stood as if they had been there nightlong, though they must have come out of their tents just at dawn; they would have roistered till the stars grew dim, then rested for a while, till it was time to greet the initiates as they came out of the circle.

Agni, leaving the cold of the stones behind, found himself face to face with his father. The king stood upright without assistance, with a fair handful of the elders at his back, and three fine strong ponies waiting beside him— one more than Agni had looked for, but that was well and more than well. They were all, as Agni had hoped, mares. People were looking askance at that, perhaps, if they thought to turn their eyes from their own kin, but Agni had asked for mares and no geldings. He had no fear of his manhood, and some little hope of bringing home a stallion.

Agni did not see Yama, nor indeed any of his elder brothers. But of younger brothers and fellow hunters and his friends and companions there were more than enough, a whole grinning pack of them, though some of the grins were strained with the aftermath of too much *kumiss*.

They all hung back in awe of the king. He embraced his son ceremonially and kissed him on both cheeks, and held him so, speaking swiftly in his ear. "Find your stallion, and come back as soon thereafter as you may. I'll be king still when you return. My word on it."

Agni stiffened, his eyes widening, but the king's grip was too strong; he could not pull away. "Listen to me," the king said, fierce and swift, as if he must say it all before anyone could grow suspicious. "The factions are forming. The wolves gather to pull down the old stag. But not before the autumn dancing. Not, if the gods will, before you come back. Come back soon, O best of my sons. While I live I can protect you. Once I am dead—"

"You won't die," Agni said, just as fiercely. "I'll come back. And you'll live years yet."

"Maybe," the king said. He slapped Agni's cheek lightly, more blessing than rebuke. "May the gods bring you a king of stallions, and bring you back safe to the tribe."

Those were the words that tradition prescribed. Agni barely eased for the speaking of them, even as he bowed and murmured the response: "May the gods grant that I come back a man."

The king let him go. He had to take his horses and mount and ride away as all the initiates did, each in his separate direction. Agni's was north and somewhat west. He was not bound to it, but it seemed as good as any. He glanced back once, at the ring of stones that seemed far smaller and less terrible in daylight than it had in the darkness, and at the men standing in a circle beyond it. The king had not moved since Agni left him. Agni's friends and kinsmen leaped and whooped and sang him on his way. He flung a grin at them, a flash of insouciance, and put a swagger in his seat on the dun mare's back, keeping it till the earth bore him out of their sight.

❖ ❖

Agni kept to the northward way, remembering what he had been told of a herd that ran on the northern plains. Where the others went, he did not know, nor was he permitted to know. Sometimes some of the initiates would hunt together, but they were not to do so until the herd was in sight. Until that time, each hunted alone.

He did not think any of the others had gone northward. There were other herds nearer, that were known to have colts of the age that was required. But Agni's spirit yearned after something greater. Even knowing that his return could be delayed, that it might be days before he came near the northern herds, he determined to win his stallion from among them.

Often as he made his way across the steppe, as he hunted his dinner and as he lay in camp of a night, he pondered the things that his father had said. He had been aware of nothing that was not as always. His brothers vied for the king's favor, as they had done since he could remember. Yama the eldest declared that he would be king. And yes, there had been rumblings that the old king should submit himself to the knife, and suffer a new king to rise in his place. But nothing greater than it ever was. Nothing to raise the hackles, to urge him to walk more warily.

And yet the king had seen fit to promise Agni that he would still be living when Agni came back. Agni's hackles did rise at that. What did the king know? And why had Agni not known it?

And what if—gods, what if Yama had discovered that his wife found greater pleasure with his brother? That would not serve Agni well among the men of the tribe. It would not serve him well at all.

It was useless to gnaw that same bone over and over, all alone with the steppe and the sky. Agni could not return until he had won his stallion. No more could he be king. He must do this. It was not a thing that he could choose, or that he might delay. Until it was done, he had no other duty, and should have no thought apart from it.

He decided on that, his third night out from the tribe. It was easier in the thinking than in the doing, but the gods were kind, after their fashion. They sent a misery of wind and rain, which absorbed his attention rather completely for the days and nights that it lasted; and when he had thought never to be dry again, the rain blew away and the sun beat down. He was dry then, dust-dry, and hot. The grass parched about him. Water he could find, but less of it, the farther he traveled; and what he could find, he offered first to the horses. If he must go thirsty, so be it. He could not do what he needed to do if he was alone and afoot.

✦ ✦

The steppe was a living thing. Bleak as it could seem, it was alive with creatures, from biting gnat to eagle on the zenith; from rabbit nibbling greenery to lion hunting the wild bull. Men in companies could sweep the steppe and never know what creatures dwelt in the grass. A man alone in that immense sea of grass, even mounted and leading a pair of horses, was as much a part of it as the wolf wandering alone, or the bird feeding on seeds of the grasses.

A man alone was also prey, and his horses sore temptation for the great predators. Agni rode warily, veering wide from lion-sign and avoiding the herd-runs of the wild cattle. Wolves he feared less. In this season they had ample young of deer and cattle to feed on, and tender young rabbits for the cubs.

But lionesses hunted greater prey to feed their offspring, and the lions, if they could be persuaded to forsake their lordly laziness, would reckon man-flesh a delicacy.

Of horse-herds he saw none. He did not fret, yet, that he had chosen the wrong path. He rode between the lion and the bull, soft as a wind in the grass, and trusted that the gods would guide him.

Sometimes he saw the great herds of wild cattle, the sweep of horns like the young moon, cows grazing and calves gamboling, and the great herd bull keeping watch over them all. He would choose a cow, a young heifer perhaps, to be his favorite; would bear her company, guard her as she nibbled on the choicest of the grasses, mount her when she invited him, and make her all his own.

Each herd seemed to have its own pride of lions. Lesser herds of deer and gazelle gathered on the edges, fine prey for a lion, all gathered together and ripe for the choosing. Just so did the tribes of men keep their cattle, their sheep and goats: to serve their needs, and to thrive and to increase at their will.

And maybe the tame cattle were not so foolish, with men to guard them and see that they were fed. Men fought off lions, and chose carefully of those that they would slaughter. They gelded the he-calves, too, so that the bull would not kill them or drive them off. Perhaps the cattle would reckon themselves fortunate.

Agni was growing antic in his solitude. He dared not speak or sing, lest the lions find him, or the bulls take exception. He made his way in silence, traveling as swiftly as the land would allow; even into the night if there was a moon. Northward, as straight as the herds and their predators would allow.

Urgency began to grow in him. The moon died and was born again, and waxed to the full. He fed himself on fruits and on seeds of the wild grasses, on rabbits and ground-dwellers and even, one or twice, a lion's leavings. His beard grew out again, itching ferociously as it did it, till his cheeks were protected from the sun once more, and his prettiness hidden as it well should be. Pretty was for a woman. A man should be strong.

+ +

The land began to change. It was a subtle change as were all such things on the steppe, but the hills were steeper, the air less fiercely warm. Water flowed more freely here. There were springs and streams, even a river or two, and a lake bounded in reeds that took him a full day and part of another to circle. The cattle were fewer here. This was a land of birds, great flocks of them that blackened the sky.

Here with his bow he ate well, and could have eaten more than well, could he have paused. But he was summoned, north and ever northward, into a country of mists and soft rain, where the grass was rich and green, and rivers broadened into chains of lakes, strung like bright stones on a thread.

There at last he found the first sign that there were horses, a scattering of prints in the mud of a lakeside, a few droppings, a day and more old. Mares, he thought, and foals: prints no more than two of his fingers wide, tiny and perfect, with a wobble in them that spoke of extreme youth. A wolfpack was following them, in hopes of catching the newborn unawares. Of lions he saw no sign, nor had since he walked into the mist. Maybe their gods did not like this country which was so different from their high desert of grass.

For mares and foals he had no use, but where they were, the stallion could not be far. He had to pause for the first dawning of excitement, a catch in the breath, a quickening of the heart. But the track of a foal was not the foal itself, nor did it promise him a stallion. He forced himself to calm, gathered his wits together, and followed the tracks along the water's edge.

.... 39 ....

Northward round the lake and deeper into the mist, Agni followed where the mares and their foals had gone. The wolves had kept their distance. A flurry of tracks told of one that had grown overbold and met the wrath of a mare. There was blood on the grass, and bits of grey fur, and the mark of a body dragging itself away to heal. The most skittish of Agni's mares snorted at it, but they were all sensible beasts. They were more interested in the horse-sign, as Agni himself was.

He smiled at it. That was a strong mare, and large of foot, too; which boded well for the size and quality of her stallion.

He rode swiftly now, but with great care, though the tracks were old. Others overlaid them as he went on. This was a herd's grazing-ground, then, and the lakes were its watering place. Smaller bands came and went within the larger one. He marked the bands of mares and foals, and the yearlings with their smaller feet and lighter traces, and the young stallions all together in a boisterous herd.

There, he thought. There.

The sun was sinking fast. He camped by the broadest of the lakes that he had found, where a ring of trees let him fashion an enclosure for the horses. A warren of rabbits provided him with dinner, and herbs grew wild along the shore, and fruit in the grass, red and sweet. They made a feast, he on the fruits of his hunt, the mares on sweet grass, as the stars came out and the moon rose.

Agni lay in a bed of fragrant grasses. The air was soft. He slid into a dream of moonlight and of a woman's face, a fall of moon-pale hair, and arms as white as snow and as warm as fire. In his dream she was never his brother's wife. She was all his own, all sleekly compliant, everything that a man could dream of.

Just before he woke, as she rode him to the gods' country for the third time, she swooped over him, laughing with delight; and her face was the face of a woman days dead.

He fell gasping into the chill dawn, shaking and gagging on the stench of her. Sweet grass and dew swept the stink away. He had spent himself in his sleep. The sweetness of the dream was all gone in horror and in humiliation.

As a wise man should, while he washed himself in the cold water of the lake, shivering and spluttering, he tried to make sense of the dream. A dream that a man remembered was the gods' sending; that, every tribesman knew.

It was simple enough to find the fear; the truth that he was given to evading, that she belonged to his brother. That, by the laws of certain gods and of his own tribe, what he did with her was a betrayal. That he could be killed for it, and she too, or maimed for their lives long.

This was a warning, then. Strange that it came now, in this place, while he hunted his stallion. He should be dreaming of horses; not of a white-faced witchy woman whose gift of the gods was to drive a man mad.

He scrubbed himself until his skin stung, and turned his face to the east where the sun hid, shrouded in mist. "Skyfather," he said. "Father Sun. Don't deny me my stallion because of a thing that is—that must be—your will. Give me my king of horses, so that I can be a king of men."

The air was still, the water flat, not a breath of wind. Birds had chittered and shrieked and sang; but for that moment they had gone silent. The horses were unwontedly still. There was no sound at all but the hiss of his breath as he drew it in, and the beating of his heart. He might have been the only living, walking thing that was in the world.

Then he moved, and the world came alive again, whisper of wind in the reeds by the lakeside, cry of bird, and somewhere, somewhere not far at all, the shrill call of a stallion.

That was his answer. With lightened heart and hollow stomach, for he would not waste the time it would take to break his fast, he scrambled clothes and belongings together, gathered the horses, and went in search of the horse that had uttered the cry.

It was not an easy hunt or a brief one. He found where the herd had settled for the night, but it was some time gone from there, leaving trampled grass and droppings behind. Somewhere in the night, wolves had brought down a foal: a weakling from what was left of it, thin and small. But the tracks of its kin were large and their stride long. There would be good horses in this herd.

It was the herd of mares, from the evidence of the foal's carcass, but the young stallions would not be far from it. Agni followed it away from that largest of the lakes, up a long and relentless slope, to a windy summit and a field of grass.

It was not the top of a hill as he had thought, but a lifting of the land itself, a new and higher plain. The grass was rich there, and streams ran through it, and some of them runneled down off the plain into the place of lakes below.

The sun came out as he stood on the height, burned away the mists and swept the dew from the grass. It was later than he had thought, nearly noon. He followed the track that had led him so far, narrow and well beaten and somewhat circuitous, as if generations of horses had made it on their quest for the best grazing.

Then at last, as the sun touched the zenith, he found the herd. He left his mares hobbled and grazing well apart from it, and crawled the last of it through the high grass, drawn by the sounds of horses at their ease: snortings, snufflings, the tearing of grass, the squeal of a mare.

There they were in a hollow just below him, in and out of a little river: mares and foals as he had known there would be, and their stallion mounted on a fine dun mare. He was a bay himself, rough-coated, heavy-boned, coarse and hammerheaded, and riddled with old scars. One eye was a puckered scar; his ears were torn. He had no beauty, but his strength was incontestable.

He was too old for Agni's choosing, too long and incontestably the king. Just so was Agni's own father. Agni, watching him, knew a stab of home-sickness.

The stallion finished his duty, slid off the mare and shook himself and went calmly off to graze. She, who was young and a beauty, cried her protest; danced and tossed her head and curled her tail over her back, demanding that he pleasure her again. He ignored her. He knew his strength, that one; and no importunate young mare was going to move him.

She, being a mare and in high heat, was not inclined to accept a refusal. She teased him. She tormented him. When he granted her no more than a lift of the head and a curl of the lip, she left him in disgust.

She did not, Agni took note, leave the herd, nor did she seek another stallion. That was strength, too; to so compel a mare. Mares did as they pleased. It took a strong stallion to master them.

Agni sighed a little. A hand of years ago, or two hands, this would have been a mount fit for a king.

And yet, thought Agni, such a sire would have sons. His mares were very fine, fat and sleek, and taller than the run of horses in the south. Most were duns and bays; a few were red chestnut. There were no greys. One of the foals, a colt, might be black when he shed his foal-coat; he was the color of mist over dark water. He was very fine, and in a hand of years would make some tribesman a great war-stallion.

He had a brother. Agni knew it in his skin. Somewhere near, the young stallions would be grazing. Not all would be this stallion's sons; some might have come from other herds, banded together in the safety of numbers, and one of them, perhaps, might be suffered to breed the old stallion's daughters, since he would not do so himself.

But it was a son of this stallion that Agni wanted, somewhere between three and five summers old. Old enough to carry a man. Young enough to accept him, once he had won the battle of wills. Some tribesmen chose younger horses, as smaller and perhaps more tractable. Yama had done that; had come home with a long yearling, and ridden him too, and lamed him with bearing the weight of so big a man before the colt was strong enough to do it. No law forbade such a thing. It only required that, in order to be reckoned a man, a tribesman must hunt and tame and ride home on a stallion from the wild herds.

Yama had a gift, Agni granted him that. He had blinded a startling number of people to the truth: that he was a weak man, a poor horseman, an indifferent hunter. Anyone else who returned with a yearling would have been laughed out of the tribe. But not Yama. Yama conducted himself as if he had won a king of stallions.

Agni meant to win such a one in truth. To ride into the camp on the back of a great lord of horses, a battle-mount for a king, a sire of herds that would be. He had dreamed death with a woman's face—but he had not dreamed defeat at the hooves of a horse.

He circled the herd. With all the cunning that he had learned in hunting the shyest of prey—for he was a lord of hunters, as Yama was not—he made himself invisible, inaudible, without scent, not even as perceptible as a wind in the grass. The old mare, the leader of the herd, raised her head and snorted at a rabbit underfoot, but not at Agni slipping past. He could have tugged at her tail, if he had been such a fool.

The hollow narrowed at its eastward end, and then widened again, growing shallow, till it was level with the plain. There on the slope, he found the young stallions. They were a boisterous lot, racing one another up to the plain and back again, meeting in mock battle, rearing and striking and feinting for each other's throats. They kept none of the order that one found in the herd of mares. They did much as they pleased, but in pairs and threes and handfuls. No self-respecting wolf would trouble them, though a lion might, if he were hungry enough. The predators, and therefore the greatest wariness, went with the mares and the weakling foals.

Agni lay in comfort, chin on folded arms, and watched the stallions play. There were no yearlings here. Those would have their own herd, and a gaunt and scraggling thing it would be, too, as they learned to live in the great world apart from their mothers. These had survived that terrible year. They were the strong ones, the princes who, if the gods were kind, would find their own mares and become kings in turn.

He found the one who must be the lesser sire, the one whom the old king permitted to breed his daughters. He was a handsome horse, tall and well made, but Agni did not like the set of his shoulder. Nor did he have the light on him that one looked for in a king. He was a lesser creature, a favorite. He would not rule when the old king's time came. He lacked the strength of will.

Agni searched among the others, looking for those who had a look of the old sire. The hammerhead was not common. The strong bones, the height, the deep slope of shoulder and the strong rounding of croup—those he found, and they were as fine as he had hoped.

One in particular drew his eye; caught it, then when it wandered away, drew it back with a toss of the head. This one was, perhaps, four summers old. He was young yet, less beautiful than he would be when he was grown; his feet were too big, his neck too snaky long. But there was a light in him, a promise of splendor.

He turned his head to snap teeth at an importunate younger brother, and Agni's breath caught. For a moment he was among the tribe again, celebrant of the sacrifice, looking into the quiet dark eye of the Stallion. This too was a red horse, a chestnut, taller and more elegant than most. But the sacrifice had had no white on him at all. This one bore on his brow a curve of white like a crescent moon.

Horse Goddess' mark, as clear as if she had risen out of the earth and drawn it with her own hand. Agni let his breath out slowly. Yes, he thought. Yes. This was the one. This was his stallion.

.... 40 ....

Agni returned to the place where he had left his mares. They were much as he had left them, grazing in the contentment of their own small herd. The spotted mare, he thought, would come into season soon. The dun sisters would not be far behind her. It was rather a wonder that none of the young stallions had found them yet.

Well; and he had been careful to leave them downwind, and they were in no need of a larger herd. He had asked for the two duns in particular, because they were indeed sisters, daughters of the king's old stallion, and they had not been parted since they were yearmates together. The spotted mare seemed pleased to be part of their company, and untempted by the scents of other herds.

And now they would do what he had hoped they would do. But first he must be certain that when they did it, he had the means to secure his stallion. He searched the whole of the country round about, noting where the herds and their offshoots grazed, how they traveled, where they paused for the night. It was a matter of days of searching, and of nights camped out of sight and scent of the young stallions.

On the day when the spotted mare was in clear but not yet full heat and the dun sisters had begun to show signs of following suit, Agni found the place that, perhaps, the gods had meant for him. It was near the plain's edge, a small deep valley with cliff-sheer sides. The entrance was narrow, but more than wide enough to admit a horse. A fall of water ran down the cliffside into a cold clear pool. A little stand of trees grew there, slender and tall, too thick in the trunk for spearshafts but admirable for building a barrier across the valley's entrance. If Agni had ventured to pray for any one particular place, he would have prayed for this.

He camped there that night, setting the mares free to graze. In the morning he set to work cutting down the trees—with thanks to the gods and to Earth Mother for giving him such a gift. Then he built a wall and a gate, with posts set deep, and branches and withies woven through them and lashed with thongs. The dun mare who had carried the burden of axe and adze, thongs and bone saw and every other thing that he had reckoned useful, won a bit of wild honeycomb for her service.

He built the wall as strong as if it must withstand a war. And so it well might, once the stallion woke to awareness of his captivity. Agni built it taller than himself and wove it tight, and made a bar for the gate.

Then at last, on the third day since he began, with the spotted mare in full heat and the dun mares close to it, he left the sisters but took the spotted mare and led her to the place where the stallions liked to graze. She was none too happy to leave the others, but once he had won the argument she was willing enough to do as he bade.

The stallions were not yet in their field, but if their pattern held, they would come to it soon. There they would find a mare all alone as it seemed, nibbling on the choicest of the grass. Agni they would neither see nor scent, buried deep in the grass close by the mare.

Or so he hoped. He had anointed himself with grass and with the mare's droppings, an odorous perfume but sweeter to stallion-nostrils than man-scent could ever be.

So disguised, in hunter's stillness, he lay waiting for the stallions' coming.

✦ ✦

They came as they always did, bright in the morning, racing one another, pausing for mock battles. The leader, Agni had seen already, was the red stallion with the goddess' mark on his brow. His friend and rival, the white-nosed bay who was suffered to breed the herd-king's daughters, was not in evidence. He was doing his duty, then.

Agni let out a slow breath. That was well, and well indeed. Of all the stallions, that one could claim the mare first; though he might fight for it, and lose. But the one he would have fought with was the one whom Agni yearned after. One or both might have been killed or maimed. And that, Agni was glad not to risk.

The herd of young stallions stopped short on the field's edge, heads up, nostrils flared, struck motionless by the sight of a lone mare in their pasture. She ignored them, though her ears flicked. She knew they were there; and, in the way of mares, chose to be oblivious to their existence.

One of the young stallions loosed a low whickering call. The mare took no notice. The red stallion however wheeled, ears flat back, and lunged at the colt who had been so bold. The colt retreated hastily. The red stallion glared at the whole pack of them. One or two might challenge, but lowered their heads, biding their time.

Satisfied, for the moment, the chestnut stepped delicately toward the mare. He was at his most beautiful, and deliberately so: nostrils wide, neck up and arched, knees lifted high. She, whose beauty was chiefly in her good sense, did not even do him the favor of a glance.

If he had been a man, Agni would have reckoned him insulted. He fluttered his nostrils at her. She made no response. He rumbled in his throat, almost a growl, almost a song.

She looked up then, just as he ventured, at the farthest stretch of his neck, to brush her nape with his breath. Her ears flattened. He quivered a little and mouthed submission. She lunged with teeth bared. He withdrew to a prudent distance. She went back to her grazing.

Agni bit down hard on laughter. There were men in plenty who maintained, often at great length, that the stallion ruled the herd and commanded the mares. Agni, who had eyes and ears, and who had grown up as brother to the Mare's servant, knew better. Therefore he had brought his little herd of mares, risking the mockery of the tribe for being a man and a prince and yet stooping to sit on the back of a lowly female. But a gelding was worse than useless for luring a stallion into a trap.

This stallion found the man-scent on the mare despite Agni's best efforts to remove it: he snorted and shook his head. But he did not turn and bolt. It was more as if he had seldom or never scented such a thing, than as if he knew and feared it.

So, thought Agni. That much was true. No tribe wandered or hunted in this country. He had found none, nor evidence of any; but they might simply be elusive. This was Horse Goddess' land in truth, and these her children, these tall beautiful horses who had no fear of man.

And if that was so, then his dream of Rudira might signify the goddess, and the death that he had seen might be his own, for violating the sanctity of her country.

No. He would not think that. He had been brought here to find this one, this red stallion with the young moon on his brow.

While Agni maundered, the stallion courted the mare. He was not headlong as some stallions were. He asked, and was polite; and if she flattened an ear or lifted a heel, he withdrew. He had sense, then, and a wise heart.

Just as she began to soften to his advances, lifting her tail and indicating that, if he asked properly, she might invite him, Agni launched himself out of the grass onto her back. The stallion shied. The mare wheeled under Agni's heel and hand, but not before she paused to stale full in the stallion's startled face.

Wise mare, wicked mare, blessed mare. The stallion was deeply taken aback by the creature that smelled of mare and had attached itself to the mare's back, but she was in full season, and he was rampant for her.

She was nothing averse to lifting that wicked tail of hers and bolting toward the haven of her herdmates. She had a fair turn of speed; not enough to outrun the chestnut, but enough to keep him preoccupied with keeping pace. The other stallions, startled or interested, trailed behind, but none came close enough to be a nuisance.

Horse Goddess was with Agni. By her good offices and the mare's own irresistible scent, Agni on the mare led the stallion straight into the trap that he had made. He leaped from her back as he passed the gate, rolling, springing to his feet, setting shoulder to the gate and heaving it shut on its lashings of strong leather. He dropped the bar into place just as the herd of young stallions came thundering up to the gate; but they veered away, nor did a heavy body crash into it.

The spotted mare stood heaving for breath some distance inside the gate. The stallion mounted her—O marvelous; he was barely winded—and bred her where she stood. She offered no resistance. If anything, Agni thought, she was amused. Such a chase she had led him, and now he strutted, beautifully certain that he had had the better of her.

He was even more delighted to discover the dun mares. They were less haughty than the spotted mare, but less ready too. He courted each, but did not mount either; he marked them, that was all, nibbled a nape, licked a shoulder, made their acquaintance as a well-bred stallion might. They liked him well enough, though they drove him off after a while, weary of his importunings.

Then at last he discovered his captivity. He was not greatly inclined to leave this place with its treasure of stallionless mares, but neither did he intend to stay in it for longer than it pleased him. He trotted back the way that he had come, and stopped in confusion. Agni, perched atop the wall, went utterly still.

The stallion explored the gate with nose and forefoot, prodding at it, starting when it shifted slightly, but it never gave way. He moved along the wall then. It was solid from cliff-face to cliff-face. Agni had made very sure of that.

One of the mares called to the others. His head snapped about. Mares, he would be thinking. Grass, and water. Contentment.

He knew no madness of confinement. Not yet. The mares would distract him for a while. Long enough, Agni hoped, to get his attention; then to begin his taming.

But for this day Agni would be a hunter and not a horsetamer. He would take refuge in stillness. He would do nothing to disturb the stallion.

The others of the stallion's herd had lingered for a while, pacing the wall, drinking deep of the scent of mares; but after a while they wandered away. None of them tried to break down or to leap the wall. Such urgency was not in them.

For the stallion trapped within, that time would come. Agni shaped a prayer to Horse Goddess, that the madness be brief and soon over.

When the stallion had settled somewhat, snatching grass uneasily just out of reach of the mares, Agni slid softly from the wall. The stallion started erect. Agni stood still. The stallion's nostrils flared; he snorted. Very, very slowly Agni moved away from the wall.

That was a bold son of the goddess. He watched with every sense alert, eyes rolling white, but he did not shy or bolt.

Agni sought the camp that he had made, moving as a hunter will, softly, softly. There was water close by, and provisions enough till he could go out to hunt. He could watch and be unseen, but senses as keen as a horse's would be aware of him, would grow accustomed to him, would begin not to fear him.

He was not particularly quiet in his camp. He moved about as he pleased. At dusk he built a fire, singing as he did it, any song that came into his head. He would make himself a part of this world, his sounds and movements as much of it as the birds in the remains of the trees, or the rabbits in the grass.

He was aware nightlong, even in his sleep, of the horses moving about, the deeper snort that was the stallion, a squeal as he ventured too close to one of the mares. He dreamed of horses, just as he should have done. Horses running. Horses at play, stallion-play that was like war.

+ +

At dawn he started awake. For a moment he knew it had all been a dream, the red stallion as much as the horses running over fields of mist and shadow. But when he raised himself, he saw them standing in the gloom: the three short stocky mares, and the taller, lighter, finer-headed stallion with his red coat gleaming faintly. He grazed a little apart from them, but restlessly, more so than he had done before.

By full morning the pacing had begun, stride and stride and stride along the wall, calling to his kin who were now far from here. Every now and then he would halt, gather himself, half-rear as if to leap the wall. But Agni had built it high and strong, and the stallion was at heart a sensible creature. He did not venture his life to climb over the barrier.

The mares distracted him somewhat. He bred the spotted mare again, a handful of times as the day wore on; and one of the dun mares importuned him, so that he could not in courtesy refuse her. Agni, sitting in his camp, reflected rather wryly that even if he failed to win this stallion, his mares would bring home much more than a memory of him.

The stallion was not won yet. Not by far. To capture him—that was simple enough. But Agni must ride him back to the tribe.

And it was already full summer. By the autumn dancing he must return—and it was many days' journey from this country to the tribe's autumn lands.

He schooled himself to patience. Haste had never been wise in training horses. Some said nonetheless that it were best to seize the captive, pull him down, break his will; then ride him into submission. But Agni had too much of the Mare's blood in him. He trusted in a gentler way.

Gentler, but also slower. And the day wore away, and the night after that, with Agni in his camp and the stallion shifting from mares to wall and back again.

The next day Agni moved his camp closer to the horses. Himself he moved even closer, little by little, till he sat close enough to touch the spotted mare. She did not object. No more did the sisters, but the stallion moved off mistrustfully, eyeing the strange creature askance.

Agni was careful not to move suddenly or to leap erect. As if this had been a foal come new to the world of men, he made himself small. Small, to a horse as to a man, offered no threat.

The mares were his willing accomplices in the taming of the stallion. They had no fear of Agni, nor any dislike either. Nor did they find this confinement unduly onerous. There was grass enough, and no long wearying traveling.

He bridled and mounted the spotted mare and rode her about. The stallion took exception to that. He lunged at the mare, as if to mount and breed her. She however was coming out of season and in no indulgent mood. She let fly with her heels. Agni clung to her mane and rode through the flurry, which though brief was fierce enough.

The stallion, chastened, withdrew. Agni rode her in a circle round the stallion, who tucked his tail and flattened his ears but offered no insolence. Agni halted the mare and slid from her back.

The stallion was perhaps twice his arm's reach away. He made that a pace shorter. The stallion eyed him and clearly considered flight, but was too curious, or too cowed by the mare's temper, to venture it.

Agni stopped. He would not press his advantage. Not yet. He retreated with care, returned to his camp, left the stallion to ponder what he had seen. And perhaps he did, at that. He did not have the look of a dull-witted beast.

By degrees and by caution Agni accustomed the stallion to his presence. He could not come close enough to touch, but he could sit a bare hand's breadth out of reach while the stallion grazed, or sit on the wall while the stallion paced and yearned, and meet no resistance, find no fear.

A stallion from a herd that knew men, that had been hunted and culled for time out of mind, would have been notably more difficult to subdue than this innocent. Nevertheless he was no docile creature. He had great pride, and no submission in him to anything that was not a mare.

Agni must subdue that pride and win that submission. For that he built a smaller enclosure within the valley, with the remains of the grove for walls. The horses watched in great interest, even the stallion. At first he shied off from the opening of the pen, too wise now to be so gulled, but when the gate did not shut and the mares came and went freely in quest of the sweeter grass within, he ventured it himself.

On the day when Agni could sit within the enclosure, nearly under the stallion's feet, and rise and not cause him to shy off, he secured the gate at last. The stallion, hearing the sound of it, leaped to the alert. A man betrayed by his own son, a child betrayed by its father, could not have been as angry as this stallion was, to have been caught again, and so easily too.

He raged. He roared round the enclosure. He flung himself at the walls. He battered them with his hooves.

They groaned, but they held. Agni had set the posts deep and woven the walls tightly; and a good half of the supports were living trees, rooted in the earth. The gate, which was weakest, Agni himself guarded, driving the horse back with the snap of a rope-end.

He waited out the stallion's rage with patience that he had learned long ago in breaking colts. It seemed to last a very long time, but by the sun it was not so long: from midmorning till noon. Then at last, in the heat of the day, the stallion stopped. His sides were heaving. His neck was flecked with foam. Leaves and bits of torn grass and clawed-up earth were tangled in his tail. Even as exhausted as he was, he would not lower his head. He would not submit.

Agni slipped over the wall into the pen. The stallion rounded on him. The flick of rope in his hand sent the horse shying back, but he returned with daunting quickness, teeth bared, half-rearing. Agni drove him back again with rope-end and swift movement and a stamp of the foot, never touching him or offering him pain. He made to whirl and kick. Agni shifted his body, flicked the rope-end, brought the horse about to face him again.

That was the game, and that was its rule: that the horse face him, focus on him, be attentive to the shifts of his body and the flicks of the rope. Kicking, lunging, biting, yielded nothing.

At last the stallion stood still. His head hung low. But, Agni thought, he was not quite spent. He was cunning in his way, and he learned swiftly. Agni moved toward him with care, rope-end at the ready, and did the thing that he had been looking to do: laid a hand on the sweat-streaming neck.

The stallion reared, wheeled, lashed out with his hind feet.

But Agni was not there. Agni was well out of reach—and the stallion found himself caught with a rope about his neck, tightening as he flung himself backward. Agni wound it swiftly round the stout sapling that he had left near the middle of the circle, secured it, and stood back.

A horse could kill himself, could break his neck, fighting such confinement. But Agni had trusted in this one's good sense, and in the game that they had played—and, yes, in the complaisance of exhaustion, though that was not perhaps as strong as it might have been. As he had hoped, the stallion did not fight long. He learned soon that if he ceased to pull back, if he moved forward, the tightness round his throat eased. Then he tried another thing, a lunge and twist, to free himself; but Agni was there, and by the gods' grace the rope held.

The stallion stood still. His eyes were fixed on Agni. Agni could not see hate in them, which rather surprised him. Wariness, yes. Anger. But something—respect? interest? Something else that almost made him smile.

By careful degrees he worked his way along the rope, keeping it firm but not tight, till again he could touch the stallion's neck. The stallion flinched a little, but did not recoil. Slowly, cautiously, Agni ran his hand down toward the shoulder. The stallion snorted but did not turn to snap. Agni rubbed the joining of neck to shoulder, which ran like a cliff's edge between a low plain and a higher one. The stallion did not give to it as a tamed horse might, but he did not pull away. Agni stroked the big flat shoulder and drew back.

The stallion watched him. He sighed a little. With a tamed horse he would end here; but if he let this one go, recapturing him would be deadly difficult. He had to press on, had to finish it. From the breast of his coat he slipped the headstall that he had made of good leather, sturdy but supple. He slipped it on before the horse could resist, and stood back, braced for war.

But the stallion only shook his head a little, eyes still fixed on him, weighing him as it seemed, taking his measure. Agni returned to stroking neck and shoulder, moving back a little now, toward the deep curve of the barrel. The stallion's coat was sleek, gleaming like copper. His mane was thick and matted. Agni rubbed the roots of it. Did the rigidity of that neck ease a little? It was difficult to tell.

Agni went on slowly, accustoming this wild thing to his touch. He had won something in the game. It was not submission. It was a kind of wary trust, a lessening of anger, a rousing of interest in what this strange creature was doing.

When Agni slipped on the hobbles, the battle was brief. The stallion had learned. Fighting only bound him tighter. Stillness gained him a kind of relief. He did venture to snap at Agni then, in annoyance; but not in the rage that had possessed him before.

Once he was hobbled and haltered, Agni loosed the rope that bound him by the neck. He reared in triumph, lunged—and nearly fell as the hobbles caught him. Agni stood back, quiet, while he regained his balance. He shook his head in frustration, rubbing and rubbing it on his foreleg, but the halter would not come off.

"Ah, brother," Agni said. "It's a defeat, but it needn't break you. The goddess meant you for this—else why did she make you so wise? I've seen horses kill themselves rather than do what you've learned to do almost willingly."

The stallion pricked his ears. He was listening. Agni babbled on at him, it did not greatly matter what. It was the sound of his voice that had caught the stallion's attention, the cadences and the timbre of it, and the thought behind it, willing calm, willing reassurance, willing him to yield to this that, after all, was his destiny.

The shadows had grown long. Agni ended the lesson at last, slipped out of the pen, went to fetch the leather buckets that he had brought, filled with water. He hung them on the pen's wall and flung cut fodder over, the best of the tall grass from the valley's far end. Then, deliberately, he went to wash and eat and rest himself.

He heard the stallion moving in the pen, from where he lay just outside of it; heard him drink, heard him nibble at the cut grass. He tried more than once to scrape the halter off, but failed. The hobbles he could not break, nor did he waste his strength in fighting them. That was a wise creature indeed, the goddess' own and no mistake.

At last Agni let himself fall into sleep. No alarm woke him. He roused once at the sound of hoofbeats, but it was only one of the mares. She came up close, blew warm breath in his hair, wandered off.

✦ ✦

Morning found the stallion still in the pen, the water nigh all drunk and the cut fodder gone. Agni renewed them both under the stallion's eye, and left him to them while he broke his own fast. But then, when he had eaten, drunk, dressed, tidied the camp, gathered and regathered his belongings, and seen the sun full into the sky, he returned to the enclosure and to the game that he had played on the day before.

The stallion remembered. He fought at first, fresh with the morning, and angry, too; but the hobbles slowed him markedly. When he ceased to fight, when he moved where Agni bade him, Agni let the hobbles go, and held his breath. But the stallion did not burst out in his freedom. He stood until Agni bade him move. He played the game still as he had learned, with a look that, had he been a man, would have told Agni that he understood.

Agni hobbled him again, met only slight resistance. Unhobbled him. Again restored the hobbles. The stallion nipped lightly at his hair, but did not fight him. He sighed faintly and went to the fence and lifted the thing that he had left there, the fleece that was his saddle.

The stallion shied at it, but not badly; and once he met the end of the rope that bound his halter, he stopped. Agni let him sniff the thing, showed it to him, stroked it along his neck. He followed it with a rolling eye, but suffered it. Agni stroked him all over with it. Then at last, with no great ado, settled it in its proper place on his back. He twitched his skin at it, but Agni's hand held it lest it fall and startle him.

When he had calmed to it, Agni drew up the girth. Little by little, degree by degree; stopping if he flinched, stroking him, soothing him with voice and hand. And when he was girthed, and had not lost his wits or his calm, Agni played the game again, accustoming him to moving with that light burden strapped to his back.

"Brother," Agni said to him, "if every tamed horse were as sensible as you, there'd be no need of whips or hobbles."

The stallion snorted lightly at that—and discovered, on examination, that a bit of honeycomb in a man's hand could have a bridle-bit hidden in it. He half-reared, threw his head about, loosed a flare of his former temper; but Agni's return to the game, and the taste of honey on his tongue, won him over yet again.

He was discovering that the game went on and on; that each new thing was more alarming than the last, but that none of it caused him pain. None did harm to aught but his freedom—and that he had lost when he followed the spotted mare into a valley that, before the man came, had been open for his coming and going.

And toward evening, as the sun sank low, Agni crowned the game with the thing for which the rest had been but prelude. He slipped onto the stallion's back.

He had not intended to do it. He had climbed up on the fence, intending simply to accustom the stallion to the sight of him up so high, and to fetch his laden pack and lay it on the saddle. But the stallion stood just so, as if he knew what to do; and Agni's leg was there; and it was the matter of a moment to slip it over the waiting back, to settle into the saddle, to pick up reins and a solid hank of mane, and to wait for what would come.

At first, nothing, except a blank astonishment.

Then the world went up in flames.

Agni rode it out. Horse Goddess held him in the palm of her hand: for more than once he knew that he had lost the battle, that he must go flying. But the stallion failed to make that one last move, that twist or that lowering of the neck or that sudden veer, which would have flung Agni from his back. Agni clung for grim life. And at last, after an eternity in the midst of the whirlwind, the stallion stopped. Agni nearly fell for sheer surprise; but caught himself, and sat breathless, still in the saddle, on the back of the stallion that he had won for his own.

✦ ✦

Agni wondered if the stallion was as astonished as he was. He would have wagered that the beast was not as dizzily happy. Or perhaps he was. His ears flicked back and forth, but less uneasy than intense, focused, learning this new thing as he had learned all the others. He was not, Agni well knew by now, a mere mute beast. He thought about things. He learned. He liked learning. It was as if he had been shaped for it. And yet Agni did not think that he or any of his forebears had ever borne a man's weight on his back. He was the first.

He would not be compelled. Persuaded, asked politely, he gave with a glad heart. Force he met with force; he was strong, stronger than any man could be.

He was like nothing so much as the Mare and her kin. And that did not surprise Agni at all. Was not he, as much as they, the goddess' own?

✦ ✦

After those first grueling days, they settled to a greater ease. The stallion learned to be groomed; to be fed from the hand; to be bridled and saddled without fuss; and to heed the will of his rider in walk and trot, canter and gallop, turn, stop, bend and wheel and dance sidewise, little by little, briefly, day by day. And when he was sure of himself in the pen, he was let out in the larger valley. Bridled at first, ridden, under Agni's will. Then free among the mares, and it was with beating heart that, after he had set the stallion loose, Agni went to fetch him to be ridden. He shied, but when Agni called he came, set his nose in Agni's hand and took up the piece of honeycomb from the palm, and let himself be haltered and groomed, bridled and saddled and ridden.

And after a handful of days in which he was so tractable, Agni knew. At last it was time. And none too soon, either. It was summer still, and hotter than ever, but the trees that were left had begun to the show the first glimmerings of red and gold. The nights though mild began to have the whisper of a chill near morning. And the stars were shifting, were wheeling from summer into autumn.

It was time, perhaps past time. On the night of the new moon Agni knew that he must go. He ate and rested for the last time in that camp. The horses, who had now to seek grazing far up the valley, on some whim had come down to watch him, all four, mares and stallion. Under their calm regard he finished his supper.

He looked up from the last of it to find the stallion standing over him. The stars were out, though the west was rimmed still with light. He looked into that calm dark eye, that somehow had lost none of its pride even as it submitted to his will, and saw in it what he had not consciously been looking for.

"Mitani," he said. And that was a name in the language of the Mare's people, that his sister had taught him when they were small, to give them a secret tongue to share between the two of them. *Goddess-blessed*, it meant, and *Son of the New Moon;* for the Mare's people had said many things in few words.

"Mitani," he said again. The stallion's ears pricked as if he recognized the name. Agni lifted his hand. The stallion lowered his nose into it and blew softly. "Mitani," Agni said, sealing it, binding it to the one who owned it.

42

In the time between the new moon and the full moon of autumn, Agni rode into the outer camp of the White Horse people. This was like nothing so much as the young stallions' herd from which he had won his Mitani. Here the young men had come leading or riding their stallions. The first who had come there had found a camp set up for them by the boys who, next year and the year after, would seek their own stallions. These had raised tents and built a campfire in the place where it had been from time out of mind, in the shallow grassy bowl near a stream that ran yearlong. A hill watched over it, crowned by a cairn of stones. An old king was buried there, or a god. He was said to guard the place, and to look after the new-made men who camped there waiting for the night of the full moon, when they would ride back together to the tribe.

Agni was one of the last to come. He rode in as he had dreamed of doing, as he had seen his elders do for the past pair of autumns, riding his stallion and leading his mares. It might be more glorious to show himself so before the whole of the tribe, but it was wonderfully sweet to hear the whoops and cheers of his agemates; to see how they came running or galloping, the latter mounted on their own stallions. Rahim had a fine bay, and Patir a spotted colt, and little Chukri had won himself a great tall heavy-bodied creature with a mild eye and an extraordinary set of stones, as big as a man's head and seeming as weighty, too.

None was as fine as Mitani, nor did any bear the new moon on his brow. Agni held himself the taller for that, and let the horse dance a little, flagging his tail and calling challenge to all these strange new stallions. *My* mares! he cried. *My* world!

Agni laughed for the joy of it. There was a place for his horses among the lines, and a strong pen for the stallion, to keep him apart from the others; for stallions would fight if they could, and not every one of them was as well won to his master's will as was Mitani. Mitani was not glad to see his prison, but he endured it. He had his mares, though none of them would permit him any liberties—they were all in foal, Agni had reason to suspect. He was reasonably content.

Agni was still smiling as his friends and kinsmen showed him the tent that had been pitched for him, with the signs of his family painted on it, and gifts within: furs to sleep in, honey mead to drink, fine new clothes and ornaments to make him beautiful, and everything that was fitting for a prince returned to his people. There was even a servant for him: a shy and tongue-tied youth whom he last recalled as a plump-faced infant with his thumb perpetually in his mouth. The infant had grown into a gangling colt of a boy, with a patchy growth of new beard, who had outgrown his thumb and taken to biting his nails instead.

The drums were beating, the dance begun. A brace of fat red deer roasted over the central fire. While the meat sizzled and the fat streamed off it and the scent of it wreathed the camp, the young men danced in an exuberant skein, out and around and inabout. So they would dance when they returned to the tribe; but this was freer, and noisier too. They succeeded, with a whoop and a roar, in circling the fire just as the deer were done. Each dropped down where he stood, sweating and grinning, and the boys brought the makings of a feast.

Agni half sat, half lay on the sunset side of the circle, warm with the dance and the welcome. Someone passed him a horn of mead. It was strong and fiery-sweet. Rahim on his right hand and Patir on his left dropped arms about his neck and shared the horn.

Nevertheless, amid all this brightness, he had to know. He had counted the number of those who were here. "Sekhar? Dushiri? Natan?" he asked.

Rahim drank deep from the horn and did not answer. Patir leaned against Agni and sighed. "Sekhar died. The stallion he was trying for kicked him in the head. Dushiri's stallion broke out of the pen he'd made for it and couldn't be caught again. Natan nobody's seen or heard from."

"He may come back," Rahim said, emerging from the depths of the drinking horn.

"The gods willing," said Patir.

Agni granted that a few moments of silence. Sekhar had been a bit of a fool, but charming in it. Dushiri's luck—ill and worse than ill—struck him as if it had been a blow. Dushiri he had been fond of. Dushiri he had ridden with, hunted with, danced with in the festivals.

And now Dushiri was gone. He could not come back to the tribe. He had failed to win his stallion. To the people of the White Horse, and therefore to the man who would be their king, he was as dead as Sekhar.

Everyone knew what happened to young men who failed to win a stallion. No tribe would receive them. They went away. They died alone.

He shivered, though the sun was still in the sky, and the air was mild. He too could have failed. His stallion could have hurt or maimed him. His pen could have broken. Anything at all could have happened, if the gods had willed it.

Yet they had not. He sat here between his two dear friends, because the gods had chosen to favor them all. Two of ten—three perhaps—was not as ill an omen as it seemed. The gods exacted a price for every gift they gave. For this one, for the joy of the man who had found his stallion, they took their share; took some of the young men in sacrifice.

It was a hard thing, but so was the world. A man learned this young, or he never learned it at all. Agni would grieve for the dead and remember them as they had been, but they were gone. No word or act of his could bring them back.

He plucked the horn from Rahim's hand, and found it still half-full of mead. He drank the lot of it, though it dizzied his head and cloyed in his throat. In the warm sweet haze he fell to the rest of the feast.

✦ ✦

Natan did not come back. The moon waxed to the full. On the day when it
would rise round and white and whole from the eastern horizon, the new-
made men of the White Horse made ready to enter the tribe. They bathed
and groomed their stallions—with much uproariousness as some of the less
thoroughly tamed, objecting to indignity, flung their masters in the mud—
and made them beautiful with plaited manes and daubs of paint and fine new
caparisons. Then they did the same for themselves.

It was a noisy thing, yet there was a hush in the heart of it, a breathless
stillness. Agni plaited Rahim's thin pale hair in the many braids he insisted
on, while Patir plaited Agni's own ruddy mane into a single thick braid.
"You'll be the prettiest of us," Patir said without envy. He was pleasant
enough to look at, and knew it, but it had never mattered greatly to him that
others were handsomer than he.

Agni shrugged. "I hope I'll be the strongest," he said.

"You likely will," said Patir. He tied off the braid with a bit of leather.
"But I wager I'll be married first."

Agni snorted. "That's no wager. Everybody knows your father agreed
with Korosh that you'd have one of his daughters once you won your stallion.
You'll even get to choose which one."

Agni glanced over his shoulder in time to see Patir's face flush crimson.
But he mustered a proper portion of bravado. "Maybe I'll choose them all."

"What, all six? Even the baby?" Rahim twitched out of Agni's grip.
"Here now, if you're going to talk instead of do something useful, at least
let me finish before the night's over."

Agni pulled him down again and went back to work. "Though why you
want to look like a blooming daisy I don't know," he muttered. And after a
pause in which Rahim steadfastly refused to speak, he said to Patir, "Don't
take the prettiest one. Take the one who meets your eye when you look at
her."

"What if that is the prettiest one?" Patir inquired.

"Then you're fortunate," said Agni.

"And you would know," Patir said.

Agni held himself still. Made himself say lightly, "What would I know?
I'm not promised from birth to one or all of Korosh's daughters."

"No, but you're no innocent in the ways of women, either," said Patir
with an arch of brow that made Agni want to slap his head off his shoulders.

"I heard on the wind," said Rahim, "that there's one in the White Horse
camp who'll be looking for you to come back."

"Or maybe she's in Red Deer tribe," said Agni through the humming
in his ears, "or Dun Cow, or—"

"Maybe," said Patir.

There they left it, nor did Agni detect any veiled glances. And yet his
heart would not stop its hammering.

It had been a perfect secret, what he did with his brother's wife. No one
had ever seen his coming or her going. There had been no rumor, and no
betrayal. She would not do it. No more had Agni.

How then?

Not at all, he answered himself. Young men liked to talk. Women were an endless preoccupation. Patir was chaffing, that was all; plying Agni with mockery.

Agni determined to be comforted. He was in no danger. Not now; not ever, if the gods were kind. And when he was back among the tribe, when he was truly a man and accepted among the priests, and certain to be king when at last his father went among the gods, then he would make a law for himself. He would take the woman who was meant for him, who made his body sing.

It was an oath of sorts, that he swore to himself. He would have Rudira. He burned to think of her.

Tonight he would walk among the tribe. And maybe, if the rites allowed—or if not, then tomorrow—he would see her again.

He leaped up, scattering his friends. "Come! Why are we dallying? We've a ride ahead of us."

✦ ✦

It was not so far, but not so near, either; nigh half a day, and a struggle in the wind and on horseback, to preserve one's beauty for the tribe. They paused just over the last hill to restore their paint and their plaits, and to brush the dust from their horses' coats.

Then at last they rode up over the crest, paused there to be seen, and galloped whooping down on the camp.

The camp was waiting for them. The men in their finery, mounted on their own stallions; women thick-shrouded in veils but allowed for this instance to see their young kin come home; children leaping, running, galloping on their ponies, dogs barking, cattle lowing, and from the herds the calls of stallions at the scent and sound and sight of strangers.

Agni found himself at the head of the riding, borne along on the back of his red stallion. People stared and pointed. He heard Horse Goddess' name, and the name of the moon, and words of wonder and envy. "Of course *he* would bring home such a horse," they said.

He laughed at that, because after all he was a prince. Mitani danced and tossed his head and shrilled deafeningly at all the horses. *I am king!* he cried. *I, and no other!*

✦ ✦

The king of the White Horse people waited for his son in the camp's center, sitting on the royal horsehide that was—Agni saw with vivid clarity—the precise color of Mitani's coat. He looked no older, if no younger, than he had when Agni left. The thing that Agni had dreaded, that the man on the horsehide would be another, and worst of all his brother Yama, had proved unfounded. His father was still king. He was still, as far as Agni could see, both strong and in possession of his wits.

He rose to welcome his son, held out his strong thin arms. Agni sprang from Mitani's back into that embrace. It was fierce; it squeezed the breath from him. And yet he laughed, no more than a gasp. "Father," he said.

"My son," said the king. He let Agni go. His eyes had moved past his son to the stallion who waited with well-schooled patience. "You did well," he said.

"Horse Goddess was kind," said Agni.

"She does love her children," the king said. He held Agni at arm's length, peering into his face. Whatever he saw there seemed to content him. He nodded and said, "Come now to the dancing. And when that's done, and the gods' rites too, we'll speak together, you and I."

Agni bent his head. It was only proper, but he meant it. He was glad to see the old man again—gladder than he had imagined he could be. He wanted to be king, oh yes. But not yet. Not for a long while yet.

+ +

They danced the sun out of the sky and sang the moon into it, deep voices of men and beating of drums and the trumpeting of stallions. Each young man was presented to the tribe, given all his names and the names of his forefathers, and honored for the victory that he had won, the stallion who would be his mount hereafter.

Agni had yet to see his brother Yama, though others of his brothers were much in evidence. Some even seemed glad to see him, and pleased that he had won such a prince of horses. Some of the new-won stallions grew fractious as the rite wore on, but Mitani stood still, head up, as a king should do; watching it all with calm interest, his only infraction an occasional call to the mares. *His* mares were safe among the rest by now, and well he knew it, as horses know.

Agni's heart was full. It was all as he had dreamed it since he was old enough to know how a man became a man. The moon shining down. The fire leaping up. The faces of the people, fixed on him, and his father intoning the names that he had been given and the names from which he sprang, back to the morning of the world. And beside him, warm and breathing and utterly alive, his stallion whom the gods had meant for him.

He was man among the men of the tribe. In the morning he could enter the circle about the king, and sit where a young man sat, and be a part of the counsels of the people. He could present himself for one of the priesthoods. He could be the leader of a warband. He could, and before too long should, take a wife. All for the winning of a stallion, and for standing before the people to be confirmed in his name and his place, and made a part of them till death should take him.

.... 43 ....

The night wore away in dancing and feasting, in singing and in laughter. Agni sat at his father's side, when he was not dancing among the men. The king was stronger and more hale to look at than he had been since Agni could remember. He looked almost young again. He even danced the Stallion

Dance with the rest of the men, whirling and stamping and shouting, shaking his long white mane and laughing, light as a boy.

Some of the new-made men were gone long before the sun rose, Agni could well imagine where. But although many a pair of eyes smiled at him over a veil, none was the color of water, below a brow as white as bone. Rudira was not among the women. He searched for her as best he could with so many eyes on him, so many people watching. Neither she nor Yama was anywhere to be seen.

No one spoke of Yama as absent. Agni saw his tent in the rounds of the dance, set where it always was, somewhat west of the king's. And yet he had not shown his face at this great rite, nor had his wife slipped away to see if her lover had returned.

That was the only stain on Agni's joy, that she could not see it. But she would know. How could she not?

Though if Rudira and Yama were in that tent together . . .

He shut away the thought. Tonight should be only splendid. He danced it into the dawn, and saw the sunrise from the king's side, leaning drunkenly on his friend Rahim. Patir, it seemed, had chosen one of Korosh's daughters after all; or had chosen to forget that he was promised to one of them, and let himself be lured away by a woman of another kindred.

It did not matter, Agni told himself. He was happy. He was back among his kin; and he would be king.

※ ※

After all the dancing and feasting, drinking and laughter, the light of day was harsh and bitterly bright. The tribe's new-made men were allowed that day's indulgence. Thereafter they had places to fill, as sons, brothers, husbands; as hunters and warriors for the tribe.

Today they could lie about, drink *kumiss,* and tell the tales of their stallion-hunts, each vying to outdo the last. Agni saw Yama after all, strutting among the men of his own age as if he had been among them all the while, taking no apparent notice of the brother who had come back with a prince of stallions. Yama was no lovelier than ever, and no more gracious. He had managed to keep about him a surprising number of men, and not all younger sons or weaklings, either. Too many reckoned his bulk authority, and listened to his bluster and called it sense.

Agni suffered no great anxiety in taking the count of Yama's following. He had expected it—had known that people would follow Yama while Agni was away. But while the king was strong, Agni's strength could only increase again; and when at last and at length the king was gone, Agni would stand higher than he had before.

Not that he intended to wait passively for people to come back. When the morning was well advanced and his head had recovered sufficiently from the effects of his night's indulgence, he sought the horselines. He found Mitani with what might have been dismaying ease, by the sound of a stallion's challenge.

The war had not yet begun. Mitani was penned alone as each of the new stallions was, but someone—by accident or intent—had failed to fasten the gate securely. Mitani had broken out and gone in search of his mares. And when he had found them, he found another stallion about to claim them.

Agni suppressed a groan. Of course it would be Yama's horse—not the yearling he had brought back from his own summer's hunt, but the one who had succeeded that one; a heavy-boned creature very like its master, and known to be of uncertain temperament. Mitani beside him seemed slender and gangling-tall, and somewhat awkward in his youth. But not weak. No, never that. Even as Agni came running, he lunged for his rival's throat.

There were people about, but no one was bold enough to come between warring stallions. Agni, who should have known better, could only think of death and maiming, of his beautiful gift of the gods torn and bleeding on the morning after he came to the tribe. With no thought but that, he bided his moment; and when the stallions in their battling came round to where he stood, he launched himself toward Mitani's back.

Mitani barely noticed. The stallions had drawn apart, circling, necks snaking, bracing for a new and deadlier lunge. The first had dealt no more than bruises. This one would draw blood.

Agni slipped the belt from about his middle and held it by one end, letting it fall along his thigh, balancing on Mitani's back. The bunching of muscles brought him to the alert.

Yama's stallion sprang first. Agni tightened his grip on sides and mane, whirled the belt up and round, and caught the charging stallion full across his tender nose. He recoiled, staggering, half-falling. Agni kicked Mitani about, utterly against the stallion's will—but his training held; thank the gods, he had not forgotten. He wheeled, snorting and snapping at Agni's leg, but obedient in his fashion.

It did not last long; but it lasted long enough. When he spun back, his rival was gone. Fled; which, had the beast been a man, he would have declared loudly, to be only prudence.

Mitani trumpeted his victory. Once Agni had been so kind as to slip from his back, he circled his mares as a proper stallion should, and herded them apart, and kept them so. No stallion challenged him, even the king. The mares were, after all, his daughters.

"He'll be king when the old one goes," someone opined. Agni did not see who it was, and it was not to his advantage to crane and peer. He had to pretend that he had not heard. To walk away with a light step, as if he had no doubts of himself or of anything else in the world.

After so long alone with no human creature about him, he felt strange, as if his skin had worn away; and now the close quarters of the tribe rubbed painfully on it. But he could not escape onto the steppe, not even to hunt; not so soon. People would take it ill. And that above all he must not permit.

He was convivial therefore. He walked through the camp. He visited friends. He was cordial to his kin. He found Patir in front of Korosh's tent with a pair of that man's sons, playing knucklebones. Patir looked as haggard as one might expect, but he grinned at Agni and tossed him the cup. "Win a round for me," he said.

Agni won one for him and another for himself, and took Patir away, not greatly to Patir's distress.

"Have you chosen a daughter yet?" Agni asked him.

He nodded, none too eagerly. "It's decided. I'm to have the eldest. She's not the prettiest, but she'll do."

"And does she have sense?"

"I can't tell," Patir said. "All I've seen of her is a pair of eyes above a veil. She never says a word."

"Then how do you know if she's pretty?"

"I asked my sisters," Patir said. He did his best not to look embarrassed.

"Ah," said Agni. "That was wise. And what did they say?"

"That the second eldest is beautiful but vapid, the third has a voice like an eagle shrieking, and the rest are too young to trouble with. But the eldest is good enough to look at, has a pleasant voice, and says she's ready to be a wife."

"Do you ever wonder," Agni mused, "if it's really the women who rule? We have to ask them everything, and when we choose wives, who else knows which one we should take?"

Patir shrugged. "It doesn't make a great deal of difference, does it? They're in the tents. We're outside. We don't have to go in unless it pleases us."

"Or unless we want to eat," Agni said, "or sleep, or wear clothes."

"We can do all of that ourselves," said Patir, "if we have to." He slanted a glance at Agni. "Are they talking wives for you, too?"

"Not yet," Agni said.

"They will," said Patir.

+ +

But not too soon, Agni thought. There had been talk, of course. There was always talk. This man's daughter or that, this one's niece, that one's granddaughter, would make a useful alliance for the king's son. No one ever spoke of beauty or of wit, or of the gift of driving a man wild.

Evening came none too soon. Agni took his daymeal with others of the new-made men, in a circle round a fire tended by Rahim's mother. She was a widow and therefore permitted to walk abroad, though she must cover her face. It was said she had been a great beauty in her day; and there were men, elders, who would have been glad to relieve her of her widowhood. But she never saw fit to accept them, and her male kin were not so bold as to compel her. She kept her own tent therefore, and looked after her daughters and her only son, and was adept at feeding hungry young men.

Everyone knew that if Rahim married, it would be outside of the tribe. His mother had long since discarded every girl in it as unworthy.

He was in comfort. Agni and the rest, waited on by Rahim's veiled and studiously demure sisters, were wondrously aware of their new manhood.

They could command and be obeyed. They could meet a girl's eyes—even if she were only Rahim's sister—and not look away, though it was as much as any's life was worth to venture more.

Agni slipped away as the night grew dark, when the mead had gone round enough to blur the keenest-sighted. He had only pretended to drink, taking a sip to warm him, no more. In the full dark he made himself a shadow, ghosting round to the tent that stood to the west of his father's.

+ +

No fire burned in front of it, but the horsetail hung limply from its peak, signifying that its master was in the camp. Agni had seen Yama earlier, sitting in a place of honor at a campfire tended by a minor clansman with a great number of brothers and cousins. All of them that Agni could see had been waiting eagerly on him.

When Agni looked for him, peering out of the shadows, he was still there. He looked well advanced in *kumiss*, and well settled in his place. He would stay there nightlong, as a man might do if he chose. Some of the new-made men had professed their intention of doing just that round Rahim's fire, because they could; because they were no longer expected to go obediently to bed in their fathers' tents.

Agni had been asking no leave but Rudira's for a long while now. Tonight he did not mean to ask it. He did not expect that he would need to.

He knew well where she slept in Yama's tent, which was nigh as large as the king's—larger in fact than it should be, as young as Yama was, and as little respected for his skill in the hunt or in war. It was like Yama, like Yama's stallion: oversized, overbearing, and hollow at the heart.

The slit in the tent's wall that Agni had made some seasons since was still there, unmended, and it seemed undiscovered. He listened outside of it as he had many a time before. The camp's sounds separated themselves, near and far, from the barking of a dog to the laughter of a woman to the lowing of a bull. But within he heard nothing, till he was ready to stoop and slip beneath the wall.

Then he heard voices, too low almost to perceive. His breath caught, but they were women's voices, and low only because they were somewhat distant. One was Rudira's. The other, it came to him after a while, belonged to Yama's mother.

Without thinking, he slipped into the scented darkness of the corner that Rudira had claimed for her own. Its walls of leather were lowered and tied, but he could see a glimmer of light through the joining. He made his way toward it, moving cautiously, without sound.

Rudira sat with Yama's mother in the common space of the women's side. Lamps were lit. The remains of a small feast lay between them. A small girlchild curled half in and half out of the lamps' light, sound asleep. She had been waiting on them earlier, perhaps.

They sat together and apparently at ease, but there was a tension in the air, such as Agni had seen between two men in war, or two stallions at battle over a mare. Their conversation had a desultory air: small things, this woman bearing, that child ill of a fever, this pair to marry and that pair at odds, and such gossip as women might be expected to exchange of an evening.

He lay beside the curtain, breathing as lightly as he could, and listened. He should never have been here, never have lingered, but there was a peculiar comfort in it, a strange kind of contentment, just to see her face, her hair silver in the lamplight, the clear line of her profile. Next to that heavyset old woman she was like a fall of bright water down the face of a crag.

Agni at first was hardly aware that the current of conversation had shifted. Its tone was much the same, idle, casual, but the words were no longer quite so harmless. "When my son is king," the old woman said, "mind you well that you do as I tell you."

Rudira arched a brow. This was no new thing to her, it was clear. "Are you so certain that he will be?"

"He will be," said the old woman.

"There are a fair few who would contest that," Rudira said.

"Ah," said Yama's mother with a gesture of dismissal. "They may talk. My son will take the king's place when the old one dies."

"He'll have to fight for it."

"Not if you do your part," the old woman said.

"What if I won't?"

"You will." Yama's mother said it with calm certainty.

The old woman left soon thereafter. Rudira sat for a while alone, narrow-eyed, contemplating the space in front of her. The tent was quiet. The other wives, if they were there, were asleep or silent behind their curtains. There were no babies, no children. The gods had not yet so blessed the lord of this tent.

Rudira sighed and rose. She stretched. Her body arched in the light gown that a woman might wear in the women's place, letting slip the shawl that had warmed her shoulders. She ran hands down over her breasts and hips, and smiled, and danced a step or two, a little dance of delight in who knew what. Perhaps no more than her own beauty.

She turned in that light-and-shadowed space, shaking her hair out of its plait till it poured like water down her back and shoulders. With a wicked glint then she wriggled out of her gown. She was naked beneath it, full white breasts, sweet rounded belly, silver tangle of her sex. Her nipples were erect, as long and large as the end of her smallest finger. She stroked them, circling them idly, smiling at some vision that only she could see.

Agni could hardly breathe. His rod was rigid, aching—remembering too keenly how long it had been since last he had a woman. *This* woman, the night before he left the tribe to hunt his stallion. Outside of dreams he had touched none since.

She danced, fancying herself alone; stroking her belly, her thighs. Slipping fingers through the curling hair that grew there, stroking herself, eyes closed, head falling back, and such a smile on her face as he knew well indeed.

The sight of her, the remembered scent, the heat of her body reflected in his, burned all thought, doubts, fears, clean out of his head. There was only she. She, and none other.

He slipped the knot of the curtain and stepped into the room where no man but the lord of the tent should ever go. It was a dizzying thing, a mad thing, and he did not care at all.

She was oblivious to him. He moved softly, slipped arms about her, kissed her ear, her neck, her shoulder. She did not flinch or stiffen. She melted into his clasp, purring in her throat.

It was he who tensed, who half pulled away. "Were you expecting some-one?"

She turned in his arms, supple, laughing softly. "Oh yes," she said. "You."

"You—" He growled at her. "You knew I was here!"

She smiled and would not answer.

"Witch," he said.

"Hush," she said, and made a sign to ward off evil. "Don't say such things."

"Then how did you know?"

"I know you," she said. She slipped the clasp of his belt and freed his rod, that felt as great as a stallion's; and pinned it between them, dancing a slow dance of hip and thigh, till he must drown himself in a kiss or groan aloud. Here, where Yama could come, or any of his wives or servants, any woman of the tribe, and see them so.

There was a wild delight in it, an edge of terror that made it so much the sweeter. She mounted him where he stood, locked legs about his middle, rode him with urgency as desperate as if she, and not he, had known no pleasure of the body since the stallion-hunt began.

Some distant part of him laughed at that. She would never have been without that pleasure, whether she took it from her husband or from her husband's brother. Or—who knew? Perhaps some other eager lover had crept through the slit in the tent-wall.

Then there was no thought in him at all. Only the heat of her body and the fierce female scent of her, and the surety. Here, with her, at last he had come home.

·············· 44 ··············

Agni went back late and in secret to his bed in his father's tent. He left Rudira all warm and purring in her sleeping furs—nor did he leave her willingly. But the night was passing, and he could not be caught in her bed. Not for her sake. Not for his own.

He had thought that he would fall direct into sleep, all his limbs and body loosed by the pleasure that they had shared. And yet he lay awake. This tent was noisier by far than Yama's. There were babies in it, and children; his brothers and his sisters, and their mothers, and the king himself with the woman whom he had chosen to keep him warm in the night. It was easier to come and go unnoticed, but harder to sleep once he had come back.

And he had, after all, remembered the words that Yama's mother spoke to Rudira. Something that Rudira must do, that would assure that Yama became king.

What, betray Agni? But if she did that, she betrayed herself; and for that she would die.

She was the white fire in his soul, the woman to his man, but he was not blind to the truth of her. She had no honor. No woman did, except perhaps Sarama. Honor was for men. For women there was only the body's urgency, and their own pleasure.

Rudira would do whatever it best pleased her to do; and she was not of the White Horse people. She had no loyalty to their king. To her husband, it seemed, she had some little semblance of it, enough at least to conspire with his mother to make him king.

And Agni had meant to remonstrate, to remind her that he would be king, and not her husband; and when he was king, he would find a way to claim her. But she had reft him of thought or sense, blinded and dizzied him with her body.

There was time yet. The king was strong, and the tribe prospered. When he died or was taken into the circle of the sacrifice, then the brothers would contest for the mastery. Agni would win it. He was the chosen one, the heir. The people would speak for him.

✦ ✦

Agni never did ask Rudira what she had been plotting with Yama's mother. She was endlessly, burningly hungry for him. On nights when he could not go to her, when some rite or gathering of the men kept him away, he might come late to his bed to find her scent in it, or a strand of her hair, or something that told him she had been there.

She never came when he could come to her. When he remonstrated with her, called her mad, bade her remember the price of such things, she would not listen. "I needed you," she would say. And that was all.

Her husband did not take her to his bed, that Agni knew of. She must be finding ways to put him off, for surely Yama would not be able to resist her. She would never say. That was a woman's secret, as was so much else that passed within the tents.

Winter closed in, hard and cold. They danced the death-dance at autumn's ending, called the spirits of the dead to be fed and warmed and feted, and laid them to rest again in the stone barrows of the people. At the dark of the year they sacrificed the black goat and the spotted bull, but no stallion; not that creature of wind and sun and the bright morning of the year.

Agni was made a priest that winter, of Skyfather and of the lords of horses. What he did in the rites of his priestmaking, what visions he saw, what words the gods spoke, he told to no one. In the spring he would wear the Stallion mask and perform in the sacrifice; would speak the words that had come down from the dawn time, and dance the steps that were as old as human memory.

So preoccupied, between his nights with Rudira and his days of learning to be a man and a priest, he saw little of his father, and thought less of it.

One day of wind and snow, when the dark of the year was past but the spring was far away, he braved the knives of wind and snow to cross the camp from the priests' tent to his father's. He had no thought but of warm mead and dry clothes, and aunts and cousins fussing over him, and a little rest of the spirit.

The priests' tent was the domain of men, crowded with the instruments of their calling, cluttered and indifferently clean. One never dared sit unless one looked first; there might be a bleached skull there, or a bundle of herbs, or the makings of a mask for the spring festivals. They ate, there, when someone remembered to cook, which was not unduly often. They kept no order that Agni could discern.

His father's tent was a haven: warm, full of light and the scents of cooking, the chatter of women and children, smiles and open arms and willing welcome. The brothers who were his rivals, the wives who schemed for their sons, would not trouble him under the king's eye. They all preserved a kind of determined amity.

That day he went in search of it. He had finished his mask for the sacrifice and laid it with those other, older masks, that priests had made in years before him. He was tired. His back ached. He was chilled to the bone. He had no thought but of the pot that hung over the fire, full of whatever the hunters had brought back the day before, and of warmed mead and warm feet, and sleep without dreams.

He found the pot and the fire in the small tent that the women put up when the wind blew high and the snow flew fast, and meat and herbs and a few savories therein. But in the tent was a heavy stillness.

He struggled to get some sense out of the brothers nearest the door, but they were babbling. The eldest of the aunts, dour Taditi, overran them with little pretense of humility. "The king fell," she said.

Agni thrust through crowding, useless people. They were all either standing and staring or standing and sniveling. No one seemed possessed of wits enough to move.

The king had fallen indeed. He had been eating his dinner, Agni saw, when the fit had taken him. Bowls were scattered, a jar of mead spilled, darkening the royal horsehide with its sticky wetness. The king lay in the middle of it.

He was still alive. His eyes burned in a face that had twisted horribly, as if some god had turned it to clay and pulled it awry. Half of it was as it had always been. The other was all melted and misshapen.

And not one of the people crowding about him had even thought to lift him out of the puddle of mead. Agni hissed in anger, bent and raised him, grunting with the effort: for he was a big man, and heavy, a dead weight. But Agni was strong enough to carry him out of the common space and into the king's own place.

People tried to follow. He heard Taditi's voice raised, piercing as a hawk's cry, driving back all but the most determined. Even those hesitated somewhat, so that Agni had time to lay his father on the bed of hides and furs, to arrange the lifeless body, and straighten as best he could the right arm, that had twisted tight and would not let go.

And all the while he did that, his father watched him, hot-eyed, furious at this thing that had struck him down. Agni could think of no words to say that would comfort him. He settled for making his father's body as comfortable as it might be, for cleaning it—for he had soiled himself, worst of humiliations, as if he had been a helpless infant—and dressing it afresh, and covering it with a clean coverlet.

He had help in the last of it, Taditi as fierce-eyed as the king and as silent as Agni, and one or two of the younger wives with their veils forgotten. And, when he was nearly done, Yama's mother, eldest of the wives, thrusting the other women aside to finish covering her husband's body. Agni she either did not deign or did not dare to touch, but neither did she look on him with any welcome. "I'll look after him now," she said. "You can go."

"I don't think so," said Agni. He sat beside his father, seeing full well that she had been about to take that place, and smiled at the woman whom he should, he supposed, think of as his enemy. When he spoke again, it was to Taditi. "Someone should make sure that all my brothers know, and the elders, too—but my brothers first."

"He may not die," Taditi said, not as if she contradicted him; simply as if she thought that he should know. "People can live years, sometimes, and even recover from such strokes of the gods' hand."

"To be sure," said Agni, though in his heart he did not believe that his father would live long, or come back again from the edge of death's country. But in front of those who watched and listened, in particular Yama's mother, he would pretend that he did believe. For his father's sake he could do no other.

To Taditi he said, "Nevertheless, my brothers must know."

She inclined her head, turned and went to do as he had not quite bidden her. One did not command Taditi. She was like a man in that, and a man who was a king.

She was his father's eldest sister, who had married long ago, but her husband had died. She had come back to her father's tent, which after a while became her brother's, and kept order in it even above his wives. She did not put herself forward, and there were many who did not know what she did or how she ruled in this tent, but Agni knew. She had brought him up when his mother died and his sister was taken away, raised him and taught him what she knew, what she judged fit for a manchild to know.

She would see that his brothers were told, and that the news was spread slowly, lest the tribe forget itself and begin to wail that its king was dead.

Not yet. He could not move or speak, but his eyes were alive. He knew where he was, and who bent over him. From the glitter in his glance, he understood the words that people spoke, too: perhaps more than any of them knew or wanted him to know.

Agni remained beside him. He did not demand it with his glance, but neither did he forbid it. Agni preferred to think that he wanted it, that he was glad of his son's presence.

The brothers began to come in ones and twos and threes. And, inevitably, Yama came. He shouldered aside the rest, thrust his way to the front, stood glowering down at Agni. "What did you do to him?" he demanded.

Agni took time for a slow breath. Now was not the moment to leap up and challenge this idiot. When he answered, he answered softly, with as much courtesy as he could muster. "Our father fell," he said, "to a stroke of the gods' hand."

"And what did you say that caused it?"

Agni gritted his teeth. "I was among the priests, performing my duties to the gods. I arrived just after he fell."

Yama grunted. "So you say." He lowered himself to one knee and bent, peering at the stricken man. "Is he awake? Can he hear us?"

Agni had long since concluded that a man could not study to be as dense as Yama was. It was a gift, a jest of the gods. Any fool could see the fury in those eyes: the one that opened wide, fixed on Yama's face, and the one that sagged as if the bone that housed it had melted with the rest.

"He is awake," Agni said levelly. "I believe that he can hear us. I pray that he will recover. Will you do as much, son of my father?"

Yama shook a fist in a face. "You watch your tongue, puppy. If you had anything to do with this, as the gods are my witness—"

"I had nothing to do with this," Agni said. "Will you come to blows over the body of a man not yet dead? Do please try to have a little respect."

Yama would have struck him then, if Taditi had not stepped between them. "Enough," she said in her harsh old woman's voice. "You may quarrel all you like, and bring the tribes down about you—but not here."

Yama drew back growling. Agni remained where he was. He permitted himself the flicker of a smile, before he turned back to the king. "Father," he said. "Shall I send these people away?"

The rage in that eye altered a little, enough perhaps for an answer. Agni sighed. "Very well. But when you begin to tire, I *will* send them out."

It was unbearably difficult to sit there, to see how his brothers alternately wept and blustered; how the best of them sat mute, and the worst babbled much as Yama had, seeking for someone to blame.

"There's no one to blame but the gods," Agni said to that, cutting across the currents of conversation.

"But someone might have—" one of the younger brothers began. He had always been Yama's echo. Agni could hardly expect him to be different now.

One of the others stopped him. "Someone didn't. I feel the gods' hand in this, and the hand of time. It grieves me—but it is what is."

Those with sense murmured agreement. Those without snarled at it. Yama dropped down at the king's side opposite Agni, and made it clear that he intended to stay there—to prevent Agni from doing whatever fancied harm Agni might do.

Very well, Agni thought. Let him amuse himself. The women had hidden when the young men came in, and so many of them, too; all but Taditi. It was she who called forth some few of them and bade them fetch food and drink for their sons and brothers. Some ate, drank, and left. Too many lingered.

And more came: the kin, the elders, men of the tribe hearing word of the king's fall, come to see him in his infirmity.

Such a thing should never have happened. People said it none too quietly as they came and went, and the king lay helpless, mute, powerless to speak in his own defense. If he had gone to the knife as some had urged him, if he had allowed himself to be sacrificed while he still had somewhat of his youthful strength, this ignominy would never have befallen him.

"It's a bad omen for the tribe," the elders muttered among themselves. "A king smitten down in the black heart of winter, and not to death but to a kind of death-in-life. It bodes ill for the time ahead of us."

Worse omen, Agni thought, to speak of it, to wake terror in hearts already much afraid. And none of them, not one, had the least care for the man who lay trapped in the prison of his body. Only for the king, and for what his fall would mean to the tribe.

Agni took the gaunt cold hand in his, the one that perhaps could still feel, and warmed it as best he could. "Father," he said, "fight this. Be strong. Your people have need of you."

And well he knew it, too, Agni saw in his eyes. He could do nothing. Not one thing. The gods had seen to that.

·············· 45 ··············

The king did not die that night, or any of the nights thereafter. He clung to life though it must be a bitter burden, speechless, helpless, half of him withering away even as his people watched. Agni never left his side; and not only because it so evidently galled his brother Yama. If the king died, he wanted to be there. If the king lived, he wanted to be part of the cause of it.

He did what he could. He rubbed life into motionless limbs. He lifted that dead weight and banked it in folded hides so that it could receive guests. He prayed with a fierce intensity, storming the gods in their ancient fastnesses, demanding that they listen. "We need him. We can't lose him. Give him back to us!"

They would not answer. Gods never would, in Agni's experience. Unless they were Horse Goddess; and she was no kin of theirs, nor friend either.

✢ ✢

Of a bitterly cold night, when by some trick of fate there was none but Agni to keep vigil over his father—Agni and Taditi, who had fallen asleep where she sat—a shadow slipped through the shadows of the tent and wafted sweetness over him. He gasped and nearly cried out, but a white hand silenced him. Rudira wrapped arms about him and clung, shivering with cold or perhaps with fear.

Without his willing it, his arms closed the embrace. She stroked herself against him. She was wrapped in leather and furs, he in coat and warm mantle, for even here the air was chill; and yet he felt the heat of her flesh as if they had both been naked.

"I missed you," she breathed in his ear. "Oh, gods, I missed you."

With a mighty effort he gathered himself together, got a grip on her arms, and thrust her away. "No," he said, fierce and low. "We can't do this. Not here!"

"Why not here?" she demanded, and none too softly either. "Who's to see? Who'll care?"

"Everyone!" Agni stepped back out of her reach, though she could easily have leaped into his arms. "Now go, before someone catches you. You can't be found here."

"Nobody's coming," she said. "*He* is busy with Indra. Fat cow. He loves her because she worships the ground he spits on."

"Father can hear you," Agni said.

"He cannot," said Rudira without a glance at the still form under its coverlet. "Soon he will not. They've decided it, you know. Since he won't go as he was supposed to, they'll see that he does it regardless."

Agni's back went stiff. "How? What will they do?"

She shrugged. "I don't know. Something in his potions. A knife under the ribs. Maybe even a sacrifice, if enough of the priests agree to it. They're all saying that it's past time; that he has to go, or the tribe will suffer."

"That's king-killing," Agni said.

"That's the law, they say."

"And how do you know this? Who has been talking?"

"My husband," she said, calm beside his intensity, as if it did not matter to her. And yet it must, if it had driven her to come here. "Some of his friends. A priest or two. A few of the elders. They meet in our tent, and they talk all day and into the night. They think it's time to make an end."

"The gods make an end," Agni said. "Men may only do so on the festivals that the gods have ordained. Not in their own time, of their own choosing. That is murder."

"They say it's not," said Rudira in her voice that was like a child's, breathy and light. "They say the gods are agreeing to it. And they say . . ." She paused as if the words were too much to utter, but in the end she spoke them. "They say that if you try to stop them, they'll do whatever they have to, to get you out of the way."

Agni was not surprised. Nor was he afraid. He had expected such a thing from the moment when he saw the king fallen. "If they kill me," he said, "the gods themselves will judge."

"I'll die if you die," she said. "You mustn't. Promise me you won't."

Agni dared not laugh, or he would offend her. "I'll do my best," he said.

She seemed to be satisfied. But she would not leave and have done. Short of carrying her out bodily and dropping her in the snow, he could not think what to do.

She slipped his guard, back into his arms again, searing him with kisses. Not for the first time—and that was not an easy thing to admit—he caught himself wishing that she had been a gentler creature. That she had not been such a white fire of a woman; so dangerous, and so irresistible.

Tonight, in this place, he could resist her. Though his father slept, or lay in a black dream that passed for sleep; though Taditi slept the sleep of the dead—nevertheless their presence gave Agni the strength to stand against her. He put her aside as gently as he could, but with immovable firmness. "Not here," he said, "and not now. Go. I'll come to you when I may. I promise."

Her face went hard and still. "You won't come," she said. "You're tired of me."

"I am not," said Agni, "and I won't quarrel here. Go, quickly, while it's still safe."

"If I go," she said, "I won't come back."

"You shouldn't," he said.

Her eyes were terrible, her rage as great perhaps as the king's; as if Agni had betrayed her as the king's body had betrayed him.

And yet he hardened his heart. For her sake he did it, even more than for his own. She could not be caught here, least of all in Agni's arms.

He saw how she willed him to relent. But he would not. She whirled in a passion of temper and ran, back the way she had come.

The air in her wake held a scent of thunder. Agni found that he had forgotten to breathe. He sucked in air till it dizzied him. His body was hot, but his rod was shrunken and cold, as if she had laid a curse on it.

Fear stabbed, that she truly had done such a thing. He thrust it away. She was in a temper, that was all, because he had never denied her before, never refused to give her what she wanted. She would wake to sense soon enough; would see that he had done it for her sake, and out of respect for the king's presence.

+ +

In the morning Patir came into the tent where Agni sat, where the king lay unchanging. He came every day, if only for a few moments, to sit with Agni and to share with him some of the gossip of the camp. He and Rahim and certain others of Agni's old friends were his eyes and ears in the tribe, and his voice too, in that they said the things he would have said if he could have left his father's side.

This morning Patir's expression, usually so cheerful, was somber. Nor did he chatter on as he most often did. He was silent, standing by the king's bed, looking down at him.

"Tell me," Agni said.

Patir hunched his shoulders as if they pained him, and relaxed them slowly. "They say he's dead," he said, "and rotting, but the cold preserves him. The cold, and his kin who won't admit that he's gone."

"My father is alive," Agni said. "Look at his eyes. He hears us. Father, listen to him! He's talking madness."

The king's eyes did not shift. They had dulled as the days passed, the rage diminished, the fierce edge blunted. There was life in them still, but it flickered low.

"It's being said," said Patir, "that it's time to end it. That there should be a second sacrifice to the Black Bull; that he should go in what dignity is left him, and not wither till there's no telling if he's alive or dead."

"Who says such a thing?" Agni demanded. "Who?"

"I think," said Patir, "that you should see and hear for yourself."

"You know I can't leave here," said Agni.

"I'll watch over him," Patir said.

Agni eyed him narrowly. This was the friend of his childhood, his year-mate, his kinsman. And he was mistrusting even this one; wondering if this was the plot, if he was to be betrayed and his father murdered for a few moments' folly.

Patir met his stare steadily, with clear-eyed innocence. Agni drew a breath, sharp enough to hurt. "Well enough then," he said. "Mind you don't move till I come back."

"Not a muscle," said Patir.

✦ ✦

Agni did not like to admit it, but when he left that space in which he had lived, eaten, slept for more days than he liked to count, he was glad. When he saw the sky again, he wanted to whirl in a wild dance.

But he did not. He walked calmly through a camp that was much as it always was. It was quieter, perhaps. Somber. Troubled by the illness of its king. But children still played, boys still galloped their ponies hither and yon, and men gathered in circles to play at knucklebones or to share a skin of *kumiss*, and to talk.

There was always talk. Talk was the sinew that knit the tribe. Chatter of this, chatter of that. Nothing to the purpose, this deep in the winter.

While the king was indisposed, the elders did what must be done, which was not much in this season. A dispute or two, perhaps; an exchange of gifts between families whose children would wed in the spring gathering.

It was all very peaceful. And yet, as Agni walked through the camp, his hackles began to rise. There were no daggers drawn, no voices raised. If there were factions, they were the same as always: the boys, the young men, the priests, the elders, Yama's pack of malcontents and Agni's friends and kin. Those last managed one way and another to join him as he walked, till there was a fair gathering of them.

That had not been Agni's intention. He could hardly hear secrets if he went escorted by a small army of men. Indeed he did hear words spoken, but of the prince and his pride, and the king's sickness, and other, lesser things.

Nevertheless from what he heard he gathered enough to understand why Patir had sent him out. This waiting time could not endure. Something must break, and soon.

But only the king could break it, by letting go or by rising from his sickness. Certain gatherings of people fell silent when Agni passed—a suspicious silence. He suspected that they had been speaking of this. That they contended among themselves that if the king would not die of his own accord, he should be sent to the gods by the will of the tribe.

Even the elders went suddenly still in Agni's presence. They sat in their circle, wrapped in their bearskins, and glowered at nothing in particular. Such was power, Agni thought: to impose silence on those incorrigible talkers.

He came as to a haven, to Rahim's father's tent. Rahim was tending the fire in front of it, and a pack of his brothers with him. They greeted Agni with loud delight. Rahim peered at him, searching his face; then nodded and sighed as if in relief. "Ah. It's you. I thought you'd turned into a woman, you've been shut up so long."

"*You* sent Patir," Agni said.

Rahim shrugged. "He sent himself. But maybe I allowed as how that wouldn't be an ill thing."

Agni squatted beside his friend. One of the brothers handed him a leg of wild goose, fresh-roasted and crackling with fat. Agni bit into it hungrily.

"What have they been feeding you?" Rahim asked him. "You look fair peaked."

"I haven't been hungry," Agni said between bites of goose.

"You should eat," said Rahim. "A man fights better if he's well fed."

"I heard," said Agni, "that it's the lean and hungry man who's more dangerous."

"Maybe he's crankier," said Rahim, "but he's weaker, too. Eat. Rakti, fetch him something to drink."

Agni gnawed the last of the meat off the bone, cracked it and sucked the marrow. When there was nothing left to glean from it, he tossed it to a waiting dog, and met Rahim's glance. "Now tell me. Where's the war?"

"Here," said Rahim.

Agni raised a brow. The others drew in closer, he noticed; maybe to listen, maybe to guard the circle. Maybe both. "Tell me," he said.

Rahim took his time about it. He waited for his brother to bring the skin of *kumiss* and the cup, to fill the cup, to hand it to Agni, who drank a sip of the fiery stuff and made as if to fling the rest in Rahim's face. Rahim grinned, not at all repentant. But when he spoke, he was as somber as he could ever be. "Word's passing round the camp. The elders are divided on it, but enough of them have agreed, that they're going to do it regardless of the rest. They're going to make another sacrifice in the dark of the moon. They'll kill the black bull. And they'll send the king to the gods on his back."

Agni nodded slowly. He was not surprised nor greatly shocked. "So. And it's three days to the dark of the moon. What if I forbid them?"

"You know well," Rahim said, "they'll laugh in your face. You may be the king's son, but you're not king yet. There are many who say you never will be. They're wanting an older man, and not a raw boy who's just won his stallion. Who, they say, has been standing in the way of the king's departure for the gods' country."

"And how am I doing that?"

"Who knows?" said Rahim. "Casting spells, maybe. Making bargains with the gods below."

Agni snorted. "I'm no sorcerer," he said, "and they're fools if they think so."

"They do recall," Rahim said, "that your mother was one of the Mare's people, and that your sister is the Mare's own servant. They think you may partake of some of that power—especially since you came back from the long hunt with a stallion of such quality, with Horse Goddess' mark on his forehead."

"And that," said Agni with a touch of temper, "should be all to the good. A king should stand above other men, and so should his horse."

"Surely," said Rahim, and the others nodded. "But some are saying that too strong or strange a stallion is maybe an ill thing."

"Yama," Agni said. He spat. "Surely; and he couldn't come home with anything better than a poor yearling, and that one dead lame in a year."

"People want to believe him," Rahim said. "It's the small spirits, the envious and the puny-minded—but there are an amazing number of them. Some are elders. It's only age that makes them elders, after all; not any kind of wisdom."

"Why, shame!" said Agni. "Age *is* wisdom."

"And we're all fools," Rahim said.

Agni prodded at the fire, stirring up a tongue of flame. "I think . . ." he said. "I think I should ask my father. Whether he wants to live; or whether he prefers to die."

"I think he'll want to die," Rahim said.

He said it a little gingerly, as if he expected Agni to rise up in rage. Agni watched the fire's dance. Diviners could see portents in the lick and leap of flames. He was no diviner. Still he could see beyond the fire to his father's face, that dreadful half-alive, half-melted thing. If it had been Agni . . . Agni would have preferred to die.

"I have to ask," he said. He stood. "I do have to ask."

Rahim nodded. "And when—if he finds a way to say yes?"

"Then that is his will," said Agni.

✦ ✦

Patir had not left the king's side since he sent Agni away. He greeted Agni calmly, but Agni thought he saw a faint, wild flicker in Patir's eyes: more than a hint of gladness to be freed from the duty he had taken on himself.

He did not leave at once—did not flee. He lingered, and Rahim who had followed Agni back to the king's tent, and a handful of the others. Their eyes were on Agni.

Agni knelt by his father's bed. It was only, he told himself, that he had been away; that he had looked on other, untwisted faces. The king was no more frail, if no less.

And yet the shadow on him was deeper. Maybe, thought Agni, he would cheat the priests, and die before the dark of the moon.

Agni bent and whispered in the king's ear. "Father. Father, listen. In three days, it's dark of the moon. They'll sacrifice the black bull then, and send you with him. But if you will it—if it's your will to live—I'll stand against them. I'll defend you."

The king did not move. No light dawned in his eyes. He lay as he had since he fell.

Agni sank back on his heels. A great weariness was on him, sudden and crushingly heavy. As if, he thought—as if the burden of the king's life had fallen on him.

The elders had taken it on themselves, but the weight and force of it had come to Agni. Which was only fitting. Agni was the son, the heir. It was his to choose, and his to ordain; because the king himself could not speak.

"Patir," Agni said. Even to himself he sounded faint and far away. "Go to the elders. Tell them to make the sacrifice. But tell them . . . the king may take his own way into the gods' country."

Patir nodded. There was something about the way he did it, as if he bent his head to a king. He took the others with him, all but Rahim, who had curled comfortably on a heap of furs, and Rahim's brother Rakti.

They were guarding Agni. They were not being obvious about it. He might not have noticed, except for the way Rahim had set himself so that anyone coming in must either step around him or fall over him, and Rakti had placed himself rather conveniently near to the store of the king's weapons.

Agni had never been guarded before. Not as a king is guarded. It was strange, like a gift, and like a burden too. It expected things of him. It asked him to be what he hoped to be. To be a king.

He shook off the tremor that came with the thought. Rahim and Rakti were his friends. They were making sure he was safe. That was all. They would have done the same in battle or on the hunt.

While they watched over him, he could rest. He stretched out beside his father's bed, meaning simply to close his eyes, to wait till Patir came back. Just until then. And then . . .

·········· 46 ··········

Agni slept deep and long. From deep sleep he passed into dream. It was strange, because he knew that he was dreaming. He knew where he was, what he did there, lying on heaped furs beside his father. And yet he was also standing on the steppe under a sky the color of dawn. There were others near him. And nearest, like a flame in that dim place, the stallion Mitani. But the stallion's eyes held a man's awareness, a man's intensity.

"Father?" Agni asked, half in wonder, half in disbelief.

The stallion bent his head. He gestured with it, and pawed. *Mount*, he said.

But even as Agni moved to obey, in the moment when he set hand to the stallion's neck, a whirlwind howled between them. Agni clutched at Mitani, wound fingers in mane, clung desperately as the storm raged about them. Mitani stood steady, unmoved.

The wind buffeted Agni, beat on him like fists. Only Mitani's strength kept him on his feet. Borne up by that strength, he lifted his head. The wind whipped his hair in his eyes, blinding him. But here in the place of dreams, he could see clearly. He saw the storm, its rage and its power. It blew from the east with battering force, surging toward the west.

And in the west, under a serene and sunset sky, a woman was sitting. She sat alone, illuminated by the sunset. Its light was no more ruddy than her hair.

Sarama. Agni did not speak the name, and yet it resounded in his skull. His sister Sarama sat at the gate of the west, her face a mask of quiet like the face of a goddess.

She did not move, nor did she speak. She seemed unaware of him. She offered nothing, no escape from the storm; and yet where she was, was stillness.

✦ ✦

Agni woke abruptly. The dream lingered, the taste of it, the bruising force of the wind; and Sarama's face.

Dreams were never simple in their meanings, but this one seemed clear enough. Sarama was safe, had come into the west. He need have no fear for her, nor fret for anyone but himself—and for their father.

He sat up in sudden dread. But the king lay as he had lain before, neither more nor less alive. Rahim and Rakti were on guard still. Taditi sat in the place she had marked for her own, fiercely and rather defiantly awake. Only her presence assured him that he had indeed slept, and not simply closed his eyes for a moment.

He rose and stretched. Yes, he had slept, and for a long while, too, by the stiffness in his body.

That was well enough. He would be the stronger for having rested. He would need to be strong. It was coming to end, this dance. Whether in two days' time, in the dark of the moon; or, if the king so chose, sooner than that. Then Agni would take what the king had laid aside. Agni would be king.

✦ ✦

Waiting was a terrible thing. On this day, perhaps because the rite had been decided on, more people came than had come in the hand of days before. Taditi let them in, muttering over it, but acceding to Agni's will in the matter. "Let them see," he said. "Let them say goodbye, if that's their wish. It's no harm to him."

And, he thought but did not say, if anyone tried to help the king on his way, Agni would know. And if that one was Yama, then Yama would be a murderer; for a man marked for the sacrifice must not be touched by any mortal hand, nor sent to his death except by his own will and his body's consent, before the time appointed.

The king was clinging to life. Waiting, perhaps. Wishing to go as a king should go, by the knife, in a flow of clean blood; not ignobly in his bed.

He clung to breath if not to consciousness, and the moon shrank and dwindled till the last feeble glimmer of it vanished in the dawn. On the day of the new moon, in cold so bitter that the air cracked like ice, the tribe prepared for the sacrifice. Priests of the Bull chose the victim from the sacred herd, a black bull, young, without white marking, without blemish. The women prepared the fires, and such feast as there could be so far into a hard winter. The men and boys and the priests of other gods gathered stones for the barrow in which king and bull would lie. It was hard labor in the cold, but it warmed them admirably, and whetted their appetites, too; for they fasted all that day, for the gods and for the king who soon would walk among them.

Agni dug stones out of stone-hard ground and fitted them together until his hands bled. Then, because his heart was uneasy, he left the rest to finish, and went back to his father's tent.

Taditi stood guard over the king. He lay unchanged, breathing faintly. "Did anyone come?" Agni asked his aunt.

She inclined her head. "Yes," she said. "Prince Yama came."

Agni raised a brow. "Did he?"

"He came," said Taditi without expression, "and looked, and saw me. And went away."

"Indeed," said Agni. "What was he carrying? Knife or vial? Or did he cast his eye on one of the pillows?"

"He had a knife," Taditi said. She smoothed the coverlet over the king's body. "You be careful, child. This one will go before the night is over—it's his time. But it's not yours."

"You think—" Agni did not say the rest. Of course she did. So did Rahim and Patir and all the rest of the young men who had been so careful to surround him since the king's fall. If he left this tent now, he would find a handful of them hanging about, always with good and sufficient reason, but never very far from him.

And here was Taditi, looking after him, too. It was a gift, such care for his life.

"We do it for the tribe," Taditi said. "The people are best served if you lead them."

Agni bent his head and was silent. He did not know what kind of king he would make; he had never been one. But he had been raised for it, and this he knew: He would be a better king than Yama.

✦ ✦

As the sun sank over the winter steppe, sere grass and windblown snow, the people gathered round the great fire that the women had made. The cold had deepened with the sun's fading. The chattering of teeth and the stamping of feet marked the gathering; but no one fled to the warmth of the tents. Every man and woman, and every child to the infant strapped to his mother's back, had come to see the king's passing.

Agni left his father to the women, as the rite prescribed. They would prepare him, wash him and clothe him and make him fit to walk among the gods. Agni could trust them to protect him. He prepared himself with care, not that it mattered what anyone but the king wore or how he plaited his hair; but the people would see, and Agni wanted them to see a man who would be a king.

As he bound off the end of his plait and reached for his best mantle, the cured hide of a bear that he had killed, a soft sound brought him about. He had leaped for his dagger before he thought.

Rudira stared wide-eyed at the blade hovering a bare hand's width from her face. Agni did not lower it at once. He wanted to, but his hand would not move. "You shouldn't be here," he hissed.

She tossed her head at that, irritable, like a mare vexed by a fly. "Why? Everyone's out by the fire." She made no great effort to lower her voice, though this was but a curtained corner of the king's tent, and the women were close by with the king. "You haven't come to me. Even after I told you."

"I couldn't," he said. "My father is going to die tonight. Or doesn't that matter to you?"

Her eyes glittered. "It doesn't matter in the least. Not to me. Though to my husband it matters a great deal. He wanted to be rid of the old man days ago. He's not happy that it's come to this."

"Why? Because it lets my father go as a king should?"

She shrugged a little, tilting her head, letting her mantle slip. She was clothed under it, but Agni well knew what was under that. His body responded like a well-trained hound, leaped to the alert and poised.

But for once his mind was stronger. It was fixed on the sacrifice, and on the king's death. She looked to him like a foolish child, shallow and self-absorbed, and growing petulant as she saw how her blandishments had failed. She was not so beautiful then. Her beauty seemed overwrought. It cloyed.

"Why did you come here now?" he demanded out of the cold place where his heart had been. "Did my brother send you?"

She did not answer that, which was her right. But she did not deny it— and that struck him deeper than he had expected.

"He knows." She did not deny that either. He seized her, shook her. "Tell me he doesn't know!"

"I can't," she said. Her voice was faint.

"How long?"

Her shrug was invisible, but he felt it under his hands. She was more the sulky child than ever.

Agni's belly cramped. If Yama knew—then he would use it. Yama was never one to refuse a weapon.

"Who told him?" Agni demanded of her. "Who betrayed us?"

"He just knew," she said. Had she always been so dull of wit? Had Agni simply been blinded by her beauty? She was extraordinarily beautiful. Whatever made a woman sheerly and fiercely desirable, she had it. The turn of her glance, the lift of her shoulder, the sweet curve of her breast under the coat—

It was a witchery. He rent his mind away from it and fixed it on the king. Through the memory of that grey maimed face, he forced himself to think of what this meant, that Yama knew what Agni had been doing with his wife.

"No," said Agni. "No, he doesn't know, or he'd be here with the knife in his hand to cut me to ribbons. He's not clever enough to lay this subtle a trap. Nor are you—though you may think you are. What are you trying to do? Keep me away from the sacrifice so that your husband makes the king-cut? Why? What care do you have for him?"

"For him, nothing," she said. "I want to be a king's wife."

And she could not marry Agni, not unless he killed her husband; and for the killing of a brother, the penalty was exile. Agni could neither dispose of Yama nor take Yama's wife for his own. That had always been so, and Agni had always known it, as had she.

She wanted to be a king's wife. It was as simple as that. Badly enough to betray Agni to death or exile or worse?

Perhaps.

And time was growing short. If she kept him here, kept him away from the sacrifice, she cost him the kingship. She might think that little enough price for him to pay, if she were married to a king, and Agni the prince remained her lover. She would not be imagining that he would refuse. One sight of her naked body and he would be hers again, heart and soul.

It was amazing, he thought, how quickly one could come to hate what one had loved.

She must have seen something in his face. She shrank back.

Time was when he would have gentled her, taken her in his arms and kissed away her fears. But the king was going to his death, and Agni must be with him when he died. Not for any woman would Agni fail in that. Least of all for this one, who had betrayed him—whether in speaking of him to her husband, or in pretending that she had. Truth or lies, with either one she had lost him.

He set her aside as if she had been a child, swept his mantle about him and strode out of the tent, into the moonless night.

⊹ ⊹

They made the sacrifice of the black bull under a vault of frosty stars, lit by the great fire. The bull was young and huge and confused as to what was wanted of him. He did not like the fire; he lowed and flung back his head, and tried to turn and bolt. The priests struggled with him, turning him, pricking him with goads until he surrendered to their will. They brought him to the fire, where the chief of them waited, armed with the knife of sacrifice. He was quick, springing on the bull, sinking the blade in the heavy throat, freeing the bright blood.

The bull sighed and toppled slowly in the space prepared for it. When at last it was dead, when the blood was drained from it and poured out before the gods, the slow drums began to beat. Set high on a bier, borne by the women of his tent, the king came for the last time before the people of his tribe.

They had set him upright, combed out his hair and his beard, and dressed him as a king. From below, in firelight, he seemed as he had been before his fall, erect and impeccably royal.

Yet he did not move. His eyes were shadowed beneath the high head-dress, the planes of his face gaunt, carved clean. He might have been a corpse borne to its grave.

Agni moved into the light. The priests of the Bull had drawn back, leaving the great carcass where it had fallen. The women brought the king beside it, lowered his bier and withdrew as the priests had. They were veiled, all of them, and yet Agni recognized the eyes of Yama's mother, and Taditi behind her, silent, watchful. There was no sign of Yama. Agni had more than half expected him to leap forth, to bellow a challenge, but there was nothing. Only silence.

He stood in the circle of light, alone but for the king. He looked down into those shadowed eyes. Perhaps the king returned his gaze. Perhaps he did not. The soul in that body was well set on the road.

If Agni would be king, he must finish what the fall had begun. He must sever the cord that bound this man to life.

He had killed men before, in battle, as any warrior must. But to kill so, in sacrifice—the sacrifice that was made only of and by a king—was nothing that he had ever done.

He must do it. The knife was in his hand, the black blade, the haft carved of bone. A priest held out the cup that was a skull, the skull of a king long dead. Agni took it slowly.

The king sat unmoving. He breathed: Agni saw the faint lifting of his breast.

He would go as a king should go, by the blade as he had lived. Agni gathered his courage in both hands. The drum beat, slow, slow. The priests began to chant the hymn of the opening of the way. For the king it would be as if a gate rose before him, opening slowly, showing before him the gods' country.

But he could not go to it unless Agni aided him. Agni tightened his fingers round the haft of the knife. The skull-cup fit closely in his hand, ready to drink the blood as it sprang. He drew a deep breath, let it go. As it fled away, steaming in the cold, Agni made the king-cut. Swift, hard, clean. The blood ran high and strong: startling in one who had been so close to death. As the life poured out of the king, the fire flared, catching the glitter of his eyes. Full into Agni's, alive, vivid—aware. And glad. Heart-glad.

•••••••••••• 47 ••••••••••••

The king was dead. Agni poured his blood on the earth to mingle with blood of the bull. Priests took up the body, wrapped it in the bull's hide, and laid it on the bier. Beside it they laid the bull's head with its great curving horns.

The people would feast on the body of the bull. Agni, fasting, aching with cold, must follow the priests away from the warmth and the light, into the cold dark. Only the women followed.

Yama did not step forward, did not challenge, did not demand that he

and not Agni go to the grave with the king's body. Agni's back ached with
the tension of waiting for it; but it never came. He went as he should properly
have done, alone with the priests and with the women of his father's tent.

They walked in starlight, unlit by lamp or torch. The path was clear
before them. The people had beaten it all the day long, going back and forth
from camp to new-raised barrow.

Now Agni saw it all but finished, rising higher than he had expected,
dark against the stars. They had built it well. It would endure, first in heaped
stones, and then when spring came, when the ground had softened, it would
be covered over and made into a hill like one born of Earth Mother herself.

They laid the king in it, wrapped in the hide of the bull, and when the
barrow was built the bull's head would mount guard over it. The bull would
look to the rising sun as the sacrifice had done since the dawn time; looking
back the way that the people had come. But the king looked westward. It
was not the way of the people, but Agni set him so, and the priests did not
contest it.

Agni could not have said why he commanded it. Because Sarama had
gone into the west, the daughter whom the king had loved. Because the tribes
had always gone westward; had always followed the sun when they looked
for new lands to conquer. So would the king do, turning his face forward
instead of back, ahead to what would be, and not behind to what had been.

They laid his precious things with him, that the women had brought: his
weapons, his shield, the trappings of his horse. They laid baskets and bowls
beside him, food for his journey, all that the people could spare. They had
brought his old stallion; the beast came willingly, and suffered the knife to
be set in his throat. He sank down at his master's feet, sighed and slipped
into death. Then they built the barrow over king and stallion and buried
them deep, and labored till dawn to do them their last honor.

As the night passed, people of the tribe came from the feasting to lay a
stone, a blessing, a prayer; to bid the king farewell. His kin came, his sons,
the elders who had been his friends and rivals. They all came, every one, with
gifts for his memory, food and drink for his spirit, tales that remembered him,
that made him live again for a little while.

Then and no sooner, Yama came. He set himself on a stone, lifted no
hand to the barrow, but held court as if he had built it himself. Only a fool
would have believed it, but there were fools enough in the world.

Agni kept his distance. Yama did not denounce him, did not stand up
and challenge him in front of the people. He did not in fact say anything at
all to Agni, or acknowledge his presence. By that Agni grew more certain
that Rudira had lied.

Women had no honor. Agni must never forget that. And Rudira had
even less than most. Rudira the beautiful, Rudira the spoiled and endlessly
indulged, Rudira who saw nothing but what she wanted, and sulked until she
had it.

He despised her. And yet the thought of her sent a rush of heat through
his body. She had lied only out of selfishness, and because she was angry;

because he had neglected her. If he went to her tomorrow, she would be as eager for him as ever, would rebuke and then forgive him, because she could not imagine that anyone would honestly wish to be free of her.

And did he? He had looked at no other woman since he met those silver eyes above the bridal veil. They had warmed to his regard, and beckoned; and within days of Yama's wedding, Agni had found himself in Rudira's arms. There had never been a woman so gifted in giving a man pleasure. He did not think there could be.

Such thoughts to think upon the grave of his father. Agni set them aside, stood on the summit of the great cairn and watched the sun come up. The bull's head rose above his own, mounted on a spearshaft. The new sun gleamed on its horns, caught its eyes and woke in them a semblance of life. It would guard its charge well, till the flesh fell from the bones, and the empty skull bleached white in wind and sun.

The king was well set on his way. Agni bowed to him one last time and spoke his own farewell, the last that the king would hear before he passed the gate into the gods' country. It was simple; Agni had never been one for great flourishes of speech. "Fare you well, king and father," he said. "May your bones rest gentle on the breast of Mother Earth. May Skyfather hold your spirit in his hand. May the gods welcome you among them, and raise you high, and make you a king as you have always been."

He looked down at the faces of the people who lingered. Many faces; a great portion of the tribe, and great honor, that they should have remained in the bitter cold. The rite would not allow him to speak again while he stood on the barrow, but he could encompass them in the sweep of his arms, could offer thanks with his eyes and his smile. Some smiled back. Others regarded him steadily, somberly, as if they weighed him and reckoned his fitness. He would, after all, be their king.

But not till the days of mourning were over. From the new moon to the full; time enough, since this thing had been expected, for word to reach the tribes over which the king had ruled, and for their elders and their warleaders to come to the kingmaking. Then it would be done. Then Agni would be king of the White Horse people.

✦ ✦

He went back alone to the tent that had been his father's, ate something perhaps—he did not afterward remember—and fell headlong into sleep. He slept the sun out of the sky and back into it again. Then at last he woke, ravenous, and found Taditi sitting by him, wafting a cup of warm mead under his nose. He swam up out of a dream that he forgot as soon as it was gone, reached blindly for the mead, drank till he was dizzy. Then she fed him, carefully as one did after fasting, until he was something close to himself again.

The world felt strange. The king was not in it. Neither the maimed and dying thing that Agni had watched over for so many days, nor the strong old man who had held the tribe in his hand. Agni caught himself looking for that one, listening for the rough-sweet voice, wondering why the accustomed place was empty.

He could sit in it. It was his right—if for no other reason than that, as favored son, he had inherited the tent and everything in it, even the women. But he could not bring himself to take them. Not yet.

Once he had risen properly and dressed and made himself presentable, he took his own place, the place that he had always had, to finish his breakfast. As he was nibbling the last bits, the women came to him there, unveiled as they might properly be before the man who was now their master. He had not known there were so many. A dozen wives, a dozen more who were concubines, and daughters innumerable, some nigh old enough to marry, others still nursing at the breast. And still there were the sons, the youngest clinging to their mothers and staring at their elder brother, the rest with the boys or the young men, or grown and married as Yama was. At least, he thought wryly, he need not consider the daughters who were married. Those belonged to their husbands, and need only be his concern if they dishonored the tribe.

Those who came to him now were his whether he was king or no, his inheritance. The wives were his to keep or to send away. The concubines likewise. The daughters he must raise till they could be married.

He was a wealthy man, who had been possessed of nothing but his weapons and his clothing and the stallion whom Horse Goddess had sent to him. He could give it all away, if it pleased him. But that would do no honor to the king his father. Or he might ask these women what they wished: to stay, to go, to belong to him or to return to their kin. It was no shame to them or to him if they left. But if they chose to remain, then he was theirs as they were his.

They paid him reverence, kneeling to him and bowing their heads, though one or two of the menchildren did so with visible reluctance. None of them would speak until he spoke first. "Very well," he said, speaking the words he had rehearsed before he came there. "I'll give you the choice now. To stay or to go. If you stay, I care for you as my father did before me. If you go, you go with no dishonor. I give you the freedom of your choosing."

He heard, or thought he heard, the whisper of a sigh. The tension in them eased, if only somewhat.

They glanced at one another. He could see the factions in the way they sat or in the way their eyes met. There seemed to be several small factions and a pair of larger ones, subtle but clear to see once one found the way of it. It was like this in battle, when enemy fought against enemy, and within each army the tribes and clans held together.

The chief of one such spoke abruptly, breaking the silence. "I go to my son," said Yama's mother, "I and my daughters."

That was defiance, since a mother might go, but her daughters should remain in their father's tent. But Agni did not mean to contest that of all choices. Whatever might come of it, whatever the woman's reason for taking herself and her offspring away, he was glad. Glad to be rid of them. Glad to be free of their hostility.

He bowed his head as he had seen the king do. "You may go," he said.

In strict propriety she should wait until all choices were made, but Yama's mother had no desire to be proper. She rose, and her daughters rose with her. Agni would have wagered that their belongings were all packed, and that those were few; that the rest had long since been carried into Yama's tent.

Memory woke in him, of this woman deep in converse with Rudira, speaking of plots and of things that should be done. He might have served himself ill by sending this of all people into the enemy's camp.

And yet if he had compelled her to stay, he would have had an enemy in his own tent. Best to let her go.

When she departed, and without a word of farewell, either, others rose also. Them too he granted leave. They would go to fathers, brothers, and no doubt new husbands when the time of mourning was over.

When they had gone, they left behind more than half of the wives and concubines and most of the daughters, and Taditi looking grimly pleased. It was an honor to Agni that so many had stayed, had chosen him over their own kin.

He would have to learn all their names. And the wives . . .

He found himself flushing. Patir had suffered enough for the choice of half a dozen sisters, and he had only had to marry one. Agni stood face to face with half a dozen wives, and all of them his by the custom of the tribe.

He knew what was expected of him. "I welcome you," he said. "I take you as my father would have wished, to be mine as you were his, and to bear my sons for the strengthening of the tribe."

They bowed to him, submissive as women should be. Not one offered him a bold glance, nor lured him with the hint of a smile. Only Taditi would look him full in the face, and she was an aunt, and could never be his wife.

He swallowed a sigh. A tentful of Rudiras would have worn him to nothing and made him unfit to be king. And yet he could not help but yearn for what he could not, and should not, have.

He put on a smile for them, and sent them back to their duties and their places. They went willingly, taking comfort perhaps in the return to daily things, in knowing that nothing would change except the face of the man who summoned them to his bed in the nights. And maybe that was not so terrible, either. He was young, after all, and not ill to look at.

He would not be expected to take up his duties until after the mourning. That was a reprieve of sorts.

The king's tent returned to its familiar round, the babble of voices, babies' cries, even a woman singing as she tended her child. Agni escaped from it into the cold and the spit of snow; to the company of his friends and his red stallion under him and the exhilaration of a hunt.

They brought back a pair of winter-gaunt deer, poor enough prey but welcome. Agni gave his share to one of the smaller tents, to the widow there, who was more than glad of it. She and her children would eat well for a handful of days, if she was thrifty, and the deer's hide would make a fine coat for one of the sons.

"Generous as always, I see," Yama said as Agni turned from the woman's tent. Agni had not seen him coming. He smiled at Agni, seeming amiable, as brother should be to brother. "Do you do it because it's well done, or because people will think it is?"

"Should it matter?" Agni walked past his brother. It was open rudeness, but Yama was choosing not to remark on it.

"It looks well," Yama said, matching step with Agni. "So you've taken his wives."

Agni smiled thinly. "Were you thinking to claim them?"

Yama shrugged. "I have enough of my own. Though if they're too great a burden for you . . ."

"I'll remember," Agni said.

"I'm going to be king," said Yama.

Agni did not pause, did not glance at him. "And how do you intend to accomplish that? I struck the king-blow. I saw the king to his grave. I claimed the king's women."

"It's the elders who elect the king," Yama said.

"The elders hold to custom," said Agni. "They honor the wishes of the one who is dead."

"Custom," said Yama, "yes. And the gods' law."

Agni's heart went still. But Yama did not say it. Did not challenge him.

Nor would he. For to challenge Agni would be to admit that he could not keep his own wife satisfied. More than honor, more than law to Yama was his precious self. Yama might strike Agni with a knife out of the dark, but he would never stand up in front of the elders of the tribes and confess himself a cuckold.

Agni, knowing that, smiled sweetly at his brother and went lightly on his way. Nor did Yama follow. Maybe he fancied that he had won. Well enough if he did, if it gave Agni a moment's peace.

48

"He's up to something else," Patir said. They had come to dinner in the tent that was now Agni's, Patir and Rahim and a fair handful of the others. To most, still as lanky as young wolves, and still unmated too, it was a matter for much staring about and some ribaldry, that Agni had become such a man of substance.

Agni bore it with such fortitude as he might. There was no ill-will in it. It was only friendship.

They sprawled at their ease in the warmth of the tent, round the fire in its hearth of stones. Some of the smoke even wound up through the opening in the roof. They were eating from the great pot and drinking the last of the summer's mead, savoring it, remembering warm air and the sweetness of honey.

But Patir's mind was fixed firmly in winter. "Yama has some plan that he's sure will make him king."

"He can't be king," said Agni, "unless I'm killed. And I don't intend to be."

"Still," said Patir, "we'd all best watch your back."

Agni laughed at him. But after they had all gone away, when Agni lay in his sleeping-furs, buried deep and wonderfully warm, the one cold thought lingered with him. They could not live in the same tribe, he and Yama. Not if one of them was king. And since that one must be Agni, Agni well might have to kill his brother.

Yama could challenge. That was custom. Agni would win. That was truth. Agni was the better fighter, the better hunter. But Yama could be treacherous; and therefore, as Patir had said, Agni must watch his back.

✦ ✦

Agni watched his back. His pack of young wolves guarded it, turn and turn about. And the elders began to come, riding off the steppe, windblown and raw with cold. They brought tales of winter even more brutal elsewhere, hunting not merely thinned and difficult but shrunk to nothing, tribes forced to wander far within their winter ranges simply to stay alive.

They had been fortunate here. There was hunting still, and the herds could find forage. Westward, the newcomers said, it grew worse, and word was that the farther one traveled, the more terrible it was.

"Skyfather is angry," said an elder of the Dun Cow as he feasted on roast kid. He sucked the meat from a bone, noisily, and wiped the grease from his beard, and licked his fingers. "No one knows why he's angry, or why he's angrier at people who live toward the sunset countries. The omens tell us nothing. The signs are all unreadable. It's as if he's lost all patience."

"All's quiet here," Agni said. "Our ill omen was the fall of our king; but the rite of the bull appeased the gods."

"Not all of us have kings ripe for the killing," the elder said. Because he was an elder, no one upbraided him for his callousness. He tossed the stripped bone to the dogs and downed a full cup of *kumiss*. "Though mind you, if every tribe sent its king to the gods, they might sit up and take notice. At least they'd have to listen to so many newcomers at once."

"That might make them even angrier," grunted an elder of the Spotted Hound.

"I can imagine," someone else said; Agni did not see who it was. "All those young fools yapping and whining at the gate."

A snort of laughter ran round the fire. Agni was mildly shocked by it. Elders could be horribly irreverent. It was a privilege of their position.

But a king had to be more reverent than any. Agni preserved such aplomb as he could, saw to another round of *kumiss*, made certain that no one lacked for food or drink or comfort. He received no thanks for it, though he would have heard, and soon, if anything had failed of perfection.

They seemed content. And tomorrow was the full moon, and the king-making. There were still a few elders absent; they were coming, messengers said, but slowly, for a storm had delayed them. The sky was clear now, and would remain clear, the priests said, until after the kingmaking.

It would be well. Agni convinced himself of that. He maintained an air of calm, or so he hoped; did the duties of a host, saw his guests provided with everything that they could wish for, and maintained judicious silence when he saw one or another of them in company with one of Yama's followers.

Tomorrow it would be done. He would take the place that had been made for him, and be what his father had raised him to be.

He could, in courtesy, leave his guests early, see them well tended, and seek out his solitude. It might have served his cause better if he had stayed, but he lacked the stomach for it.

He half expected to find Rudira in his bed, sulky as ever and demanding that he atone for his sins of neglect. But his bed was empty. Tomorrow one of the king's wives—his wives—would fill it. Tonight he had it to himself.

Briefly and rather wildly he thought of slipping out, of finding the opening in Yama's tent, of winning Rudira's forgiveness. It would take the whole night long, and promises of nights to come, but he could do it.

And if his brother caught him tonight of all nights, he would lose everything that he had lived for. He dropped onto his furs, wrapped them about him, sank gratefully into their warmth. His body would have been glad of another warmth, soft arms, supple hips. He groaned and rolled onto his face. He would not—would not—go to Rudira.

One night. Only one night. Tomorrow, when he was king, he would let himself think of her again.

✦ ✦

On the morning of the kingmaking, the elders gathered in a tent raised for them, heated with a fire burning sweet herbs. The latecomers had come in near sunrise, having ridden through the night; all but the men of the Red Deer. Those would come or they would not. The kingmaking would not wait for them.

Agni had no part in their council. Even if he had been of age to sit among them, they would have excluded him, because he was the chief cause of their deliberations.

They would, he knew, settle other business first, disputes and petitions, matters of the clans and of the tribes that looked to the White Horse. Last of all they would consider the matter that had brought them here, the making of a king.

The women of the king's tent had arranged a diversion for Agni. It was a gift and a marvel. They had set up a small tent beside the larger one and lit a fire inside, and set over it a cauldron, and filled that with water from the river. Taditi fetched him to it with a command that he was not inclined to disobey, and the youngest wives and concubines drew him in, giggling like silly girls.

A bath in winter. Some might reckon it an invitation to catch one's death of cold. But hot water on winter-chilled body, and steam to draw out a whole season's worth of sweat and dirt and the inevitable vermin, and herbs for sweetness, and a salve that Taditi had made, worked with slow strokes into clean skin, were pure bliss. Agni almost did not mind that these women saw him naked, and remarked on it too. They were not displeased, he gathered. "So smooth," one of them marveled, stroking his back and sides as if he had been a horse.

They groomed him as if he had been one, too, washed and combed his hair and plaited it with feathers and bright beads, trimmed his beard and dressed him in clothes that were all new, even to the belt and the boots. They were made of finest leather, and a little of the woven cloth that traders brought from the west and the south, ornamented with beads and with clever stitchery. The coat was a wonder of fine work, embroidered with the great tales of the tribes: men on horses riding out of the sunrise, women bearing burdens and carrying children on their backs, men at war and at peace, the sacrifice of the Stallion and the dance of the spring festival, and the king on his sacred horsehide above the gathering of the people.

It was a wonderful coat, a glorious coat, a coat for a king. Agni stood up in it with pride and a kind of awe. The labor of kingship he had always known, and the power that it brought with it, but the splendor was a new thing. His father had cared little for pomps and shows. He had been a plain man, if never simple.

Agni might choose to be beautiful. Sometimes. For his own pleasure and for the honor of his people.

He smiled at the women whose gift this was. "I thank you," he said. The words were little enough, but he thought they understood. "Go on," Taditi said with the roughness that in her always masked great emotion. "Show the men what a king you'll make."

✦ ✦

Agni went out as casually as he could. As he had more than half expected, his friends were waiting for him, a guard of honor round the tent that the women had raised. They were remarkably handsome, too, he noticed, fresh-plaited hair and best coats and new boots here and there. They whistled and hooted at Agni. "O beautiful!" Rakti warbled. "O light of our eyes!"

Agni chased him down and thumped him, but the others were quicker on their feet; and he did not want to spoil his wonderful new coat. He settled for a glare and a snarl all round, which they met with a singular lack of concern.

"Come," said Patir with a touch of impatience. "We have to be there when the elders come out."

They all knew that very well, and said so, too; but they did not dally longer.

✦ ✦

For all their haste, it was a long while before the tentflap opened and the chief of the elders of the White Horse led the rest blinking into the hard bright daylight. The people had gathered in the open space before the tent. They had, one way and another, contrived to give Agni and the young men the foremost places.

Agni saw Yama off to the side, surrounded by the usual flock of sycophants. He did not look at all cast down, though he had an air of tension about him, a tautness that drew Agni's companions in close and set them on watch.

The sun mounted to the zenith and sank with winter's swiftness. It had been almost warm; but as the shadows lengthened, the cold closed in.

The men of the Red Deer had come, people were saying, just before Agni came out. They had paused to speak to no one, had ridden straight to the tent and left their horses for the boys to look after, and disappeared within. Their faces had been grim.

As the hours lengthened, anticipation turned to curiosity, and curiosity to apprehension. There should have been no such delay. At noon the chief of the elders of the White Horse should have come out of the tent with the others after him, and lifted the staff of his office, and named the one who had been chosen to be king.

But he had not done so, and the elders of the Red Deer had come in late and at last, just before he should have done it. The people hummed with conjecture. War, perhaps. Wrath of the gods. Some other terror, or some dispute so great that the kingmaking must wait upon it.

But what that dispute could be, no one professed to know. There had been no rumor of war, no contention between tribes, nothing but a hard winter and a slain king.

Agni ran the same gamut as the others, but on him the burden lay heavier. He could not imagine that they delayed for difficulty in choosing a king. It was some matter of the Red Deer, then.

One who was not an elder should not intrude on the elders at such a time as this. And yet the people were waiting. Which the elders must know very well. And yet . . .

He had stepped forward, he had determined to approach the tent and to inquire within, when the flap lifted at last.

A sigh ran through the people, marked by a chattering of teeth.

The chief of elders of the White Horse stepped into the sunlight, but one step only. No others followed him. His face was grim. His eyes passed over the gathering, but they were oddly blind. When they found Agni, they came alive; but not with joy. "Agni," he said, "son of Rama son of Tukni of the White Horse people. Come here."

It was not the call to kingship. It was like the beating of the drum at the king's sacrifice, dark and slow. In a rising murmur and in a kind of numbed obedience, Agni went as he was bidden. The elder retreated, beckoning him sharply, summoning him into the tent.

It was dark within, blind dark after the glare of daylight. There was a fire, and light through the opening in the roof, but smoke so filled that space, and the stink of it and of unwashed humanity was so strong, that for a stretching while Agni was as one blinded and deafened and reft of his senses.

But they came back, if slowly. He stood where he had been led, inside the circle of elders, near the fire that flared suddenly, illuminating faces. Not one looked on him with gladness.

He began to grow, not afraid, but alarmed. This was not a matter of the tribes. This was something to do with himself, with something that he had done.

Yama. Rudira.

But if he was to be denounced, Yama should be here. And Yama was outside, unsummoned, nor did anyone leave to fetch him.

Men came round the fire, strangers wearing the stitched and beaded signs of the Red Deer. Agni remembered vaguely one or two of their faces. Two of them were young, which surprised him; too young to be elders. They looked on him as if he were their bitter enemy.

"Yes," said the youngest, who was somewhat older than Agni himself. "Yes, that is the one."

A low murmur ran round the circle, a rumble like a growl. Agni stiffened at the sound of it. "And who may you be?" he demanded. "Have I done you injury? By the gods, if I had, surely I would remember it."

The stranger's lip curled. "Would you now? And would it matter to you if you had?"

One of his elders laid a hand on his shoulder, silencing him. That one's glance was no more friendly, but his words were rather less intemperate. "You are Agni son of Rama of the White Horse people?"

Agni bit back the first retort which came to his head, that if he had answered to that summons, surely he must be the one who had been summoned. He drew a breath, calmed himself, answered quietly. "I am the king's son of the White Horse tribe. And you are?"

The elder did not answer that. "Agni son of Rama, you are charged with crimes against our people."

Agni stood very still. "I do not recall," he said, "that I have ever committed injury against a man of the Red Deer."

"Man, no," said the young man. He was shaking, Agni saw, and not with cold. With anger. "But a woman dishonored and defiled, the daughter of a chieftain, wife of an elder, taken by force—"

Memory struck like a blow to the belly. Spring gathering, a wedding, a pair of green eyes glinting boldly on him, luring him away from the dancing and the firelight.

She had been a maiden—no doubt of that at all. And she had worn her hair as an unmarried woman will, loose beneath her headdress.

He had never asked her name or known her lineage, nor, trusting the evidence before him, troubled to fret that she might be another man's wife. It had not been the most pleasant of meetings, nor had they parted excessively well.

Agni had forgotten her within moments of her leaving him, all memory of her burned away in the heat of Rudira's body. But that he would not speak of.

He almost laughed. His greatest fear had always been that he would be caught in dishonor with a married woman—and so he had. But not with the one he had expected, his brother's wife Rudira. With a woman who had, in ways both subtle and wicked, concealed what she was.

He drew a breath, gathered the words, spoke them calmly. "I do recall that a girl of the Red Deer accosted me at my brother's wedding. She was a maiden, I can swear to that. And she wore her hair loose, as a maiden will. She was no man's wife."

The young man of the Red Deer burst out almost before Agni was finished, overrunning the last of his words. "She was the wife of Bapu the Hunter, whom a wild ox gored, and who could not enjoy a woman in the normal way thereafter. She was still his wife—and she would never lie, or conceal it, or pretend to be an unmarried woman. *You* lie, prince of the White Horse. You seized her out of the shadows while she watched the dancing, carried her off and raped her, and left her bleeding and all dishonored. Look at your face! You don't remember that, do you? You don't even remember!"

"I don't remember," Agni said with deliberate calm, "because it never happened. She was standing in the shadows, yes, while I danced with the young men. She made an assignation. I went to it. I never took her by force. She asked, and I gave what she asked."

"That is a lie!" the young man cried. "My sister was seized and taken and ravished, and left to make her own way back to her husband's tent."

"And if that were so," Agni demanded, "where is her husband? Why is he not here? Why was it left to you, and why did you wait till now to charge me with it? Both of you should have come in the morning, faced me and challenged me, and called for a reckoning."

The young man spat on the ground at his feet. "Bapu the Hunter is dead. He suffered much from his old wound. The shock of her return, the horror of her dishonor, prostrated him. He fell ill and died. And she told no one else, not then. Her grief was too great, her shame too deep. She hid it from us. We noticed how she was always weeping, but women do such things when they are widowed, and she had seemed fond of her husband. But then she delivered herself of a child, she who should have been untouched; who was to be given in the spring to a prince of the High Hills people, and he had been much concerned that she come to him a maiden. He would never have raised her bastard."

"I am sorry for that," Agni said, "but she said not one word of her husband or her kin. She came to me as a woman unwed. I took her as she asked. If she had come to me when she knew she was with child, I would have taken her in. I am honorable when I know that I have need to be. I will take her in now, if you ask it."

"No," said the man of the Red Deer. "You are lying. You have raped an elder's wife, a chieftain's daughter. The elder is dead because of it. Our chieftain died of an apoplexy when word was brought to him that his favorite, the light of his eyes, the daughter whom he loved above the rest, had delivered herself of a daughter. She is dead. The birthing killed her. *You* killed her, man of the White Horse. That is the charge I raise against you. Murder, and dishonor of my family and my tribe, and blood feud on you and all your kin unless I am given satisfaction."

Agni reeled at the blow of her death, though he had not known her at all, except in the body. The rest of it seemed like something from a story, tragedy heaped on tragedy. But it had nothing to do with him. She had snared him with a lie, with seeming to be what she was not.

He forced himself to focus, to hear the rest of the words that her brother spoke. "I will give satisfaction," he said, "in whatever measure I may. But I did not rape her, nor knowingly trample on her honor or the honor of her kin. I am not her murderer."

"She swore on her dying soul," said her brother, "and on the souls of her mother and her father before her, and on the soul of her husband who had died of the shock, that you had done so. She swore it to the priests and sealed it in her own heart's blood. And then, man of the White Horse—then she died."

There was a silence. Agni turned about slowly. There was no oath greater than the oath of one who was dying, sworn before priests and sealed in blood. And there was one of the priests to whom she must have sworn it, carrying the sign of it, the polished bone of an ox, carved with the gods' eyes and stained dark with old blood.

It was the seal of a lie. Though why a woman should hate him so much, should trap him with a lie, then pursue him beyond the grave, he could not imagine. Maybe—yes, maybe she had hoped to snare a prince, and dreamed of shedding her eunuch of a husband and making herself wife to a king. Had she seen where he went after? Had she watched him with Rudira, and seen how great his pleasure was, and hated him for it? Or had it simply been that she had conceived when she had never thought to do such a thing, and had borne her dishonor, and had looked for revenge on the man with whom she had wrought it?

With a woman, there was no telling. And she was dead.

"The child," Agni said. "Is it—"

"We took it to the steppe," the woman's brother said, "and left it."

Agni held himself still, forced himself to think clearly. Of course they had cast the child out. It was ill-begotten, and a girl. There was no place for such among the tribes, least of all in a hard winter.

He looked from face to face around the circle. He had been tried, he could see. And he had been condemned. By the oath of a dying woman, by a lie against which he had no defense. He had told no one of that assignation, not even Rudira. It had been a secret, swiftly done, nigh as swiftly forgotten. He had had a dozen such since his beard began to come in. All the young men did.

"I do not know," he said slowly, "why she lied. And yet she did. She sought me out. She summoned me to her. For what came of it I am sorry, but she never came to me, nor asked me for help. If she had, I would have given it. That I swear by my father's spirit."

"Maybe you believe that," said the chief of elders of the White Horse, who was his own kinsman: speaking heavily, with evident regret. "Still there is the oath that she swore, and the grief that her family suffers, and its great dishonor. Three of its own have died for this. The shame will blacken the tribe forever after."

Agni kept his head up, though his belly had cramped into a knot. "I

acted in as much honor as I knew to act. I granted a woman what she asked,
as she urgently asked it, during a time when such things are, if not approved
of, then at least regarded with indulgence. That I am guilty I do not deny.
That I am guilty of such great transgression as I am accused of, I most firmly
refuse to accept."

"We have only your word for that," said the chief of the elders. "And
this." He tilted his head toward the bloodstained bone. "Against this you
have no defense. The law grants you none. You must pay as the law demands."

The knot in Agni's middle clenched tighter yet. "With my life?"

"No." That was the woman's brother, thick with disgust. "*I* asked it,
but they refused to grant it."

"Then," said Agni, "I'll pay whatever penalty you ask. Horses, cattle—"

"No," the man of the Red Deer said again. "I will take nothing from
you."

Agni spread his hands. He must not allow them to see anger in him, or
to suspect the slightest sign of fear. "Then what will you have? What can I
do?"

"Leave," the other said. "Be banished. Go away from the tribes forever."

Agni swayed on his feet. Death he could contemplate. Heavy fines in
cattle, in horses, in wealth of whatever kind—those he could pay. But this—

He turned his eyes on the chief of elders of his own tribe. "Did you grant
him this?"

"We persuaded him to accept it."

The elder said it without joy, but without wavering, either.

Agni shook his head, as if so simple a movement could sway all these
gathered elders. "I can't go away. I have to be king. My father—"

"If your father had known what you were," said someone whom he did
not know, wearing the signs of the Black Stallion, "he would have cast you
out himself."

"But I am not—" Agni stopped. No one believed him. Even those who
looked on him with sympathy, who appeared to grieve for the judgment that
they had made, still reckoned him an ill creature, a man who had not only
taken another man's wife, but who had done so against her will. If she had
indeed been what she pretended, a young woman seeking a husband among
the dancers, and if there had been no charge of rape, he would have borne
the burden of her death, and owed forfeit to her kin. But she had been an
elder's wife. And she had a claimed a thing, perhaps to salvage what honor
she had left, that he had never done nor dreamed of doing.

It had not even been a pleasant meeting. He had obliged her out of
courtesy, and forgotten her as soon as she was gone. He could not remember
her face. Green eyes—yes, he remembered those. But of the rest, nothing.

He looked at the world that had been so bright, at his wonderful coat
that had been made for a king, at the circle of elders who had proclaimed
his sentence. A sentence against which he had no appeal. If he had been
struck down by a bolt from heaven, he could not have been destroyed so
swiftly.

So this, he thought with distant clarity, was why Yama had not risen to challenge him, nor interfered in the old king's death and burial. And yet, how could this have been Yama's doing? Yama was never so subtle or so perfectly cruel. Yama's mother, his sisters—maybe. But if they had done this, they were more terrible than he had ever imagined. They could find a wife who was a maiden, and persuade her to act out the lie—promising her a new husband, a prince, who would take her out of guilt but keep her and give her honor. Then, somehow, they proved to her that such could never be, and taught her to hate him, and drove her to her death; and so destroyed the one who stood between Yama and the kingship.

No. He could not believe such a thing, even of Yama-diti. Because if he believed it, then he must believe that Rudira had played some part in it. That what he had heard in Yama's tent that night after he came back with his stallion was a pact between the prince's mother and the prince's youngest wife. That they had acted together to destroy Agni, so that Rudira could be a king's wife.

No. And no again. This was the gods' doing. Only gods could lift him so high, and give him so much farther to fall.

He turned blindly. "I must speak to the people," he said. "I must—"

"No," said the chief of elders. "You will say nothing. You are outcast."

"But who will be king?"

"That will be settled," the elder said.

"Promise me," said Agni. "Promise me that it won't be—"

"We promise you nothing," said the elder. "We owe you nothing. You are no longer one of us."

With each word, the blow struck harder. Agni had been numb, unbelieving. Now he woke to sensation—and that sensation was pain.

.... 49 ....

Of all the ways in which Agni could have lost the kingship, this was the one he had never expected. The irony was exquisite. If he had lost it for Rudira— that, he would have understood. But to lose it for this, for an hour's encounter, for the folly of obliging a woman who had demanded it of him, was beyond anything he had thought to fear.

His own elders condemned him in sorrow that seemed unfeigned, but they would not alter their judgment. They brought him out of the tent into the glare of the day, to the shouts and cheering of the people, which died down raggedly as those closest saw the grim faces, and marked how Agni was brought before them: as a captive and not as a king. They had not asked to bind his hands. But they gripped him by the arms and thrust him into the light, and held him as the silence spread.

Then they stripped him. They reft him of his beautiful coat. They snatched away his ornaments, even to the beads and the feathers in his hair. They laid his body bare before the people. And all the while they did it, they proclaimed aloud the tale of his crime—the lie that had been sealed with a dying woman's oath.

He, the part of him that thought, that reasoned as a man can reason, had gone away. He was nothing, no one. He had no name. They had taken it. He had no tribe, no kin. All that he was, all that was left of him, was outcast.

They drove him out with whips and stones and clods of earth and close-packed snow. They made a passage through their midst and pursued him down it, out, away, onto the steppe.

Barefoot, naked in the bitter cold of winter, bruised and bleeding and numb in the heart, still he walked erect out of the camp. He stumbled, rocking at blows, but he did not fall, nor did he flinch or grovel. That much he could show them in his ruin: a straight back and unmarred pride.

Pride carried him away from the camp of the White Horse people. Pride kept him on his feet until the last of them had fallen away, weary of the pursuit. And pride took him farther, and farther again, till the cold was set in his bones, and the dark had swooped down on him and taken him out of the world.

✦ ✦

Agni swam out of sleep. Through the blur of its leaving, he saw faces. Patir; Rahim. Taditi frowning down at him, looking as severe as she ever had when he was a scapegrace child.

He frowned back at her. "I had the most horrible—" He yawned, stretched; gasped. Dreams did not ache in every bone, or catch on ribs that must be broken.

"You didn't dream it," she said, harsh as ever, and as little inclined to soften the blow.

He tried to scramble up, but he was as weak as a newborn foal. "What are you doing here? Where is this? If they cast me out, and you are seen with me—"

"—we'll be cast out." Patir seemed unruffled by the prospect. "We're camped by the high tor. You've been wandering in a fever for a night and a day. The kingmaking went on after all, though some of the elders tried to stop it."

"And they chose Yama." The taste of it was bitter in Agni's throat. "He did this. I don't know how, but he did it." And yet he suspected. Rudira, Yama's mother—women had their own world, their own wars. If somehow they had discovered what Agni had done with the woman of the Red Deer, and conspired with her, even persuaded her to do what she had done, then all the rest would have been inevitable.

None of the others disputed with him. He looked about, seeing at last where he was: in a tent, and not a particularly small one, with all the comforts one could ask for; and most of those his own. "How—" he began.

Patir looked inexpressibly smug. "Sheer brilliance," he said. He caught Taditi's eye and flushed. "Hers, not ours."

She nodded grimly. "I had a feeling in my bones," she said. "When the elders didn't come out when they should have, I packed everything I could. I told these puppies to be ready. And I waited."

"And you never told me?" Agni demanded.

She refused to be cowed. "You would have wanted to do something foolish. So did the rest of them, but them I could threaten. They weren't eager to face your wrath if my bones were wrong."

Agni shut his mouth tight.

She nodded, approving. "Yes, be sensible. I was. As soon as the word came, we did what was necessary."

"We gathered everything," said Patir, "and took our horses and rode out while the people were in disarray. We found you where she said we would, blue with cold but burning with fever, and brought you here."

"You should never have done it," Agni said.

"That's gratitude," said Taditi to the others. "When are you going to tell him how many of the people wouldn't follow Yama?"

Agni sat bolt upright. He gasped, he reeled, but he stayed there. "How many—"

"It's only the hunting party," Rahim said. "And some of their brothers and cousins."

"Rather many of their brothers and cousins," Taditi said. "With such of the herds as they could claim for themselves, and tents and belongings, weapons, horses, whatever they were able to ride away with. You can thank the gods this new king is a fool, or he'd have thought of ways to stop them."

Agni sat with his body jangling, stabbing with pain, and tried to fit his mind around both his exile and the number of men who had gone to it with him. So terrible a thing, the ruin of everything that he was—and yet, by gods' will and the will of his friends, he found himself chieftain of a tribe.

Nor was it a lie, a false comfort lest he will himself to death. He insisted till they surrendered, struggled to his feet and stumbled out of the tent, leaning on Rahim and Patir. And there was a camp of goodly size, campfires, herds of cattle, horses, men performing duties as they must in a camp of warriors, since there were no women to do it for them. Taditi was the only one.

"I had no desire to live in a tent that was ruled by Yama-diti," she said.

He looked out over this camp that, without even knowing it, he had made. His eyes brimmed and overflowed. One stroke, one lie, had cast him out of the tribe; yet here was a tribe that had chosen him, that had left its own in order to follow him.

"I don't understand," he said.

"What's difficult?" said Rahim. "They made Yama king."

"But the people," Agni said. "Your honor, your name, your kin—"

"There's no honor in a lie sworn as truth," Patir said.

"It could be true," said Agni.

Patir shook his head. "Most men, yes. Not you. Because . . ."

"Because," Taditi said when Patir could not say it, "you've never in your life taken a woman who was not willing, nor had any need. And you've had eyes for only one, this past year and more. She's a shallow, spiteful thing, and she wanted to be married to a king. She told her husband's mother of you, of what you'd done that she reckoned a betrayal. All the rest came of that."

Agni opened his mouth, shut it again.

Taditi shook her head. "There's no fool like a fool in love. It was an open secret, puppy. All the women knew. Even a few of the men."

"I saw you," Rahim confessed, "creeping out to meet her once."

"And he told me," said Patir, "and one way and another the others had wind of it. We agreed to keep it a secret, but to keep a watch on her. None of us trusted her. Her kin have a name for treachery."

"I feel," said Agni after a stretching while, "as if I must be the only fool in the world."

"All young men are fools," Taditi said. "Now come back in and lie down. You've a bit of mending to do yet."

Agni did not want to go back into the smoky dimness of the tent, but they were stronger than he, and he was wobbling on his feet. Taditi fed him, though what it was he did not afterward recall. Somewhere between bite and sip he fell into a heavy sleep.

His dreams were dark: fire and shouting, grim faces circling, voices repeating the rite of his exile. Rudira came in her glimmering white nakedness, and took him as a man takes a woman, headlong, and no pause to ask his leave. He struggled, but she was too strong. As she held him, as she drained him dry, her face shifted and changed, until he looked into a face he had nearly forgotten. The face of the woman of the Red Deer. And she grinned at him, and her grin was the grin of a skull.

He woke gasping, battling the furs that wrapped him. He fought his way out of them and lay on the icy floor of the tent and struggled to breathe calmly. These were not true dreams. Only fear-dreams. So he told himself.

He crawled back into the furs, shivering as if he would never be warm again. Somewhere in his sleep it had all come home to him. The numbness was gone. He was cast out of the tribe, his kingship taken from him before he could properly lay hand on it. Everything that he was and had been was gone.

He should have been dead. And yet he lay here in comfort, looked after by the aunt who had tended him when he was small, and a whole pack of idiots camped about him, waiting for him to tell them what to do. That could not be at all to Yama's liking.

Yet Yama could do nothing. Unless Agni took the army that had followed him and led it against the people, Yama was powerless. Agni had been made as nothing, was invisible, did not exist. The tribe could not go to war against nothingness.

Agni was not comforted. The heart of him, the indissoluble center, was gone. He had been born and raised in the White Horse people. When he named himself, he was Agni son of Rama of the White Horse. Now that was taken away. He was outcast. He had no family, no tribe. Even his name had been taken away, though that clung stubbornly and refused to go—like the friends and allies who had followed him and so destroyed themselves.

His fault. He did not know how or understand why, but somehow he had bound them to him beyond the dissolution of his bonds to tribe and kin. It was not supposed to have happened. When a man was cast out, he lost everything. His friends, his allies, shut him out of mind and memory. They were not supposed to follow him.

He must have cast a spell on them. Maybe it was as some people had whispered, that his mother had been a sorcerer of great power; and maybe after all he, and not only Sarama, had inherited that power.

He snorted in his wrapping of furs, and sneezed. That was nonsense. He had no power but what any man had.

"Then why?"

He asked it of Taditi, whom he found in the other half of the tent, behind a curtain, grinding grain into flour. She had come away with riches, a whole packtrain worth from the look of it.

She looked up when he lifted the curtain, and at first did not answer his question. When she did, she did it sidewise. "Have you ever wondered why Yama of all your brothers reckoned himself most fit to be king?"

"He's the eldest," Agni said promptly, "even if he was begotten of a prince and not a ruling king. And he's a fool."

"And he has a strong-willed mother." She bent her back to the grinding of stone on stone. "And a wife who wants to be a king's wife."

Agni scowled. His head ached. Strangely, for a moment he heard Sarama's voice, observing acidly that yes, indeed, thinking was a difficult thing. "Yama's a weakling. I knew that. But even with such a man as king, the tribe is the tribe. No one simply leaves it."

"There was nothing simple about our leaving," Taditi said.

"You shouldn't have done it," he said.

"Probably not," she said. She swept flour from the stone into a jar, spread a new handful of grain, set to grinding it again. "It's as well you don't understand why people follow you. If you did, it might go to your head."

He blinked.

She ground the grain, stroke by steady stroke. Her body in the coat and the well-worn skirt, her greying hair plaited and wound tight about her head, had no beauty in them. She never had been beautiful. And yet she was the strongest human creature Agni knew. Stronger than his father had ever been.

And in the west, if the traveler's tale was true, a woman could be a king. It was outrageous and preposterous, but the rumor of it had sent Sarama into the sunset countries. If there were or could be such people, Taditi might have been king. And what sort of king she might have made—

Agni had lost his wits with his tribe. Men ruled the tribe. So had the gods ordained. Women ruled men. So people said, but softly, and not where too many could hear.

"You didn't want to live in a tent ruled by Yama-diti," Agni said. "You said that. But the others—"

"The others made a choice," she said.

"And did you encourage them to make it?"

She brushed another heap of flour into the jar, wiped the stone clean. She sat on her heels, staring down at it, as if she could read signs there, or omens, or the answers to his questions. "They didn't need any encouragement," she said. "They had already considered what the tribe would be under Yama as king. You would have to leave, they all knew that. They weren't prepared for an out-casting; but when it fell on us all, they held to their choice."

"They should not have," Agni said.

"It was rather a wild impulse," she granted him, "when it came to it. Patir and Rahim would have done it regardless, for love of you. The rest were caught up in the heat of the moment. None of them believed that you of all people would have to force a woman. Not with so many both willing and eager. They were in a fine and tearing rage."

"And now they would have cooled down," Agni said, "and it will be dawning on them that they can't go back."

"There is that," Taditi said.

"I have to go out," he said. "Do I have a mantle? Or a coat?"

"You have both," she said. She rose stiffly and stretched. He waited with carefully schooled patience, and with courtesy that she herself had taught him. He won no praise for it. It was expected.

She brought him his own mantle of bearskin, and his good leather coat, too. He needed both. It was rawly cold, the sky heavy, lowering, threatening snow. His loyal tribesmen kept somewhat of a raffish air, like a pack of boys on a raid, but there was an aimlessness to them, a kind of prowling restless-ness, that did not bode well.

It was no more than Agni had expected. Though his body creaked as badly as Taditi's, he circled the camp, and visited each fire, and each tent, too, if he was invited; and he nearly always was. Most of their names he knew, or their kin. Their number rather took him aback. There were nearly two score of them, which would be nigh every man of the tribe at or about the age of hunting his stallion, and some younger, too, no more than boys; even a few who were older, men who for one reason or another had had nothing to bind them to the tribe. All gathered here for Agni's sake, and looked to him as their chieftain.

Food they had, for a while, for both man and beast. There was hunting round about. No tribe claimed this country, though both the White Horse and the Dun Cow hunted in it in the spring. It was well chosen.

There was even a sheltered place for the horses, a bowl of a valley with a stream running through it, its center unfrozen despite the cold. There was grass beneath the snow, and tender saplings to nibble on.

Agni found Mitani there, and somewhat to his surprise, the mares that Mitani had claimed for his own. The stallion's peal of welcome deafened him, and for some unfathomable reason made him burst into tears.

Mitani roared up to him in a stinging spray of snow. He caught mane as the stallion wheeled, let the force of the motion swing him onto the warm back. Mitani neither started nor bucked, though Agni had not done such a thing before—should not do it now, either, but a spirit of wildness was in him. He was making no more sense than anyone else, than anything that had happened since the kingmaking that had gone so terribly awry.

He circled the camp as the first flakes of snow began to fall. Mitani was fresh, lively, snorting and dancing: making himself beautiful for people to marvel at.

And as Agni rode, as the snow thickened, as he bound the camp tightly in the circle of his riding, it came to him with the strength of a true dream: what it was that the gods wanted of him. Why they had caused him to be cast out. Why so many strong young warriors had followed him.

The west. The sunset countries. The place where a woman could be king. Where Sarama had gone—and where she had forbidden Agni to go.

But that had been before he was cast out, when their father was still alive and whole, when Agni had place and kin and kingship. Now that was all gone. Agni was free. He could go where he chose, unless he chose to go back to the White Horse people. With the tribe that had gathered about him, a tribe of fighting men, he could do whatever he pleased. Raid, wage war, conquer tribes, take their women, carve out a kingdom for himself.

The gods had given him the means. Yet now, as the snow flew about him, blinding him with whiteness, he knew that they had not given it to him for any simple purpose. They had sent his sister before him into the west. Now he must follow.

A land where a woman could be king. A land that knew no war. It would be rich, and ripe for the taking. It was all but in his hand. He could see it from Mitani's back, limned in the snow: a vision of light, warmth, greenery. Winter would never be so harsh there, nor its privations as terrible.

He was almost warm, thinking of it, looking out across the camp of what would be his army, as the snow closed in and covered it all. In the spring, he thought, they would go. They would sweep the western tribes before them. They would fall on the sunset countries and take them. And Agni would, after all, be a king.

II

THE LADY'S OWN

·············· 50 ··············

SARAMA HAD THOUGHT herself with child in the autumn, but just as she was sure of it, her courses came and swept away whatever life had begun in her. That was the Lady's will and her doing. Sarama could accept that. But she could not stop grieving for the child who would never be.

She did not speak of it to anyone. Danu might have grieved with her; and she did not want him to do that. He was too well content to be in Three Birds again. He was happy, even in the thing that she made him do, the instruction in fighting and in the ways of war.

For his sake she kept her sorrow to herself. He was greatly preoccupied between the ruling of his Mother's house and the barest raw beginning of a fighting force.

It was bare indeed, and as raw as Sarama had ever seen. These people looked on fighting as a thing that only animals did. Men—human creatures—settled their differences without blows or bloodshed. They could only with difficulty bring themselves to strike, and then without force; and if by chance a blow fell hard enough to sway an opponent, the one who had struck the blow was tearfully apologetic.

And yet as hunters they were admirably skilled. They might mourn the prey after it was dead, but they pursued it with implacable purpose and slew it both swiftly and cleanly. If they could learn to think as hunters, hunters of men, they might begin to have some defense against the war that was coming.

✢ ✢

That winter was the gentlest Sarama had ever known. Except when she was traveling from Larchwood to Three Birds, she was warm, out of the wind, in comfort unless she chose otherwise. There was enough to eat, and a great plenty in the feasts of the dark of the year and of midwinter and, most wonderful of all, in the very early spring, when the snow began to melt and the rivers to run free again. They had their flocks and herds and a great store of the grain that they planted and encouraged to grow. Hunger was a thing that few of them knew.

In the spring her courses paused again. She did not hope or even think much on it, as if the thinking itself might cause the child to slip away. It almost frightened her, how much she wanted this child to live. Better not to turn her mind to it at all; to let the Lady work her will.

Every morning unless it rained or snowed, Sarama went to an open field just outside of the city. There gathered the ones whom Danu had chosen, who might make warriors. They were the hunters, the runners and messengers, the tenders of herds who had defended them well against wolves. Most knew the bow and had some skill with the spear. They would happily shoot arrows and cast spears from sunrise to sunset, but when it came to fighting hand to hand, they took to it badly.

Danu was no better at it than the rest. Sarama tried not to be angry with him, or to lose patience. That was difficult. He could madden her with his stubbornness, hunch those big shoulders and lower those black brows and look more like a bull than ever. He and the one they actually called the Bull—Kosti-the-Bull, his name was—would have been mighty warriors in the tribes. In the Lady's country they were known for their prowess with women, or for their skill in keeping a Mother's house in order. They were fast on their feet, powerful with the spear, could bend a longer, stronger bow than anyone else. And yet when set face to face with wooden swords, they turned into simpering idiots.

"I'll hurt him," Kosti said when Sarama urged him to strike harder.

"Not if he blocks the stroke," she said for the hundredth time. "Now strike. Strike hard."

He lifted his sword—lovely grip, beautiful balance—and delivered a love-pat that would have done justice to a slip of a girl. Sarama growled and snatched the sword out of Danu's hand and leaped on Kosti, whirling the wooden blade, raining blows.

And he dropped his own sword and covered his head with his hands and backed away, pure coward; except that cowards whimpered and wept, and he was simply defending himself and refusing, flatly refusing, to fight back.

"The horsemen will kill you!" she raged at him. "They'll cut you to pieces. They won't care if you won't hit back. They'll laugh, that's all, and hew your head from your neck."

Kosti lowered his head and said nothing. She whirled on Danu. "Hold up your sword. Defend yourself. *Now!*"

He used his sword to protect his head, at least, though he would not strike, only parry. Sarama flung down her blade in disgust. "Let's only hope that you can fight them off with bows and spears; because if they come in any closer, you've lost the war."

Danu, like Kosti, did not argue with her. Men never did here. She flung herself onto the Mare's back, and left them all to their practicing and to their complete inability to strike a blow in anger. No one even slapped a child here. As far as she could tell, the children did as they pleased, but what they pleased to do was never anything reprehensible. People simply were not people in this place. They were something subtly and infuriatingly different.

✦ ✦

Danu came to bed earlier than usual that night. Sarama was still undressing when he came in.

Even when she was utterly out of patience with him, the sight of him could make her heart beat hard. He could not seem to learn to strike back when someone struck at him, but he had learned easily and quickly to take her when she wanted to be taken. To come to her as he did now, to take her in his arms, to kiss her till she gasped. He bent his head and teased her nipples with his tongue. She shivered and caught her breath. They were tender, a tenderness that was new, that made his touch almost too much to bear.

Just when she must cry out or push him away, he had mercy. He left her breasts and worked his way down slowly down the curve of her belly, coaxing her to open her thighs. She arched her back against his bracing hands.

He lowered her to the bed with effortless strength, all quivering as she was, ready to shout or to rage at him if he did not finish it. He raised himself over her. She locked legs about his middle and impaled herself on him. The

size, the shape of him were exactly as they should be. Were made for her.
Were hers, as she was his.

+ +

He tried always to stay awake for a while after, a courtesy of his people, and
one that she had learned to value. She cradled his head on her breast, tangling
fingers in his thick curling hair. His own fingers wandered wickedly between
her thighs, stroking just enough to keep the warmth alive. She gave herself
up to it for a while, rocking with pleasure on pleasure.

But her mind was gnawing on a thing, and even his loving could not
persuade it to let go. "It's nearly spring," she said. "By summer they'll be
here, if we're seeing true, and if they really are coming."

"They are coming," he said.

"And none of you can fight," she said. "You must be lacking something,
some gift, something in the spirit."

"Ill spirit," he said. "That's what we call a person who strikes another
person with intent to harm. Ill spirit, demon, one whose face is turned away
from the Lady."

"It's going to kill you," she said.

"Maybe," he said, "when the horsemen come, when they ride at us, we'll
forget. We'll be as we are with wolves or with the wild boar. We'll be able
to strike."

"You had better pray for that," said Sarama. "There's no hope for you
else."

He sighed. "We do try, Sarama."

"Surely," she said. "And you fail."

"I'm sorry," he said.

"Never be sorry," she said. "Just learn to fight."

+ +

Danu might never be of any use as a swordsman, but one thing Sarama was
determined that he should know. She waited till a warm day of honest spring,
just before the planting time. The snow was gone except from shaded hollows, and the rivers ran high and free. The first green had begun to spring
on the hillsides. Then when he had gone to the practice-field, with the colt
following as he always did, Sarama rode the Mare to the field. No one remarked on that. She often did it; it would have been more worth noting if
she had not.

But this time, instead of watching from the field's edge for a while and
then setting the Mare free to do as she pleased, Sarama rode the Mare to the
part of the field in which the archers practiced their craft. Danu was stringing
his heavy bow, making light work of it, with a glance at Sarama as she came
between him and the sun.

"Leave that," she said, "and come here."

He was obedient as she had expected. But when she slid from the Mare's
back and said, "Mount," he would not move.

"Mount," she said again.

"No," he said.

"Maybe you won't fight," she said, "but you will learn to ride. Now mount. Like so." And she showed him: clasp mane, leap, swing leg, and so astride. The Mare was patient, which was not always her way.

Danu glowered at them both. "What earthly use is there for me in learning to ride?"

"Every use in the world," said Sarama from beside the Mare. She pointed with her chin toward the colt, who grazed nearby. He had grown in the winter, a little taller, much broader and deeper. He was as tall as the Mare now, and would be a larger horse altogether.

"Come another spring," she said, "you'll be riding him."

"Oh, no," said Danu. "No, I am not—"

"Among the tribes," she said, "when a youth wishes to become a man, he goes out for a whole summer and seeks his stallion. And when he finds the one who will be his, he captures it and tames it and rides it back in the full moon of autumn. And so is he reckoned a man among the horsemen."

"I don't want to be a man among the horsemen," Danu said.

"Ah," she said, "but some would say you already are—or will be once you ride this colt. He is your stallion. He looks to no one else, nor has any desire to. When he's older and stronger, he'll grieve if you won't ride him. It's what he was born to do."

"You can ride him," Danu said.

"No," said Sarama. "I belong to the Mare. That is *your* colt."

His face set. He was going to be stubborn. Sarama met his glare with one fully as baleful. "You're afraid," she said.

"I am not," he said too quickly.

Ah, she thought: so he did have that kind of pride, after all. "You don't want to look like a fool," she said, "because I've been riding since before I could walk, and you've never done it. You don't want the others to see how you fumble."

"I do not!" he declared. And, wonder of wonders, he stepped up to the Mare and got a grip on her mane and managed, one way and another, to get a leg over her. It was not graceful and it did not delight her, but she stood for it, by the Lady's blessing.

He sat on her back with an expression almost of shock, as if he had done it without thinking at all, and could not imagine what to do next. Sarama let him think about it for a while, and grow accustomed to the feel of it: to be sitting so high, with a living body under him. The Mare stamped at a fly. Danu gasped and clutched her mane.

"Relax," Sarama said. "When she moves, flow with her. Now touch her with your leg, so. Yes. Don't clutch! Flow. Let her walk. Let her carry you."

She had never seen a grown man before who was not born to the saddle. It was faintly absurd, but she knew better than to smile. He had a little talent for it, and more willingness than she might have expected, once he had been shamed into trying it. It was not like fighting. Fighting was altogether against his nature. But riding the Mare—that, as she had seen and he seemed startled to discover, was a great joy and pleasure. To be carried by a willing creature, to consider that creature's comfort, to flow with it, to be a part of it, to feel the wind in one's hair, was a thing he could not have conceived of until he did it. She watched the smile break out, the grin of incredulous delight.

"Oh," he said as the Mare walked sedately across the field. "Oh, this is wonderful."

"Isn't it?" said Sarama. "Now turn her. Touch her with your leg: yes, so. Ask with the rein. Think of turning."

He did as she bade, and the Mare turned. And again; and again. And halted, too, when Sarama showed him how to ask, and started again. Over and over, till Sarama ended it—capriciously, he must have thought, for he frowned at her. But he was obedient.

He gasped as he slid to the ground. His knees buckled. He clutched at the Mare. His look of astonishment was so pure and so profound that Sarama bit hard on laughter. "I never knew I had muscles *there*," he said.

"It gets easier," she said. "Walk, now. Stretch. Don't stand still. You'll stiffen."

"You make it look so easy," he said.

"I could ride before I could walk," said Sarama. "Now walk."

He walked. "And what did you do, then, if you were too young to walk?"

"I crawled," she said. She walked beside him as he limped back down the field, and the Mare on his other side, concerned for him. She had not meant him to hurt.

The archers and the spear-fighters, male and female, and even the few who tried to fight with the sword, all watched him in awe that must have gratified him. He had ridden the Mare. He had done a thing that none of their kind had ever done.

And he would do it again and again, until he was master of it. And then, Sarama thought, if there was time before the war came, she would teach him to shoot that bow of his from horseback. And then, maybe, he would be a warrior after all.

·············· 51 ··············

Spring grew green and rich in the Lady's country. Danu danced in the planting festival, and sowed his own seed in the furrow, with every other man whom the Lady called to the task. Sarama had never seen the fields tilled and sown; her people took what their gods gave, from the steppe and from the hunt, nor knew either planting or harvesting. She helped as she might, but she was as clumsy in that as Danu had been and still was on the Mare's back.

He could not confess that he was glad. It was one thing he could do that she could not, one thing in which he had the advantage. It was not a thought that he would ever boast of, or be proud of, either.

She had, one way and another, become a power in the city. People reckoned that she must be a Mother. The Lady spoke to her through the moon-colored Mare; and she carried herself, conducted herself, as a Mother might. She was not aware of it, that Danu could tell. It was simply what she was.

She had not taught anyone else to ride the Mare. No one else asked, either. People were not terrified of the two horses here as they had been in Larchwood, but they stood in awe of them. Horses belonged to the Lady. Anyone who rode them must be hers, too.

Now when Danu went to the market, the men sitting in their alleyway between the stalls greeted him warmly enough, but with a hint of distance. He had grown away from them. He belonged to the woman from the east, and to the Lady.

That hurt, a little, even knowing that his closest friends from the days before had as little time to sit about and talk as Danu did. They were in the practice-field or waiting on the Mother, learning new duties for when the war came.

"If it ever comes," said one of the grey uncles in the market, on the day when the boats came down the river. The traders had come back at last with all their wonderful things, shells and colored stones, painted pots, furs, dye-stuffs for the weavers, nuggets of gold and bits of copper, all to trade for the fine weavings and the intricately painted pots of Three Birds.

The traders, who came from the south and the west, knew no rumor of horsemen or of a terrible thing called war. All was well in the world, they said, the cities rich, the people content. The omens were for a rich summer and a good harvest.

Sarama had told Danu of a thing that people could do in war, the building of a wall to protect a shrine or a sacred place. Three Birds and the cities to the east of it were the wall of the Lady's country, its protection against the horsemen. If they fell, that fair summer would open the road for the conquerors, and the harvest would feed them.

It hurt his head to think of people who would take and keep, and never share. But the ache grew less as time went on. He was hardening to the truth, to the harshness of Sarama's world. Some might say that he was being corrupted.

+ +

Danu traded a bolt of his best weaving, the intricate and many-colored cloth for which Three Birds was famous, for an arm-ring of hammered gold. It was richer and more intricate than the one he always wore, incised with the Lady's spirals, gleaming and beautiful. As he ended the bargaining and handed over the bolt of cloth, Tilia appeared next to him, linked arms with him and smiled at the trader, and said to Danu, "How lovely! Is it for me?"

Danu gave her a look. He tucked the armlet into his pouch, thanked the trader courteously, and left her booth. Tilia followed perforce.

"She'll like it," his sister said when his silence showed no sign of breaking. "Is there an occasion? Are you celebrating?"

"Isn't it enough that she is, and that she chose me?" Danu asked.

Tilia raised a brow. "Ah! Such wisdom. She should give you a gift. I'll tell her how it is here."

"You will not," Danu said. "In her tribe, men give the gifts. She says I'd be reckoned a man there, because of the colt. Even if I do have no aptitude for fighting hand to hand."

"Her people are strange," Tilia said. "You really think they're coming."

"I don't think it will be long," said Danu. "Can you feel it? It's strongest just before dawn. The earth growls in its sleep."

"I don't hear such things the way you do," Tilia said. Her voice was flat. Danu could not tell if she resented it, or if she was accepting an unpalatable truth.

"I wish," said Danu, "that it were you and not I. I never wanted to be the Lady's servant."

"You know what they say," she said. "The ones who want it are the least fit for it."

He snorted. "I don't feel fit at all."

"I don't think anyone does." She paused to admire a potter's wares. "When do you think she's going to tell you about the baby?"

Danu could hardly admit to surprise. Tilia might not hear the Lady's voice, but she had eyes that saw farther than some. "She'll tell me when she's ready," he said.

"Not that she needs to," said Tilia. "But, you know, you'll be uncle to it, since she has no other kin here. She should give you a little warning."

"In the tribes, it's the man who sired the child, who claims it and gives it his name." Danu stooped to examine the intricacies of a painted bowl. With his eyes on the interlaced spirals, he said, "They even have a word for him, that has a meaning like *mother* to us."

"Imagine that," Tilia said. "A man taking credit for the making of a baby. Not that he doesn't have something to do with it, but a few moments' pleasure against nine months of bearing and all the pain of delivering—they *are* strange people."

"She still thinks we don't know what a man does to make a child," said Danu, "because we have no word for what he is to the child after, except uncle and friend. No word like their *father*."

"I should think that such a word would give a man too much power," Tilia mused. "If he gets a name from those few moments in the night, and a claim on the woman who gives it to him—who's to tell where the end of it will be?"

"Men who rule," he said, "and who take what isn't theirs, and make a glory of war." He turned away from the potter's stall, nearly colliding with a handful of passersby.

Somehow he found his way out of the market into one of the quieter circles. On a deserted doorstep where flowers grew in a pot, the first of the spring, he sank down and lowered his head into his hands.

Tilia had followed him. How not? She sat beside him. "You won't turn into one of those just because you're learning to fight, or because she lets you ride her Mare."

He raised his head. "How do you know? How can you be certain?"

"Because I know you," she said. She touched his cheek, then slapped him lightly, just hard enough to sting. "Remember this when you're tempted to become a horseman. You belong to the Lady. She shines in everything that you do. She won't let you fall to the horsemen's gods."

"But what if I want to be a *father?*" he said. "What if I want that?"

"How many uncles do you know who were mothers' bedmates when their children were conceived? I suppose they're fathers, too. They raise the children, teach them what they need to know, make them fit to serve the Lady. Would you do anything different?"

Danu shook his head.

"So," said Tilia. "What are you moping about?"

"Things are changing," he said. "The life we've lived for generations out of count, the ways we've held to, the very way we think—it's all going to be gone. Changed. Made different."

She shivered herself; he saw her. But she betrayed no fear. "If things are changing, then it's laid on us to make sure that they change for the better—or that if the worst does happen, it's less terrible than it might have been."

He could not think of anything useful to say to that.

She struck him on the shoulder with a hard fist. "Look at yourself! You've learned about war. You've learned about this thing called a father. You're riding horses. You've changed. And you're still you. You're still Danu."

"Am I?"

"As near as makes no matter," said Tilia.

✦ ✦

She left him with much to think on. Not all of it was dark. That much she had given him.

He thought on it while he did his duties in the Mother's house, and while he practiced on the field, and while he crept toward mastery of riding the Mare. He even thought on it while he lay in Sarama's arms, though she gave him little enough time for thinking.

She ripened with the summer's coming, a bloom that one who knew could not mistake. Her breasts were fuller. Her belly rounded. And one night, while they lay side by side, he felt a flutter that woke in him a sudden, incredulous joy.

He looked up into her startlement. She looked as if she would retreat, coiling into herself, turning away from him. But he would not let her go. "I've known," he said.

Her hand sought her middle. He did not think she was aware that she did it. "How—?"

"One knows," he said, "if one can see. You were afraid to tell me. Why?"

She shrugged. He thought she might not answer, but after a long pause she said, "I was afraid it might die. And . . . you might tire of me. And not want to—"

He shocked himself by understanding. "Is that how it is in the tribes? A woman gets with child, and the man she chose—who chose her—turns his back on her and goes elsewhere?"

"No," she said. "No, it's not like that. It's . . . she grows huge and unlovely, and he leaves her to grow the child in peace. He has other wives. You—I suppose you have to get another woman to choose you. Since—"

"That is the most appalling thing I have ever heard."

She stared at him. He did not suppose she had ever seen him angry before. He seldom was. But this—it gnawed at his belly.

He tried to make it clear to her. "When a woman is with child, when she swells with the Lady's gift, she is the most perfect that she will ever be. She is the living image of the Lady. All that the Lady is, is embodied in her. She is sacred; she is blessed.

"And the man whom she graces with her regard—he shares the blessing. He stands beside her. He supports her when the weight of the child grows heavy. When the birthing time comes, he is there; she bears her child in his arms, and he takes it, and consecrates it to the Lady. Then he too is blessed, and beloved of the Lady."

Sarama frowned. "The man—the father?"

Danu shook his head. "No. The man whom she chooses. It may be the one who was with her the night the Lady kindled a child in her. Or it may not. She may choose that one for his beauty or his wit or his gift of pleasing a woman. But the one who stands beside her, who will be uncle to the child— that one she chooses for his gentleness and his strength. He will raise the child, you see. Only the best and the most steadfast may do that."

"I—can choose another man?" Sarama asked, as if she could not believe such a thing. "I have to choose another? What if I don't want to?"

"You don't have to," Danu said as patiently as he could. "You can if you wish. It's your right. Your duty to the child, to give it an uncle who will raise it properly, chide it when it needs chiding, indulge it when it needs indulging, teach it the ways of the people. That one need not be the one who shares your bed in the nights. He is for your pleasure. The uncle is for the child's sake."

"Like—" She was trying; struggling, but trying. "Like when a man has a beautiful wife, but she has little skill for being a mother. So he gives his son a nurse, one of his other wives maybe, or a sister, or a daughter—someone who can raise it as it should be raised."

"Only sons? What does he do with daughters?"

"Daughters don't matter," she said.

"Daughters are everything here," Danu said.

"I hope it is a daughter," said Sarama fiercely. "I want it to be a daughter. And here of all places in the world—here she can be all that she was meant to be."

Unless the horsemen won the war, and only sons were allowed to matter. But Danu did not say it. Saying it would give it too much strength.

Instead he said, "I've been asked often to be a woman's bedmate, but never to raise her child. I'll not be wounded if you find another."

She took his face in her hands, tangling her fingers in his beard, so that he could not move or look away. Her eyes burned on him, as if she limned the lines of him in fire. "Why hasn't anyone asked? Because you're beautiful? Does beauty forbid a man to bring up a child?"

"I don't know," he said. "Do you think it does?"

"I think," she said. "I think . . . I wouldn't know where to look for a nurse for this baby. You'll have to do."

"I could find—"

Her finger stopped him. "Don't be ridiculous. I want *you*. Maybe it's a terribly ill choice, but it's my choice. Are you going to argue with it?"

"No," he said. "Oh, no."

"Why?" she demanded. "Because you were brought up never to argue with a woman?"

"And because I want it," he said. "Yes, I want it. I want this child in my arms. I want to be its uncle. And—and its father. There's never been a father in the Lady's country before. I'll be the first. I pray I'll do it well, and not shame her or harm her people."

She kissed his brow, his cheeks, his lips. "You will always do well," she said.

That was the Lady in her, speaking through her. He felt the power of the blessing, the strength of that regard. It swayed him, buffeted him as if it had been a great wind. It swept his heart clean, and emptied him of doubts.

Those would come back. He knew that. And yet for this night he was pure in his faith, content in the Lady's arms, blessed and beloved.

············· 52 ·············

After the time of the sowing, when the first green shoots had thickened and begun to grow tall, just at the threshold of summer, a guest came to Three Birds. Sarama had been in the temple, resting in the quiet, content in the Lady's arms. As she came out she met the Mother coming in, bent on the same errand. They paused on the threshold. The Mother's smile was warm: astonishing always after the coldness that Sarama had known in Larchwood. Here Sarama was welcome. Here she was even, if not loved, then looked on with affection. Maybe it was for Danu's sake; maybe, after so long, a little for her own.

They did not say anything of consequence, she and the Mother. They seldom needed to. There was understanding between them. The Mother was more like her son than maybe he knew. His beauty he must have had from the father that no one here would acknowledge, but the rest of him was hers. Gentleness and strength. Yes. And a warmth that people came to as if it had been a fire on the hearth. All that family had it, even blunt uncompromising Tilia.

Sarama, whose spirit blew hot and cold in the winds of the world, luxuriated briefly in that warmth. It made the day brighter. The true wonder of it was that the more she shared it, the more of it she had.

The Mother went out about her business. Sarama went in about her own.

She found Danu at the bread-baking. The flour was ground, the bread made and set beside the hearth to rise. He greeted her with a swift and brilliant smile, but he did not leave his duties. Nor had she expected him to. She wanted to watch him, that was all, and maybe lend a hand if he needed one. She had learned some while since where one might sit or stand and be out of the way. He was used to it now, no longer so self-conscious. The others, the menservants and the Mother's acolytes, reckoned Sarama a madwoman, but a harmless one. They were glad of another hand now and then, and not inclined to object that it was Sarama's.

It was a comfortable place to be on this bright morning. It would be warm later, but it was cool still. The sun shone through the opened shutters. The breeze that blew in was fresh, and sweetened the air inside. The smoky closeness of winter was nearly all gone.

As she lent a hand with the cleaning of a fine catch of fish from the river, one of Danu's sisters called from the outermost room. She put a lilt in it that spoke of strangers in the house, guests from elsewhere—traders, Sarama expected; they all stopped here to pay courtesy to the Mother.

✢ ✢

If these were traders, they had precious little to trade. There were three of them, two strapping and silent women, and a third of less bulk and even less volubility.

Sarama knew them all. The silent ones had come to Three Birds with her in the winter, and had left as soon as they arrived, eager to return to their own city. The one whose escort they were had not grown less wintry in her expression since spring warmed the earth.

"Catin," Danu said in what sounded like honest surprise. He slanted a look at this servant, a brow at that. They moved quickly to lead the guests in, to relieve them of their packs and their walking-staves, to ply them with food and drink and every comfort that the house had to offer.

Then at last he could sit with them and ask the question that had been burning in all their minds. "What brings you to Three Birds?"

Catin had not looked at Sarama past the first, sweeping glance that took in the whole of her, and stopped and held at the swelling of her belly. Yet as she answered Danu, her eye flashed sidewise at Sarama. "News," she said, "and a warning. With the new moon, a message came from the forest people."

"The forest people?" Danu's brows were raised. "What, a message from a myth?"

"They are real," Sarama said without thinking, and before Catin could speak. "Strange people. Their language is nothing like yours, or ever like mine. They look—different. Like stones: heavy and solid, as if they grew out of the earth."

"Yes," Catin said, as if the word had been startled out of her. "How did you know them? Are they a legend to you, too?"

"I saw them," Sarama said. "I was a guest in one of their villages. Two of them guided me to your country."

"No," said Catin, and the almost-warmth that had been between them, however briefly, was gone. "They would never do such a thing. Their world is even more fragile than ours. And the news they bring—they can never have welcomed it. Horsemen massing on their eastern borders. Camps spread as far as the eye can see. And more coming, day after day."

Sarama had expected it. Had waited for it. And yet . . . "So soon?"

"The forest people say," Catin said, "that the gods from the steppe sent out the call, and all the tribes have answered."

So soon. This time Sarama did not say it. Catin sounded grimly pleased, as if she was glad to be proved right; to know that Sarama had indeed come leading the war behind her.

The others did not seem quite to understand what this meant. Even Danu was much too calm. He said, "Gods can move quickly when mortals are willing."

"But," Sarama said, "when I left, there was no—"

"You left," said Catin. "What was to keep the rest of the tribes from following you?"

"The Lady," said Sarama.

"And did she promise you that? I saw people learning to fight as I walked into the city. Why teach them, if she'll keep the tribes away?"

"You can," said Sarama, "either castigate me for bringing the war or condemn me for trying to keep it away. Not both at once."

"Ah!" said Catin. "You speak well."

Sarama gritted her teeth at the condescension in Catin's tone. "I have had good teachers," she said sweetly.

"He is, isn't he?" Catin sat back in the chair that was reserved for guests and sipped the sweet mead, first of that year and very fine.

In the uncomfortable silence, Danu said rather too brightly, "The Mother should be here soon. Will you be staying long?"

"Long enough to sleep," she said. "Then I have to go back."

Danu nodded. He showed admirable restraint in not remarking that her city would have great need now of lessons in fighting.

Sarama could hardly say it if he would not. She held her peace therefore, and waited impatiently for the Mother to come and set them all free of this uncomfortable gathering.

The Mother came at length with stately grace and freed Sarama and Danu to escape to the inner rooms. The servants fled behind them.

"I don't know why," Sarama said when they had taken shelter in the kitchen, "but I simply cannot like that woman."

Danu sighed. "I think the dreams so overwhelm her that she sees nothing else. And she thinks of you as the cause of them."

"I am not," said Sarama.

"Knowingly," he said, "no. Nor willingly."

Sarama opened her mouth, but shut it again.

He inspected the pot that hung over the fire, tasted its contents, crumbled in a little of something dried, green, and fragrant. He had not looked on her with hatred, nor did he seem greatly troubled.

"You think I led them here," Sarama said.

"I think," he said, "that once the westward way was opened, others would think to follow."

"I wasn't the first," she said. "There was the man who brought horses to Larchwood."

"Yes," said Danu. "You followed him. Why wouldn't others follow you?"

"The gods send them."

"And the Lady sent you ahead, to prepare us." Everything, it seemed, was in order. He turned to face Sarama. "Only Catin tries to lay blame, and Larchwood follows her because she'll be its Mother when her time comes. We lay no blame here in Three Birds. What is, is. If you hadn't come to teach us how to fight, we might have no hope at all."

"You think they'd have come?" Sarama asked. "Without me?"

"You said it," said Danu. "A traveler was here before you. He told tales everywhere. Yes? And if you heard him, then others must have as well. There's fertile ground there for such seeds to grow in."

Sarama looked about. She had learned to see this place as simply itself. But if she tried, she could still see with a tribesman's eyes. So many things in this one small room, and some that she might not even have recognized, intricate and strange. Riches: a copper pot, a carved wooden box, a great heap of painted bowls. And, more than anything else, the larder full and it was barely summer, a wealth of things to eat. These people never went hungry, even in the dead of winter. Such was a tribesman's dream, to live in a land so rich that he could eat well the year round, nor suffer unduly in the achieving of it.

Danu brushed her cheek lightly with his finger. She shivered at the touch, and caught herself in the beginning of a smile. He warmed her with his own. "We'll not send you away," he said. "That I can promise you."

"You can?" she asked.

He nodded. "The Mother said. You'll be guest and friend here for as long as it pleases you."

"Even when the war comes?"

"We'll need you most of all then," he said.

"I hope you remember that," she said, "when you see what war is. Words can't describe it. You have to see."

"I won't forget," he said.

"Maybe," said Sarama.

III

SHEPHERD OF MEN

AGNI BROKE CAMP within a handful of days after he was cast out of the tribe, as soon as he could ride and not fall dizzy from Mitani's back. The gods favored him with a run of warmth, a false breath of spring. There was more and deeper winter on the far side of it, but bright sun and soft breezes sped him on his way.

He rode due west, as Sarama had done before him. His journey in truth was shorter than hers; the high tor stood at the western edge of the hunting grounds, looking out toward the sunset.

Sarama must have ridden as a hunter rides, because none of the tribes camped along the way had seen or heard of her. Agni made no secret of his coming. He could hardly have done so, with twoscore and a handful of men, a great herd of horses, a herd of cattle, and Taditi riding demurely veiled on the back of an ox. They were a tribe, and they traveled as such.

A tribe on another tribe's lands was, in most instances, a call to war. But Agni rode under the sign of the gods' messenger: the horns and the tail of a white bull. He had sacrificed it on the night before their departure from the high tor, with his own hands had led the beast up the steep hill and onto the summit, and there slit its throat. The blood had sprung red and steaming on melting snow and bare brown earth, and all the omens had been good.

Under the bull's horns and its tasseled tail, Agni could ride openly through the lands of every tribe. He could enter its camp, walk unmolested where a stranger would far more likely be killed, face its chieftain or its king and deliver the message that the gods had given him while he slept atop the tor, with the bull's hide wrapped about him. Skyfather's emissary had come to him in his dream, the raven of battle with its glossy black feathers. "We give you the sunset," it had said to him. "Go now and take it, and hold it in Our name."

Agni told the tale of that dream, and conveyed the message that went with it. "The sunset countries are ours for the taking. Come, ride with me. Ride and conquer."

And the chieftains nodded wisely, and the elders murmured in wonder, and the tribe did not break camp in the morning when Agni left it. But beyond the camp and the herds, just out of sight of the tents, inevitably Agni would find a company waiting for him. The young men, the wild of heart, the bored and the headstrong and the men without wives or inheritance to bind them to the tribe, were ready and eager to follow a man whom the gods had sent to them.

He made no secret of his coming, nor of his exile either. "Best they know what they're following," he said to Patir as they rode away from the camp of a clan that called itself the White Bear. "I'll not lie or hide. I'm doing as the gods bid me."

Patir nodded a little abstractedly. "We'd better hope the newcomers start thinking about feeding themselves. There's nigh a hundred of them now, and a wide stretch of steppe ahead of us."

"I'll see that they think of it," Rahim said, and Taditi nodded.

Agni was left with nothing to say, and no promise to make. It was all done for him. Time was when he would have been angry, but at the moment, as he thought on what he was and what he was doing, all that came to him was laughter.

The others did not try to understand. Agni supposed he had been saying and doing strange things since he woke by the high tor and found himself both exile and chieftain. He had felt strange. His world had shattered, and these were the shards: an army of dreamers, a red stallion with a crescent moon on his brow, and the sun riding low ahead of him, beckoning him onward.

With a hundred men at his back, he was stronger than many kings. But he would not let them call him by that name. "I'll earn it," he said. "I've sworn as much. But I'm not a king yet."

They called him by the name that his father had given him, therefore, the simple name, without title or mark of respect. And that became a mark of respect in its own right.

+ +

None of the people Agni met knew anything of Sarama, until he came to the camp of the Stormwolves. They were a strong tribe in their part of the steppe, under a chieftain hardly older than Agni. His name was Gauan. He of all the chieftains and kings heard Agni out as eagerly as one of the young rakehells on the fringes, leaning forward, nodding at this observation or that, rapt in the tale that Agni told.

When Agni was done Gauan said, "I've seen a face like yours before."

Agni leaned forward himself. "What? My face? On a woman, by any chance?"

Gauan's delight was palpable. "Why, yes! So you're the brother she never quite failed to admit to."

"Why would she—" Agni did not finish that. Instead he asked, "Was she well? Had she traveled safely?"

"Perfectly so," Gauan said, "from everything that I could tell. We gave her escort as far as we could. I would have followed her to the ends of the world, but I was going to my wedding."

"Would you follow her now?" asked Agni.

Gauan rubbed his chin under the thick ruddy beard. Of course he hesitated. He was the lord of a tribe. Women and children looked to him for protection. The riches of his people, its herds, its sons, its stores of weapons, were his to guard. He could not simply take horse and ride in pursuit of a dream.

And yet he said, "My wedding is long over, and my wife is suitably with child. Yes, I would follow Horse Goddess' servant. I should like to see that she came safe into the sunset country."

"I too," said Agni, as much prayer as answer.

And in the morning the warband of the Stormwolves rode with Agni's gathering, leaving the women and children behind, and a reluctant company of men to defend them. Then Agni knew that this was real; that it was no dream or delusion. Truly, as he lived and breathed, he was leading an army that meant to conquer the west.

✦ ✦

If the west did not conquer his army. Past the borders of Gauan's country for the first time he saw the shadow that was the great wood. The tribes within sight of it were restless, stirring already before he ever reached them. They had had their own dreams, their own summonings. Their fear of the wood was deep, their tales of it harrowing, yet they had mustered their courage before the faces of their gods. They had made their own gathering, massed their own army.

Agni came to it warily, stepping softly. A false word, an ill-conceived action, could strike a spark that flared into war.

He had tribes in his army who had been bitter enemies before they made common cause with the march to the west. These new tribes, none of whom he had ever known before, were as uncertain in their temper as bears in the spring. It well might please them better to slake their thirst for blood with the slaughter of strangers from the east, than to face the wood that they had feared all their lives long.

He took great care to ride into that camp with his weapons secured out of reach. His people were watching him closely, the archers with bows ready to hand, but these strangers would not see that. They would see a man riding all but alone, unarmed, with nothing to mark him a king. He had argued that even with Taditi, insisted that he put on no airs, assume no dignity beyond what any man could claim. It should be enough that he had an army at his back.

He would never confess to her how tight his throat was as he rode into the camp, or how taut the muscles were across his shoulders. An arrow or a thrown spear could have cut him down in an instant.

So many faces. So many strangers. They had made no pretense of excitement, nor did any of them quicken his pace to see the easterners ride in. And yet they all were there, opening a passage for him. He could not turn aside from the straight path, must ride direct to the camp's center.

Since that had been his intention, he made no effort to contest it. He smiled at those whose eyes met his—not many; they were all staring, but not into his face. He put on every appearance of ease, as if he came to a camp of friends.

The elders and the leaders waited for him in the center. They were not all young, though even the eldest looked to be still of fighting age. These were warleaders, commanders of armies. From the weathering of their faces and the count of their scars, they had seen more wars and raids than Agni had ever dreamed of.

Such men among the eastern tribes had told him that he was a fool; that he had no hope of piercing the wood, let alone of conquering a country that only one man of the tribes had ever seen. If that one was lying or had stretched the truth, Agni and his army might find themselves standing at the edge of a precipice, or worse, facing a tribe to which war was breath and life. War was glory, but people in the east were rather fond of peace. After all, it let them enjoy the fruits of war.

In front of these dour men with their hard faces and stony eyes, he slid from Mitani's back. The stallion stood where Agni left him, patient, as he had been taught. Agni walked forward a step, two, three. He could feel his own men behind him, but hemmed in by greater numbers than their own. If it came to a fight, it would not go well for them.

He turned his mind away from that. He stood here because he had been guided to this place; because every night in dreams, the gods urged him onward. Surely these people believed in dreams. How else could the gods speak to them?

He halted just out of their reach and let his eyes pass over each face. Every tribe had its own features by which one might know its people, but they were all of much the same stamp: narrow, high-cheeked, hawk-nosed. They were fair or red or brown for the most part; blue-eyed or grey or green or, rarely, pale brown or amber like Agni's own. Few were dark, and those few were known to have foreign blood.

There were a number of dark faces here, men not as tall as some but broad and strong, and their faces were heavy, as if carved out of stone. Their hair was black, their eyes dark. Perhaps because they were so dark, they seemed to regard Agni with more mistrust than most.

He considered putting on a grim face, but that would be too much like the rest. He relaxed therefore, smiled, said easily as a man might among friends, "A fair day and a warm welcome to you, men of the west."

Some of them blinked. Others seemed taken aback. The greeting should have been theirs to utter, but they had sat silent, saying nothing.

Maybe Agni's presence had driven words out of their heads. He turned in his place, looking about at a camp that spread as wide as a gathering of tribes. "I see," he said, "that the gods have spoken to you, too. Are you ready? Will you go into the west?"

One of the grimmest of them all, a black-browed man with a great scar that rent his face in two, said in a voice like stone grinding on stone, "Are you all so light-minded, you in the east?"

Agni laughed. "And are you all so dour, you in the west? Is it the wood that does it to you? Come, be glad. Skyfather is calling you. He lays his blessing on you."

"Earth Mother is not greatly pleased," the grim one said.

"She should be," said Agni, "if the gods call us to war. Blood is meat and drink to her. It makes her rich; it nourishes the green and growing things."

"Yes," said the grim warleader. "The grass is never so green as on an old battlefield." He looked Agni over, a black look under black brows. "You're but a boy. How much blood have you shed in battle?"

"Enough," said Agni with his own flash of darkness. "If I say I hope we can win the sunset countries with little bloodshed, will you still ride with me?"

"Do you fancy that you'll lead us?"

Agni met that level stare. "I know that the gods set me in front of the rest. If their blessing holds, I'll be a king in the sunset country. But I'm not a king yet. Nor do I ask to be. I only ask that you ride with me."

"Even to death, or the world's ending?"

"Wherever the gods decree."

The warleader nodded, grim as ever, but a spark had brightened his eye. "I'll do it. I don't speak for the rest, but I'm willing."

The others glanced at one another. It was all agreed, Agni knew that. They were only feigning this last debate, to keep the stranger off balance. He could not tell whether they would go as the dark-browed warleader had said he would go. Many looked as if they would refuse.

Yet, after what no doubt they reckoned a judicious pause, they nodded, one after another. "We'll go," one said, a man as fair as the other was dark, so fair that though he was a man of middle years he had hardly more beard than a boy. He stroked what there was of it, nodding, frowning at Agni. "Yes, we'll brave the dark places. But not in your name. You we don't know."

"You know Skyfather," Agni said, "and the Thunderer, and the lords of the storm. I ride in their names. And you?"

"For Skyfather and for the burning god and for the lords of blood and battle," the fair man said, "we ride together."

"That will do," said the dark man.

It would more than do. But Agni could not in wisdom let them see how relieved he was. He smiled, nodded, did his best to look as if he had never expected any other choice.

·············· 54 ··············

The armies of west and east settled together in camp, if briefly, for time was passing. Agni as the leader of the eastern tribes was admitted among the warleaders, but they made it clear that if he would be more than they, he must earn it.

He was not inclined to argue that. These were seasoned men, men of power and substance, rich in cattle and horses. He beside them was a ragtag boy with a pack of restless young wolves. But if they could make common cause, then that was all that was needed. The gods led them. Nothing else need matter.

Taditi did not happen to agree. These men had brought women with them, a few only, favorite wives or bold-spirited concubines to keep them warm of nights. She went among the tents—prowling, Agni would not quite call it—and came back with a face as grim as the dark warleader's, and even less forgiving of youthful follies. "You are too humble," she said.

Agni mimed vast astonishment. "Why, aunt! I've never been accused of humility before."

"You've been accused of idiocy more than once," she said. "It never hurt you badly, but you never led an army before, either. They're saying in the tents that the men are laughing together at the eastern boy, and telling one another that you'll be an easy one to command. You're no one to reckon with, they say, you with your callow boys and your meek manner."

"You're trying to provoke me," Agni said.

"If the truth provokes you," said Taditi, "then I'm not the one to regret it."

Agni propped himself on his elbow in the heaped furs of his bed. He would not gratify her with a flash of temper.

" 'Callow'? They said that?"

"And meek," she said, "and no threat to any man. The women reckon you pleasant to look at. You might even make a man if you lift your head a little and look their husbands in the eye."

That stung. It must have shown on his face: Taditi's laughter was like a lash of cold rain. "I'm the youngest of them by a hand of years," he said. "I've never led more than a double handful in war. Should I declare myself king, and give them honest cause to laugh at me?"

"Carry yourself like a king," she said, "and the rest will follow."

The taste of bitterness filled his mouth. "What, as I carried myself when they cast me out of the tribe?"

"Stop that," she said, sharp as a slap. "You were conspired against. And you will be again, unless you act against it. You owe respect to your elders, but those elders owe you respect as the gods' own. They've no leader here, no one man who hears them out and then decides for them all. They'll quarrel and scatter before they come through the wood."

"They have a leader," Agni said. "The dark man, the one I spoke to—"

"He speaks for them more often than not," she said, "but his tribe is small and his strength limited. There's also some doubt as to his loyalty. Do you mark how different he looks? He's kin to the forest people. He speaks their language and can command them to a degree, but if it comes to a choice between the tribes and the forest people, no one knows which he'll choose."

"Well then," Agni said. "The fair one, the one everyone's eyes seemed to rest on. Surely he can command them when he's so minded."

"Not he nor any other of the western tribesmen," Taditi said. "Why do you think the gods sent you? They need someone from outside, one of them but set apart, with the strength of will to hold them together, and a little magic, too."

Agni snorted. "Will I may have. I've been called stubborn often enough. But there's no magic in me."

"You don't need feathers and chants and a bone flute to bring men to your call. You did it among the White Horse people and in most of the tribes to the west of it. Now do it here."

"But I don't know what I did."

"Does that matter? Just do it."

✦ ✦

Taditi had always been much too wise to endure. Agni lay awake longer than he meant to, chewing over the things she had said. Ridiculous to expect a raw boy to set himself above seasoned warleaders. Worse than ridiculous to castigate him for acting as a youth of his age should do.

And yet how proper was anything that he did? He was exiled. He should be nameless, friendless, hunted wherever he dared to show his face. Not lying in comfort in a tent, with a woman to tend him and a whole army to do his bidding. He the outcast lived as well as he ever had when he was a prince; and had a greater following, too.

It was all skewed about at the gods' whim. And if he had misheard them, or never heard them at all, and all this riding was a delusion—

That path he dared not walk. He had not asked any of the youth of the White Horse to follow him when he fled the tribe. They had done it of their own accord. He must trust that what he did, he did by the gods' will.

And if he did that, then he must do as Taditi urged him to do. He must carry himself like a king. Even if it ended as it had at the kingmaking, he could not fail to do it.

These people knew what he was and why he had left his tribe. He had made no secret of it. No more had they dwelt on it. It was not their tribe nor their dishonor. If he made enemies they would crush him with this thing, but while they remained his friends, they chose to ignore it.

The world was not a simple place. And by some jest of the gods, Agni had been set high in it. They gave him no choice in the end but to do as they willed.

✦ ✦

Walk like a king, Taditi had said. Think like one. Expect that people would do as Agni bade them, and never doubt that they would obey.

It was no more or less than he had been taught to do, as his father's son. Here where he had not been born to rule, where he must earn it, he walked into the circle of elders as the sun rose on a fair morning. He had seen as he came there how no one seemed inclined to move. They might be camped in this place for the summer, for all that he could tell.

He had learned that the dark warleader's name was Tillu and the fair one's was Anshan. Agni spoke to Tillu, who sat as a leader sits, despite what Taditi had said of him. "Tell me, man of the Stone Tree people. Can the people of the wood be persuaded to guide us through it?"

There was murmuring, as he had expected, against the upstart who would not take his proper place on the edge of the circle and listen meekly to the words of his elders. But Tillu answered him straightly enough, with no apparent reluctance. "Some may. Are you asking me to see to it?"

"I am asking," Agni said, "that we prepare to ride as soon as may be, but that we not ride blind. If there is a way through the wood, if we may come through it safely and in good time, can we find it?"

"We may try," Tillu said.

+ +

Agni left the elders to their leisure. He did not doubt that once he was gone, they were not merciful. But if Tillu did as Agni asked, and if in doing it he speeded their departure, Agni did not care what the rest said or thought.

Aside from the warleaders, this was an army of young men. So were all armies. Men who did not fight well died before their beards went grey. The greatest numbers were always the boys and the new-made men. These were Agni's own agemates, agemates in the hundreds that he had brought to this gathering. With them he was at ease. If they were hostile, he could face them down.

Mostly they were not. He walked through the camp with Rahim and Patir, Gauan and a handful of the others who had come here with him, and as he walked he gathered a band of young men. They followed him here as their fellows had on the steppe. He did not think he did anything or said anything apart from greeting this one, smiling at that one, watching as another practiced hurling his spear through a ring no larger than a man's hand, and cheering when he succeeded. It was nothing he made himself do. His father had taught him the way of it when he was small, how to be welcomed among the people, till it was as natural to him as the breath he drew.

If it would bring these people together and persuade them to begin the ride into the west, then Agni would do it till the sun went down, and into the night; and rise at dawn and carry on with it, till he knew the name of every tribe here, and the names of many of its men, too. Names were part of a man's soul. If one had a man's name, one had his attention. Then one could become his master—or his friend.

On the second day since Agni came into the camp, the elder Tillu paid him the honor of seeking him out. Agni was inspecting the horses, seeing to their feet, marking those that were looking a little worn and those that had taken this wound or that on the road or in the herd. Mitani was taking an interest, following just behind him, thrusting an inquisitive nose between Agni and the bruised hoof that he was tending. He laughed and thrust it away. As it retreated, he met Tillu's dark stare.

Agni kept the smile. Maybe Tillu warmed to it a little. On that terrible scarred face it was hard to tell. Agni finished tending the hoof, left the horse to his rider, straightened and said, "A fair morning to you, man of the Stone Tree."

"And to you, man of the eastern tribes," Tillu said. He tilted a brow at Mitani. "That one thinks the world of you."

"And I of him," Agni said, stroking the sleek red neck. Mitani lipped his hand, found nothing there, nipped and wheeled and fled in mock terror at the blow that never even began.

Agni grinned to see him go. Even Tillu proved himself capable of a wintry smile. "If your king of horses will let you go," he said, "there's somewhat that you should see."

Agni nodded to Rahim, who moved on to the next of the waiting horses, and began the inspection that Agni had set aside. Rahim would do well. Agni followed Tillu, and Patir followed them both, and a handful of young men who might simply have been curious, but who were conveniently well armed.

Tillu marked that, too, with a glance and a raise of the brows. Agni met the glance with a bland expression. He had not asked to be guarded. They did it because they chose to—as Mitani followed him. That was unusual in that the stallion did not wander off as they left the horselines, but continued in Agni's wake.

Tillu led them all through the camp toward the looming shadow of the wood. Agni had found that his eye tended to slip away from it, to see it but not to see it, as if it were a shape of living darkness. Yet from so close it was only a wall of trees, with outriders straggling along the hillside and clustering by the stream.

In the shade of such a copse, men were sitting. Agni did not at first see what was strange about them, except that they were all dark-haired men. They were dressed in tanned hides, and not a great deal of those in the warmth of the morning. Most of what he had taken for rough-tanned leather, he saw as he came closer, was their own skin, weatherworn and thick with black hair.

One was even naked, though that was not immediately obvious: he wore belt and baldric, long bone-hafted knife and slung bow, and his burly chest was hung about with ornaments of feather and stone and bone. His head was crowned with the skull and ears and branching antlers of a stag. Its hide, hooves and all, hung down like a cloak. He looked as if he had been embraced by the shell of the deer.

His body was thick-carved with scars, knotted and roped with them. Whorls of blue and black made a mask of his face. It was, beneath the patternings, a face like Tillu's, but heavier, stonier. Tillu, Agni could see then, was a halfling of these people, his features fined and—if one could believe it—softened by the crossing of eastern blood. This was the pure breed, one of Earth Mother's own, like a man carved out of stone.

As Agni took in the sight of him, so he took in the sight of Agni. Agni could not tell what he was thinking. His face was empty of expression, his eyes black stones. Whether he saw a king or a callow boy, a man like himself or a creature of another kind than his own, Agni did not know.

Tillu beside this one was as familiar as any tribesman. "These men will guide us," he said.

"And do they ask anything in return?" Agni inquired.

Tillu regarded him blankly. "Ask? They? They do it because we ask it."

The man in the deer's hide spoke. His words were alien, scattered with gurglings and clicks, like water muttering to itself in its sleep. Tillu heard him out with an expression that told Agni he understood.

When the speech was ended, Tillu said a little slowly, "This is a priest. He sees farther than other men see, and understands the speech of birds. He says to you: 'We guide you through the wood to serve ourselves. Promise to harm nothing, to touch nothing, to conquer nothing. Your gods have conceived a lust for the White Goddess' country, but our country is no part of it. We will not be conquered. Promise.' "

Agni frowned. "And if I won't promise?"

Tillu spoke in that language like water running over stones. The priest answered briefly. Tillu said, "No promise, no guide."

"That is reasonable," Agni said. "But they must guide us well and safely and by the shortest way, and promise no harm after."

The priest could promise that. Agni gave his own word in return. The priest listened intently to Agni's words; by which Agni knew that he understood the speech of the tribes, though he might not choose to speak it. He answered even as Tillu opened his mouth, but in his own tongue. Tillu said, "We follow *you*. Not the others. You. If the others go another way or try to break the word you've given, they have no guides. Only you."

"Why?" Agni asked.

Was that the glimmer of a smile? "Because," said the priest through Tillu, "we wish it so."

That was simple enough. Taditi would be pleased, Agni thought. She might even give him a few moments' peace.

.... 55 ....

Whether the elders would or no, on the fourth day since Agni came to the camp by the wood, all the young men struck their tents and readied to ride. Their guides were waiting. Agni's own following champed at the bit. When he came out to the horselines, he found Patir at Mitani's bridle and the chief of the guides standing with the patience of a stone. The priest was dressed, or not dressed, just as he had been before, man's body emerging from the hide of a stag. Agni's men looked askance at him. He was a strange, wild figure, a spirit of the wood.

Agni grasped mane and swung onto Mitani's back. The stallion was in motion even as Agni settled, fresh and eager and none too unwilling to venture the shadows of the trees. He would not suffer another horse to go before him, unless it were a mare; and men of the tribes did not ride mares.

They were bound to foot-pace, since their guides either would not or could not ride. But they were swift on their feet and tireless, and could run as fast as a horse might comfortably go, there amid the trees and the tangled undergrowth. The paths were narrow and twisted. The branches closed in overhead, shutting out the sky.

Agni, looking back, could see no more than the first dozen of his following. He could hear farther than that, but sounds were strangely muffled here, lost in the whispering of leaves. This might be a trap, might be treachery too perfect to escape: catch the horsemen in the wood, cut them off from one another, cut them down before they could move to defend themselves.

They could not always ride, either. Where trees grew close or branches hung low, they must perforce dismount and lead their horses.

Agni on the march liked to ride back and forth along the line, to keep count of his men, to see that the baggage was safe, to share a song or a story. Here he was bound to the lead, with only the priest ahead of him. For all he knew, the dozen men he could see and the dozen more that he could hear were all that had followed him. All the rest might have remained in the open country under the blessed vault of the sky.

He had bought this with his word and with his conviction that the gods had led him into the west. He did not know if he even traveled westward. All directions were the same under the trees.

He must trust in the gods and in his guide. And when a clearing opened with startling suddenness, wide and sunlit and sweet with grass and flowers, he could draw aside and count the men who rode or walked through it. Their beginning he knew; he had been in it. Their end was lost in the dimness of the trees.

As Agni sat Mitani and Mitani grazed, well content with the respite, Tillu rode out of the trees and curved round to his side. The warleader of the Stone Tree was mounted on a horse as thick and massive as himself, a heavy-headed black with feathered hooves, such as one sometimes found wandering away to the northward. It was taller than Mitani and far more strongly built, but seemed remarkably placid for a stallion.

Tillu sat at ease on the broad back, watching the army ride past.

"You've been in the wood before," Agni said without taking his eyes from them.

"Once or twice," Tillu said. "My mother was a captive from one of the forest clans. My father took her not for her beauty—she had none—but for her power in the clan. Women rule here. You may widen your eyes at it, but it is so."

"I widen my eyes," Agni said, "because I've heard the same of the western people. Do they exist after all? Or are these the ones the travellers tell of?"

"Oh no," said Tillu. "The forest people are another people altogether. It's said they were made before the dawn of the world, even before the gods; when Earth Mother was alone, and hungered for company. So she made the people out of clay and stone, taught them to speak, gave them the gifts that she had then to give. The grey light of dawn was theirs, and the chill of morning. But when she made the sun, she took it into her head to refine her creation. Then she made a new race of men, and made them beautiful. She put fire in them; but it was too strong for them, burned and consumed them. So she made them again, but set a core of clay in them, a vessel for the fire; and what was pure fire, she shaped into the gods."

Agni heard him out in wonder. "You know great and secret things," he said.

"My mother was a clan-mother," Tillu said. "And yes, as you asked, there are people beyond the wood, between the trees and the sunset. It's called the Lady's country. The Lady is Earth Mother. They know no other gods. That, the forest people say, is because they were made between the dawn and the daylight. They remember the time before there were gods. They worship none but Earth Mother, because the gods came late and were made of the leavings of their own creation."

"And women rule them," Agni said.

"Oh yes," said Tillu. "They'll find you appalling. The forest people do. They're gentle people, too gentle for the likes of us. But for the terror of the wood, they'd all be dead long ago. The tribes would have overrun and killed them."

"Or made pacts with them," Agni said, "to leave them unharmed, and overrun and kill someone else."

"Can you blame them for that?" Tillu asked.

Agni shrugged. "It's war. One does what one must."

"Precisely," said Tillu.

✦ ✦

When night closed in, the men of the steppe found themselves in a world they had never imagined. There were no stars beneath that canopy of branches, no moonlight; only a black and whispering dark. It was full of rustlings and murmurings, far-off howls, the shriek of something dying.

So many men could not camp within sight of each other. Their guides led them to a chain of clearings and showed them where there was wood to burn, water to drink. For the horses' sake they pitched tents under the trees, leaving the grass clear. Even that was little enough.

By pausing in clearings, Agni had worked his way well back along the army's length. Now as dusk grew dim beneath the branches he looked for his own people again. He found them just short of full dark, camped on a fire-seared hillside where the grass grew green and rich amid the charred stumps of trees. They were in greater comfort than some, with more space and therefore more sky, and better grass for the horses.

He squatted beside the fire, next to Taditi, who tended a fine haunch of venison on a spit. The rest of the deer roasted nearby, over Gauan's fire. "Lucky shot," he called across the darkening space.

"Wasn't luck," Taditi muttered. "Was sharp wits and a sharp eye. We'll need a strong share of that if we're to come out of this place."

"I hate it," said Patir. He was lying on the grass staring up at the stars. "It makes my skin creep."

"People are laying wagers whether the whole world is forest," Rahim said from across the fire, "and whether the sunset country is clear of trees."

"It had better be," Patir said darkly. "If I see a tree there, by the gods, I'll cut it down and burn it."

"Earth Mother might object to that," Tillu said, taking shape out of the darkness and sitting on his heels by the fire. An antlered figure loomed behind him. Agni saw fingers flick in a gesture against ill spirits, but it was only the priest in the stag's hide.

He was watching Agni. Agni smiled brightly at him and turned his glance on Tillu. "How long will we be in the wood?" he asked.

Tillu shrugged. "As long as it takes. Five days? Eight?"

"Eight days?" Patir howled like a dog. *"Ai!* We'll all run mad."

"Pray," said a voice like stones shifting.

They all stared at the priest. He stood unmoving, his face shadowed by the stag's crown.

"Pray to the gods," Tillu said, "and think of sunlight. It's open country where we're going, though you," he said to Patir, "may find a tree or six to burn."

"Let it come soon," said Patir.

✦ ✦

No one went mad, though tempers frayed and men were sore tempted to quarrel with one another. Agni rode tirelessly up and down the army, in and out of its camps, soothing and stroking and coaxing people to be sensible. He slept, he supposed, though not happily. There were dreams, and they were dark, full of murmurings and whisperings like the forest he slept in. If he came through it, he would wait long before he went near it again.

Even beyond men's troubles, the horses were less than happy. They could forage, but poorly; they were not deer, to thrive on leaves and twigs and bits of forest flotsam. Water they had; the wood was laced with streams and little rivers. But grass was scarce, and there was not enough of it for so many horses. They could not linger much longer if they were to be strong enough to carry men to battle.

Not a few of those men wondered, sometimes too loudly, if they were being led in circles, weakened for the slaughter. Agni hoped that they were not. The priest's steps were sure in these tangled places. His fellows appeared and disappeared—scouts, Agni guessed, with word of the way ahead. Each evening found them in a clearing that showed no sign of men's presence before, or along a riverbank where only the tracks of wild beasts marred the soft earth.

They never saw a camp or gathering place of the forest people. They were being led away from such, Agni suspected. He would have done the same if he had been leading the warriors of gathered tribes through his people's country. Warriors were never to be trusted.

These were not warriors. They were hunters, and perhaps more than one was a priest. They guided their charges through the wood with silent skill. Their women were not to be seen, nor their children. They were all men of indeterminate age, some more gnarled than others. None spoke the language of the tribes. Only the priest seemed to understand it.

It was like the rite the boys endured when their voices first began to deepen, when they passed from boys to young men, and began their long schooling in the men's arts. They went into the barrows of their ancestors, deep within the tribe's lands, and remained there from dusk until dawn. In the rite they went back to the womb's darkness and there sought visions; and when the visions were done, they crawled through the narrow passage into the first light of morning, and so were reborn into the world and the tribe.

Here the gathering of warriors slept each night in the womb of the forest, and crawled each day through the narrow ways. But they never saw the open country. They were never born again into the world.

Agni's mind was slipping. He had to struggle to remember the count of days. Six? No, seven. Five? Four?

"Seven," Taditi said when he asked. Nothing dismayed her, not even the crashing in the night that proved, by the signs they found come morning, to be the passing of a herd of aurochs. If it had veered aside, it would have pounded their camp to dust.

Taditi had no fear of the dark or of the shadows under the trees. She professed to be rather more pleased than not to be spared the glare of the sun. But then she was a woman. She had grown up in the dimness of the tents, closed in by walls. Walls of trees, walls of a tent, it mattered little to her.

Agni had never thought before that a woman might have an advantage over a man. It was a strange thing to think, in this strange place.

✦ ✦

As seemed to happen each night, Tillu appeared at the campfire in time to share whatever was to be had, which that night was a brace of rabbits and a string of wood-doves wrapped in leaves and roasted. The priest was with him for the first time since that first night; where he had been between, Agni did not know nor venture to ask.

They ate hungrily. Agni and the others of his people were seldom hungry now. They ate because they must, but they had begun to doubt even that. But Tillu and his kinsman seemed well content. When they had eaten their fill and belched politely, Tillu said to Agni, "The priest has somewhat to ask."

Agni raised a brow. He had eaten one of the doves, but it had tasted of ashes. It sat heavy in his stomach.

The priest spoke briefly. When he fell silent, Tillu said, "He says, you were not born alone. The stars say so. Where is the other one, the one you were born with?"

Agni blinked. Of all questions he had expected, this was one of the last. "The other—my sister?"

The priest nodded as if he had hoped for such an answer. "Your sister," Tillu said for him, "yes. Where is she?"

"She went west," Agni said, "ahead of me."

The priest nodded again and smiled, and did a strange thing: he patted Agni on the shoulder. If he had been anyone Agni understood, Agni would have said that he offered sympathy. Though for what—"Is she dead? Are you telling me that? Did this place kill her?"

The priest shook his head. He looked pleased, and not as if he grieved for any loss. He patted Agni's shoulder once more and vanished into the night.

Tillu had not moved. Agni rounded on him. "What was that? Why did he ask about my sister?"

"He reads the stars," Tillu said. "He says that your star is twofold, and one is brighter than the other. I think he wants to know which one."

"She's not dead, is she?" Agni demanded. "She's not sick? Or dying?"

"I don't know," said Tillu. "No one asks priests why they do what they do."

That was eminently true, but Agni did not have to like it. He went to bed soon after, snarling, and lay awake too long, fretting over his sister.

Which no doubt was exactly as the priest intended. That one liked to trouble a man's sleep, Agni thought. He had a look about him, as if there were more gods in him than he could easily carry. Sarama had it, too. Had had it. Still had it, by the gods, and would have it till she grew vastly old.

"Horse Goddess," Agni whispered into the dark. "Lady, protect her. Keep her till I come."

56

On the eighth day, as Tillu had predicted, they reached the wood's edge. It was a gradual thing, a thinning of trees, a greater frequency of clearings, and sun so bright that it dazzled them. And then at last through the thin and straggling treetrunks they saw open country, a long roll of hillside and the gleam of water in a river.

Green country. Fair country. Country that lay naked beneath the sky. It was more beautiful than a woman. Agni felt his body rouse to it: startling, a little, as if he had been deathly ill or dead, and had come to life again.

Just so he had been when he saw the sun in the morning after he came out of the barrow. He had been naked then and rampant for all the men of the tribe to see; but none of them had laughed, except to admire his spirit.

There had been no woman for him just then. No more was there one now. He shifted on Mitani's back, and turned to look over his shoulder. His people emerged from the wood in ones and twos and threes, with their pack-horses and their led horses. They should have been a brave sight. They looked like children emerging sleepy from a tent, blinking and squinting, some rubbing their eyes. If the forest people had had a mind for treachery, or if this country had known war, they could have been cut down where they stood.

But as they woke to the truth, first one and then another looked about in amazement; astonishment; joy. A whoop rang out. One of the men of the White Horse kicked his mount into a gallop, shrieking like a mad thing, taking the hillside by storm.

His gladness spread like sparks from a fire. Between one breath and the next, the whole yelling mob of them had surged into motion.

Mitani jibbed and reared, but Agni was not moved to join that wild ride.

He should have been leading it. He knew that. Nevertheless he held his place, looking back, searching the shadows for signs of a heavy-browed face, or a stag's crown of antlers in the season when a living stag wore only velvet.

He did not see them, nor Tillu the halfling either. The forest people had fulfilled their promise. They had not lingered after. No farewell; no tidy ending. Simply their absence.

Agni did not know why he lingered himself, when he knew that there was no reason. Mitani was growing frankly angry. He sighed at last and let the stallion go. Mitani bucked for spite, twisted, nigh unseated his rider. But Agni had ridden out worse, and Mitani was too eager to catch his fellows, to put his heart into it. He smoothed into a gallop.

✦ ✦

It came to Agni, as the wind sang in his ears and tugged at his hair, that he should have kept the priest as a guide. The man knew this country, surely. He knew where they should go, and how they should speak to the people there.

But he was gone. Agni had no guide now but the gods.

Well then. First he must gather his scattered people and pray that none of them had run afoul of someone from this country. War was best fought if one had the advantage of surprise. And though tales said that war was not known in the sunset country, Agni did not want just now to trust to tales.

None of them ran far. Just far enough to be truly away from the trees, and to see that this was a green and lovely country. The horses saw that even sooner than the men. They were none too eager to gallop when they could crop the rich green grass.

In a little while that whole rolling field between the forest and the river was dotted with grazing horses. Their riders had slipped from their backs to lie in the grass, or had gone down to drink from the river. A few, Agni was pleased to see, had begun the making of a camp.

He gathered a handful of his own young men and sent them out to scout and to bring back what game they could. The others set to tending the horses and pitching camp. It was still early in the day, but they were all agreed, with no word spoken: they should stop, rest, let their horses graze. And, if they could, the elders and the warleaders should gather to plan the war.

The western tribesmen camped next to but not among Agni's men of the east. Agni pondered very briefly before he ventured to send messengers to their leaders, inviting them politely to visit him in his camp. He hinted at mead, and at *kumiss*.

Taditi had worked wonders with what was left of their provender, in expectation that this country would feed them well and amply. It was a wager of sorts, that they would not starve before they hunted and gathered all that they needed. Or, of course, won it in battle.

Agni settled in front of his tent on the bear's hide that was his sleeping fur, and kept company with Rahim and Patir, Gauan and some of his warriors, and various of his tribesmen. They came and went as they pleased, babbling with the pleasure of sun and grass and sky, and the dizzy delight of having come at last to the place they had been seeking.

"Do you think we'll find cities?" they kept asking. "Will there be copper? Cattle? Women?"

To be sure, Agni thought, this place seemed empty enough. He saw no great gatherings of people, no tents of stone such as the tales told of. Only grass and river and a scattering of trees which Patir had not yet made a move to burn.

One by one as the day wore away, the elders and the warleaders happened by. It was not because Agni asked, they made it clear, but because it pleased them to wander this way. His mead, his *kumiss,* the venison toward evening, for one of the hunters had found a herd of deer grazing on the edges of the wood, drew the westerners to his campfire. They lingered for the mead and for the company.

As the shadows grew long and the sun sank over the hills to the westward, Agni observed rather idly, "If we're to fight a war, we might consider how we'll do it."

"Ride," said a warleader with the features of the forest people, but startling pale eyes. "Fight. Kill. Take what we win."

"Certainly," said Agni. "And what will we do with it once we have it?"

"Use it," the warleader answered, "and when it's finished, ride away."

"We could ride clear into the sunset," one of his fellows said. "Right past the world's edge."

"What, and fall off?" Rahim shook his head. "I'm not minded to go as far as the edge. A rich tribe, beautiful women, copper for the taking—all those will well content me."

"If there's any such thing," growled a man who sat just out of the light. Agni saw a pale blur of face, a glitter of eyes, but little else. "What if this country's empty?"

"It's not empty," said Tillu, making his way through the seated men to settle beside Agni. This, his manner said, was his proper place, and he would face down any who challenged him for it.

Rahim, who had been gently but distinctly thrust aside, shrugged and reached for another collop of venison. There would be payment later, his glance said, but for the moment he was content to let be.

Agni suppressed a sigh. Horses were much simpler than men. They tolerated one another, or they fought. They did not bide their time, or form factions that could trouble their herd-leader's mind both now and later.

Tillu, who seemed to have ambitions to lead this herd of men, went on with what he had begun on the circle's edge. "There are people here," he said. "Hundreds. Hundreds of hundreds. The forest people led us to a region that's little frequented, so that we can gather our forces and take them by surprise. But there are people here, oh yes. And cities. And cattle and copper and gold. All the riches that a man can dream of."

"I should like to see them," said the unbeliever.

"Ride half a day's journey north or south or west, and you'll see," Tillu said.

"I intend to," said the unbeliever.

"So should we all," Agni said, "but we should do it together, and we should know beforehand how we'll go about taking whatever we find."

He held his breath. They all stared at him, but even the unbeliever was silent. He breathed out slowly. Think like a king. Yes. Like a king. When he could trust his voice to be firm, he said, "We'll camp here tomorrow, if you will, and see which of our scouts come back, and what they've found. Once we know, we'll agree which direction is best, and ride in it. Some of us will lead, and fall on whatever camp or city we find. Others will come behind to secure it. Then we'll leave men in it to hold it, and after we've taken what we please, we'll go on to the next. And the next. In this country, if the tales are true, every man can be a king. And every king that we find will be a woman."

They laughed at that, mocking the thought of it. But Tillu did not laugh. He said, low enough that only Agni and those closest to him could hear, "Women rule the forest people. I've seen it. And they say that women rule here. That their only god is Earth Mother, and they worship her with rites of gold and blood."

"All the easier for us to take and hold them," Gauan said. "Is it true, then? They know nothing of war?"

"So it's said," said Tillu.

Gauan shook his head in amazement. "I don't know if I'll believe that even when I see it. But if it does happen to be so—what a gods' gift for us."

"And where are their men?" someone wondered.

"I'll wager they're all geldings," Gauan said, "except the few they keep for stud."

Nervous laughter ran round the circle. "Maybe the women are bearded," said a man across the fire from Agni. "Maybe they walk like men, and look like men, but when you catch them in bed—if you can stand to kiss those hairy cheeks—they're as female as they need to be."

"I like a smooth skin," Gauan said, "and a pretty face."

"Razors!" the other sang out. "We'll all carry razors and shave every bearded face we find. If it's soft, if it's pretty, if the body's cleft below—it's ours to take."

"Just be sure the cleft is in front and not in back," someone else advised.

They whooped at that.

Agni would have been interested to hear how far they would take this flight of fancy, but someone tugged at his sleeve. It was Patir, who had gone to relieve himself. "Muti's back," he said.

Even as Agni rose, a prickling in his belly warned him to yawn, to stretch, to mutter something about too much *kumiss* and not enough bladder. No one noticed, even Tillu. He slipped away easily after all, following Patir round his tent and into the cool sweetness of the night.

The air was different here. Grass scented it. The wind moved freely, unhampered by trees. The sky was clear overhead. The moon was thin but waxing, shedding a pale light on the faces of not only Muti but his two brothers who had gone out with him. And in the midst of them a stranger. It seemed to be male, and young, too young to have grown a beard.

Agni refused to share the foolishness that reigned still around the fire, from the sound of it: ribald laughter, and a shout as if at a particularly clever sally. This in front of him was a boy or a very young man, small among the tribesmen, with a shock of curly hair, very dark, and big dark eyes. They were wide, but Agni saw no fear in them.

He turned to Muti. "Well?"

Muti grinned. The boy smiled tentatively back. "We found him just over the hill," Muti said, "herding a flock of goats—which, before you ask, we took possession of; they're back with the cattle. He's simple, maybe. He's yet to say a word that any of us can understand."

"Has he said a word at all?" Agni asked.

"Plenty," said Muti. "All in gibberish."

As if he had understood, the boy spoke. They were words, Agni could tell, and they appeared to have meaning, but it was none that Agni could find. He jabbed his chin at the younger of Muti's brothers. "Fetch me someone who understands this language."

"But," said the brother, whose name at the moment Agni could not recall, "I don't—there isn't—"

"Find one," Agni said. The brother grumbled, but he went.

Which left Agni with the boy. Agni looked him up and down. He returned the favor. He was not afraid. He looked about him with bright-eyed interest, though his eye kept returning to Agni as if captivated. Agni did not know what there was to marvel at. If the boy's dark-haired people had never seen a redheaded or light-eyed man before, still by now he would have seen his fill of them: Muti was as red as the metal called copper, and his brothers were sandy-fair, and they were all blue-eyed. Agni in moonlight should look almost as dark as a man of this country.

There was no telling what the boy was thinking, and no asking him till someone should come who had some knowledge of his language. Agni turned to Muti. "Come into the tent. No, not there! This way."

Muti's eyebrows went up, but he did not argue when Agni led him in under the tent-wall, creeping in the back as Agni had been used to creep in to visit Rudira.

No, not that thought. Agni knocked it down and set his foot on it. He emerged into the lamplit dimness of the tent. It was close quarters with Muti and the boy, but Agni was not minded just yet to show him to the elders round the fire.

The boy was as interested in the tent as in everything else, and as fearless. He sat where Agni pointed, tucked up his feet and smiled as if he were a guest in a friend's tent.

"Now," Agni said to Muti, "tell me where you found him."

Muti was never as comfortable as the boy. He squatted on his heels as if ready to leap and bolt, and said, "He was herding goats on a hill half a day's walk from here. We captured him and brought him back."

"Without resistance?" Agni asked.

"None at all," said Muti. "He walked right up to us. We were on foot, there. When he saw our horses he seemed taken aback, but he didn't give us any trouble."

"No war," Agni murmured. "No fear." He had never imagined that one might lead to the other. If men did not kill men, if there were no warriors, no raids, no tribe doing battle with tribe, then what would any man be afraid of? Wolves, maybe. Lions. Winter. But not other men, even strangers.

Not to be afraid of strangers. It was like a story from the gods' country, from a place where there was no suffering.

And Agni might be maundering, building whole worlds on a mind too simple to know fear. He brought himself back into the world, saw that the boy was fed—venison and mead he seemed to know, and to find good. He was not trying to escape, did not try to follow Muti when Muti went to fetch food and drink for him. He seemed as content as a tamed puppy or a hand-raised foal to stay where he was put.

Muti's brother did not come back. Agni felt sleep creeping up on him. The boy was sitting on his sleeping-roll. He sighed, shrugged, wrapped his arms about himself and leaned lightly against the tent-wall and let himself drift as he did in the saddle, upright but dreaming.

When he opened his eyes again, people were whispering. He blinked, and squinted. Light dazzled him: morning light through the flap of the tent, and a shadow athwart it. Muti's voice said, "He's asleep. Can you wait?"

"I'm awake," Agni said. As his eyes grew used to the light, he saw the boy curled on the bed, sound asleep, and Muti with his brother, staring, apparently struck dumb.

"Well?" Agni asked. "Did you find someone who understands this language?"

Muti's brother nodded, but doubtfully. "Lord Tillu says he understands the trader's argot. He's not sure if it will do, but he's willing to try."

"I hope you told him to let me be the judge of that," Agni said.

Muti's brother rolled his eyes. "That I did, though he didn't take it very kindly. He's outside. Shall I send him in?"

"No," Agni said. "I'll come out. Bid him wait. And be polite."

Muti's brother looked a little affronted, but he went to do Agni's bidding.

Most interesting, Agni thought. He had expected some tribesman or hanger-on, or maybe a stray woodman. That Tillu should offer himself for this office—he was ambitious, was Tillu. Which might not be altogether a bad thing.

Agni levered himself to his feet. He was stiff with sitting nightlong. He stretched every muscle, groaning a little, catching the boy's glance in the middle of it. The boy was awake and upright and his eyes were wide.

Agni began to wonder, out of nowhere in particular, whether this was a boy at all. Moonlight softened a face, but daylight sharpened all its edges. This one seemed to have none. It was a smooth rounded face, pretty in its way, if one inclined toward blunt nose and full cheeks.

A girl alone, herding goats within reach of an army?

But if they knew no war, then maybe they knew no bands of marauders. No sudden attacks. No rape. A girl might be safe with her goats in the hillside, at least from men. Wolves and lions would not care what or who she was.

Muti and his brother were waiting. With a last glance at the boy—girl?— Agni stepped out into the full light of morning.

His campfire was ashes, all but a few embers over which Taditi crouched, coaxing them into flame. Men were out and about, but Agni saw no elders. They would all be sleeping off the mead and the *kumiss*.

Tillu was sitting outside by the campfire, eating a bowl of something savory. It proved, when Taditi handed Agni a bowl of it, to be a stew of dried meat and herbs. Agni settled in comfort beside the western tribesman, and they ate for a while in amity.

But the foreigner was waiting inside the tent, and he—or more likely she—weighed heavy on Agni's mind. He said rather abruptly, "You think you speak the language of this country."

Tillu did not appear to take offense. He licked the bowl clean and laid it politely down in front of him, and bowed to Taditi. Taditi sniffed and took the bowl away. Still with glinting eyes as if she greatly amused him, he said to Agni, "I think I may have a few words, if the tongue the traders speak is like the one they speak here."

"There is that," Agni said. "Well then; you're welcome to try. Come into the tent."

Tillu nodded amiably and rose, and at Agni's gesture preceded him back into the dimness.

The girl—Agni was sure of that, entering behind Tillu, seeing the face anew—was sitting where he had left her, head cocked, alert but quiet. Her eyes fixed on Tillu in a kind of panicked fascination. Agni hissed at himself for not thinking of what a woman might make of that face with its great hideous scar.

She did not shriek, at least, or cower, though her glance leaped to Agni and held, as if she took some pleasure or some comfort in his presence. If nothing else, she would find him prettier to look at.

"Tell her," Agni said, keeping his voice gentle lest he alarm her further, "that we are men of the east, and we've heard of her country, and have come to see it for ourselves."

Tillu frowned as if in concentration. Then he spoke a few words, haltingly. The girl appeared to listen, but Agni could not tell if she understood. Nor did she answer.

Tillu spoke again. This time she must have made some sense of it: her lips twitched. She spoke briefly, with an intonation that indicated she was speaking to a child, and not an intelligent one either.

Tillu's brows went up. "She says," the man said, "that now you see this country, you can go home."

Agni laughed, more with relief than with mirth; because after all here was someone who could speak to this stranger. "I don't think so," he said. "Yet. Ask her if her people are near, and would they be hospitable to guests? We've need of food and such."

The glance Tillu shot him asked if he had gone out of his mind. Was this not a war? Agni met it with a bland stare. Tillu sighed but chose visibly not to argue. He spoke, this time with more confidence and fewer hesitations. The girl answered. He said, "She says her people are where her people are, and you're welcome to visit their markets."

"I would like that," Agni said. "She'll guide us. Tell her."

She was duly told; and she nodded, as an innocent will, wide-eyed, trusting him. Agni smiled at her. She smiled back. She was very pretty, once one grew accustomed to round cheeks and round eyes. She was not shy, either, nor modest; she carried herself like a boy.

"Do you have a name?" Agni asked her through Tillu.

She nodded broadly, with a flicker of laughter. "Maya," she said.

"Maya," Agni said. She favored him with a broad smile. "We'll go," he said, "to your market."

"Now?" Tillu asked on his own account, with a touch of incredulity.

"Now," said Agni. "When better?"

Tillu shrugged as if say that it was Agni's foolishness and he had no part of it, and spoke to the girl. She looked not at all dismayed. Her glance at Agni was bright and bold. She slipped past him out of the tent, with a word that must have meant "Come."

.... 57 ....

Led by the girl Maya, Agni set out for the gathering place of her people—the city, as he had been told it was called. Rather a mob followed them. Tillu of course, because he was Agni's voice in this place. Patir and Rahim were not to be left behind, nor was Gauan, and they brought hangers-on of various sorts. There must have been three dozen of them, all mounted, for what man would be caught afoot when he could ride? And of course they were all armed, for who went abroad without sword and spear, bow and shield?

They were a warlike company, then, and none too sedate. Maya was quick on her feet, but once they had left the camp behind, Agni halted and caught her eye, and beckoned. She blanched, maybe, but she was a bold creature. She took his hand and made herself light and scrambled up behind him. Mitani was wary but quiet. She had the wits to sit still and not cling too tightly, though Agni could feel the tension in her. It made her quiver just perceptibly, and made Mitani switch his tail and snort.

Mitani carried her nonetheless, and she relaxed slowly. She pointed the way when Agni hesitated, otherwise leaned lightly against him. He was aware of her through the coat that she wore, and his own leather tunic: the shape of her body, the small round breasts pressing against his back. As they rode onward, her hand began to work mischief. It crept under his tunic, found the string that bound his trousers, tugged it loose and darted beneath.

He clapped his hand against hers. Her laughter bubbled against his back.

Even Rudira had never been so bold—no, not even when they were private together. And he was riding at the head of a middling large war-party, with every eye on him, and laughter enough if any knew what this impudent child was doing.

Agni extricated her hand from his clothes and pressed it firmly against his middle, where the belt made a wall between her mischief and his skin.

She sighed gustily and appeared to surrender, but Agni was twinborn with Sarama. He had learned never to trust a woman with a mind of her own.

And to be sure, as they rode up a long hill, she began to nibble his ear. Little gusts of laughter tickled him between the sharp nips, a mix of pain and pleasure that made him want to howl. He must not think of what she was making him think of. He *must* not.

He had been long seasons without a woman. None had offered herself among the tribes, nor had he been offered any. The consolation that some took on long marches or in war, to turn to one another, was not one that Agni had ever found pleasing.

And here was a woman pressed close to him for all to see, teasing and tormenting him with hands that were far too clever for so young a child as she seemed to be. Denied the swift road to his manly parts, she took the long way round across his back and shoulders. She took it long indeed, and she took it slow, and she found the spot along his spine that made him shiver, and the one along his ribs that made him twitch and curse.

She was mad, he decided. What sane woman would do such a thing in front of three dozen men? And laugh while she did it?

When they reached the hill's summit, high up against the sky, she had a little mercy. She slid from Mitani's back to stand in the high grass and to spread her arms to all before her.

"My country," Tillu said for her. "My people."

Agni had already guessed that was what she had said. If he turned and looked behind, he saw a rolling green country, empty of habitation, lapping up against the forest's knees. But in front of him down the long slope was pure strangeness: a skein of what looked like camps, but camps grown vast and set in wood and stone. Each wore a girdle of patchwork green and brown, rings of fields where the fruits of the earth must grow at man's will and not simply at the will of the gods. Or so Tillu said. Agni could see no pressing reason to disbelieve him.

It was a great marvel and a strangeness, and more than strange. There were so many of these cities. They strung like beads along the river, and danced in their circles on the hilltops and in the wooded valleys.

Things moved on the river: boats, Tillu said, using a word that Maya had spoken. They were built of wood and of hollowed trees, some with tents pitched on them, and people sat or stood in them and drove them with poles and oars—another word for which Agni had had no meaning before, nor had much now; but when he came to the river he would see. And there were people on roads between the cities, too, on paths beaten down by the passage of countless feet. More people than Agni had known were in the world.

"This is only an outland country," Maya said through Tillu. "There are more people west of here, and much greater cities."

Agni sucked in his breath and did his best not to look amazed. She might be lying, to strike him with fear and awe. But he thought not. She was too calm about it, not furtive at all as people were when they lied.

He straightened his shoulders and said to Maya, "Come." She took his outstretched hand and climbed up behind him, more adeptly this time, and with less stiffening and clutching. Agni, who wanted to go stiff and clutch at something familiar himself, sent Mitani down the hill. The others followed, some slowly, some with great insouciance, refusing to be astonished by this broad new world.

✦ ✦

The nearest of the cities was Maya's city. There were, she said with gestures, ten tens of people in it—very few, her manner professed, but she was proud of it nonetheless. It was built in circles, though the houses were square-sided, all facing inward toward one that was higher and more ornate than the others. It seemed to be a king's house, covered with signs that must be sacred, with carved beams and bright paint.

They rode through the fields that were plowed in curves and circles, sprouting with green, precise and ordered. People were doing things in the fields, digging or plucking or rooting in the earth beneath the young grain. They all came erect as the tribesmen rode past, wide eyes, pale faces, a murmur that followed them.

Agni had seen goats in outlying fields, and cattle and sheep. But no horses. Theirs were the only ones: the first, maybe, that had walked in this part of the world.

People were standing just past the first of the houses, at ease but alert, like guards. Yet they were unarmed. In all their rich and beautifully colored clothing, he saw not one knife or spear, no bow, no weapon of war. Maybe their bodies were their weapons. They were all women, dark as Maya was dark, and most were plump, and one or two were grossly fat. As fat as any tribesman could dream of being in a year of impossible richness, when there was nothing to do but lie about and sip from the honeycomb.

Then Agni truly believed that the traveler's tales were true. No one dressed so, stood so, looked so, who lived as tribesmen lived. These people were rich. They lived soft and without fear.

And women ruled them. Agni saw men in the fields, but they hung back. Women came forward, bolder than Agni had ever seen, staring openly and murmuring to one another. None quite dared come close enough to touch the horses, but while Agni gaped like a fool at the city and its people, they had closed in all about. The only way open was ahead, toward what must be the elders.

Strange to think of them so, all these women, standing monumental and calm. Something about them made Agni think of Taditi, and of the Old Woman.

One was not the tallest, but she was the most monumental, vast breasts, vast thighs, face as vastly calm as the face of the moon. She stood among the others, but something in the way she stood, in the way the others stood about her, made her their center.

Agni swung his leg over Mitani's neck and slid lightly to the ground. The women watched in silence. He beckoned. "Tillu. Talk to them if you will. Tell them that we come to trade with them."

Tillu nodded, and spoke to them. The one of great presence replied in a deep sweet voice. Tillu said, "She says that you are welcome, and that you are her guests in this city. She's called the Mother. That's her name and her title. You're to call her that."

"My mother is dead," Agni said—and where that came from, he could not have told.

Nor had he meant Tillu to render it into that other language, but it was done before Agni could stop it. The Mother stepped forward and laid her hand on Agni's arm.

"She says," said Tillu, "that she is sorry, and that you should not be. All mothers are one Mother. They are all the Goddess."

"The Old Woman said that," Agni said. He shook himself. "Tell her we thank her, and we'll visit the market, if she gives us leave."

She inclined her head as if she had been a king. Then in her own person she led him into her city.

✦ ✦

"I hope you're being clever," Patir said in Agni's ear as they stood in a market that would have been a great wonder in a gathering of tribes. And this was a city reckoned no larger than a clan-gathering on the steppe.

Agni raised a brow at Patir. "You think we should fall on them with fire and slaughter?"

"I think these people know nothing of war," Patir said.

"So I see," Agni said. "I also see that they are very rich, and very complacent. Wouldn't you choose to conquer without bloodshed, if you could?"

"Easy pickings," Patir said. He sifted through a bowl of bright stones, picking out the brightest, turning them to make them sparkle. "It's too easy."

"These people have never known war," Agni said. "Look at them. We're strangers; we're armed. We rode in on horses. And they smile at us and offer us whatever they have."

"They're buying us off," said Patir. "They're cowards."

"They're innocents," Agni said.

"Is there a difference?" Patir let the stones fall back into the bowl, and went on down the line of stalls to a trader in woven cloth. There were spread weavings more elaborate than Agni had known was possible, bright as flowers, some rough, some smooth, some a mingling of both. Agni would have reckoned them fit for kings, but even the children wore such marvels of the weaver's art, playing carelessly in the dust and mud, with no one to rebuke them for dirtying their beautiful coats.

There were more traders in cloth, and traders in pots of wonderful artistry, and traders in things to eat—most of which Agni could not even name—and among them women who offered the ruddy wonder of copper, and even more wonderful than that, the bright gleam of gold. It was like sunlight given substance, cool and smooth to the hand, and startlingly heavy. Agni marveled at a great twisted ring of it, a ring for the throat, as the trader indicated with a gesture and a smile, with knobs of amber ornamenting the ends. It clasped his neck as if made for it, and sat cool and heavy on his shoulders.

"It is yours," Tillu said, appearing beside him, speaking for the Mother, whom Agni had seen just a moment before at the far end of the market. She could move quickly for a woman so huge, and lightly too. For himself Tillu added, "Amazing. The amber's the same color as your eyes. She knows it, too. She's got her eye on you, my lord."

Agni did not dignify that with a response. He ran his finger round the curve of the ring, cherishing the feel of it. Then he frowned. "This is a thing of great price, an ornament for a king."

Agni thought Tillu might be too caught up in his teasing to repeat the words, but he had a fair sense of his own importance. He spoke; and the Mother nodded, eyes on Agni.

"You must want something in return," he said to her.

Once she had heard that in her own tongue, the Mother nodded. "Yes," she said. "Bring none of your war here." The word she used, though strangely altered, was Agni's own, in his own language. His eyes widened slightly at that. She went on, and Tillu spoke for her, stumbling, searching for words, because this was not trade-talk or guide-talk; this was the conversation of kings.

"If you will go on," she said, "and let us be, then you may have your fill of whatever you please. It is riches you wish, yes? Not blood."

"Riches," Agni said, "and kingship."

She frowned slightly. "A man cannot be a Mother," she said.

"What—" Agni fixed a hard stare on Tillu. "What did you say to her?"

Tillu spread his hands and sighed. "I said what I could say. There's no word for king here—nothing for a man who rules over the people. The only word close to it is the word for Mother."

"Ah," said Agni. He reflected on that, while the Mother waited, patient. "Tell her that a woman cannot be a king."

"But there's no word for—"

"Teach her a new word," Agni said. "And ask her where she learned the word for war."

"King," she said, softening it, twisting it a little, making it sound like the other words she spoke. "That is—a man who rules, yes? Men never rule here."

"So I gathered," Agni said. "And the word for war?"

"It is the word for what is," she said. Nor would she say more than that. Instead she said, "Come with me. Be a guest in my house tonight."

Agni could see that he was not well advised to refuse. Equally clearly he could see that Patir and Rahim and Gauan had drawn in close, and that they liked this not at all.

Agni inclined his head to the Mother, to his friends' manifest distress. But if he was to take this country, he must know how best to go about it.

"She tried to *buy* you," Rahim said as the Mother led them out of the market. "These people have no honor."

Agni, who was still wearing the golden torque, shrugged with more nonchalance than he felt. "You expected otherwise? These are women ruling women. When did a woman ever have honor?"

That silenced Rahim, though clearly it did not satisfy him. Nothing but war in the manner of the tribes would do that. And that, they would not get here.

"These people are unarmed," Patir said. "I doubt they even know how to fight. If they have no honor, then what have we if we kill them? They have no defense against us."

Agni nodded. "Yes. Yes, you see it. There must be a way in honor to take this country."

"Take it as you take a woman," said Gauan. "If she's willing, take her gently and with all good will. But if she's not—then take her as you may, and let her learn to accept you."

Someone hissed. Rahim maybe, warning Gauan of delicate ground. But although Agni had been cast out of the White Horse for taking a woman who was unwilling, he had never done such a thing, nor ever intended to. He said to Gauan, "You may have the right of it. These are women, after all. Surely a woman is a woman, even if she rules a city."

"That is a fine figure of a woman," Tillu observed, watching the Mother as she walked ahead of them. "I wonder, do they take men as we take women?"

"You don't know?" Rahim asked.

Tillu shrugged. "Well. The traders tell tales, but who knows which of them are true?" And though Rahim begged him to tell the tales, he shook his head and laughed, and would not tell even one.

Agni, listening to them, felt his cheeks go hot. The girl Maya had vanished somewhere between the edge of the city and its market. As wonderful a creature as this Mother was, when Agni's nether parts grew hard, it was the girl he thought of and not the woman. The woman was too much like Earth Mother; too close to the goddess' self.

✦ ✦

Her house was as large as a clan-chieftain's tent, made of wood and painted inside and out. It was hung and carpeted with more of the wonderful weavings, and full of treasures, fine pots and chests and furnishings made of wood and carved and again painted. Agni saw an outer room with a loom laid out on the floor, and an inner room with shutters open to the sunlight. There were others deeper in, but those he was not shown, not just yet.

It was strange to look up and see wooden beams overhead: like being in the forest, but lighter, brighter, because the sun was allowed to come in. With the Mother and a handful of younger women and girls who must be her daughters, there was only room for Agni and Patir, Rahim and Tillu. The rest, except for half a dozen of his own men of the White Horse, he sent back to the camp with word that he was safe, and to wait. Gauan went with them to lead them, not particularly willingly. He had been spinning great webs of fancy with Rahim, boasting of the wine he would drink and the women he would win. He was sore disappointed to be sent back to the company of men.

The half-dozen who stayed behind camped with the horses on the grassy hillside near to the Mother's house, though she offered another house for them. "They prefer to sleep under the sky," Agni said, which was true. The Mother did not argue, nor did she seem greatly afraid of armed men so close to her house. For that matter his three dozen had failed to dismay her; but he reckoned it wise not to burden her with the feeding of them all.

They went back laden with foodstuffs and with treasures, that they would show off to the rest. Those who stayed were even more richly endowed and even better fed. The four who were guests with Agni in the Mother's house were richest of all. They feasted like kings: a whole kid roasted and served on a great platter, nested in fruits and steaming grain, and bread finer than Agni had ever seen before, and honeycomb, and mead, and wine that came, the Mother said, from the south.

They ate and drank well, but not till they fell into a stupor. They were too wise for that. None of the women seemed disappointed or in any way dismayed.

It was not the liveliest feast Agni had ever sat to. There was a woman who sang, and a pair of young men came in and danced a stilted, stately dance. Those were the only men Agni had seen up close. All the rest were women.

He made bold to ask the Mother: "Where are your men? Do you have any but these two?"

When the question was made clear to her, she neither blanched nor laughed. She responded calmly, "We have as many men as anyone else. Men cooked this dinner that you eat so happily. Some are hunting, herding, travelling abroad."

"You have sons?" Agni asked. "A husband—husbands?"

There was a word, it appeared, for sons, but the other left Tillu baffled and struggling to explain. The Mother's reply was clear enough. "I am blessed by the Lady: all my children are daughters. No man shares my bed now. The last one I chose, chose to go back to his own mother. I've seen none since whom I would invite into my bed. Until," she said, "tonight."

There was no mistaking the import of her glance, even before Tillu rendered the words so that Agni could understand.

"Don't," Patir muttered under his breath. "There's the trap. A net, a rope, all her brothers with knives . . ."

"I don't think so," Agni said, not taking his eyes from the Mother's face. For all the number of her daughters, she was not so very old. Her hair was black and glossy, her skin unlined. She was, in her way, quite beautiful.

As if she had taken the thought from his head, she said through the greatly amused Tillu, "You are beautiful, man of the east, like the red deer in autumn. Will you worship the Lady with me?"

Agni's cheeks were afire, but he nodded. Patir growled, barely to be heard. Agni reckoned that more jealousy than fear for Agni's safety. Rahim was openly envious.

The Mother's smile lit the room. She rose and held out her hand. Agni barely hesitated before he took it.

There was indeed a room beyond the rooms that Agni had been shown, and one beyond that from which came the scents of roasting meat and honey sweetness. This one to which the Mother led him appeared to be her own, nearly filled with a great soft bed. Lamps were lit, hanging from the beams, shedding a mellow light across the coverlet; for it was dusk without. Somehow, while Agni was otherwise occupied, the sun had gone to his rest, and night had fallen.

Tillu had rather pointedly not been invited to follow, nor had he gone so far as to offer. The last Agni saw of him, he was grinning broadly. He found all of this much too amusing for Agni's peace of mind.

And here was Agni, and here was the woman, with but one common word between them; and that word was war.

Words were little enough between a man and a woman. Rudira had been used to chatter overmuch, though Agni had never ventured to say so.

There was nothing that this one could say, that he could understand. All that she needed to convey, she did with glances and smiles, and with her hands divesting him of his clothes before he could muster will to object. He shivered though the room was warm, naked in front of this woman with her wise, wise eyes.

She was small: her head came just to his breastbone. And yet she must have outweighed him by a fair fraction. He, who was no small or narrow-shouldered man, felt like a stripling beside her.

Her hands marveled at his skin, how milky white where coat and trousers covered it, how smooth to the touch, even with its dusting of red-golden hairs. The men she had had before, she let him know with gestures and with glances, had been less tall but more massive, broad-shouldered, deep-chested, and thickly furred with black hair. He was lovely, her hands said, like a young stag. And such hair; such eyes, golden as the amber in the torque that she had given him, outlandish, wonderful.

No woman had worshipped him with her hands before. Kissing and stroking, yes, but not this sheer delight in the touch and the feel of him. She ran hands over his face, shook his hair out of its braid and buried her fingers in it, and stroked his shoulders, his breast, his belly and loins and thighs. His manly organ ached with stiffness, and yet he made no move toward her. She stroked him, kissed him and teased him with her tongue, till he gasped and pulled away.

She laughed at that, not cruelly; warm rich laughter, as if she understood him perfectly, and did not blame him, either. He had never been laughed at so before. It made him angry, and yet it made him eager. He reached boldly and found the fastenings of the garment that she wore, and worked them free.

He had expected layer on layer, but under the long coat or tunic she wore only a skirt woven of scarlet cords, wrapped about her buttocks and her thighs but baring the thick curls below and the great dark-nippled breasts above, as rich as this country she lived in, and as extravagant in that richness. He had seen no infant in the house, nor heard one, and yet her breasts were heavy with milk.

Her eyes invited him; her hand on her nipple pressed forth a drop. With a kind of antic terror, he bent his head and sucked as a child would, as he could just remember doing. Her milk was warm and faintly sweet.

He struggled not to gag on it. She did not try to hold him, did not catch at him even when he scrambled backward away from her. He could leave, her manner said, if he must. Or he could stay.

He was not a coward. This was not his country or his language or his way of taking a woman. Maybe Patir had the right of it: maybe he should simply set his knife to this woman's throat, take her place and her power, and show these people what a king could be.

Or maybe he would gather his courage and advance on her and take her in his arms and kiss her till she gasped; and while she was catching her breath, spread her thighs and take her standing, fierce as a stallion on a mare in season. And like a mare in season, she opened to him willingly, took him strong and took him deep. It was like a battle, strength against strength.

He must be stronger. This strength must yield to his. He bore her backward onto the softness of the bed. She gave way, but willingly—too willingly. She allowed him to be the stronger.

Just so had he tamed Mitani—and the way he did it would not have sat well with many a horsetamer of the tribes. Agni might well have indulged in a flash of anger, but rueful mirth overwhelmed it. It was a fault he had, that he saw more than one side of everything. That came from his mother's people, Taditi liked to tell him. They were all strange.

And here he lay in a billow of bed, with Earth Mother's own living flesh beneath him, and his body carrying on in perfect contentment while his mind wandered afield. She was as apt to his bidding as a fine mare, and as wanton as a mare in season. And every bit of it she did because she chose, and not because he forced it on her.

She stroked him with light and teasing hands, clasping his buttocks, driving him deeper, holding him tight as her body stiffened and surged. And when she had touched the height of her pleasure, she slipped free of him and smiled, stroked his hair, and went peacefully to sleep.

He lay beside her, as alone as if she had cast him out on the steppe. His body quivered, taut still, unsatisfied. Furtively, shamefully, he finished it. He spent himself with no little spite, in the mounded coverlets. She never stirred.

But when he made to rise, her arm circled his middle, and her eyes, wide awake and very much aware, smiled into his.

He could break free. She was not as strong as that, nor her grip so tight. It was her smile that held him, and the levelness of her gaze. She knew him as women always seemed to do: inside and out, heart and soul and body.

But she did not know that part of him which reflected on winning a kingdom. He could not see it anywhere in her eyes. That was a men's thing, a thing of Skyfather's will and shaping. Earth Mother knew nothing of it.

He knew then what he would do. It had been coming to him since he saw this country, but now he was sure of it. His hand went to the collar about his neck, the heavy golden thing, warm with the warmth of his skin.

Her eyes followed his hand. They asked a question. He nodded.

Her smile was blazing bright. She pulled him to her, covered him with kisses. And while he was still gaping at her, taken aback by the force of her gladness, she coaxed and teased and persuaded his member to come erect again. Then she satisified him as he had satisfied her, with exuberance that left him gasping.

And that, he thought, was what it was to be a bought creature. It might also be what it was to be a king, or the beginning of a king.

✦ ✦

In a country that did not know war but that knew trade very well, there appeared to be no dishonor in prompt surrender. As early as the morning after Agni came into that first town, women came bearing gifts of gold and copper, fine pottery, fat cattle and sheep heavy with wool, rich weavings, bright shells, stones, beads and baubles, all the wealth of this fabulously wealthy country. With it they hoped to buy his goodwill, and to spare themselves the edge of his spear.

He found them more than willing to feed and house his people, to give them whatever they asked.

"Even women," Rahim said in wonder. He had gone with the women from a city not far away, to discover if they were indeed as willing as they seemed to offer their hospitality. He came back with a mildly stunned look about him. "There's no end to them," he said, "and no limit. Women everywhere—and all it needs is a glance. They have no fathers to forbid, no brothers to defend them. They can do whatever they please. And if they decide to take a man right where he stands, then they do it, and no one finds it strange."

They were on the road then, Agni and those closest to him, riding to a city that was said to be greater than the others, the greatest in that region. It too lay near the wood, but farther south, in a gentler and yet more wooded country than that to which they had first come. They traveled in a shifting escort of dark-eyed people, and most of those women or girls. The boys hung back, shy and seeming somewhat afraid.

If Agni ruled as king over them, they would learn to be bold as boys should be. He tilted a brow at Rahim. "Are you still irked with me because I won't give you a war?"

"I still think that the men are getting restless," Rahim said, "and spoiling for a fight. But if they can have women instead, any women they want—"

"They'll grow soft," Patir said, "and be fair prey for the men we never see. We're being fattened for the slaughter. Can't you see it?"

"I don't think so," Agni said. "These people are innocents. They'll let us rule them if we refrain from killing them. Which in our minds makes them cowards, but in theirs . . . who knows? I think they know nothing of honor or dishonor. All they know is prosperity. Everything that they do, they do to preserve that."

"They're weak," Rahim said. "They're soft. They're delighted beyond words by the sight of a man who's a man."

"What, are all theirs geldings?" Gauan lolled on his horse's back. He had a fondness for the wine of this country, too much of one perhaps. Agni had not seen him other than sotted since they were given a whole ox-train laden with jars in return for the safety of a city some days' journey south and west. "I'll wager they cut the boys when they're young, the way we geld colts, and only keep the best for stud. We are the best they've ever seen."

"They do love your yellow hair," Taditi said. She had appeared that morning mounted on one of the geldings from the remounts' herd, and riding him not too badly either. "I want to see these cities," she had informed Agni. "I'm tired of skulking in your tent."

Agni knew better than to take issue with her in front of his people. She was veiled, at least, as a woman should be, and she wore a properly modest robe, albeit with trousers and boots beneath. She had ridden in silence, keeping well behind him, until just now. He looked to find her close beside him, her eyes as bold as if she had been a woman of this country, and in front of his men, too.

She dared him to reprimand her. He opened his mouth to do just that, but shut it again.

Rahim seemed undismayed by her forwardness. "It's not just yellow hair that lures them. Red hair, too. Brown, even. Anything that isn't what they've looked at every day. We're a new thing. We're wonderful."

"You are full of yourself," she said.

He laughed. "I'm richer than I ever dreamed. Last night I had myself a whole hand of women. How can I not be happy?"

"The gods bless us," Agni said. "They've laid this country in our hands. It's their will that makes it so simple."

"Earth Mother will have somewhat to say of that," muttered Patir. Taditi shot him a glance of wintry approval.

Agni wondered if he should feel beleaguered. It was difficult, riding in the sunlight, in the cool of morning and knowing it would be fiercely hot later. This green and settled country with its tilled fields and its dark-eyed people was beginning to seem a little less strange. They came out of their fields and villages to stare at the horsemen riding by, and once or twice he understood a word of what they said to one another. They called a horse a horse, as they called war by the name he knew.

Often they brought gifts, running to meet him on the road, offering him whatever they had that was rich or unusual or beautiful. Flowers, sometimes, woven in garlands, or a soft-fleeced lamb, or a platter of sweet cakes. The young women stared at him boldly, the boys shyly: more boys and even men as he rode on, or maybe he had learned to notice them. They effaced themselves well in fields or among the houses, as women were supposed to do on the steppe.

Not all or even many of the men who rode with him were as wary as Patir. Most trusted in the gods and in these people's ignorance of aught but the word for war. This was the country of the blessed, given to them as a gift. Why might gods not give gifts to men whom they loved? Earth Mother might object, but she was only one, and she was old. The gods were younger, stronger, nearer to the world of the living.

So assured, and basking in sunlight, Agni entered the greatest of the cities that he had seen, a city of ten hundreds of people, or so he was told. Its circles stretched wide across a shallow valley, watered by a river and a blue bowl of lake. The high house in its center, which he knew now for their goddess' holy place, rose to thrice the height of a man, with a high peaked roof and a painted gable.

Its Mother was old and growing feeble. Her heir was no child herself, mother of many daughters. If they had been sons and if she had been a king's wife, she would have been reckoned a great lady among the tribes.

The Mother and her heir had no great beauty, but the heir's daughters were each lovelier than the last. In that house, over a feast of roast mutton and sweet wine, Agni discovered the joys and alarms of a man too eagerly sought after. He had heard of men quarrelling over a woman, but women did not, that he knew of, quarrel over a man. Or if they did, they kept it among themselves; not open and rather excessively lively, with the object of their attentions caught in the middle.

It was quite scandalous. Agni would gladly have left them to it, but that would have offended the Mother. Nor was he a coward, to run away from a pack of women. He gritted his teeth and endured, even when they stroked and petted him, tugged his hair, glared at sisters who had found a choicer part of him to torment.

Worse, his friends were laughing at him. They had their own flocks of admirers, eager beauties who had never heard of either shyness or circum- spection. Rahim in particular reveled in it, and mocked Agni for a fool, to be so discomfited. "You could marry them all," he said, "and never want for warm nights again."

Agni's eyes rolled. "I want wives, not ravening she-wolves."

"Indulge them," said Rahim. "Cherish them. Sing praises to the gods who set such delights in the world."

Agni's response was more a yelp than a word, as the contention for his favors swelled into open battle. They did not strike and claw at one another. They made him their weapon instead, tugged and stroked, clutched and pulled.

Just as he tensed to shake free, the Mother spoke a word. All his tor- mentors stopped at once. Their expressions were sullen. They were far from happy, but they were obedient. They settled for clinging close and for glaring at one another across his body. He wondered if he would be forced to choose one or more of them, or if they would insist that he take them all.

As seemed to be the custom in this country, the feast ended before a feast among the tribes would have well begun. In an exchange of fierce glares, the eldest of the daughters rose and held out her hand to Agni. It was her right, her manner said, and she did not expect to be refused.

She was very beautiful. Agni was not unwilling, but he was wary, casting a doubtful eye on the rest of the daughters. They scowled and sulked, but none contested the right of the eldest to claim the prize.

Agni wondered what would happen if he pointed to another of the daughters—if he would break some law of these people, or give unpardonable offense.

They were all beautiful. And all, he was sure, were skilled in pleasing a man. It seemed to be a matter of pride among them.

With a faint sigh he yielded to their custom, took the hand that he was offered and went where she led. He happened to notice as he left that Patir had taken the hand of another dark-eyed beauty, but Rahim sat alone, and Gauan too far gone in wine to care. He was rather surprised at Rahim. Women did indeed love his yellow hair.

Then Agni was gone, taken away into an inner room, and his mind had space for little else but dark eyes and clever hands and breasts as ripe and sweet as the fruits with which she teased him, tempting him, slipping them into her own mouth just as he began to taste them. Her lips were stained red; her breath was fragrant. Her kisses were rich with sweetness.

They made an art of bedplay here, as men among the tribes made an art of war. Agni could learn to crave it, if he allowed himself to slip so far. As of course he would not do. He was only half a fool.

·············· 59 ··············

Agni woke abruptly. It was dark but for the flicker of a lamp. He was alone. He lay for a while confused, remembering slowly where he was, and beginning to wonder what had become of the woman with the clever hands and the berry-sweetened kisses.

Then he heard it again, what must have roused him: an outcry without. Voices raised in anger or indignation. Women's voices, and a man's rising above them, striving to drown them out.

Rahim. And words that were almost clear. That sounded almost like, "She was asking for it. They're all asking for it. Gods, make her stop!" And a woman's voice either keening or cursing, Agni could not tell which.

He found them in one of the outer rooms: a crowd of staring, babbling people, and Rahim in the midst of it, and one of the Mother's daughters. She was cursing indeed, railing at Rahim, while two of her sisters held her back from leaping on him.

Agni caught sight of Tillu in the back of the gathering, snared him with a fierce glance and brought him thrusting through the press. "Tell me," Agni said.

Tillu's eyes were glittering; he looked as if he had been diving into the wine. But Agni smelled none of it on him. "It's the girl," he said in a tone so neutral it was flat—as if he were taking excessive care to be a voice and not a man. "She says he forced her."

"I did not!" Rahim cried; for Tillu's words had sounded loud in sudden silence. "All the women here are willing. Every one."

"And why," Agni asked, "does she say that you forced her?"

Rahim shrugged broadly. As he turned to catch the light, Agni saw the rich purple of a bruise about his eye, and a split and bleeding lip. "I heard her in here," he said, "rummaging about, making more noise than she needed to. What was that for, if not to see if someone was listening?"

"She said that she had come to look for a blanket, because one of her sisters stole her own," Tillu said. "And he crept up on her from behind and wouldn't let her go."

"Women struggle," Rahim said. "It's their way. When they say no, they want you to hear yes."

"Then he forced her," said Tillu. "She fought, which she seems to think is a terrible thing, and he laughed and went on thrusting himself at her."

"Is that true?" Agni asked Rahim. His voice sounded dim and far away.

Rahim did not seem to hear anything strange. "She was wriggling and writhing fit to drive a man mad. They're hot-blooded, these western women. She even struck me—see? With her fist."

"She was fighting you," Agni said, cold and still. "And you forced her. I was cast out of the tribe on suspicion of just such a thing. What makes you think that I shouldn't do the same to you?"

Even yet Rahim was barely dismayed. "That was a woman of the Red Deer, with a father and brothers and an ancient fool of a husband. This one has no men about her at all. And if she did—what would it matter? She's no woman of the tribes. She's as wanton as they all are here." He paused. "Maybe this is it. Maybe this is the trap we've been dreading. She's looking for a war, and finding it in me."

He was much too delighted with the thought. Agni said to him, "Then you don't deny that she resisted you?"

"She was teasing," Rahim said. "How could she be unwilling? She was naked—she *is* naked. Look at her! She's thrusting herself at you even while she curses me. They all do that, don't they? All the women. They all want you."

Agni did not see that she was thrusting herself at anyone. She was trying, as best he could see, to escape her sisters' hands and fling herself on Rahim. From the look in her eye, she meant to kill him.

"Tillu," Agni said, "speak to her for me. Ask her if it is true. If this man raped her."

Her eyes burned as Tillu spoke. She nodded vehemently, with such a snap that her teeth clicked together. She spat a mouthful of words.

"She says," said Tillu, "that she fought him from beginning to end. He only laughed at her. She wants—" He paused to draw a breath. "She wants him killed."

Agni held himself very still, made himself speak very steadily. "I thought these people knew nothing of bloodshed."

Tillu spoke as steadily as Agni had, with an overlay of gentleness that Agni found most interesting. The girl answered with calm all the more striking after the heat of her anger. "When a dog is rabid or a bull runs mad, we grant it the Lady's mercy. We kill it. When a man forces himself on a woman, there is no worse offense, and no greater madness. Him too we grant the Lady's mercy."

At last Rahim seemed to understand the gravity of what he had done. He blanched, who had been ruddy with indignation. "She *asked* for it!"

"She says not," Agni said. "Your face is testimony to the truth. These people do not strike blows—and yet this one struck to draw blood."

"And how willing *was* that woman of the Red Deer?"

Agni looked into Rahim's face. This had been his friend. Was still, beneath it all. And yet, looking at him, Agni saw the wreck of this thing that Agni had begun. To take all this country, to be given its wealth without need to shed blood for it—to hold and defend it, and make it strong—Agni had seen it in dreams since he came out of the wood.

He tried to find words to make Rahim understand. "If she had been a woman of the tribe, would you have done such a thing? Would you have dared?"

"She is not of the tribe," Rahim said. "Do you understand? These are not people. They're nothing to do with us."

"They are everything to do with us," Agni said. "We're outcast. Has it struck you even yet, what that means? We can't go back to the White Horse. We'll be killed if we try. We have to make our own tribe, and gather our own people."

"So we have done," said Rahim. "We brought them with us: men of all the tribes that we passed. Those are ours. These are conquered people. They're ours to do with as we will."

"There are," Agni said, "uncounted numbers of them. I count three hundreds of us."

"And none of them can do more than bruise a man's face."

Agni shook his head. "You'll never think like a king."

"I think like a man of the tribes," Rahim said.

Agni stood in impasse. Out of the cold place in his center he said, "Patir. Take this man and secure him. Tillu: if you will, find the Mother. She's not in the house or she'd have heard this yowling."

They both did his bidding, and quickly. Even Rahim. The others, the Mother's daughters, had gone silent, staring at Agni. He did not know why. His face could not be as terrible as that.

It must be his quiet, and the anger that blew cold in him. If they could sense it, they might walk shy of it.

Even the daughter who had been outraged was sitting in silence. She had a bruised look, a darkness about the eyes, that he had never seen before. Certainly not in the woman of the Red Deer, who had importuned him until he gave way.

In war, men took women. That was the way of it. But even Rahim had not called this war. War was a hot thing, a madness of the blood. This was cold. It was folly, and none the less grim for that Rahim had not meant to err as terribly as he had.

✦ ✦

The Mother came at last—from the temple, Tillu said, where she had gone in response to a dream.

"Better if she had stayed," Agni said, "if this was what she dreamed of."

She nodded when she understood his words: heavily, with her eyes on her daughter. The girl had drawn into a knot. There was blood where she had been sitting, bright flecks of it. She rocked and shivered.

"Dear gods," Agni said. "Tillu. Ask the Mother. Was this girl a virgin?"

It took rather a while for the Mother to understand. When she did, she shook her head, eyes wide as if she had never heard of such a thing. "She's not," Tillu said. "She says no woman has pain of—that. They see to it when the girls are young."

"Then," said Agni, "she had best look to her daughter. She's hurt, I think."

"Sweet Lady," the Mother said; and more that was too swift for Tillu to render into Agni's language. He managed the heart of it: "She is with child. If this has harmed the baby—the one who harmed it will pay the price. The price, she says—the price is his life."

"Is that not already forfeit under your law?" Agni asked her.

"There might have been a lesser mercy," the Mother said. "But if she loses the child, there is none for him but the Lady's own."

Her voice was calm. She would not yield in this.

And if Agni compelled her to yield, what would come of it? She had no warriors, no weapons, no knowledge of fighting. She might curse him and all that he did, but he had his own gods, younger and stronger than her Lady.

Those gods would have it be simple. His people were his people. These were other. They had no honor, nor did his own honor touch them. He was free with them to do whatever he pleased.

But he had been raised to be a king. A king looked after the people over whom he found himself. That was the first lesson he had learned from his father.

He needed another mind, other eyes. He needed keener wits than he had, just now. "Tillu," he said, "I need you to be my messenger one last time. Find Taditi. Bring her quickly."

Tillu glanced at the Mother. She sat silent beside her daughter, holding her, stroking her sweat-dampened hair. There were no words that Agni could say that would move her. Tillu sighed, shook his head, and consented once more to do Agni's bidding.

✦ ✦

Taditi appeared almost as soon as Agni had summoned her. "No magic," she said in the face of his surprise. "The story's out. Where have you put Rahim?"

"In a room here," Agni answered, "with Patir to keep him there."

"That wasn't badly done," she said. She brushed past him to kneel beside the Mother. The Mother took her in in one long glance; seemed to see a spirit like her own; bent her head and sighed, and spread hands over her daughter's body.

"No," said Taditi as if the Mother could understand. "This is not well done at all."

"Is she—" Agni began.

"Yes," said Taditi. "She's losing it. Are you going to stand and watch, or are you going to do something useful?"

Agni tensed to bolt, but held himself still. "That's Rahim's life if the baby dies. If I give way to these people. If I don't—"

"If you don't, you don't think you can hold this country. What makes you think you're holding it now? You're an unwelcome guest, plied with everything they can think of to persuade you to move on. You haven't held a single town. You've gone where they've led you, and let them lure you deeper into their country. How is that a conquest? What have you done but see the sights?"

"You are telling me," Agni said, "that I should bring war on them. That I should force them as Rahim forced this woman."

"I am telling you that you've been trusting too much in the gods and too little in your own wits. What do you want here? Do you want to travel from town to town, taking what each will give, then moving on, all the way to the end of the world? That's what they'll have you do."

"What does that have to do with Rahim's mistake?"

"I suppose it was an honest mistake," Taditi said. "Or honest idiocy at least. It's costing a life, maybe two. Three, if you submit him to these people's justice."

"I don't have to," Agni said. "They know nothing of fighting. If they curse us, I'll invoke our own gods. There's nothing they can do to us."

"Nothing," said Taditi, "except refuse to welcome you anywhere you go. They won't feed you, lodge you, give you comfort. You'll be outcast here as you were among the tribes."

"But here," said Agni, "I can take what I need, and hold it by force of arms."

"Surely," she said. "Three hundreds of you. Uncounted multitudes of them. Maybe they won't fight—maybe they can't. What will you wager that they won't set their bodies between you and whatever you reach for? How many can you kill before you sicken with it? How ruthless are you prepared to be?"

Agni had brought her here to say such things to him—to speak the words that no one else had the wits or the courage to say. He did not have to like what she said, nor be glad that she had said it. "You're telling me that I have to let them kill Rahim."

"I'm not telling you anything," she said, "but that your fool of a friend has struck a spark that can burn to ashes everything that you hope for here. What do you hope for? Do you even know?"

"I hope," said Agni, "I want—the gods want me to be king. They cast me out of my tribe. They sent me here. Now, for a few moments' play, we lose it all."

"That was not play," Taditi said with startling venom. She drove Agni back with it, till the wall caught him. Her face filled his world. "Understand something, boy. I love you, I've loved you since you were born. I raised you after your mother died. I brought you up, as much as anyone did. But this was no mere error. It was not play. It was sheer wanton heedlessness. I say let him die for it."

"He didn't know," said Agni, and hated himself: it came out weak, little better than a whine.

"He knew the price you paid for a rape you never committed. It should have occurred to him that this was rape, too. He's not a simple fool. He was born to be a chieftain, to be head of a clan. He should have understood."

"You are merciless," Agni said.

"I believe," she said, "in this country they call it the Lady's mercy."

Agni's head was pounding. He rolled it against the wall, taking what pleasure he could in the movement. Behind Taditi he saw women gathering, heard sounds that made his heart grow cold. Their goddess was not going to spare anyone. She was taking the child even as Agni cowered there, taking it back to herself.

Just so had Earth Mother done with the woman of the Red Deer. But that had been no fault of Agni's, except in that he had fathered the child. It had lived and died out of his knowledge, and its mother with it.

Rahim had done a worse thing than that. He had begun no life, only ended it. A warrior who killed in war, who took a woman captive, who slew her menchildren lest they grow up to be his enemies—he was an honorable man, with the honor of war. There was no honor in this. There was no glory. Only blood and pain.

And how could Agni understand, when no one else could?

"Maybe because you have more wits than most," Taditi answered him. "And maybe because your mother was Horse Goddess' own. Through her you come of a different blood. Sometimes when you catch yourself off guard you don't think as the others do. You see differently. You understand things that leave the other tribesmen baffled."

"*You* are of the tribes," Agni said, thrusting the words at her. "How do you know these things?"

"I'm a woman," Taditi said. She stepped back, freeing him from the weight of her shadow. "You want me to tell you what to think. I tell you what I think. If you want to be a king, you have to have thoughts of your own. You'll find a way out of this tangle."

"Alone?"

"However you best may."

✦ ✦

Agni left them all to it, the girl weeping as she gave up her baby's life in blood, the women weeping with her, and Taditi standing in grim silence. He would have liked to see what happened when they noticed her, but he had to go away. He had to escape those walls.

It was very early morning, just short of sunrise, cool but with a promise of strong heat later. Barefoot, bare-chested, in the trousers that he had snatched when he was roused from sleep, he was comfortable enough.

There were people about, a surprising number of them. Most, to his amazement, were men. They dandled children or stood about with floured hands as if they had come from the baking; or they were armed as if for the hunt. They surrounded the Mother's house, staring at it, dark-eyed and silent.

He was aware, abruptly, that he had no weapon. Even his meat-knife lay forgotten in the room where he had slept. He had no defense but his hands.

This country had corrupted him indeed, if he would leave his bed without at least a knife. He half-turned to go back, to fetch all his weapons, but he could not go back into that house. If that was cowardice, so be it. He would trust in these innocents, that none would rise and slaughter him in the place of the fool Rahim.

He walked through them, and they made no move to stop him. In the camp just beyond, his people were beginning to stir. Some had come out to stare, a few with drawn knives, watchful; but none offered provocation.

He did not enter the camp but walked past it. They called to him from it. "Agni! Agni prince! Is it true? Is there a war?"

"Not yet," he called back.

"We heard that they killed Rahim," someone said.

"Rahim is alive," said Agni, more grimly than he wanted to; but he could not lighten his voice. "Stay here, be quiet. Don't provoke anything. Wait till I come back."

"Where are you going?" That was Tillu, freed of messages and charges but clearly ready to go wherever Agni went.

Agni looked him in the face. "I'm going to talk to the gods. I must go alone."

"Unarmed? Half naked?"

"As the gods call me," Agni said. "Look after my people here. See that they stay out of trouble."

"First tell them what happened," Tillu said, "or they'll be running riot in the city."

Agni's brows went up. "You didn't tell them?"

"It's not mine to tell," said Tillu.

Agni sighed. No, it was not. It was Agni's burden, and his choice: to bear it in silence while the rumors ran rampant, or to afflict his people with the truth.

He raised his voice for all nearby to hear. "Rahim took a woman who wasn't willing. She was pregnant; she's losing the child. Their law demands his life if the child dies."

A murmur ran through the tribesmen. There was a growl in it, a shiver of danger. Agni pitched his voice to quell it. "I go to ask the gods what to do. Do nothing till I come back. Swear to it."

Tillu, who was closest, swore for them all. Not everyone was glad that he did it, but once it was done, no one tried to undo it.

Agni nodded in the face of their silence, and walked away from them. No one moved to follow.

·············· 60 ··············

Mitani was grazing with others of the horses in the field near the camp. Agni took him as he was, with halter and rope, and rode him away from the city, up a long hill that rose above the lake. As he rode the sun came up, shedding a long golden light across that green country.

At the hill's summit he slid from Mitani's back, hobbled him and left him to graze. Agni sat at the very top, with all the world spread out below: field and wood, river and lake, and the circles of cities stretching as far as he could see. Some were larger, some smaller, but each signified untold hundreds of people. And every one worshipped Earth Mother, ignorant of the younger gods: men in submission to women, and women ruling like kings.

While he sat there, a flock of birds rose fluttering and chattering from a little grove of trees. Just as they reached the level of his eyes, a dark shape hurtled down out of the sun. A hawk, too swift almost to see. Straight in front of Agni he struck. Feathers flew. He plummeted a dizzying distance, clear to the ground below, and in each claw he gripped a dying bird.

Agni let his breath out slowly. The gods were seldom so clear in their omens, or so prompt with them, either.

Take this country, yes. Make himself lord of it. Rule it as the hawk ruled the lesser creatures of the air. And what of Rahim?

To that they gave him no answer, or none that he could perceive. A man of the tribes would punish Rahim, but mildly: a few blows with a horseman's whip, or the taking of one of his horses. He had, after all, committed no crime against one of his people.

But Agni could not forget the girl's face, how she had looked at him, how she had doubled up in pain as her womb began to empty itself. And Rahim in his incomprehension, heedless arrogant boy, could not at all understand what he had done. Agni had loved him, still loved him. But this transgression Agni could not forgive.

Agni had never thought of himself as an implacable man. He was a man whom women loved, whom men were pleased to call friend. This hard cold thing that he felt inside of himself, that was new. It was as heavy as the collar that he still wore, that he seldom took off, the twisted ring of gold and amber. It came from the same place, from the people of this country. It had the weight of an oath, though he had sworn none; or none that he was aware of.

Was that what these people had bought from him? Not only his quiescence, but a portion of his honor? And with it, his loyalty?

He shivered in the sun. The wind tugged playfully at his hair, that was all loose, fallen out of its braid. He raked it out of his face and drew up his knees and set his chin on them, knotted tight, glaring into blue infinity. The world was not supposed to be complicated. He was supposed to be king of the White Horse people, to sire a son to be king after him, to rule the tribe and lead its wars, and when his time came, to go into the earth in the sacrifice of kings.

He should not be here on this hilltop in the sunset country, contemplating the death of his friend. His friend who was irretrievably simple. Who would never understand why he had to die.

That was what it was to be a king. He could hear his father's voice saying it. "A king must choose for the people," Rama had said. "Not for one man, or even for several, but for them all."

"Even these people who are no kin of mine at all?" Agni asked of the sky.

The sun shone down. The birds sang, returned to their copse and their contentment now that they had given due sacrifice to their lord the hawk. Mitani grazed peacefully. Now and then he snorted or stamped at a fly.

Agni unknotted and lay flat on the grass. His trousers bound him, hot leather, a swiftly waxing annoyance. He peeled out of them and lay naked. The sun pressed on him like a hand. He felt the heat of it on his fair skin, but it was pleasant, with just a hint of edge to keep it from cloying.

He spread his arms to brace himself against the wheeling of the heavens. If he let go, he would fall into the sun.

His tribe was taken from him. He was cut off from his kin. He was outcast for a crime that he had never committed. He had not let himself think of it, not once his new tribe began to gather to him. But here, in the wake of Rahim's folly, he could no longer run away from it.

Either he took this country and ruled it, or he turned and fled and withered into nothing. Flight had a greater allure than he liked to admit. An outcast, a nameless man, a creature without presence or life or substance in the world—how restful. The gods could do nothing but kill him; and that would be a welcome thing.

He had been born to be a king. Such a king: lying on a hilltop, naked but for a collar of gold. His rod had stiffened and come erect, as if in challenge to the sun. Earth Mother held him in her warm embrace.

He turned as one in a dream, and as in a dream she took him in her arms. He made slow love to her, in the warmth and the green coolness of her body, face buried in breasts that smelled richly of earth and grass and flowers. She whispered in a voice as soft as the wind, stroked him with a touch as light as air. When at last the seed burst out of him, hot and potent, a great sigh escaped her.

He lay on the grass, spent. The sun was hot on his back; burning. The grass was bruised beneath him. He was all stained with it.

He rose stiffly, stumbling. It was a long rocky way down to the lake, but to the lake he was determined to go. He did not try to mount or ride Mitani. The stallion slipped his hobble with disturbing ease and followed.

Agni skidded down the last of the slope, fell and rolled, and plunged gasping into icy water. It was as cold as snowmelt, and clean. It scoured the stains from his body and the confusion from his mind. It cast him on the stony shore, with the sun to dry him and his stallion bending over him, sniffing curiously at his hair.

He pulled himself up and onto Mitani's back. Mitani shifted a little, uneasy, but at the touch of Agni's hand on his neck he quieted. "I'm well, brother," Agni said, and did his best to believe it.

He sat on that warm damp back, looked up at the steep slope down which he had come, and considered that his trousers were at the top of it, and he as naked as he was born. He found that he did not care. He might when the numbness of body and spirit went away, when he woke to the doubled pain of the sun's burning and bare skin on horsehair, but like a priest in a rite, he felt nothing. It was a sacrifice.

He rode back as he was, and as he rode the sun dried him. The city was quiet. Too quiet, maybe. People were not out and about as they should be on as fine a day as this. They stayed close to their houses and to each other, and fell silent when he rode by.

Maybe that was only bemusement. He must have been a wild sight.

His own people had kept to their camp as he had commanded. He did not pause to praise them, nor did he set them free. They followed him nonetheless, silent as the people of the city were.

The Mother's house was most quiet of all. No sound came out of it; none of the wailing that would have marked a death among the tribes. Only a bleak silence.

Agni left Mitani on the doorstep, took a steadying breath and stepped into the dimness of walls and roof. The house was full of people, and yet it smelled of emptiness. Empty heart, empty soul.

The hawk had taken two birds. Agni remembered that, seeing the still figure in the midst of the women. The girl had died, bled out her life while he played lover to the earth.

Her Mother sat at her head, still and heavy as stone. Agni looked about for Tillu. For once the western chieftain was nowhere to be seen. Nor was there time to hunt for him. Agni met that flat dark stare and said deliberately in the only tongue he knew, "You will have your justice. That I swear to you. But you will pay for it. This city is mine, and all that is in it. I take it in return for the life of a fool."

Taditi, who understood, fixed him with an unreadable stare. Agni could not escape it, but his eyes were on the Mother. He spoke with signs, as best he could. "The man will die. I promise you. But your city belongs to me."

The Mother did not respond. Nor did it matter. Agni left her and went in search of Rahim.

Patir and Gauan had looked after him well, had kept him shut in a storeroom. It was not an ill prison, filled as it was with wine and bread and fine things to eat, smoked meats, cheeses, fruits in jars and in barrels. Rahim had indulged rather freely in the wine, and fed himself well. He greeted Agni with a broad wine-reeking grin. "Ho, brother! Been seducing the ladies, have you? You forgot your trousers somewhere."

"On a hilltop," Agni said, "under Skyfather's eye."

"Don't we all," said Rahim. He held out a jar. "Wine?"

Agni ignored him, though the scent of it was sweet. "The gods spoke to me," he said. "I've taken this city and made it mine."

"About time," Rahim said.

"I have also," said Agni, "sworn a vow to the Mother that she will have justice. The child is dead, Rahim. And so is its mother."

Rahim tilted his head and squinted. "Ah," he said in winy sorrow. "That's a shame. She was a beauty. Sweet, too. Even fighting."

Agni's heart twisted. He had told himself that he could do this, that the gods commanded it; that he was a king born. That he could be hard, and he could be cold. He could do what he must do. But this drunken fool whom he had known since he was a child, who had been playmate and agemate and companion in war and on the hunt, who had followed him into exile without a word of protest, who was dearer to him than his blood brothers—this idiot, this destroyer of innocents, looked at him with wide watery eyes and shook him to the roots of his resolve.

He had sworn an oath. The gods had witnessed it. Earth Mother had taken it and sealed it with his seed. A life for a life. One life now for two. Justice, and no mercy. Mercy had died when the child died.

Agni must make Rahim understand. The gods did not require it, but for his own soul's sake he must do it. He said, "She's dead, Rahim. You killed her. By the laws of our people and hers, your life is forfeit."

"Of course it's not," Rahim said. "She's not one of us. I'm sorry she died, but she shouldn't have tempted me."

"She did nothing," said Agni. "You raped her. She is dead because of it."

"I said I was sorry," Rahim said.

"Of course you are sorry!" Agni flared at him. "You couldn't control yourself, and you'll die for it."

"You won't kill me," said Rahim. "You'll send me somewhere else till it all blows over. It will, you know. Everything does."

"Not this," Agni said.

"Yes, this," said Rahim. "Come, we'll play a game. You'll pretend to put me to death, and I'll fall down convincingly, and you'll smuggle me away, and—"

"No," Agni said.

"What do you mean, no? You can't kill me. What have I done to you?"

"Angered the gods," Agni said. "Betrayed the trust I had in you. I might have expected it of another man, some young idiot from a western tribe, with more balls than sense. But you, Rahim. You I trusted."

"I won't do it again," Rahim said. "On that you have my word."

He did mean it. If Agni could have softened, he would have softened then. But the wind of the gods blew through him, shrill and cold. He said, "No. You won't do it again. You'll be dead."

Rahim laughed as if at a jest, but his laughter faded before it was well begun. At last, thought Agni, through the haze of wine and cocksurety, he caught a glimmer of the truth.

He did not want to see it. Agni watched him try again to laugh, and fail; watched his eyes widen, then narrow. "*You* can do this? After what the tribe did to you?"

"I was innocent," Agni said. He stepped back. At the signal, young men of the western tribes crowded into the room, took Rahim by the arms while he stood amazed, and half-dragged, half-carried him out. He was too stunned to struggle.

✦ ✦

They brought him into the sunlight, blinking, ruffled, unkempt from his night of captivity. There would be no dignity for him, no more than there had been for the woman who was dead.

The people of the city had gathered in front of the Mother's house. They made no sound as they saw Rahim. That in its way was more terrible than any snarl of anger.

He put on a swagger for them, a reckless bravado. He did not believe it even yet, Agni thought. Maybe he never would.

People came out behind them: the Mother and her daughters, bearing the body of their sister. The silence grew deeper still, and more ominous.

There would be a rite, Agni supposed. Words. Anger fed to fever-pitch. And then, in whatever way their law decreed, they would kill him. Bare hands, he supposed, or flung stones.

He could not bear it. He whirled, snatched the spear from Gauan's hand, whirled back and about. The moment was blindingly swift and yet eerily slow. In it he met Rahim's eyes; saw the astonishment there, and the disbelief. And at the last, as the spearhead bit flesh and bone, nothing at all. Only the empty dark.

············· 61 ·············

Rahim was dead before he struck the ground. Agni set his foot on the body with a kind of numb horror, and pulled the spear free. It did not come easily. Its head had lodged in bone.

That was a petty thing, and ugly, and slower than Agni could easily endure. But he could not leave the spear in the body. This was his friend, the brother of his heart, the blessed fool who had gone too far.

At last the spear was free. He laid it down carefully and straightened Rahim's limbs, as if he could wake and find himself all twisted. When Rahim was as tidy as he could be, Agni straightened. "Bring me his horse," he said.

It was Gauan who obeyed, Gauan who was not of Agni's tribe or people. Agni could not meet the eyes of Patir who had stood beyond him. There was no altering this, and no softening it. It must all be done as the gods willed.

It seemed a long while before Gauan came back leading Rahim's fine bay stallion, and yet the sun had hardly moved. The stallion was nervous, snorting at the people gathered about the Mother's house, and shying at the scent of blood.

Agni took his rein from Gauan, soothed and gentled him until he would stand, if wild-eyed. Agni stroked him, murmured to him. Slowly he eased; little by little he lowered his nose into Agni's hand. "Brother," Agni said. "Go with my brother. Bear him company among the gods as you bore him company here below. Let him walk with pride, though an error bought him his death."

The stallion sighed and leaned lightly on Agni's shoulder. Agni set his teeth; firmed his heart and mind, and thrust with the spear that had killed Rahim.

It was a clean death, a pure sacrifice. The stallion sank down slowly and without panic, as if into sleep. When the life was gone from him, Agni completed the rite as it was done among the tribes: took the head to set on watch over Rahim's grave, and flayed the body, and stripped it of its hide. No one moved to help or to interfere, which was right and proper. This was Agni's doing, all of it; his right and his fault. His the praise for it, if any was to be had. His the blame. No one else would bear the burden.

Agni's people took away the flayed carcass, emptied as it was of life and potency. They would dine on it tonight. Then they would complete the rite, as if it had been a great sacrifice.

Now, in the hard light of morning, Agni spread the hide in front of the Mother's house and sat on it as a king sits. He called to Tillu, careful always not to treat the chieftain as an errand-boy or a servant, and waited as Tillu found it in himself to oblige. This could not go on, Agni thought remotely. Either these people would learn his language, or he would learn theirs.

Whatever he intended to do, for this moment he had to trust to Tillu's tongue and his considerable wits. "Tell the Mother," Agni said, "that this is my city, and that I have paid for it in the blood of my friend. She will consider all debts paid and all justice done."

Tillu's brows rose at that, but he refrained from comment. He spoke to the Mother.

She sat by her daughter's body as if she had lost the will to move. She did not answer in words. She spread her hands. *As you will,* the gesture said.

✢ ✢

Agni sat on the new-flayed horsehide and spoke, and when he spoke, people obeyed. Just so simple was it to be a king. He saw Rahim taken away for the burial. He saw the Mother's daughter taken likewise, though he did not know if they would bury her, burn her, or lay her out for the birds of the air. She vanished into the temple, and the elders of the women with her, and the Mother walking heavy and slow. He sent then for the rest of his people, and bade them come to him in this place.

Somewhere in the midst of it he was brought food, drink, clothing for his body. It was not his well-worn and comfortably redolent leather but garments made all new, woven of the beautiful cloth that was so common here. From naked wild man he found himself transformed into the image of a king.

It was a cold and splendid thing, to be at last what he had waited for so long to be. And though people crowded about, pressing in close, he was alone. The blood of his friend stained his hands. His heart was heavy with grief, walled away and consciously forgotten until he could stop to think of it. The other of his dearest friends, Patir, who had been even more beloved than Rahim, was nowhere that Agni could see. If he had gone away, if he had turned his back on Agni for what he had done to Rahim, Agni would not fault him in the slightest.

At evening, under the waning moon, they sent Rahim to his long sleep. They built a barrow for him on a hill beside the river and laid his weapons in it, his belongings that he had loved, and provisions for the journey into the gods' country. Then when they had closed the earth's gate upon him, they set his stallion's head on a spear and left it to watch over the grave.

Some of the people from the city lingered to watch them. Men mostly, and children, silent and still. What they thought, Agni could not imagine. They did not seem glad that Rahim was dead. They did not seem to feel anything at all.

He did not discover what the women did with the dead woman's body. Once it had disappeared into the temple, it did not reappear again. That was a women's rite, he could well see, and forbidden to men.

He was not minded to set foot in the temple. Let the women keep their secrets for yet a while.

✦ ✦

He had no sleep that night, though he stumbled into the Mother's house near dawn and fell onto the bed that he had left—was it the full round of the day and night past? There was no willing woman to share it with him. They were all in the temple still.

He lay aching in his bones, his eyes burning dry, and watched the morning brighten slowly beyond the window. There was an empty place inside him where Rahim had been. He caught himself wondering how many such places there would be before he went to the knife, when he was old and could be king no longer.

At full morning he rose stiffly, stifling a groan, and made himself as presentable as he could. Breakfast was laid out for him, the bread fresh and warm, the wine cool in an earthen jar. He ate a little, drank a little. So strengthened, he went out to face the sunlight.

The rest of his people were coming, and would be in the city before the sun touched the zenith. The women of the city were still nowhere in evidence. Patir was waiting for him, sitting in the shade of the Mother's house, beside but carefully not on the bay horsehide that had, the morning before, belonged to Rahim's stallion.

Agni sat on the horsehide. It would need to be taken soon, cured and tanned, or it would rot where it lay. But for the moment it sufficed. "I thought you had gone," he said.

Patir shrugged. He had a knife and a bit of bone that he was carving into a shape that might be horse or deer or maybe, if one squinted just so, a man. It was careful work, and it absorbed much of his attention. But Agni did not commit the error of thinking him distracted.

Agni did not press him. People came, seeing Agni there, and wanted this and that. Some of it was silliness, men indulging in the luxury of a king to do their thinking for them, but Agni was patient. Much of what a king did was silliness. People needed it, and him. In its way it made them stronger.

All the while he did what a king does, he kept half an eye on Patir. Patir finished what looked to be a dagger-handle: a man, yes, crowned with horns like a stag, rampantly and exuberantly male. He leaned out over the horsehide and dropped the carving into Agni's lap.

It was a gift. Agni did not reckon that it was tribute. It fit his palm with lovely exactness. He would have a blade made for it, a wonderful blade, a blade of copper, such as no lord of the tribes had ever had.

He slanted a glance at Patir. Patir was watching him. "How much do you hate me?" Agni asked him.

Patir scowled. "Why not ask me how much I hate him?"

"Do you?"

"No," said Patir. He stabbed at the earth with his knife, over and over, as if it had been living flesh. "Sometimes he could be the—worst—idiot."

Agni bent his head.

"Do you know what he did to you?" Patir demanded. "Look at you! He made you a king."

A snort of laughter escaped before Agni could stop it.

Patir stabbed at the earth, stabbed and stabbed at it. "For all I know he meant to do that. Rahim was the gods' own fool. But he loved you. He would have done anything for you."

"Except keep his hands off a woman."

Patir's glance burned. "What do you know of that? They always want you."

"Not if you ask the Red Deer people," Agni said. He turned Patir's carving in his hands, smoothing his thumb along the curve of it. "I'm going to find the greatest city in these parts, the mother city. I'm going to take it and rule in it."

"That would be Larchwood," Patir said. And as Agni stared at him: "Tillu's been talking to people. They say that Larchwood is the greatest city in these parts, and its Mother is the wisest. They also say . . ." He paused. Agni waited. He said, "They say that the word for war came from Larchwood."

"It came from the steppe," Agni said. His eyes narrowed. "Do you suppose . . ."

"It's near the wood, they say: nearer than this place, but farther to the south. If travelers came through there, they might have brought their words with them."

"Yes," said Agni. "It's Larchwood we need, then. And I wonder—"

"If she was there? Or is still?"

"Sarama," Agni said. "Yes. There's been no word of her. I won't believe she died in the wood, or is trapped there and can't come out."

Patir did not respond to that. Agni let it slip into the silence. After a while he said, "We'll ride in the morning."

"Yes," Patir said.

It was not as it had been when Rahim was alive, when their friendship ran clear and bright between them. But it was better than hate.

·············· 62 ··············

Almost as soon as Agni's tribesmen had come to the city, they rode out of it again. Agni had conceived an urgency, a need to see this place called Larchwood—where he might find, or find word of, his sister. They said no farewells. They simply left. They took with them whatever they could carry. Copper and gold, and lesser treasures too. But no women. That lesson, for however a brief a time, they had learned. It was sealed in stone and crowned with a stallion's head, Rahim's grave where he would sleep till the world ended.

They rode south and somewhat east, through the cities and their attendant towns and villages. People watched them but did not approach. The cities were quiet, the way open, the message clear. Whatever they took, they took freely. No one offered protest. But they were not made welcome as they had been before. They were allowed to ride through, but not invited to linger. Nothing came to them as a gift. It was left for them to take.

In this way the tribes lured prides of lions away from their hunting runs, or diverted a stampede of wild oxen from their camps. Agni chose not to challenge it. It suited his purpose to drive direct for his goal, and it pleased him well enough to find no obstacle in his way.

He was careful not to relax his guard. These people did not fight; they yielded. They gave way rather than contest for mastery. But even they might rebel at last, might stand fast against him, even move to defend themselves. Then he must be ready for war.

His people were growing cocky, and more so the farther they rode from Rahim's barrow and his death. If Agni did not find a fight to give them, and soon, they might rear up and bolt. But he was not ready yet to slip the rein. He held them in tight, led them onward, pressed toward Larchwood at speed that left them too breathless to rebel.

They came to it at last on a day of mist and rain, a soft grey day that muted even the highest of spirits. The world closed in; distances shrank. Hills vanished beneath a veil of cloud. They felt rather than saw the wood draw in close again, the cold green breath of trees wafting out at them, bringing memories of the long ride westward.

Agni shivered in his splendid new coat. Larchwood, he had been warned, was a woodland city, built in and about groves of trees. At that, when he came to it, it was not so closely hemmed in as he had expected. There was open land in plenty, and more so toward the river. There as elsewhere, boats should have crowded along the banks, and people should have been coming and going in the bustle and hum of a western city in the summer. But there were only a few boats. The city was quiet, winter-quiet, muted and still.

He rode in without asking leave, led his people as straight as the curving ways would allow, to the city's center and the temple that marked it. Indeed this was the greatest of the cities that he had seen, circle upon circle. It had not seemed so large when he rode into it, masked as it was in trees; but like the forest itself, it went on and on.

Still the forest had ended at last, and this city yielded up its center. Its people made no move to hold him back. They stood in doorways and beside walls, watching, saying nothing.

Here for the first time Agni saw a glimmer of fear. It was subtle, but he did not think that he mistook it. They were afraid of the horses. No one else had betrayed such a thing. Only these people. Only here.

The city's heart was empty and quiet. No one waited there, except for a small figure sitting outside the temple. It was a child; male, Agni rather thought, though it was hard to tell. As Agni halted, with the others drawing up as they could behind and the ranks to the rear spreading cautiously outward toward the city's edges, the child rose from whatever game it had been playing, and stood staring.

Here was no fear. Here was the kind of naked yearning that Agni had seen in boys of the tribe watching the men on their stallions. He had known it himself, and not so long ago, either.

It was striking in this place, among these people. Without thinking, without calculation, Agni held out his hand.

The child grinned, as bold and brash a manchild as Agni had seen, and leaped happily up behind Agni. He had sat a horse before. There could be no doubt of it.

And then he said in words that Agni could understand, "My name is Mika. What is yours?"

Agni swallowed his first response, which was to demand where in all the world this child had learned to speak the language of the tribes. Time enough for that. First he answered, "My name is Agni. You're not afraid of me."

Mika laughed as a child could, with a kind of bubbling glee. "I'm not afraid of anything. Are you bringing war?"

"Only if people bring war to me," Agni said.

"We don't do that," said Mika.

"I see you don't," Agni said. And then he asked it: "Where did you learn to speak my language?"

"A man came," said Mika, "and he had a horse. He talked a lot. I listened. Then he went away. And she came, and I listened some more. It was easy."

"She?" Agni asked when Mika did not go on, in a kind of dizzy hope.

"Sarama," said Mika.

Agni had been prepared for that, and still the breath rushed out of his lungs. He slipped from Mitani's back, intending to do it, but not perhaps so bonelessly as that. Mika stayed where he was, happily, regarding Agni with bright-eyed fascination. "She looks like you," he said.

"She is my sister," said Agni. He wanted to seize Mika and shake him till his teeth rattled. But he stood still. "She's here?"

"She's in Three Birds," said Mika. "So is the Mother. And Catin." Whoever or whatever that was. "They all left. They said war was coming."

"Sarama? Sarama left? Was she a captive? Had they hurt her?"

"She went with Danu," said Mika. "From Three Birds. Catin hates her. I don't like Catin. I like Sarama. Did you come looking for her?"

"Yes," Agni said, because it was simplest, and it was true enough. "The Mother is gone? Who rules here?"

"Nobody," said Mika.

"They just left?" Agni demanded. "Just walked away?"

Mika nodded.

"I will never understand these people," Agni muttered.

"It could be a trap," said Patir behind him.

"It could," Agni conceded. He turned slowly, taking in the city, such of it as he could see. Strange to know how much more there was, and to think that he had seen only a small portion of it.

He stopped abruptly and said to Patir, "We'll carry on as if we have no worry in the world. I'll rest in the Mother's house. Post guards there and bid the rest pitch camp near the river, and see that everyone's fed. We'll see just how docile this city wants to be."

"We don't want to fight," Mika said. "The Mother is afraid to."

"Is that why she ran away?" Agni asked him.

He shook his head, wide-eyed. "Oh, no. She went to the Mother in Three Birds. The Mother in Three Birds is the wisest in the world."

Agni pondered that, but said nothing directly of it. "You speak my language well," he said.

"I listen," said Mika. "That's all."

"The gods have given you a gift," Agni said. "Come with me."

Mika was happy to oblige, though he did not like to leave Mitani. Mitani, eager to shed his gear and roll, was rather too pleased to take his leave of Agni and Mika both and follow Patir back through the circles of the city.

Agni had hoped to keep him nearby, but there was nowhere for him to graze here. The houses were too close together, the grass too sparse beneath the trees. Agni would have to hope that if anything came upon him it would come from without, and would have to pass his guards long before it came to him.

+ +

The Mother's house was not deserted: there were people in it, servants from their look and bearing. They received Agni less than joyfully, but they did not drive him out, nor did they fail in their duties. It seemed to be a matter of pride.

This would do. He settled in the house as if it had been his tent, took the largest of the sleeping rooms for his own and left the rest for the men who rode closest to him. There were no women in the house, he could not help but notice. All the servants were men.

He could reflect that they were being permitted to conquer this country. Or he could conquer it as he best could, and trust in the gods for the rest.

Toward evening, as the servants prepared the daymeal, he summoned the elders to him. He refused to consider that they would not come.

And indeed, well before darkness fell, they were all gathered in the Mother's house, sharing the daymeal that the servants had made. They were no more submissive than ever, nor any more cheerful, either. Tillu said it for them all: "Riches are all very well, and so is an easy conquest. But the young men need a fight. We can only send them out hunting for so long—and with so many cities crowded together here, there's precious little game to be had."

"Or if we can't give them blood," said an elder from one of the western tribes, "women would appease them. For a while. But what good is a warrior without a war?"

"These people won't fight," someone else said. "They're like sand and water. Push and they give way. Strike and they scatter."

"They do take well to being ruled," Tillu observed.

"Aye," growled one of the elders, "and what good is that?"

"Plenty," Tillu shot back, "if it gives us everything we ask for. Copper. Gold. Willing women."

"War?"

"Maybe," said Tillu, "if we take enough, push hard enough."

Agni did not like the direction that was taking. "Listen to me," he said: and it was gratifying to see how they all turned at the sound of his voice. "We have restless young men and a country that won't fight. That's certain. Now suppose we find a way to keep them occupied. I'm not minded to dissipate our forces by scattering them over this country. But if I send them out by clans and kin-bands and tell them to secure the cities—and bind them with oaths to provoke no killing—how busy do you think I can keep them? More than that: if I tell them to muster the men, to turn them into warriors, and raise from them a force to defend all this country, they'll be months, years, in the doing of it."

"And then?" said Tillu. "What then? If they teach these people to fight, they've raised a force to cast us all down and drive us out."

"No," said Agni. "No, that's not what they'll do. Listen now: how long do you think it will be before the tribes learn what we've learned? Once they know how rich this country is, they'll all be turning westward, hoping to take a part of it for themselves. But we hold it. It's ours. *Our* country."

"Ah," said Tillu, trailing off to a long sigh. Agni watched comprehension dawn in the rest of them: slowly in a few, but in the end it came to them all.

"We'll have all the fighting we could ask for," Gauan said. "But not now. Not this moment, when we're most likely to need it. It may be years before the tribes come after us."

"The longer the better," Agni said, "and the more time we have to make this country strong enough to face whatever comes."

Eyes gleamed round the circle. There were doubters in plenty, growling at his folly, but his will for the moment was stronger than theirs.

"You know what you're doing," Patir said, drawling the words from where he sat by the wall. "You're turning this whole country upside down. Once you teach its men to fight, they'll never be the same."

"Do you think that's an ill thing?" Agni asked him: honestly, because he wanted to know.

"I don't think you can turn back the sun," Patir answered, "and for a surety the gods have shown us what they want of us."

Agni nodded. "They've given us this country, and its people with it. If we're strong enough, we'll hold it. If not . . . we die. We all die in the end. But I choose to die a king."

"I'd rather die old," Tillu muttered. He raked fingers through his beard. "This is a very large thing you're thinking of. It's not just a raid—gallop in, grab whatever you can find, gallop out again."

"Is that all you thought it was?" Agni asked.

Tillu shrugged. "How often does a tribe take over another tribe's lands? It happens—raid begets raid, and we're all driven westward. But this isn't the steppe, and these aren't tribes. These are people unlike any we've ever seen. They live in cities. Their tents are made of wood and stone. They don't follow the herds from season to season. They stay where they are, like trees. We'll have to change, too, if we're to live with them. We can't turn them all into tribes of horsemen."

"Nor should we want to," Agni said. "Think of it, Tillu. These people live where they live, always. They make Earth Mother give them her fruits. They eat whatever they like, whenever they want it. We can travel among them as tribesmen should, take what they have to give, and never lack for anything. We can take what's best of both our worlds."

"It will make us soft," said one of the doubters. His fellows nodded, agreeing with him.

"You can go back to the steppe," Agni said, "and live as hard as you like. But the rest of the tribes will follow me westward, because the gods have led them. There is no turning back. We've done what we've done. This sunset country is ours now, and the lands of the east will be full of strangers. It's always been so. Remember the tales you heard when you were a boy. Remember where your tribe's lands were then. Haven't we all seen our hunting runs shift, and move as the sun moves? The gods are driving us westward—driving us here."

"I wonder," murmured Patir, "what happens when we've gone as far west as we can go? Will we find ourselves looking at the sunrise, and driving the eastern tribes ahead of us, back in a long circle?"

"We'll fall off the edge of the world," Gauan said.

"You're mad," said the doubter.

"And so are you," said Gauan, "or you'd never have come with the rest of us." He grinned, making the words light, inviting them all to laugh with him. A few even obliged.

No one said anything precise, or agreed on anything, but when the last of the wine was drunk, when the last elder had fallen asleep where he sat, Agni knew that they would acquiesce to whatever he did. There would be enough for all of them to do, even without the pleasure of a battle.

IV

WARRIORS AND WOMEN

STRIKE, FEINT, WHIRL and strike. Strike again, parry, stamp, whirl, strike.

Danu could do it in his sleep. He did it every morning with staves in the practice-field; and after that he shot arrows at targets. His dreams were full of arrows flying, horses galloping, men shouting in a language that he heard—yes, even in his sleep.

And yet there was no shadow of war on Three Birds. The summer burgeoned richly, swelling ripe to the harvest. Traders came and went. Travelers passed through on their way to other cities, or to visit this one that was the greatest in this part of the Lady's country.

Catin, having delivered her message, had gone back to Larchwood. Then for a long while the east was silent, and no word came.

At midsummer the quiet broke. It was no one Danu knew, a runner from Widewater well to the north of Larchwood, but the message was the one that he had dreaded. "Horsemen," the woman said. "Riders on horses, hundreds of them, spreading like a plague over the towns to the east of us. We give them whatever they ask for, and even what they don't ask for, but they won't stop. They keep coming. They stayed in a village called White Oak, but one of them raped a woman there, and her baby died. He was given the Lady's mercy. Then they went on."

When Sarama heard that, she went white and still. She was still carrying the child, her belly just beginning to round with it: invisible under the coats or the gowns that she wore like any woman of Three Birds, but well perceptible to Danu's hand when he lay with her in the nights.

At word of the horsemen's coming and the death of the one who had committed the only crime for which a man could die in this country, she left the Mother's house and disappeared. Danu found her much later, after hunting everywhere that he could think of. He had not thought to look in the room they shared, within those narrow walls, with the window that looked out to the temple.

She sat with her arms folded on the windowframe, chin resting on them, staring out at nothing. He had never seen her so still.

He touched her in honest fear, lest he find her reft of substance, turned into air and mist. But she was solid and warm, with her straight silken hair the color of tarnished copper, and the flecks of sun-kisses across her nose. He wrapped his arms about her, cradled her.

She did not move into his embrace, but neither did she resist it. She lay against him with a sigh. He kissed her hair. It smelled of herbs and of sunlight, and a little, always, of horses. "No one will touch your child," he said.

She twisted a little so that he could see her face, and the frown on it. "I'm not afraid of that. I'd kill any man who touched me unless I wanted it."

"Then what?" asked Danu. "What scares you?"

"Imminence," she said. And when he stared, puzzled, not quite understanding: "It's coming. The thing I came to warn you of, the thing that maybe I brought to you—it's here. It's in the Lady's country."

"You're afraid of war? Of dying?"

"No," she said. "Of men on horses. Of—" She broke off. "Did you hear what the woman from Widewater said? About the chief of the horsemen—the one they've made their king?"

Danu nodded. "A young man. Very young—too young, one would think, to carry such authority. He rides a red horse with the new moon on its brow."

"And he is a red man himself," she said almost impatiently, "but a coppery red, lighter than mine, and his eyes are the color of amber, which is strange and rather frightening when he stares hard at a person. And he is tall, one of the tallest of the riders, but lean, and yet wide in the shoulders. His beard is still a young man's beard, patchy in places, and he wears his hair in a braid, thick as a man's wrist."

Danu's brows went up. "She didn't say all that. The red hair, the yellow eyes, that's all she said. And that he has a nose like the curve of the young moon."

She tilted her head up, with her nose like the arch of a newborn moon, and fixed him with those leaf-green eyes. "Yes," she said. "His name is Agni. I was born first. He came clasping my foot in his hand."

"Your brother?" Danu had not expected that. "You're twinborn?"

She nodded.

He drew a breath. "Among us . . . twins are sacred. They're the Lady's own."

"Yes," said Sarama. "I don't understand. Our tribe hunts far to the east—very far. He was to be king of it. How can he have come here? I told him not to follow me. I made him promise."

"And did he?"

"No," she said. "He never—quite—" She shivered in his arms, caught at him and clung. "I didn't want it to be true. I didn't want Catin to be telling the truth. I did bring the war. I am the cause of it."

"I think it would have come without you," Danu said, and he did believe it. "It was coming, you told me, before you ever went westward. People were thinking of braving the wood. Someone would have led them into it, and even through it. And if you hadn't been here first, we'd never have learned how to fight."

She shook her head, but she did not argue with him. He held her for as long as she would let him, which was a surprising while.

When she pulled away, he did not try to hold her. She drew herself to her feet. "I have to talk to the messenger. Is she still here?"

"She has to go on to the Long Bridge," Danu said, "but she's agreed to stay the night."

"Good," said Sarama a bit distractedly. "Good."

✦ ✦

Danu did not hear what Sarama said to the messenger. He had duties in the house, and thereafter was caught up in looking after some of the children for his brother Tanis. When he came back to the Mother's house, it was dusk. The lamps were lit in the doorways, the stars coming out overhead. It was a beautiful night, warm and sweet-scented, fragrant with bread baking, meat roasting, spices wafting from kitchen fires. Somewhere a woman was singing, and a child laughed, sweet and high.

Sarama was taking the daymeal with the Mother and her daughters. She seemed calm, much as she always was, smiling at something that one of the daughters said. But she did not glance at Danu when he came to sit beside her, nor did she come to his bed after. She had gone to the temple where he could not follow.

That grieved him. It should not have. Of course she would commune with the Lady. She had much grief to bear, and much guilt. But he, foolish mortal, wanted her to commune with him—to come to him for comfort.

It was a foolish thing to do, but he went to the temple, sat on the doorstep and clasped his knees and waited there, while the stars came out and the moon came up and the city went still around him. He emptied his mind of thought as the city's circles emptied of people. He practiced an art that the Mother had taught him. He schooled himself to simply be.

Sleep came on him while he sat there. Her step woke him abruptly and completely. She paused beside him, a tall shadow, with the moon turning her face to a white glimmer. "Danu?" she said. She sounded half asleep herself.

He unfolded stiffly and stood. She touched him, ran hands along his shoulders as if to assure herself that he was there. "Danu? What's wrong? Is someone sick?"

"No," he said.

"Is there a new message? Has someone come?"

"No," he said again.

"Ah," she said, as if suddenly she understood. "You were afraid for me."

He did not say anything.

She stroked his cheek, brushing fingers through his beard. "It is my brother leading the horsemen. The messenger told me enough that I could be sure of it. I'm not going to run off to him."

"I wasn't afraid of that," Danu said. "I was afraid it might break your spirit."

"What, that he followed me after all? That's as the Lady wills—or as she allowed the gods to do."

He laced his hands behind her. She leaned into them as she loved to do of late. She said it eased her back. She was not greatly pregnant yet, but the child's weight could drag at her, unbalancing her slightness.

The Mother said that she was broad enough to carry a child, but she seemed so slender, no wider than a boy. He fretted over that, too, though he would never let her know it.

"They'll come this way," she said, "before too long. Everybody comes here. It's the greatest of the cities."

"There are greater ones," he said, "away west and south. But hereabouts . . . yes. We're the Mother city. So you think there will be war."

"He hasn't done any fighting," she said. "People have offered him gifts, persuaded him to go on past their cities. If he can keep his men in hand, if none of them breaks loose and raids the villages, he well may bring no war at all."

"Then what?" said Danu. "What does he want?"

"I think he wants to be king," Sarama said.

Danu raised his brows. "A king? A man set over us?"

"That's what he was raised to be," she said.

"But the dreams," said Danu. "Mine, Catin's—if all he wants is to sit on a horsehide and tell people what to do, where's all the fire and terror?"

"I don't know," Sarama said. She sounded troubled. "Agni is a great hunter. Men love him. Women, too. He's been strong in war, but he's never been as hot for it as some. Though he'd throttle me for saying it, I think he'd rather tame a horse than kill a man."

"But he would kill one," Danu said, "if he were driven to it."

"Even you would do that," said Sarama. She silenced him before he could protest. "The Lady tells me nothing but that he's in her country. It's as if—she's glad. How can she be glad? He wants to be king."

"I never tried to understand the Lady," Danu said.

"I can't help but try." She sighed heavily.

"Will you be glad to see your brother?" he asked when she did not go on.

She blinked. "What? Glad? Of course I'll be glad. But I don't want him *here*."

"I should like to see him," Danu said.

"I can imagine," she said as if it had just occurred to her, "that he would be fascinated to see you."

He frowned.

She clasped him tight, and startled him with a ripple of laughter. "My dear beautiful man, among the tribes a woman's man is chosen for her by her kin. Her male kin. Her father, if she has one living. Her brothers. She most certainly does not choose her own, and above all she does not come to her brother with a man's child in her belly, and that man no one he has ever seen before."

"Dear Lady," Danu said. He thought perhaps he should be appalled. It was difficult. She, after all, had chosen him. He could never regret that. "What will he want to do to you?"

"Nothing," she said, "if I can help it. If not . . . he'll likely not kill me. I don't think. He might want to geld you. Kill you. Demand that you take me as your wife, and make my honor yours."

"Wife?" said Danu, struggling with the word in her language.

"Woman who belongs to you," she said. "Woman who lives in your tent, bears your children, does your bidding."

Danu laughed incredulously. "You? Belong to me? And how can you bear *my* children? They're yours."

"That," she said, "is going to baffle my brother to no end."

"I am baffled," Danu said.

She patted his cheek. "I'm sure you are," she said.

He did not like this mood of hers. At least, he thought, it was brighter than it had been before. "Tell me what you're laughing at," he said.

"Myself," she answered. "No, don't glare at me! I doubt my brother will kill you, and he knows that if he gelds you I'll do the same to him. He's going to insist that I marry you." And before he could ask: "Marry is to make me your wife. To take me and say that you own me, and to accept my honor as yours."

"I can't do that," Danu said.

"And I'll have to promise to take no other man while you live. You have no need to promise the same. A man may take as many wives as he likes."

"I won't make you do that," said Danu, "and he can't force me. I don't care if he tries to fight me. All of this is appalling. The Lady will never allow it."

"That's why I was laughing," she said. "Because I know you, and I know him. If you don't kill each other, you'll be fast friends."

"I'll never understand him," Danu said, "nor he me."

"I hope you may," she said.

"If he's like you, I never will."

She shook her head, drew him to her and kissed him. "You are a wonder and a marvel, and I wish to the gods I had never led my brother to this country. He's going to change it—more than I ever could. Because I can teach you how to fight, but he gives you reason to do it. I can feel the younger gods in him. They'll destroy the Lady if they can, and set this country under their heel."

"They'll never touch the Lady," Danu said. "You never need fear that."

"But they can touch you," she said. "They can touch your country. And then—"

"And then we shall be stronger. We can do that, Sarama. Soft is strong. Like spidersilk. Like water, wearing away stone."

"You are so sure," she said.

He was not; but he was standing on the step of the Lady's house. It must be she who spoke in him.

It comforted Sarama, or seemed to. That was all he wanted.

As inevitably as snow in winter, in the wake of the messenger from the east came the Mother and her daughters of Larchwood, fleeing the coming of the horsemen. Others like them had come westward, but only they had come as far as Three Birds. Only they feared war so much that they ran as far as they expected it to go.

Their Mother came with them, but Catin led them. It was her fear that brought them. Her urgency drove them on.

"You should go farther," Sarama said to her. "Go all the way to the world's edge. Maybe the horsemen won't follow."

Sarama had not meant to speak with Catin. But after the dance and the feast of welcome, when the Mother's house had been turned upside down to make room for its guests, the two of them happened to meet between the house and the temple. Sarama had taken refuge in the Lady's house for a while, and like a coward evaded Catin's bitter dislike. But she had come back because she was too proud to stay away, and because she had left Danu to face Catin alone. Not that he could not fend for himself, but she should have been there. She should have stood beside him.

As the Lady's luck would have it, she met Catin halfway between house and temple, under a grey and misty sky. The tenders of the fields had been singing thanks to the Lady for her gift of rain after so many days of sun— blessing her for bringing relief to parched earth. Sarama had only begun to understand what the world and its weather were to people who made the earth grow and bear fruit. She was not so glad of rain, that turned roads to mud and made riding a misery.

It was only mist now, more pleasant than not on her cheeks. Catin had not even worn a mantle against it. She stopped at sight of Sarama, and thought transparently of turning and walking away. But like Sarama she had her pride. She said, "So I was right. Are you still denying it?"

"No," said Sarama. "That's my brother leading the horsemen. Did you know that?"

Catin's eyes widened. So: no one had told her. Not that anyone knew, except the messenger who had gone on to the Long Bridge, and Danu. Danu had kept silent. Sarama was not surprised.

She watched Catin's surprise transmute into a kind of glee. "He followed you. Did you tell him to do it? What did you promise him?"

"Actually," Sarama said, "I forbade him. He came regardless."

"How very disobedient," said Catin.

"Horsemen are like that," Sarama said. "They don't listen to women."

"That is the women's fault. They should keep their men in hand."

"So they should," said Sarama. "Did you ever think of doing it, instead of running away?"

That stung: Catin's eyes glittered. "We came to take counsel with the Mother of Three Birds, and to ask her help in standing against the horsemen."

"While the horsemen take your city that you left behind." Sarama shook her head. "You should have stayed. He's not fighting or killing. He might even have been worth your choosing. Aren't you curious to know what a man of the tribes is like?"

"Whipcord and wire," said Catin, "and a powerful stink. They never bathe after the midwife dips them in mare's milk and hands them to their mothers."

"Ah," said Sarama. "You have seen them."

Catin shook her head tightly. "I've heard what people say of them. One of them forced a woman. She was carrying a baby. It died. Have you ever heard of such a monster?"

Sarama smiled her sweetest smile. "I'm sure it was an honest mistake."

Catin hissed. "Only an outlander would make light of such things."

"Surely," said Sarama. "I think you came here to taunt me. Why do you dislike me so much? Do you want Danu as badly as that?"

"You took him away from me," said Catin.

"You cast him off," Sarama said. "You nigh to broke his heart. Can you fault me for wanting to comfort him?"

"You did that," said Catin with a long, raking glance.

Sarama met that glance and laughed. "Imagine! I'm quarrelling over a man. He'd be horrified if he knew. He's such a proper man of his people."

"You don't deserve him."

"Probably not," said Sarama. "Now say it. Say that you expect me to take my Mare and ride away and lead the horsemen here, and make them bring war to the people who cherished me as one of themselves."

"You're fond of mockery, aren't you?" said Catin.

"Not as fond of it as you." Sarama shrugged, sighed, walked past her.

As she had more than half expected, Catin caught at her arm, pulling her about. She gave to it as if it had been a horse's leap and shy. Catin seemed a little startled at the lack of resistance. She put Sarama in mind, just then, of a young and headstrong mare, fiercely mistrustful of strangers and fiercely protective of her own. It did not make her easier to like, but it bolstered Sarama's patience.

Catin did not seem to know what to do with Sarama now that she had caught her. Sarama did not help her; she stood quietly, waiting for Catin's grip to slacken.

"I'll be watching you," Catin said. "Every moment of every day, and every night, too, that you walk abroad from your bed. If you even think of running to your brother, I'll know. I'll stop you."

"I am not going to run to my brother," Sarama said. "I'm not going to send for him, either. If he comes here—I'll welcome him. But only if he comes in peace."

"I don't believe you," said Catin.

Sarama shrugged. "The truth doesn't depend on your belief. Now will you let me go? I'm wanted in the Mother's house."

"And I am wanted in the temple," Catin said, thrusting Sarama away. "Go, laugh at me. And remember that I'm watching you."

"I won't ever forget," Sarama said.

Danu was standing in the doorway of the Mother's house, silent and invisible until she stood in front of him. She started and nearly leaped on him before she knew who it was.

He regarded her without fear of the knife she pressed to his throat, frowning a little as he searched her face. "You're ill," he said.

Slowly Sarama lowered the knife, sheathed it, breathed deep. "Not ill," she said. "Troubled."

"Tilia will speak to Catin," Danu said. He spoke quietly, but there was a growl in it, too soft almost to hear.

"No," said Sarama, quickly. "No, don't tell Tilia. She'll trample Catin flat."

"She'll tell Catin to let you be," Danu said. "Catin's dreams are too strong for her spirit. They twist her in ways that I don't like. She's decided that you are bent on destroying us. Nothing that any of us says will dissuade her from it."

"For all any of you knows, that is the truth."

Danu shook his head. "She doesn't understand. She thinks she knows what you are, what the dreams mean. But she hears too many voices. She can't tell which is true and which is false."

"How do you know that I can, either?"

"I know," Danu said with certainty that Sarama could envy—if she had not wanted to slap it out of him.

"Don't trust me," she said. "Don't believe me. Catin is wise in that. She knows that I'm the enemy."

"You are not," Danu said, unshakable.

"You do love me," Sarama said. She meant it, and not with irony.

"I do love you," he said in all seriousness. "Now come inside. Everybody's quiet. I kept a jar of the honeyed wine for you."

She held him before he turned to lead her within. "Tell me. Tell me the truth. Do you trust me?"

"Why should I not?" he asked, as innocent as a newborn child.

"Maybe," she said, "because my brother and others of my kin and kind are riding toward you with swords."

"*You* are not," he said. "You're teaching us to fight."

"Catin trusts too little," Sarama said. "You trust too much. Is there no balance in the world?"

"The Mother has balance," Danu said. "Tilia may—she's difficult sometimes to predict."

"Ah," said Sarama: a sound half of disgust and half of unwilling amusement. "And I'm a fool, too, because I chose you. We'll all be fools together. My brother will be so appalled, he'll turn and run from the sight of us."

Danu rolled his eyes at that, which made her laugh; and that was no ill way to regard the whole of it.

65

Agni held his men in a delicate balance, poised between conquest and war. They went out as he commanded, took towns and villages, exacted tribute in treasure. There were too few of them to settle in any one place, or to hold any single city. They trusted to speed, and to ceaseless motion. If there had been resistance, they would have crushed it. But there never was.

He lingered a few days in Larchwood, long enough for all three of his mares to foal: the dun sisters on the same night, their spotted cousin the day after. Two fillies and a colt, red dun or red chestnut, stamped each in the image of its father. Then when they were big enough to travel, drawn by the same restlessness that had brought him so far, he left the city behind, took his horsemen and rode toward the setting sun.

Summer deepened about him. The days were breathlessly hot, the nights still and warm and abuzz with biting flies. The westward cities crowded ever closer together, in ever greater numbers of people. He rode straight; those who had followed him came and went, hunting in widening circles but always returning. They all ate like kings, and dressed like them, too.

It was a glorious riding, but with an edge to it, a shortening of temper. They had seen the new moon in Larchwood. As it swelled to the full, they came through a skein of villages to a town that proclaimed its wealth with a fluttering of banners and a ringing of what Agni learned were called bells. They were made of copper, and they made a sweet sound.

To be so rich, he thought: to be able to delight one's fancy with precious copper, to shape it into a ripple of music.

Here at last he could not simply ride into the town and take what he pleased. People stood across the road, women most of them, with hunting spears and blades of peculiar shapes and sizes, that must be knives for cutting meat and butchering cattle and, perhaps, mowing grain in the fields. Their faces were grim, their feet set firmly in the road, their bodies walling it from side to side.

Agni halted in front of them. His people drew up behind, tall on their horses, towering over these women on foot. "Mika," he said to the child who rode behind him, "tell them to let us pass."

"They're not going to," Mika said.

Agni sighed faintly. Tillu had opinions and was not shy in expressing them, but he never argued as this child did. Neither had he spoken as well for Agni, or been so keenly aware of these people's minds: how they thought, what they meant by the words they spoke. "Just tell them," Agni said.

Mika told them—or so Agni could suppose. One of the women in the front rank answered in a harsh clear voice. Agni knew the word: "No."

"Tell her that if she resists, it is an act of war. And in war, people die."

"She says she knows," Mika said when he had spoken and been answered.

"Very well," Agni said. He turned Mitani about and raised his voice.

"We ride forward. Don't strike unless someone strikes you first. Use your horses' weight to drive them back. This town is ours. We will take it."

They all nodded. He caught and held any eye that gleamed too brightly, and stared it down. When he was satisfied that they would do as he bade them, he turned again and rode Mitani toward the line. It did not waver, which spoke well for these people's bravery and badly for their common sense.

Very deliberately he kept his spear on his saddle and his long knife in its sheath. He simply rode forward. Mitani hesitated, unwilling to trample living flesh; but Agni urged him on. He could feel the weight of his warriors behind him, their numbers smaller than the people gathered here, but strong, and mounted on horses.

The line stiffened against the weight of them, but it could not hold. It weakened and wavered and broke.

Agni was through, and the road was clear, his warriors quickening their pace behind him.

He did not see how it began. He heard a sound that he knew too well at first to understand. The song of an arrow, the soft thud as it struck flesh; the cry of a wounded man. But as he turned, he saw as in a dream the raising of a spear, the woman—it was a woman, he could not mistake her—driving it into the body of a horseman who pushed past her.

One blow bred another. The tautness of waiting shattered. With a howl of pure glee, Agni's warriors leaped into the fight.

Agni drew breath to bellow at them, to command them to stop. But the words never escaped. The people of this town, the Lady's people, were fighting—not well, but fighting it certainly was. Their archers were particularly dangerous. Maybe for them it was easier, because they need not stand face to face with a man before they shot him.

Agni waded in. He slipped his spear from its lashings and struck with the butt of it, fending off wild blows, ducking arrows that flew overhead. It was an untidy, unlovely melee, no order or reason in it, but blood enough. Patir was down—off his horse but on his feet, staggering, bleeding from a wound in his forehead. Past him Gauan lay unmoving, his yellow hair stained scarlet.

Dead. Agni sat Mitani above him, staring down at his bruised and broken face. Someone must have had a stone, and smitten him with it. His expression, what there was of it, was enormously surprised.

Agni bent low, leaning far out of Mitani's saddle, and trailed his fingers in Gauan's blood. He tasted it, the sweet strong taste.

He straightened. His mind was very clear. He called to as many of his people as could hear, and beckoned them to him, away from that travesty of a battle. "Come," he called. "Come with me!"

✦ ✦

They took the town with fire and blood, swept over it and devoured it. They took its women and children. Any who fought them, they killed. They made war in the Lady's country, made a sacrifice of blood to the red gods, the war-gods. They poured it out on the earth in Earth Mother's name, that the grass grow rich and the rains fall steady, and make the people strong.

Agni sat in the Mother's house. She was dead, killed in the fight on the road. Her daughter, her heir, lay badly wounded, with women tending her. Agni did not mean for her to die, unless the gods willed it. His heart was all cleansed, all empty. Blood had washed it clean.

In a little while he must see to Gauan's burial. No other horseman had died; only the prince of the Stormwolf people, that amiable man who had ridden so often at Agni's side. Friends they had not been, not as he and Patir were, or as he had been with Rahim. But they had ridden far together, and shared many a campfire of an evening. Agni would miss his familiar presence, his light touch with a jest, the way he had of coaxing people to smile when they were inclined to be surly.

It should be easier than losing Rahim. Rahim he had killed with his own hand. But dead was dead. There was no calling Gauan back. He was gone.

Agni looked round him at this house so like every other Mother's house, as if, like the temples of the Lady, Mothers' houses were prescribed by rite and custom. The hangings just so, the carpets thus, the furnishings in this order and no other. All Mothers, these people believed, were faces of the Lady. And she, it seemed, liked all her houses to be alike.

He was tired of that sameness. If he ever paused long enough to do it, he would remake a Mother's house into a king's tent. He would cast out the furnishings, pull down the hangings, hide the harsh wooden walls behind softer walls of leather or woven cloth.

Tonight he endured it as it was, because there was no time to change it. Outside, in the town, his men celebrated noisily. They had all been spoiling for a fight. This easy victory suited them well. They had women, willing or unwilling, and wine and mead, and here and there a wound to brag of. This was war as they had been raised to wage it.

He had caught some of them hoping that there would be more armed townspeople farther on; that this would not be the only fight or the only honest victory in this strange conquest.

"And where are we going?" Patir asked Agni over the remains of a dinner prepared and served by silent, tight-lipped men. "Will we just keep riding westward till we find the edge of the world?"

Agni had not honestly thought about it. "I suppose we could do that," he said. "Or we could find a city that suited us and take it to live in as if it were our summer hunting lands; and in the winter we'll go elsewhere—maybe back to Larchwood, maybe farther west, wherever we please to go."

"We could," said Patir, "take what we've won and go back to the steppe."

"And where would we go?" Agni asked him. "We're outcast from the White Horse. Everywhere else we're likely to go, some tribe or clan has claimed it. We'd have to wage war, conquer a tribe. Wouldn't you rather stay here, where no one knows how to fight, and the whole country's ours for the taking?"

"It's settled country," Patir said. "Cities everywhere you look. You can't ride half a day without coming across half a dozen villages. There's no room to breathe."

"There's hardly room on the steppe," said Agni, "particularly in the westward lands. The world's filling up with people."

"It's too full here." Patir stretched out, propped up on his elbow, and sighed.

"Are you asking to go back?" Agni asked.

"No," said Patir. "You like it here."

"I do not," Agni said.

"You do." Patir grinned at Agni's glare. "You like a country full of women who talk back to you."

"So does Taditi," Agni said. "If I go, she'll stay. She's already told me that."

Patir did not ask how Agni could let her be so insolent. He knew Taditi. "Have you ever wondered if she's warming her bed with fine young things while we take our pick of the women?"

Agni sucked in a breath. It was supposed to be a word, but none came out. Taditi? Disporting herself with doe-eyed youths?

"She's a woman," Patir said, "and she's not as old as all that. Mika told me the men rather like her looks. She's too thin by far, they think, but they admire her strength, and her seat on a horse."

"These men are all like women," Agni said. "They giggle and simper like girls. I'm surprised none of them has asked me into his bed."

"They are weaklings." Patir lay flat and stretched, arching his back and yawning loudly. "Ah! I could sleep till winter."

"You can't," Agni said. "We have to bury Gauan."

That sobered Patir, for a little while. "His kin want to declare blood feud against this whole country."

"They'll settle for taking their revenge on this town," Agni said.

"Why?" Patir asked. And when Agni lifted a brow, not certain of the meaning: "Why are you so easy on these people? We've found we can provoke them into a fight. That makes this honorable war. Why won't you let it happen as it happens?"

"Because I want to rule this country, not destroy it," Agni said.

"You are a strange one," said Patir. He sprang to his feet. "Come. We've a barrow to raise."

Agni rose more slowly. Sometimes it seemed that whatever Patir said was only half of it; that Rahim should be there to complete it. And now Gauan was gone. More would go if these hotheads had their way; till this country with its crowding people and its relentless refusal to fight, overwhelmed and consumed the last of them.

He considered explaining that to Patir, but Patir was nigh gone already. He held his peace instead, and went to lay Gauan on Earth Mother's breast.

············· 66 ·············

Of course it was Catin who had the news first. A town called Wild Rose had given way to its fear and determined to stand against the horsemen. They had killed a horseman, and for that a whole dozen of them had died and many more been wounded, and their town taken as a prize of war.

"You see?" cried Catin to the assembled people of Three Birds. "This is what comes upon you. *This* is what comes of fighting."

"If you don't fight," Sarama said, raising her voice only a little, but enough to carry, "they'll only go on till they find someone who will."

"So they'll stop," said someone from among the crowd. "They've taken Wild Rose. They'll be content."

"No," said Sarama. "Wild Rose is little more than a village. A king of the horsemen will want a city worthy of his kingly presence. He'll take whatever comes between himself and such a city, but he won't let it turn him aside. Once he comes to that mother of cities—*then* he'll stop."

"Three Birds is the mother of cities in this part of the world," Danu said.

"We can make sure that he stops here," Sarama said. "We may even turn him back. He can't have many men with him. Everyone agrees, these are men, not tribes with women and children. He'll be stretched thin, so far from the steppe, and with so many towns and cities in back of him for him to hold. If we stand fast—"

"If we stand fast," said Catin, "we die, and he runs over us. Why not just give him what he wants? Then he'll go away."

"I don't think so," Sarama said.

"You don't make sense," said Catin.

Sarama bared her teeth. Danu spoke smoothly and easily in her silence. "I think she means that the horsemen will come to Three Birds because no city is greater—and if we fight them they'll cut us apart, but if we don't fight them they'll take us and break us. They'll stop here whatever we do. If we can push them back, maybe they'll give up their war."

"It won't be that easy," Sarama said, "but the rest is true enough. He may look for us to be cowed because of what he did to Wild Rose. He may meet further resistance as he comes toward us, but it won't stop or even slow him. It will give his men something to do—and that he'll regard as a blessing."

"Why bless him?" Catin demanded. "Let's offer him nothing. No fight. No bribes to go away."

"Then he'll simply take what he pleases," said Sarama. She turned away from Catin. "You may dream as you like. I'm going to see that our fighters are ready for whatever comes."

⚜ ⚜

They were ready; but what came first was a wave of the Lady's people. Townsfolk and villagers, struck to horror by the killing in Wild Rose, fled the horsemen's advance. There was a little resistance, they said, a few of the younger women and men refusing to run away, but wise people gathered their belongings and set off westward.

They did not mean to stop in Three Birds. Like Sarama they had seen that it was the greatest of the cities and the most likely to draw the horsemen's eye. They would rest there for a night or a day, but they would go on; would travel westward till their fear was gone away, or till they came to the edge of the world.

People in Three Birds, Sarama was pleased to note, did not run away. Some elected to go on trading ventures or to visit kin in cities well away from the horsemen's advance, but no one actually, openly fled.

The same could not be said of the people from Larchwood. As seemed to be their ancestral way, once they had clear sight of danger, they set themselves as far away from it as they could go. Catin professed that someone must bring warning to the west, as if every trader and traveler could not have done it as well as she. Her Mother was weary, though she insisted that she was not ill. She was content to go wherever her daughter led her.

Good riddance, Sarama thought. Let them take their fear and their doomsaying elsewhere, and leave Three Birds to fight its battle as it had long prepared to do.

The fighters whom she had labored so long to train were as ready as they would ever be. She had raised such defenses as the Mother and the elders would allow: had set a mob of young men and women to digging a ditch on the sunrise side, all round the edges of the fields, deep enough and wide enough to give a horseman pause. At the bottom of it she had them set sharpened stakes. It was an ugly thing, but then, as she said to Tilia, war was ugly. And since the city could not pick itself up and move, and since the people on foot could never match the pace of men on horseback, there had to be some way to stop the horsemen; some barrier that they could not cross.

"Therefore," Sarama said, standing on the edge of it, "this."

Tilia peered down at the stakes with an expression half of awe and half of horror. "If anyone falls on these . . ."

"Yes," said Sarama.

"I think I hate this thing called war," Tilia said.

"Most women do," said Sarama. "The men reckon it a grand game. No man is a man unless he's won his stallion and proved himself in war."

"Is that what they're doing?" Tilia asked. "Proving themselves?"
Sarama nodded.

Tilia snorted. "All they prove to me is that they're savages."

"They don't care what *you* think," Sarama said. "You're a woman."

"Then they should care very much indeed," said Tilia.

Sarama bit her tongue. It was going to be interesting when Tilia and Agni stood face to face. Each so sure of the world's admiration. Each raised from birth to rule over the people. And each convinced that the other's race and sex were by far the lesser.

+ +

Danu seemed unruffled, impervious to the fog of fear that hung over the city. And yet it was he who said to the Mother of a morning, when the horsemen were no more than two days' ride outside of Three Birds, "It's too dark in the soul here. Let's hold a festival. Let's dance the dark away."

It was a mad thing to do, as if they celebrated a victory before the battle was even fought; and foolish too, if the horsemen came on quicker than expected, and found them all drowned in wine. But the Mother gave it her blessing, and the city flung itself into the doing of it. There was desperation in their eagerness, but an honest pleasure, too. They had not had a festival since spring. It was time and more than time to build the Lady-fires, to prepare a feast, to put on their best clothes and ornaments and come out as the sun rode low, late in the long summer day.

For tonight they forgot fear. They forgot the war. They sang, they danced together. And some sooner, some later, disappeared two by two into the shadows, all of them who were old enough and some whom Sarama would have thought too young to think of such things. Even the Mother, that placid mountain of a woman, beckoned to the one called Kosti-the-Bull, and went away with him.

Sarama did not see what anyone saw in Kosti. He was a gentle soul, soft-handed with the children, but much too much like his namesake the bull for Sarama's taste. Danu beside him seemed almost lightly built, and beautiful in it.

He had thrown himself into preparations for the festival as if no one else could do as much or as well as he. Sarama had expected him to bury himself among the cooks and the servants, but when the feast was spread and the wine had begun to go round, he came out among the dancers. In the sweet skirling of the pipes and the beating of drums, he stamped out a rhythm that set all their hearts to pounding.

Sarama's had had a fair beginning at the sight of him. People here were modest as they should be, except in festivals. In festivals, one's best clothes were the ones that came off most quickly—or that never went on at all.

He had on a kind of kilt, a skirt like those the women wore under their gowns, with long fringes from which hung bright beads and bits of carved wood and bone, and copper bells that chimed sweetly in the lulls of the music. The rest of him was bare, the Lady's signs painted on his arms and breast and legs, long sweeping curves and spirals, dizzying and holy. When he began his hair was knotted tight at his nape, but as he leaped and whirled, stamped and spun, it escaped its bindings and tumbled down his back.

He was beautiful, beautiful and wild. He had half-masked his face, flat curve of white, dark wells of eyes. So the people of the Lady's country sig-nified their gods or their strong spirits. This was a young god, swift and light of foot, wooing the earth with his dancing.

Wooing Sarama, too. The turn of his head, the breadth of his shoulders limned in firelight, made her breath come quick, her heart beat hard. She wanted to run her hand down that strong smooth back, and kiss the furrow of it, and taste the salt of his sweat.

She drew a shuddering breath. He danced, tireless, to the beating of the drums. He was dancing defiance. He mimed the horsemen, their horses galloping, curvetting, tossing their manes. He mimed battle as Sarama had taught him, leap, thrust, retreat. He mimed the strut of the conqueror, the arrogant lift of the chin, the thrust and roll of the hips that made Sarama choke on laughter. He was more like a tribesman drunk on his own splendor than maybe he knew: exact, to the life, who had never seen a man of the tribes in the flesh.

He ended the dance with that wicked thrust, on a single, bone-jarring beat of the drum. The fire flared suddenly, startling them all. When their eyes cleared, he was gone.

✦ ✦

Sarama found him where she had expected, down by the river washing the sweat and the paint from his body. Moonlight and starlight and a faint light from the fire turned him to a shape of glimmer and darkness. The night was caught in his hair, shadow deeper than shadow.

She watched him with great satisfaction. He had dropped his kilt to bathe. He took his time about it, long lazy strokes, sweetening himself with a potion of herbs and sand and somewhat else that she did not know, that was a marvel for making a body clean. Its scent, sharp and sweet, drifted to Sarama.

She followed it as if it had been a wishing laid on her, a yearning for the warmth of his skin. It was as as warm as she could wish it to be, damp and fragrant. He turned in her arms, still a little breathless, laughing as she ate him alive with kisses.

She pulled back. "You did that to drive me wild."

"I did it to wake you up," he conceded, "but I did it for the people, too. So they'll remember."

"I don't want to remember," she said. "Not tonight. Make me forget."

"I want to remember," he said.

"I don't."

"Then I'll remember," said Danu, "and you can forget."

"Women are supposed to be this accommodating among the tribes," Sarama said. "Men are supposed to be intransigent."

"I am being intransigent," he said. "I'm exasperating you to no end."

She peered at him in the moonlight. He was not feigning his antic mood. His eyes were bright, his teeth glinting as he laughed. He was exasperating. Indeed.

She pulled away. "Go pleasure yourself tonight. I'll be dreaming of war."

He caught her before she had gone a step, and held her with that effortless strength of his. She stared at him. She had not expected him to do so manly a thing.

"You will dream," he said, "if you dream at all, of sunlight and quiet. And maybe, a little, of me. Now come here."

A command. How startling. Sarama was already, perforce, in obedience. He drew her closer, folded his arms about her, and said softly in her ear, "Hold on now. Hold tight. Remember nothing but moonlight and starlight and the dance that the Lady taught me."

And that dance, she thought, was all the distraction she could ask for. His body against hers, the clean warm scent of him, the wild curling of his hair as it dried, the heat that rose in him, found a heat in her to match it. The child leaped in her belly. It danced as its father had danced, in joy that defied terror.

He bore her back and down, and laid her in the grass. Its sweet scent filled her nostrils. He took her gently—*he* took *her*, as he never had before; as she had despaired of teaching him. He did it with a kind of astonishment, as if he had not expected it, either.

Just as he slackened, as the enormity of it struck him, she wrapped arms and legs about him, round the blessed curve of the child, and held him tight, warm and hard inside her. She rocked gently to keep him so. "You are a wonder," she said, "and a marvel. If you get yourself killed doing what's necessary for this city, I'll hunt you through all the dark lands, hunt you down and haunt you."

He could not answer just then. Nor, in a moment, could she.

✦ ✦

When the heat had cooled, the urgency subsided, she cradled him in her arms. His hair was all a tangle. She would be half the morning unsnarling it, and with him champing at the bit to be about his duties.

It would keep him close, which was not an ill thing. She resisted the temptation to ruffle it further. He would never thank her for that.

"I do love you," she said. "Believe that."

"I don't simply believe. I know." He kissed the curve of her breast.

She shivered at the touch. "Stop that," she said. "Listen. I want you to be sure. I'm not going to go running to the horsemen. I won't betray any of you. This is my place now, and these are my people. *You* are my people."

"Yes," he said.

"You can't be so sure of me," she said. "It's not reasonable."

"And yet you ask me to be sure?" He teased her breast with his tongue, a bit of wickedness that got him slapped; but he only laughed.

"I know what you'll say," she said. "The heart knows. I suppose it does. But except for Catin, none of you people is wary enough, ever, or sure enough of your own mortality."

"We are very sure of that," he said with fair to middling gravity. "Don't mistake clarity for idiocy, or the Lady's calm for a fool's oblivion. We know what lies ahead of us. Death for some of us, maybe. Maybe not. Whichever it is, we're ready for it. We trust ourselves to the Lady."

"Is that why you danced tonight?"

He nodded. "And because I wanted you to want me."

"To choose you," she said. "Again. As if I could ever fail to."

"I hope you never do," he said.

She clasped him tightly, till he gasped and protested. She eased a little. "Don't change," she said. "Don't ever be other than you are."

.... 67 ....

Mika wanted to learn to ride a horse. He was insistent on it. Agni was inclined to indulge him. If nothing else, Mitani would be glad to be relieved of the burden.

Since the battle, most of the people of this country did not even try to stand and fight. Either their villages were empty, their people fled, or a few ill-schooled young persons tried to make a stand. They always failed. This country was Agni's, and no one seemed to doubt it, or to be much inclined to defend it.

And yet those who lingered professed a belief in the city to the west, the mother of cities, this place called Three Birds. Some power seemed to reside there, some force that would hold back the horsemen. People thought of it as a wall to hide behind.

"Its Mother is wise," Mika said when Agni asked, "and strong in the Lady's spirit."

"We're stronger," said Agni.

"Maybe," Mika said with the air of one who is determined to be polite.

Agni forbore to upbraid him for it. Mika had kept his innocence even through the red roar of battle. Fear he had none. He was a strong spirit himself, and a bright one.

+ +

"He's plotting against you," Tillu said.

He had come to Agni's tent in the evening, professing to carry a message that would not wait. But when he had come in and been given wine and sweet cakes and such courtesy as was due his rank and station, he had nothing more to offer than baseless fears. "That boy is your enemy," he said. "He spies for his own kind. He'll harm you if he can. He might even kill you."

"Maybe," Agni said. He had been resting when Tillu came and demanded entry, closer to sleep than he had been in more days than he liked to count.

He yawned, but Tillu was in no mood to care for subtleties. "My lord," he said. "Think. You don't know that he can be trusted. He's not one of us. He wants to ride horses in order to steal one. Then he'll go back all the more quickly to the women who rule him."

"I do think," Agni said. "I think maybe you're jealous."

Tillu stiffened.

Maybe this was not wise, and maybe Agni was too tired to judge rightly, but he had trusted this man. He still did, enough to speak freely. "You are, aren't you? You were my voice to the people of this country. You labored long at it, and lowered yourself greatly, even stooping to run messages for me. Then came this slip of a child with his ready tongue and his outrageous manners, and took it all away. I thought you would be glad to be a prince again."

"I am glad," Tillu growled. "I'm angry, too. Do you think that little of me? Do you judge me so poorly? I've no need to be jealous of a child, no matter how close he may cling to you. I know his kind, and I know what they can do. He'll betray you if he can. Why not? You're no kin of his."

"He's not a tribesman," Agni said. "He doesn't think as tribesmen think. I'm safe from him. I'm sure of it."

"You're cocky," said Tillu. "Have a care you don't get yourself killed."

"I am always careful," Agni said. He made himself smile and slap Tillu lightly on the shoulder. "Come, my friend. It warms my heart to see you fret so for me; and I'm grateful for it. But I'm in no danger."

"You are in great danger." Tillu stood. "At least remember what I said. And let Patir set a guard on you."

"Patir always has a guard on me," said Agni.

"Then have him double it."

"I'll speak to him," Agni said. "Will that set your mind at rest?"

"Not much," said Tillu. But he seemed to understand that he would get no more from Agni. Not tonight.

+ +

When Tillu had gone, Agni could not compose himself to sleep. Tillu's concern was honest, and that warmed him, but he did not believe for a moment that there was any cause for it. Nonetheless it jangled at him. It made him remember where he was, in what country. And while Mika was not his enemy—of that he was heart-certain—the same could never be said of the rest of Mika's people. In all that country, only here were people who wished Agni well.

There was still a little light in the sky. He went hunting something—he did not overmuch care what.

Not all the women were gone from this town in which they had camped, nor was any of those unwilling. They lingered, it seemed, out of curiosity and in despite of fear. Having done nothing to harm the horsemen, they found themselves unharmed in return.

One was tending a thing that Agni had learned to call an oven, baking bread that lured him with its fragrance. She was plump and dark-eyed as nearly all the women were here, but prettier than most. She smiled at the sight of him, with a look that he could not mistake. No enmity here, and no revulsion either.

She offered him a loaf still warm from the baking. He bit into it. She watched him eat, still smiling. He was well and modestly dressed, but under those eyes he might have been naked.

Men had looked at women so, it was said, before Earth Mother taught the women to veil themselves and live sequestered in tents. No wonder the goddess had so protected them. Women were weak, and men excessively strong. A man who wanted a woman would take her and care nothing for her family or her honor—as Agni was said to have done to the woman of the Red Deer.

And here was a woman regarding him just so, as if she would leap on him and have her way with him, and never ask his leave.

It should have left him cold, or made him angry. Tonight, in the mood that possessed him, he was inclined to oblige her. These women took men of their own choosing, and had their will of them, too. He had not given himself up to one of them, not yet. Not entirely. Tonight maybe he would do it.

Rudira, when he thought of her at all, now seemed a weak shadow of the women here. All her wantonness had been mostly boredom and the petulance of a spoiled child. If he had not been her husband's brother, and the one Yama hated the most at that, Agni wondered if she would even have noticed him.

That was a hard thought. He had never dared think it before. But with those wanton black eyes burning on him, the memory of wanton grey eyes was dim and pale.

He ate the last of the loaf. She leaned toward him, reached out a hand, brushed the crumbs from his beard. He held still. Her smile changed. She stroked fingers through his hair as they all loved to do here, captivated by the color and the feel of it: so much softer than her own, and so straight.

She took him by the hand. He let out a breath. She tugged. He followed her as if he had been one of the meek men of this country. It was almost alarmingly easy; as if his will lost itself somewhere, and had no life or presence apart from hers.

She led him inside the house that stood nearest the bread-oven. It was a small house, bare and rather mean, but it was clean. By the light of a lamp she undressed him, cooing over him. She loved his shoulders, his breast with its sparse red hairs, his skin that was milk-white where the sun seldom touched it. She particularly loved his manly parts, cradled them in her hands as if they had been rare stones, and stroked his tall shaft till he gasped aloud. Still smiling that perpetual smile, she mounted and rode him as capably as any horseman.

He could lie still in shock, or he could try to give her such pleasure as she would take. It was all the same to her. She used him as a man might use a woman, as a thing for her pleasure; and no regard for his pride. She made of him a plaything, dandled him and petted him, and when he had brought her to the summit, after she had wrung every drop of pleasure from it, she rose and smoothed her gown over her hips and her heavy thighs, and left him without a glance.

She did not come back. He had not honestly expected her to, but it was a disappointment nonetheless. Even here, he had grown accustomed to women looking on him with liking, wanting to linger, professing themselves well pleased with what he had to give.

He dragged himself up after a while and went back toward his tent; but he passed it, went to the stream that flowed along the edge of the field. He washed himself in it over and over, scrubbing till his skin was raw. Even then he did not feel clean.

✦ ✦

He slept a little, maybe. He was up before dawn, rousing his people, driving them to break camp and ride before the sun was well up. Mika had his own horse now, more or less: one of the remounts, an ugly-headed, thick-furred creature of indeterminate color. He called it a name in his own tongue that, he said, meant Fierce Lion, and clung to its back with more determination than skill.

Lion was a very small horse and terribly short-legged, but he had a decent turn of speed. He could keep pace with Mitani for a while, as he did this morning. Mika had never yet failed to be bright-eyed and wide awake, even at ungodly hours. He met Agni's bleared scowl with wide eyes and irrepressible grin.

Agni looked him straight in the eye and said, "Tell me you're not spying for the Mothers of this country."

Mika barely blinked. "What is spying?" he asked.

"Watching," Agni said. "Listening. Sending word to the enemy of all one sees, so that the enemy can destroy the people whom the spy calls friend."

"That is a horrible thing to do," Mika said. "Who would do such a thing?"

"A spy," Agni said.

"Then I am not one," said Mika. "I watch and I listen, because I can hardly help it, but I'd never talk to an enemy. What would I do that for? It would hurt you."

"War is about hurting people," Agni said.

"Yes," said Mika, unwontedly somber. "I don't like war."

"Your people are all strange," Agni muttered.

Mika's ears were sharp. He said, "You don't like it either. Everybody's dreams said you'd come in a storm of fire. You haven't brought much fire at all."

"It's wasteful," Agni said. "One burns, slays, sheds blood, not for pleasure, but to gain what's necessary. Then one stops."

"Some of your men like the killing," Mika said.

"There's glory in it," said Agni.

"They like it," Mika said. "The way you like it when a woman chooses you."

"I choose a woman," Agni said a little more fiercely than he intended.

Mika graciously and visibly did not contradict him. "They like it that way. It makes their rods stiff."

"And what do you know of that, puppy?" Agni asked him.

Mika shrugged elaborately. "Maybe I'm not all *that* young."

"No: maybe you're younger."

Mika made a rude noise, kicked his horse into a scrambling gallop, and gave Agni a taste of his dust.

Agni spat it out and laughed. "That's no spy," he said.

Patir, who had been riding behind them the whole time, came up beside Agni and watched the boy on his shaggy rug of a horse, racing their own shadow down the long open road. "He may not know he is," he said.

Agni shot him a glance. "Don't tell me you believe that."

"Maybe I don't," Patir said. "But think of it a little differently. This child is an innocent. He'd see no harm in riding to a city ahead of us and telling its Mother everything we intend to do to it. He'd never understand how that might harm us—and he'd be sure the Mother wanted to know."

"We'll tell him not to tell anyone," Agni said. "He's honorable in his way. He'll keep his word."

"I don't doubt it," said Patir.

They rode on for a while. In back of them, people were singing: a song of warriors on the march, advancing from victory to victory. Agni joined in the chorus till it trailed off in favor of an uproarious drinking song.

Then as if there had been no interruption, Patir said, "Tillu means well."

Agni nodded. "He's a good man. I trust him. But he's seeing betrayal where there is none."

"He's fond of you," said Patir. "He frets maybe more than he ought. All of us do."

Agni could hardly contest that. "All of you? Westerners too?"

"More of them than you'd think." Patir slapped at a fly on his horse's neck. "And do you think this great city, this Three Birds, will fight us? Or will it lie down and open its legs?"

"I hope it does neither," said Agni.

"Then what?"

"I should like," said Agni, "to find my sister there and ruling it, holding it for me."

Patir snorted, but softly. "What makes you think she'd do such a thing?"

Agni shrugged. "It's a pretty dream. More likely she'd fortify it and hold it against me."

"Or stand aside and let what will happen, happen."

"Probably," Agni said. "The Mare's servants have done it for time out of mind. They were like these people, you know, in the beginning. Women ruled by women; men sent apart as young stallions are from the herd. They fought to defend themselves, but never waged wars among their tribes. When the eastern tribes came on them, they held where they could, but they judged it wiser to bend like grass in the wind."

"They're all gone now," Patir said, "except for your sister. And you."

Agni thought about that. He had never reckoned himself one of the Mare's people. She was a goddess for women. And yet, after all, her blood was in his veins. He was twinborn with the last of her servants. Maybe he was part of her, the last man of her people.

Strange thought to think, riding this path beaten by countless feet, in this country that none of his kind had seen before now. And maybe Sarama was waiting for him in the city with the odd name, or maybe she had gone on to the edge of the world. He would know when he came there.

The horsemen were coming. Herdsmen in the easternmost fields, wandering almost as far as the next city, had met with people fleeing more urgently than before. The horsemen had taken Two Rivers. They rested there, but the word was clear: they had only paused. They were coming to Three Birds.

The defenses were as near to finished as they could be. Sarama set scouts and sentries along the borders, sharp-eyed children and herdsmen who were skilled in the use of bow and spear. The defenders in the city were ready, waiting for the word that the horsemen had passed the borders.

Sarama rode the Mare for a while, and showed Danu how to pare and trim the colt's feet, which had overgrown themselves. He did not seem, as others did, to find her calm unreasonable. But then Danu was a calm man himself. As calm as a Mother, she would say when she wanted to make him blush and sputter. He was never comfortable with the thought that he might be as strong or as blessed as a woman.

The colt took lively exception to their meddling with his feet. When they had won the day and sent him bouncing and snorting off with his feet much improved, Tilia rose from the stone on which she had sat watching, and walked with them toward the borders. The colt, belying his display of temper, veered round and followed, and the Mare in his wake, calm but alert.

Sarama kept half an eye on her. She had been restless for a day or two now, and irritable, snapping at the colt if he came too close. She knew what was in the wind.

Tilia watched her, too, and with fair perception. "What's she smelling? All the stallions?"

"Hundreds of them," Sarama agreed.

"And no mares? What foolishness. How can they make more horses?"

"They don't," Sarama said. "On the steppe they raid for more, or go home to the tribe and turn them out with the mares in season."

"They won't be raiding for more here," Tilia said, "and there's only one Mare. That's not very provident of them."

"War is not about providence," said Sarama.

"I can see that it isn't." Tilia strode through the tall grass of the easternmost field, moving light and moving fast. She was one of the better fighters, when she deigned to be. She had a keen eye and a strong arm, and a fine aim with the bow. Sarama thought she might be ruthless in a battle; might well bring herself to kill, for her people's sake.

Danu, Sarama was less sure of. He walked behind his sister, lighter than she and quicker, with an effortless strength; but he lacked her edge. He was a gentler creature.

Most men were, when they did not egg each other on. Women in the tribes kept secret what was open knowledge here: that for sheer relentless ferocity, there was nothing like a woman.

The border was quiet. Tilia went back to the city to see that the fighters were ready and in their places. Sarama lingered for a little while, looking out across peaceful country, rolling green hills, little rivers flowing into the greater one that rolled past Three Birds, and a scattering of towns and villages in the hollows and along the rivers. Hereafter, if war stayed in this place, they would learn to build on hilltops and in places that could be defended.

Maybe war would not stay. Maybe the tribesmen would be driven out. Sarama had prayed for it in the temple this morning. She belonged to the Lady now, and to the Lady's country. She wished peace on it, and freedom from war. It might never have either, now that war had followed her here. But she could pray. The Lady might see fit to listen.

✦ ✦

The day stretched ahead of them. The sun reached its zenith and hung there. When after an endless while it began to sink, a runner came with the word they had been waiting for. "Horsemen! They've passed the Mother-hill. There are hundreds of them—they're thick as locusts."

Three Birds maintained its calm. Its fighters, ranked behind the ditch that warded the eastern road, sat or lounged at ease. They had taken a little bread and cheese, and drunk a wine made of fruits and flowers that was supposed to make them strong. It made them a little giddy, but no one seemed far gone in it. They had heard the tales of the city that had fought. They were better prepared by far, and they knew how to fight. They were still, and wisely, on guard.

Sarama had let the Mare loose to graze along the ditch. But something, somewhat past noon, led her to call the Mare to her.

They came on slowly for a band of marauders, hardly faster than a walk. They were not as thick as locusts, but they were numerous; more than Sarama had expected. She saw banners and tokens of a great gathering of tribes, some that she knew, many that she did not. Someone—Agni?—had swept the steppe, and brought in every young rakehell that had ever vexed a tribe.

Not all of them were so very young, at that. There was a grizzled beard here and there, the face of priest or elder or a warrior who had outlived his battle-brothers.

She came to him last, the one she had been aware of from the moment the first rank of horsemen came over the hill. He had grown. His shoulders were broader, his beard thicker. He rode the stallion who must have come to him at the Lady's bidding, a tall red beauty with a crescent moon on his brow.

She had forgotten how tall a man could be, or how keenly carved her people's faces were. Even their pale skin, their eyes blue or grey or green or Agni's rare amber, their hair yellow or red or fair brown, were strange after brown faces, dark eyes, blue-black curling hair. Did she look as odd as that to the people here?

The horsemen rode down the hill, spreading out across the fields, trampling the grain that was near to harvest. Maybe they did not know that it was planted with care and great labor, and its loss would mean a lean winter. Certainly they did not care.

When the earth opened in front of them they stopped, the foremost starting, shying, tangling the ranks behind. The line bent like a bow, recoiling. But Agni sat his red stallion on the edge of the ditch, staring down at the stakes as Tilia had not so long ago. His expression was difficult to read. Maybe it was surprise. Maybe, even, admiration.

He looked up. Sarama met his glance. His eyes widened slightly: not surprise, that. Greeting, of a sort. Gladness? Maybe. Neither could escape the fact that they faced one another across a deep ditch filled with sharpened stakes.

He was the enemy. And yet he was her brother. The sight of him was like cool water in summer's heat. She had been a stranger among strangers, even those she had come to love. This was her own blood, her own kin.

She doubted that he felt the same. He was a man, after all. He was, she could see, a king—and of more tribes than the one that he had been born to rule.

She spoke across the barrier, not loudly, but loud enough for him to hear. "Good day, brother. Have you come to conquer us?"

" 'Us'?" He raised his brows. "Are you their king, then?"

"Not likely," said Sarama.

"Good," he said, "because I'd not like to fight you for it."

"Would you do that?"

He nodded. "This is the place the gods have led me to. I saw it in dreams every night as I rode here. It's just as I dreamed."

"Even this?" Sarama tilted her head toward the ditch.

"No," he said. "But there was fire and war in my dream, and a rattling of spears. Did you muster these fighters? Can they actually fight?"

"We can fight."

Sarama started. Danu's voice was deep and deceptively soft, pitched to carry. It was utterly unlike him to put himself forward, still less to speak as if he were, by his lights, a woman.

But then this was a man who faced them. Danu must find him unbearably presumptuous.

Agni looked him up and down. "So. Do they all speak a decent human language here?"

"Only some of us," Danu said. He had stepped out of the line of fighters, spear in hand. He leaned on it with ease that was insolence, hip cocked, chin up, and a such a look about him that Sarama wished for a leash and a whip, to bring him to heel.

Agni was no better. There was no mistaking the challenge in his glance. Young males—hounds, bulls, or stallions; they were all the same. "And who are you? Are you anyone of note among these people?"

"Probably not," said Danu. "I'm the Mother's son."

"Ah," said Agni. "A prince."

"A man," Danu said. "No more, if no less."

Sarama rode the Mare between them, treading delicately on the edge of the ditch. "Enough," she said. "Take your men away, brother. Find another city to be king in. This one is not for you."

"But it is," Agni said. "I'm going to take it."

"You may try," said Sarama.

"You'd fight me?"

"Yes," Sarama said. Her heart was not as steady as her voice, but that was stone, and sufficient.

"You'd betray your own kin?"

"Yes," she said again.

His eyes narrowed. He was a stranger then, a man she knew and yet did not know at all.

He had seen at last the shape of her in the enveloping coat. He could not fail to see how Danu stood, how he glared across that barbed space. "So," he said. "That's the way of it. If he's the Mother's son here, will you be Mother when the old one dies? Is that how it's done?"

"No," she said.

"No?" He arched a brow. "I don't believe you. I think we're rivals here. Aren't we?"

"We are whatever you force us to be." Sarama backed the Mare away from the edge, holding his gaze, half wishing he might follow it and tumble into the ditch. But he did not move.

Not so the men behind him. They were shifting, restlessly as it seemed, but as she focused on them she saw a method in it. Spearmen to the front. Archers to the rear, stringing bows, fitting arrow to string.

They would fight. Agni might weaken in the last instant, but Sarama doubted that he would try to overrule them. They would call him fool and coward, words that no man could bear to hear.

She flicked her hand in the signal that she had agreed on with her own fighters. She did not look back to see what they did. They would be readying spears, stringing bows in their own turn. Hand to hand it could not be, not across three manlengths' width of bristling trench, but thrown spears and well-aimed arrows could wound and kill well enough.

The moment stretched. The air had a taste of heated copper, of blood and of fire. Neither would give the signal that would loose the arrows. Strings could only stretch so long; archers' arms were strong, but not strong enough to hold arrow nocked to string forever. And yet Sarama could not find in her the word that would begin the fight. No more, it seemed, could Agni.

A stir behind her almost—but not quite—brought her about. She would not turn her back on the horsemen.

They were staring at something in back of her, something that began in the distance and drew steadily closer. Sarama heard a flutter as of birds' wings, and the voices of birds.

The horsemen wore such a look of blank astonishment that Sarama dared to look over her shoulder.

It was only the Mother of Three Birds with the flock of her daughters. Her acolytes preceded them. A few of her sons followed, and others of the people behind. But what had struck the horsemen dumb was the escort that went with them: a shifting, twittering flock of bright-winged birds.

The birds had come out of the Lady's wood to follow the Mother. Three white doves circled above her. She walked in stately calm, as if she went about every day in a cloud of wings.

Sarama's fighters parted before her. Sarama half expected her to walk right over the ditch, to float on air or to sprout wings and fly like one of the birds, but her daughters set hand and shoulder to the bridge of wood that had been made to lie across the trench, swung it up and round and over to the other side. Then, as calmly as ever, the Mother walked across and stood in front of Agni.

He sat tall on his tall horse, and she was not a particularly tall woman. Still she towered before him. She said clearly in the language of his own people, that Sarama had not even known she knew, "Be welcome, king of the horsemen, in Three Birds."

Sarama swayed on the Mare's back. No one else seemed stunned, but most on this side could not understand the language of the tribes. The horsemen wore expressions half of smugness, half of disappointment. They had been hoping for a fight, but they had been too wise, their faces said, to honestly expect one.

And there was the Mother face to face with Agni, for he had slid from his stallion's back. He was still much taller than she. She admired his height openly, as women did here. They were never circumspect about a man's attractions.

"Come," she said to him, and led him back across the bridge.

His men hesitated briefly, much too briefly for Sarama to persuade anyone to overset the bridge. It was wide enough for two to ride abreast, or for three to walk leading their horses. And so they did, all of them, leaving no one behind. They were not fools, to be trapped on the far side of a city's defenses, with no way to come through if the people of the city chose to cut them off.

So much, thought Sarama, for the defending of Three Birds. In but a moment's time, the Mother had set it all at naught, had given up the city without so much as a murmur.

And her people said nothing against her. Even Sarama's fighters, even Danu, bowed their heads and acquiesced. A Mother could not choose wrongly, could not betray her people to an enemy. There was no space in their minds for such a thing.

.... 69 ....

Agni would never confess even to Sarama—especially to Sarama—how truly astonished he was, to be given this of all cities as a gift. He looked for a trap, for a subterfuge that would destroy him and all his men, but there was none. The city was open to him. The Mother led him through the circles and the curving ways, to her house that was the largest he had yet seen.

A great tribe of people lived in it, filling its many rooms. They broke camp and shifted elsewhere with all apparent willingness, to make space for him and for as many of his people as could be persuaded to sleep under a roof. The rest camped in a field just outside the city, on the westward side, where no ditch had been dug or defenses raised.

She was a great personage, this Mother of Three Birds. Her house was richer than Agni could have imagined, back on the steppe. There were even copper vessels, and in the room that he was given, there was an image of the goddess of these people, and it was made of gold.

They feasted in the fashion of this country, with a richness and a variety that were almost too much to conceive of. There were different kinds of wine, he discovered, and different ways to bake bread, and an art to herbs and sweetness that made every bite a novelty and a marvel. And yet for those who needed the refuge of simplicity, there was a whole ox roasted without embellishment, and bread very like that which they made on the steppe from the ground seeds of the wild grasses.

Sarama must have taught them to do that. Agni did not see or speak to her. For that matter, there were not as many women about the Mother as he remembered from the field. The servants were men, as they had been elsewhere. The one who had stood so close to Sarama was rather excessively in evidence. He was, Agni began to understand, the chief of the Mother's servants—what in a king's tent would have been the first of his wives or the foremost of his daughters.

He did not carry himself like a woman, or like an effeminate either. He was respectful without servility to the Mother and to the others of the women. To the guests he was perfectly and pointedly polite.

Agni studied him beneath lowered lids. Something about him must be extraordinary, if Sarama had let him take her to his bed. Agni could see nothing but a man of these people, pleasanter to look at than most, with shoulders as broad as the span of an aurochs' horns, and a curly black beard. He spoke the language of the tribes well, better than Mika did. But then he had had better teaching.

Agni disliked him intensely. He must know what Agni was, not only the king of the horsemen but Sarama's own brother, but he treated Agni as he did all the rest. The same courtesy. The same distance. He offered nothing that he did not give to every other guest in his mother's house.

A tribesman would never have been so calm. A man who filled a woman's belly without her kinsmen's consent was either a gelding or dead. Here, it appeared, such things were of no consequence. Certainly this man had no shame of it, and no fear of the kinsman, either.

+ +

When the feast was done, when they were all filled to bursting and awash in wine, Agni went to a solitary bed. No woman presented herself to him or to any other. The women were gone.

Agni struggled with that understanding, through a haze of wine. Women gone. Only men in a silent house, and children from the sound of it: somewhere not too far away, a baby cried. No woman's voice or presence.

This was the thing he had half dreaded. This was the reckoning. The women would come, would—

He walked, he thought, not badly, with steps only a little uncertain, out of the room with its golden goddess-image. He stepped carefully over fallen bodies of his men. Some were upright, if one were charitable.

One was full awake, aware, and behind him. And he had companions. Patir had kept his head. So too Mika, and Taditi whom Agni had not remembered as staying with them in that house at all. He had thought her with the baggage as she had chosen to be since—when? At least since the city that offered them a fight. Wild Rose, that was its name: now crushed and trodden underfoot.

Still Taditi was here, dressed as a rider but decently veiled. With such an escort he could venture the halls of the Lord of Skulls himself, the dark god who danced on the field of war. And was that his face, grinning out of the moon's blind eye?

Agni walked in the moonlit city. It was quieter here than it would ever be in a camp of the tribes. Few people in this country kept dogs, and most of those herdsmen and hunters. City folk as a race had little use for them.

Therefore there was no barking and yapping to herald his passage, nor anyone out or about so late. He did not know where to go, precisely, but the temple in the city's heart seemed a useful beginning.

It was dark and empty. He thought briefly of going within, of breaking the ban on men in the goddess' place; but as more than once before, he lacked the stomach for it. He wandered on past to the darkness of trees that stood, of all places, in this city's heart. It was as broad as the camp of a tribe, thick-woven with branches.

Through the branches Agni saw a glimmer of light. He followed it, and the others followed him, soft-footed on the leafmold. The ways were twisting and narrow, but no more so than they had been in the great wood between the steppe and the Lady's country.

It was not so very far through this wall of trees. Its center was a broad open space, a circle of moonlit grass.

There were the women, all of them surely, a circle within the circle. His breath caught at the sight of them. They were all as near naked as made no matter, hair flowing loose over moon-whitened shoulders. They moved in a slow dance to no music that he could hear, breasts swaying, hips swinging, till the cords of their skirts rippled and swirled. It was the most purely sensual dance that he had ever looked on, and yet there was nothing lascivious about it. It was pure female, pure worship of the goddess who had wrought women and men and all the pleasures of the flesh.

This was no sight that they meant man to see. They were making a great magic, women's magic: drawing down the moon. It shivered in his blood.

But he was the king of the horsemen, Skyfather's own. Day vanquished night. The sun made the moon grow pale. No woman was ever strong enough to stand against a man.

Mika was shuddering with terror. Only Agni's strong grip kept him from wheeling and bolting. "What is this?" Agni demanded in a whisper.

Mika could not answer. It was Taditi who said, "They're calling on the moon to make them strong."

"To destroy us?"

Taditi's face was hidden in shadow, but her voice was as dry as it had ever been when he was being an idiot child. "These people don't think like men."

"Then what are they doing?"

"Facing what they have to face," Taditi said. "They've accepted you. It can't be easy to be conquered."

Agni wanted to fling doubt in her face, but his eye was drawn inexorably toward the dance of the women. One had swayed and circled to the center, one whose belly was as round as the moon. Her hair was dark in the pallid light, but a different darkness than the rest. She spread her arms wide and let her head fall back. Her skin was as white as the moon's own face. Her breasts were like milk. She was more beautiful than he had ever known, and unreachably remote.

He began to understand Mika's terror. But he was neither child nor male of this country. With fear came the hot flare of anger. His sister had turned traitor to her tribe and people. And now he saw her standing as a person of power among the enemy.

His mind willed to stride forward, to seize her, to carry her off where she belonged. But his body was frozen where it stood. Under the sun he could have done it. Under the moon he had no such power.

Nonetheless the moon could not drive him away, nor could the sight of so many women dancing the moon's glory. He did not believe that it could strike him blind, or that he would go mad. He was stronger than that. He watched it through to its end, till the long skein unwound itself and the dancers wandered apart. They did not speak to one another. They simply went away, as if they had done all that they intended, and saw no need for idle chatter.

Sarama did not come to Agni, or anywhere near him. But he was barred from going after her. He recognized the woman who stood in his way. She was the perfect shape of one of their goddess-images, great breasts, great curving hips, great swell of thighs. But unlike the images, her face was no blank immortal mask. This was vivid life, scowling at him, looking on him with little liking and less admiration. She planted her fists on those ample hips and spat words at him.

Mika was gone, vanished. There was no one to tell Agni what those words meant. But he could well guess, from her expression and the way she spoke them. She was not at all pleased that he had intruded on the women's magic.

He did not even think before he did the thing he had always done with angry women: relaxed, lounged a bit, put on his most winning smile.

It won nothing from her. She cursed him with a glance, turned on her heel and stalked away through the dappling of moonlight.

She was, he thought, rather amazingly beautiful. His taste had always run to the very slender and the very fair. She was as far from either as it was possible to be. And yet she set his blood to singing.

He sighed faintly. That she despised him, he had no doubt at all.

He was not accustomed to being despised. Hated, yes; his own brother
hated him. But women had always doted on him.

✦ ✦

These women had no earthly use for him. He learned quickly—almost before
the sun was up—what it was to be king in Three Birds. People did as he
asked, waited on him as they must judge proper, but there was no warmth
in it. No one sought him out. No one came to him as one comes to a king.
That they left to the tribesmen.

He refused to be dismayed. He would wait them out. The Mother had
left her house to him and gone to live elsewhere—not far at all, he discovered,
and in the same circle of the city. Some of her servants had stayed behind.
But not, rather to his relief, the one he disliked so cordially. Not the man
who shared Sarama's bed.

Nor Sarama either, for the matter of that. Agni met her coming out of
the house that the Mother had taken, the second morning after he came to
Three Birds. She was dressed to ride, with her hair in a plait, as modest as if
she had never danced bare-breasted in the moonlight.

She could hardly fail to notice him, since he blocked her path. When she
stepped sideways, he stepped with her. She sighed audibly and stood still.
"What do you want?" she demanded.

"Is that all you'll give me?" he shot back. "A cold glance and a hard
word?"

She arched a brow in the way she had had since she was old enough to
find him exasperating. "You come as a conqueror. Should I be falling at your
feet? Are you asking that I be grateful?."

"Ah," he said. "*You* were not happy that the Mother surrendered to
us."

"I was not happy," she said with quivering calm. "We were going to
drive you back."

"I might have argued that," he said.

"I'm sure," said Sarama.

This time when she stepped round him, he let her. He turned with her
and walked beside her. She did not run away from him, but neither did she
match her steps to his. She did as she pleased. He could follow or not, as it
pleased him.

He chose to follow. "Maybe," he said after a while, "the Mother acknowledges that Skyfather is stronger than her Lady."

"He may think he is," said Sarama.

"He made me king here," Agni said.

"The Mother allows you to be king here." She looked as if she would
be stopping there, but after a moment she could not resist adding, "She is a
mother. So is the Lady. And won't a mother choose to indulge her child, if
she sees fit?"

"I never knew you despised us," Agni said.

She shot him a glance of pure annoyance. "I don't despise you."

"You hate me, then. Why? Because I came here?"

"I am angry with you," she said, biting off the words. "Why? What possessed you? You had a whole tribe to be king of, back among the White Horse people. Or wouldn't the old man die soon enough for you?"

Agni could not fault her for saying such things. She did not know. And yet each word was pain, like the stabbing of thorns in tender flesh.

He did his best to hide the pain, to speak levelly, even lightly. "The old man is dead. He died in the winter."

That took her aback. She was too angry, still, to be gentle. "So you left the tribe to its own devices and went chasing a traveler's tale?"

"As you did?" He caught her glance and held it. "Listen to me, and listen well. I know you forbade me to follow you. But I was driven out, and when men stopped driving me, the gods took up the goad."

"Driven out?" There: he had her attention at last, and some of her old fierceness on his behalf. "What did they do to you?"

"They accused me of a thing I never did. Of taking a woman by force, and getting her with child, and being her death."

He held his breath. Her face had grown terrible. If she believed the lie, if she condemned him, he did not know what he would do. Fall on his spear, maybe.

She said, soft and very precise as she did when she was purely, sheerly angry, "Whoever believed that of you was a perfect idiot."

"Yama believed it," Agni said.

"Yama is king?"

He nodded. The taste in his mouth was bitter.

There was a pause. They had walked out past the last circle of the city and come to the rings of fields about it. She slowed, plucked a stalk of wheat that was taller and thicker and richer than any wild grain that Agni had seen, and stripped it of its grains. She chewed on them, frowning at the air. "So," she said at last. "He did it to you, to seize your inheritance. Or his mother did. I doubt he's clever enough to do up his own trousers, let alone plot to destroy a prince."

"His mother," said Agni. And made himself say the rest: "And one of his wives."

She did not ask which one. For that small mercy Agni was grateful. "They drove you out. And you did the only thing you could think of, which was to come running to me."

"That was not what I did at all."

She planted fists on hips and thrust out her chin. "You did too."

"Did not."

"Did too."

He did not know which of them burst out laughing first. She fell on him as she had always done, bore him back and down, and sat on him till he cried for mercy. She did not let him up then, either, but grinned down at him with all her old wickedness.

He reared up, overpowered her, rolled through the green wheat.

They fetched up against a pair of feet. Sturdy feet, solidly planted on the rich earth. Agni looked up. Danu stared down.

Agni grinned and bounded to his feet, and held out his hand. Sarama took it with no evidence of embarrassment and let him pull her to her feet. They stood hand in hand like scapegrace children, but Agni was determined to be no more discomfited than Sarama.

She at least had stopped fixing him with the cold stare that had so dismayed him. It was much as it had been when they were younger, the two of them against the world, and none to come between them.

But this man was the father of her child. It could not be the same, nor could it be as simple. Sarama slipped her hand out of Agni's grip even as he slackened it, and said to Danu in the language of the tribes, "Good morning, man of Three Birds."

"Good morning, woman of the horsemen," Danu said in a rather acceptable accent. "And man of the horsemen," he added after a pause.

Agni inclined his head. He would be civil for his sister's sake.

Sarama saw: her eye glinted sidelong. "We're going to ride," she said. "Will you come?"

Danu nodded. Agni almost laughed. It was obvious what he was doing: protecting his woman from the interloper. Did he think that they had been doing more than playing like pups in a litter? Was he perhaps jealous of his woman's own brother?

Maybe he had cause, though it was not as he might think. No lover could be what Agni was to Sarama: twinborn, brother and blood kin.

But neither could Agni be to her what this man was. Agni glowered at Danu, who glowered obligingly back.

"Stop that," she said, setting her body between them. "I'll not have you fighting over me, now or later. Will you swear to that?"

Agni did not want to. Nor, patently, did Danu. But she made them swear. It did not increase the amity between them, but it forced a truce.

✦ ✦

Danu could ride as he could speak the tongue of the tribes: not exceptionally well, not as one who has done it from childhood, but well enough for use. Well enough indeed to ride the Mare, who by law and custom should carry none but Sarama.

Agni did not have to suffer that. He sent one of the boys to the remounts and had him bring back something suitable: a big-bodied gelding, rather plain but sturdy and sound. "My gift to you," Agni said, he hoped without irony.

Danu accepted the horse with fair grace. The colt—his colt—was much less pleased. When Danu mounted the gelding, the colt lunged at the beast, jealous to the bone and making no pretense about it.

Danu was openly astonished. It was Sarama who headed off the angry colt, setting the Mare between and bidding him remember his place. He veered off with ears flat back, casting baleful glances at the horse who dared to carry his man.

"Now you see," Agni said rather dryly, "why some of us use our remounts less often than we should."

"I don't ride him," Danu said. "Sarama says not to, till he's older."

"*He* doesn't understand that," Agni said. "The Mare he endures, because she's a mare, and the Mare."

"This is going to be difficult," Danu said.

"He'll resign himself to it." Sarama cut off what else either of them would have said. "Here, try your gelding's paces. Yes, just as I taught you with the Mare. A little harder, there; he's not as soft to the touch as she is. Yes, yes. Just so."

Agni followed on Mitani, watching the two of them. They did not act like lovers: no clinging to one another, no languishing glances. And yet there was no denying the shape of her, or the care she took with the Mare, sitting lightly, venturing nothing outrageous. Her pupil could not have done it in any case, but that would not have stopped Sarama.

So much was different. And yet so much was the same. Sarama had not forgiven Agni for coming here—but she seemed to have decided to accept it. There was, after all, no changing it.

·············· 70 ··············

Agni did not want to leave Sarama alone with her lover, but a boy came running with somewhat that Agni must do, and there was no evading it. That led to something else, and then to something else again, the cares of kingship catching and holding him till well after sunset.

He went to bed alone as before. As before, the women were all elsewhere—but tonight they were in their own houses. He had expressly forbidden his men to seek them out. If they sought out this man or that—well, and what man was strong enough, or fool enough, to resist?

No one had sought him out. The Mother had made it rather clear by her distance that she had no such ambitions. The younger women seemed less than enthralled with him. Nor had he been drawn to any one of them.

He caught himself thinking unaccountably of the Mother's heir, the one whose name was Tilia. If this had been a conquered tribe, Agni would have taken her to wife. That was custom for a conqueror, to take the conquered chieftain's eldest daughter, and others of his daughters too if he were so inclined. With that marriage, that joining of his blood to theirs, he became fully and completely king of the tribe.

And suppose, Agni thought, that he did this. That he married the Mother's heir. The people would have to accept him then. Would they not? They could hardly ignore him if he stood beside their own ruler.

He lay on his back in the darkened room, listening to the sounds of people sleeping about him: Patir's soft snore, Mika's toss and murmur, Taditi's slightly rough breathing. He could marry that sullen, beautiful woman. Oh yes, he could do that. There was nothing in marriage that required a woman to love her husband, only to honor and obey him. Even that one could be taught to do as much, surely.

His blood quickened at the thought of her in his bed—in this bed, a warm and ample armful. She might not come willingly, but she would stay because she wished to. He had a gift for that; in solitude, to himself, he could admit it.

He went to sleep greatly pleased with himself, and dreamed of her—glaring at him and bidding him begone, but she had no power to banish him. Only Skyfather had that.

It was, he decided, a good enough omen. He carried it with him into waking, and set out at once to find the Mother.

✦ ✦

She sat on the step of the house that she had taken, in a circle of children, instructing them in something that held them rapt. They were not, Agni was interested to note, all or even mostly female. Small boys had teaching, too, it seemed, just as the girls did. It was very different from the tribes.

Agni had been learning a little of these people's language—by accident, almost, as Tillu and later Mika spoke for him, and he, standing idly by, began to listen for the words, to try to match them to the ones that he had spoken. It was a scattered, ill-matched collection he had, but sometimes it made a little sense.

The Mother was speaking simple words, words that children could understand. Agni found he could fit them together as often as not. They were stories, teaching-tales: why the thunder rolled, and what made the rain. Skyfather had no part in it here. It was all the Lady, and the winds who were her servants, and the rain that waited on her pleasure.

He was noticed; there was no way he could not be. But the Mother did not pause for him, nor did the children cease their listening. He crouched on his heels just outside of the circle, and listened to the stories. They grew easier for a while; then his head began to ache. It was difficult, making sense of words in a language that he barely knew.

The Mother ended her teaching soon after he tired of it. The children were greatly disappointed, but she was adamant. "That's enough for today," she said. "Now go, show your mothers how you've learned to serve the Lady."

They left then, with many glances back. All but Agni. He had not brought anyone with him who could speak the language. He began to think that he had done a foolish thing.

The Mother said, "Come here."

A woman did not command a man; it was not done. And yet Agni obeyed her, because it pleased him. He settled on one knee beside her, searching her face as she searched his. She seemed to like what she saw: her eyes glinted a little. She was not as old as Taditi, though she was still old enough to be his mother. He could see her daughter Tilia in her, but rather more of her son, the beauty blurred and thickened by age but still perceptible.

What she saw in him he could not tell. Strangeness, maybe. A likeness to his sister—whether that was good or ill. He could see no hatred in her. She did not have the look of a conquered creature.

And yet she had given him this city. She must know what she had done, and at least begin to understand it.

She let him know by signs that she wanted him to help her up. He did it for courtesy, as he would with an aunt or a grandmother. Her grip was warm and surprisingly strong, but soft, as if she did not know or did not care to know her strength.

In that she was like all her people. She walked, and he walked with her. It was clear soon enough that she was taking him toward the temple. She did not take him into it—rather to his disappointment; no man ever walked there, that much he had been assured of. But there had never been a king in this city before, either.

She led him past that carved and painted marvel, rounding the curve of the city and turning outward from it. He had not been in that part before. It was as like the rest as one part of the wood was like another, painted wooden houses, sturdy dark-haired people, few dogs and no horses, and all the cattle were out in the fields. Men did not strut like warriors here, nor did women creep softly in veils. Children were much the same as they were in the tribes, naked most of them, playing noisily in packs and running hither and yon.

The girlchildren were noisier, here where no one warned them to be modest. The boys were not permitted such freedom. Agni heard one bold manchild let out a blood-curdling whoop. It cut off abruptly at the snap of a word from a man who sat on a doorstep. He was a great bull of a man with a wonderful curly beard and a deep drumroll of a voice. Among the tribes he would have been a notable warrior. Here it seemed he was relegated to the care of children.

He greeted the Mother with an inclination of the head, and Agni with a flat stare. The Mother took little notice of him. Agni followed suit, as a king should. He felt the dark eyes on him for as long as he was in sight.

They went a little farther, to a house shaded by the spreading branches of a tree. Tilia was in it, and Sarama, sitting with a handful of young women, making arrows as women in the tribes would make coats for their men.

Agni's coming wrought a great silence. The Mother strode through it as if it had been a field of tall grass, bore Agni with her and sat in a place that opened before her. King's art, that, and splendidly done.

She made no particular move, but Sarama came and sat at her feet, a little clumsy with the weight of the child. The Mother spoke to her, words that again Agni almost understood. Sarama set them in his own language— in hers, if she would remember it. "Tell us what you came to tell."

Agni kept his eyes on the Mother, but he was keenly aware of the other eyes on him, and one pair in particular, regarding him steadily. He did not flatter himself that she took any pleasure in the sight of him.

He would have much preferred to speak to the Mother alone. But if she wished it to be as it was, then so be it. He said what he had to say, without the flourishes of words that would have softened it for a tribesman. "I've come to ask for your daughter."

Sarama's brows went up at that, but she spoke words that, as near as Agni could tell, were the right ones. The Mother responded only a little less briefly. "Really? Which daughter? And why?"

"Your eldest daughter," Agni answered, "to be my wife."

"Wife," said the Mother, using the word Agni had used, as Sarama had also. There was no such word in her language, it seemed. "That is—a kind of servant, yes?"

Sarama was choosing not to explain. She left that burden on Agni. "It is a woman who shares a man's bed, bears his sons, looks after his tent."

"Ah," said the Mother. "Here, a man does those things, except for the bearing of children; but he may raise such of those as a woman has. Is that what you would call him, then? A wife?"

"A wife is a woman," Agni said. "A man is her lord—her husband. He protects her and shelters her from harm. She honors and obeys him."

"I think," said the Mother, "that a wife would be a rather distressing thing to be. And you are asking me to give you my heir for such an office?"

Here, thought Agni. Here was the heart of it. "Among my people," he said carefully, "when a tribe is conquered by another, the conquering king takes the highest-ranked daughter of the fallen king, and makes her his wife. That seals the conquest and marks the joining of tribes."

"He chooses the fallen king's heir." The Mother pondered that. "A man, choosing a woman. That is against nature."

"Not among my people," Agni said. "Have you no such custom here?"

"We don't conquer." That was Tilia, breaking in in words that Agni could understand. The rest were in her own language, too fast almost for Sarama to follow, but follow Sarama did. She seemed to be taking a grim pleasure in it. "What makes you think I could possibly want to be your house-servant? I am the heir of Three Birds. I will be Mother here when my time comes. How do you dare to dream that you can choose *me*?"

"Because," Agni answered sweetly, "I conquered you."

"You were given what you thought to take." Tilia had risen from her seat, had come to face him, bristling. "I say no," she said, again in the language of the tribes. "I say no, and no again. I will not choose you."

"But I choose you," Agni said. He turned again toward the Mother. "I am thinking," he said, "that for whatever reason, and by your Lady's will, you gave this city to me. I take it as the gift it is, but it has no love for me, and no inclination to do as I bid it. Your daughter now, your heir, is all that I am not. She can preserve the peace, speak to the people, guide me in ruling them as a wise king rules. Without her I'll do what I must, but if that is to subdue this city by force, then that I'll do. Do you understand?"

"I understand," the Mother said. "You ask me to give a thing that is not mine to give, for a purpose that few will see."

"And yet," said Agni, "you do have a thing called marriage. The Great Marriage. Yes?"

He heard a sharp intake of breath. Tilia's, perhaps. The Mother was very still. "That is for gods," she said, "and the children of gods."

"Kings among the tribes," he said, "are reckoned children of the gods."

"But not by us," said the Mother.

"Now that I am here," Agni said gently, "you will have to change your reckoning. There are new gods in your country. New men. New ways of seeing the world."

She was silent. It was Tilia who said, "I don't want to see the world differently. Why do you want me? What do you hope to gain by it?"

"Kingship in truth," he answered promptly, once Sarama had given the words to him.

"It would serve us well to refuse," Tilia said.

"No," said Agni. "You don't know what conquest is. Not really. You don't want to know. If you do this, you'll be safe from it."

"We are already conquered," Tilia said bitterly. "I don't wish to be any more vanquished than I am."

"And yet you will be, if you aren't wise."

"I don't want to be wise," said Tilia. "I don't want to be a *wife*." She put such a twist in the word that Agni could taste the sourness of it.

"It needn't be so ill," he said. "After all, what becomes of a woman in the Great Marriage?"

"The woman is Mother of mothers," the Mother said before Tilia could answer.

"And the man?" Agni asked.

"He's reckoned greatly wise, and the Lady favors him."

"That's all?"

"That's great honor," Tilia said. "He's looked up to as if he were a woman."

Sarama was enjoying this much too much. Agni leveled a glare on her. He said, "You mean he becomes an elder. He gains presence in the city."

Tilia nodded—not gladly, but she did not appear to be one who savored a lie.

"So you see," Agni said. "This gives me rank that I lacked before, and a voice among your people."

"It profits you," she said. "It does nothing for me."

"It protects you from whatever comes after. More horsemen," said Agni. "There's no escaping that. The westward gate is open. They will come."

"If they're all like you, what does it matter? They'll come, we'll give in to them, they'll fancy themselves great conquerors, and we'll go on as we have before."

"And every one who comes here," said Agni, "supposing that the war doesn't run right over you as it undertakes to destroy me, will come looking for you. It's the custom. The conquering king takes the conquered king's daughter. Not all or even most will stop to ask. They'll simply take."

"They can't do that," said Tilia.

"They can do whatever they have in mind to do. They are warriors. You are not."

None of these people seemed able to understand such a thing. Even Sarama seemed in sympathy with her brother for once. She spoke on her own behalf, clear enough and simple enough for him to understand. "He's telling the truth. I don't like it, either, but that doesn't change it."

Tilia was set against them both. Nor would the Mother speak to her, to command her as a father would have done among the tribes. That seemed not to be the way here.

Agni rose. He had said as much as he could say. He bent his head to the Mother, and bent it somewhat less deeply at Tilia. Then he left them.

············· 71 ·············

Agni could be patient. He was a hunter. As he had hunted the antelope and the aurochs and the wild birds of the steppe, so he hunted Tilia. He watched. He waited. He intruded on her consciousness only as much as it served his purpose.

He could not hunt her every moment of every day. He had his men to look after, furred and feathered game to hunt, and a country to learn the ruling of. It was different, ruling cities—particularly cities that had no desire to be ruled. But rule he must. It was an urgency in him, greater as the summer waned. They must be made strong, must learn to face the truth, that he was only the beginning. Those who followed would be far less gentle than he had been.

It was difficult going. He rode round about the towns and cities near Three Birds, made himself known to their Mothers, showed his face in their streets and in their markets. As he had been elsewhere, he was given whatever he cast his eye on, as if that alone would make him go away.

He had no such intention. The Mother's house of Three Birds, that at first had seemed so strange and so constricted within its rigid walls, grew familiar, and then almost pleasant. He was learning to hear the wind in the eaves, and to accept the silence of it in the walls.

His men in tents were less happy than he, constricted by the closeness of the cities here. Much riding about and much hunting, and the warming of the women toward them, kept them somewhat in hand.

✦ ✦

"You could give them something to do."

Agni had come back from settling a quarrel in the camp, something petty that had grown out of all bounds and stopped just short of bloodshed. He was looking for a little quiet, and maybe something pleasant to eat. The one who brought it to him was Tilia herself, speaking words that he could understand.

He seized on that first. "You've been studying my language."

She shrugged. "It amused me," she said. The words were oddly formed, and sometimes she stumbled, but her meaning was clear enough. "Your people are not amused. They want to fight."

"Fighting is what they do," said Agni.

"All the time? They never stop?"

"Sometimes," he said, "one would think so." He did not know if she caught the subtleties of that. She seemed to be waiting for him to say more. "They have to be kept busy," he said.

"I said that," she said.

She had caught him as he was about to fling himself onto a heap of rugs and furs. He did it with a kind of recklessness, because she was watching him.

She sat more decorously, tucking up her feet, which was not a thing that a woman should do in the presence of a king; but she would not think of such a thing. Maybe a man did not do it here in the presence of a Mother's heir.

"Tell me what you would have these men do," he said.

She shrugged a little, not coyly, but not sullenly either. "I would teach them things. Teach them to speak our language. Teach them to build a house, make a pot, weave on a loom."

"Women's work," Agni said.

Her brows arched. She had an admirable way with them. "Certainly. And so much the more honorable than men's work. Yes?"

No. Agni did not say the word. Her glance stopped him.

"Think," she said. "How people will think of them. If they act like— like people. Not like conquerors."

"A little fear is a good thing," Agni said.

"You are afraid of what they will do if they don't—if—" She stopped, searching for the words.

He offered such of them as he could think of. "If they don't have a fight to keep them busy?"

She nodded. "You are afraid. They kill then. Don't they?"

"And other things," Agni said.

"So," she said. "Teach them to be busy."

"And send them elsewhere?" Agni half said, half asked. "Send them to the towns to learn—and to be present, to hold or to defend as need commands. Yes. Yes, they've been pleased to do that. But don't ask them to look after the children."

"Oh no," she said with no irony that he could detect. "I would never ask them to do a thing as hard as that."

Agni wondered if he should be insulted. Probably; but he did not think that she would care.

There was a silence. It stretched. She seemed comfortable in it. He was reminded, without her saying a word or making a move, that this had been her house before it was his. Maybe he was sitting in her accustomed place.

It was a magic of sorts, he supposed. A wishing laid on him, a subtlety of stillness.

He refused to be caught in it. The jar was where he remembered, half-full of wine, and there was a loaf wrapped in a cloth, left from the morning. He brought them both to where he had been sitting; and because he had been raised to courtesy, he offered her a share of each.

She accepted them, which rather surprised him. None of these people had a gift for enmity.

Maybe they did not need one. This too-perfect comfort, this ease in his presence, began to gall him. She had no awe of him, and no fear either. Her glance was bold. She carried her head high. She was as forthright as a man, with a man's confidence, and his certainty that the world would yield to his will.

And yet she was as womanly a woman as had ever sat across from him sharing bread and strong sweet wine. The shape of her was as rich as this land she lived in. The woven fabric of her gown stretched tight across her full breasts and showed clearly the broad swell of her hips. She would bear strong sons and beautiful, with her great doe-eyes and her ripe red lips.

She had no coyness, no arts of allurement, yet she was utterly alluring. His hands twitched, yearning for the sweet curves of her body. Her skin would be as soft as sleep, her hair as sleek as water running over stones. She would meet him as he came to her, open herself to him, take him inside her . . .

He came to himself with a snap. Dream though he might, truth was a colder thing. She had come here, which might be encouraging, and might not. But she was far from asking him into her bed, still less agreeing to be his wife.

Still. She was here. They finished the bread together, and the last of the wine. He had to go out again, and soon. There were people waiting, a quarrel to settle in the camp. But he lingered.

She showed no sign of leaving. It was he who had to rise, stretch, consider what to say. In the end he said nothing, only nodded. She nodded back. Whatever that might mean.

+ +

Sarama refused to join in the hunt. "I will not force any woman to be a wife," she said.

He had caught her well afield, both of them mounted, and the Mare in season: she teased Mitani shamelessly, and tried his patience with it. Agni kept him in hand. To Sarama, who was making no such effort, he said, "I said nothing of force. I'll win her, and win her fairly."

"Then you'll win her without me."

"Why?" he demanded.

"Because," she said, "I'll not be party to the subjection of a friend."

"Subjection? What makes you think I would ever—"

"Oh come," she said. "You want to bend her to your will. She'll never let you. Nor will I help you conquer her."

Agni might have hit her if they had not been mounted, and if the Mare had not just then chosen to squeal and strike at Mitani for the great crime of walking beside her. When they had untangled that, Agni's temper had cooled not at all, but his urge to strike had vanished somewhere amid the Mare's eruption of temper. He spoke through gritted teeth. "Once you knew me. When did you forget what I am?"

"When you called yourself king of this country."

"I'm still your brother."

She nodded with no reluctance that he could see. "And I still won't help you snare Tilia."

"Then I'll do it myself," he said in a fine flare of temper. He wheeled his stallion about and sent him plunging back toward the city.

She let him go for a little distance. But when he had slowed, she was there, and the Mare flattening her ears and snaking her neck at Mitani. "Brother," said Sarama, "give it up. You'll find wives enough among the tribes, once they recognize you as a king among kings. You don't need one of these women who know nothing of submission."

"Women like you?" he asked. "Women like that?"

"Women who won't be wives."

"Then what are you to the Mother's son?" Agni demanded of her.

"*I* chose *him*," said Sarama.

"Ah," said Agni, and let her make of that what she would. She had given him something. Maybe she knew it; maybe she did not. There was a thing he had needed, that maybe now he had.

✦ ✦

A man could not be a wife, and a king could not submit to a woman. Particularly if that king was Agni, with the memory of a night when he had tried to be like the men of this country. It soiled him still, that recollection.

Nevertheless a hunter could let the prey come to him. A horseman could convince the untried colt that he obeyed by his own will.

Agni set out to seduce this woman as he had seduced Mitani. He was there where she was, as much as he might be: fletching arrows or weaving cloth with the young women, dancing in front of the temple on a festival day, dining with the Mother of an evening. He would happen past. He might pause, or he might not. He would let her see him. He had heard that she liked a tall man and a man with a fine free stride. He had heard too that she fancied a sweet voice. He could sing when he was minded to; and maybe when she was nearby to listen.

She could not help but notice him. What she thought, she was not telling. She happened by on her own, sometimes when he was resting in the house that had been her Mother's, more often when he sat on the horsehide and settled affairs for his men. Her people never came to him. His came often, as they properly should, to pay their respects, to bring him word of his people who had gone far afield, to bid him settle quarrels and confirm alliances.

She would come in the midst of this, hovering about the edges, not seeming to watch, but inescapably present. She was testing her skill in their language, she would say if anyone asked. Agni made sure that someone did ask—and he laughed at the answer. That might have driven a tribesman away, but she stayed where she was. She had pride and to spare, but it was a different kind of pride. She would face even laughter, before she would retreat.

They danced around one another. There were other broad-hipped beauties casting eyes on Agni, but he was in no mood for them. He wanted Tilia. He wanted her, he realized, very much.

He dreamed on a night of thunder and of rain, between the crashing of the thunder and the pounding of the rain. It was different inside a house, under a roof. He kept waking, or dreaming that he waked, and falling fast asleep again.

Somewhere between waking and sleep, on the edge of the dream-country, he stood in a field of grass the color of mist and rain. The sky was the soft sky of morning, casting a grey veil across the sun.

Someone walked toward him through the colorless grass under the colorless sky. No more color was in the stranger than in the rest of the world. It was a shrouded shape, a woman's perhaps, for that was a woman's veil and mantle. It seemed not quite solid; it shimmered a little as it moved, as mist will when the wind scatters it.

Agni waited for it. He was bound to the earth, still and solid as a stone. A stone's weight dragged at his shoulders, his arms and legs. He could not have moved even if he had willed to.

As the shape drew closer he saw more clearly that it was a woman's. The face was hidden altogether in veils, but the wind molded the mantle to the unmistakable curve of hip and breast.

He could see it very clearly, even the taut nipples, and the navel in the smooth rounded belly, and the soft mound at the meeting of the thighs. It was no such goddess-glory as the women here, more slender by far though womanly enough. It was, he thought with the detachment of dream, a woman of the tribes: taller, narrower, more quick and yet less strong in its movements.

It stopped just out of his reach. He could not see its face at all. Veils and mist obscured it.

It stretched out its arms. Its hands were white, white as bone, with long restless fingers. They made him think of the roots of trees, or of weeds reaching up through water, weaving and swaying. And yet there was something about them that made him think of death, of the worms that prey on carrion, and of bleached bone.

Dreams were great magic and great portents. One did not contest a dream. And yet Agni yearned to escape from this one. Thrice now he had dreamed a white horror of a woman. Thrice he had been given this omen, warning, whatever it was.

He could not move at all. His skin shuddered at the approach of those unearthly fingers. They never touched him, never quite.

A voice spoke to him out of the veils. It was a woman's voice, clear, not unpleasant: eerie coming from such strangeness. He knew it very well, and knowing it, searched the veils for sign of Rudira's face. But there was only grey blankness.

"Agni," she said. "King of the outcast people, lord of the tribes that went into the west. Did you hope that none would follow you?"

The dream compelled him; it roused his tongue to answer. "I hoped for nothing. I went where the gods led."

She laughed, her old familiar laugh, sweet and lilting. "You went where I made you go. I wanted to be a king's wife. Through you I won it."

"And it tastes of ashes?" Agni could not help but ask.

She laughed again, a ripple like bright water, but with shadows stirring beneath. "It tastes of honey from the comb. Did I harm you, after all? We both have what we wanted. You are a king, and I am a king's wife."

"You betrayed me," said Agni.

"I gave you into the gods' hands." She swayed closer. Her veils melted as such things will in dreams. She was all as he remembered her, skin as white as new milk, hair as pale as moonlight, eyes like rain on clear water. She who had seemed richly curved among the women of the tribes, now seemed slight and even fragile, with her high round breasts and her narrow waist and her hips hardly wider than a boy's.

Yet still he could not see her face. Her body he remembered vividly. So many days, such a stretch of seasons since he had held her in his arms, and he remembered every line of her. Her scent, her softness, even the way her hair grew on her forehead—everything was as clear as if he had lain with her just this morning.

She took him into her as she had always done, with a kind of breathless leap and cling, wrapping legs about him, holding him tight when he would have recoiled in startlement. Her grip was soft but very strong, stronger than it had ever been in the waking world. Resistance only made her cling the closer. She roused him as only she had ever been able to do, and warmed him to burning.

There was no woman like her. Even as he knew with perfect clarity what she was, that she had no honor nor knew the meaning of loyalty—still he wanted her. Even when she had drained him dry, milked him of his seed and left him gasping, her body made his blood sing.

It was a madness, a demon in him. A demon with her face.

He covered her with kisses—with, he thought, clever intent. But she arched away as he drew near to her face, swayed and wove and turned, so that he never touched her lips or her cheeks. Her hands were as light as kisses, as strong as blows. She shaped him as Earth Mother shaped the world, molded all of clay, soft and malleable in her fingers.

He did not want to be molded. He wanted to take her as one can in dreams, again and again, no weariness, no need to rest. But she held all the power. Her strong white hands, her drifting veils, were image and trappings of great magic.

The Rudira of the waking world was rumored to be a witch of a line of witches; and for a certainty she had power to drive a man mad. But she had never been as this dream-Rudira was. This was the earth's own power, goddess-power. It thrummed in his bones.

"You would take the woman of the Lady's people in the Great Marriage," she said, cooing the words as if to a loved child. "And do you believe that the Lady would approve of such a thing?"

"Skyfather wills it," Agni said.

"Ah," she said. "He is her son. They are all her sons, the gods, or her sons' sons. She let them loose when they were born, let them run as they pleased. But she will bring them back to hand."

"Not through me," Agni said.

"If you take the Mother's heir to wife, she will hold you in the palm of her hand."

"Skyfather holds his hand over me," Agni said.

She swayed closer. "You want her?" Her voice was a whisper. "You lust after her?"

"I want her country," he said. "I want her people's loyalty."

"And you want her," said Rudira.

He could not lie to a dream. "She is beautiful," he said.

"More beautiful than I?"

"No one is more beautiful than you," he said, and he meant it. But when he had said it, he remembered a smooth brown face, a pair of eyes as great as a doe's but never as gentle, a tumble of blue-black hair. Beside that, this woman of the tribes seemed thin and bloodless. Her body that had seemed so ripely curved was pared to the bone, her breasts shrunken, her ribs sharp-carved beneath the skin.

He reached again for the veil; looked again to be thwarted. But before she slipped away, his hand caught at fabric as softly yielding as mist. It shredded and tore. He looked into her face.

No flesh at all. White bone, black pits of eyes, the ceaseless, relentless grin of the death's-head. Laughter echoed from the hollow skull. "Am I not beautiful?" her voice demanded, sweet as ever. "Am I not the fairest of all the living?"

It was sweet, that voice, and yet it was not Rudira's. For a stretching while he did not know it. But it did not mean him to escape so easily. In the shadows on the naked bone, he saw another face than Rudira's. A face less beautiful and less sleekly sure of itself. The face of a woman of the Red Deer, a woman who died because of the child that he had set in her.

"You are dead," he said. "You were laid to rest. Begone! You have no power over me."

She laughed at him, sweet and terrible. Her laughter followed him all the way out of the dream-place and into the land of the living. He woke with the memory of it echoing in his skull.

.... 72 ....

The coming of the horsemen changed everything. And yet if one lived from moment to moment, the Lady's world was much as it had always been. Then one looked up and met eyes that were blue or grey or green or even, occasionally, amber, set in a narrow blade-nosed face. The women thought them handsome, these tall narrow men with their pale skin and their odd-colored hair. In Danu's eyes they were frankly ugly.

He did not know why he disliked them so intensely. They had not brought the horrors of his dreams. They were here, that was all, eating what they were fed, filling the fields with their camp. The harvest promised to be rich enough to feed these extra mouths; no one expected a lean winter after all, though it would not be as fat or the storehouses as full as in other good years.

So far the horsemen had taken little that was not given them, nor shown aught worse than bad manners and ignorance of proper courtesy. Sarama had warned the women to expect rudeness beyond their easy belief, and there had been some of that. But nothing so grievous as to require the Lady's mercy.

Catin and the Mother and the people of Larchwood were gone. They had left as the horsemen drew near to Three Birds, gone away westward to, they said, warn the cities beyond. Tilia had not been charitable in her opinion of their departure. "We won't see them again," she had said when the last straggler had climbed the hill to the west and disappeared.

"I think we will," Danu said. "Catin will come back. She won't be able to help herself. She has to face this dream, face it and let it make her stronger."

"She's not strong enough to begin with," said Tilia, "to think of being stronger."

Danu did not argue with her. She believed what she believed. He knew what he knew. And the horsemen came, and they forgot that they had come near a quarrel over Catin.

Now, with the horsemen here and showing no sign of going on, Danu understood a little how Catin could so dislike Sarama. Danu loved the Mare's servant. But Sarama's brother—now there was a man who made him bristle and snarl.

Sarama did not see why they should so dislike one another. "You could be friends," she said. "He's not a ruthless warmonger as some are; mostly he's like me, though he'd be hard pressed to admit it. He can tell you all the stories, what I teethed on and how I used to quarrel, and what I was like before my breasts budded. All the things a brother knows."

"I don't need to know them," Danu said.

It was a rare quiet moment at midday. She had come back to the house they were living in, for what reason he had not happened to ask. He was bringing in the washing, overseeing the line of servants and acolytes and some of his brothers and sisters as they brought up new-dried armloads from the field by the river. The outer room of this smaller, crowded house was full of the scent of sun and grass and new-washed cloth.

Sarama pressed against the wall to let Beki pass with a billowing heap of bedding. Danu's second in the house warmed her with a smile. She returned it somewhat abstractedly. "I think you're jealous," she said to Danu.

"Probably," he said. "I know he is. What is his trouble? Is he angry because you didn't ask his leave before you chose me?"

Her glance was a little surprised, a little pleased—and it stung a little, because of what else it said. He had startled her by understanding this thing about the tribes; as if he had neither wits nor perception, nor could learn her customs as she had learned his. "Yes," she said. "Yes, he's unhappy—more with me than with you. If he were other than he is, he could have killed you and flogged me, and so preserved the honor of the tribe."

"He is generous, then," Danu said. "And merciful."

"And you dislike him as much as ever."

He shrugged uncomfortably. "He makes me feel as if I'm less than I am."

"Ah," she said, as if that explained it all. She did not linger much longer; she went out while he was settling the disposal of a great amount of bedding in a house somewhat too small for as many people as were living in it. Which, he reflected uncharitably, was another cause to dislike the king of the horsemen, for displacing them all and never acting as if he understood the sacrifice.

It was all very petty. He should master himself and practice discipline, grow strong enough in his spirit to be, if not friendly, then suitably amiable toward Sarama's brother. Even if the man had gone so far as to ask for Tilia as a wife.

✦ ✦

Not long after Sarama left, when the washing was put away as best it might be and Danu was considering the prospect of a few moments to himself, Tilia came in as Sarama had, as women had a way of doing: taking no notice of the bustle around them, aiming straight for Danu and bidding him wait on their pleasure. Which, with Tilia, was to take refuge in the kitchen garden. There among the lettuces and the peas on their vines and the beans growing up over the wall, she said, "I'm going to give the horseman what he wants."

Danu had no words to say to that.

"Don't look so flattened," she said. "You had to have known I'd give in. He won't let go till he has what he's asking for."

"He's asking for you," Danu said. His tongue stumbled a bit still, but it did his bidding.

"Yes," she said. "He wants me."

"Do you want him?"

She narrowed her eyes—as if she had any need, now, to think on her answer. "If he were passing through as he did elsewhere, and if he were behaving himself with reasonable propriety, I'd have taken him to my bed long since."

"You like him," Danu said. He did not mean his voice to sound so flat.

"He interests me," she said.

"Enough to bind yourself to him in the Great Marriage?"

"There," she said. "There, you see? You can think like him. Think like *me*. He will bind himself to me. That may be more than he bargained for."

"And he can't escape it once it's done." Danu felt his lips stretch in a slow smile. "You are wicked."

She stooped and plucked a lettuce and nibbled on it reflectively. "That's what the Mother said."

Danu raised a brow. "Does she disapprove?"

"Not at all," Tilia said. "She says the horsemen will learn to understand a different kind of power. I'm to teach it to that one first—since he reckons himself higher than a Mother."

"He could kill you," said Danu, "if he became very angry."

"So will any animal if it's mishandled," she said, as calm as ever. "I'll remember what he is. Don't fret for me on that account."

"Maybe I'll spare a little fret for him," Danu said. "He's a proud man. You'll break his pride."

"If that's the way of it," she said, "then so be it."

✦ ✦

Tilia went away as Sarama had, with precious little pause for farewell. Danu considered indulging in resentment, but none of them—for he reckoned Agni with the rest—would trouble to notice or to care. They would all do what they pleased to do. His wanting or not wanting meant nothing to them.

In that mood, and rather inevitably, he came on Agni himself near the hayfield that had become a camp. Danu was going to ride the horse he had been given, a bit of generosity that he understood all too well: he must not embarrass Sarama's kin by failing in that essential art.

Agni also was afoot, and seemed to be going to find his own horse, the red stallion that ruled the herds as Agni ruled the men who had followed him. He greeted Danu with a nod, amiable enough if not precisely warm; but these tribesmen were always cool with strangers. It was because, Sarama had told Danu once, any stranger might be bent on killing. "Animals are like that," Danu had said then. "Not humans." She had shrugged and gone on thinking thoughts that no one of the Lady's country could bear to think.

Agni's greeting was warm enough for what it was. He seemed to bear Danu no enmity.

Danu said it straight out, without preamble and without embellishment. "My sister is going to give you what you ask for."

Agni stopped short. Danu was gratified to see the shock that came first, and to see how long it took him to ease back into his usual insouciance. "Is she?" he asked at last, with a touch of breathlessness still. "And what price is she going to put on?"

"Price?" Danu did not need to pretend incomprehension. He honestly did not understand.

"Price," Agni said with carefully nurtured patience. "What she expects in return, if she gives me what I ask for."

"She'll get your promise to hold off the horsemen who come after, and your voice in their counsels—while she goes on as she always has, being the heir of Three Birds."

"So," said Agni. "She expects to go on. What if she discovers that our wives live in the tents and never go out?"

"You'll not ask that of her," Danu said, and hoped he sounded as if he believed it. "She's no caged bird, nor ever will be."

"And you," Agni said. "Are you?"

The shift took Danu somewhat aback. But his wits were quick enough, and the answer was on his tongue before the pause could stretch too long. "Our men aren't kept as your women are. None of us knows such confinement."

"A wise man wouldn't tell me such a thing," Agni said. "I might use it against you."

"You won't," Danu said.

Those strange eyes, the color of amber under the ruddy brows, flashed on him in something that was not quite anger. "How do you know? What makes you trust me?"

Danu did not know how to answer that. "What makes you trust no one?" he demanded in return.

An odd expression crossed Agni's face, half sad, half wry. "Our worlds are so different," he said. And abruptly: "Ride with me."

Danu did not want to ride with a man who had ridden since he was old enough to sit up, and who had no cause to be kind to a fledgling horseman. But there was no graceful way to refuse—and no way, either, to quell the uprush of pride that made him answer before he thought, "Yes. Yes, I'll ride with you."

+ +

After they had caught and readied their horses, and fended off horsemen who came to ask this or that of their king, and disposed of one or two who seemed determined to guard Agni against a dangerous stranger, they rode out westward. Danu had no particular aim in mind; simply to ride, because Sarama had told him to do that, and do it every day, till it was as natural to him as walking.

It was still a beastly uncomfortable way to get about; but Danu had admitted long since that it was faster than going afoot. He was, maybe, growing a little less awkward. He did not need to cling quite so tightly with knees and hands. He was learning, a little, to follow the movement beneath him, to loosen his hips and back and let the horse do the rest.

Agni's ease and comfort stung him with envy. *He* never tensed or lost his balance. He rode as if he were a part of his horse, smooth and effortless, riding out an eruption at some trifle or other, and never so much as shifting on his stallion's back. Danu knew too well how difficult that was.

Agni said nothing of Danu's lack of skill, nor, to be fair, implied it either. He accepted it, as far as Danu could see, without either approval or disapproval. It simply was.

In that he was like his sister. But then, as Tilia had said, they were very much alike.

It did not make Danu like him any better.

They spoke little as they rode, and then of lesser things: the flight of a bird, the warmth of the air, the buzzing of bees in a flowery field. Danu marked those and where they flew, for later; to raid their nest and capture their honey.

He knew a stab of startlement at that, a flash of guilt. He was thinking like a horseman again. Thinking of fighting and taking. And yet that was what one did with honey. One took it. One left a little for the bees, but the rest was lawful booty.

Just so must the horsemen think of the Lady's country. Its riches were there to be won. They did not ask if they had a right to win any such thing. They simply did it.

He looked at the king of the horsemen with eyes that saw a little differently; that maybe understood him. It was not a comfortable understanding. Danu could not even flee from it. He had changed too much. He was not the placid and all too complacent creature who had been so shocked by dreams of fire, nor yet the complaisant one who had followed Catin to Larchwood and there come face to face with the Mare's servant.

It seemed that Agni wanted simply to ride, to go as far as he could, though certainly not as fast as he could, not with Danu dragging at his tail. Nevertheless he set a pace that left Danu breathless, clinging for his life to his horse's mane, and his horse straining to match the effortless long stride of Agni's stallion. It was terrifying, and yet it was wonderful: the surge and thrust of great muscles beneath him, the strong scent of sweat, the wind singing in his ears, whipping his heavy braid straight out behind him.

They stopped at last for nothing that Danu did. His horse had no more speed left in him, and Agni's seemed minded to pause beside an eddy of the river for a nibble of summer-ripened grass. Danu sat on the sweat-soaked back and simply breathed.

The horseman looked as if he had been out for a canter on a summer's morning, a little windblown but much at ease otherwise. Danu wondered if that was hate he felt, or simply envy. Envy, he hoped. Hate was a thing of men who fought in wars. Not of the Lady's sons and daughters.

Envy, then. He could envy that ease and that air of perfect calm, so like a Mother's and yet so different. It must come with the office, with speaking for the Lady, or for one's gods, before the people.

Agni said, "You don't ride badly."

"I ride terribly," Danu said.

Agni laughed, sharp and short and a little surprised. "No, not terribly at all, for one who came to it so late."

"Your sister is a good teacher."

Danu waited for the amber eyes to darken, for the brows to knit; but something, maybe wind and sunlight, had muted Agni's usual resentment at Danu's daring to speak of Sarama. Agni was almost amiable as he said, "She's a better rider than I am. Always has been."

"And you will admit it?"

Agni seemed as surprised as Sarama was, to be asked such a thing. These horsemen did not say what they thought, when they thought it. Danu had a great deal of difficulty understanding that, but it was so.

As with Sarama, Agni was startled into an honest response. "I don't have any pride to protect, with you."

"Because I have none?"

Agni drew breath as if to deny it, but said instead, "You aren't as our people are."

"No," Danu said.

"She likes that in you."

"I think it puzzles her."

"Women like to be mystified," Agni said.

"She doesn't like it at all," Danu said. "It makes her angry. Then she snarls at me. And after she's done snarling . . ."

He could have said the rest to the brother of a woman from this country. But not to this one. Even the suggestion made Agni's eyes darken.

"Yes," Danu said before Agni could speak. "You could kill me or worse. But that's in your country. This is mine. And in mine, women are free of themselves, and no man would dare to tell them how to behave."

That made Agni frown, but it was a different kind of frown, directed not at Danu but at something outside of them both. Danu let the silence grow, till Agni broke it. "This is not your country now. It is mine."

Danu was too polite to shake his head or to contradict Agni directly. He said, "The Lady is strong, and the Mothers partake of her strength."

"They gave in to me," Agni said.

"They bent like wheat before the wind," said Danu. "When the wind passes, the wheat grows straight again."

"This wind won't pass," Agni said.

"It might grow gentler."

"Don't hope too much," said Agni, roughly enough to raise Danu's brows.

"You don't like it when people think you gentle," Danu said. "You're afraid it means you're soft."

"My people would say that," Agni said.

"Your people see the world strangely." Danu slid from his horse's back and stretched, groaning a little. He did not know that he could or would mount again. And if he could not, then by the Lady he would walk, and Agni could go or stay as he pleased.

Agni chose to slide down as well, far more gracefully and without the sounds of pain. He was a great deal taller than Danu, but rather less broad. Danu refused to be made small beside him.

He noticed. His expression altered slightly. Maybe he was amused. Maybe not. "So," he said. "You have a little pride after all."

"You're a man," Danu said.

"And are you?"

"My body says I am."

"There's more to it than that."

"What?" asked Danu. "Killing people? We don't do that here."

"You didn't do it. That will change."

"Not if we can help it."

"You won't be able to," Agni said.

"You want that to be true."

Agni's eyes went a little wild. "Here. Wrestle with me."

Danu was tired and his bones ached, and his tender parts chafed abominably. He was in no mood to play a game, least of all with this man.

And yet, as Agni had observed, he had a glimmer of pride. Of all the things that fighting was, this, the matching of body and body, was least displeasing to the Lady. She judged strength by it, and judged a man's wits, too. Some among her people were not ill versed in it—Kosti-the-Bull not the least of them. And Danu, though he made no vaunt of it. Maybe Sarama did not even know. She had never asked.

There were, when he paused to think, a number of such things that he had kept to himself. And Agni was waiting, his lip starting to curl, sure that the soft foreigner was going to turn tail and run.

Danu let himself go still. His feet were solid on the summer-parched earth. He felt the pulse of it in his blood, the beating of the Lady's own heart. He drew in a breath of warm sweet air overlaid with a pungency that was the horseman, a mingled scent of man and leather and horses.

Thought emptied out of him; doubt, fear, fretting over things that might never be. When he was pure being and pure will, he leaped.

The horseman reeled backward, overborne by Danu's weight. He crashed bruisingly to the ground, taken all off guard, but even yet beginning to fight back. He was quick and he was strong, but Danu had expected both. Danu sat on Agni's chest until the horseman stopped trying to twist free, and said mildly, "Whatever you wanted this to settle, I hope this settles it."

Agni regarded him in pure astonishment. No anger, Danu was interested to see. Another of the horsemen would have been angry—enough maybe to kill. "So that's what you do," Agni said. "Your body's your weapon."

"We do it for pleasure," Danu said, "and because it's better than galloping about killing people."

Agni accorded him an ironic salute, somewhat hampered by Danu's weight on his chest. "Ah! Well struck. Now will you try another round? Fighting fair this time?"

"What is fair?" Danu asked. But he let Agni up and gave him time to compose himself. Agni put aside his belt and his baldric and the weapons that he carried as if he might be killed at any moment, and stripped off tunic and shirt, and fussed unduly in Danu's opinion. When at great length he showed himself ready, Danu fell on him again and flattened him again.

"You have no skill at all," Danu said.

"You never let me show it," Agni snapped, not too feebly for a man who had had the breath knocked out of him twice running.

"Ah," said Danu. "You want to play, not to win. Well then. Up. Give me a game worth playing."

He could do that, after all, and with the strength of temper, too. But Danu was quicker and stronger, and flattened him a third time. This time Danu was breathing lightly, and the wind cooled the sweat on his cheeks and brow. Agni was running with it, his bare breast and arms gleaming. He wriggled like a fish in Danu's grip, and nearly as slippery as one, too.

Danu picked Agni up, not as effortlessly as he might have liked Agni to think, and heaved him into the river.

Agni came up roaring. Danu laughed at him, and only laughed the harder when Agni seized him and tripped him and pitched him into the water. He had to throttle his laughter before he choked on it; but when he had thrashed and flailed his way to air again, he let it out in a full-throated peal.

"You are mad," Agni said. He was standing waist-deep in the river, well and prudently out of Danu's reach.

Danu grinned at him. "I was hating you," he said by way of explanation, "for being so at ease on a horse."

"So you can best me thrice out of three," Agni said. "I still don't like you."

Ah, Danu thought: at last, honesty. "Nor I you," he said.

"We'll never be friends," said Agni.

"No," said Danu.

"But something else," Agni said. "That, we seem to have fallen into. Almost—brothers."

Danu considered that. He liked it no more than he liked Agni. And yet it had a degree of truth in it. Enough maybe to go on with.

He nodded. "Yes," he said. "Yes. After a fashion, brothers."

.... 73 ....

Agni did not know what Danu had done, if anything, to soften Tilia's resistance; but it was so. When he came back from that odd and humiliating skirmish, he found her sitting serenely in the room he slept in. Her hands were folded in her lap. Her eyes were cast down, as demure as any woman of the tribes should undertake to be.

She was not alone. The boy Mika was with her, all eyes and raw nerves. Agni had meant to wait her out; but Mika was as spooky as a whipped colt. "What did you do to Mika?" he demanded.

"Nothing," she said. She seemed unperturbed by the abruptness of the attack—not at all like Agni in the wake of Danu's onslaught.

Mika nodded vehemently. "She didn't do a thing. She—she just—"

"I asked him to speak for me if I stumble," she said, barely stumbling at all.

"He looks as if you beat him," Agni said—not wisely, and he knew it.

Her lips tightened a fraction, but her calm did not break. "I'm a Mother's heir," she said. "He's a boychild. And he knows it too well."

Mika dipped his head, but not before he had nodded again, nearly thumping his meager chest with his chin. He mumbled something: apology, Agni thought.

"Never apologize to a woman," Agni said to him. "It only diminishes you."

She could not have understood all of that, but she understood enough.

"You think you can win me?" she said. "Is that what you do? *Win* a woman? You're not doing it well at all."

"So what do you do?" he demanded. "Do you try to win a man? Or do you just point to him and say, 'You. Now. Come'?"

She laughed. It was pure mirth, untainted with anger or perceptible dislike. It made him think of Danu rising up out of the river, white teeth gleaming, laughing as if there were nothing in the world more hilarious than being pitched into an icy river.

All these people were mad, Agni decided. Since madness was sacred, and since a wise man never stood in the way of true insanity, he waited till Tilia was done with her high amusement at his expense. Then he waited longer, till she recovered such wits as she had.

"Mika," she said, "say it."

Mika blanched and stammered, but he mastered himself before Agni could move to do it for him. He spoke haltingly at first, but thereafter with growing confidence, as the words he had been taught rolled out of him.

"She—she wants me to speak for her, because she's a fair novice in this language you speak, but I've been at it longer. And I'm younger, you know. And the Lady has given me the gift. So she asks—she tells me to say to you: Man of the horsemen, what you ask is presumptuous beyond bearing, and I should laugh in your face. But the Lady speaks to me, and she tells me that the winds of the world are changing. That a storm is coming down on us, and you are but the wind that blows before it. But wind can be strong in itself, stronger than the lightning or the rain. A blast of it can topple a forest, or lift up a river and cast it on dry land.

"I have no desire to be poured out like water, or be left in a bed of mud and gasping fishes. I'll ride with you on the storm, horseman. I'll make the Great Marriage with you as you ask me to do.

"Now I ask you," Mika said, and Agni heard Tilia clear behind the words, even as he saw her face as she listened, with its wide dark eyes and its firm chin. "Do you know what this is that you ask? Do you understand what the rite is, and what it will do to us both?"

He was to answer that. He did, slowly, because it seemed to matter a great deal to her. "We have marriage among my people."

"*Great* Marriage," Tilia said, speaking for herself, thus granting Mika a reprieve. "What you speak of—a man takes a woman, the woman obeys the man, she bears his children, she keeps his tent—that's what a man does when a woman asks him to be the keeper of her house. That's not the Great Marriage." She inclined her head toward Mika.

He spoke hastily, babbling the first few words, but again he calmed as he went on. He was a brave child, was Mika, and gods-gifted. "The Great Marriage is the Lady's strongest rite. It partakes of everything that she is, and everything that she wishes for her people. It makes a woman and a man one. It sets them in the center of the circle, and the circle encompasses them, and they give the circle its power. Once that rite is done, there is no sundering the two so joined. There is no walking away, horseman. No changing it once it's done. The vows you take in that rite, you take for as long as your soul shall live." He paused. Tilia nodded again, bidding him go on. "Will you do this, then? Will you even go so far?"

"Will you?" Agni asked her directly.

"It may be the saving of this city," she said.

"That's all?" Agni did not like to admit it, but the stab in his belly was not anger. It was disappointment. "If I were elderly and ugly and walked with a limp, would it be the same to you?"

"You are not those things," she said.

"Does it matter that I'm not?"

"Of course it matters," she said.

"So," Agni said. "You want me, a little."

"Any woman would," she said with the breathtaking bluntness that seemed to mark all her people. She rose, and without farewell or further word, left the room.

It seemed empty without her in it. Mika had sunk back against the wall. His breath was coming a little quickly; his face was greenish pale.

"There now," Agni said as to a skittish colt. "There. She's gone. And I won't eat you."

"You're sure?"

Agni sighed gustily. "I don't think I'm hungry. I don't know if I dare to be hungry."

"Yes," Mika said in all seriousness. "She's a Mother's heir, you see. That's what Mothers and Mothers' heirs do."

"I am going to tame her," Agni said.

"She'll tame you first," said Mika.

"We'll see about that," Agni said. Mika clearly did not believe him; equally clearly he decided not to argue with such a perfection of folly.

Maybe it was folly. Maybe, by the gods, it was not.

✦ ✦

Patir said nothing at all, which proved to Agni that he was of Mika's mind: Agni was mad to press this thing. Taditi however made her opinion known in words as cutting as they were clear. "You marry that woman, you'll never be the same again. She'll have you bitted and bridled and broken to saddle."

Agni did his best to be reasonable. "She will only do that if I let her."

"She'll see to it that you do the letting." Taditi folded her arms and set her chin and looked terrifyingly grim. "It's one thing to take the chieftain's daughter—that's tradition, and wisdom mostly, if a man wants to be king. But this isn't the steppe. These people have no such customs, and no mind to adopt them. You think you want to take this woman in order to make you one of them—to win their acceptance. You'll win nothing but the gelding's portion, once she gets her claws in you."

Agni shook his head stubbornly. "She'll come round. You'll see. After all, she gave in. She swore she'd do no such thing. I'll be her master yet. Be sure of it."

Taditi went off muttering about arrogance and young idiocy. Agni forbore to take her to task for it. She had always been outspoken. Here, in this country of outspoken women, she seemed if anything rather subdued.

She was not altogether comfortable here. Agni had been surprised to realize that. He would have thought that she would be at ease among people who were so much like her; but she had tired of the gentle, complaisant men, and the women irritated her with their boldness that far outmatched her own.

Still she had to endure, because Agni had no intention of leaving. Where would he go, after all? His tribe was barred to him. He had no mind to battle for a kingship on the steppe. This place, this title that he held—yes, this woman whom he meant to make his own—all were as they should be. He knew it in his belly, where one knew the deepest certainties.

The others would acquiesce in the end, because he was king, and because the gods were moving in him. Even Tilia knew it, and Tilia was the Lady's child.

·············· 74 ··············

They made the Great Marriage under the first moon of autumn, a slender crescent hanging in the sky at sunset. Agni's tribesmen, the people of Three Birds, traders who had come by the roads and on the river, everyone who had heard of the thing that was to be done, all came to see the king of the horsemen swear the great vows with the Mother's heir of Three Birds.

Agni wore the coat that had been made for him when he was to be king of the White Horse people. Taditi had taken it when she left the tribe, and kept it for him—at what cost, she refused to tell him. She brought it out as he prepared to dress, and put aside the much lesser garment that he had meant to wear, and clothed him in the coat that was fit for a king. "Now we'll make you beautiful," she said.

She did her best. He went out scrubbed clean, his beard clipped close, his hair plaited tight and wound with beads and thread-thin strands of copper. There was a gift waiting for him from the Mother herself: a glorious thing, a collar of gold, heavy and gleaming, and an armlet of the same metal. They, with the torque that he had been given in that first of his conquered cities, weighed him down with splendor.

He was to wear no weapon. On that, the Mother had been most firm. No spear in his hand, no bow at his back, not even a knife at his belt. He must go to the Lady as one of her children, washed clean of blood.

If it would make him truly king in Three Birds, he would do it. The price was not too high. No one would threaten him here.

He walked out of the house that had been the Mother's, into the long light of evening. The circles of the city were empty. They were all by the river, gathered in a great throng beside the curl and glisten of the water. Agni had thought to ride there, but these were not horsemen. They asked that he come afoot. He did it because he was too proud to refuse, walking gingerly in his boots that were made to ride in.

He was aware of Taditi behind him, following him as she would never have done in the camp of a tribe. She was freer here by far, though she was quiet about it.

So escorted, he came with the last light of sunset to the field by the river. It was black and teeming with people, and set with torches like stars. A line of these guided him inward down a path left open for him. Eyes gleamed on him, catching the torchlight. Pale blurs of faces turned to follow him.

Under all those eyes he strode out as a man should. He walked alone: Taditi had slipped away amid the crowd. Where he walked was light. The rest was darkness. His back prickled with the consciousness of it; of being utterly exposed, clear to any eye that saw, but of the people who surrounded him, he saw only shadows.

It was a test, he told himself. A proof of his courage. To do as he had been raised and trained never to do; to make himself vulnerable, and not to flinch at it.

A murmur of voices had greeted and followed him, but as he walked on it subsided into silence. In that silence he became aware all at once of the beating of his heart, the hiss of his breath, the sound of his feet striking the ground. Somewhere deep in it, a new sound grew. At first it seemed to come from the blood, a faint high singing, but as it grew in intensity, he knew it was no part of his body. It was a pipe, thin and high and twittering as a bird's call. Just as he recognized it, another joined it, deeper, like a woman's voice crooning wordlessly to a sleeping child. A drum wove into it, echoing the beat of Agni's own pulse, but with a roll as of thunder. Then amid the thunder came a sound like the falling of rain, drop by drop tinkling into a pool: the music of plucked strings.

Birdcall and woman's croon, thunder and rain: all the spirit of Three Birds caught and held in that mingled music. It carried him to the riverbank, to a half-moon of torches that sprang suddenly alight, blinding him. When he could see again, he saw the shapes standing among the torches. Broad shadow-shapes like stones set in the turf by the roll of water: heavy shoulders, heavy breasts—for they were naked but for the blood-red skirts that women wore here. Their faces were blank, smooth oval masks, long slits of eyes.

Agni quelled the shudder of fear. Priests—priestesses—here went masked as they did among the tribes, masks that transformed their wearers into blank images of divinity.

It was eerie and strangely arousing to see those naked and powerfully female bodies and those sexless, featureless faces. Their skirts clothed them, not as women's gowns did on the steppe, to protect their modesty, but to draw the eye to their sex. Not for concealment, but to flaunt their beauty. All of it, even its most secret places.

The masked women had stood still as the light first fell on them, but as Agni approached they began to move in a slow swaying dance. Their circle opened, swaying outward till it had taken Agni into itself and drawn him to its center.

There at last, stepping from deep shadow into the ruddy golden light of the torches, was Tilia. Agni looked for the Mother, but there was only Tilia, and no way to tell which of the dancers was the ruler of Three Birds. If any of them was.

Tilia was dressed, or not dressed, as the others were. But she wore no mask. Her hair flowed free down her back and over her breasts and shoulders, framing the broad oval of her face. It was unmistakably her face, unmasked and unconcealed, and yet it was as blank as one of the masks. No joy, no resentment. Not even welcome, though when he had paused in front of her, she took his hands in hers. Her grip was warm and firm, no tremor in it. Agni fought to achieve the same.

The dancers circled them, flickering from shadow into light and from light into shadow. How anyone beyond could see, Agni could not imagine.

Even as the thought touched him, the circle spun outward, wheeling like a flock of birds, scattering in the rolling of drums and the sudden shrilling of the pipes. Agni stood alone with Tilia under the starlit sky, and a circle of open grass about them, but beyond it the great dark ring of people, thick as trees in the forest.

Then at last the Mother came forward, surrounded by acolytes with lamps that cast a gentler light than the torches. Each lamp was shaped like a bird. The young girls held them as if they had been birds indeed, cradling them, cherishing each fragile flame.

In that soft light, the Mother was as perfectly herself, as unmistakably human, as the dancers had been inhuman. She wore the same skirt, flaunted the same bare breasts, but her face was bare, her hair as free as her daughter's was, and her head was crowned with woven stalks of grain. Her eyes on Agni were warm, the first warmth that he had seen in any of them since he came down to the river. She even smiled, which made his heart quiver unaccountably.

Agni's hands were still joined to Tilia's even yet across a space of stillness. The Mother laid her own over them. Her hands were light; yet Agni felt the force of them as he could feel the sun's strength on his face at midday. Just so had he seen a smith in the city, smelting copper in a forge. Fire had melted the lumpen ingot as ice melts into water. Then the smith had added another ingot, and it had melted into the first, till there was a single pool of molten copper.

Agni met Tilia's eyes. They were wider than usual, and fixed on his face. Did he look as wild as that?

And still there was no word spoken. Only the music, and that had faded to a murmur.

The Mother's voice rippled over it, rich and sweet. Tilia murmured the words in Agni's own tongue, or as much of it as she had: a gift, and a great one. "My children," the Mother said, with Tilia as her echo, "look at one another. See what you see. Look deep. Look long. And look well. This you must see with every day that passes, from now until your death."

Agni's belly tightened. To take, to hold, to be master of a woman—that, he knew. This—it bound them both. As the Mother had said: until death.

"Look," she said. "Know this one beside whom you will walk, with whom you will bear and raise children, whose life will be your life, whose heart your heart. Look, and understand."

Agni looked. He could not have done otherwise, even had he willed to. He saw a face limned in lamplight, the arch of dark brows, and eyes too dark to read. He saw beauty of a kind that his people never knew; darker, smoother, broader. He saw the night in her eyes, and stars caught in her hair. He saw himself reflected as in a dark pool: narrow face, blade of nose, sunburnt cheeks and ruddy hair and eyes the color of amber, like a lion's, or like a goat's.

He did not want to see how she saw him, even with a noble arc of horns and a fine long beard. He peered past that so-mocking image, far into the shadows where thoughts darted like fishes in a pool. He hunted her as he would hunt the red deer in a deep wood.

He found her in a singing silence, not sitting as he had expected, motionless as the image of a goddess, but standing erect, on guard, with a bow in her hand, and an arrow ready to nock to the string. So warlike. So bold, and yet so much afraid.

Within him too she must find much the same; he on his tall red horse with spear and bow and long wicked knife. Marriage was a kind of war, he supposed: the Great Marriage more than most.

The Mother's voice sounded soft in his ears. "See," she said. "How different, and how very like. Such is my creation. Such is beauty, twofold: sun and moon, dark and light, woman and man. Be two now. Be two who are one."

Hand locked in hand. Eye locked on eye. Heart beating—not quite together. Agni's breath shuddered as his heart leaped, wavered, steadied. Beating as hers beat, stroke for stroke.

Words slipped away. The music, that had gone on unnoticed, swelled to fill the world. Voices wove into it, voices of women, voices of men, singing in no language that he knew, perhaps in no language at all: a ripple of pure sound. This was the song the stars sang; the song that swelled with the waters in spring, and fell silent with them under the weight of winter's cold. But even in silence it went on, more beautiful than anything of earth.

This was like no rite he had ever known. It bound without oaths. It asked nothing of him, and yet it asked everything. To be one. No word of master or servant, man or woman, husband or wife. Simply—one.

He was not asked to accept or reject what was laid on him. Gods did not ask such things. They commanded. Mortals obeyed.

If he could have escaped, he should have done it long ago. His presence here was binding enough, and his hand in hers was all the oath that he was expected to swear. He was breathing as hard as he was, and her hands were no longer quite so steady.

"So mote it be," said the Mother, spreading her arms to embrace them both.

Agni's instinct cried to him to shrink and bolt. But he was stronger than that. He stood his ground. The Mother's warmth wrapped him about. Her breath was sweet. She smiled and kissed his brow, and kissed her daughter's, and gently but irresistibly turned them to face one another.

There could be no doubt of what she wanted. Agni had never kissed a woman in the light before, in front of strangers. It froze him with shyness.

Tilia had no such scruples. She moved almost too quick to see, caught him and held him and kissed him till he gasped.

When she would have let him go, he caught her as she had caught him, and kissed her with all his art and passion. Her eyes were wide. He laughed as he drew back, laughed and embraced her and spun her about in sudden, wild elation. It came from nowhere and everywhere, like the music. It was probably terror, but it felt like mad glee.

And everyone was laughing, singing, whirling in the same dance, the whole great crowd of them under the stars. All that had been solemn was suddenly wild with joy. They crowned Agni and Tilia with flowers, wound them with garlands about necks and arms and bodies; took them up and carried them, singing, far along the line of the river to a place as new as this morning.

It was a house made of green boughs, built under the branches of a great tree, with a smaller river flowing past it. From the greater river one could see only the loom of the tree's crown. The house one could not see at all, nor the stream, nor the field of grass about it. It was a lovely place, and secret, and it was clear what Agni was expected to do here.

The throng did not linger as it would have on the steppe, though from what Agni could gather, their songs were quite as bawdy. They danced in a long winding skein, an endless line of them, round and round about the hut of branches, down along the stream, and back the way they had come.

.... 75 ....

Silence came slowly in the fading sounds of voices, pipes and drums and stamping of feet. The acolytes had left their lamps behind, a half-circle of them outside the house, and one glimmering within. Agni stood wrapped in flowers, feeling hot and rather tired.

He gathered his wits about him and mustered strength to step over the lamp in front of him and explore the house. Tilia caught him with his foot in midair. "No," she said. "Not that way."

He lowered his foot. He had a brief, rebellious thought of entering the circle regardless, but he had sworn to undergo the rite in its proper form.

Tilia took his hand. "Now," she said. "Jump."

Agni felt a perfect fool, but jump he did, hand in hand with her, as high and far as they both could go. Right over the lamp, from darkness into light, from the great world to the shelter of the house. They came down lightly, still handlinked, turning face to face in the ring of light.

Tilia was smiling. At last. And at him, too, with no constraint that he could perceive. She looked him up and down with every appearance of pleasure. "Such a beautiful man," she said.

Agni flushed. "And you," he managed to say. "So beautiful."

"Yes," she said. There was no modesty in her. She tugged him with her into the fragrant dimness of the hut. It was all bark-brown and leafy green within. The bed was of sweet grasses under a woven coverlet. Jars along the wall yielded wine and mead, fruits cured in honey, cheeses, dried fish and cured meat.

Agni looked round from tasting the last. "How long are we supposed to stay here?"

Tilia shrugged. "Until it's time to leave," she said.

"What, days? Months? Years?"

"As long as we need," she said.

These people were like that. Vague; frustrating.

Agni did not mean to be frustrated on this of all nights. He shrugged as she had, and tried to mimic her calm. "Well then," he said. Which was all he could think of to say.

"Indeed," said Tilia.

He drew a breath, let it go. Did she do the same? He stepped toward her, just as she moved toward him. They nearly collided: a snort of laughter, quickly suppressed. Her eyes were dancing with it.

She was nothing like Rudira, not in any slightest respect. Even the heat of her was different. Cleaner, somehow. Lighter. She had washed herself in a mingling of scents, herb-green, flower-sweet. Her skin was as soft as a child's. He traced the line of her cheek, of her shoulder, of her breast. Her nipples were large and dark, like her eyes. He traced the spiral of the dance about them. She shivered a little with pleasure, and caught his hands when they would have withdrawn. Her back arched. Her breasts flowed over his palms, soft and yet surprisingly firm.

And all the while he was lost in her and she should have been lost in the things that he did to her, she was finding and loosing the fastenings of his clothing, freeing him from it, all of it. The air was soft on his skin. Her hands were light, tickling and teasing. They had no need to stroke his shaft erect. It was raised long since, straight as a spear. She circled it with her fingers. He quivered. Her grip tightened: soft, soft, but with a promise of strength. He stilled. Her fingers loosened. She smiled.

Trapped. And yet so was she, her breasts in his hands, her body arching toward his. She kissed him deep, just till he strained for breath, then outlined his body in kisses. All of it, crown to ankle, down the heart-side and up the other, and back round to his lips again. Each kiss was like the lick of a flame.

He had never felt as he felt now: as if his bones would flare to ash, and all for the touch of a woman's lips. Rudira had heated him to burning. Beside this, she had been ice and dry bones.

Tilia drew back a little, searching his face. Not as she had when the Mother commanded her, but as if this time she did it for herself. To see what he was. To understand him, if she could. If any of her kind could understand one of his.

She seemed more sure than he that she could do it. She traced his face with her fingers, marking each line of it. She raked nails lightly through his beard and played with his hair. Its straightness seemed to fascinate her. She extricated it from its braid and coiled a strand of it round her finger, and watched as it sprang free.

He slipped fingers through her mass of black curls. They caught and tangled, thick as tendrils of vine in a wood or roots of grass on the steppe. Yet they were softer by far, like nothing that he knew a name for. Sleep, maybe. Curls of mist in the morning. The first tender grass of spring, winding round his fingers.

He learned to know her fingerbreadth by fingerbreadth, from crown to soles. She had a mole on her shoulder, and a whorl of dark down in the small of her back. The down of her legs and arms was heavier, but still soft; not at all like the black mat of her sex, with its crisp curls concealing the tender pink lips. The scent and taste of her were subtly different than the women he had known, even those of this country: salt-sweet as they all were, but more sweet than salt.

She had no shyness, nothing that one would call modesty. Where his touch gave her pleasure, she arched into it, purring in her throat. He, who had learned silence in his nights with Rudira, caught himself gasping audibly as without warning she rolled him onto his back and mounted him.

He matched her rhythm, finding it strong and deep, slower than he was used to, like a surge of water in a lake. He rode it like water, slow undulant motion, almost like a man in a dream. But dreams were never as vivid as this, even the dreams from which one woke having spent one's seed, pouring it out on Earth Mother's belly.

One could burn swiftly, as he had with Rudira; flare like a torch and cool almost at once thereafter. Or one could burn slowly, fire that grew stronger as it burned, nor consumed the flesh about it. She brought him to a shout of triumph and a slow descent thereafter, heartbeat by heartbeat into a quivering stillness.

She sat astride him still, though he had slipped from her, slack as a man must ever be after he has spent his seed. Her face drifted above him, past the deep swell of her breasts. She was smiling, a smile that made him think of cream.

Some madness in him, some imp or demon, brought him awake all at once. He seized her, spun her, sat astride her as a moment ago she had sat astride him. Her smile barely wavered, though her eyes were wide. He was exhausted, drained dry, and yet he could not resist. He kissed those warm ripe lips. Those cheeks. That broad brow beneath the peak of night-black hair. That firm round throat, those shoulders, those breasts, that belly made for carrying children. Sons. Strong sons for a king of men.

And, he thought in a kind of wonder, no one would come to challenge him, no one threaten him with death or worse for daring to touch this woman. She was his wife. His first wife, his royal woman, who would, the gods willing, bear his heir.

She would do that. All her people cherished children deeply, and made as many, as often as they could.

His joy darkened abruptly. How many children had she had? How many men had she—and would she—

"Tell me this," he said. "This Great Marriage. Will you be—taking men after this?"

"Of course," she said.

"That's not our custom," he said: taking pride in his calmness, in his strength in not seizing her and shaking her and shouting at her for saying that terrible thing. *Of course*—as if oaths and marriage meant nothing at all.

From that thought he asked her, "Then what did we do? What is the Great Marriage, if it's not to keep one only for the other?"

"Me only for you," she said with dismaying perception. "You for whatever woman pleases you."

"That's the gods' way," he said. "A man loves many women, sires many sons. A woman loves one man, bears his sons, submits to his will."

"It is not the Lady's way," she said.

"Then what? What is this Great Marriage? *I* am to touch no other woman, while you have your pick of the men?"

"No," she said. "It's not about who—*has* anyone. It's the spirits together. What they talk of. How they raise children. What house they keep, and who lives in it. Everything that matters."

"That's what a wife does," he said, "and knows no other man than her husband."

"Here," she said, "a husband does it, too."

He sank down beside her on the sweet-scented bed. He could, in a little while, take her again by storm. His body was unconcerned with the follies of the mind. It wanted her more than ever, now it had had a taste of her.

She seemed of much the same mind. Her hand wandered teasingly down his breast and belly to the waking beast below. She held it gently in a warm hand, even as she frowned at the things they had said to one another.

No woman had ever talked to him so, with bodily passion but a cool clarity of mind. It tangled him in confusion. He wanted to be angry; he wanted to understand. He was all in knots.

She sweetened it to simplicity. She roused him again. He rolled her onto her back; she clamped legs about his middle. Her frown lingered. It fanned his own temper, drew him the tighter. He took her hard. She growled in her throat, half lust, half laughter. She matched his every thrust. She raked nails down his back. She bit his neck, and laughed when he yelped.

It was love like war, snarling and tumbling from end to end of the hut and out under the stars. They fetched up against the treebole, Agni pressed to the roughness of its bark, and Tilia stone-heavy on top of him. Nor was she in any haste to relieve him of her weight. She had him in her power, and well she knew it.

He groaned. She lightened herself a little for that, but trapped him still, veiling him in her hair. Her skin was hot against his. Her scent was musk and flowers—stronger now, richer, dizzying to the senses. "I shall teach you," she said, "to be a great lover. Then all the women will vie to choose you."

"I am not going to teach you anything," he said, rough in his throat, "that will make my men any more eager to get their hands on you than they already are."

"I do thank you for that," she said as if she meant it.

He tried again to shift away from the knob of root that dug into his back. This time she let him go. He came up from beneath her and knelt in the mold of leaves and grass. She smiled in the lamplight and the starlight, and reached, and smoothed a trailing lock of hair out of his face. The gesture touched him strangely. More than anything that she had done, it warmed his heart.

Maybe, he began to think, this was not folly. Maybe it could be as he had hoped, king and king's wife, ruling cities that looked to them willingly. And maybe, if the gods favored him, he would win her favor—as if he needed to win it. But he wanted it. He wanted her to look at him always as she was looking at him now, with tenderness that he had never seen before. As if after all she felt a flicker of fondness for him, and a promise, maybe, of more.

And why that should matter, when all that he need think of was his possession of her, he did not know. He had been in this country too long; and Sarama and Taditi before that had taught him to think strange things. He was, when it came to it, a middling poor likeness of a tribesman.

That was a thought he had never thought to have, even when he was cast out. That he who had so prided himself in being a man among men of the tribe, had become—something different. Something that could make a thing called the Great Marriage with a woman who reckoned herself a king's heir, and look at himself and at her, and know but a faint urge to run howling back to the steppe.

This country had conquered him, in its way. And yet, he thought as Tilia sighed and fell asleep with her head lolling heavy on his breast, he was still Agni—was still the king of the horsemen. No rite or vow or binding could alter that.

LADY OF

HORSES

I

CONQUERING THE CONQUERORS

IN THE WINTER of the year that the horsemen came to Three Birds, Sarama bore a daughter in what the women reckoned a swift and easy birthing—the Lady's gift, and blessed, they said. Sarama, who had labored most of the night, dared not imagine what a long or a difficult birthing was like. It should be enough to lie exhausted in a clean and sweet-scented bed, and her daughter in her arms, and the father of her daughter holding them both in his embrace.

Just so he had held her when the child was born, all the hours of it, tireless, uncomplaining even when she screamed and swore. "*Your* fault!" she remembered shrilling at him. "*You* did this!"

She had been even angrier when some of the women laughed, and the midwife said, "Surely. And you, too. It takes two, child. Now stop your tantrum and *push*."

She was so furious that she obeyed—and to her utter surprise, brought the baby into the light then and there, red squalling flailing creature like the embodiment of her own temper.

The baby was still rather red, and Sarama could not have begun to call her pleasant to look at. And yet she was the most beautiful thing in the world. She slept against her mother's breast, all clean and warm and soft. She had dark hair, a great deal of it, and a face more round than oval, and a bud of a mouth that pursed, seeking the breast even in her sleep. Sarama dared to hope that she would grow up beautiful: as beautiful as her father.

Danu bent over them both. He touched the baby's hair with a finger—such a large finger, and such a small head, and so gentle a touch. "What will you name her?" he asked softly.

"Rani," Sarama answered at once. Then: "Unless you'd rather something else."

"No," he said. "Oh, no. The mother names the child. Or don't the tribesmen—?"

"The father names his sons," she said. "The mother is permitted to name the daughters, if he permits them to live."

Danu shivered. She had told him before how the tribes culled their youngest and weakest in lean seasons, and how a father might choose not to raise his daughters. He had been horrified then; he was horrified now. She freed a hand, lifted it to touch his face. "There," she said. "There. You are her father, no? And you permit her to live. So I name her. Her name is Rani."

"Rani," he said. "It's a pretty name."

"A noble one, too. It means something like Mother, and something like King, and something like both put together. She'll shine brightly in the world."

"Yes," he said. His eyes were on the child, his voice soft. "So little a creature, to matter so much."

"So strong a man, to be so smitten." She strained a little over the baby's head, just to the point of pain, and kissed the part of him that she could reach: his shoulder, as it happened. She sank back with a sigh into the support of his arm. He eased her down. If he had been solicitous she would have been annoyed, but he did it matter-of-factly, because after all she had just given birth to a baby.

She could not imagine any man of the tribes making himself into a birthing-stool for one of his women, bearing her as she bore the child, and enduring every grueling hour of it with no more respite than the woman herself had. Even Agni—Tilia had not conceived yet, that anyone knew of. And when she did, and Agni discovered what was expected of him, he would be appalled. Birthing was a woman's rite. A man had no part in it at all.

Sarama was glad that her man was not a tribesman. That he was here, hollow-eyed and pale about the lips with tiredness, holding her and her daughter—their daughter—in the strong circle of his arms. Too often she thought of him with a little condescension, as something less than a man, because he was so gentle and so soft-spoken and so very respectful of women. She had no shame of him, nor did she despise him, but he was not a man as her brother was, or her brother's following.

Now as he held her, his body making a wall against the world, she knew a prickle of shame. There was nothing weak about this man. He was a wonder and a marvel, though he would blush if she said so.

Beyond the warm wall of him, the world began again to touch on her: people coming in, stepping softly, but bright-eyed, eager to see the baby. The Mother, Tilia, some of the elders from the city. A diffident handful of Danu's brothers, big men all and strong, but almost too shy to lift their eyes to Sarama. And, last and at some remove, Agni.

Her brother wore kingship well. He had always taken for granted that when he spoke, men would listen. Here in the Lady's country it was more to the purpose that women should listen, but as Tilia's consort in the Great Marriage he had gained what he looked for. He was listened to. He could speak wherever Tilia spoke, and be heard.

Neither he nor Tilia was given to displays of the gentler sort, but there was an ease between them that Sarama could not mistake. They got on well together. He had not, that Sarama knew of, gone wandering in search of other women, and Tilia had not chosen any but Agni since the Great Marriage. They seemed well content with one another.

If she honestly needed to know, she could ask Tilia. Agni . . .

On the steppe, even after long time apart, Sarama and Agni had been as close as only the twinborn could be. Here, something lay between them. It was not only Danu, or Rani, or both. It went deeper. It had somewhat to do, Sarama thought, with the country itself; with the defense that Sarama had mounted against the horsemen, and the choice that she had made, to be one of the Lady's people. Agni had never faulted her for it, but neither had he forgiven her. She was born to the tribes. She should be loyal to them.

She was born to the Mare's people. That was a thing that he had never understood. The Old Woman had taken her away when she was small. Agni had been left behind, manchild that he was and firstborn son of his father's kingship. Sarama the daughter, elder though she might be, was of no account to the reckoning of kingship. Agni was the prince, the heir. He would be king when his father was dead.

Agni was the king's son by birth and upbringing. Sarama belonged to the Mare. And the Mare was a face of the goddess, that same power who was Lady of the Birds and Lady of the Deer, and Earth Mother too. The Lady's country was Sarama's country, as much as if Sarama had been born and bred to it.

Sarama did not see what profit there could be in saying such things. Agni was all prickly pride. He would not care to hear her defense.

Yet he had come to look on her daughter—mere female though Rani might be. He brought with him a breath of clean air and horses, as if he had come in from the fields. He bent with no constraint that Sarama could discern, and kissed her on both cheeks, and said, "Well done, sister, and a great victory. She'll be a great power in this world."

Just so, or nearly, did a man greet his wife or his kinswoman when she had given a son to the tribe. Agni's eyes glinted, daring her to remark on it. She smiled at him and said, "I thank you, brother. We've named her Rani. Would you like to hold her?"

Agni's expression of shock made her laugh, but he was a bold creature. He took the child from Danu's hands, none too clumsily either, and held her as he might have held a puppy. It served the purpose. He regarded her half in alarm, half in dawning amazement. "Gods," he said. "She's little."

"She'll grow," Danu said.

"Young things do," said Agni. The constraint between them was less pronounced than usual. Danu was too tired, Agni too captivated with the baby to indulge it.

Sarama was not one to smile warmly at the sight of such amity, but she sighed a little in relief. She was always afraid that those two would quarrel, although they never did. They preserved a teeth-gritted civility, but with an edge of tension.

At a glance and a gesture from Danu, Agni sat beside the bed, still holding Rani in his arms. No one else asked to hold her. That privilege was given a man first. The women would wait till there was no man present.

Sarama wondered if Agni knew that. If he did, he was not inclined to grant them the reprieve. He was staying, his manner said, for as long as it suited him.

He seemed comfortable in the manner of a man of this country, cradling a child while the women settled to a round of quiet chatter. Sarama slipped half into a dream, lulled by the sound of it. She was aware, dimly, of Danu's body beside her, warm welcome presence, and the slow surge of his breathing as he too slid into sleep. It was a deeply peaceful sound.

Sarama was blessed: in her man, in her child, in her kin. Without knowing precisely why she did it, she stretched out a hand. Agni widened his eyes a little at her touch, but did not shake it off. She smiled sleepily. After all, she thought. After all, her brother was her brother.

.... 77 ....

Agni came back late from the Mother's house, seeking not the house he slept in but the camp of his tribes. It was deep midwinter and bitterly cold, but never as cold as it could be on the steppe; this was a milder country altogether. His men were out and about with little care for the cold or the wind, though the snow that threatened, and the early dark, would quell them soon enough.

They greeted him as they always did, nodding or smiling or calling his name. He did not preserve the royal distance that his father had. It was not in him, and he saw no profit in it.

Winter had cooled the blood in most of them. They were not so eager now to fight, or even to ride about the country. Of those who had gone to hold cities elsewhere, some had come back, and others sent messengers as often as the weather or the roads would allow. Word was that winter to the eastward was much worse than here. It would be a cruel season on the steppe, after a dry summer and a rainless autumn.

In this rich country, vexed by little more than the cold, Agni had begun to consider the dangers of soft living. He had his men out in all weathers, riding, shooting, mock-fighting; and the Lady's people, too, though most of those did their fighting on foot.

He had spared Sarama a score of horses with which she had, until she grew too big with the child, been teaching the pick of her troops to ride. When Sarama found herself confined to gentler pursuits, Taditi had surprised everyone by announcing that she would take the Lady's riders in hand. She had done it, too, and was teaching the best of those the beginnings of mounted archery—an art that Agni had not even known she knew.

She was in the camp just now, tending the fire in front of the tent that was Agni's when he stayed among the tribesmen. She had a brace of fat rabbits and a yearling deer turning on spits, and a pot of something fragrant with herbs.

Agni squatted beside her, watching her. She greeted him with a nod and a grunt, but kept most of her attention for the pot, to which she was adding pieces of this and bits of that. She looked content—as much as Taditi ever could. The sourness that had been in her for a while, the sense that she endured her days here rather than enjoyed them, was gone. Had been gone, now he thought of it, since she took to training the riders.

Why, he thought: Taditi needed somewhat to do. She had been living with Agni in the Mother's former house, but there was nothing for her to do there. First the menservants and then, after the Great Marriage, Tilia, had done what needed to be done. There was only so much that she could do in a king's tent that was seldom if ever occupied by the king. But to make riders out of lifelong walkers, and to teach them to shoot from horseback as well— that was a challenge. It brought her alive again.

That was a new thought for a tribesman, that a woman could be as eager to be up and doing as a man. Sarama had always been like that, but that was Sarama. Taditi was of the tribes, born and bred, and though blunt-spoken and undeniably formidable, was still, after all, a woman.

Agni's head ached a great deal these days, as it struggled to think thoughts that were alien to it. Tilia had a way of contradicting everything that he thought he knew, just by being herself. Sometimes he thought he could not bear any more; he would snap, he would break. But he never did.

Still without speaking to him, Taditi filled a bowl and set it in his hands. Its warmth was greatly welcome, the scent and taste of it delectable, herbs and roots and meat and a bit of fruit all stewed together. They filled his belly and warmed him from the inside out.

When he had finished the bowl and received another, Taditi spoke at last. "Aren't you going to tell us?"

"What?" said Agni.

"Sarama," she said with a snap of impatience.

"But don't you know—"

"We know she had a daughter," Patir said, appearing behind Taditi, and Tillu's terrible scarred face behind him, and a crowd of others, faces of kin and of western strangers, all fixed on him. Patir went on speaking for them. "All we know is the bare fact. Give us a story."

Agni looked at them all. With a sound that was half sigh, half laughter, he said, "It is a daughter, she looks like her father, and Sarama is resting well. I didn't linger overlong. She'll be brought out and presented to Earth Mother on the third day, it's said. Then you'll all see her."

"The baby will be the Mare's servant in her time," Taditi observed. "That's a fine thing, to see the line go on."

"Imagine," said Tukri of the White Horse. "A daughter, and she matters in the world."

"Daughters do, here," Agni said. He shifted a little, making room for Patir to dip from the pot, and some of the others with him. They sat or knelt or squatted together, eating Taditi's excellent stew and after it the rabbits and the deer, and washing it down with honeyed wine.

As Agni finished a cup, someone touched his shoulder. He recognized one of the westerners: a man of the Golden Aurochs, notable for the white streak in his hair and the bear's claws that he wore as a necklace. He had a pleading look about him now, and a wheedle in his tone. "My lord, not to trouble you, but Modron and I, we had a wager, and he says he won, and I say I won, and—"

Agni levered himself to his feet. That was the king's part: to judge even petty things, because they mattered to the people. He went to settle the wager between Modron and the Bearcub, and after that was the beginning of a blood feud between cousins from the Stormwolf people, and a rash of contentions both greater and smaller, as if the resolving of one only bred a dozen more.

When at last he came back to Taditi's circle, he was seeing the camp in a different light—and not only because the sun had set in ice and fire. Its quiet was deceptive; the peace that had lain on it, that he had thought ran deep, was as shallow as a flicker of light on water.

It was nothing as obvious as a war. The tribes were not feuding. No one had killed anyone, or quarreled badly enough to endanger a life. And yet the little conflicts, the arguments, the wagers won and lost, the restless feet and twitching hands and the tempers too easily frayed, came together into a single, greater thing.

Agni was not at all surprised when he had settled beside the fire to find himself face to face with yet another gathering of men. These were elders of the tribes, men of rank and substance, though Agni noticed that Tillu, while present, was not joined with them. Nor were others who held themselves closest to Agni. These were lesser men, or men who had kept their own counsels.

Agni did not move, nor did he allow his expression to change. But inside he had drawn taut, as one does before battle.

There were preliminaries. More wine. A confection of honeyed fruit, a gift from one of the Lady's cities. The last of the sunset died from the sky. Clouds veiled the stars. Beyond the fire's warmth, the air was bitter.

Those on the circle's edge must be numbed with cold. But no one wandered off. Agni, wrapped in his bearskin and close by the fire, was in as much comfort as he ever needed to be.

One of the elders, a man of the White Bear whose name, as Agni recalled, was Hagen, spoke at last and evidently for them all. "Lord king, it's winter yet, and deep in it. But spring comes soon enough."

Agni lifted brows at that. "Indeed," he said.

"Surely," said Hagen with no appearance of discomfort. This was the counsel of elders, meandering, indirect, skirting round and round the point. "Warm days will be welcome, and nights that don't freeze us to the bone."

His fellows nodded as if he had uttered great wisdom.

Hagen sighed. "No, it's not long at all before the grass grows green again, and the soft winds blow across the steppe. Then the spring fawns will come, and the calves, and the foals in the horse-herds."

"And the young men will grow restless," said another of the elders, "and dream of raiding, of cattle and horses and fine strapping women fit to bear them strong sons."

"Not," said Hagen, "that they don't have much of that here. But the wind on the grass, the sky free above one, and room to gallop—those things are the more precious the longer one lives away from them."

That was as direct as an elder was likely to be, this early in a council. Which, Agni thought, proved the seriousness of it, and the strength of the concern that had brought them here.

He read it well enough. "You want to go home," he said.

The elders regarded him in silence. They could not reprove him: it was a king's privilege to be abrupt. But they could make it clear that they were not ready yet to be so direct.

He sighed and warmed his hands at the fire, and determined to be patient.

At length Hagen said, "We would be content to live in this land of plenty forever. But our young men . . ."

His companions nodded, a wagling of beards round the circle, a gleam of eyes as they watched Agni. Agni held still. This was a test. He had expected it long before now, but the strangeness of the wood and then of the Lady's country, and the confusion of a conquest that had had little to do with war, had diverted them. Now it seemed they had leisure to challenge him.

He let them drag it out as they pleased, now that he knew what they were doing. He could be as patient as a hunter needed to be. He turned his eyes to the fire, resting his spirit in the dance of the flames.

At length Hagen said what he had come to say. "Our young men are asking to end this war that never began. They want to take the booty that they've won, the gold and copper and such women as will go, and go home, back to their own lands and their own people."

"All of them?" Agni inquired.

"A good number of them," Hagen said.

Agni nodded. "Yes. Yes, I can see that some would be homesick. It's very different here."

"Too different," Hagen said.

"You do understand," said Agni, "that all the tribes will come westward in the end. They'll have to. Already they're pressed close against the wood. If they don't break through, they'll have nowhere to go."

"They can fight back," said one of the other elders.

"For a while," said Agni. "But the east presses hard upon us. It's like the wind and the storm. It blows as it blows, and there's no defense against it."

"There's nothing for us here," Hagen said. "We've taken everything we can carry. If we ride back eastward as soon as the spring breaks, we'll be in our own lands by the Great Sacrifice."

"Indeed," said Agni. "Have you heard that it's been a bitter winter? It will be a lean sacrifice. Your people will be hard put to feed the lot of you."

"We'll take all the provisions we can take," Hagen said. "We'll come bearing great gifts. They'll make us kings."

"I am already a king," Agni said, "and I say they're coming here. They'll have to. The steppe won't feed them. They'll hear of this country, how rich, how easy to live in. They'll come, and we'll all have our war."

"Yes," said Hagen, "but when? This year? Ten years from now? Our young men have been away from their people for a year. If it's the will of the tribes to come back—so be it. But until that happens, they want to go home."

"I can't stop them," Agni said.

Hagen looked at him with something close to hope. "You'll go? You'll lead us back?"

"I didn't say that," he said. "If they want to go, let them go. I am staying here. This is the country that I won, that gave itself to me. It's mine. I'm not leaving it for the next man to take as he pleases."

"And if we all go away?"

"I'll not be left alone," Agni said. "My own kin will stay. The rest may go or stay, as they choose."

"You don't care?" That was a hanger-on, a man much younger than the elders, and somewhat gone in wine from the sound of him.

"I care greatly," Agni answered him. "I will not provoke a war among our people, or force any man to stay who would rather go."

The elders glanced at one another. Agni wondered if any of them had had a wager. "You think you can hold this country without us?" one demanded.

"I can try," said Agni.

"Idiot," said yet another, and not to Agni. "He can't go back. He's cast out. He knew when he came that he was here to stay. Hasn't he even taken the she-king's daughter to wife?"

Agni spoke before they could murmur of betrayal. "I could be king on the steppe. I choose to be king here. Those who are loyal will stay. Those who are not will go. What more need any of us do?"

He caught and held each pair of eyes, and made each fall. He *was* king. While they sat in front of him, drinking his wine and enjoying the warmth of his fire, they were subject to his will. What they chose to do or think elsewhere was between them and their gods, and the oaths that they had sworn to Agni as king.

When the last of them had yielded, even Hagen, Agni nodded and allowed himself a thin new moon of a smile. "Tell your men," he said, "that I set them free. To go where the winter is far more bitter than here, or to stay in warmth and in comfort. And come the summer . . . a war to delight any warrior's heart."

"You can't promise a war that soon," Hagen said, startled out of his submission.

"Why not?" said Agni. "Your men will go back. They're fat, sleek, loaded with riches. Their people will look, will see how well they've prospered, and determine to go in search of such riches for themselves. They'll bring the war straight to me—in haste, and without long preparation. I'll give those who stay enough fighting to content even the fiercest."

There was a silence. Agni could not tell what they were thinking. None would raise his eyes, even Hagen who spoke for them all. Who said, at length, "You are both clever and farsighted."

That was praise. Agni did not acknowledge it. A king did not. He expected it; he took it as tribute. He rose, wrapping himself more tightly in his mantle. "I give you goodnight, sirs."

No one tried to hold him back. He walked erect and haughty long after they could have seen him in the dark, lest one of them had followed him. Only when he was well away, and well within the circles of the city, did he let himself relax.

He reeled against a house-wall, caught it and let it hold him up. He had not meant his knees to let go quite so completely. It was exhaustion: the long fret while Sarama was brought to bed of her daughter, and a long day's hunting before that, and kingship pressing in close when he had looked to find—what?

Kingship. If he had wanted to rest in peace, he would not have gone to the camp. People were always at him there, demanding that he do their thinking for them.

He had meant to spend the night in his tent. But by the time he remembered that, he was far away from the camp, and it would cost his pride too much to go back. He went on as he had begun. The gods were guiding him, maybe. Or Earth Mother, whose country this was; who, for whatever unfathomable purpose, had chosen to make him king in this place.

It was never wise to try to understand the gods.

.... 78 ....

Tilia woke when Agni came in. She had been sleeping, but lightly, uneasy in his absence. And that was a thing that she had never expected, that when he was not in her bed, she should feel cold and distressingly alone.

He was not the lover that Kosti was, or even that Beki had been, who was so ordinary to look at but who was a wonder and a marvel in a woman's arms. He was not too ill to the eye, though one could wish for a little less nose, a little more flesh about the cheeks and jaw. His eyes were no proper color for a man's, although they would have looked admirable in a goat.

And for all of that, when he stood in the light of the one lamp that she had left burning, he was exactly as beautiful as he needed to be. She watched him through her lashes, feigning sleep, while he paused to bask in the room's warmth—for it was in back of the kitchen, and the hearth heated its small space in wondrous fashion. In summer it would be intolerable. Now, in winter, it was bliss.

He shed his heavy mantle, and everything beneath it, too. He was narrower than a man of her people, except in the shoulders; leaner, rangier, with long ropes of muscles, and legs bowed from a long life on a horse's back. His skin was as white as milk, freckled where the sun had touched it. He did not grow the pelt that men of her people tended to grow; his was sparse, like a woman's. But there was nothing female about his body.

She liked to watch him when he did not know she was doing it. He put aside constraint then, and forgot to hold himself as his people believed a man should, particularly a man who was a king. Then he looked younger, less royally sure of himself. She could see the boy he must have been, awkward and gangling but with a peculiar grace. He put her in mind of one of his horses, with his long face and his long legs and his loose-jointed gait.

Once he was naked, he stretched and yawned and shook his hair out of its braid. His hair was wonderful, much brighter than his sister's, the color of somewhat tarnished copper. It was thick and straight, like a horse's mane, but much softer. He took no great notice of it except to rake it out of his face. He was frowning at the air, pondering something that troubled him.

Whatever it was, he put it aside to slip into the bed beside her. His body was warm, fire-warm. He smelled of wine and smoke and frosty air, horses and wool and man—not too terribly much of that last. He had taken well to the cleanliness that the Lady enjoined on her people; a little to Tilia's surprise, at first, until she came to know him. He was not a savage by nature. He was, in fact, quite a civilized creature.

She slipped arms about him. It was gratifying how quickly he roused to her touch. She took him inside her, rocking slowly, without urgency; warmth without heat and pleasure without—for the moment—passion.

This was a thing that she had had to teach him. He had only known the stallion's way: seize, thrust, have done. He did not speak of it, but she saw what she could not mistake. There had been a woman in his tribe—more than one, as how not, but this one in particular had marked him deep enough to scar. She had ridden him as Tilia had seen some of the tribesmen ride their horses, too fast and too hard and with too little regard for his spirit. She had had no patience for the gentler ways of a woman with a man.

Tilia had a great deal of patience, when it suited her—little as her brother, for one, might have believed it. And Agni had found in himself a talent for restraint. One could, with such an art, prolong one's pleasure for most of a night if one were so inclined.

Neither of them was so minded tonight. Her pace quickened just as he began to thrust deeper, long strokes, slow still but growing swifter, and strong. Neither had yet said a word.

His breath caught first. Hers followed soon after. They clung tightly, flesh on sweat-slicked flesh. He was still inside her. She held him as long as she could, as if she could bind them into one creature.

But the world could never stand still, nor even pause for long. He slipped out of her and lay beside her, breathing a little quickly even yet. She kissed him wherever she could reach.

He laughed at that, with a touch of breathlessness. "Will you eat me alive?" he asked her.

"Every bite," she said. He had spoken in her language. She spoke in his. It was a game they played, to sharpen their wits. She was better at it than he was. He never stopped trying to best her. She rather liked that. It was good for a man to try to match a woman. Not that he ever could, but the trying helped strengthen his spirit.

He lay a little apart from her but still in her arms as she was in his, the better to see her face. She traced with a finger the line of his cheekbone, the sharp clean line of his jaw. His beard was soft, a young man's beard. He kept it clipped close, as if he reckoned it somewhat of a nuisance; though he would have been greatly angry if she had said such a thing. These horsemen were inordinately proud of the things they had that no woman did. Beards. No breasts. And the great thrusting thing that was a man's most useful possession—of that, they made an enormous fuss. As if a woman lacked something because her parts were tucked safely away, and as if it were an advantage to have it all hanging in front of them, dangling and bulging and getting in the way.

He was, for a man, a lovely creature. She said as much. He growled, but he had learned not to grow angry when she reminded him of his proper place in the world. He liked to dream that she would submit to him, or at least allow him to impose his will on her. Sometimes it was amusing to indulge him. Other times, as now, she chose the truth instead.

"Sometimes," he said, "I wonder why you trouble with men at all. You could keep them in villages of their own, and go there in season, and get daughters from them and leave the sons, and never be vexed by them else."

She traced the Lady's symbols on his breast, circle and spiral and narrow oval and, for him if he only knew, the shape that meant man. She laid her hand on that, where she had drawn it over his heart, and said, "What a marvelous idea, to set the men apart. Is that what your people do? Especially the young men? Like the horses? We live all tangled together here. It's untidy, but it does seem to suit us."

"You'll never be in awe of me, will you?"

She raised herself on her arms. His eyes widened. He was always a little taken aback by her beauty. She swooped to steal a kiss, and hovered over him, smiling with great contentment. "No man will ever awe me. Even you. But if any could come close . . ."

"You're just saying that."

"What, sulking?" She teased him with her breasts, brushing them across his chest, slipping away when he tried to catch her. "Beautiful man," she said.

He leaped, taking her by surprise, and overset her. She laughed. These men were ridiculously proud of their strength; as if the force of a man's arm were all he needed in the world. She yielded like water, she made herself all soft, she gave him nothing to fight against; so that when they had tumbled to a halt, she was as she had been before, and he was flat on his back, winded, glowering at her.

"Admit it," she said. "You'll never overcome me. But you might—indeed you might—learn to stand beside me."

"Or behind you?"

"Not you," she said.

"A man should stand above a woman."

She had argued that with him before. He wanted to argue it again, but she had no intention of letting him. She diverted him instead. She settled herself comfortably beside him. She let him hold her, which he loved to do. She said, "Tell me what's troubling you."

He sputtered a little, but this was not the first time she had caught him sidewise. He answered her sensibly enough, considering. "How do you know something's troubling me?"

"I know you," she said.

"You know too much." He was growling. She waited him out. At length he said, "All right then. It's the tribes—the westerners mainly. They want to go home."

"Yes," she said.

"You knew?"

She shrugged. "One could see. They've been leaving in ones and twos and threes. The winter stopped them, but one finds them in the fields to the eastward, yearning unmistakably. Are you surprised?"

"No," he said. "Of course not. I was expecting this. It's only . . . I was hoping it would take a while longer."

"Patience doesn't appear to be a great virtue in the tribes."

"Usually we can wait till spring," Agni said a little dryly.

"You think they'll all go back?"

"No," he said. "I think that some will go, and they'll find the aftermath of a hard winter, and everyone will see how fat and rich they are, and by full summer the tribes will be overrunning this country again."

"You won't stop them," she said. It was not a question.

"I don't think I can." She lifted her head from his breast. He was staring into the dark beyond the lamp's glow. "It's not going to stop now. It's going to go on and on. There's been no escaping it since that traveler brought his mare to Larchwood, then went back to the steppe with his copper knife and his stories."

"You followed the stories," she said.

"So will the others."

She laid her head on his breast again and took his rod in her hand. It swelled to fill her grasp. She stroked it, smiling as he twitched and caught his breath. But there was no smile in the words she spoke. "This time it will be war."

"Yes," he said.

"You aren't eager for it?"

He stiffened. She stroked a little harder. He sighed. The tension stayed in him, but transmuted. His speech was a little breathless. "I'm not as bloodthirsty as some."

She set herself to pleasuring him, because it was her pleasure, and because she needed to think about what he had said. Nothing in it was startling or unexpected. But that he saw it and spoke of it—that made it real. That gave it power.

In the last moment, she took him into herself, that none of him be spent. She wondered if he knew how completely he had given himself to her. Most likely not. He must always fancy that he was the stronger, that he was lord and master and she must, in the end, defer to him.

One could become adept at catering to such delusions. Tilia thought about that while he slept, snoring softly. She could feel him inside her still. Warmth; a kind of presence. Maybe—maybe at last—

Maybe. It was not the best of times to bring a child into the world, but it was all the time she had. And fitting that it should begin now, so soon after his sister had borne a daughter before the Lady. They were all making a new world, mingling the blood of the cities and the steppe, the Lady's children and the Mare's children and the children of the wild horsemen.

.... 79 ....

After a winter that was reckoned harsh in this gentle country, came a mild spring: warm days, chilly nights, soft rain to wash away the snow and wake the sleeping earth. Tribesmen began to take horse and ride eastward. Fewer went than the elders had predicted, but somewhat more than Agni had hoped. They did not all go at once. They left alone or in bands of three or four. They took as much wealth as they could carry; nor did Agni try to prevent them, though he forbade them to take more than two remounts apiece.

"There's our trouble," he said to Sarama on a brisk morning after a night of rain. He had gone to survey the horse-herds, and met her on her way to ride with Taditi's archers. She was riding one of the stallions from the White Horse herds; for the Mare was great with foal, holding court among the herds like a king's first wife, and doing no work but that of waiting for the birth.

Agni paused with Sarama on a rise above the long field in which the horses grazed. She nodded at his observation, looking out over what seemed to be, what was, a great number of horses. "Too many stallions and geldings. Too few mares."

"It's not anything people think of," he said. "On the steppe, when one raids, one captures the enemy's wealth, his women, his horses. Here—there are no horses."

"Your mares are in foal, yes?" she said.

"All three of them," he said. "And there's the Mare, too; and a few others here and there. But not enough. If we're to live here, we have to have horses."

"Yes," she said. She had not taken her eyes from the herd. The stallion fretted under her. He was young and not well disciplined, and he did not suffer Mitani well at all. Mitani, like the king he was, ignored the young fool and busied himself with a clump of grass.

The young stallion squealed, bucked, skittered sideways. Sarama made no effort to stop him. Agni opened his mouth to say more, but shut it again. She hardly noticed. Her mind was gone already, riding with Taditi and the archers. Her body was not slow to follow it.

Agni let her go. He knew better than to think that his trouble concerned her more than a little. The world she lived in touched only occasionally on anyone else's, and even more seldom since Rani was born.

He shrugged, sighed. He had not honestly expected Sarama to solve his problem for him. The answer was obvious in any case. There were no mares here. There were mares on the steppe.

"Someone should go and bring back a herd of mares," said a voice behind him, shaping his thought into words.

He looked over his shoulder at Patir. His friend sat easily on the back of his spotted stallion, surveying the herd as Sarama had done. But his eyes were alert, keen, taking count of the mares, the foals, even the three yearlings who had been born in the conquest of the Lady's country. "A raid," he said, "as great as any I've heard of in stories. Not just to seize a few horses, but to take and bring back a great wealth of them."

"Would you go?" Agni asked him.

Patir's glance lit with eagerness, but he hesitated. Agni's brows went up. "Ah," he said. "Who is she?"

Patir the insouciant, Patir the unshakably composed, was blushing like a girl. "What makes you think—"

"What's her name?" Agni asked.

Patir looked down in remarkable confusion. "All right," he muttered. "All right. Her name is Chana."

"Ah," said Agni.

Patir shot him a blazing glance. "Fine one you are to laugh at me, with what you've got filling your bed."

"I could kill you for that," Agni said mildly.

"You could. And then you'd have to find someone else to round up your mares for you."

"So you'll do it," Agni said. "Even if Chana objects?"

"Does it matter if she does?"

"She may think so."

Patir shook his head. "Chana won't. Chana is different. She likes it when I command her as a man should command a woman. It's tiresome, she says, to rule the world. She finds it restful to let me do it."

"And you believe her?"

"She'd never lie to me."

Agni could hardly contest that, since he had never met the woman. But that any female of this country would willingly submit herself to a man, even a man as pleasant to the eye and the spirit as Patir, taxed his credulity sorely.

Nevertheless he had noticed a number of dark-eyed women in the camp, rather a large number when he stopped to think. It seemed that there had been none all through the autumn and much of the winter. Now suddenly there were a dozen or two. Or three. Four?

Agni rode as he had intended, then sat on his bay horsehide for his day's stint of being formally king. And as he rode and judged and listened, he watched. He counted.

There were women everywhere, or nearly. Some were rather obviously living in tents. Others seemed to be visiting, or to be indulging curiosity. They were tending fires, mending garments, even looking after the cattle. All things that women or children would do in any camp of a tribe.

And yet these were women of the Lady's country, dark-eyed, dark-haired, more often plump than not. The one standing framed by the flap of Patir's tent was a beauty, small-boned and delicate—striking among these sturdy people. She did not conceal her face behind a veil as a tribeswoman would have done, nor did she duck her head and vanish when she felt his eyes on her. She smiled, dazzling him.

Shocking. Bold beyond belief. Agni wondered what she would do if he grinned back at her. Not that he intended to try. Not from the king's horsehide, and not in front of Patir.

He ended the hour of judgment rather short of its full span, and sought out Taditi, whom he had seen walking back from the horselines with her bow in her hand. He found her in the tent, putting bow and arrows away, and rubbing the string with fat to keep it supple before she coiled it and laid it in its case. She glanced at him but did not pause. He squatted near the flap, where the sun slanted in to warm him, and waited till she came and sat on her heels beside him.

From where he was, he could see a fair arc of camp, and the women coming and going, and men too. "How long has this been going on?" he demanded abruptly.

"What?" said Taditi, rather reasonably in the circumstances. "My riding and shooting? I thought you knew I'd been doing it since the winter."

"Of course I knew," he said. "I don't mean that. I mean this. All these women. Where are they coming from? When did they start coming here?"

"Ah," said Taditi, reminding him somewhat forcibly of how exasperated Tilia could be when he used the same expression. It could make one feel a right fool.

Taditi ignored his scowl. "So you finally noticed. Some of the men have a wager. It's been going on since winter—since a little after your sister's baby was born."

"Why? Why just then?"

"Who knows?" said Taditi. "Suddenly it's a fashion. Leave the city, find a tribesman, look after his tent. I expect we'll see a good number of dark-eyed babies come winter."

Agni seized on the one thing that honestly mattered. "It's a *fashion*? That's all it is?"

"It seems so," she said.

Agni sank back onto his heels. "And does that fashion also partake of the woman's submitting her will to the man's? Simply for the novelty of it?"

"My," she said. "You are perceptive."

Agni had learned long ago not to lose his temper when Taditi spoke to sting. "And I suppose it's all the rage to have one's own tribesman, just like the Mother's heir."

"That should bother you?" said Taditi. "It serves you well, I should think. It binds these women to your men, and mingles our blood with theirs."

"I'm not bothered," he said. "I'm wondering how long it will last."

"A long while," said Taditi, "if your men have any wits at all. Has it struck you yet that if these women learn to act like women of the tribes, they might come to think like proper women, too? And then they're yours, bound to you and to the gods."

Agni shivered a little. Sometimes Taditi spoke as if the gods were in her, too; or maybe Earth Mother spoke to her as if she had been a Mother of this country.

"Fashion can become custom," Taditi said as if to herself. "I remember when I was a girl, how we all wore our hair loose as they still do in the dancing at festivals. Then someone took it into her head to wear a crown of braids—because, she said, it got her hair up out of the way. In no time at all, every unmarried girl was wearing her hair up except in the dancing. Now it's custom, as if from the dawn time: braids wound around the head for young women without husbands, and braids down the back or coiled at the nape for married women. All because of a fashion that everyone thought would be gone in a season."

"Obviously it was practical," Agni said. "Now tell me what's practical about one of these women giving up her power in the world."

"How do you know any of them is doing that?" Taditi inquired. "Not, mind, that they aren't discovering how easy it can be to let someone else do their thinking for them."

"That's what Patir said. That they're finding it restful."

Taditi nodded. "Just so. A mind is like a body, as you know perfectly well. It has to keep working, or it grows fat and slow. This that they're doing—it's easy. It lets them be lazy. And it gives you the power you need to make this country yours beyond any doubt. If you win its women, if their children grow up in the ways of the tribes—you've won, not only for this little hour in the sun, but for the generations after you."

"And you," said Agni. "You don't approve."

"I don't approve or disapprove. I see what is. This is a greater victory than any in battle."

"If we can hold it. If they don't all get tired of the game and go back to their own ways. And," said Agni, "if they don't conquer us while we preen ourselves for conquering them."

Taditi shrugged. "There is that. I think, if you stay here, you'll end up winning as much as you lose. Particularly if you keep the advantage over these innocents."

"I don't know how innocent they are," Agni said darkly. "They're only learning to fight—but they can twist a man in knots."

"Really? I should study them." Taditi straightened—creaking less than Agni did, which was a little distressing—and set to filling the pot for the daymeal.

Agni stayed where he was. He had much to think on. Horses, and women. War. Warriors. Spring and all that it meant: festival and sacrifices, dancing and feasting. These people had a festival of their own; that much he had discovered from listening here and there. It seemed to have something to do with planting the fields and making the grain grow, and eating a great deal, and women choosing men and going off with them to make a sacrifice of themselves to Earth Mother.

He began to wonder as he sat there, whether there might be a way to mingle the festivals. It was a peculiar thought, and disturbing. The festivals were the festivals, and had been since the dawn time. It was a great ill thing to change them.

But Taditi's tale of women and their fashions had set his mind on a track as daring as it was strange. All things began somewhere—even festivals. Surely those had begun in the dawn time, or so it was said. But was this not a dawn of its own? There had never been horsemen in this country before. They were changing the world. And if the world changed—might not custom change also?

He clasped his knees and rocked. People would object. People objected to changes; and changes in sacred things were, to most, unthinkable. It must be the Mare's blood in Agni that made him so different. If people objected strongly enough, they well might kill him. Or they would refuse to follow him, to perform the rites as he had altered them. He was but a king, after all, and the gods' servant. He was not a god himself.

✦ ✦

"There is a way," said Danu.

Agni did not know how it happened that he had told Danu, of all people, what he was thinking of. He had gone in search of Sarama or Tilia or even the Mother, and found the Mother's son looking after the baby. It was a warm morning, almost summer-warm, and Danu had brought his daughter out onto the doorstep. She was tiny still, but not as wizened as she had been when she was born.

Agni peered into her face. She startled him: she peered back. He grimaced at her. She smiled as sweetly as her mother ever could, and with much the same air of distraction, too.

"Here," Danu said.

Agni found himself with an armful of baby. For lack of greater inspiration, he cradled her as he had seen her father do, and rocked her. She sighed and smacked her lips and went to sleep.

"Amazing," Danu said. "She howls for everyone else but me."

"She knows her kin," said Agni.

Danu smiled, leaning back against the house-wall. It was always a little startling to see him with baby in arms or spoon in hand, doing women's work. That strong face, those heavy shoulders, should have marked a great warrior. Nor was he at all an ill hand with bow or boar-spear; but it was obvious that he preferred this gentler occupation.

And Agni found himself unburdening to this man whom he did not like and whom he most certainly did not admire. Danu heard him out with evident attention. When Agni was done he said, "There is a way. If you make your sacrifice and we make ours, and we all come together after and dance till dawn, might not both sides be satisfied?"

"That's not a mingling," Agni said.

"It's as much as anybody will accept. You know that or you'd not have asked me."

Sometimes Agni could not fathom these people's logic. The men thought like women, and the women thought like nothing he could put a name to. And yet, rather to his dismay, Danu made perfect sense. "You don't think we can make a new rite."

"I think time can change much," Danu said, "but there hasn't been enough of it yet. If we dance together—that's enough. For now."

The baby stirred in Agni's arms, annoyed that he had stopped rocking her to talk to her father. He did as she clearly bade, watching her face, seeing Sarama in the shape of the chin, the molding of the brow; but the rest was Danu. "Our children will make a rite of their own," he said.

"I think so." Danu seemed calm about it. He walked close to the Lady always; probably he had seen it all already, and schooled himself to accept it.

Agni had had the answer he was looking for, but he lingered for a while. It was pleasant here, warm in the sun, with the baby asleep and her father humming softly to himself. The world and its troubles seemed far away.

This must be what it was to be one of the Lady's children. Sunlit peace. Never any doubts, and few fears. Their nights were moonlit and full of stars. Dark things never walked there.

Agni shook himself, lightly lest he wake the baby. Nothing was ever as simple as that, even here.

He handed Rani to her father, who took her smoothly, so that she never stirred. Danu smiled. Agni found himself smiling back, and still smiling as he walked away.

He did not like Danu at all. And yet the man was wise in his way, and he was pleasant company. All things considered.

················· 80 ·················

Camp and city held their festivals on the same days, by agreement between Agni and the Mother. Great Sacrifice and Spring Planting, sacrifice of blood and sacrifice of wine and seed, one in the camp, one in the city—and dancing all together after.

That was the pact they made. Agni was reasonably certain that the rites would go as they should go. But the dancing might be more difficult. He made sure that word was spread: any man caught taking a woman against her will, no matter how mild the protest, would be seized and punished according to the magnitude of his crime. Even to gelding or death, if the offense warranted.

"And if one of the women takes one of us against his will?" one wag wanted to know.

"They'll pray over her," said someone else, "and make her live in his tent for a month."

The men who were near seemed to find that vastly funny. Agni failed to see the humor in it. There was nothing amusing about rape. Rahim had died for it. Agni had been outcast for an accusation of it.

Memories were short, and it had been a fair while since anyone enjoyed a festival. Agni hoped that his prohibition would be enough—and that the Mother would bid her women be cautious.

✦ ✦

The first sacrifice, sacrifice of the Hound, went as it should go. The Hound died well. His blood flowed red on this alien earth. And in the dancing after, there was no trouble that Agni could discern. So too the second day, the sacrifice of the Bull, and the second dance. As freely as the wine flowed, as easily as the people went back and forth from camp to city, still no one ventured beyond the limits that had been set.

Last year Agni had been an exile in search of a dream that the gods had laid on him. There had been no Great Sacrifice in his camp. The year before . . . Sarama had come back on the day of the Bull, this day indeed, and Agni had looked ahead to the taking of his stallion and the gaining of the kingship.

Now he sat on the royal horsehide in the circle of elders, and it was not as dull as he remembered. He could have risen and joined the dance; the king was not forbidden. In a little while he would. At the moment he was content to sit as a king sits, and to watch the dance wind its skein through the camp and out into the city.

They danced too, the Lady's people, a spiral dance remarkably like the dance of the Sacrifice. There was the beginning of a common rite. He saw how it was, men and women dancing together, dark heads and fair, hand linked with hand under the waxing moon. Here, he thought. Here it began. And maybe someday their rites would mingle, too, as they mingled in the dance.

Somewhere in the city, Tilia and the Mother sat as Agni was sitting, or so he supposed. Agni wondered if Tilia found it as dull as he had when he was the heir and not the king. Or maybe they performed a rite in the temple, one of their women's rites that no man was allowed to see. There were a great many of those. He would be surprised, after all, if there was not one tonight.

He rose at last when the moon rode high overhead, but he did not go to join the dancers. He wandered off instead, first to relieve himself, then simply to walk along the river. The air was soft, no touch of frost—much softer than it would be on the steppe, this early in the year. Scents of tilled earth, new grass, spring flowers, rose up with the dewfall, strong enough to dizzy him.

He wandered out past the horse-herds, past the pen where the Stallion waited, the one who had been chosen for tomorrow's sacrifice. The priests—and Agni among them—had chosen a black this year, all night-dark without glimmer of white. He was a shadow on shadow in the night, a soft snort, the stamp of a hoof on the yielding ground. Agni bowed low to him. He pawed restlessly, begging to be let out, to run with his fellows under the moon. "Tomorrow," Agni said to him, "O blessed, you'll run the fields in the gods' country. Then you'll never be bound again."

"So that is a royal sacrifice."

Agni caught himself before he wheeled and bolted. Tilia was standing next to him as if she had been there from the beginning. She wore what women wore here in festivals, the skirt that was their sacred garment, that they won when they came to womanhood; she was bare else, as they always were before their goddess, with her hair all loose and her breasts like twin moons, round and full.

She slipped her arm through his, leaning her head against his shoulder, as beautifully trusting as a child. But that was no child's body pressed lightly against his, and no child's voice either that said, "Come worship the Lady with me."

Agni was more than glad to oblige, but he paused. "In the fields? In the—the burrows?"

"Furrows," she said with a ripple of laughter. "Where we'll sow the seeds of the harvest in the morning. Tonight we'll sow another kind of seed."

He caught himself blushing. Thank the gods, it was too dark for her to see. "You people are so—close to the earth."

"Earthy," she said. "How not? We're Earth Mother's own."

She tugged at him. Agni followed. "You came for me," he said.

"Yes," she said.

"You didn't have to. Did you? You could have taken anyone you pleased."

"I wanted you."

Agni drew a slow breath. He did not want her to know how dizzily happy she had made him. Of course she had come to him. She was his wife. And yet . . .

And yet her custom had not required it, and she would not have cared if Agni had objected to her taking another man. She had chosen Agni because she wanted him, not because she was required to do it.

Such a world this was, that he should be trying not to grin like a mad thing because his own wife wanted him in her bed. Or, as it happened, in a furrow near the river, in the rich scent of turned earth, under the high vault of the stars. She lay in the furrow, all mingled with the earth, and bade him take her so.

He remembered a day on a high hilltop, not long after he took Three Birds; how Earth Mother had come to him and bidden him love her. This was Earth Mother's child, warm flesh and welcoming arms, mortal beyond a doubt, and yet all the sweeter for it. Her body that he had come to know so well, her scent with its hint of spices, wrapped him about. He held himself above her, looking down at her. So beautiful, so perfectly matched and mated, body joined to body in the moon's glimmer.

She arched under him, taking him deep into herself. He gasped. Of its own accord, his body quickened its pace. The end of it took him by surprise; seized him and shook him and left him limp on the earth.

The night air was cool on his fevered skin. He rolled onto his back, baring his body to the moon.

Tilia lay propped on her elbow beside him, drinking in the sight of him. Her smile was rich and warm, like cream. "I wanted *you*," she said as if their conversation had not been interrupted. And then: "I want to watch your sacrifice tomorrow."

His stomach clenched. The warmth of release vanished. He was cold, cold and baffled. "What? Why? Don't you have rites of your own?"

"They don't require my presence," she said.

"So why?"

"I want to see," she said.

"There's blood," he said. "There's killing."

"I know," said Tilia.

"*I* have to do the killing. I'm the priest of the sacrifice. It has to be the king, you see. Or the king's heir."

"I know," she said. "Your sister told me."

"Why? So that you can hate me?"

She answered that with silence, which maybe was the best that it deserved.

He drew a deep and calming breath. "Did she also tell you that women don't attend the sacrifice?"

"Women from the tents," she said. "The Lady's servants are another matter."

"Then I may attend the rite in the temple?"

She bridled. "No man attends—" She broke off. "That's different."

"How is it different?"

"Because it's a women's rite," she said.

"This is a men's rite," said Agni.

She hissed. She was not going to see it. But Agni was not going to give in, either. "A bargain," he said. "You come to the sacrifice of the Stallion. I go to the Lady's rite."

"We could just come," she said.

"So could I," said Agni.

There: impasse.

She sat up suddenly, curling into a knot. "You don't make anything easy," she said.

He widened his eyes. "Well then. Who'd have thought it? Here you've been wearing us away like water on stone, and now the stone seems a little hard. This is what a bargain is. A trade. If you give, I give. If you take, I take something else. You come to the sacrifice, I go to the temple."

"I can't give you that," she said.

"Then who can? The Mother?"

"If the Lady speaks through her."

"Then I'll ask the Mother," he said, "in the morning."

She unknotted. "And if she says no?"

"No bargain," he said.

"You are a hard man," said Tilia.

"No," he said. "I'm as soft as water, for a tribesman. It's your men who are softer yet."

"Men should be soft," she said. "If they're not . . . they have so little strength of will, and so much strength of body. They do whatever they take it into their heads to do. Steal, rape, kill."

He shook his head, not to deny what she said, but to shake it out of his mind. He must not grow angry. Not now. What she said, he had heard before, from her, from others of these women. For all he knew or cared, it was the perfect truth.

But he was making a world here. He had to remember that. There was no little pride, too, in proving that a man could be as strong in spirit as a woman.

Therefore he held his peace except to say, "I'll speak with the Mother."

She nodded. The little distance between them might have been as broad as the steppe.

He rose and gathered his clothes together. She watched him but did not try to stop him. He would sleep in his tent tonight. She would come there, or she would not. That was hers to choose.

Maybe he was a hard man after all. Good, then. He was a proper tribesman.

+ +

Agni approached the Mother with something very close to trepidation. She heard him out with that air of hers, as if nothing had ever surprised her or could surprise her. And when he was done, she said, "Yes."

His teeth clicked together. "Yes?"

"Yes, you may watch the rite."

"But—"

She sat in unruffled serenity, sitting as she-king over the planting as Agni had sat as king over the dancing. "You may watch," she said, "from the door. You may not speak. You would be advised not to move. Be eyes only. Be nothing else."

"I won't go blind? I won't be struck dead?"

"Does that happen in your country?"

Her eyes were not even on Agni. He followed the line of her gaze, out over the southern field, the Lady's field, where row after row of people—men, women, children—sowed seed in the tilled earth. The day before, they had harrowed it; and the day before that, broken the sods, plowed and turned it. They had made a rite of it, made this field sacred, the first field and the field that would make the pattern for all the others.

He watched the sowers in the lead, the people behind them closing the furrows, and the children with great fans of leaves or sheets of cloth, driving the birds away. Just after a chattering flock had erupted into the air, Agni answered the Mother's question. "It doesn't happen here? There's no punishment for the man who trespasses on the Lady's rite?"

"No man would do such a thing."

"Not even for temptation? To see what is so secret that he's never to be part of it?"

"No," said the Mother.

"And you say that men are undisciplined."

"We teach them to control themselves," the Mother said.

"But you won't let them stand face to face with the Lady."

Her smile, though faint, reminded him distinctly of Tilia at her most recalcitrant. "The Lady is wherever her children are. Male children as much as female."

"But only women may enter her most sacred places."

"And only a man may enter a woman's most secret places. Should we alter that, too? Or object to it?"

"Yet you will allow me in the temple," Agni said before matters got any more out of hand. He hoped that she could not see how he blushed; though that was a vain hope, with his fair skin.

She forbore to remark on it, which was a mercy. She said, "The world changes. A man sets foot in the temple, and women see blood sacrifice in a field that was once theirs. The Lady wills this; for what reason, no one mortal knows."

"And you never fail to do as the Lady wills."

"That is my duty and my office," she said.

"And do you never doubt? Ever? At all?"

"Does it matter if I do?"

"To me it does."

She regarded him for a moment. He watched her reflect that to his people he was as she was: first of them all, leader and guide, and sacrifice too if need be. She did not approve of his holding such an office, male that he was and ill-schooled in the arts of serenity, but she could hardly deny that he held it.

When she spoke, it was to the office and not to the man. "Yes. Yes, I doubt, and I fear, too. The Lady speaks to me, but not always in ways that I can understand. I must interpret her signs and omens, and hope that I interpret them rightly. And always I must preserve the image of calm, because if a Mother is frightened, her people will be terrified."

"Yes," Agni said. "Except that for us, it's not calm we cultivate; it's stern authority, and the image of strength."

"Will you look stronger if you see how we worship the Lady?"

"I will look stronger if I trade what your daughter asked, for a favor of equal value."

"Ah," said the Mother. "It's all bargains and trade. And seeming strength."

"Isn't that what ruling is?"

"Some of it," she said. And after a pause: "We gather in the temple at moonrise."

"We sacrifice the Stallion at noon," he said.

She nodded. He nodded. It was not perfect amity, but it was agreement. It would do.

.... 81 ....

The Stallion died as the sun touched its zenith. He did not come quietly, but struggled and fought; he made a war of his sacrifice. Agni hardly needed an omen so clear, but it seemed the gods were determined to leave no doubt. This bloodless conquest would not endure. Blood would come, and battle.

The Stallion died as an enemy dies, fighting his death. Agni conquered because he must; because he could do no other.

He earned this new and royal horsehide. And when it was taken and the sacrifice all completed, the old hide, the hide of the stallion that had been Rahim's, was folded and blessed and given to the gods on the pyre of the sacrifice. The smoke of it was rank, rising to blue heaven.

Even an ill sacrifice was sweet to the gods. Some of the tribesmen were afraid; Agni saw the rolling of eyes and the flicking of fingers in signs against evil. They were blaming the women who stood apart, raised on a hilltop, watching. Ill luck, the men said, and the gods' curse, that a company of females should lay eyes on the men's rite.

It was not the women's fault that the gods were driving all the tribes into the west. They were no more to be blamed for it than the grass that catches the lightning and sets the steppe afire.

He did what he could to calm his people, by spreading word that the omens were never as ill as they seemed; that they were simply a promise of war. Had not they all been hoping for just such a thing? Some believed him, he could hope. The rest would be quiet for fear of seeming cowardly.

Wine soothed them soon enough, wine and sunlight and the heat of the dancing. There were women in the dancing, more of them even than Agni remembered, and every one seemed eager to find herself a tribesman to play wife to. That was the fashion, the thing that all the young women were doing this season, for the novelty of it.

Let fashion become custom; then let them all become one people. Agni did not make a prayer of that, not exactly. But if the gods chose to take it so, then he would not object.

✦ ✦

Somewhat before moonrise, when the dancing and the feasting were in full cry, Agni slipped away from his place in the king's circle.

He put off his festival garments, his beautiful coat, his ornaments of beads and feathers. The torque of gold and amber he kept, because he was seldom without it. He put on riding clothes, plain and meant for use, and plaited his hair tightly behind him. No one was in his tent to help him, not even Taditi. He was completely alone.

But when he came out, blinking in the light of torches, he found Patir and Taditi both, and somewhat to his surprise, the westerner Tillu. And, keeping to the shadows but not carefully enough, the boy Mika.

"I don't think I'm to go in company," Agni said.

"The women did," said Taditi. "There must have been three hands of women on that hill—ruining the sacrifice, if you ask the odd fool."

Agni considered that, and considered forbidding them all to venture past the camp. But Taditi had the right of it. The women had come in force to see the Stallion die. Why should he not attend their rite with his small company? One of whom, he could not help but reflect, was a woman.

He nodded curtly. Taditi did not weaken into an expression, and Tillu's scars did not allow much of one at all, but Patir was biting back a grin. He always had loved to see Agni bested by his aunt.

Agni showed Patir a fine set of teeth, and set his face toward the city and the temple. They followed. He would have been astonished if they had not.

✦ ✦

It was daylight still, the hour between sunset and dark, when the light is too clear almost for earth, when the west is stained with blood but the stars have begun to glimmer in the vault of heaven. Agni walked down silent streets, past closed doors and shuttered windows. The city had shut itself up tight—as if none of its people dared walk abroad for fear of the Lady's wrath.

How very strange to keep a festival by shutting oneself in one's house and hiding from the moon. How like a city of women.

Lights glimmered outside the temple: lamps hung from the beams and set on the steps, shedding a soft glow into the street. They looked from a distance like a fall of stars.

So many beauties here; so many strange things. Agni stepped into the circle of light. The door of the temple was open, an oblong of darkness. He thrust down a stab of fear, the terror of descent into night. There was light inside—there must be.

There was not. It was blind dark and full of whispers. Agni stopped just inside the door, still within reach of the lamps. His following did not even go so far. The edge of his glance caught Mika's face, stark white. How much courage it took a manchild of this country to come here for this purpose, Agni could well imagine.

Agni held his ground just inside the door. His hand had gone to his belt where his knife hung, and clenched tight round the hilt.

The whispers grew louder, imperceptibly, until he realized that he did not have to strain to hear them. There were words in them, a rhythm like a chant. Slowly it swelled. Women's voices, low and sweet. A chittering as of birds. The thin wailing of a pipe. A sound of plucked strings, and the beating of a drum.

As subtly as the silence had lifted, the darkness faded away. Lamps shone within as they shone without. They illumined nothing more mysterious than a room of wooden walls floored with stone. The Lady sat at the end as the Mother sat in her house, squat and holy. There were heaped pots about her, the most beautiful that the potters made, and the first flowers of the spring, and a sower's bag bulging with seed, and other things that Agni could not quite see.

The temple was full of women. They were all masked as they had been in the Lady's wood, that day when he trespassed on their rite. Now, no longer a trespasser, he saw them again in the garb of their goddess, faceless and nameless. Their bodies were painted in black and red and white, a dizzying pattern of spirals round breast and belly and thighs.

They did nothing to allure him, did not move, did not acknowledge his presence. And yet his rod was hard and painful against his belly. His breath came short, his heart beat fast. The air thrummed. They were raising the powers, the same powers that woke the earth in spring. Their bodies were full of it, burgeoning with it.

Women's rite. Women's magic. Small wonder that they had suffered him to see it: no little power of his could weaken this of theirs. Was it mercy, that they forbade their men to enter the temple or share in its rites?

No; the men knew already what weaklings they were.

Agni had not meant the thought to be so bitter. He must remember— must keep in mind the glare of the sunlight, the bright red of blood, the strength of the Stallion as he fought his death. That too was power, as strong in the daylight as was this one under the moon. Two faces. Two powers. Two sides of the world.

The women danced, stately as trees in the wind; dipped, swayed, circled. He remembered that dance from the Lady's grove, though it was smaller here, constrained within walls. It wound its spirals before the goddess' image, round and round, tighter and tighter, till it burst in a flurry of sound: music and voices both.

So they sealed the planting and blessed the harvest that was to come. But as yet they were not done. Each woman whirled alone, spinning in a kind of divine abandon, and none ever touched another, nor collided, nor stumbled into the walls.

One spun from altar to door. Her hand caught Agni as he stood all unwary, caught and held him fast, and spun him with her into the temple itself. The dance bred its own force. He could not stop it. He spun as the stars spun, as the sun wheeled on his daily course. Round and round, and irresistible.

It was Tilia gripping his hands, her body that he knew so well, the feel of her skin, the scent of her, the way she held herself as she danced. They whirled together from end to end of the temple, from side to side and round in a great circle. He was aware, dimly, that the others had stopped; that they had linked hands round the walls and left Agni with Tilia in the middle.

This could not be the common rite. If no man could enter the temple . . .

✦ ✦

"It's the Great Marriage," Tilia said. "It changes everything."

"So it's not a new thing or even very unusual," Agni said.

They had gone from the rite to an astonishing and quite splendid festival. For when the women came out of the temple, the city came alive with light: lamps and torches everywhere, in every street, round about every house. The city was lit almost as if it were day. Its people came out with dancing and singing, with laughter and merrymaking. Dark and quiet shattered as if they had never been.

Agni sat next to Tilia in the garden of the Mother's house, in a blaze of torches, and ate things of marvelous complexity, for which he had no name. But wine he knew, and roast lamb, and bread fresh from the baking, and cakes made with honey. Tilia fed him because it suited her fancy, pressing on him both the strangely delicious and the merely strange.

She explained it, too, after her fashion. "The Great Marriage is rare and wonderful. It gives a man rights and powers that he would never otherwise have. And it makes the rite of the planting stronger, if he dances the dance with the woman whom the Lady has bound to him."

"And what if I hadn't asked to come?" Agni demanded. "What then?"

"We'd have gone on as we always have," she said. "Your presence was a great gift."

"I meant it to be a bargain. A kind of defiance."

"That, too," she said. Her eyes glinted. She was laughing at him.

He was too tired and too mellow with wine to be angry. He spared a snarl, for pride, but no more than that. She dipped a bit of bread in honey and offered it to him. He had to take it or have a lapful of honey. She pursued it with a kiss, sipping honey from his lips.

Here, in front of her kin, her brothers, even her mother. Agni had seldom been so mortified. And she never knew or seemed to notice. Mercifully she drew back, distracted by somewhat or other, some word that one of her sisters spoke. Then Danu came in with the servants, bearing yet another course in this endless feast.

Agni's embarrassment faded a little. No one after all had so much as looked askance. People here were not modest as they were among the tribes. Nor were they shy of touching one another in public. This thing that man and woman did together, they had no shame of it. It was a sacred thing, a rite of their goddess.

Agni was a more modest creature. He could not help it. He kept a little distance, held himself somewhat apart, and Tilia let him be. He doubted that she noticed particularly; she was distracted with some of the children.

Women, he thought. Even women of the tribes could never let men get the better of them. He began to wonder, rather dangerously, whether women kept to the tents of their own will because it pleased them, and not because their men required it. Just as the young women were doing in his own camp: following a fashion, fashion become firm custom, but among themselves they had nothing but mockery for the men who imagined that they ruled the world.

Bitter thoughts again; women's magic, twisting his perceptions. He hoped that the Sacrifice had unbalanced the women as badly as they had unbalanced him. Somehow he doubted it.

Tilia did not even give him the satisfaction of conquering her in their bed. It was full of children doing things that no child among the tribes would dare to do, and laughing while they did it; when they were caught, they only laughed the harder. Agni turned away from them in disgust. His tent was safe—was sanctuary, deep among his own people. He was so dismayed, and so shaken, that he did not notice till he was in the tent, that Tilia had not followed him. For all he knew, she had leaped into bed with the children, and joined in the revelry.

Agni lay alone in the chill of the late night. His body was cold, but his temper warmed him. He had not been ill advised to go to the temple. He told himself that, sternly. But it had done strange things to him, had made him see in ways that were not comfortable. Not in the least.

Here was peace. Here was the world as he had always known it, walled in leather, with the smell and sound of horses close by. This was his world. Not that other. He might rule it, he might name himself king of it, but he was no true part of it. Nor, here in the dark, did he believe that he ever could be.

·············· 82 ··············

Patir left on the morning after the Stallion's sacrifice. He took with him a dozen young men of the White Horse, strong horsemen all and intrepid raiders. They would bring back mares for Agni—"Safe, sound, and in foal," Patir promised.

They took with them the memory of an omen. In the night, while Agni nursed his bitterness and Tilia did whatever Tilia did, the Mare had foaled of a filly. Then, to everyone's profound astonishment—even Sarama's—of a colt. Twins were rarer by far among horses than among men, and twins that were born alive, that lived and thrived, were rarer yet. These were small but they were strong, and stood and nursed as quickly almost as if each had been born alone.

That was a great portent, a gift of the gods. It heartened Patir and his men enormously. It roused the spirits of the camp, that had been dampened by the Stallion's resistance to his sacrifice. War, and fruitful herds—those were joyful omens to a tribesman.

Agni saw Patir off and lingered on the camp's edge, watching the riders dwindle into distance and vanish over the long hill to the eastward. Then for a while longer he stood there. He had a whole mingled tribe at his back, and some of the elders close by, and Tillu, who was, when it came to it, a friend, but his brother in spirit, the friend of his youth, was gone; gone to hunt mares as they both had gone in search of stallions. And Agni must stay behind, must strengthen the defenses in this country, and prepare it to face the war that the gods had promised.

It was a great charge. And Agni would have given it all to be riding with Patir, back to the steppe. Back home.

This was home. He stiffened his back, turned on his heel and walked firmly away from the eastward road. That was his no longer. He had made his choice. He was bound here. He would live and die here.

That was the omen he saw in the Mare's foals. He sought them out, and found them in a sheltered valley. Sarama was with them, and Danu, and somewhat to Agni's surprise, Tilia. The Mare grazed as placidly as Agni had ever seen her, while her offspring discovered the delights of the world.

The filly would be grey, Agni thought; she had the signs, a salting of white about the eyes. But the colt might not. And they were both duns, as far as one could tell: striped backs, mouse-colored coats, manes that might be black when they were older.

Agni caught Sarama eyeing Danu's young stallion balefully. She could hardly have failed to know who had sired these foals. At the time when the Mare could have been bred, there was only the colt in all this country. But knowing and seeing were different things.

"They're fine foals," Agni said, and not simply because he felt compelled to defend the colt. They were indeed, as their father was. Maybe he was not goddess-born, and maybe his mother had been a mere traveler's mount, but he was well made and strong. If a tribesman had come back from his hunt with such a stallion, he would have been reckoned fortunate.

All of which Sarama knew perfectly well, but she had never been a reasonable creature. She was rather proud of it, too, as a woman could be: ever contrary. Such unreason let her dote openly on the offspring while glaring at the sire. "After all," she said, "they're their mother's children."

"Indeed," Agni said gravely.

She knew he was mocking her: her glance was burning cold. But she did not choose to go to war with him. He was glad. There was war enough coming, without his being at daggers drawn with his own sister.

✦ ✦

The year began with rites and omens. It went on in a kind of clenched-teeth quiet. Those tribesmen who had yearned to go home were gone. The rest stayed, which was well; there was much to do. Agni had consulted with his elders and with the Mother and elders of Three Birds, and from those councils he came to a greater one, a gathering of Mothers from the towns and cities as far eastward as Larchwood itself. The Mother of Larchwood was gone, vanished into the west, but Mothers who had looked to her looked now to the Mother of Three Birds and, inevitably, to the king of the horsemen.

Agni told them what he, and they, would do. They would make their cities strong. They would dig moats such as Sarama had dug here, made deadly to horse and horseman. Most would line the pits with sharpened stakes. One or two, suitably situated, could divert streams into the moat, and build a wall of water between themselves and the war.

No one argued with him, or rebuked him for presumption. All those who might have done that were gone, fled out of reach of the horsemen. And so they would be, as long as Agni and his people stood in the way.

After they had taken counsel together in the Lady's grove, they gathered in the field between the camp and the city for a festival of welcome. There had been a great number of festivals in Three Birds that year. Agni never ceased to marvel at the ease with which this country gave of its bounty. Even in the depths of winter, when times were as lean as they ever were, no one was hungry. No one suffered.

Now as summer swelled about them, even the camp dogs were fat, lolling in the sun. Agni had had to command his men to practice their riding and shooting and fighting, to send them on hunts and drive them like cattle, to keep them from becoming as lazy as the dogs.

Today however was a feast-day. People of the city and men of the camp had joined forces to welcome the Mothers to Three Birds. It was rather wonderful to see them together, managing to understand one another, and working in amity as far as Agni could see.

His black horsehide, new with the spring, was spread in the shade of a tall tree. He would go to it in time, but for a little while he was minded to wander about while the guests found their places and settled in comfort. The Mothers took little enough notice of him when he was not sitting in front of them. He did not think they meant any rudeness. He was a man. He was of little account beyond his narrow sphere.

Time was when that would have angered him terribly. Now he was merely amused. They need only notice him when it served his purpose. If they chose to keep their arrogance else, then so they might.

It was a peculiar kind of kingship, but it had made him lord of this country. He held the reins of it even as he wandered with seeming idleness, listening, speaking if he was spoken to, testing the temper of this gathering.

Traders, seeing an opportunity for rich trade, had left their stalls in the market and their boats on the river, and set up shop in a corner near the Mothers' gathering. They would never have dared do such a thing in a festival of the Lady, but there was nothing sacred here; only the saving of the people from the war that was coming.

Agni circled round them toward the eastward end of the camp. A stranger had caught his eye, a face he had not seen before. This was neither a trader nor the member of a Mother's following. She had the look of one who had traveled far, much worn and somewhat strained about the eyes. Agni saw nothing extraordinary about her, dark-haired and dark-eyed creature that she was, except that she was thin, as women here took great pains not to be, and except for her eyes. They lifted to him as he approached, and he nearly missed his step.

There were gods in her. Great powers stared out of her eyes, piercing him where he stood. She was so full of them that there was nothing of the simple self left; till she blinked and swayed and looked at him as a woman might, especially in this country. She liked what she saw—before she remembered to think of him as an enemy.

"You," she said. "Who are you?"

"Agni," he answered. It was the first thing that came into his head.

"So you understand me," she said.

"A little," he said.

People came and went around them. They all recognized Agni, or seemed to, but none was minded to call on him as one calls on a king. It was a reprieve of sorts. He was not often given this gift, to be a man like any other.

This woman honestly did not know who he was. After all, how could she? He boasted no more splendor than many a tribesman, except for the gold about his neck.

As if the thought had touched her, she stretched out her hand and brushed the torque with a finger. "This is fine work. Did you steal it? Or conquer it?"

"It was given to me," he said.

"In payment for what?"

"I think you know," he said.

Her lips tightened. "It all comes to that. We trade gold for our cities' safety. You take what your whim bids you take, and nothing stops you."

"That is changing," Agni said.

"Yes," she said. "The conqueror must hold what he's conquered. He'll defend it against the ones who come after. But still it was ours before it was his."

"You do hate us," he said, "don't you?"

"No," she said, and she did not say it altogether willingly. "You are the burden the Lady has laid on us. We suffer you. We don't love you."

"I suppose," he said, "that is reasonable."

"Catin!"

She stiffened at the sound of the name. Agni half spun. He had never been so glad to see Danu before.

Danu greeted Agni with a glance and a tilt of the head, but his eyes were on the woman called Catin. "What brings you back?" he asked her.

She shrugged, lifted her hand, managed with the gesture to take in the whole of it, city and camp and the festival between. "One hears," she said, "of what is happening in the eastern cities."

"Such as yours?"

Agni had never heard Danu sound quite so cold before. Danu was a warm man, even with Agni, whom he had no reason to like.

Catin kept her head up, but to Agni's eye she seemed to shrink a little. "We do what we must. Larchwood is safe. Isn't it?"

"Yes," Danu said. "Because the horsemen protect it."

"So I've heard." She flicked a glance at Agni. "Its Mother is dead."

Danu's bent his head. "May the Lady keep her," he said.

"She was not supposed to die," Catin said fiercely. "She was supposed to stand fast, to be patient, till the horsemen had tired of their game and gone away."

"The horsemen are not going to tire of their game," Danu said. He paused. Catin said nothing. He said, "Then you are—"

"No," she said.

"No? But—"

"There is no Mother in Larchwood," she said, "nor will be hereafter. Larchwood belongs to the horsemen."

"You gave it up," Danu said.

"We were afraid," said Catin.

Danu greeted that with silence. It was a perfectly expressionless silence, and yet it said everything that it needed to say.

"It's not your place to judge," she said.

"No," he said. "It's not."

She laughed, a sound utterly without mirth, and turned and walked away.

Agni stood with Danu where she had left them. After a suitable while he said, "She's mad."

Danu nodded. He was as calm as ever, but Agni thought he saw a flicker of pain. "Your sister says," said Danu, "that gods speak through her. Too many gods, all clamoring at once. They eat away at her spirit."

"Yes," said Agni. "I saw."

"You—" Danu shook his head. "I always forget. You're of that blood, too."

"What, I see too far? Or not far enough?"

"You see what Sarama sees," Danu said. "You hear the Lady—and your gods, too. But it hasn't broken your spirit."

Agni shrugged uncomfortably. "They speak to me. Not through me."

"Yes," said Danu as if Agni had spoken a revelation. "Yes, that's the way of it. You are like a Mother. She—she wasn't strong enough. She was always so much afraid."

"Of what? The gods?"

"The dreams," Danu said. "We all dreamed, you see. Blood and fire. Dreams that we learned to call war."

Agni looked at him. The dreams he knew of, and the portents of war. But he had not understood, not quite, what they might mean to one who had never known that men could kill men, or find glory in it. A person—a woman—might break under the force of it.

All about them people laughed, danced, sang. If any of them was afraid, if any of them dreamed terror, there was no memory of it now, or none that any would admit. They saw the sunlight, and turned their minds away from the dark.

Agni could will to do that. And so he would, in a little while. But as he stood with Danu, with the man who in the way of the tribes was to be thought of as his brother, he looked the dark full in the face. It held no fear for him. War was glory; blood was sacrifice. And if he died in war, the gods took him to themselves and raised him up, and made him a great lord among the dead.

He did not think that Danu would understand any of this. Yet Danu was not afraid, either. No one in Three Birds seemed to be. For most it was innocence. For Danu, the only word that came easily to Agni's mind was courage.

"Should I let her wander loose?" Agni asked, speaking of Catin. "She'll spread fear."

"A little fear is not an ill thing," Danu said.

Particularly, Agni thought, among these rampant innocents. He bent his head to Danu's wisdom. Danu smiled, saluted Agni as a tribesman might— with insouciance that could only be deliberate—and left Agni to make his way back to the circle of elders.

83

One early morning near the end of summer, Sarama went hunting with some of the women who had learned to ride and shoot. She left her bed a little reluctantly, with Danu in it, and Rani well sated with nursing. Sarama's breasts would ache again before she came back, but Rani would do well enough. One of the women would feed her with her own, Danu's sister Mareka perhaps. Mareka had milk enough for six.

The Mare, fortunate creature, had weaned her twins some time ago. She had not forgotten them, but they were her charge no longer. They ran with the other young ones, the half-dozen who had been born in the camp that spring— improvident men, not to bring a herd of mares with all their vaunting stallions.

The Mare was free of herself and her charge, restless, eager to run. Sarama held her in for the moment. Even so, the others had fallen behind, all but Taditi, who could ride as well as any tribesman. Practice, she had said when Sarama asked, and defiance. She had been an infamous hoyden in her youth.

"Was that why no one married you?" Sarama had asked her—months ago now.

Taditi had laughed with honest mirth. "Oh, no! You'd have thought so, wouldn't you? But they were all after me. I was the king's daughter, after all. And I was interesting. I turned them all away. I had no desire to belong to a man."

"I . . . am sorry I never took the trouble to know you," Sarama had said.

"Ah," said Taditi, waving away guilt. "You couldn't have known. I was of no account, an elderly aunt in the king's tent."

"You raised my brother."

"But not you." Taditi slapped her lightly. "Stop that. It's no good wallowing in it."

Nor was it, Sarama thought as they rode side by side in the rising morning. She had not known Taditi then, but she knew her now, and had come to admire her. She was like the Old Woman; like the Mother of Three Birds. Strong.

✦ ✦

They hunted eastward, where the best game was, in the hunting runs near the new-walled town called Thorn. Here in a tumbled country of hill and wood, too rough and stony for farming, deer and boar and wild cattle roamed the copses and coverts, and birds flocked thick about a marshy lake. They were hunting birds, as the best practice for the archers, and bringing down a fair number, too.

At noon they paused to rest. Some had brought somewhat to eat, bread and fruit and cheese, or hard-baked cakes that people made for long journeys. A few seized the time to snatch a little sleep.

Taditi had set guards because in war such would be needed. Nothing more dangerous than a boar was likely to come on them here; but it was wise, she said, to make a habit of being wary.

Sarama was not one of those set on guard, but she was restless. She had been pent up in the city for much too long.

Her breasts were aching. The Mother had shown her how to press out the milk, and she had done that once already since the morning. She would do it again before they went on with the hunt. But for the moment the ache was tolerable. It reminded her of her daughter, the warm milky scent of her, the way she caught at the nipple when it was given her, tugging hard, a pleasure that was just short of pain. Sarama wanted her suddenly, fiercely, with an intensity that took her aback. Yes, a mother loved her child—but Sarama had never known how powerful that love was.

She walked the edges of the circle that they had made. It was not a camp, it was too brief, but it had shape and purpose. The women set on guard were out of sight: practicing their scouting, Sarama supposed. She hoped that they were not practicing their sleeping. Even after so long and under Taditi's firm hand, the young women of Three Birds did not take easily to the arts of war. They were inclined to forget such minor things as staying awake while on guard.

Sarama was tired, a little, but not enough to trouble her. It was a fine day, cool for the season, sweet still with scents from the rain that had fallen the day before. The sky was clear, with a scud of clouds; a light wind blew, just enough to cool her cheeks. If she climbed to the top of the hill to the northward, she would see the town in its raw new palisade. But from here the world seemed empty of cities.

She sat on a stone and turned her face eastward. She could not see the wood; the land was too tumbled and rose too steep between. But she knew it was there.

She did not think about it often. Nothing about it had pleased her more than leaving it. And yet if the tribes would come, they would come through the wood. By now they would hardly need guides; the path through it was a beaten road. It would be a road in truth before they were done. Trees would fall, the sky open overhead, and tribes come through in a long relentless stream.

As if her half-dream had shaped itself into flesh, a mounted company rode over the eastward hill. Sarama watched without alarm. So: had Agni sent some of his men hunting, too? That would be like him, to guard his sister by means of a training exercise.

They must have left earlier than Sarama's company had, to be coming back westward already. Or maybe they had overshot their charges. They halted on the hillside as if they had just seen the gathering of women and horses. She did not recognize any of them, or their horses either; but they were rather far away still.

Habit older than her time in the Lady's country had brought her feet under her and tensed her body as if for a fight. Her hands had sought her bow and strung it.

No, she did not recognize these men who, having surveyed the camp, had begun to ride forward again. They had the look of a raiding party, young rakehells with an air of ragged insouciance. Their clothes were much worn, their horses lean and ribby. They were, she realized with a shock, in quite ordinary condition for riders on the steppe. She had grown used to fine coats, woven cloth, and horses fat with rich fodder.

Had she been as ragtag and filthy as these men were? The wind was blowing from the east, bringing with it a powerful reek of unwashed bodies.

Gods; she had grown soft.

It had not dawned on these strangers yet, perhaps, that these were women. As they came within earshot, the man in the lead raised a shout, a cry of welcome. Sarama rose in response and waved her arms. Then she called the Mare, and called to the women behind her: "Strangers! On guard!"

It was gratifying to see how quickly the circle of idlers became an armed company. No one wasted time fetching the horses. Bows strung, spears at the ready, they faced the strangers from behind a wall of weapons.

Sarama stayed where she was. Her bow was strung, an arrow in her hand, but she had not yet nocked it to the string. She was not afraid. On the steppe, alone, she would have been. But with a company of armed women behind her and the Mare at her side, she had no fear of anything that these men could do.

They came on carefully, as strangers would on the steppe, riding with hands well away from weapons. She watched it dawn on them that she and all her companions were women. It spoke well for them that no one broke ranks to try a little rapine. They were sensible, it seemed. Or the sight of so many weapons made them so.

"It's true, then," she heard one of them say, the one just behind the leader. "This is a country of women."

"Women who fight," said a man nearby him. "That's not in any tale we heard."

"Ah," said the first. "Well. Tales can twist the truth."

Sarama smiled. "A fair day and a fine welcome," she said, "and what brings you to this part of the world?"

The riders halted well within bowshot but out of reach of a thrown spear. Their leader came on, alone but for the two who had spoken. They reminded Sarama rather poignantly of Agni as he had been in the tribe, with Patir and Rahim always at his back.

These were not such princely men as that; in fact they seemed rather callow. But they had courage. They stopped in front of her. Their stallions were greatly interested in the Mare, but she pinned her ears and warned them off. She was in foal again and taking no nonsense from any male.

"My name is Buran," the leader said, "and I come from the Tall Grass people."

"And I am Sarama," she said, "and I am Horse Goddess' servant."

Ah: they had heard of her. Jaws dropped. Heads bent. Buran the leader sprang from his horse and knelt at her feet as if she had been a king or a goddess. "Lady! The gods are kind. And can you tell us where we may find the king of the sunset country?"

"What, Agni?" She had not heard that name given him before, but for a certainty there was only one man in this country who called himself a king.

"Yes," Buran said. "The sunset king."

She considered the hunt, the hour, her freedom. She sighed a little. She said, "I can take you to him."

Such innocents they were, and so easily delighted. They cheered as if they had won a battle. Which maybe they had. The wood was behind them, this country before them, and not one among them could know the language of the Lady's people—and they had ridden straight to Sarama.

Not everyone was minded to return to the hunt, now that there were strangers to look warlike in front of. Sarama returned to Three Birds with ample escort of women as well as men—because, said Kina, who was as fierce as anyone ever was among the Lady's people, raw boys fresh off the steppe might forget themselves. They had no discipline, after all, and Sarama was too evidently a woman.

Sarama could see no profit in correcting the child. She was glad enough of the company, and pleased too, because it showed the beginnings of warlike caution.

Not that these boys were likely to venture anything impertinent. They were too utterly in awe of everything and everyone they saw. They had ridden into a legend, and they were nigh overcome by the wonder of it.

"So they're telling stories about us on the steppe?" Sarama asked Buran.

He nodded, eyes wide. "Oh, yes, lady. Wonderful stories. Is it true that the women all want men, all the time? And that bread grows on trees?"

"They know how to make the grain grow," Sarama said, "so that they have bread whenever they want it. As for the women . . . warn your men. The women are willing, yes, but if a woman says no, no is what she means. And the penalty for rape is death."

Buran swallowed visibly. "We . . . heard that the king killed his own brother for taking a woman that he'd won in battle. So that's true?"

"True enough," Sarama said. "Watch well. And bid your men take care. This is a land of riches, but it has its laws. Any who breaks them must pay the penalty."

Not only Buran had heard. The others were listening. She hoped they were heeding it. Agni would not thank her for bringing in trouble. And trouble it would be, if these strangers did not keep discipline.

They were only the beginning. "More will come," Buran said, "some from far away. The winter was hard, and there's been little rain this summer. The rivers run low. There was wildfire in Stormwolf country, and a plague among the cattle of the Golden Aurochs. The gods have cursed the steppe, it's said. They're driving the people westward."

"It's something in the sunrise country," one of the others said. "Something's driving tribes into the west. Drought, it's said. Plague. It gets worse the farther eastward you go."

"The gods want us to come here," said Buran. "This is the country that they've made for us."

Sarama refrained from comment. She could not help reflecting that if tribe after tribe came westward, there would be no room for all of them. They would heap like waves, rise up and crash down and shatter everything in their path.

She had seen the floods in the spring, when the rivers broke their bonds of ice: great walls of water and flotsam, roaring with terrible force. As often as not they overflowed their banks and spread out onto the steppe. The unwary could drown, their tents and camps swept away. That was the gods' power, too. And far too much like what she saw in this one young man with his wide eyes and his head full of legends.

One did what one could. If one could. One moved away from the water, raised a wall against it if there was time, fought it as one could, and prayed that that would be enough.

·············· 84 ··············

It had been a rich summer, not the richest that anyone could remember, but rich enough that no one had any great fears of feeding herself through the winter. Even with the trickle of tribesmen coming in search of the sunset king, there was grain enough in the storehouses. The cattle were fat, the goats and sheep plentiful, and a great store of fodder laid in with the harvest.

Nevertheless the omens were bad. Birds flocked early, gathered and flew—fled, some thought—into the south. The people brought in the harvest just ahead of a great storm. Even the tribesmen were pressed into service, grumbling and snarling about grubbing in the dirt, but Agni flogged them on with words and mockery—the same words and the same mockery with which Sarama, and then Taditi, had prevailed on him to command his proud horsemen to turn farmer. The last baskets of threshed emmer wheat went into the storehouse amid a spatter of cold rain.

The harvest festival was a wet and foreshortened thing. The women held the full rite in the temple, but the dancing and feasting were all washed away in the rain.

Agni had threatened to do his sulking in his tent, and nurse the blisters, too, from wielding a sickle day and night. Tilia was hardly surprised to find him in their room in the Mother's house, the room behind the kitchen that though tiny, airless, and ghastly hot in the summer, was undisputably their own.

It was pleasant tonight, with the lamps lit and fresh coverlets on the bed, and warmth from the kitchen fire driving away the rain's damp. Agni had even managed to wash himself somehow, probably by standing in the rain. He would have been terribly angry if she had remarked on it, but he had become a fastidious man.

She had shaken rain from her mantle already when she entered the house, but still it dripped on the floor. She spread it over the chest that took up all of the room that was not filled with bed, and laughed at his expression. He never grew accustomed to the Lady's garment, the skirt that marked a woman—and marked her very well, too. Sometimes she liked to take him while she wore it, and laugh at his mingled shock and excitement. He was very shy when it came to women.

Tonight she unwound the skirt, which was as wet as her mantle, and spread it to dry, and leaped into the bed's warmth. He yowled. "*Ai!* Woman, you're *freezing!*"

Brilliant observation; she was shivering convulsively, and her teeth were chattering. She clung tightly. After his first yelp of outrage, he remembered what a bold brave tribesman he was, and clasped her close, rubbing warmth into her body. In a little while, not only his hands performed the office. She rocked with him, not too slowly, not too quickly; an easy rhythm, like one of his horses in the gait that he called canter.

Someday maybe she would ride one. Others of the women were making a great fashion of it. It was better, Tilia allowed, than that other fashion, to play at being women of the tribes, complete with meek submission and confinement to the tents. Though not much better. Riding was part of fighting; of learning the ways of war.

She shut her mind away from that, and let her body be her world. The Lady's gift swelled slowly. She prolonged it as much as she might, because while it went on she need not think. But he was only a man, and his strength had its limits. She took the last of the gift just as his breath caught. Her whoop of glee covered any sound he might have made, but he was never a noisy lover. He had learned to be silent. It was a necessity in a tent, she supposed, with the walls so thin and everyone living on top of one another.

He slept soon after, which to his credit he did not often do. Tilia was content to lie warm beside him, with her body thrumming still, and his breathing soft in her ear. Her hand had come to rest over her belly. The Mother had said—a woman could know. Tilia never had, though she had conceived before, and lost the child before it was real enough to do more than interrupt her courses.

This time she knew. Deep inside her, the seed was taking root. She shaped a prayer to the Lady, a prayer without words. It was pure will. *Let this one live. Let it be born. Let it grow up and grow strong.*

✦ ✦

Tilia was happy therefore, a happiness too deep to speak of, while the rain fell and the river rose—unheard of in this season—and the fields turned to mud and the roads to mire, and tempers shortened to snapping. Then came the sun, but with it the cold. Water turned to ice, mud to something remarkably like stone.

The trickle of tribesmen had slowed and then stopped. Then on the wings of a new storm, a storm that blackened the whole of the northern horizon, came a new and very great riding. Men, two dozen and more. And horses.

Horses in hundreds: mares, foals, a stallion or two that would not be left behind.

Patir who had gone out from the Lady's country in the spring—Patir had come back, bringing with him the mares that he had promised. There were more than Agni had dared to hope, more maybe than the land could support. But he would find a way. There were cities enough, and there would be fodder enough, particularly if he sent the horses to winter pastures.

As he watched them come in under a lowering sky, he was aware that another watched with him. Sarama had ridden out of the city, and come to see the arrival that had been so long awaited. Just as Agni turned to greet her, the Mare's head flew up. She loosed a peal that drowned any sound he might have uttered.

And an echo came back, manifold. Among the oncoming herds, one band of mares had held itself somewhat apart. Agni was not aware of it until his eye was drawn to it.

His breath caught. They were all greys, from very young and nearly black, to snow-white with age. They were not so greatly different from the rest in shape or size, and yet there was a fineness to them, a clarity of line that one found only in the best of horses.

The Mare's kin had come into the west of the world. They had left the Goddess' hill, perhaps for all of time, and come to their sister, and to their sister's servant.

"How in the world—?" Agni wondered aloud.

"Not for him," Sarama said, tilting her head at Patir where he oversaw the drovers. "For Horse Goddess. And for her." She stroked the Mare's neck, smoothing the long smoke-grey mane.

The Mare ignored her. She was fixed, intent on her sisters and aunts and cousins. She tossed her head, and snorted lightly. "Yes," Sarama said in the tone she reserved for the Mare and maybe—though Agni rather doubted it—for Danu when they were alone together, "yes, beloved."

The Mare sprang into a gallop, with Sarama clinging, laughing, to her neck. Agni watched them go, and watched the reunion, the mares calling to the Mare, and the Mare running, mane and tail streaming, to be reunited with her kin.

When they were all gone, the mares and the Mare lost among the herds again, Agni drew a faint sigh. He had given no thought at all to the Mare's people, no more than any horseman did; they were no thing of man or of men's concerns. But to have them here, in this country that he had taken, was a blessing, and a great one. Horse Goddess had sent her own children to swell his herds. Maybe, after all, she had some care for him, for the younger born, the mere and unregarded male.

He laughed shortly. No, of course not. The herd had come for the Mare, as Sarama had said. It had never come for him, nor for any of his doing.

Still it was a great thing, and he was glad of it. It rounded out the world. It made his conquest complete.

✦ ✦

For this day and for the days after, however long the storm lasted, Agni saw the mares settled in Three Birds' own winter pasture, in the sheltered valley with its stream that ran too swift to freeze, and its grass that grew all winter long, green beneath the snow. Agni rode back with the others who had ridden to help, in the teeth of a gale. By the time he came to his tent, it had begun to snow.

Taditi was looking after Patir, feeding him from the pot and plying him with wine. She had always been fond of Patir. He was wrapped in one of Agni's coats, with Agni's bearskin over it.

He grinned as Agni ducked into the tent. His grin seemed enormous, too large for his face. He was thinned to the bone. There were new scars on his arms, knife-cuts from the look of them, and more probably where coat and mantle covered him. He walked with a hitch in his step. But it was a jaunty gait nonetheless. He was greatly pleased with himself.

"Hard battles?" Agni asked him.

He shrugged. "A few. Most seemed glad to have fewer mouths to feed."

"Is it bad?"

Patir's face sobered. "Not—as bad as it could be. But close. Last winter was cruel. The spring rains didn't come. Then it was a dry summer. There was a fire on the steppe—you heard of that?"

Agni nodded.

"Well," said Patir. "So you know the most of it. All portents are for a winter worse than the last one. People are dreaming of the west. They call you the sunset king, and some are starting to talk as if you're a god."

"I've gathered that," Agni said. "We've had our own invasion, boys from the tribes, looking for legends. I disappoint them, I think. I'm too young. And I don't tower up to heaven."

Behind them, where she was putting together their dinner, Taditi snorted. "That's not what I'm hearing. They'll make a hero-god out of anyone. And you do have the same air that horse of yours does: you know how pretty you are. Young males are remarkably easily swayed by such things."

Patir laughed at Agni's expression. "See! And I believe her, too."

"The more fool you," muttered Agni.

He was glad for the reprieve of dinner. Patir fell to it with singleminded determination. He had not, he professed between the bread and the venison, eaten so well since he left Three Birds in the spring. Agni wondered if he had eaten much at all. A man could live on mares' milk and bootleather, but he was hardly likely to thrive on it.

Agni, well-fleshed and comfortable, dressed in the rich weavings of this country and ornamented with gold, began to feel soft, as he had not felt in a while. He would eat less, he promised himself, and spend more time in the practice-field, even when the weather was dismal. War did not wait upon clear skies and gentle sunlight. A wise chieftain waged it in snow and in bitter rain, when the enemy was most off guard.

Not that there would be any riding or fighting tonight. A wind had come up with the evening, tugging at the tent's walls, making them billow and sway. The storm was on them.

✦ ✦

It raged for three days. The tents held against it, most of them; those that did not were old or worn or ill secured. In the city the houses stood fast, but one of the storehouses, and one of the largest at that, had the mishap to stand in the shade of a tree. Under the weight of wind and snow, the tree shattered, and took the storehouse with it—and a great store of grain and fodder, fruits and wine and provender laid by against the winter.

It was not a terrible disaster, but it promised a leaner season than they had hoped for, with so many people in city and camp. They salvaged what they could, once they could make their way through the snow. It heaped and drifted to the rafters of the houses, covered over the tents and would have taken them down had not the tribesmen or the women who lived with them labored to keep the tent-roofs clear.

And that was only the first storm of the winter. None thereafter was quite so long or so fierce, but they came hard on one another, storm after storm, with seldom a respite between. The flocks and herds began to suffer. Not only the herdsmen made camp in the winter pastures, but such of the peo-ple—tribesmen as well as people of the city—who had the will or the skill to look after the animals.

After the storms came cold so fierce that it snapped trees in two and turned even the swiftest-running streams to ice. Beasts of the wild and birds froze where they slept. Then followed a thaw, which would have been a great relief, except that it brought with it a wave of sickness. What snow and cold had been unable to do, the sickness did: it laid low both man and beast. Some died, though not as many as might have died on the steppe. The healers were strong here, and their art greater than it was among the tribes. Their herbs and simples, their potions and prayers, did what good any mortal rem-edies could. And yet there was death, in the city, in the camp, and in the pastures among the herds.

It was a cruel winter, the most cruel in memory. And when the spring came, warm with sweetness, came also the first new travelers from the tribes; and they brought the word that been so long awaited.

War. The tribes were gathering. The steppe had killed the weak and con-vinced the strong. Their way was westward. Their fate was to conquer, to overrun the Lady's country and take it for their own.

Just so had the gods spoken to Agni, and just so had he done. But now he was king in the Lady's country, and it had, inevitably, become his own. He was the one whom the tribes would conquer. He was the focus of their war.

He was ready, as ready as he could ever be. Now he must wait, and hold fast, and pray to his own gods and to the goddess of these people, that he would have the victory.

II

WAR

CATIN HAD COME and gone from Three Birds throughout all of that year, even into the winter, when no one else was mad enough to venture the roads. She even came, once, walking on the snow-laden ice of the river, stayed for a day or two, left again without a word. The tribes knew her like, as did the cities: one of the Lady's children, wandering and mad. People listened to her ramblings, because they were holy, and some were omens. Many were not; but that was the task and challenge, to tell which was which.

When she was in Three Birds, she liked to ride with the women who were meant to be fighters. She would not take up a weapon. "That's not for me," she said. But she rode as well as a tribesman—even Taditi admitted as much. She had a way with horses; she could speak to them and they would seem to listen. Even the Mare had some little use for her, for whom all the world but Sarama was an endless nuisance.

In the spring after that grim winter, when the snow still lurked in the hollows but the grass had begun to grow green, Catin came back to Three Birds. The first anyone saw of her was on the back of a mare who had lost her foal in the winter. The mare had recovered well enough, but had been much cast down. Now, under Catin, she arched her neck and danced a little, and taunted the stallions.

One of those stallions was Danu's colt, or so people persisted in calling him. He was well grown now, somewhat gawky still but solid and strong. The winter had not troubled him enough to notice, though he was ribby as they all were, men as well as beasts. He was not as tall as Agni's Mitani, but he promised to be somewhat larger, with his deep chest and his broad hind-quarters.

Sarama had informed Danu that it was time. The colt was ready to be ridden, and Danu would ride him. Danu had too ingrained a habit of obe-dience. He tried to argue, to protest that he was no fit rider for a horse so young, but Sarama overrode him. "He is your stallion. You will ride him. If you fall, we'll be there to catch you."

Danu was not afraid of falling. He was afraid of ruining an innocent. But Sarama would never understand that. She had grown up in a world full of horses. She could not imagine what it was like to have discovered the beasts when one was already grown, and to have learned to ride after one's bones and muscles were fully formed. All the things that she did without thinking, that were honed to instinct, he had to remember, one by one. If he forgot one, it might be the most important, the crucial thing that, undone, would destroy the rest.

But Sarama would not hear of his refusing. "He's your stallion," she said. "It's your duty to ride him."

Therefore he was standing in the field, in the new green grass, and eyeing the colt. The colt, who was now a young stallion, had been taking liberties with the mares, and had the scars to show for it. He approached Danu with his head up and his ears back, with intent that was clear to read. If he could not win a mare with his charming manners, he would overwhelm a man with his strength.

Danu faced him down. He was a brave spirit, but not brave enough to tempt fortune. He lowered his head, with a snake and snap to see if after all he might still win; but Danu was ready for him. He backed down swiftly then, and yielded to the inevitable.

Sarama was grinning. So was her brother, whom Danu had not heard coming, and a gathering of people from both city and tribes. By the Lady; did they think this was a festival?

He could walk away. But if he did that, he would only have it to face again. He straightened his shoulders resolutely and made himself think only and wholly of the colt. The colt never took much notice of people apart from Danu and, on occasion, Sarama.

Once Danu had begun, it grew easier. The bridle with its bit of leather and bone, the saddle-fleece, were familiar; the colt had worn them both before. Sarama was there to hold the bridle. And there was that broad back, and the colt standing still, waiting. He knew what he was doing. He was wondering, from the tilt of his ears, what was taking Danu so long.

Danu took a deep breath, grasped mane, and mounted. The colt staggered a little; Danu was not a small man. But the colt steadied. He even, after a pause, essayed a step, then two. And thus, with remarkable ease and no fuss, he carried a rider.

Danu's cheeks ached. He was, he discovered, grinning like a fool.

And Sarama was smiling. "You see?" she said.

✦ ✦

Just as Danu was ending his first ride on his own stallion—and being applauded for it, too, by tribesmen who had much to say of a man becoming a man at last—Catin appeared, bareback on the mouse-colored mare. The colt was full of himself, strutting before the rest, because he was, at last, a man's own stallion. The arrival of a mare raised his tail over his back and set him to trumpeting.

When he had loosed the last peal, Catin lowered her hands from her ears. "That's well," she said as if they had all been conversing for some little while. "You'll need him when you fight the men from the steppe."

She was talking to Danu. He saw the gods crowding in her eyes. Because of that, and because, as Sarama too often said, he was much too polite a creature, he did not roar out in protest. He said mildly, "I have no intention of fighting any man, horseman or otherwise."

"And yet you will," said Catin. She turned those eyes on Agni. "And you, my king. You will fail when the horsemen come. Unless you learn to think like a woman."

"And how is that?" asked Agni with remarkable aplomb.

"If you need to ask, you need badly to know." She clapped heels to the mare's sides. The mare wheeled and leaped into a gallop.

There was an enormous silence. Agni drew a deep breath and let it out slowly. Then he said, "Well, brother. If I do your fighting for you, will you do my thinking for me?"

Danu met those eyes that were, at the moment, so much like a lion's. Agni was jesting, but Danu had no mirth in him. "You should ask that of Tilia," he said. "Or of your sister."

"Or Catin?" Agni was not to be quelled by such a dullard as Danu was. He wheeled about, as full of strut as a stallion, and said to all of those who watched and listened, "Ah! But you see, we don't know *which* god is speaking through her."

"It's all of them," Danu said. "At once."

"Then no wonder she's mad." Agni vaulted onto his stallion's back. Mitani was not at all reluctant to show them his paces.

Danu watched. He had grown past envy, which pleased him rather. He could take in the pure pleasure of it, the man and the horse moving together like one being. Danu would never be so splendid on a horse. He had come too late to it.

And yet he had won his stallion. He would take his man next, he supposed, and be a perfect mockery of a tribesman.

✦ ✦

He did not plan it or even want it, but he rode back to the city with Agni, he on the gelding that he had been riding for so long—and his colt was not pleased with that, either. But however proud of himself the horse might be, he was very young still, and his back was weak.

"He'll grow," Agni said, "and be strong. You have a horseman's wisdom, you know."

"Almost as if I'd been born to it?"

Agni slanted a glance at Danu. "I'm not making fun of you."

"No," said Danu. "It is the truth, isn't it? And yet our children will grow up knowing both the Lady of the Birds and the Lady of Horses."

"And thinking like women?"

"That troubles you, doesn't it?"

Agni did not try to deny it. "Some say I already do. If I didn't, I'd have taken this country with fire and sword, and never tried to speak its language or marry one of its women."

"There's more to it than that," Danu said.

"I'm sure," said Agni. They had mounted the long hill that looked down on the city. He paused there, and Danu paused with him.

"Look," Agni said. "What do you see?"

"Home," said Danu.

Agni nodded. "Yes. I—I see strangeness grown familiar, and a place that belongs to me, but I'm not sure yet that I belong to it. But the steppe is mine no longer. I can't go back to it. I have no place that I can, beyond all doubt, call home."

"This is home," Danu said. "Where your kin are. Where Tilia is." He thought for a moment. It was not his to say, not really, but it seemed necessary, just then. He could say that the Lady commanded him. He said, "Tilia is going to be a mother, you know."

"Yes, I know that," Agni said a little sharply. "She's going to be a Mother. She's the Mother's heir."

"No," said Danu. "She's going to be a mother. To bear a child. To make you—I suppose—a father. Since that is the way you think."

At last he had managed to evoke astonishment in the king of the horsemen. "She never told me!"

"Need she have?"

Agni looked like a horse about to bite. But he held himself still.

Danu looked down, a little ashamed. "No. I shouldn't have said that. Sarama was surprised, too, that I knew and she hadn't told me. I could see. As could you, if you knew how. They don't teach you that, do they, among the tribes?"

"It's a thing of the women's side," Agni said with the hint of a growl.

"Not here," Danu said.

He watched Agni ponder that, and watched the rest of it dawn on him at last: what Danu had told him. What it meant. It was a while before he spoke. When he did, it was to say a thing that Danu had never expected from a tribesman. "She hasn't before. Has she?"

Danu understood, but widened his eyes nonetheless.

"Had a child," Agni said. "She hasn't been a mother before. Has she?"

"No," said Danu.

"Why?"

Danu shrugged. "The Lady knows."

"Did she think she was barren?"

Danu could not lie, and he had little talent for prevarication. He nodded.

"Would that stop her from being Mother in her time?"

Danu nodded again.

There was no telling what Agni was thinking. He perceived more than Danu had given him credit for, but what he thought of it, how it felt and tasted to him, Danu could not tell.

After what seemed a long while, Agni said, "She knew, didn't she? Or hoped. What the Great Marriage would do."

"What *you* would do," said Danu. "There was a foreseeing, I've heard. A whisper among the elders: that the Mother's heir would get no children save by a man of another people."

Agni laughed. There was little mirth in it. "So that's what I was meant for. To be stud-horse to the Mother's heir."

"Isn't that what a king takes wives for? To be his broodmares and bear his sons?"

"Then we're well matched," Agni said.

"And you're resentful. Why? You should be glad."

"Yes," said Agni. He touched heel to Mitani's side. The stallion moved forward, down the long slope.

Danu's gelding followed with no prompting.

Agni spoke to the air ahead of him, but the words were meant for Danu. "Why did you tell me this?"

"Because it was laid on me."

Mitani halted. Agni turned on his back. "Would she have told me?"

"It becomes obvious," Danu said.

"And I have to learn to think like that?" Agni snorted in disgust.

"Ah," said Danu mildly. "One must learn to see. To observe. And to understand. I suppose that's difficult."

"Not as difficult as keeping myself from thumping you." Agni wheeled Mitani full about and sent him curvetting in a circle around Danu on his mercifully calm gelding.

Danu should be apprehensive, he supposed, and wondering if this was the battle that Catin had foretold for him: face to face already with this man from the steppe. But Agni was a little less angry than, however unwillingly, amused. With a whoop that startled Danu nigh out of his skin, he whirled again and plunged at the gallop toward the city.

He was going to confront Tilia. Danu might not come alive or unflayed from his own encounter with her, but he was not sorry he had said what he had said. He had caught the shock; Tilia, he hoped, would have all the joy.

·········· 86 ··········

With Tilia carrying his child—which she stubbornly persisted in calling hers and hers alone, but he had some hope of waking her to greater sense—Agni understood at last what made a man fight most fiercely. It was more than glory, and more than the exhilaration of danger. It was the heart-deep, bone-solid certainty that he would do anything, anything at all, to keep his own blood safe. The woman he had taken in earnest of this land, the child within her who was his own, his flesh, were all the world. And everything that was his or hers, he would protect to the death.

Somehow, without his noticing it, she had become a necessity. If duty kept him in the camp, he caught himself looking about for her, or reaching for her in the night, or looking for her beside him when he woke in the morning. He only breathed truly easily when she was in his sight.

She did not seem to respond in kind. Her farewells were light, her greetings calm, as if she had not missed him at all. She had much to do, not only in Three Birds but in the towns to the eastward: calling their people together, seeing that they were provisioned, and even making sure that they tended to the defenses, the walls and the ditches and the troops of fighters.

She was gone as often as she was present, refusing to ride—that was not her fate, she said firmly—but accepting a guard of horsemen or mounted women. Often it was Sarama and Taditi and their archers; sometimes it was a company of young men from the camp. They vied to be chosen to ride with the king's wife. It was a great honor and a great trust.

And Agni found himself bound to Three Birds. If he contemplated riding about, or for that matter accompanying Tilia on her travels, he ran afoul of this duty or that, or someone had a dispute for him to judge, or a deputation had arrived from one of the cities with messages that only he could answer. He never managed to escape. Even when he tried to slip away at dawn with a small company of horsemen, there was the Mother of Two Rivers waiting for him outside his tent, bidding him judge a quarrel between one of her elders and a clan-chieftain.

He did that to the evident satisfaction of the Mother and the elder, if not of the chieftain against whom Agni had laid down the judgment. He had taken a store of gold that was not his to take, and from the temple yet. Agni could hardly find him innocent of wrongdoing.

When they were gone and with them most of the day, Agni sat for a while on his black horsehide. The others were gone away, both elders and hangers-on. He was, for once, alone.

And he was king at last of the Lady's people as well as the horsemen. This was not the first judgment he had been asked to make for people from the cities, but it was the first that had come between a Mother and a lord of the tribes. And they had asked him to judge, not the Mother of Three Birds or the council of the Mothers. They had come to him as king, and accepted his judgment.

He was not fool enough to think that it would have gone so well if he had found in favor of the chieftain. But the gods and the Lady had been kind. It had not even been a difficult verdict. There would be grumblings in the camp tonight, but he was not afraid of those. He was strong enough to quell them. And that too was the mark of his kingship.

He rose at last, stretched and sighed. Everyone else was free to come and go, but the king must stay. For the first time he felt what his father must have felt, the weight of the burden, the strain of being the center.

And Tilia was somewhere off to the eastward, sublimely unconcerned by the danger to herself or her child. Sarama was with her, but Sarama at least had left her daughter behind. Rani stayed with her father, as safe as child could be.

It was an absurd thing to do, maybe, but Agni went in search of his sister's lover. He found there an uncritical welcome, the open hospitality of all these people, and even a little rest. People still came to him, but not as easily or as quickly as in the camp.

He ate his dinner in the garden of the Mother's house, in the fading light of evening, with his sister's daughter in his lap. Several of the Mother's daughters and sons were there, and a great crowd of children. But Rani wanted her uncle. She was very firm about it, and objected loudly to the suggestion that she play with her agemates.

Agni was content with her presence. She was warm and clean, and she patently adored him. He had no doubt that she would grow up to be as contrary as her mother, but in her youth she was a perfect and worshipful female.

He slept in that house, in the bed that smelled of Tilia. He dreamed of her. She was not making love to him, or even paying much attention to him at all, and yet he was greatly comforted. Tilia flinging herself at him and begging him to love her, love her till she cried for mercy, would have discomfited him sorely.

Far better to see her in the dream-country as she was when awake, weaving a fabric of all the colors of earth and sky, and conversing with Sarama and Taditi and a shadowy company of women. He never quite heard what they spoke of, but he knew no pressing need to hear it. The comfort was in the sound of her voice, in the sight of her face, in the perfect dailiness of it all.

Such a dull creature he had become, that he could be so warmed by a dream of nothing in particular. If she had walked out of it just as he woke, he would have taken her by storm.

He woke alone, washed and dressed and ate. As he sat in the Mother's garden as he had the night before, warmed by the rising sun, he contemplated the day's duties and sighed. He was greatly, almost irresistibly tempted to cast them all aside and escape to a daylong hunt. But he was too irrevocably a king. The royal horsehide called him, and the royal burden.

He would have gone to them somewhat since, except that Rani had come out in the arms of one of her father's youngest brothers, and she had insisted anew that Agni and only Agni be her resting place in the sun. He had fed himself; now he fed her. She was still nursing from whichever of her aunts was convenient, but she had begun to demand richer meat. She took bread and fruit and cheese in such bites as her few teeth would allow, and made a great mess of it, too; then laughed uproariously as her father swooped down to sponge her clean.

Agni was hard pressed to keep a grip on the damp wriggle of her. As she came nigh to leaping out of his arms, he looked up at the shift of a shadow, into Tilia's face. She leaped to catch Rani. Their hands touched. A spark leaped, starting Agni but not, it seemed, Tilia. She swung Rani deftly into her arms.

With the child between them, there was no seizing her as he sorely wanted to do, and kissing her till they both were dizzy. Agni discovered that he was smiling, blinking like an idiot in the sun, warmed through by her simple presence. Part of him wanted to rise up and bolt, run far away from such a sickness. The rest was too deeply content to move. She had come back. She was safe. And tonight . . .

✦ ✦

The night came none too soon. Agni left the camp rather more quickly than some of his men would have liked, but still too late to share the dinner in the Mother's house. Nonetheless they were all still gathered in the common room, with the shutters open to let in the sweet air of a summer's evening, and twists of herbs burning in the windows to keep the biting insects at bay.

Tilia and the Mother were sitting side by side. Agni had not seen them look so very like before. The child had deepened Tilia's presence as well as her body. She was coming to the serenity that the Mother wore as easily as her own skin.

A place opened for him near but not beside them, between Sarama and Danu. Rani, half asleep in her father's lap, crawled into Agni's.

It was a strange council of war. And yet that was indubitably what it was. Tilia had come back with word from farther east. Messengers had brought news from the forest people. The horsemen were coming. They had gathered on the forest's westward edge; their kin among the secret people had done as kin could not but do, and made pact to guide them. Just so had the westward kin, the kin who shared blood with the Lady's people, brought word where it could best be heeded.

"They'll be guided toward Larchwood," Tilia said. "It has the best defenses, and is the most ready."

She had learned to think like a warrior. So had they all, however much against their will.

"We could," said Agni, "discard this waiting. If I gathered all my forces from the cities as well as the camps, and sent them into the east, caught the tribes unguarded, and waged our war there—"

"If you did," Tilia said, "you'd fall. It's all the tribes, the messages say. Remember what you told us: that when numbers are small, the best course is to build a wall and stand behind it."

"This many horsemen will break down the wall and trample it flat."

"But," said Tilia, "think. How many cities, how many towns there are in this country. How many of us there are. The first city may fall, and the second. Even the tenth. But each one will wear the invaders thinner, weary them more. By the eleventh, they may be weak enough to overcome."

Those were Agni's own words, his own counsel turned round and held up like a shield. He had thought it wise when he first taught it. Now, so close to the war, he was not so certain.

"Don't waver," Tilia said. "It's here the battle will be. We've directed everything to that end. The road is marked, the cities chosen for sacrifice, and everything made ready. We'll stand or fall here. Didn't we agree on that long ago?"

"We might change our plan," he said. "If any part of it fails—"

"It won't," she said.

Her confidence was sublime. Someday, Agni thought, he would see her shaken; would find her baffled by some ordinary human thing.

None of these people appeared to have the least doubt that they should stand and wait. They were city people, people of the settled places. Of course they knew how to stand still.

He had thought he did; he had conceived the plan in a great surety that it was best for this country and for these people. But his instinct in the end was to take horse and ride, to attack rather than defend.

Instinct was no use here. This was a different country; a different world. That difference would be its salvation.

This time. And after . . .

No need to think of that. Not now. He had been their nightmare, their dream of blood and fire. And now he was preparing to defend them against a true threat of blood, and certain fire.

✦ ✦

Tilia was eager for him that night, all but snatching him out of the gathering and carrying him off to their bed. He was delighted to give as he was given, body to body, with an urgency that made the world vanish away. There was only she, her flesh on his flesh, her arms enfolding him, her eyes gazing dark into his. Her scent, her warmth, the taste of her lips, snatched away memory and silenced fear.

But even they could not go on forever. They lay as close as they could lie, and their child between. Agni felt it then, the bird-flutter, the movement within that promised life. His breath caught.

She laughed in his ear, rich and deeply pleased with herself. "What, horseman! Haven't you ever felt a baby kick before?"

"Not one of mine," he said.

"Ah," she said, "yes. You'll want a share in this."

"And shouldn't I have one?"

"A few moments' loving," she said: "you had that."

"And will have it again," he said, "and yet again, if you and the Lady are kind. Are you going to ask your brother to raise this child?"

"Why, should I?"

"I know," said Agni, "that your men raise the children. He's in this house, he's raising one of his own. Why not a second?"

She raised her head from his breast to look into his face. "Are you asking to choose who will raise my baby?"

The words were harmless enough, but there was something dangerous in the way she said them.

Agni trod as if on the hunt, on leaves that might rustle and put the game to flight. "I am asking," he said, "whom you will choose."

"What if I chose you?"

He blinked. "You'd never do that."

"Why?"

Simple. Devastating. "Because," he said, "I have no gift or training for it."

"No man does," she said.

"Your brother—"

"My brother is remarkable," she said. "I don't know if I want him raising my child."

"And isn't it the mother's brother who often does it?"

"I have seven brothers," she said.

"But—"

"If I chose you," she said, "would you be horrified?"

"I'd be surprised. One can't be a king with a baby in one's lap."

"It seems to me that you were doing just that this evening."

"That was here," he said, "not among the horsemen."

"Then you don't want to raise my child. You only want to be its father."

"A father raises—" He broke off. "It's different."

"Yes, it is," she said.

Agni sat up. He breathed deep. He mustered such calm as he could find. "Are we quarreling?" he asked her.

"Are we?" she asked in return.

"You are infuriating."

"So are you."

He could not tell if she was laughing at him. He rather suspected that she was. "I . . . would like it very much if your brother Danu raised our—your child."

"I'll remember that," she said, "when the time comes." And then: "You don't even like him."

"One doesn't need to like one's brother," said Agni, "only to trust him."

She nodded. Either that made sense to her, or she understood it well enough. "I used to torment him, you know. He was always so quiet, and so painfully shy. I'd set the other girls to teasing him. They'd tell him he was the one they'd choose for their first man. Then they'd laugh when he blushed."

"And was he? Did any of them choose him?"

"Most did," she admitted. "It's a great honor. And of course, the more chose him, the more wanted to choose him. It became rather a fashion. Kosti was stronger and could go on longer, and Beki was better skilled, but Danu was a little of both. And he's so pretty. He was beautiful then, before his beard hid most of his face. Much as you must have been," she said, "when you first became a man."

He was blushing: his cheeks were fiery hot. She laughed as the women had laughed at Danu. "You see? It was the same for you. No wonder you don't like him—and no wonder you trust him."

Agni did not even want to understand all the meanings of that. "So this brother of yours is a man of . . . great experience."

"He's been chosen often," she said. "Though not since your sister came. One knows, you see, when a man doesn't want to be chosen."

"I'm glad," he said.

"Was that a growl?" she asked. "I thought your men were supposed to—*take* many women."

She had used the word that the tribesmen used, because there was no exact mate of it in her own language.

"When it's one's sister," Agni said, "one wants her man to treat her well."

"And if he doesn't?"

"That depends. One might upbraid him. Or one might kill him."

"I won't have you killing my brother," said Tilia. Her voice was light, but there was stone beneath, both dark and hard.

"Fortunately he doesn't need killing," Agni said.

"Good," said Tilia.

"Do you know," he said, "I think you could kill, if you had to. I'm not sure he could."

"Oh, he could. Any of us could." Tilia looked no happier than he would expect, to tell that particular truth.

He took her in his arms, not for any particular reason, and certainly for no sign of weakness on her part. It seemed right, that was all. She sighed and rested against him. Neither slept, not for a long while; but there was peace enough in their silence.

·············· 87 ··············

The horsemen came out of the wood on the day of midsummer, when the Lady's power was at its strongest; when the fires of her festival burned on the hilltops, and the people danced in rings about them. The festival that was in Larchwood was a festival of fire, fire and blood. For these horsemen did not come cautiously, none knowing what he would find until he found it. They had guides who had ridden here before. They knew where to go. Nor did they show any such softness as Agni had been subject to. They came in war, and they came in search of blood.

They had the look of starving wolves, the messengers said. They seized, they took, they slew. Larchwood's walls barely deterred them. They simply went around, and raided the lesser towns, those with weaker walls or none, but ample stores and plentiful herds.

Agni would not leave Three Birds. He had determined to lure the enemy there, and fight on his own ground. But he could not prevent Sarama and Taditi and the archers from riding to see for themselves what the messengers had spoken of.

Long before they came to Larchwood, they began to meet the people fleeing. The last retreat had been orderly compared to this; people afraid but not desperate, simply removing themselves to safer cities. These were the flotsam of war. Some had been burned with fire, others wounded by arrow or spear. They had left their dead.

The tales they told were terrible. Sarama and Taditi had heard such tales before, but the women from Three Birds were white with shock. They had insisted that they knew war, because they had seen the coming of Agni's horsemen. Now at last they understood how mild that conquest had been. One town taken by force. One woman raped, and her attacker punished with death.

This truly was war, in fire and slaughter. Any who fought was dead or taken. Of that, Sarama had not the slightest doubt. Agni had withdrawn all his men to Three Birds and the towns immediately about it. The cities and towns to the east had been cast on their own devices. They were a sacrifice, a blood offering on behalf of the greater cities beyond.

Those who fled would find welcome in the westward cities. The dead would be mourned, the first great slaughter that had been in this part of the world; the first war that these people had ever known.

Grim Taditi grew grimmer as they rode toward the rising sun. They rode with all caution, as warriors should in the enemy's lands.

Probably they had no need to be so careful. The enemy were finding this country a blessedly easy conquest; not dull, as Agni's men had found it, for there was fighting enough, and killing, but no great challenge, either. They were not looking for spies or raiders. They were taking what they pleased to take, and killing where it pleased them to kill.

And they were passing by the walled cities, ignoring them. If the people of the lesser towns had sense, they would take refuge in the cities; but most had no desire to huddle behind walls while the enemy raged without. When they ran, they ran far away.

✦ ✦

The horsemen had ridden round Greenfields between Larchwood and Two Rivers, and taken the ring of towns just beyond, and there paused to rest and tend such wounds as they had. They had taken with them everything they could carry, from every town that they took. Great mounds of booty lay out in the open, that must have strained the back of every ox and every remount that they had brought or been able to steal. And every man had a new cup, a skull-cup, that marked his prowess as a warrior.

Sarama left the bulk of the company well concealed in a copse of trees, and crept up a hill from which she could spy on the camp. It was a great camp. How great, she had not known until she saw it.

Beside this, all Agni's gathered tribesmen were but a scant handful. His had been the castoffs of their people, the restless young men, the warriors in search of a war. These were the tribes themselves.

There were even women: veiled figures in the shadows of tents, though she saw no children. She recognized standards and banners. Stormwolf, White Bear, Golden Aurochs. Raindance, Red Deer, Black River, and a dozen others. And, unmistakably in the center, the White Horse.

Her throat tightened as she stared at that moon-pale horsetail streaming out on the wind. They were not her people, not any longer, but she had grown up on the edges of them. She could not see them here and remain unmoved.

Taditi stirred beside her. "I'm going down," she said.

Sarama rounded on her. She did not flinch. She was dressed as Sarama had never yet seen her in this country, in a woman's gown, with both head and face covered. Sarama had forgotten how like a shadow a woman could look, who showed nothing of herself but her eyes.

Still Sarama said, "You can't. What if you're caught?"

Taditi laughed in her veil. "Who'll see me? I'm a woman. And don't you want to know exactly what these people are up to?"

"Not if it kills you," said Sarama.

Taditi shrugged. She crept along the edge of the crest, quiet as any hunter, and vanished into a hollow. When Sarama saw her again, she was a shadow ghosting through the outermost herds, working her way inward.

There was nothing Sarama could do, nor if Taditi was properly cautious would Sarama see anything in the camp; and yet she stayed where she was. She watched the warriors come and go. She saw a stallion breed a mare—these conquerors had thought to bring the means to make new horses. And she saw the circle of men near the White Horse banner, men who even at this distance seemed older, heavier than the young warriors round about. They were holding a council. She strained to hear, but she was too far away.

She could not see particularly well, either, but she had little doubt of the man who seemed to be sitting where the king would sit. There was no mistaking that bulk or that bluster.

Yama seemed to have made himself king of more than his single tribe. Sarama peered under her hand, willing it to be another man, some one of the elders who happened to be thickset and fair-haired and given to a certain broadness of gesture; or some king of another tribe than the White Horse. But her eyes persisted in informing her that that was indeed her father's son, the man whom she supposed she must call her brother.

Either Yama had outgrown his tendency to be a fool, or the rest of the tribes were idiots. Even if he had not been what he was, he was young; he was new to his office. He should have deferred to one of his elders among the kings.

For there were other kings there. Each had his mark of rank: headdress, mantle, ornamented spear. But only one sat where all the others must face him, on a horsehide, with a gleam of gold about his neck and arms and brow.

Sarama could not help but remember Agni in his torque of gold and amber, sitting cross-legged on his black horsehide. He never kept much state apart from the torque and the hide, nor put on airs beyond what people expected of him as king. She had heard some of the more callow horsemen complain that their king was too modest; he was not kingly enough.

They would have loved Yama. Even sitting down, he strutted. She watched him hold forth, inaudible at this distance, but his gestures told her all she needed to know. He was boasting. Yama had always loved to boast.

She watched till she could bear it no longer, and until she was sure that she would not see where Taditi had gone. Then she left the hilltop, returned to the rest of the company, and set herself grimly to wait. If Taditi had not come back by morning, she would venture the camp herself. She could creep and lurk and be a worthless woman as easily as Taditi could, if she was forced to it.

✦ ✦

Taditi came back long before morning. Sarama woke with a start from an uneasy doze, to find a shadow looming over her. It stooped, and lowered itself with a faint creaking of bones, and said in Taditi's rough familiar voice, "You've done well. I almost couldn't find you."

"Then maybe the enemy's scouts won't, either," said Sarama.

"No worry of that. There aren't any."

"They're that arrogant?"

"They're that sure of where your brother is. They mean to strip the country of its wealth, then take him in his lair."

"Just as we thought they'd do."

"Yes," Taditi said. She dipped from the pot over the tiny shielded fire, and sipped and nibbled at herbs and stewed rabbit. "This is better than anything they had."

"There aren't any women to do their cooking for them?"

Taditi's eyes gleamed in the flicker of firelight. "There are women. But most of them are more suited to keeping a man warm in bed than to keeping his belly filled."

"So," said Sarama.

"So," said Taditi. "I don't suppose you saw who was sitting as king."

"Yama."

"Yama," Taditi said.

"Have they all gone mad? Or have the gods wrought a miracle? Have they transformed Yama into a king?"

"Yama is just as he always was."

"Then why?"

Taditi sighed. "When tribes gather together, they seldom choose the king who can rule them with a strong hand. They choose the one who will give them the freest rein, and interfere the least with their own kings' whims."

Sarama knew that. She had learned it as a lesson, as lore from long ago. It had been—how many lifetimes since the tribes gathered in such numbers?

"Then they don't have a leader," she said. "They'll go wherever they take it into their heads to go."

"For the moment, they're all agreed to conquer these cities and end with Three Birds. And Agni, of course. They're calling him the Outcast, and telling one another that he's no true king."

"They would," said Sarama. She drew her knees up and clasped them. It was a mild night, quite lovely in fact, neither too warm nor too cold. Yet she felt a chill, a shiver beneath the skin. "Yama will want his skull for a cup."

"Set in gold," said Taditi. "He was singing it out for everyone to hear. Did you know he brought his mother and his sisters? And one of his wives?"

"So that they can gloat over Agni's downfall?"

"So that they can do his thinking for him," Taditi said. She paused. She had never in her life spoken diffidently, nor did she do so now, but her words came a little slowly, and seemed a little more carefully chosen than they were wont to be. "You do know why he was cast out."

"Of course," said Sarama. "The woman from the Red Deer. The lies she swore to before she died."

"Do you know to whom she swore them?"

"Her father and brothers, I should think," Sarama said, "and the priest who attended her dying."

"That's what your brother thinks, isn't it?"

"Wouldn't anyone?"

"Yes," said Taditi. "Except that if she was prevailed on to lie even to swearing a great oath, could you possibly expect anything else to be true, either?"

"I . . . suppose not," said Sarama.

Taditi nodded briskly. "I wasn't thinking, either. The more fool I. I had my suspicions, but I never thought . . . well." She drew herself up short, took a breath, said it direct. "Yama's mother and his youngest wife had word of this woman among the Red Deer, how she was married to a eunuch and restless in it. They prevailed on her to seduce your brother, spun a great tale of his desire for her, and promised her that he would marry her if she disposed of her husband. But after she'd done what she'd agreed to do, two things happened. She saw your brother walk away from her, and she followed him. She saw him go to another assignation that he clearly liked much better, and knew how she'd been lied to about his love and loyalty. And as she stumbled away from that, Yama came on her and gave her honest reason to tell her husband that a prince of the White Horse had taken her by force."

Sarama was not surprised. Agni had suspected as much, though he had only said so under the influence of a great deal of wine. "So the rest of it was like a mountain falling: a few small stones gathered other, larger ones, till my brother was buried in an avalanche. But," she said, "why swear against him? Why not against the one who actually raped her?"

"Jealousy," Taditi said. "Anger. Who knows what she was thinking, there at the last? She might have blamed him for being the cause of it all, as people will when they're pushed to the edge. She had nothing left to gain then, and nothing to lose. There's a great freedom in that, you know. You can do anything then. Anything at all."

There was a silence. Sarama thought of Agni, how he had known all that, or guessed it, and still kept the brightness of his spirit. "He's a strong man," she said.

"For a man," Taditi agreed, "he is." She paused. Her eyes on Sarama were sharp. "You don't know the rest of it, do you?"

Sarama frowned. "What are you saying?"

"You know what I'm saying."

"No," said Sarama. "I want you to tell me."

"Very well," said Taditi with a snap of annoyance. "Agni your brother and Yama's wife Rudira were lovers for a year before Agni was cast out."

"A year?" Sarama could not say she was shocked; it made sense when she thought on it, from things that Agni had said, glances he had cast. So too did all the rest make sense: Yama, Yama-diti, and yes, that sad child of the Red Deer. *Poor Agni*, she almost said, but stopped herself. No; there was nothing poor about her brother, great fool that he had been, and great price that he had paid. "They must have begun on the night she was married to Yama."

"Very nearly," Taditi said. "She cast eyes on Agni at the wedding, and claimed him when it was over. He never protested too strongly. Why would he? She's a beauty."

"He might have considered what would have happened if Yama had caught him at it."

Taditi snorted. "You think he didn't? She was like a drug to him; like wine. She has a name in some quarters as a witch, though I never noticed any particular talents in that direction. All the witchery she ever needed was her body."

"And her face," said Sarama. "I remember her now. A white-faced woman, with eyes as pale as water. She was with the king when I was last in the camp, when I decided to go away. She stared at me."

"Looking to see your brother in you, I suppose," Taditi said.

"Is she that besotted with him?"

"Maybe," Taditi said. "It's known she wanted to be a king's wife—and she never stopped for an instant in betraying your brother."

"But she never accused him of the thing that would have killed him. She let another woman accuse him. A woman of another tribe, so that he'd be exiled but he wouldn't be put to death. Maybe in her mind that was a kindness."

"What, she did it for his own good?" Taditi shook her head. "She might even see it that way. She's a strange one. Rather stupid really, but very clever when she sees something that she wants. Mostly what she wants is a man, the prettier the better. Or if not a man, then something pretty to wear. She's found her element here. She was dripping gold and trying on gowns when I saw her."

"You were in Yama's tent?"

Taditi laughed at her alarm. "There, there! The tent is enormous—it's your father's old one—and no one saw me at all."

"You don't know that," Sarama said. She suppressed an urge to leap up and begin striking camp. It was dark enough and the camp was well enough hidden that it was hardly likely a hunter would find them before morning.

They would leave as soon as it was light. For the rest of the night, there was nothing they could do that they had not done, either posting guards or concealing their camp from passing eyes.

She rested as she could. The night was dark, no moon to brighten it. The trees concealed the stars. More than once she woke with a start, certain that she was in the wood again, and all the rest—Danu, their daughter, the horsemen and their conquest—no more than a dream. Then a horse would snort or a woman murmur in her sleep, and Sarama would sigh and relax slowly. It was no dream. It was real. And even with blood and battle ahead of her, she would far rather this than the endless shadows of the wood.

.... 88 ....

Even with the fear of discovery knotting in her belly, Sarama turned aside from the straight road home to ride through one of the towns that the horsemen had sacked and abandoned. It was emptied of the living, and yet it was grimly alive with beasts and birds, fattening on the flesh of the slain.

The stink of it struck the riders well out in the fields, and thickened as they rode closer. Their horses, bred in the tribes, snorted and skittered but did not turn and bolt.

Only Sarama's will held most of the archers behind her. She heard retching, but would not turn to see who it was. It spared the woman's pride, and it spared her own.

Fire had leveled much of the town and been a pyre for many of the dead: the sweet-savory stink of roasting flesh overlaid the smell of death and burning. Sarama rode with her eyes open, seeing but unseeing, as one learned to do in war.

So these women would learn, as she undertook to teach them. They must know what was coming; why they had trained so long and so hard, and what they must defend against. Charred and blackened walls, blackened and twisted bodies, the white gleam of bone in a flyblown face. Women, children, men flung together and heaped like firewood, half burned, half rotted, abandoned without mercy and without pity.

"They are not human, who did this," said one of the boldest of the archers, stocky outspoken Galia who could draw as strong a bow as a man. Nothing had ever frightened her, that Sarama knew of, nor was she weak in the stomach. Yet this sickened her.

"They're all too human," Taditi said.

"This is what happens when men are allowed to rule," said Galia.

Sarama could not argue with that, and Taditi chose not to. They passed through the rest of the ruins in silence, the silence of grief overlaid with the simmer of anger.

The archers would take this memory home with them. It would make them stronger when the battle came. Sarama caught herself grieving for innocence. Even the brightest spirits had gone all dark. It was a long while, and a long way in the sunlight, before any of them smiled again.

✢ ✢

It was no longer the fashion in Three Birds for women to play at being women of the tribes. Some stayed in the tents because they had conceived a fondness for the men they had chosen, but most returned to the city and to the companies that would stand to its defense. Tales of horror told by people fleeing westward were dismaying, but little more. Tales told by their own people, people they had known from childhood, struck fiercely home.

Agni still doubted that the Lady's children could learn to kill. They would turn tail and run, he was unhappily certain, once they had a sight of blood.

But he had a deeper trouble than that. "You were sure?" he asked his sister and his aunt, over and over. "It was Yama riding as king?"

Over and over Taditi said, "Yes. It was Yama. You don't think I'd know him?" And on the dozenth repetition, she added acidly, "Don't tell me you don't know how your own kind think. He's their puppet on a stick."

"He's coming for me," Agni said. He heard her, but her words had little meaning. "Whatever people are saying, whatever their reason for raising him up—he persuaded them to do it because I did it. I gathered the tribes, too. I led them westward."

"They were looking to the sunset countries long before you ever dreamed of coming here," Taditi said.

"Yes, but why should Yama trouble with it? White Horse lands are—were—far enough east that the people need never pass the wood. They could simply inherit the lands that the western tribes left behind."

"Not if it's as bad on the steppe as people say," Sarama said. "What would they eat? How would they live? No; they had to come here. The gods scoured the steppe clean, so that they'd not be tempted to linger."

"What, even the gods?" Agni's mouth twisted. "You know what that makes me, don't you? I'm the lure sent ahead of the hunt. I've drawn the whole pack to the quarry."

"Don't wallow in it," Taditi said. "You don't have time. They can't be far behind us, even at the speed they must be making, as loaded down with spoils as they are."

"Someone in the army will come to his senses," Agni said, "and command people to leave their booty lying; they'll get more and far better here."

"Here is where we want them," Sarama said. She did not sound excessively happy, but neither did she seem cast down. "And we were worried that they might not come to the bait."

"I didn't expect that *I* would be the bait," Agni muttered.

⊹ ⊹

All that any of them could do, they had done. They had only to wait.

Agni had never waited well. Everyone else had ample to do to shore up the defenses and to hone the skills that battle would call for; or just as important as those, to carry on the daily tasks that kept people in comfort: baking bread, washing clothes, tending children. But Agni had wrought too well. His own task had been to apportion each task as it best might be; but once that was done, there was nothing to do but sit and look kingly, and wait for the enemy to come.

Too many of the elders took open pleasure in sitting and being looked after, but Agni was not an elder yet. He was young still—very young, if truth be told—and he had a great need to be up and doing.

He found occupation at last in a rather unexpected place: in a smith's workshop, tending the bellows to her terse instructions. She was not in the least impressed that the king of the horsemen himself was laboring in her forge. Her apprentice was gone, galloping about on the back of a horse, as she put it. It was only fair that the man whose fault it was should have taken the girl's place, if only for an hour.

She was working gold that day, not copper as one might have expected. There was a row of copper knives awaiting the finishing polish, beautiful things, sharp and deadly, but her chief concern was with the spinning of a gleaming golden wire. It was simple work, quite tedious, and yet it absorbed the mind.

She spun the golden wire as the gods might spin the fate of the world, stretching it impossibly long, winding it round a spool as Agni had seen weavers wind the thread of their spinning. Such thread had never clothed a human body. This would be for beauty's sake, and no more—if never any less.

Patir found him there, to the smith's visible disgust. "Just when he showed signs of learning how," she said.

But she could not keep him with her, not with the news that Patir brought. "Scouts are in. They're coming."

Agni had no need to ask his meaning. It was the matter of a moment to lay down the bellows, bow politely to the smith, and bolt into the sunlight.

+ +

It was still a long while before the enemy could reach Three Birds. They had been seen west of Two Rivers, had passed by it without turning aside to take it. Danu was not sorry to hear that. He was fond of the Mother of Two Rivers, whom he had known since they were children. If she and her people were safe, then a little more of the world was as it should be.

That night everyone was advised to sleep, but almost no one could. One of the few was Rani, whom Danu had dosed with a little mead mixed in goat's milk. She might have been fretful to be put to bed in the temple, as unfamiliar as that place would be, but as safe as any in the city; but she was nodding as he carried her there, and sound asleep when one of the Lady's acolytes took her from him to carry her within.

"Even for this, they won't let a man in the temple," Sarama said.

He had heard her coming, felt her on his skin. As he turned, she stepped into his arms and clung tight. It was brief, and nigh squeezed the breath out of him. Then she was gone again, standing at a little distance, seeming remote and rather cold. "You still won't do the sensible thing and take her to the Long Bridge?"

"No," he said as he had been saying for days now. "If she isn't safe here, she'll be safe nowhere that the horsemen can reach. And they will reach as far as the sunset itself, unless we stop them now."

"But she might—" Sarama stopped, and bit her lip. He had heard that, too; that Rani might at least live a little longer—as if she could live without ever knowing her mother; for Sarama would not leave this place until the battle was fought.

"Let's not quarrel now," she said. "Not now. Let's go—let's go somewhere—"

"Yes," he said, since she could not finish. She made no move to go; he led her therefore, not far, but far enough to rest her spirit a little.

The house into which he led her was empty. The people who had lived in it had gone westward, except two of the daughters, who rode and camped with the archers. Everything within was clean, tidy, ready for its owners to return. They would not mind that he took refuge here for Sarama's sake.

She looked as if she might protest, but he silenced her with a finger on her lips. There was wine stored in a jar, and a cheese wrapped close in a cloth, even a round of the bread that people made for journeys, made of nuts and dried fruit and grains both crushed and whole. It was not new made, but it was the better for that, rich and sweet.

They made a feast in that empty house, with the long light of the day's end slanting through the opened shutters. The quiet, startling at first after the hum and tumult of a city preparing for attack, grew till it filled them as it filled the house. Danu watched the tension ease in Sarama, the stiffness fade from her body, the taut lines smooth from her face. She was never pretty as anyone would reckon it—as her brother was, if one admitted the truth; features that in him were drawn as clean as the edge of a blade, seemed too strong for her woman's face. And yet she was beautiful, an odd fierce beauty that only grew the stronger, the more the years touched her. She was not a pretty woman, nor had been a pretty child; but when she was old, none of that would matter. Only the beauty would remain.

They had not said a word since they came into the house, nor needed any. Danu left the place where he had been sitting, knelt at her feet and laid his head in her lap, and sighed as she bent to close him within her arms. In that space, not so long ago, her daughter had slept coiled in the womb. Now Rani slept in the temple, safe in the Lady's arms, with the rest of the children.

Danu had never minded before that he was forbidden to enter the temple. It was the women's place, their sanctuary. But they had taken Sarama's daughter—his daughter. He wanted her back.

Foolishness. Sarama slipped down from the bench to her knees, arms still about him. Her breathing had quickened, but it was no quicker than his own.

They were alone here, as they never were; all alone in a house empty of people. Anything they did or said, no one else would hear. No one even knew where they were. It was wonderful; wicked.

She laughed as he took her—*he* took *her*, which was just as she wished it. Such a strange language, hers was, to say he took, when in truth it was he who gave and she who took. He rose above her; she lay beneath, all joyfully open to him, and laughing that sweet wild laughter. It sounded as the wind must sound on the steppe, or the rain on the endless expanses of grass.

She did not want him to be gentle. She dared him to be as a stallion is, as the stag in his season. He was trained to gentleness as a tribesman trained for war. Yet he had learned to fight. He could seize her, too, and drive deep, and impale her as if on a spear. She gasped; but before he could recoil, she clutched him tight. He could move nowhere but within her.

And he remembered what the tribesmen never did: that it was the mare who accepted the stallion, and the doe who allowed the stag to fall upon her. With the faintest of sighs, he let his body do what it clamored to do. To take her swift and hard, no measure to it, no long slow ascent into pleasure. He went up like a burning brand, in a shower of sparks.

And when they were gone, he lay beside her, cold and ashamed. She lifted herself over him as a little before he had risen over her. She was smiling, the same warm rich smile as when they had loved all night. She kissed the corner of his mouth. "There, there. Why so glum?"

"I—" he said. "I didn't—"

"What? Love me long enough? Are you as proud as that?"

"I didn't please you," he said. There: the truth. And the shame of it, too.

She seemed remarkably unperturbed. "You *are* that proud. No, my beloved, you did not fail to please me. Not in the slightest."

"But—"

"Hush," she said. And he obeyed, because he was raised to obey. She knew that, too: she began to laugh again, irresistibly. Even he could not cling to his pride in the face of such mirth.

It was not an ill thing, he supposed, to find both love and laughter on the eve of war.

·············· 89 ··············

They came with the sun, rising over the eastward hills, rank on rank of them, and their shadows marching long ahead of them. There seemed no end to them. Nor were they either weary or laden down as Agni had hoped they would be. They were flush with victory, greedy for spoils, as if there could never be enough in the world to sate their hunger.

Everything was ready for them, everyone sent to her place. Agni had risen before dawn as he always did, dressed and broken his fast in his ordinary way. Tilia was already gone. The rulers of the women had gathered in the night to make what magic they could.

As Agni came out of his tent, fed and ready to face the sky, the Mother's song rang out faint and piercing clear. The sun climbed over the horizon, and the enemy with it.

Agni did not hasten even then, even with the city struck to a kind of quiet panic and the camp humming with excitement. Battle—battle at last.

The hum was much less than it would have been the day before. All the tents were pitched as always, the fires lit in front of them, everything from a distance as it should be. But most of the tents were empty, and the westward horse-herds, out of sight of the enemy, were much depleted or gone, carrying warriors where Agni had bidden them go.

Mitani was waiting by the horselines, bridled, saddled with his best fleece, and beads and luck-feathers woven into his mane. Patir stood near, but it was the child Mika who held the rein.

Agni leveled a glance on him. "Why aren't you in the temple?"

Mika's head tossed as if he had been a horse himself, and his eyes glittered. "I'm not a baby! I have twelve summers. That's old enough to fight. Tillu said so."

"I don't see Tillu," said Agni: and it was well he did not, because the elder of the Stone Tree people should be leading the army that was gone out.

"What are you going to do," Mika demanded, "make him say he really said that? He did. I heard him."

"You bullied it out of him, no doubt," Agni said. "And do you even know how to fight?"

Mika nodded vigorously. "I can shoot. I'm a very good shot."

Agni sighed. He knew that look too well. If he forbade, the brat would come regardless, and get himself killed trying to prove that he really could fight.

"Well then," Agni said. "You come. But you stay with me. If I tell you to go elsewhere, you go. Not one word against it. Promise me."

"I promise," Mika said without a tremor.

Agni nodded shortly, turned, put the child out of his mind. He sprang onto Mitani's back. Mitani was fresh and rather headstrong. It was a fine few moments before he would settle.

By the time Mitani would agree to walk, if not sedately, out of the camp, it was time. The deep throbbing voice of a ram's horn sang from the city, from the summit of its temple. The enemy had come within bowshot of the ditch.

The camp roused behind him. The city would be waking, too, though it also was much depleted, and not only by people fleeing westward. Those who were left in it, who were not bound to look after the children or to tend the houses and the holy places, took weapon and followed Agni eastward, to the ditch that had become the boundary of the city.

He had had it widened and set with more and deadlier stakes. A wall of brush and bundled grass rose on this side of it, chin-high on the men of this country, somewhat over chest-high on Agni. Already many of the city's fighters were there, waiting with admirable patience for word to string their bows or ready their throwing-spears.

Agni's horsemen rode calmly out and spread along the barrier. From beyond it would seem that only they were there; the archers were invisible. Every man wore his best battle finery, and some had painted their faces in fierce patterns, stripped off their coats and painted their bodies, too, to make them more terrible to look at.

Agni was quite plain in comparison. He wore no paint. But he wore the coat that he had worn to the kingmaking, though it was a warm coat and the day was already sweltering, and he wore the golden torque that he always wore, that some were calling his mark of kingship.

When Mitani had reached the barrier, he agreed at last to stand still, though it was a very active stillness: head up, neck arched, snorting gently at the wall of strangers that came toward him out of the sunrise. They seemed to fill the whole of that valley, to advance like a river in flood and spread wide as it found its passage blocked.

Agni had ample time to discern and mark the banners. Just as Sarama had said: they were all here. All the tribes that he knew of, and more that he had never heard of. Their numbers were overwhelming; daunting. And not one of them looked either weary or cast down.

Nevertheless, he thought, they had come a long way. They had fought, perhaps more often than they expected. They had spent their strength in sacking the towns left open for them. Some maybe had even left, gone back to the steppe or elected to stay in one of the eastward cities rather than continue the advance.

But they looked deadly, and they looked eager to seize this of all cities. This that had been great enough, and rich enough, to become the camp of the gathered tribes; that held the outcast himself, the nameless and kinless man who had made himself a king.

That kinless man, whose name had refused to go away when he was exiled, sat his stallion unmoving. The archers were watching him, alert for his signal. But he was not ready yet to give it. He was looking for one banner amid the many, and one face beneath it.

There. Not in the lead as a proper king would be, but in the middle, with a wall of other tribes before him and a wall of tribes behind. Prudent; cowardly. Just so would Agni expect Yama to do.

Yama was not visible amid so many mounted men. That rather suprised Agni. He would have expected his brother to be borne above the heads of the rest, or to travel in a blaze of gold. There was gold in plenty, and some of it heaped to excess; surely a man so weighted down could not lift his arms to fight. But which of the gleaming princelings was Yama, Agni could not tell. They were all strutting fools.

He drew a deep breath. His heart was beating hard. His palms were damp. He was not afraid, nothing so shameful. He was ready, that was all. Prepared for whatever would come.

Closer and closer the enemy came. The archers held their fire. The signal, the clear horncall that they all had agreed on, was in Agni's own hands, the horn hung from his saddle, waiting for him to lift it. But he did not, though eyes rolled at him, and horses began to champ and fret. He waited.

A trickle of sweat ran down his back. He could not regret insisting on this coat of all that he might have worn, but he would be wonderfully glad to strip for battle.

He had his own standard now. Patir lifted it as the enemy came to halt at last: a hoop of beaten gold set on a spearshaft. Beads and plates of gold and copper hung from it, suspended on strings of tight-plaited horsehair. They chimed as the wind caught them, and the flame of them went up to heaven.

He felt the eyes of all that army turn and fix on him, caught by the splendor of his standard. He sat no straighter, nor did he lift his chin any higher. Let them see him at ease, unperturbed by their advance. And please the gods, let them not see him crimson and sweating and wishing he had had the sense to leave the coat behind.

When the full weight of their attention was on him, when they were as thoroughly distracted as he could expect them to be, he lifted the horn at last and blew a long wailing note. It was, as it happened, the call one used in Three Birds to proclaim that the quarry in a hunt had been brought to bay. Patir's snort behind him let him know that his friend had recognized it.

As the notes of the horn died away, bowstrings sang. Arrows flew. And out of the woods to right and left, and from the hill behind, came all the forces that Agni had made ready. Men of the tribes, mounted women, people of the city on foot with bows and spears. They did not have to fight well. They simply had to be numerous.

It was hard and cold, that thought. Sarama was out there, riding with the warrior women, and Taditi no doubt beside her. Danu, whom he did not like but trusted to the bone, was somewhere among the cityfolk. And here was Agni with Patir, waiting still, watching the massed tribesmen discover that they had, at last, found a battle. He heard a whoop, a yell of pure glee.

They were trapped and rather thoroughly surprised, but they were hundreds strong. They divided into tribes and clans, smaller knots of fighting men amid the greater mass of them, and chose each his enemy. That, Agni had expected, had hoped for. Many small bands were easier to strike or to disregard than one great massed wall of men. One did the same when hunting beasts in herds: divided them, the better to conquer.

A king with any skill in hunting would have known what this was that Agni did, and seen that it did not happen. But Yama made no move to prevent his army from scattering. His own men closed in a circle about him, shielded him from arrows and turned spears outward against attack. But no one ventured within reach of them.

In a very little time, what had been a fallow field was transformed into the field of battle. Shouts, cries, the ring of metal that was new in the world; shrieks of men and horses wounded; battle-songs from those with breath to sing. Bright scarlet of blood. Men falling. Horses dying.

Battle. And as the knots of fighting men, women, horses spun away, there was Yama in the middle, untouched. Maybe he began to understand that he was singled out. If so, he did not know what to do about it.

Now. Agni nodded to the ones who waited, strong men and women of the city. With a sound perhaps of relief, some of them drew aside the barrier. The rest lifted up the bridge and swung it down. It was a great thing, greater almost than they could do. At the summit of its ascent it wavered. They braced with all their strength. For a stretching moment it looked ready to fall back; but they prevailed. It swept round and crashed to the ground, secure on the far side of the ditch.

It was all Agni could do to hold Mitani. The stallion danced on his hindlegs, wheeling and snorting. Agni cursed him under his breath and drove him forward. When his forefeet clattered on the bridge, he nigh went up again. But Agni was ready for that. He clapped heels to rigid sides and sent Mitani plunging across. A booming of hooves on wood, a blur of deep-dug ditch and deadly stakes; then Earth Mother lay underfoot once more, and the field was clear for a little way before him, and his own men, his friends and kin, were crowding at his back.

He gave them room to come across the bridge. Just as the last horse was firm on solid ground, the people behind hauled the bridge back, leaving them with one way home: straight ahead through the enemy, till they could win to the northward road.

"It's a beautiful day to die," said Patir, reining his spotted stallion to a halt beside Agni. He had the look he always had before a fight, wild and a little glazed, with a grin that came and went irresistibly. He always said the same thing, too: for luck, he maintained.

And Agni always made the same reply: "It's a better day to live."

And a grand fight, Rahim would have said, third in their chorus. But Rahim was dead. They left his part to silence.

Agni called himself to order. Yama's company had not moved in all this while; they stood like a walled city, bristling with spears. No doubt they thought to wait out the battle, let the rest do their fighting for them, and claim the prize when all was done.

Agni had no intention of letting them do any such thing. He wheeled Mitani to face his men, his best, his strongest, his own; his kin who had come with him all the way from the White Horse. There was battle all about them, tribe against tribe, Lady's children against men of the steppe. But here was a matter for family. White Horse against White Horse. King born against the one who had betrayed him into exile.

This would do for a battle. Oh, yes. It would do indeed.

·············· 90 ··············

Danu went out long before dawn, hours before the Mother sang the sun into sky. The stars were out in their myriads. So were the insects that plagued the night; even an ointment of pungent herbs could not keep them altogether at bay. He found the rest of those he was supposed to meet, by the sounds of slapping and the occasional soft curse. They were all gathered by the ditch, ready to cross it when the last of them had come.

Although the horsemen were camped well away to the east, no one ventured a light. Night-eyes and starlight were ample for most; those who were night-blind held close to their more fortunate kin.

Danu could see very well. He lent his hand to a smallish woman who proved by her voice and the glimmer of her face to be Chana—not so eager now to be a tribesman's woman, not since these new horsemen came with their fire and slaughter. He had heard that her tribesman had objected to her going, had commanded her to stay. If he had asked, she might have agreed. But since he had not, she was here, one of the company that marched to fight for Three Birds.

It seemed a very long time before everyone was there, the bridge was lowered, and all of them had gone across. The bridge's tenders hauled it back and restored the barrier of brush, making a wall against the enemy.

They went quickly, in a long line, running as hunters run. They all knew what they were to do. Agni had tried to insist that one of them lead, but no one wanted the burden. If in the heat of battle it came to one of them in particular, so it would. Agni had muttered something about impossible idiots, but no one had seen fit to notice.

In any event they were well on their way, armed and supplied as hunters turned warriors, and everyone knew where they were going. Danu was not a particularly fast runner, but he was steady, and he could run for as long as he needed to. He was content to run among the last of them, keeping to an easy lope. No use in wasting his strength now, or tripping or twisting an ankle in the dark. He meant to face this battle with his eyes wide open and his strength at its fullest. Because, no matter how reluctant he might be, he had learned to fight for precisely this. He had no intention of running away from it.

They were all of the same mind. Late-night musings in solitude and noontide reflections in the market were all done with. There was only the truth to face. Whether any of them could do what had to be done. Whether they could bring themselves to fight; to wound. To kill.

After the first few dozen strides, Danu had found the rhythm of his pace, easy and all but mindless. His breath came easy, his legs moved without stiffness.

Many of the women ran naked but for their crimson skirts. The men were more modest, but there was no great need to be. He stripped off his tunic as he went, thrusting it into the pack with his provisions, his spare bowstrings, and the few odd bits that he had judged might be useful. The night air was soft on his bare skin. Biting creatures were less pleased to seize on moving prey; he had no great fear for his tender parts.

It would have been pleasant, this running from dark into dawn, if not for what waited at the end of it. He turned his mind away from that while the night lasted, let himself be content with the surge and flex of muscles, the steady pumping of his heart, the drawing in of breath only to be let out again. So must a horse run, for the joy of running. So must the colt do—the young stallion that everyone insisted was his. He had left that one safe among the herds. Mounted fighting he could do, but he could not bear it if the colt was hurt.

And so he ran with the foot-fighters, and the colt grazed and played and plagued the mares, and never knew what he was missing.

✦ ✦

Dawn was greying the sky when they came to the place where they would wait upon the enemy. Some went to the northern copses, others to the grove to the south, there to hide till the horn called them out to the battle. Danu happened to be among those who went north, which was a little farther but the cover was better. The boar that used to make the place terrible had been killed that summer—by Kosti, who had been sore baffled when the horsemen offered him an outpouring of admiration for the feat. The beast had been ravaging farmsteads in the village beyond the wood, and had nigh killed a man who had gone to gather firewood. Kosti had happened to be hunting out that way, and the Lady had blessed him; she had allowed him to give the boar her mercy. It was only sensible that she should do so. Everyone knew that Kosti was the strongest man in Three Birds.

The horsemen had acted as if Kosti should take credit for that strength. It embarrassed Kosti terribly, and made him the butt of a jest or two round the market.

Danu was glad, just then, that Kosti had subjected himself to such embarrassment. The boar's wood was dark and deep, and much too tangled to admit a man on horseback. But for a hunter with good night-eyes and light feet it was penetrable enough.

They found a clearing not far in, a place to rest and wait. Most slept under the lightening sky. A few of the women took the time to paint themselves in the Lady's patterns, painting them thick as if for a great festival, circles and spirals round breasts and belly, and wide staring eyes on their foreheads, and a coil of serpents on legs and arms. They took great care about it, with others waking as the morning went on, and taking up the paints for themselves.

Danu took his turn as the sun moved into the sky. Chana helped him, and his sister Mareka. They were not merciful. His beauty he lived with; it was nothing he could help. But women were not often given opportunity to comment on all of it—or to decide that while Kosti was bigger, Danu was made more to measure.

"No wonder your outlander won't share you," Chana said, rubbing his rod for luck, and clapping her hands as it rose to greet her.

And to think, thought Danu, that he had daydreamed once of her choosing him. She was lovely in her smallness, and would be delicious in his arms. At the moment she was threatening to paint his rod, which did not endear her to him at all. He slapped her hands away, rose over Mareka's protests, and stalked off to finish in peace. Their laughter followed him.

They could laugh all they liked at that distance. He painted himself as for the dance, and passed the pots to his brother Tanis, who always woke latest and surly, and was no different this morning. His weapons were ready, he had seen to that before. Nothing was left but to wait.

✦ ✦

The ram's horn blew both sooner and later than Danu had expected. Sooner, because no one had thought the enemy would come so early in the morning. Later, because they had all known long since that the horsemen were coming. It was a rumble in the earth, the sound and sense of a great herd of horses. But a herd alone, unridden, never came on so straight, with such evident purpose.

They were not to move until the second signal. The first waiting had been difficult. The second was excruciating. It was not so terribly long by the sun. By the spirit's time it was half of eternity.

Danu was one of those inclined to slip out to the wood's edge, to see what could be seen, so that the rest could be ready when the call came. The horsemen were just riding past, rank on rank of them, gleaming with stolen gold, draped in fine weavings. They looked like nothing that Danu had seen before.

He had seen Agni's riders, and they had been a wild enough sight when first they came. But these were wilder. It was death, he thought. Death in their eyes, and blood on their souls. Agni had come to conquer. These had come to kill.

Something inside Danu went cold. He was not aware of it at first, except as a silence of the spirit: as if a voice that had spoken to him lifelong had gone mute.

It was not the Lady's voice. She was there still, her wind breathing in his ear, her breast against his as he lay in hiding and watched the horsemen ride by. For a moment he felt her arms about him, warm and strong.

He folded his arms and rested his chin on them. The horsemen rode on by, down to the dark line of defenses. They could see all that he could see, and they spoke of it, heedlessly, as if none of them cared that they might be spied on. They were arrogant, Sarama had said. They had heard of Agni's easy conquest. They expected just the same—and never a thought that the people might have learned, not just to fight, but to wage war.

Agni was gods-gifted, Sarama said. He could see the pattern of a war as a weaver could see the pattern in a loom half-threaded: with an eye that saw past the moment to the moments that could be. Danu had not found a way to tell her that he saw nothing remarkable in that. He hunted so, and danced so. And even, on occasion, so persuaded a woman to court him.

Well then: Agni had a gift for war. Danu did not, nor wanted one, but all the plan as Agni had unfolded it seemed simple in its essence. Other people called it deadly complicated.

He sighed, but softly lest after all there be scouts or spies within earshot. Down below, the army had halted. Agni had come out of the city: Danu saw the flame of his standard like a second sun. Soon, thought Danu.

✦ ✦

Now.

The horn's song was piercing, and won a snort from Danu. Brought to bay, was it? Yes; one could say that of the city, with so many horsemen fighting over it.

He rose up out of his hiding place. Already the first of his fellows emerged from the wood.

He ran this time for life and breath, but with care still, because he must fight when he was done. He saw how those to the north had kept together, but those to the south ran more raggedly. Of the riders who should have come round from the east, for too long a while he saw no sign. Then the first of them rode over the hill; but before he could see who it was, he had to watch where he was running, or fall and break his neck.

The horsemen had scattered as Agni had said they would, dividing into smaller companies. There were still an ungodly number of them, and every one raised from infancy with a weapon in his hand.

You've hunted from a child. Taditi's voice, both harsh and sweet, with no slightest hint of softness in it. *You've killed in order to live. That's what war is. Only you're not killing the boar or the defenseless deer. You're killing men who have a burning desire to kill you.*

He had not wanted to listen when she told him that. Now he could not get the words out of his head. They pursued him straight down the hill into a knot of men on horses.

Horses. *Aim for the horses if your nerve fails you. Think of the wolf culling the herd.*

Danu aimed for the horses. Tanis was close by, and Mareka and Chana and Beki, and threescore more of his friends and kin. That was a tribe.

Friends, kin. And there was the enemy, thickset dun horse shying at Danu, Danu shying from the stroke that would sever its hamstring, knowing something, learning something that he had never wanted to learn. He could not aim for a horse. But a man—a man with death in his eyes and a bone knife in his hand—a man he could leap upon. Could strike with a copper blade that he had hoped never to use. Could—kill.

A stag died no differently. Killing was killing. And yet, to kill a man—

A shadow flickered in the corner of his eye. His body spun all by itself, knife stabbing at air that, somehow, thickened into flesh. A spear thrust where a moment before his head had been. He clawed his way up it to the man who clutched at it, too shocked to let go.

And these called themselves fierce warriors.

Danu backed away from that thought, from the contempt in it, the dark hard thing that was not himself. Was not Danu. Was—the Lady knew what. But it was not Danu.

The knife that had been pointed to thrust, he reversed and thrust into its sheath instead. He seized the spearhaft and heaved, flinging the rider from the horse. With a rather sublime lack of good sense, he hauled himself onto the animal's back.

It was a smaller beast than he was used to, and thin enough that its backbone clove upward even through the heaped fleeces of its saddle. But it was a horse, and it agreed to do as he asked it, once it had got over its startlement at being relieved of its more familiar rider.

From a horse he could fight as he had been trained to, as he had expected to: as an archer. He could hardly be mistaken for a tribesman, wild naked man with dizzying patterns painted on his breast and face and arms. But he could ride, and that took them aback; and somehow he was riding round the lot of them, calling his kinsfolk together. Some of them came limping, some did not come. Chana, Tanis—the fighting must have carried them away. Yes, it must have.

This was battle. Heat, dust. Stink of sweat, blood, entrails ripped and trampled. Smell of death, death above all.

And yet much of it was a surprising stillness. People resting, people licking their wounds. People gathering to reckon losses, and to settle on targets. Danu looked into faces that must mirror his own. There was death in them now, death in their eyes.

The stillness shattered. A horde of yelling horsemen thundered down on them. With a strange and potent clarity, Danu saw their banner, a wolf's head fixed in a snarl, and the men beneath it much the same, all in wolfskin mantles and reeking to high heaven.

They had no more mercy than winter wolves. They fell on that company, all of them on foot but Danu. He saw Beki fall; saw the stone axe cleave his skull. Saw how the spirit left him, wailing its shock, and the man who had killed him laughed and wheeled his horse and sprang upon another.

But Danu was there, mounted as the tribesman was mounted, with a spear and a copper-bladed knife and no intention at all of letting him kill another of the Lady's children. It was nothing Danu decided. It was deeper than teaching. One stood one's ground. One looked death in the face. Then when it struck, one struck back. Spear straight to the heart. The other veered, but he was not fast enough, never fast enough. Danu thrust the spearpoint home.

The dead man's weight pulled Danu from his stolen horse. He fell as best he could, bruised and a little winded, but had no time to lie there, no time to indulge himself. Hooves pounded deathly near. He rolled, knotted, snatched the spear and staggered to his feet. Edged stone whistled past his ear. He spun, stabbing, whirling in a terrible dance, the dance of the dark god on the burning ground, the dance that was death.

.... 91 ....

The sun ascended in a smoke and reek of battle. Sarama's archers, having done their part to show the enemy that he was surrounded, had drawn back over the crest of the eastward hill. They would fight again when there was need; but Agni had been insistent that they hold themselves in reserve.

Agni was being a wise lord of warriors, but he was also protecting a company of women. He had never been so careful with the foot-fighters, who were nigh as many men as women. And one of whom was Danu, because like a fool he did not trust his seat on a horse, and he would not risk his colt in battle.

Sarama would never have tried to prevent a man from going to a fight. In that much, she was of the tribes. And yet, waiting, lurking out of sight, creeping out to see how the battle fared, she wished devoutly that she had ordered Danu to stay at home. He might even have obeyed her.

And that was why she had not done it. For pride, because a man who would not fight was not, after all, a man.

He was down there somewhere, fighting for his life, while she lay about in the rising heat of the day. The horses cropped grass in peace. Most of the archers seized the chance to rest.

At last Sarama could not bear it. The sun had risen toward noon, and the heat had risen with it. But the battle had abated not at all. Nor would it, that she could see. The enemy was not in the least daunted. It was a young warrior's delight, a grand fight, and the prize hovering in front of them: the city within its defenses, as beautiful as a woman, and to these men perhaps more alluring.

Sarama had to move. To do something. The Mare was not excessively willing to leave the sweet grass of the meadow, but she yielded to persuasion.

As Sarama swung onto her back, one or two of the others roused to curiosity. "Where are you going?" Taditi demanded, direct as always.

Sarama shrugged. "We're not doing any good here. I thought . . . we might find their camp. I'll wager it's ill defended. If we can take it, we'll strike a harder blow than maybe they expect."

"They expect nothing of us," Taditi said, not bitterly; it was the truth. "Agni wanted us at the enemy's back."

"And won't we be, if we're holding the camp?"

It was not particularly clever persuasion, but not only Sarama had perceived Agni's purpose. Taditi looked round at the circle of eager faces, frowned, shrugged, sighed. "Very well. Pray our luck holds, and we don't fail him by being elsewhere when he needs us here."

"He needs us on the path of the enemy's retreat," Sarama said. "The camp is the first place they'll go. And they'll find us in it, holding it against them."

That made sense even to Taditi. They were up, mounted, and ready to ride in remarkably little time; and glad, too, after all, to be doing something. Rather too late, Sarama hoped that it was not madness; that she had chosen rightly. That the force driving her was the Lady, and not some prankster among the gods.

❖ ❖

The horsemen had made little effort to hide their camp, no more than they had when Sarama found it before. It was a little better defended: a few boys with spears, and warriors who had been wounded but still could ride and wield a spear. Sarama had little fear of them. The women with her, still new to battle, she did not trust completely; not yet. But they would do what they could.

They fell on the camp as the enemy had tried to fall on the city, in a headlong charge.

And it did not resist. The defenders drew back, would not strike. There was nothing to fight.

By the time Sarama realized what was happening, they were deep in the camp and the defenders had closed in behind them. She berated herself for a fool, for a blazing and arrogant idiot.

Just as she wheeled the Mare about and opened her mouth to call the rest together, a familiar voice said, "Sarama! What are you doing here?"

For an instant she was not surprised at all. It was very much the sort of thing that Tilia would say.

Tilia.

Sarama stared into that of all faces, standing in front of her in the midst of the enemy's camp. And not as a prisoner, either. There were others behind her: elders of Three Birds, Mothers of the towns nearby, and the Mother of Three Birds herself, as serene as ever.

"What are *you* doing here?" Sarama demanded of them all.

Tilia answered, as Sarama had expected. "Somebody had to do something about the camp," she said.

"But you were safe in the city."

"We wanted your brother to think so." Tilia shook her head. "That man. You'd think a woman was as weak as a baby, the way he carries on."

Sarama's thoughts exactly, when she had taken it into her head to capture the camp. She sat mute on the Mare's back. Slowly the rest of it came clear. The people standing about, tribesmen and veiled women, with no look in them of defeat, but none of victory, either. The men were armed. None made a move to threaten the women.

They did not believe it. That was the root of their quiet. They could not credit the truth, that they had been conquered by a handful of women, and only a few of those even carried a knife, let alone bow or spear.

Sarama could well imagine how it had gone. The Mother and the rest had walked serenely in, stared down the defenders, and informed the camp that it was become a stronghold of the Lady's people. The Mother had done much the same when Agni came to Three Birds. Sarama wondered if the birds had come this time, too, to strike people mute with wonder.

Maybe Agni should have let the Mother face the whole army herself, instead of resorting to battle. It would have cost him all his pride, but it might have succeeded.

No, Sarama thought. The gods of war would not have allowed it. But here, where were only women and the young and the wounded, the Lady's voice could be more clearly heard.

"Come," said the Mother.

She was speaking to Sarama. Taditi followed because she chose. The others, Sarama sent to the camp's edges, to hold it if the army should come back.

✦ ✦

The camp was quiet. Unearthly quiet, now that Sarama stopped to notice. People stood about, but no one spoke. They watched the Mother as the rabbit watches the hawk.

They were terrified of her. Goddess knew what tales people had told of her, what powers ascribed to her. That she had come here so calmly, so utterly without fear, must only have proved that the stories were true.

The center, the king-place, belonged to the White Horse. It was piercing, the familiarity of that tent and the tents about it. They had stood in every camp that she remembered, in just this order, each according to the rank and standing of the men who owned it.

There were only women here. None uncovered her face, though there was no man to see. They stood outside of tents or peered through the flaps, wary eyes, furtive postures, trained from childhood to creep about in shadows. These bold barefaced women, many of them bare-breasted, would be shocking, even appalling.

The Mother stopped in front of the king's tent. "I should like to go in," she said.

Sarama blinked, startled. "You haven't—" She broke off. "Why are you asking me?"

"This was yours once," the Mother said.

"No," said Sarama. "Never. It's the king's tent. I belong to the Mare."

The Mother smiled at the Mare and stroked the sleek grey neck. But she spoke to Sarama. "You never lived here?"

"Only when I was in camp," Sarama said, "and never for longer than I could help."

"So," said the Mother. "Give me leave to go in."

"Can I prevent you?"

"Yes," the Mother said.

Sarama sighed a little. For days—months—she could convince herself that she understood the people whom she had chosen for her own. Then one of them said something, did something, that was utterly incomprehensible; and she knew that she was an outlander. Would always be an outlander. Would never be anything else.

The thought passed like a gust of chill wind. Sarama lifted the tentflap and held it aside. "Be welcome in my father's tent," she said. Which was courtesy of the tribes, and pleasing to the Mother: she smiled as she bent her head and entered.

The moment went by with blinding swiftness, and yet in memory it was crawlingly slow. The Mother smiling, stooping. The blade—grey flint, gleaming as it caught a shaft of sun, plunging down. The hand that gripped the blade, slender fingers, very white, heavy with rings, and massive golden armlet. So much weight of gold drove the knife into the lowered neck, drove it deep, and half clove it asunder.

All in the space between two breaths, between two beats of the heart. The Mother's body fell, lifeless long before it struck the ground.

Nobody else saw, at first. Only Sarama who was closest. The Mother had vanished into the dimness of the tent. Sarama stood stone-still. All her vaunt of being a warrior, all her swiftness and her strength, and she was powerless to move.

A shadow crossed her: Tilia, walking blindly in the Mother's wake. Sarama had moved before she thought, wrapped arms about that solid body and flung it reeling back.

Taditi grunted as Tilia careened into her, but braced and held her ground. She was not hopelessly shocked as Sarama had been. Her wits were about her, her eyes sharp. She steadied Tilia, who was sputtering with anger, and shook her till she fell silent.

Sarama slipped her knife from its sheath, her lovely new copper knife with its blade so wonderfully keen, and crouched, every sense alert. No sound came from within the tent. She drew a sudden breath and feinted.

The pale hand flicked out again. Sarama caught it, striking swift as a snake, and twisted it. The flint knife dropped. Sarama hauled the murderous creature into the light.

It was a woman, of course: a wan pale slip of a thing with eyes as colorless as water. She snarled at Sarama and spat words that Sarama did not trouble herself to listen to. She had no doubt that they were curses. "Be quiet," she said. And when the woman would not obey, she slapped that bone-white face. The cursing died to a hiss. Sarama shook her till that too stopped.

"Rudira," Taditi said. Her voice was flat.

Sarama's eyes widened a fraction. *This* was the woman who had so bewitched Agni, the woman who had betrayed him because she wanted to be a king's wife? She had a certain beauty, Sarama supposed, if one's taste ran to milk and water. For all that she had killed the Mother of Three Birds and wrought the gods knew what in consequence, she had no more power in her than is in a snake that slithers in the grass. Just like a snake, she had struck out of hiding.

And the Mother was dead, with no warning, no foreseeing. Not even a premonition.

Tilia had won free of Taditi's grip, or been let go. She plucked Rudira out of Sarama's hands, nor did Sarama try overly hard to keep her. If Tilia had killed her, Sarama would not have wept.

But Tilia did no such thing. Clearly Rudira expected to die: she lifted her chin, bared her white throat. Tilia ignored her; set her aside, lifting her as easily as if she had been a child, and left her there, and knelt at the Mother's side, half in the light, half in the darkness of the tent.

Sarama held her breath. But no new death fell out of the shadows. There were people inside: Sarama could hear them breathing. None of them moved to come out.

Nor did Rudira move to kill the daughter as she had killed the mother. She stood rubbing the wrist that Sarama had gripped so hard, whimpering a little as if it pained her. Sarama did not doubt that it did, nor doubt at all that she whimpered as a clever child does, to melt its nurse's cold heart.

Sarama's heart would never melt. Not for this one. She turned her back on Rudira, contemptuously, and braved the shadows.

It was only dark for a little while. Then it was dim, the dimness of a tent lit by lamps, odorous and close. Women's world, Sarama used to think when she was younger; but it was no world that she had ever submitted to. Nor would she now. "Yama-diti," she said, clear and cold. "Do you know what your son's wife has done?"

Yama's mother remained where she had been sitting, illumined by a cluster of lamps that with a shock Sarama recognized. She had seen it in the Mother's house in Larchwood, seen and marveled at it, for its branches were made of copper.

She must not be distracted. She focused her mind and set herself to hear that Yama-diti would say.

It was not so much, but it was enough. "She thought she defended us."

"So she did," Sarama said. "Straight into the bitterest blood-feud of them all. That was the Mother of this city—the king of this country. The one you see out there, kneeling by her: that is her heir, who is now Mother. Who is wife to my brother. Who is king above the kings who are in this land."

Yama-diti heard her out in silence, in a stillness that made her think of Mothers; but Mothers were serene. This was not serenity.

She was afraid, Sarama thought. That terrible old woman—all her haughtiness was fear.

And yet fear could make a person deadly. Fear had killed the Mother, and might well kill the rest of them before this day was ended.

Yama-diti spoke at last, in a dry cool voice. "So. It's true. He's alive."

"You hoped that he wouldn't be?"

Yama-diti shrugged slightly. "It would be convenient if he were dead. That's his wife out there, is it? Wise of him to marry the king's daughter. Does he know where she is now—she and the baby in her belly?"

Sarama held herself still. Tilia had power enough in her to turn aside a curse, and certainly to keep her baby safe. And yet Sarama's back prickled. Her hackles were up like a dog's. "You lose an advantage in this country," she said. "Nobody here doubts a woman's ability to think. People will know who rules in this army."

"Then I won't need to pretend, will I?"

"Except to your son."

Yama-diti permitted herself a thin smile. "He serves his purpose."

"And when he no longer does? Will you kill him yourself, or have someone do it for you?"

"I am sorry that my son's wife was such a murderous fool," Yama-diti said, "but I am not another."

"No," said Sarama. "You think before you kill."

"So do you," said Yama-diti.

Sarama looked her full in the face. For a wonder, she returned the stare. Sarama said, "I will advise my brother to kill you."

"Why not do it now? I could commit any number of treacheries before I come to him. Or he may die in battle."

"Or both?" Sarama shook her head. "I don't think so. He'll win. And he'll want to be the one to judge you. You harmed him first, long before you harmed any of us."

"You're a fool," said Yama-diti.

"Maybe," said Sarama.

.... 92 ....

Agni rode headlong into battle. It was not too great a distance, but far enough; and Mitani was fresh, and had exhausted his patience. Even amid the clamor of so great a battle, the thunder of that charge overwhelmed the rest. Agni howled as he rode, howled like a wolf.

He did not care at all if he died. He cared that he should die well—and that he should take Yama with him.

Poor wretch of a king Yama might be, but his men were loyal. They were Agni's blood kin, his brothers, young men who had grown up with him in the tribe. But it was his tribe no longer, and they had turned their backs on him. They had cast him out.

Bitterness drove him. It strengthened his spear-arm. It made his long knife the more deadly. Men fought him. He was barely aware of them, except that they stood between himself and his prey.

Yama was in excellent flesh. The others had eaten well since they came to this country, but they had still the look of men who had lived too harsh for too long: a greyness to the skin, a haggardness in the face. But not Yama. He had never lacked for anything.

An axe whirled in Agni's face. He struck it aside with the butt of his spear. His arm rang with the blow and went briefly numb. He took no notice. He was wounded, maybe. There was a sensation like pain, somewhere far away. It did not matter.

He broke through. His men, his yearbrother Patir, defended his back. He stood in a circle empty of aught but Yama. It was a surprisingly large circle, and the grass in it astonishingly green. It was only a little trampled.

Yama regarded him without fear; with nothing more potent than exasperation. "By the gods," he said testily, "you don't even have the decency to be dead."

"What, you didn't know I was alive?"

Yama scowled. "There was supposed to be a king here. Not you."

"It was always said," said Agni, "that I was born to be king. Even your mother couldn't keep me from it."

"What does my mother have to—"

"Oh come," said Agni. "Don't play the fool. We all know who tells you what to do and say and think."

"*I* decide what I will think," Yama said with a haughty lift of the head.

"After your mother has told you what it should be," said Agni. He bared his teeth. It was not a smile. "Or is it someone else who rules you? Is it one of your sisters? A wife? Which of your women teaches you to play the king?"

Yama growled in his throat. "*My* women stay safe in my tent. Where are yours, little brother? Or do you even have any?"

"At least," said Agni with poisonous sweetness, "I can get them for the asking. They come willingly, and stay willingly. I've never had need to force a one of them."

"And for that you were exiled," Yama mocked him.

"That was a lie," Agni said. "And well you know it. It was you who raped that girl, wasn't it? The oath she swore was the truth. She was forced by a prince of the White Horse. The rest was lies and distortions and misdirection—but its core was true."

Yama laughed. He had no remorse, no more than Rahim had had. "So you guessed it, little brother. I'd not have thought you had it in you."

"I know your mother," Agni said.

"And my youngest wife," said Yama. "You know her very well indeed. Don't you?"

Here on the field of battle, outcast and condemned, Agni could laugh aloud, freer than Yama had, and with more genuine mirth. But he sobered quickly, and tilted his head, and regarded his brother with half a frown. "You know," he said, "I never did understand why you didn't denounce me for that and have done. It would have finished me just as completely, and a great deal more simply."

"Oh, no," Yama said. "That would have brought me down, too. This way I got my revenge, or as much as the tribes would allow. And you knew the real reason. Did it hurt, little brother? Did it burn your heart?"

Agni did not dignify that with a response. All at once, and quite completely, he had had enough of chatter. It was time to end it—one way or the other.

He freed his knife from its sheath. He dropped his spear. Madness, yes; but it was too long. He wanted to press in close, to feel the life ebb from that body. To know that this one of all his brothers, this one who had betrayed him most grievously, was dead.

Yama suffered from no such yearning. He shortened his spear and stabbed. Agni just barely evaded it. Yama stabbed again. Agni ducked behind Mitani's neck and sent him sidling away, slipping from his back when the stallion was apart and safe, and leaping upon Yama.

They crashed to the ground together, Yama beneath, Agni atop. Yama lashed like a snake, flailing blindly. His fist caught Agni above the ear and nigh stunned him. But Agni's weight was enough to hold him. Agni drove it downward. Yama grunted.

He looked down at a face that he had known since he could remember. There was nothing familiar about it at all. This man had taken everything that he was, or allowed it to be taken. He was sweating, scarlet, but there was a pallor beneath. He was afraid. Agni was sweating, too. He had forgotten that he still wore the kingly coat that he had meant for defiance, and for a reminder.

Yama heaved upward. Agni lurched and nearly fell. But he held on. Yama began to fight in earnest.

It was an ugly, dusty, bruising fight. Yama dived for his knife. Agni hammered it out of his hand and kicked it far away. He scrambled for it. Agni lunged after him. They rolled on the bloodied earth, hammering at one another, pure blind animosity. It was years broad, years deep.

Yama clawed at Agni's eyes. Agni struck him half senseless. And hauled him up and held him, shaking him furiously till he stood on his feet: not steadily, not with dignity, but when Agni let him go, he did not fall. "Now fight!" Agni raged at him. "Fight like a king, damn you. Fight like a man!"

Yama growled and lunged. He had a knife, smaller than the other, which had no doubt been hidden in his coat. Agni ducked aside. He felt it pass, so close it hissed in the leather of his coat; but it never touched skin.

He groped at his belt. Sheath—no knife. His knife gleamed on the ground, close and yet impossibly far, with Yama between. Yama saw him empty-handed, and laughed, and taunted him—words that blew away on the wind of battle, but Agni saw the mockery in his face.

Yama stabbed. Agni stumbled back. The blow to his head had struck harder than he knew. It slowed him. It made his mind wander.

While Agni wavered, a shadow leaped out of the sun. It was small and very quick. It might not have been there at all, except that it had Agni's knife in its hand.

A name spoke itself in Agni's mind. *Mika.* He had forgotten the child completely; had, if he thought at all, trusted Mika to stay out of the thick of the fight.

Never trust a boychild who fancied himself a man. The thought was wry, edging toward appalled. Agni had no power to move, and no strength either.

Not so Yama. Yama laughed and batted the boy aside. It was an easy gesture, effortless, and utterly contemptuous. The soft snap that followed on it did not strike Agni at first with its meaning. But as he saw the body fall, saw how bonelessly it fell, he knew. He did not believe it, or want to believe it. But there was no mistaking it. Yama had broken the child's neck.

A great howl welled up, but it never escaped. Agni would not give Yama the satisfaction.

His sight had cleared a little. Enough that he saw the knife glinting beside Mika's body. The knife—he must have the knife. He danced clumsily aside as Yama leaped yet again. Yama was playing. Drawing out the kill. He was sure that he had it. Oh, indeed. Most certainly sure.

Fool.

Agni ducked, rolled, dived—missed. But his hand, groping desperately, felt the bite of a blade. He set his teeth and twitched it to him, found the hilt, came up in a graceless surge. He met Yama turning to strike the killing blow. Bore him back. Thrust deep—and, for Mika, twisted.

Such surprise on that face. Such sudden lack of malice.

Agni looked down. The hilt was in his hand, clapped close to Yama's side. And no blade—no blade at all to see.

Yama slipped out of Agni's grasp. He dragged the knife down with him, sunk deep in his breast, piercing his heart.

Agni stood swaying. This unsteadiness should be passing. Yet it seemed to be growing worse. He was not wounded. Was he? Just—tired. Yes.

And there was Mika. Agni wanted to carry him into the city, but this was a battle, and he was deep in it. He laid the body out as comfortably as he might, and covered it with his coat, the coat that he had thought so splendid before he saw the weavings of the Lady's country.

It was still beautiful. It wrapped all of Mika, covered him well. It would keep him warm even in death.

With the broad blade of a broken spear, with both of Yama's knives, Agni dug a grave for him. It was not deep, but deep enough. Nor was it large, nor need it be. Mika had always slept curled in a knot with his head pillowed on his hands. Agni laid him so, nestled in earth, and turf laid over him for a coverlet. "Sleep well," Agni said to him. "Sleep in your Lady's arms."

He staggered up. His face was wet. He was filthy, smeared with earth. He scrubbed it off as best he could, slipping in and out of clarity. Sometimes he saw very clearly. Sometimes he saw nothing at all.

He was in the middle of a battle. He could not sleep now, or fall into a stupor. There was not even time to mourn for Mika. He found a spear some-where—white horsetail hung from it, lifting in the wind. It was Yama's spear. The royal spear. The spear that only the king could bear, that was the battle-standard of the White Horse people.

It held Agni up. And there was Mitani, looking as if he had been waiting for a long time, and fretting unregarded: eyes fixed on him, ears up. His nostrils flared, fluttering with a soft inquiring sound. Agni was on his back, no memory of getting there, but Mitani was much steadier on his feet than Agni had been on his own.

Agni lifted the spear, because he did not want to drag the horsetail in the dust. There was a strap on the saddle-fleece to hold the spearbutt in place. It slipped in easily, and the spear was suddenly much less unwieldy.

Mitani had never had a spear hanging thus above his head before. He snorted and danced sidewise.

Agni could not see very well and could not seem to think at all, but he could ride in his sleep. He took Mitani in hand. The stallion was unwontedly headstrong. He wanted to dance; to circle snorting, tossing his head.

It was remarkably quiet. There was still clamor away somewhere, but not close in. And yet there were people. Many and many of them. Eyes staring at him: dark eyes and light, people of this country and men of the tribes. No one was fighting.

A face swam toward him out of a dazzle of sunlight. Agni smiled in great relief. "Patir," he said.

"My lord," said Patir, who only talked so when he wanted to be exasperating. But there was no lightness in his voice, or in his face either.

Agni peered at him. "Patir. Have we lost the battle?"

Patir looked startled. "My lord! Don't you—" He stopped, peered closer, and said in a tone much more like his own, "Agni, are you hurt?"

Agni shrugged a little. "I'm dizzy. I keep wanting to fall asleep. It's just a headache. We have lost, haven't we?"

"You *are* hurt," Patir said.

He came in close, calling out to others of the White Horse exiles, but Agni slapped them off. "Stop it! Get back to the fight. It's still hours to sundown. We'll win it yet."

"We *have* won it," Patir said sharply. "Or you have. Who hit you? Yama? You hit him back, it seems. He's dead."

"Mika's dead," Agni said. "He died. Yama killed him."

"And you killed Yama," Patir said. "You killed the king."

Oh, Agni's wits were slow indeed. He had only thought of killing Yama— of taking vengeance for Mika; ending the fight that had been between him and his brother since they were children. He had never stopped to think of what it meant.

A king who killed a king won all that was in that king's possession. Which, since it was Yama, was the whole of that army. All the tribes and clans. All the horses and the herds. The women, the children. The spoils that they had won. Everything.

Agni had known this. He had hoped, prayed for it. But when it had come upon him, he had been too fuddled to notice.

Agni's head was clearing a little, with Patir's eyes on him and the others crowding behind. The noise of battle had receded even further, as word traveled outward. People had only to look up to see Agni on his red stallion with the white horsetail floating over him.

He looked out over a field of slaughter. Grass stained red with blood. Cries of the wounded, and keening of women over the dead.

This was glory. This was kingship. Blood bought it. Blood paid for it.

The gods of war were sated, and their servants the gorecrows thronged to the sacrifice.

A fierce white heat flared up in Agni. It was the war-gods' fire, the burning of their joy. He swept up the spear and whirled it about his head and sang, a song of triumph.

III

BEGINNINGS

.... 93 ....

THE KING OF the horsemen rode into the camp in the first dimming of evening. The sun was high, but the shadows had shifted and begun to grow long. The heat was breathless, the wind gone, the sun's hand heavy with sleep. But no one slept, not on this day, unless it were the dead.

Agni had stood beside Yama's body as the men of the king's warband lifted it up and carried it off the field. He was calm, empty of either hate or grief. Even anger was gone. He had won. He had what his father had meant him to have, the name and office of the king.

The camp was waiting for its king to come back. Agni had forbidden any to bring word. He would bring it himself, give Yama's body into its mother's hands, and take her surrender as he had taken that of all the kings and chieftains who had followed Yama to the battle. How many of those were regretting their choice of king, Agni could well see. If they had not chosen Agni's own brother and enemy, they might still be fighting, and victory close to hand.

There was a great sweetness in that knowledge. Agni entered the camp in the cloud of it, and found a terrible silence.

There were dark faces amid the fair. Women of Three Birds stood among the women of the tribes. There was no mistaking what had happened here. While Agni was winning the battle, Sarama's archers had taken the camp.

There was no gladness in them, no light of joy. Agni had rather expected that of these unwarlike people set face to face with war. But such somber faces, such heavy silence, made the skin between his shoulders tighten.

The cause was deeper in, where he was riding in any case. As he speeded his pace, he heard the whispers behind him. The women had recognized the body on its bier of cloaks and spearshafts. None of them raised her voice in a keen. That was a notable thing. One learned much of a king's standing in a tribe, by such tribute as the women of his tribe gave or failed to give him.

Agni passed through the camp's center to the king-place. There was the camp of the White Horse, a sight as piercing as memory, and yet oddly remote. It was not Agni's camp, not any longer. His own was west of here, on the other side of the hill, in a field outside of Three Birds.

Women of Three Birds were waiting for him there as they had been on the camp's edge. He saw archers with their bows, Taditi and Sarama, and—which he had not expected—elders and acolytes of the city and the temple. And Tilia, kneeling outside of the king's tent. The Mother lay in front of her. There was nothing of sleep in that heavy body. Only death.

Agni's heart constricted. His throat was dry. It was only a woman, part of him insisted. King she might have been in the reckoning of her people, but she was conquered. She had had no power but what he chose to give her.

And yet she had been the Mother. And she was dead. Of all the deaths that he had seen that day, this was the last that he had expected. She was not supposed to die. She was supposed to keep safe in the city, and come out in a cloud of birds when the fighting was over, and heal what could be healed, and teach the earth to grow green again.

He surprised himself with grief. He sank down beside her, bent and laid his hand on her breast over the silent heart. The cause of her death was unmistakable. Tribesman's knife: blade of flint, hilt of carved bone.

He met Tilia's gaze over the cooling body. He expected grief, and found it in plenty. Yet he had not expected to find serenity. Anger, rather. Bleakness. Yet Tilia was as serene as the Mother had ever been. It was a little cold, that serenity, but there was no mistaking it.

"Tell me how," he said.

Tilia did not answer. It was Sarama who said, "She asked me to admit her to the king's tent. I didn't know—I think—she knew. She knew what she was doing. But why?"

There was a wail in that, though tightly reined in. Taditi gripped her shoulder and said, "It was Yama's wife. The white bone of a woman. Rudira."

Agni started as if struck. "Ru—" He took himself in hand with all the strength he had. Made himself stop shaking. Said as calmly as he could, "Where is she?"

A cluster of the archers stirred, drawing his eye. A figure erupted from them and flung itself at Agni.

Only Sarama was quick enough. Her knife slashed. Rudira darted aside, but not far enough. With a cry she stumbled and fell.

Agni caught her. It was madness, he knew it, yet he had seen no weapon in her hand. And he had heard a word in her cry: the sound of his name.

She lay in his arms, gasping, whimpering with pain. Her odd pale beauty had not changed, nor had she. She was still Rudira. His body, remembering the heat of her, quickened in response, but his heart was cold. "Why?" he asked her. "Why did you do it?"

She carried on with her whimpering for a while, but he was not taken in. She swallowed the last of it and stroked his cheek, wincing at the pain in her side. "I thought—I was—it was an enemy. I couldn't let her in the tent."

"Yama-diti said the same," Taditi said. "I suppose it's true. She couldn't have known who it was that was coming in."

"She knew," said Sarama, clear and cold.

Rudira clung to Agni with sudden strength. But her eyes were on Sarama, glaring at her. "You hate me. Everyone hates me. But you can't do anything to me. I belong to him. I'm his wife."

Sarama's eyes widened, but no wider than Agni's own. "Are you now?" said Sarama.

Rudira held Agni in a deathgrip. "Yes. Yes, I am. Aren't I? Tell them, my lord. Tell them I am."

Agni opened his mouth, shut it again. Nothing that he could think of to say would be of any use.

Tilia astonished them all with a ripple of clear laughter. "By the Lady! You all look so dumbfounded. So tell us, king of the horsemen. Are you married to this woman?"

"No," Agni said. Then more vehemently, "No, I am not. She was married to my brother."

"He is dead," Rudira said. "I am the king's wife. I must be the king's wife. You are the king. How can I not be your wife? As," she said with sweet reason, "we have been to one another for lo these several years."

Agni heard her with much less horror than he might have expected. The women who heard were neither surprised nor shocked. Nor, as far as he could tell, were the men who had followed him. Was there anyone who had not known what he was to Rudira?

With a kind of revulsion, Agni laid Rudira down, and not with great gentleness, either. He had to pry her hands loose and hold them tightly to keep them from locking behind his neck.

She arched her back and flaunted her breasts at him; but he had only to lift his eyes to see better. "Husband," Rudira said. "Beloved."

"You're mad," he said.

"Oh, no," said Tilia. "She's quite sane. Just . . . slantwise."

"I must be a king's wife," Rudira said.

"You'll be nothing," said Agni, "because you killed the Mother of Three Birds."

"She was an enemy," said Rudira.

She made him think, piercingly, of Rahim. The same simplicity. The same incomprehension. The same unmistakable failure to understand what she had done.

Rahim he had loved. Rudira . . .

Love had never been a part of it. Lust, oh yes. His body sang to be near her. If it had had its way, he would have fallen on her then and there, and taken her by storm.

But his heart did not want her at all. "You'll die," he said, and there was no more pain in the words than if she had been a tribesman who had fallen afoul of the laws. Pain enough, that was, but not as it would have been for one he loved.

It was Tilia who asked, "Why?"

He stared at her.

She repeated the question. "Why? Why will she die?"

"Why— Because she killed the Mother."

"That's no reason," Tilia said.

Agni gaped like a fish. "But—she killed—"

"She didn't know," Tilia said.

"You can't let her live. She'll try to kill you."

"I don't think so," said Tilia. She came and knelt beside Rudira, looking her in the face. "That was my Mother you killed," she said.

"Do you want me to be sorry?" Rudira asked.

"No," Tilia said. "I want you to know. And that," she said, tilting her head toward Agni, "is mine. Are you thinking that I'll share him?"

Rudira's eyes narrowed. "He was mine first."

"I married him," Tilia said.

"Of course you did," said Rudira. "He needed you. He couldn't be king here without you."

"He could," Tilia said, "but this way was easier."

Rudira sat up. She had forgotten that Agni stood near her, and could hear every word. She had also, it seemed, forgotten that she was wounded. "He belongs to *me*," she said.

"I don't think so," said Tilia.

"I'll kill you too," Rudira said.

Tilia laughed. Agni tensed to leap, for Rudira's expression was murderous; but she did not spring on Tilia.

Any hope he might have had of mastering this debacle was long gone. And there was Yama all forgotten, and the Mother unregarded, and these two women deciding his fate. He could give in to rage, or he could rise and see that both Yama and the Mother were cared for as they deserved. Yama as king, for after all he had been that; and the Mother as befit her rank and office.

He did not delude himself that either Tilia or Rudira was chastened by his actions. Rudira was not to be punished, as far as he could see. There had been a brief moment when he might have overcome her, but that was past. Tilia appeared to bear her no rancor. And that was the strangest of all the things he had seen in this country: that a Mother should be dead, and the one who had killed her was not even rebuked for it.

"She'll pay," a voice said above him. He looked up startled. Catin looked down from the back of her mare. She was as ragged and insouciant as ever, sitting cross-legged on the broad rump, and the horse did not even turn an ear.

"She'll pay," Catin repeated. "Have no doubt of it. You may not understand the price, but she will."

"What, to give me up?"

Catin looked long at him, then shook her head. "Man," she said. "Irredeemably a man."

"I should be ashamed of that?"

"It might do your spirit good." She stood on the dun mare's rump, as steady as if it had been a level floor, and stretched her arms to the sky. "Look!" she cried. "The world's changing. Do you feel it under your feet? Do you taste it on the back of your tongue?"

"I see it clear enough," Agni said.

"You barely see your rod in front of your belly." She somersaulted off the mare's back, bounding lightly, impossibly, to her feet. "Rudira," she said. "Rudira, destroyer of worlds, come and talk to me."

There was the mad greeting the mad, dark woman face to face with bone-white over the Mother's lifeless body. Rudira had even less use for this tattered vagabond than for the Mother's heir—now, before the Lady, Mother indeed—of Three Birds. She sneered at Catin. Catin grinned at her. "Run away with me," she said.

"I'd rather die," Rudira said.

"Certainly," said Catin. "But we're going to run away first."

"I am staying here. That man is mine. I am not giving him up."

Catin half-turned over her shoulder and looked Agni up and down, a long raking sweep. "Why, child, whatever for? He's pretty, I grant you, but there's a surfeit of pretty men in the world. Come with me and you can have them all."

"Are they all kings?"

"In their own minds they are," said Catin.

"I must have a king," Rudira said. "Nothing less is worthy of me."

"Every man you choose is a king," said Catin. "Think of it. How splendid you make them. How they fall over one another to love you."

Rudira preened. "So they do. But, stranger, what do you gain from it?"

"Amusement," Catin said.

Rudira's brows drew together. "You'll not laugh at me."

"Never you," said Catin. "No, not ever."

"Well then," Rudira said. "I'll make my own kings. But that one—he is so lovely. I want him."

"Who's to say you won't have him?" Catin laid her arm about Rudira's shoulders, close as a sister. "Come, see, there's the most delightful young thing among the Stormwolves. He took a wound—a scratch, little more—but he's in great need of comforting. Because, you see"—and she lowered her voice almost to inaudibility—"he's afraid he might not be able to love a woman again."

"What," said Rudira in shock, "is he wounded *there?*"

"Of course not," said Catin, "but too close for him to tell the difference. We can show him very well, don't you think?"

"Exceptionally well," said Rudira.

⁜ ⁜

Agni watched them go in a kind of disbelief. Of all the strange things he had seen, this was the strangest. And, now it was too late, the most dismaying. He should have kept Rudira here. He should have seen her punished according to the laws of the tribes. For that, for killing an enemy so treacherously, she would have died.

He called himself back to his senses. There was more than enough to do besides fret over a pair of madwomen. A king and a Mother were dead. A battle had ended in blood and slaughter. There were armies to see to, terms to offer. A world to change—that much Catin had seen clearly.

A great part of him wanted to run after Rudira, to seize her, throttle her—to tumble her in the grass. But enough of him was king, and enough of him was sane, that he turned his back on the dwindling sight of her and set his face toward the duties of his kingship.

·············· 94 ··············

The world had shaken on its foundations. And when it was still again, the battle was over. Agni had won it. The tribesmen would make great legends of it, but Sarama could see the dazed look on his face. He did not believe it yet, not really. He was numb.

He could have cast his brother Yama to the dogs. It would not be the first time a victorious king had done that to a vanquished enemy—particularly an enemy whom he had detested for his life long. But Agni had never had the art of cruelty. He gave Yama a king's burial before all the gathered tribes, and raised his barrow with all proper honor. It was atonement, maybe. Agni would never admit it, but Sarama knew her brother.

And while he did as a king must for a fallen king, the Lady's people saw their Mother to her rest. It was a rite of silence, a giving of her body to the earth that had borne it. There were no dirges, no great processionals, no displays of fire and splendor. She made her way on the shoulders of her children, down from the horsemen's camp, over the eastward hill and across the field of battle, and so into the city over the bridge that spanned the pit of spears. Her people, all that lived and could walk, came slowly in her wake.

They passed to the Lady's grove. The men and boys hung back on the edges of the trees. The women went on into the green and peaceful circle that neither blood nor war had ever touched, until now. Until a Mother was laid within the earth, the first Mother that had ever died of treachery, in an act of war.

A woman of wealth in a city as rich as Three Birds might be buried with gold and with beautiful things that she had loved. But a Mother belonged to the Lady. Her rite was old, older than memory. She went into the earth naked as she had been born. No work of hands adorned her. Her bed was made of flowers, and flowers covered her.

They laid her to sleep in a waft of sweetness, and covered her over with green turves. Then as the moon rose above the trees that ringed the grove, her sisters and daughters, her kin, her friends, the women of her city, danced to honor her memory.

Tilia led the dance as was her duty. A vast quiet had filled her when she saw the Mother dead at her feet: an emptiness that was not serenity, nor yet acceptance.

The dance anchored her to the world again. It made her real; confirmed her in the truth. The Mother was dead. *She* was the Mother. When she came out of this grove, her name would be taken away. She would be no longer Tilia. She would be Three Birds, and Three Birds would live in her, in her body, just as her child grew and stirred and dreamed of the world into which it would be born.

She could refuse it. There was no disgrace in that. She could give it to Mareka or to one of the elders; to women who had borne and suckled a plenitude of children. She had yet to suckle even one. Some might cry out that she was not worthy. And maybe they would be right; but the Mother— her Mother who was dead—had named her heir. She must trust the Lady. She would take what she was given. She would be the Mother of Three Birds.

Agni would call her arrogant. Strange sunlit thought for that dance in the moonlight. His face came clear in her memory. She danced the spiral dance around it, around him. His quick laughter, his quick temper. The lift of his chin when he caught sight of someone he knew. The long clean line of his back. His beauty that was nothing like a woman's.

She made a gift of that memory to the Mother who was dead: a beautiful young man to keep her company in her long sleep; a warmth of sunlight to brighten the dark. His spirit would not miss the little bit of it that she took. Nor, she thought, would he mind too greatly that she had done it. He had honored the Mother, too. Maybe, in his way, he had loved her.

+ +

Sarama elected to see the Mother to her rest, and to leave Yama to the men who had fought him and the men who had fought under him. And yet as she danced the Lady's dance, it gave her no peace. Danu's face kept intruding on her memory. Danu's voice kept sounding in her ear, speaking words that she could never quite understand.

She had not seen him anywhere. Not in the camp, not among the people who had followed the Mother to the grove. There were companies abroad on the battlefield, gathering and tending the wounded and looking after the dead. He must be among those companies. Not among the dead. She would know if he had died. Surely, by the Lady, she would know.

She left the dance and the grove before the moon was well risen. She had honored the Mother as much as she could. The Mother would not mind too terribly that she had left so early. The Mother had loved all her children, but Danu had been closest of all to her heart, except for Tilia.

The Mare would have been happy to crop grass on the edge of the Lady's field, but she offered no more than a token protest when Sarama asked her to bear bridle and saddle-fleece again. Sarama was none too delighted to be back in the saddle, either; she was tired, and her bones ached. But she would sleep in no bed unless it had Danu in it.

Impulse and a kind of crazy hope led her to the Mother's house. People were in it, sleeping or awake, but not Danu. Only Rani was asleep in the arms of Danu's brother Tanis. Sarama did not try to wake either of them. Rani would only want her mother to stay, and cry when Sarama left. Or worse—she would call for her father, and Sarama could not provide him.

Danu was not in the city. No one had seen him leave the battlefield. The last anyone knew, he had been among the fighters sent to lay an ambush. Some of those had come back, wounded or whole, but none recalled seeing the Mother's son past the first disposal of forces. He had gone north to the old boar-coverts. That much appeared to be certain.

Sarama returned to the field. It was a strange bleak place under the moon, a field of the dead and dying, and shadow-shapes moving among them. The dead of the tribes would burn on a pyre, come sunrise, and their ashes be buried thereafter. The dead of the city would lie unburned in the earth. Now, in the night, people labored to find and separate them, and to give the mercy-stroke to such of the wounded as they found.

None of the black-bearded men was Danu, nor had he been found among the dead. Sarama rode slowly over that field, peering in the moonlight. Some of the searchers had torches, but she did not wish to be encumbered with one. The moon was bright enough.

The farther from the city she went, the more of the dead were yet un-claimed. Wounded there were none. That was a mercy, perhaps. And yet, if no one lived, then Danu—

He was alive. She would not let him be dead. She searched for him with a kind of desperate care, pausing beside each body and making certain that it was not his. She found Beki who had been Danu's second in the Mother's house, and Chana who had amused herself for a while with Agni's yearbrother Patir. They had taken ample escort with them into the gods' country: men and horses, even a warhound that had died with its teeth sunk in Beki's throat. Sarama had not known that any of the tribesmen had brought warhounds. They were an eastern affectation, and little known on the western steppe.

She slipped from the Mare's back and left her to follow or to stay, as she chose. The soft sound of her footfalls trailed after Sarama.

These were people whom Sarama knew, these dark-haired dead. The horsemen were all strangers, their banner unfamiliar. They had all fought hard, died hard.

She found him in the thick of it. There was a horse down, and a knot of tribesmen. And beneath them a hand that she knew, and a golden armlet gleaming pallid in the moonlight. She would remember later the thought that came to her, the dull wonder. No one had taken the gold from him.

She reached to touch it. It was cool. But the hand—

Warm. It was warm. Not very; not as if it surged with life. But it was not as cold as death, either.

With sudden fury she attacked the heaped bodies, lifting them, hurling them away. In her right mind she could never have done it. Now, the moon filled her. It made her strong.

The last dead tribesman fell bonelessly to the side. Danu lay sprawled on the trampled grass. He was naked but for belt and baldric, and his body was wound about with livid scars.

He had painted himself richly, as if this war were a dance. Only a few of the marks on him were blood. That was darker than the paint, and thicker, and its patterns had no order in them. She could not see what was fresh and what was dried.

Her hand lay trembling on his breast. It was cool, unmoving. She stroked fingers through the curly fleece of it. He never stirred. Her fingers clawed; raked hard, almost hard enough to draw blood.

Nothing.

A great wail rose up in her. He was not dead. He was *not*. He did not dare be dead.

His lips were as cool as the rest of him. Cool, not cold. He tasted of blood and earth.

In a kind of madness, she stripped off her garments, her coat, her trousers, and all her weapons. The night air was chill on her skin.

She covered him with her body, all of him that she could. She gave him her warmth. She stroked him, rubbed the cold out of him. She took his soft cool rod in her hand and struggled to wake it. She cursed him, raged at him, hated him for refusing to stir. He was refusing. She knew it. "Wake up, damn you!" she railed at him. "Wake up and look at me!"

She was being unreasonable. A distant part of her was aware of it, but she was not inclined to care. He had not died. She would not let him.

At first, when something about him changed, she hardly noticed it. She was too preoccupied. And yet in a little while there could be no mistaking it. The thing that had lain limp in her hand was coming alive. It was warming, growing. Rising up as a man might rise from the dead.

A breath shuddered as he drew it in. Another followed it, racking his body. He arched against Sarama's hand. She took him inside herself. Blindly, without mind or will, he took the rhythm of that dance, the oldest of them all.

He stiffened and shuddered. Dying—damn him—

No. Not unless the Lady's gift was a kind of death. His eyes snapped open. He gasped. She caught his breath before it escaped, and gave it back to him. All the life, all the strength that she had to spare, she poured into him. He was warm, warm to burning.

His arms closed about her with blessed, bruising strength. He rolled, flinging her onto her back, rising above her. His eyes were clouded, yet as she met them, slowly they cleared. He saw her; knew her. Knew what she had done. He blushed darkly in the moonlight.

She laughed for joy, and because he was so terribly shocked. "I couldn't think of any other way," she said.

"I'm sure you couldn't." His voice was deep and sweet. It was the most wonderful sound in the world.

"I wouldn't let you die," she said. "I wouldn't let you dare."

He frowned. The shadow had come back to his eyes, but there was no confusion there. Not any longer. "I—wanted—" His frown deepened. "I killed. I killed men. I killed—many—"

"You fought in a war," she said.

"But I wasn't supposed to be good at it!"

She let the echoes die. None of the dead started awake. The moon stared down, cold and serene. Softly after his great roar of anguish she said, "Get up."

He stared at her.

She sharpened her voice a little. "Up. Get up. Now."

His habit of obedience had not left him. He staggered to his feet. A hiss escaped him. He was wounded. Not to death, but not lightly either. He must be dizzy with loss of blood, and with the sudden and manifold stabbings of pain.

She could not be merciful. Not until he was strong in his spirit again. She rose as he had risen, and braced him as he swayed. He needed to eat, drink. He needed to sleep somewhere apart from a heap of the dead.

He did not want to do any of those things. He wanted to stay on the field, to bury the dead, to wallow in his self-disgust.

She would not let him. "Don't you go away from me," she said fiercely. "I need you. Rani needs you. Your sister needs you. The whole world needs you."

"Then let the world take care of itself."

That was so utterly unlike him that she froze. He nearly escaped her; but she was not as easily dismayed as that. She pulled him back to face her. "I *won't* let you go."

"Maybe I don't want to stay."

"I don't care."

His eyes blazed on her. She was glad. Heat was life. Heat of temper would bring him back to himself.

She tugged at him. He staggered after. The Mare was grazing close by. Sarama got him onto her back, cursing him when he resisted, striking him as if he had been a recalcitrant child. He was acting like a tribesman. "And you know better," she snapped at him.

That quelled him. He sagged on the Mare's back, clutched mane before he fell. "I don't—I can't—"

"Be quiet," she said. And for a wonder he obeyed.

Of all the places that she could take him, the enemy's former camp was closest. It was safe, she reckoned, and she had seen Taditi in the king's tent before she went in search of Danu. He might lose his wits again in a camp of the horsemen, but she had to hope that that was past.

✦ ✦

He seemed calm enough, and unshaken when he saw where she was taking him. The camp was quiet, most of its people away seeing Yama to his grave. But Taditi was in the king's tent as Sarama had hoped, and she knew at a glance what was needed of her. She brought wine, food, water to wash Danu and a blanket to wrap him, and a calm presence that brooked no nonsense. Between the two of them they saw him cleaned and fed and settled in a quiet corner. He had sworn that he would not sleep, but sleep took him almost as soon as he lay down.

Sarama stayed with him. There was much that she could have been doing, but nothing that mattered as much as this. No one who mattered as this one man did. Not her brother, not her kin. Not even her daughter.

She would never make a king, nor ever a Mother. A king could not leave all his people for one man alone, or a Mother cast aside duty to watch over her beloved. Sarama, who had done both, sat on her heels in the tent's dimness and watched him sleep. When he stirred uneasily or murmured, she spoke softly to him. And when the black dreams struck, she lay beside him and held him till they passed, through the long hours from deep night into morning.

She slept herself then, a little. She woke to find him open-eyed, regarding her with a dark and unreadable stare. "Good morning," she said.

His brow lifted. "Is it morning?"

She nodded.

"It's still night here," he said.

"We're in the king's tent of the White Horse," Sarama said. "I brought you here because it was closest."

"No," he said. "No. *Here*." His fist struck his breast over the heart. "I didn't dream it, did I? I fought. I killed people."

"You helped to save your city."

"Yes." It was a sigh. "I don't want to be proud of what I did."

"Are you?"

His eyelids lowered. His lips set. "I don't . . . want to."

She touched him softly, brushing fingers over brow and cheeks. "Beloved," she said.

He shivered. His eyes closed tight. "None of us who fought there will ever be the same again. We've lost something, Sarama. We'll never get it back."

"I know," she said softly. "I know."

"And," he said, and his eyes opened, and they were darker even than before, "do you know the other thing? The thing that eats my spirit? I would do it again. Every bit of it. Every drop of blood. Because if I, if we, had not done it, our city might have fallen."

"It would have fallen," Sarama said. "Agni couldn't have held them off. His men were too few. He'd have fallen himself, and maybe died. And Yama would be king in Three Birds."

"It does matter," said Danu. "Doesn't it? Which horseman calls himself king. I would rather Agni, who made the Great Marriage with Tilia, than the man who made a path of slaughter to our eastward door."

"Yes," said Sarama.

"But I am not glad of it," he said fiercely. "I can't be glad of it. No one can ask me to be."

"No one will," she said. She raised herself up. "Come, enough. The sun's up. Yama is in his grave. We've a world to put together again. Will you lie here and mourn the breaking, or help me mend it?"

He glared at her in quite unwonted resentment—signs of a temper that she had hardly known he had. But he had not changed as much as that. He mastered himself; he rose to his feet. He looked down at his nakedness and blushed a little, but he was not one to stop for a bit of modesty.

Sarama was pleased to offer him garments that Taditi had found and laid out the night before: coat and trousers of fine-tanned leather, and a shirt woven in this country.

Danu looked at them, measured them against his body. They were a fair fit. "Yama's?" he asked.

"Does that bother you?"

"No," he said. "No." He took them, put them on. He looked well in them—better than Yama would have done. There were boots, too, a little large but passable, and a belt, and a knife that he quietly but firmly put aside.

He was still Danu. It would be a while before he realized it; but Sarama, seeing the knife laid on the chest beside the bed, knew it for a surety. Nothing, not even war, could corrupt the spirit that was in him.

··············· 95 ···············

With day would come the judgment. But in the time between dawn and full morning, Agni looked for refuge in sleep. He made his way to the king's tent in the camp of the White Horse, found a corner that had no one in it, and let the darkness take him. A fleeting thought, that he was outcast from this place, that he could be killed for trespassing here, touched him and flickered away. If anyone wanted to slit his throat while he slept, then so be it. He was far too tired to care.

A soft touch roused him. Fingers stroking him; the feather-brush of kisses. He smiled, still in great part asleep, and reached to fill his arms with Tilia's warm ample body.

What stirred in his embrace was a slighter figure by far. He snapped awake, already in motion, recoiling against the wall of the tent.

Rudira lay where he had left her, in a tumble of pale hair, pale skin, pale impudent breasts. She laughed at his expression. "What, my love! Weren't you expecting me?"

"Get out," said Agni. His voice was thick.

She moved only to prop herself on her elbow and fix him with a steady regard. "Do you know, the boys Catin showed me—they were only boys. None of them was you."

"Get out," Agni said again. "I don't want you here."

"Of course you don't," she said. "You're angry with me. You think I'm all kinds of monstrosity."

"Aren't you? By the gods, woman! You betrayed me, exiled me, murdered my ally. Do you think I'd ever want you near me again?"

"Some part of you does," she said with an arch glance downward.

He took no notice of that, or of the ache in his loins, either. "You have no heart," he said. "Your spirit is an empty thing. All you know, all you see, is that you want to be a king's wife."

"And won't I be?"

"I have a wife," he said.

"Certainly," she said. "She's a king now, too. I saw her. She won't have time to spare for you. She'll be much too busy being king."

Agni's heart constricted. Rudira had a tongue like a snake, both subtle and poisonous. That she spoke the truth, after her fashion, only made her the more deadly.

He had let her live when he should have killed her. He could fall on her now, seize her, snap that slender neck in his hands. But his blood was not so cold, nor his strength of will so great. He would only fail.

And she knew it. Her smile was sweetly mocking. "Come, my love. Surrender. I'll share you with her. You don't love her, after all. How can you? Fat cow. But she's made you a king. That's a fine thing for a woman to do."

Agni drew breath to tell her how very wrong she was. But he thought better of it. She would only call him deluded; and she might do something rash. She had killed one Mother of Three Birds. She would think nothing of killing another.

He shifted, moving toward her. Her smile turned gleeful. He made as if to take her in his arms; veered and rolled and came to his feet well beyond her. As it dawned on her what he had done, he snatched up such garments as came to hand, and made his escape.

It was the coward's way, but no other was of any use with Rudira. The daylight offered refuge, morning light over a camp so familiar it struck him with pain. Camp of the White Horse in the gathering of tribes, and each clan-standard where it had always been, and Taditi tending the king's fire as she had done since he could remember. The only difference was the standard next to the white horsetail, the flame of gold that marked the first king of the Lady's country, the first lord of horsemen to rule where only women had ruled before.

Taditi greeted him with the rake of a glance, and gave him a cup that proved to be filled with much-watered wine. There was bread to go with it, and cheese. "It's not much," she said, "but it's all you're getting till you send people out to forage."

"The city can provide," he said, "and we'll cull the cattle. How hungry is everyone?"

"Not at all," she said, "yet. They've been seen to."

With a faint sigh he drank his wine, ate his bread and cheese. The camp had come to life as he sat there. Men came out of tents, yawning and stretching. Women went about their shadowy business. No one looked particularly cast down. And no one came to fling him out. People who passed offered him respect as one did to a king, an inclination of the head, sometimes a greeting, a soft "My lord." Just as if he had never been exiled. As if he had been king here since the old king died.

So did people school themselves in war, to accept what its fortunes might bring. Conquest; defeat. Return of a man whose name had been taken away, who had been made as nothing, yet who had won them all in battle.

It was only sensible to accept the inevitable; to greet him as their king. To let him be what he should have been from the beginning.

Fortunes of war. Agni drank down the last of the wine. People were hovering, not quite trying to draw his attention. Some were familiar: elders and warleaders, clan-chieftains and lesser kings. A few bore the marks of wounds. They were his. He had conquered them. Now they waited on his pleasure.

A king could let them wait about for most of the day, then suffer them to approach him as he sat in the circle of judgment. But Agni was not a particularly kingly king. He tilted his head. First one, then another, then the lot of them came to sit round the fire. No one needed its warmth, for the day was hot even so early, but what it signified was greater than simple comfort.

They were vanquished, and he had not yet spoken his judgment over them. Until he did, they could only speak if he spoke first. But no words came to him. He sat, feeling faintly like a fool, while the silence stretched.

As he sat there, others came. Those indeed he knew, and by name. Patir his yearbrother, Tillu with his terribly scarred face. Elders of the western tribes, young men and battle-captains of Agni's own eastern people. They claimed places nearest Agni, and no one dared contest it. Kings and elders who had been displaced, moved aside without protest. That too was the fortune of war.

Patir settled on one side of Agni, Tillu on the other. Patir said, "All's done on the field. The healers have the wounded in the city. They're expected to live, the gods and the Lady willing."

Agni bowed his head. "Thanks be," he said. "And the dead?"

"All sent to their rest," Patir answered. He yawned cavernously and stretched. "Ah! I could use a little myself."

"You haven't slept?"

"A little," Patir said. "When this is over I'll sleep from new moon to new moon, and let the work look after itself."

"So shall we all." Agni looked round the circle of faces. To his own people he was an easy burden, their own king and friend, whom they had chosen of their free will. As far as he knew, they were content with the choice. The strangers who had come to take this country now found themselves taken instead, and no certainty of what he would do to them. He might kill them. Blood-feud did not touch a conquering king. Or he might restore them to all that they had had before.

He finished his bread and cheese, drank the last of his wine. When he rose, some made as if to rise with him. He waved them down. "Stay," he said.

And they stayed. They obeyed. It came to him then, the full force of it, breaking at last through the wall of numbness that had been about him. What he had done. What he had won.

And could he hold it?

No doubts. No weakness. He held himself erect as he walked away.

✦ ✦

He did not go far. He only wanted a little peace. When he went back, he must judge them all, all the men who had come from the east. He was not going to kill them. He never had intended to. But what else he might do . . .

He walked out past the camp's edge, up the hill that sheltered it from the battlefield. That was as Patir had said, cleared as much as it could be. Two mounds rose on it, one crowned with spears, one with flowers. Dead of the horsemen, dead of the Lady's people. Carrion birds squabbled over scraps, remnants that had been forgotten.

The grass was all trampled and torn and stained dark with blood and mud. It would grow back richer than ever. That great gift the gods had given, that Earth Mother grew most fruitful on the field of death.

Agni sat on the hillside. The sun beat down, but the wind eased the strength of it. His body was a pattern of aches, bruises and small wounds. None of them mattered. Nor did the ache in his loins. But the memory of Rudira's hands on his skin—

At first he thought he was dreaming it. But someone had come up beside him and sat there in silence; and when he looked, he saw that it was Tilia.

She neither touched him nor spoke to him, and yet her presence warmed him through. After a while he said, "I thought you had to stay in the city. Until—"

"I came where I was needed," she said.

"But the Mother—"

"She sleeps," said Tilia.

Agni shut his mouth carefully. Her words were gentle, but they were as firm as a slap. The Mother was dead. Her story was ended.

After a moment Agni said, "You hold her place now."

She nodded.

"Will that—"

"No," she said.

"I hate when you do that."

Her glance was as unrepentant as it had ever been, and as brightly wicked, too. It comforted him. "And you're king now," she said. "Really king."

"That won't change me," he said.

Her brow arched. "Did I ask if it would?"

Maddening. Wonderful. He smiled; but memory intruded, like the rake of nails down his back. "Gods," he said. "I should have killed her."

"You should not," said Tilia.

"I can't keep her here. She's like a child or an animal. She's as treacherous as a spring wind. She'll kill you if it suits her whim, or kill me, or betray us both."

"Leave her to us," Tilia said.

Agni shook his head. "No. I can't do that."

"Why not? You people talk of the men's side, the women's side. This is a thing of the women's side. We'll deal with her. You go, do what men do, be king."

"But she is *my* mistake."

"How arrogant," said Tilia, "and how perfectly like you. She is a whole world's mistake. Your world made her. Let my world heal her."

"But—"

Her dark glance silenced him. "Go," she said. "They're waiting for you."

Certainly they were. Agni had bound them to it. He bent toward her, kissed her lightly. She looked a little startled, and a little pleased. He leaped up lightly and held out his hand. She let him draw her to her feet. Hand in hand they walked down the hill into the camp.

·············· 96 ··············

Agni the king sat in judgment over the men from the east. It was a sight the tribes had never seen before. Not only the king under his golden standard with his golden torque about his neck, but the woman who sat beside him and the women who sat and stood where elders should. Women unveiled, unconstrained, conducting themselves as equals in the council of the tribes.

Tilia sat on the black horsehide, upright and still. Her gown was of the finest weaving, a pattern of red and green and white, and her ornaments were gold.

Agni's coat was of the same weft as her gown, but his belt and trousers and boots were a tribesman's. He wore a weapon as a horseman should, a long knife sheathed in leather and hafted in carved bone. Its blade was copper, forged in Three Birds. He was of both worlds. So must his people be, if they were to live as the gods ordained.

Agni's own people had settled themselves among the women with a kind of cocky defiance. Patir was one of the last of them to appear. He would have taken a place close to Agni but somewhat away from the elders; but Agni caught his eye. His brow rose. Agni nodded slightly. With a careful lack of expression but a spring in his step, he took the place of honor, the place given to the captain of the king's warband, standing at his right hand and upholding the golden standard.

The lords and chieftains of the invading tribes advanced to stand before the king. They eyed the Mother and elders of Three Birds with little liking, and the elders and chieftains of Agni's following with little greater pleasure. Those that were of their own people were the young, the reckless, the outcast; and now they sat in judgment over their own fathers, brothers, princes.

It should not have been so. If they had chosen another king, Agni might have been standing before them, waiting as they waited, compelled by custom and the laws of the tribes to abide by their sentence.

He let them wait for it. He knew already what he would say, but he wanted to study their faces, to see who and what they were. Some he knew, men of the White Horse and of its brother tribes. Others came from farther away, north and south perhaps, even east. They had all come in search of wealth, gold and copper, fine weavings, willing women. And yes, war.

War they had had. The rest . . .

He spoke at last in the murmurous silence. "Men of the tribes," he said. "Dreamers of riches. Slayers of women and children, destroyers of cities. You belong to me now. I am your king by right of conquest. Do you accept me?"

Silence.

Agni would not repeat what he had said. To do so would have been weakness. He sat as a king sits, gleaming in gold, with his wife of the Great Marriage beside him and his yearbrother on guard at his right hand. He let them see that. He let them remember what he could do if they refused him.

It would be a brief fight. His own men were few, and theirs a multitude.

But custom held them. Law bound them. First one, then another came slowly forward, dropped stiffly to his knees, bowed on his face. Not one refused. Not even those of the White Horse, though they came late and slow. And when each man of the White Horse rose, he looked into Agni's face, looked hard and long.

He bore their scrutiny. He had no shame of what he was or had done. Nor had he committed the crime for which his people had cast him out.

Maybe they saw that. Maybe they simply accepted the inevitable. He had defeated their king. He had won them and all that was theirs.

Before he was outcast, he had been their prince, their king who would be. He watched them remember. He watched them choose. To follow him. To take him as their king.

When they had risen and drawn back, a great tension drained out of him. It had been there, if he had known it, since he was driven from the tribe. He had made his own tribe and people, but these were his kin. That they accepted him—it mattered. It mattered very much indeed.

When Agni had received the last of their tribute, he rose. He spread his arms. He called them all—every one—to the festival. Victors and vanquished mingled; enemies that had been were transformed into allies. Even blood-feuds were laid aside.

In the morning the feuds would come back. Enemies would remember that they hated one another. But they would be one army, one great gathering of tribes. Then Agni must see that they were given places to camp, grazing for their herds, occupation for their men.

The Lady's country was wide. It could sustain them. As for what they could do: all that they had burned and broken, they could mend, and whatever they had destroyed, they could build anew. That would be the work of years. Then when war came again from the steppe, they would be ready. There would never again be such easy conquest as Agni had found, or as Yama had met in his turn.

All that would come when it came. For this day, they kept festival.

✦ ✦

But Agni was not quite done with his judging. There was still a matter that he would not leave to the women.

Yama-diti had secluded herself with her daughters in a tent beside the king's tent. It was small and rather tattered: such a tent as a poor relation would claim, or a discredited wife. Agni did not succumb to the pathos of it. That Yama-diti was deeply bereaved, he did not doubt. But she was never either poor or powerless.

He had her summoned to him in the king's tent, because a king did not go to a woman unless it was her bed he sought. He waited where his father the old king had been accustomed to receive his wives and daughters, in the common space, the high wide center of the tent. It was brighter and airier than he remembered, with the tentflap fastened back and banks of lamps lit—more lamps than they had ever had in the old time.

He was not in the least surprised to see Rudira enter with the woman and her daughters. In front of them Yama's widow at least observed an appearance of circumspection. When they had been brought in, Patir who had been his messenger, and Tillu who had attached himself to the company, both stood on guard at Agni's back. Agni had not asked them to do that, but neither did he forbid. He did not particularly wish to be alone with these of all women.

At a gesture from Agni, the women sat. Yama-diti and her daughters were modestly attired in the manner of the tribes, but Rudira wore fabric of this country woven as thin and pale as mist. She kept her eyes lowered, her hands in her lap. He elected not to see how her nipples tightened under the gown, or how she arched ever so subtly so that he would be sure to notice.

The tentflap was lifted still. Taditi came to stand in it, half blocking the bright flood of light from without, but not so much that it failed to shine full on the unveiled faces of Yama-diti and her companions. Rudira blinked and cowered, shielding her eyes. Agni did not recall that he had ever seen her in full daylight. Only in dim places, in shadows, or under stars or moon.

The sun did not destroy her as they said it would destroy a witch, but neither did she bask in it. Not as Yama-diti did, like an old serpent coiled at ease on a stone, fixing Agni with a flat glittering stare.

Agni could not speak the words that would have been proper to a woman whose son had died. Not when it had been Agni who killed him. Agni could muster no grief, no regret that he had done it. Brother in blood Yama had been, but in the spirit he had never been aught but an enemy.

This woman had borne him, raised him, taught him bitter and envious hatred of any who had what he had not. Agni they had hated above all, because though he was younger born, he was the firstborn son of Rama the king. Yama was eldest of the princes, but Agni was the heir, who would be king in his turn.

Yama had never been the enemy. Not truly. The mind that ruled him, the will that bent him, was here. Rudira wanted to be a king's wife, would do anything at all to gain it. Yama-diti wanted to be a king's mother: to hold power as a woman must among the tribes; to rule through the son of her body.

Agni had pardoned the men who fought against him. This one he could not pardon. She had not merely fought. She had conspired to destroy him.

When he spoke, he spoke to the point. "I can't let you live," he said.

Yama-diti neither stirred nor flinched. One of the daughters began to weep softly, the easy tears of a woman who hopes to melt a man's heart.

But Agni's was set in stone. "You may choose," he said. "Poison in the cup, or the spears of my warband under the sky."

"The spear is a man's death," Yama-diti said.

"You were a king's wife. That honor is allowed you, to die like a man."

"And if I choose neither?"

"I choose," Agni said.

"Poison," said Yama-diti without hesitation. "I do not wish to die like a man."

Agni inclined his head.

"But," said Yama-diti, "I ask a thing of you. My daughters had nothing to do with what was done to you. They are your sisters, the children of your father. Let them live."

"Why?" Agni asked. "They're your creatures. They have no minds or will apart from you."

"Then give them to a man who can master them." Yama-diti's eyes glittered, stabbing the air in back of Agni's shoulder. "Give them to him."

Agni glanced back at Tillu. Yama-diti's eyes, the force of her regard, shook him out of comfort and away from familiarity. For a moment he saw Tillu as a stranger would: the terrible scars in a face that had never been beautiful, even in youth and unmarred. It was the face of a forest man overlaid with a faint cast of the tribes, strong as old stone. A blade had cloven it in a fight long ago, Tillu had told him. It had healed, but he would never lose the marks, the nose broken and split, the lip twisted in a perpetual snarl.

Agni blinked, and his sight cleared again. He saw the eyes above the scars, and the spirit in them. A good man, a man wise after his fashion, and loyal to the king whom he had chosen to follow.

Agni raised his brows. Tillu lowered his. "Your choice," Agni said.

Tillu nodded. "They're a king's daughters," he said, "and a king's sisters. Their breeding is good. I'm less sure of their tempers—but my eldest wife is a strong woman. She'll teach them manners."

Agni watched the sisters. The one who had wept was sitting narrow-eyed, her tears forgotten. The other regarded Tillu in a kind of horror.

Idiots. If they reckoned it punishment to be given to a good and loyal man who would treat them far better than they deserved, then so be it. "Watch your back," he said to Tillu, "and eat nothing that either of them serves you. And give their children to other women to raise."

"I'll tame them," Tillu said, "never you fear. They'll be eating from my hand."

"Biting it, rather," Agni muttered, but Tillu only laughed. He was not at all unhappy with this prize that he had been given. He might be a little less than pleased with their faces; they were sour creatures, with their mother's strong chin and her hawk's nose. But faces mattered little when a man was getting sons, and blood mattered much. In one stroke of an old woman's mockery, Tillu had become kinsman to the king.

Yama-diti's expression betrayed nothing. If she had hoped to be denied, to take her daughters into death with her, she had been disappointed. Yet Agni rather suspected that she had hoped for this. It would be like her to bind her daughters to a man so ugly that few women would go to him willingly, but whose heart was good and who would treat them well. He would get sons on them, and daughters. She was dead by her own choice, but she would live on in her children's children.

Taditi was waiting. Agni caught her eye. She came forward with the cup and set it in his hand. He caught the strong sweet scent of wine, and the other thing beneath it, both bitter and pungent.

Yama-diti's eyes fixed on it. Had she expected him to wait, to send her away, to give her time to work more mischief? Or had it simply come home to her that this was the reckoning?

Agni held out the cup. She had to raise herself to take it, kneeling in front of him. Her fingers brushed his as they closed on the cup. It was a skull-cup, and new, still faintly rose-tinted with the blood that had given it life. It had yet to be carved or painted or bound with gold as Agni intended.

A shudder ran through her. She knew whose skull this had been. Agni met her eyes over the curve of it.

She took it in both her hands, trembling just visibly. She had great courage; far more than her son had ever had. Eyes still locked with Agni's, she raised the cup of her son's skull to her lips, and drank long and deep.

Taditi had brewed the poison well, and brewed it strong. For a stretching moment Yama-diti sat still, as if she felt nothing. Then it struck, hard and sudden like a spear to the vitals. She fell, convulsed.

No one moved to catch her or to aid her. Her daughters, who might have done so, clutched at one another and stared.

She died alone as all of them watched. It was ugly but it was swift. It was as much mercy as Agni could give, and more than she deserved.

When it was over, when she lay still at last, heavy with the stench of death, the women of the king's tent came to take her away. None met Agni's gaze. He knew most of them: they had elected to belong to him before he was driven out. The rest must be wives taken since Yama made himself king, or Yama's own elder wives. There were no children. Yama had sired no sons, nor daughters either.

Not one of all those women shed a tear for Yama-diti. Even her daughters were dry-eyed. They would take her and bury her in the women's rite, and relegate her to silence. Her spirit would not haunt them. Taditi had promised Agni that. Whatever malice lingered, the women would cleanse the world of it.

It was, when he thought about it, remarkably like the burial of a Mother. And for all that he had hated her, and as glad as he was that she was dead, this much he could concede. She had, in her way, been a woman of great power and strength of will. Even in death she had yielded to no one.

✦ ✦

And when it was done, when she was taken away and her daughters had gone with Tillu to be his wives and servants, there was still Rudira. Patir had stayed, and Taditi come back from seeing to Yama-diti's rites. Rudira had not moved at all, nor spoken. She had no intention, it was all too clear, of surrendering herself to the women. She was Agni's burden. Agni and Agni alone must judge and sentence her.

Agni regarded her in a kind of despair. The rest of Yama's wives were a simple matter. Most had been the old king's, and briefly Agni's. Agni could take one or all of them. Or, if he so chose, men of the tribes would take them and be honored, as Tillu was, because of who they were and had been. But Rudira he did not trust, nor would ever trust. Rudira wanted to be a king's wife.

The skull-cup lay where Taditi had set it after Yama-diti fell, not far from Agni's foot. There was still a little wine left in it, a dark stain on the white bone. Agni could bid Rudira drink it. She might even obey.

He could not marry her. He could not give her to someone else. No more could he kill her. It was a perfect dilemma. Maybe if he chose at random, said the first thing that came into his head—

"Ah! There you are."

Agni blinked. A shadow swelled in the light from without, and shrank into the madwoman Catin. Her eyes were on Rudira; the rest of them might never have been there at all. "What are you doing here? You don't belong in this place."

Agni could not read Rudira's expression. It might be relief; it might be annoyance. Or it might be something else altogether. "I want to belong to him," she said, sliding a glance at Agni.

"Why? He doesn't want you." Catin crouched beside her. "Really, you don't need him. It's a wide world, and he's bound himself to such a tiny corner of it."

"But I want him," Rudira said.

"Whatever for? Besides the obvious, of course. He's pretty, but I've seen prettier. His rod is lovely, neither too large nor too small, and he's even learned to please a woman with it; but the world is full of men who know how to please a woman."

"He's a king," Rudira said.

"What, that again? Silly. Here, get up. Come ride with me."

"But I don't—"

"You're much too pale," Catin said, "and much too thin. You need the sun and the wind, and air that's not been shut inside of a tent."

"But—"

"Come," said Catin. "I've a mind to ride to the world's edge and see what lies beyond it. Haven't you ever wondered? Don't you want to see?"

Rudira stared at her, pale eyes wide. They were all staring. Catin took not the slightest notice. "I'm going," she said.

"But why do you want—" Rudira began.

"Never ask why," Catin said. "Just come."

Rudira's face twisted as if in pain. "I'm afraid," she said.

"Ah, child," said Catin with rough gentleness, "of course you are. You don't even know what you are, still less what to do about it."

"What am I?"

"That, no one can tell you. You have to see for yourself."

"You're mad," said Rudira.

Catin smiled. "Of course I am. Come to the world's edge with me."

Rudira wavered visibly, on the verge of diving into hiding, or worse, into Agni's arms. But Catin held out her hand. Rudira stared at it. It did not move. She clasped it, a desperate leap, as if she had been drowning. Catin pulled her up, but gently, and drew her into the light.

She stood blinking at it, tears streaming down her cheeks. But after an incredulous while she straightened. Her eyes cleared. She lifted her face, turned it to the sky.

Suddenly she laughed. There was pain in it, and no little terror. But it was honest laughter. Now it was she who led Catin, half running, laughing in the sun.

Long after they were gone, Agni sat unmoving, and the others with him. At last Patir said, "Only a god could be so incomprehensible."

"Incalculable," Agni said.

"What's difficult about it?" said Taditi. "They're both exactly as mad as they need to be. That's very sane, sometimes. Catin knows that you can't keep Rudira here. Rudira doesn't know anything worth knowing. She's been set free of the world. She'll not trouble you after this. You were all the brightness she knew. Now she has the sun itself."

"I don't understand you, either," said Agni.

And yet, in a way, he did. If he had lived all of his life inside of a tent, and if his spirit yearned for the light, but did not know either what it yearned for or why . . . he might have been as Rudira was. He too might have reached for such light as he could find, and not reckoned the cost.

.... 97 ....

The Mother of Three Birds, whom Agni had never learned not to call Tilia, became a mother at last in the autumn of the year. It was harvest time, the golden time, when summer lingered in the days, but the nights were sharp with frost.

Sarama was out with the archers as she often was that autumn, running the king's messages from town to town, or reminding the scattered tribes that they were to keep his laws. There were horsemen everywhere that war had touched, healing what they had harmed, and mending what they had broken. Not all of them were pleased to be so constrained; but Sarama's company of grim-faced women on fast horses, armed with bows and deadly of aim, had proved to be the king's best weapon against young tribesmen's arrogance.

Girls and women were coming out of the towns and cities, begging to learn to ride and shoot. Sarama had a handful of them with her that day as she rode back to Three Birds from a long month's riding about. They were mounted awkwardly on remounts, and not all were as glad to be riding as they had thought to be; it was not a comfortable thing to learn, in the beginning. But she had some hope of these. The fires of war had swept over them and tempered them like gold in the forge.

She was steppe-born, bred to wander lifelong and never settle in any one place. But as every tribe had its camps to which it returned season after season, she had Three Birds. She was not always sorry to leave it, particularly since the walls had begun to go up about it, warding it against war thereafter, but she was never aught but glad to come back. Her friends were there, her kin, her daughter—and Danu, who was her heart's center.

She came from the east this time, all the way from Larchwood, where Tillu had made himself lord and guardian of the eastward borders. He had done well for himself, king's friend that he was, and husband to the king's sisters. Through his kin in the wood he knew all that passed there, and much that passed on the steppe beyond. All was quiet, the flood of tribes stilled. They would all have time, and perhaps much of it, before war came back into this country.

Unless of course they wrought it themselves. But Sarama had no expectation of that. Not this year, and not the next. Thereafter . . . the Lady knew.

She was thinking of this as she topped the hill and looked down on the city. The field between had almost healed. The grass upon it was very green, and flowers grew on the mounds where the dead slept. The pit of spears with its bridge was still there, and Agni's wall rising just beyond it. He was building in earth and stone. Already it was breast-high to people standing behind it.

She could still see the city, its circles, its high peaked roofs, and the temple rising above them all. And, riding up from the bridge, a lone man on a dun horse, with a much smaller figure riding in front of him.

Her heart leaped. As if to match it, the Mare half-reared. Sarama let her go, plunging down at a gallop. A pealing cry rang out: Danu's stallion fighting the bit, till Danu surrendered as Sarama had, and set the stallion free to run.

They met on the field where the grass grew thick, swirling about one another. Sarama was laughing, dizzy with wind and speed. Rani called out to her: "Mama, Mama, Mama!"

They spun to a halt. Rani leaped into her mother's arms. Sarama held her tight, drinking in the sun-warmed child-scent, till she wriggled and squawked in protest. Reluctantly Sarama loosened her grip, and let Rani slide down astride the Mare's neck. Rani clasped her about the middle and clung, babbling happily: a headlong mingling of words and baby-talk.

Sarama met Danu's gaze over the tangle of dark curls. She was grinning, she realized, like a perfect fool.

And so was he. He was beautiful. He sat his stallion now with easy grace, not quite as one who had ridden before he could walk, but close enough. "You've been practicing," she said.

He shrugged a little. "I have your honor to think of."

"And your own pride?"

He shrugged again, a roll of wide shoulders. She would have loved to stroke them, to trace their width in kisses.

Tonight. His glance knew what she was thinking: it warmed till she came nigh to springing on him then and there, and never mind the baby between.

But she was wise after all, rather wiser than she sometimes liked to be. She kept to her place as he kept to his, and took note of his expression as he recalled what had brought him out to greet her. "The Mother," he said. "It's time."

Sarama's head emptied of everything, even Danu. "But—it's early."

"Not so early," he said, "and all's well. But since you've come, she would like—"

"Yes." Sarama flung the word over her shoulder. The Mare was already a dozen long strides closer to the city than she had been before.

The dun stallion was hard on her heels. Rani whooped with glee. She loved a gallop, that one. No doubt of it: she was her mother's child.

+ +

Tilia—the Mother—had gone into the birthing-room in the morning. The child was coming, but not for a while yet.

Tilia looked tired and ruffled and no more distressed than she should. Agni was much less composed. His beard looked red as fire against his white cheeks. His eyes were wild.

"You look," said Sarama, "like a spooked colt."

He glowered at her. "What, are you laughing at me? I've never even seen a baby born before."

"You've foaled mares," Sarama said. "It's not so different. It just takes a great deal longer."

"Mares aren't foaling *my* child."

"Stop that," Tilia said before Sarama could muster a retort. "I need him and I want you, but if you're going to squabble, you can do it somewhere else."

Agni looked down, sulky as a boy. Sarama felt no little bit sullen herself. They were both excessively well rebuked.

Agni laughed first. That was a remarkable thing; unheard of. But so was seeing the king of the horsemen in the birthing-room with the woman who carried his child. Sarama would have laid wagers that he would never do such a thing. But for Tilia he had done it. Oh, he loved her indeed, so to overcome the strictures of custom and apprehension and pure male pride.

+ +

Their daughter was born just before sunset, and their son not long after, just on the threshold of the night. They were dark children, but Sarama suspected in her bones that the son's eyes would be amber when he was older. Agni looked on them as fathers had, perhaps, since the morning of the world: half in awe and half in incredulity. He could not stop looking at them, or touching them, or counting fingers and toes. "They're perfect," he said, and more than once.

"Of course they are," said Tilia. She was vastly and luminously happy. To be barren for so long, and when at last she came to it, to bear two—that was a great thing, and proof to any who might have doubted, that she was fit to be Mother in Three Birds.

Her gladness blessed them all. Sarama drew back with Danu, leaving them to each other: Agni in his wonder, Tilia in her deep and singing joy.

Danu's arm slipped about Sarama's middle. He had learned, and very well, to act as well as to be acted upon. He set a kiss in the hollow of her neck and shoulder. "And shall we make ourselves another?" he murmured in her ear.

She smiled sidelong. "Would you like to?"

"With all my heart."

"And some of the rest of you, too."

He laughed, soft and deep. But his mind had wandered somewhat afield. "Would you have thought it? Those two, of all people that could have been. She's tamed the king of the horsemen."

"And he has conquered the Mother of the cityfolk." Sarama laid her head on his shoulder as she had wanted to do since he came riding toward her across the healing battlefield. "Are you conquered, beloved? And am I a tamed thing?"

"Do you want to be?"

"I want . . ." She slipped a hand beneath his coat, but only to let it rest there. People were coming, crowding to look on the wonder and to share the blessing: twin children born to the Mother in her city, and to the king who had joined with her in the Great Marriage. They took no notice of the two in the shadows, nor listened to the words that they murmured to one another.

"I want to be blessed," Sarama said. "To be yours as you are mine. To go out as the Lady calls me, and to come back, and you are here."

"Always," he said. "I am always here."

"Promise?"

"By my heart," he said.

"You know," she said, "what this is. What all of it is. We were what we were. Horsemen. Gods' children. Bound to the Lady of Horses. And you were unlike anything we had ever known. We never understood you—maybe never will. And yet, look at us. We've come together. We've made something new."

"Something that knows the meaning of war."

He did not often go as dark as that, or as quickly. She brushed his lips with hers, to warm them, and wrapped her arms about him and held him tight. "All things have a price. Would you go back altogether to what you were?"

He shivered, but he shook his head. "No. Not without you."

Sarama drew back until she could see his face. Shadow lay half across it, but his eyes were clear. They saw farther than they wanted to see, and deeper, too. "You've grown strong," she said.

"No. I've grown hard."

"Strong," said Sarama. "You'll never be a hard man. Not you. Just as I'll never be gentle, nor those two yonder be aught but proud. We change, the world changes. But what's in the heart of us, that holds fast."

"Pray the Lady it be so," Danu said, "for if it's not, then all this world of ours that was so beautiful—it will die. Nor will it ever be reborn."

"The Lady won't die," Sarama said. "Listen to her. Listen! She's older than the gods. When all of them are gone, she will remain. So too her children. They'll change; there's no help for that. But they'll never vanish from the world."

Danu's eyes were as dark as ever. He was not comforted, not wholly. He had seen too much for that; too much war, too much death.

So had they all. As Sarama moved to speak again, a baby's cry silenced her. One of the Mother's children, of the king's children, had roused and was proclaiming its presence in the world. It was a strong cry, and swiftly doubled, more shout of triumph than wail of anguish. The world was pain, it declared, and yet the world was joy. Hunger; satiation. Sorrow and gladness.

She let their voices speak for her. He was a wise creature, when he allowed himself to be. She watched the light come back into his face.

He traced the line of her cheek with his finger. "Shall we make a son this time?"

"If you want one."

"I would like that," he said gravely, but with a glint in it.

"Then we should set about it," she said.

"Now?"

"Will there ever be a better time?"

He lifted his head and peered into the birthing-room. Sarama half-turned herself to see what he was seeing. The babies' cries had quieted. The Mother had them both at the breast, and people all about, a great crowd of them as it seemed, and not all people of the city, either. Patir was there, and Taditi, and others that she knew from the king's camp. In a little while, from the look on Agni's face, they would all be sent away so that Tilia and the children could rest. But for the moment they were there, two worlds, two peoples, all together in this one blessed place.

Sarama glanced at Danu. His eye met hers. He nodded. Laughter bubbled up in her. His own echoed it. He swept her up and kissed her soundly. "Now," he said.

"Now," she agreed with great contentment.

AUTHOR'S NOTE

PERHAPS THE MOST unexpected discovery for a novelist working in prehistory these days, particularly if the novelist has had the sort of classical education that regards the civilizations of Mesopotamia— Sumeria and Ur of the Chaldees—as the very beginnings of civilized culture, is that Sumer and Ur are in fact quite young as cities go. Long before either of them, a large area in what is now eastern Europe and western Asia, and even as far west as the "heel" of Italy, saw the rise of innumerable towns and cities. Archeologists have found settlements large enough to match a medieval city, in clusters as close as within a kilometer apart, a population of quite remarkable density—and dating from 7000 B.C. until about 3000 B.C. Even predynastic Egypt does not go back so far.

Interpretation of these cultures is difficult and controversial. One interpretation in particular has been both avidly embraced and bitterly excoriated: that of Marija Gimbutas, who coined the term "Old Europe," and whose monumental body of archeological and scholarly work operates on the assumption that these Neolithic city-states were centers of peace-loving, Goddess-worshipping people ruled by women and innocent of war. Particularly in her book *The Civilizations of the Goddess: The World of Old Europe* (San Francisco, 1991), as well as in *The Goddesses and Gods of Old Europe: Myths and Cult Images* (Berkeley, 1982) and *The Language of the Goddess* (San Francisco, 1991), along with numerous articles, she assembles an impressive collection of archeological evidence to support her thesis. However the scholar may feel about her interpretation, for a novelist it is pure gold. Add to this the discovery of a second motherlode in Riane Eisler's *The Chalice and the Blade* (San Francisco, 1987), along with Margaret Ehrenberg's *Women in Prehistory* (Norman, OK, 1989) and the wonderful examination of the history of weaving in Elizabeth Wayland Barber, *Women's Work: The First 20,000 Years* (New York, 1994), and a picture emerges of a tremendously rich and sophisticated people who were, perhaps, totally different in mind and emphasis than any later Western culture.

This novel began as a prehistoric epic about women and horses. Its original inspiration was an item that appeared in the newspapers, on the discovery of bit wear on the jaw of a horse dating from about 4000 B.C. This was

493

based on an article by David W. Anthony and Dorcas Brown, "The Origin of Horseback Riding," in *Scientific American* 256 (1991), along with subsequent articles including David W. Anthony's "Horse, Wagon, and Chariot: Indo-European Languages and Archaeology," in *Antiquity* 69 (1995). Professors Anthony and Brown, with others, have concluded that there is clear evidence for the riding of horses with bits of either leather or bone as early as 4000 B.C., and possibly earlier—predating the first evidence of the chariot by some thousand years.

It so happens that these dates are significant in the history of Old Europe. These are the dates—between 4500 and about 3000 B.C.—when the civilization of Gimbutas' "Old Europe" was invaded and eventually either assimilated or destroyed by tribes of pastoral nomads. These nomads, it must be noted, were horsemen. First as riders and later as warriors in chariots, they overwhelmed the cities and swept westward until, after several millennia, they came to a halt in the isles of Britain and Ireland. Professor Anthony suggested that a novelist well might consider the first contact of these two cultures, Old Europe and the steppe nomads called the Kurgans, either around 4500 or around 3500 B.C. I chose the earlier date, the invasion of riders on horses rather than in chariots.

I have taken great and perhaps unconscionable liberties with the archeological and geographical evidence, but considerably fewer with the technology and daily details, as far as they are known. Readers in search of the "true" story would do well to go to Gimbutas, to Anthony, and to other scholars of Neolithic Europe and Asia. The basis however is the Kurgan invasion of the Cucuteni peoples of the area south of what is now Kiev, beginning around the Volga and the Don and sweeping south and west toward the Dnieper and the Dniester rivers.

In the way of all epics, I have simplified the long and complex story, and focused it on one small area and one rather symbolic geography. The wood between the steppe and the Lady's country could as well have been a river or a mountain range. That there was some barrier which had to be crossed before the warriors from the steppe could overwhelm the Goddess' country, seems likely. I should note here that the people of the wood have a basis in archeological evidence; there is some indication of Cro-Magnon survivals in this region, and further indication that these early humans interbred with the peoples of the steppe. Tillu and his kin, or people very like them, well may have existed.

The geography I invented or heavily adapted, but the cultures are based on Gimbutas and on the Rig Veda. The latter, the great Indian sacred cycle, is one of the sources and inspirations of Anthony and Brown's work on early equestrian societies. If one treats it as legend rather than myth, it becomes a fascinating historical source, a depiction of a culture that must have been based originally on the Kurgans. In the meeting of so strongly male-dominated and warlike a society with a society that worshipped a Mother Goddess and that did not until quite late—after the invasions had begun—appear to make or use weapons of war, I found my story and my characters.